# GRAVE
# MISTAKE
### and two other
### *GREAT MYSTERIES*

# BOOKS BY NGAIO MARSH

Artists in Crime
Death in a White Tie
Overture to Death
Death at the Bar
Death and the Dancing Footman
Colour Scheme
Died in the Wool
Final Curtain
A Wreath for Rivera
Night at the Vulcan
Spinsters in Jeopardy
Scales of Justice
Death of a Fool
Singing in the Shrouds

False Scent
Hand in Glove
Dead Water
Black Beech and Honeydew
Killer Dolphin
Clutch of Constables
A Man Lay Dead
The Nursing Home Murder
Tied up in Tinsel
Vintage Murder
When in Rome
Black as He's Painted
Last Ditch
Grave Mistake

# GRAVE MISTAKE
## and two other GREAT MYSTERIES

## Ngaio Marsh

Little, Brown and Company     Boston     Toronto

# Contents

GRAVE MISTAKE

I

SPINSTERS IN JEOPARDY

215

OVERTURE TO DEATH

437

# GRAVE
# MISTAKE

*For Gerald Lascelles*

# Cast of Characters

| | |
|---|---|
| Verity Preston | of Keys House, Upper Quintern |
| The Hon. Mrs. Foster (Sybil) | of Quintern Place, Upper Quintern |
| Claude Carter | her stepson |
| Prunella Foster | her daughter |
| Bruce Gardener | her gardener |
| Mrs. Black | his sister |
| The Reverend Mr. Walter Cloudsley | Vicar of St. Crispin's-in-Quintern |
| Nikolas Markos | of Mardling Manor, Upper Quintern |
| Gideon Markos | his son |
| Jim Jobbin | of Upper Quintern Village |
| Mrs. Jim | his wife; domestic helper |
| Dr. Field-Innis, M.B. | of Great Quintern |
| Mrs. Field-Innis | his wife |
| Basil Schramm (né Smythe) | Medical incumbent, Greengages Hotel |
| Sister Jackson | his assistant |

4

| | |
|---|---|
| G. M. Johnson | Housemaids, Greengages Hotel |
| Marleena Briggs | |
| The Manager | Greengages Hotel |
| Daft Artie | Upper Quintern Village |
| Young Mr. Rattisbon | Solicitor |
| Chief Superintendent Roderick Alleyn | C.I.D. |
| Detective-Inspector Fox | C.I.D. |
| Detective-Sergeant Thompson | C.I.D.; photographic expert |
| Detective-Sergeant Bailey | C.I.D.; fingerprint expert |
| Sergeant McGuiness | Upper Quintern Police Force |
| P.C. Dance | Upper Quintern Police Force |
| A coroner | |
| A waiter | |

# Contents

| Chapter I | Upper Quintern | 7 |
| Chapter II | Greengages (I) | 28 |
| Chapter III | Alleyn | 53 |
| Chapter IV | Routine | 80 |
| Chapter V | Greengages (II) Room 20 | 107 |
| Chapter VI | Point Marked X | 129 |
| Chapter VII | Graveyard (I) | 152 |
| Chapter VIII | Graveyard (II) | 177 |
| Chapter IX | Graveyard (III) | 194 |

# CHAPTER I

# Upper Quintern

## I

"BRING ME," sang the ladies of Upper Quintern, "my Bow of Burning Gold."

"Bring me," itemized The Hon. Mrs. Foster, sailing up into a thready descant, "my Arrows of Desire."

"Bring me," stipulated the Vicar's wife, adjusting her pince-nez and improvising into seconds, "my Chariot of Fire."

Mrs. Jim Jobbin sang with the rest. She had a high soprano and a sense of humour and it crossed her mind to wonder what Mrs. Foster would do with Arrows of Desire or how nice Miss Preston of Keys House would manage a Spear, or how the Vicar's wife would make out in a Chariot of Fire. Or for a matter of that how she herself, hard-working creature that she was, could ever be said to rest or stay her hand much less build Jerusalem here in Upper Quintern or anywhere else in England's green and pleasant land.

Still it was a good tune and the words were spirited if a little far-fetched.

Now they were reading the minutes of the last meeting and presently there would be a competition and a short talk from the Vicar, who had visited Rome with an open mind.

Mrs. Jim, as she was always called in the district, looked round the drawing-room with a practised eye. She herself had "turned it out" that morning and Mrs. Foster had done the flowers, picking white prunus-japonica with a more lavish hand than she would have dared to use had she known that McBride, her bad-tempered jobbing gardener, was on the watch.

Mrs. Jim pulled herself together as the chairwoman, using a special voice, said she knew they would all want to express their sympathy with Mrs. Black in her recent sad loss. The ladies murmured and a little uncertain woman in a corner offered soundless acknowledgement.

Then followed the competition. You had to fill in the names of ladies present in answer to what were called cryptic clues. Mrs. Jim was mildly amused but didn't score very highly. She guessed her own name for which the clue was: "She doesn't work out." "Jobb-in." Quite neat but inaccurate, she thought, because her professional jobs were, after all, never "in." Twice a week she obliged Mrs. Foster here at Quintern Place, where her niece Beryl was a regular. Twice a week she went to Mardling Manor to augment the indoor staff. And twice a week, including Saturdays, she helped Miss Preston at Keys House. From these activities she arrived home in time to get the children's tea and her voracious husband's supper. And when Miss Preston gave one of her rare parties, Mrs. Jobbin helped out in the kitchen, partly because she could do with the extra money but mostly because she liked Miss Preston.

Mrs. Foster she regarded as being a bit daft: always thinking she was ill and turning on the gushing act to show how nice she could be to the village.

Now the Vicar, having taken a nervy look at the Vatican City, was well on his way to the Forum. Mrs. Jobbin made a good-natured effort to keep him company.

Verity Preston stretched out her long corduroy legs, looked at her boots and wondered why she was there. She was fifty years old but carried about her an air of youth. This was not achieved by manipulation: rather it was as if, inside her middle-aged body, her spirit had neglected to grow old. Until five years ago she had worked in the theatre, on the production side. Then her father, an eminent heart specialist, had died and left Keys House to her with just enough money to enable her to live in it and write plays, which she did from time to time with tolerable success.

She had been born at Keys, she supposed she would die there, and she had gradually fallen into a semi-detached acceptance of the rhythms of life at Upper Quintern, which in spite of war, bombs, crises and inflations had not changed all that much since her childhood. The great difference was that, with the exception of Mr. Nikolas Markos, a newcomer to the district, the gentry had very much less money nowadays and, again with the exception of Mr. Markos, no resident domestic help. Just Mrs. Jim, her niece Beryl, and some dozen lesser ladies who were precariously available and all in hot demand. Mrs. Foster was cunning in securing their services and was thought to cheat by using bribery. She was known, privately, as The Pirate.

It was recognized on all hands that Mrs. Jim was utterly impervious to bribery. Mrs. Foster had tried it once and had invoked a reaction that made her go red in the face whenever she thought of it. It was only by pleading the onset of a genuine attack of lumbago that she had induced Mrs. Jim to return.

Mrs. Foster was a dedicated hypochondriac and nobody would have believed in the lumbago if McBride, the Upper Quintern jobbing gardener, had not confided that he had come across her on the gravelled drive, wearing her best tweeds, hat and gloves and crawling on all fours toward the house. She had been incontinently smitten on her way to the garage.

The Vicar saw himself off at the Leonardo da Vinci airport, said his visit had given him much food for thought and ended on a note of ecumenical wistfulness.

Tea was announced and a mass move to the dining-room accomplished.

"Hullo, Syb," said Verity Preston. "Can I help?"

"Darling!" cried Mrs. Foster. "*Would* you? Would you pour? I simply can't cope. *Such* arthritis! In the wrists."

"Sickening for you."

"Honestly: *too* much. Not a wink all night and this party hanging over one, and Prue's off somewhere watching hang-gliding" (Prunella was Mrs. Foster's daughter) "so she's no use. And to put the final pot on it, ghastly McBride's given notice. Imagine!"

"*McBride* has? Why?"

"He *says* he feels ill. If you ask me it's bloodymindedness."

"Did you have words?" Verity suggested, rapidly filling up cups for ladies to carry off on trays.

"Sort of. Over my picking the japonica. This morning."

"Is he still here? Now?"

"Don't ask me. Probably flounced off. Except that he hasn't been paid. I wouldn't put it past him to be sulking in the toolshed."

"I must say I hope he won't extend his embargo to take me in."

"Oh, dear me, no!" said Mrs. Foster with a hint of acidity. "You're his adored Miss Preston. You, my dear, can't do wrong in McBride's bleary eyes."

"I wish I could believe you. Where will you go for honey, Syb? Advertise or what? Or eat humble pie?"

"Never that! Not on your life! Mrs. *Black!*" cried Mrs. Foster in a voice mellifluous with cordiality, *"how* good of you to come. *Where* are you sitting? Over there, are you? *Good.* Who's died?" she muttered as Mrs. Black moved away. "Why were we told to sympathize?"

"Her husband."

"That's all right then. I wasn't overdoing it."

"Her brother's arrived to live with her."

"He wouldn't happen to be a gardener, I suppose."

Verity put down the tea-pot and stared at her. "You won't believe this," she said, "but I rather think I heard someone say he would. Mrs. Jim, it was. Yes, I'm sure. A gardener."

"My dear! I wonder if he's any good. My dear, *what* a smack in the eye that would be for McBride. Would it be all right to tackle Mrs. Black now, do you think? Just to find out?"

"Well—"

"Darling, you know me. I'll be the soul of tact."

"I bet you will," said Verity.

She watched Mrs. Foster insinuate herself plumply through the crowd. The din was too great for anything she said to be audible but Verity could guess at the compliments sprinkled upon the Vicar, who was a good-looking man, the playful badinage with the village. And all the time, while her pampered little hands dangled from her wrists, Mrs. Foster's pink coiffure tacked this way and that, making toward Mrs. Black, who sat in her bereavement upon a chair at the far end of the room.

Verity, greatly entertained, watched the encounter, the gradual response, the ineffable concern, the wide-open china-blue stare, the compassionate shakes of the head and, finally, the withdrawal of both ladies from the dining-room, no doubt into Syb's boudoir. "Now," thought Verity, "she'll put in the hard tackle."

Abruptly, she was aware of herself being under observation.

Mrs. Jim Jobbin was looking at her and with such a lively expression on her face that Verity felt inclined to wink. It struck her that of all the company present—county, gentry, trade and village, operating within their age-old class structure—it was for Mrs. Jim that she felt the most genuine respect.

Verity poured herself a cup of tea and began, because it was expected of her, to circulate. She was a shy woman but her work in the theatre had helped her to deal with this disadvantage. Moreover, she took a vivid interest in her fellow creatures.

"Miss Preston," Mr. Nikolas Markos had said, the only time they had met, "I believe you look upon us all as raw material," and his black eyes had snapped at her. Although this remark was a variant of the idiotic "don't put me in it," it had not induced the usual irritation. Verity, in fact, had been wondering at that very moment if she could build a black comedy round Upper Quintern ingredients.

She reached the french windows that opened on lawns, walks, rosegardens and an enchanting view across the Weald of Kent.

A little removed from the nearest group, she sipped her tea and gazed with satisfaction at this prospect. She thought that the English landscape, more perhaps than any other, is dyed in the heraldic colours of its own history. It is *there*, she thought, and until it disintegrates, earth, rock, trees, grass: turf by turf, leaf by leaf and blade by blade, it will remain imperturbably itself. To it, she thought, the reed really *is* as the oak and she found the notion reassuring.

She redirected her gaze from the distant prospect to the foreground and became aware of a human rump, elevated above a box hedge in the rose-garden.

The trousers were unmistakable: pepper-and-salt, shapeless, earthy and bestowed upon Angus McBride or purchased by him at some longforgotten jumble sale. He must be doubled up over a treasured seedling, thought Verity. Perhaps he had forgiven Sybil Foster or perhaps, with his lowland Scots rectitude, he was working out his time.

"Lovely view, isn't it?" said the Vicar. He had come alongside Verity, unobserved.

"Isn't it? Although at the moment I was looking at the person behind the box hedge."

"McBride," said the Vicar.

"I thought so, by the trousers."

"I know so. They were once my own."

"Does it," Verity asked, after a longish pause, "strike you that he is sustaining an exacting pose for a very long time?"

"Now you mention it."

"He hasn't stirred."

"Rapt, perhaps, over the wonders of nature," joked the Vicar.

"Perhaps. But he must be doubled over at the waist like a two-foot rule."

"One would say so, certainly."

"He gave Sybil notice this morning on account of health."

"Could he be feeling faint, poor fellow," hazarded the Vicar, "and putting his head between his knees?" And after a moment: "I think I'll go and see."

"I'll come with you," said Verity. "I wanted to look at the rose-garden, in any case."

They went out by the french window and crossed the lawn. The sun had come out and a charming little breeze touched their faces.

As they neared the box hedge the Vicar, who was over six feet tall, said in a strange voice: "It's very odd."

"What is?" Verity asked. Her heart, unaccountably, had begun to knock at her ribs.

"His head's in the wheelbarrow. I fear," said the Vicar, "he's fainted."

But McBride had gone further than that. He was dead.

## II

He had died, the doctor said, of a heart attack and his condition was such that it might have happened anytime over the last year or so. He was thought to have raised the handles of the barrow, been smitten and tipped forward, head first, into the load of compost with which it was filled.

Verity Preston was really sorry. McBride was often maddening and sometimes rude but they shared a love of old-fashioned roses and respected each other. When she had influenza he brought her primroses in a jampot and climbed a ladder to put them on her windowsill. She was touched.

An immediate result of his death was a rush for the services of Mrs. Black's newly arrived brother. Sybil Foster got in first, having already paved the way with his sister. On the very morning after McBride's death, with what Verity Preston considered indecent haste, she paid a follow-up visit to Mrs. Black's cottage under cover of a visit of condolence. Ridiculously inept, Verity considered, as Mr. Black had been dead for at least three weeks and there had been all those fulsomely redundant expressions of sympathy only the previous afternoon. She'd even had the nerve to take white japonica.

When she got home she rang up Verity.

"My dear," she raved, "he's *perfect. So* sweet with that dreary little sister and *such* good manners with me. Called one Madam which is more than—well, never mind. He knew at once what would suit and said he could sense I had an understanding of the 'bonny wee flooers.' He's a Scot."

"Clearly," said Verity.

"But quite a different *kind* of Scot from McBride. Highland, I should think. Anyway—very superior."

"What's he charge?"

"A little bit more," said Sybil rapidly, "but, my dear, the *difference!*"

"References?"

"Any number. They're in his luggage and haven't arrived yet. *Very* grand, I gather."

"So you've taken him on?"

"Darling! What do you think? Mondays and Thursdays. All day. He'll tell me if it needs more. It well may. After all, it's been shamefully neglected—I know you won't agree, of course."

"I suppose I'd better do something about him."

"You'd better hurry. Everybody will be grabbing. I hear Mr. Markos is a man short up at Mardling. Not that I think my Gardener would take an under-gardener's job."

"What's he called?"

"Who?"

"Your gardener."

"You've just said it. Gardener."

"You're joking."

Sybil made an exasperated noise into the receiver.

"So he's gardener-Gardener," said Verity. "Does he hyphenate it?"

"Very funny."

"Oh, come *on*, Syb!"

"All right, my dear, you may scoff. Wait till you see him."

Verity saw him three evenings later. Mrs. Black's cottage was a short distance along the lane from Keys House and she walked to it at six-thirty, by which time Mrs. Black had given her brother his tea. She was a mimbling little woman meekly supporting the prestige of recent widowhood. Perhaps with the object of entrenching herself in this state she spoke in a whimper.

Verity could hear television blaring in the back parlour and said she was sorry to interrupt. Mrs. Black, alluding to her brother as Mr. Gardener, said without conviction that she supposed it didn't matter and she'd tell him he was wanted.

She left the room. Verity stood at the window and saw that the flower-beds had been recently dug over and wondered if it was Mr. Gardener's doing.

He came in: a huge sandy man with a trim golden beard, wide mouth and blue eyes, set far apart, and slightly, not unattractively, strabismic. Altogether a personable figure. He contemplated Verity quizzically from aloft, his head thrown back and slightly to one side and his eyes half-closed.

"I didna just catch the name," he said, "Ma-am."

Verity told him her name and he said: Ou aye, and would she no' tak' a seat.

She said she wouldn't keep him a moment and asked if he could give her one day's gardening a week.

"That'll be the residence a wee piece up the lane, I'm thinking. It's a bonny garden you have there, ma-am. I've taken a keek at it through the entrance. It has what I call perrrsonality. Would it be all of an acre that you have there, now, and an orchard, foreby?"

"Yes. But most of it's grass and that's looked after by a contractor," explained Verity and felt angrily that she was adopting an apologetic, almost a cringing, attitude.

"Ou aye," said Mr. Gardener again. He beamed down upon her. "And I can see fine that it's highly prized by its leddy-mistress."

Verity mumbled self-consciously.

They got down to tin-tacks. Gardener's baggage had arrived. He produced glowing references from, as Sybil had said, grand employers, and photographs of their quellingly superior grounds. He was accustomed, he said, to having at the verra least a young laddie working under him but realized that in coming to keep his sister company in her berrreavement, puir lassie, he would be obliged to dra' in his horns a wee. Ou, aye.

They arrived at wages. No wonder, thought Verity, that Sybil had hurried over the topic: Mr. Gardener required almost twice the pay of Angus McBride. Verity told herself she ought to say she would let him know in the morning and was just about to do so when he mentioned that Friday was the only day he had left and in a panic she suddenly closed with him.

He said he would be glad to work for her. He said he sensed they would get along fine. The general impression was that he preferred to work at a derisive wage for somebody he fancied rather than for a pride of uncongenial millionaires and/or noblemen, however open-handed.

On that note they parted.

Verity walked up the lane through the scents and sounds of a spring evening. She told herself that she could afford Gardener, that clearly he was a highly experienced man and that she would have kicked herself all round her lovely garden if she'd funked employing him and fallen back on the grossly incompetent services of the only other jobbing gardener now available in the district.

But when she had gone in at her gate and walked between burgeoning lime trees up to her house, Verity, being an honest-minded creature, admitted to herself that she had taken a scunner on Mr. Gardener.

As soon as she opened her front door she heard the telephone ringing. It was Sybil, avid to know if Verity had secured his services. When she learnt that the deed had been done she adopted an irritatingly complacent air as if she herself had scored some kind of triumph.

Verity often wondered how it had come about that she and Sybil seemed to be such close friends. They had known each other all their lives, of course, and when they were small had shared the same governess. But later on, when Verity was in London and Sybil, already a young widow, had married her well-heeled, short-lived stockbroker, they seldom met. It was after Sybil was again widowed, being left with Prunella and a highly unsatisfactory stepson from her first marriage, that they picked up the threads of their friendship. Really, they had little in common.

Their friendship, in fact, was a sort of hardy perennial, reappearing when it was least expected to do so.

The horticultural analogy occurred to Verity while Sybil gushed away about Gardener. He had started with her that very day, it transpired, and, my dear, the *difference!* And the *imagination!* And the *work:* the sheer *hard work.* She raved on. She really is a bit of an ass, is poor old Syb, Verity thought.

"And don't you find his Scots *rather* beguiling?" Sybil was asking.

"Why doesn't his sister do it?"

"Do what, dear?"

"Talk Scots?"

"Good Heavens, Verity, how should I know? Because she came south and married a man of Kent, I daresay. Black spoke broad Kentish."

"So he did," agreed Verity pacifically.

"I've got news for you."

"Have you?"

"You'll never guess. An invitation. From *Mardling Manor*, no less," said Sybil in a put-on drawing-room-comedy voice.

"Really?"

"For dinner. Next Wednesday. He rang up this morning. Rather unconventional if one's to stickle, I suppose, but that sort of tommy-rot's as dead as the dodo in my book. And we *have* met. When he lent Mardling for that hospital fund-raising garden-party. Nobody went inside, of course. I'm told lashings of lolly have been poured out—

redecorated, darling, from attic to cellar. You were there, weren't you? At the garden-party?"

"Yes."

"Yes. I was sure you were. Rather intriguing, I thought, didn't you?"

"I hardly spoke to him," said Verity inaccurately.

"I hoped you'd been asked," said Sybil much more inaccurately.

"Not I. I expect you'll have gorgeous grub."

"I don't know that it's a *party*."

"Just you?"

"My dear. Surely not! But no. Prue's come home. She's met the son somewhere and so she's been asked: to balance him, I suppose. Well," said Sybil on a dashing note, "we shall see what we shall see."

"Have a lovely time. How's the arthritis?"

"Oh, *you* know. Pretty ghastly, but I'm learning to live with it. Nothing else to be done, is there? If it's not that it's my migraine."

"I thought Dr. Field-Innis had given you something for the migraine."

"Hopeless, my dear. If you ask me Field-Innis is getting beyond it. *And* he's become very off-hand, I don't mind telling you."

Verity half-listened to the so-familiar plaints. Over the years Sybil had consulted a procession of general practitioners and in each instance enthusiasm had dwindled into discontent. It was only because there were none handy, Verity sometimes thought, that Syb had escaped falling into the hands of some plausible quack.

"—and I had considered," she was saying, "taking myself off to Greengages for a fortnight. It does quite buck me up, that place."

"Yes: why don't you?"

"I think I'd like to just be *here*, though, while Mr. Gardener gets the place into shape."

"One calls him 'Mr. Gardener,' then?"

"Verity, he *is* very superior. Anyway, I hate those old snobby distinctions. You don't, evidently."

"I'll call him the Duke of Plaza-Toro if he'll get rid of my weeds."

"I really must go," Sybil suddenly decided as if Verity had been preventing her from doing so. "I can't make up my mind about Greengages."

Greengages was an astronomically expensive establishment: a hotel with a resident doctor and a sort of valetudinarian sideline where weight was reduced by the exaction of a deadly diet while appetites were stimulated by compulsory walks over a rather dreary countryside. If Sybil decided to go there, Verity would be expected to drive through twenty miles of dense traffic to take a luncheon of inflationary soup and a concoction of liver and tomatoes garnished with mushrooms to which she was uproariously allergic.

She had no sooner hung up her receiver than the telephone rang again.

"Damn," said Verity, who hankered after her cold duck and salad and the telly.

A vibrant male voice asked if she were herself and on learning that she was, said it was Nikolas Markos speaking.

"Is this a bad time to ring you up?" Mr. Markos asked. "Are you telly-watching or thinking about your dinner, for instance?"

"Not quite yet."

"But almost, I suspect. I'll be quick. Would you like to dine here next Wednesday? I've been trying to get you all day. Say you will, like a kind creature. Will you?"

He spoke as if they were old friends and Verity, accustomed to this sort of approach in the theatre, responded.

"Yes," she said. "I will. I'd like to. Thank you. What time?"

## III

Nobody in Upper Quintern knew much about Nikolas Markos. He was reputed to be fabulously rich, widowed and a financier. Oil was mentioned as the almost inescapable background. When Mardling Manor came on the market Mr. Markos had bought it and when Verity went to dine with him, had been in residence, off and on, for about four months.

Mardling was an ugly house. It had been built in mid-Victorian times on the site of a Jacobean mansion. It was large, pepper-potted and highly inconvenient: not a patch on Sybil Foster's Quintern Place, which was exquisite. The best that could be said of Mardling was that, however hideous, it looked clumsily important both inside and out.

As Verity drove up she saw Sybil's Mercedes parked alongside a number of other cars. The front door opened before she got to it and revealed that obsolete phenomenon, a manservant.

While she was being relieved of her coat she saw that even the ugliest of halls can be made beautiful by beautiful possessions. Mr. Markos had covered the greater part of the stupidly carved walls with smoky tapestries. These melted upward into an almost invisible gallery and relinquished the dominant position above an enormous fireplace to a picture. Such a picture! An imperious quattrocento man, life-size, ablaze in a scarlet cloak on a round-rumped charger. The rider pointed his sword at an immaculate little Tuscan town.

Verity was so struck with the picture that she was scarcely conscious that behind her a door had opened and closed.

"Ah!" said Nikolas Markos, "you like my arrogant equestrian? Or are you merely surprised by him?"

"Both," said Verity.

His handshake was quick and perfunctory. He wore a green velvet coat. His hair was dark, short and curly at the back. His complexion was sallow and his eyes black. His mouth, under a slight moustache, seemed to contradict the almost too plushy ensemble: it was slim-lipped and, Verity thought, extremely firm.

"Is it an Uccello?" she asked, turning back to the picture.

"I like to think so, but it's a borderline case. 'School of' is all the pundits will allow me."

"It's extraordinarily exciting."

"Isn't it, just? I'm glad you like it. And delighted, by the way, that you've come."

Verity was overtaken by one of her moments of middle-aged shyness. "Oh. Good," she mumbled.

"We're nine for dinner: my son, Gideon, a Dr. Basil Schramm who's yet to arrive, and you know all the rest: Mrs. Foster and her daughter, the Vicar (*she's* indisposed) and Dr. and Mrs. Field-Innis. Come and join them."

Verity's recollection of the drawing-room at Mardling was of a great ungainly apartment, over-furnished and nearly always chilly. She found herself in a bird's-egg blue and white room, sparkling with firelight and a welcoming elegance.

There, expansively on a sofa, was Sybil at her most feminine, and that was saying a great deal. Hair, face, pampered little hands, jewels, dress and, if you got close enough, scent—they all came together like the ingredients of some exotic pudding. She fluttered a minute handkerchief at Verity and pulled an arch grimace.

"This is Gideon," said Mr. Markos.

He was even darker than his father and startlingly handsome. "My dear, an Adonis," Sybil was to say of him and later was to add that there was "something" wrong and that she was never deceived, she sensed it at once, let Verity mark her words. When asked to explain herself she said it didn't matter but she always *knew*. Verity thought that she knew, too. Sybil was hell-bent on her daughter Prunella encouraging the advances of a hereditary peer with the unlikely name of Swingletree and took an instant dislike to any attractive young man who hove into view.

Gideon looked about twenty, was poised and had nice manners. His

black hair was not very long and was well kept. Like his father he wore
a velvet coat. The only note of extravagance was in the frilled shirt and
flowing tie. These lent a final touch to what might have been an unendurably romantic appearance but Gideon had enough natural manner
to get away with them.

He had been talking to Prunella Foster, who was like her mother at
the same age: ravishingly pretty and a great talker. Verity never knew
what Prunella talked about as she always spoke in a whisper. She nodded a lot and gave mysterious little smiles and, because it was the fashion of the moment, seemed to be dressed in expensive rags partly composed of a patchwork quilt. Under this supposedly evening attire she
wore a little pair of bucket boots.

Dr. Field-Innis was an old Upper Quintern hand. The younger son
of a brigadier, he had taken to medicine instead of arms and had married a lady who sometimes won point-to-points and more often fell off.

The Vicar was called Walter Cloudsley, and ministered, a little
sadly, to twenty parishioners in a very beautiful old church that had
once housed three hundred.

Altogether, Verity thought, this was a predictable Upper Quintern
dinner-party with an unpredictable host in a highly exceptional setting.

They drank champagne cocktails.

Sybil, sparkling, told Mr. Markos how clever he was and went into
an ecstasy over the house. She had a talent that never failed to tickle
Verity's fancy for making the most unexceptionable remark to a gentleman sound as if it carried some frisky innuendo. She sketched an invitation for him to join her on the sofa but he seemed not to notice it. He
stood over her and replied in kind. "Later on," Verity thought, "she
will tell me, he's a man of the world."

He moved to his hearthrug and surveyed his guests with an air of
satisfaction. "This is great fun," he said. "My first Quintern venture.
Really, it's a kind of christening party for the house, isn't it? What a
good thing you could come, Vicar."

"I certainly give it my blessing," the Vicar hardily countered. He was
enjoying a second champagne cocktail.

"And, by the way, the party won't be undiluted Quintern. There's
somebody still to come. I do hope he's not going to be late. He's a man
I ran across in New York, a Doctor Basil Schramm. I found him—" Mr.
Markos paused and an odd little smile touched his mouth, "quite interesting. He rang up out of a clear sky this morning, saying he was
going to take up a practice somewhere in our part of the world and was
driving there this evening. We discovered that his route would bring
him through Upper Quintern and on the spur of the moment I asked

him to dine. He'll unbalance the table a bit but I hope nobody's going to blench at that."

"An American?" asked Mrs. Field-Innis. She had a hoarse voice.

"He's Swiss by birth, I fancy."

"Is he taking a locum," asked Dr. Field-Innis, "or a permanent practice?"

"The latter I supposed. At some hotel or nursing home or convalescent place or something of the sort. Green—something."

"*Not* 'gages'!" cried Sybil, softly clapping her hands.

"I knew it made me think of indigestion. Greengages it is," said Mr. Markos.

"Oh," said Dr. Field-Innis. "That place."

Much was made of this coincidence, if it could be so called. The conversation drifted to gardeners. Sybil excitedly introduced her find. Mr. Markos became grand signorial and, when Gideon asked if they hadn't taken on a new man, said they had but he didn't know what he was called. Verity, who, apolitical at heart, drifted guiltily from left to right and back again, felt her redder hackles rising. She found that Mr. Markos was looking at her in a manner that gave her the sense of having been rumbled.

Presently he drew a chair up to hers.

"I very much enjoyed your play," he said. "Your best, up to date, I thought."

"Did you? Good."

"It's very clever of you to be civilized as well as penetrating. I wanted to ask you, though—"

He talked intelligently about her play. It suddenly dawned on Verity that there was nobody in Upper Quintern with whom she ever discussed her work and she felt as if she spoke the right lines in the wrong theatre. She heard herself eagerly discussing her play and fetched up abruptly.

"I'm talking shop," she said. "Sorry."

"Why? What's wrong with shop? Particularly when your shop's one of the arts."

"Is yours?"

"Oh," he said, "mine's as dull as ditchwater." He looked at his watch. "Schramm *is* late," he said. "Lost in the Weald of Kent, I daresay. We shall not wait for him. Tell me—"

He started off again. The butler came in. Verity expected him to announce dinner but he said, "Dr. Schramm, sir."

When Dr. Schramm walked into the room it seemed to shift a little.

Her mouth dried. She waited through an unreckoned interval for Nikolas Markos to arrive at her as he performed the introductions.

"But we have already met," said Dr. Schramm. "Some time ago."

## IV

Twenty-five years to be exact, Verity thought. It was ludicrous—grotesque almost—after twenty-five years, to be put out by his reappearance.

"Somebody should say: 'what a small world,'" said Dr. Schramm.

He had always made remarks like that. And laughed like that and touched his moustache.

"He didn't know me at first," she thought. "That'll larn me."

He had moved on toward the fire with Mr. Markos and been given, in quick succession, two cocktails. Verity heard him explain how he'd missed the turn-off to Upper Quintern.

"But why 'Schramm,'" she wondered. "He could have hyphenated himself if 'Smythe' wasn't good enough. And 'Doctor'? So he qualified after all."

"Very difficult country," Mrs. Field-Innis said. She had been speaking for some time.

"Very," Verity agreed fervently and was stared at.

Dinner was announced.

She was afraid they might find themselves together at the table but after, or so she fancied, a moment's hesitation, Mr. Markos put Schramm between Sybil and Dr. Field-Innis, who was on Verity's right with the Vicar on her left. Mr. Markos himself was on Sybil's right. It was a round table.

She managed quite well at dinner. The Vicar was at all times prolific in discourse and being of necessity, as well as by choice, of an abstemious habit, he was a little flown with unaccustomed wine. Dr. Field-Innis was also in talkative form. He coruscated with anecdotes concerning high jinks in his student days.

On his far side, Dr. Schramm, whose glass had been twice replenished, was much engaged with Sybil Foster, which meant that he was turned away from Dr. Field-Innis and Verity. He bent toward Sybil, laughed a great deal at everything she said and established an atmosphere of flirtatious understanding. This stabbed Verity with the remembrance of long-healed injuries. It had been his technique when he wished to show her how much another woman pleased him. He had used it at the theatre in the second row of the stalls, prolonging his laughter beyond the rest of the audience so that she, as well as the actress concerned, might become aware of him. She realized that even now, idiotically after twenty-five years, he aimed his performance at her.

Sybil, she knew, although she had not looked at them, was bringing out her armory of delighted giggles and upward glances.

"And then," said the Vicar, who had returned to Rome, "there was the Villa Julia. I can't describe to you—"

In turning to him, Verity found herself under observation from her host. Perhaps because the Vicar had now arrived at the Etruscans, it occurred to Verity that there was something knowing about Mr. Markos's smile. You wouldn't diddle that one in a hurry, she thought.

Evidently he had asked Mrs. Field-Innis to act as hostess. When the port had gone round once she surveyed the ladies and barked out orders to retire.

Back in the drawing-room it became evident that Dr. Schramm had made an impression. Sybil lost no time in tackling Verity. Why, she asked, had she never been told about him? Had Verity known him well? Was he married?

"I've no idea. It was a thousand years ago," Verity said. "He was one of my father's students, I think. I ran up against him at some training-hospital party as far as I can remember."

Remember? He had watched her for half the evening and then, when an "Excuse me" dance came along, had relieved her of an unwieldy first-year student and monopolized her for the rest of the evening.

She turned to the young Prunella, whose godmother she was, and asked what she was up to these days, and made what she could of a reply that for all she heard of it might have been in mime.

"Did you catch any of that?" asked Prunella's mother wearily.

Prunella giggled. Verity reminded herself that the child had taken second class honours in English at Somerville.

"I think I may be getting deaf," she said.

Prunella shook her head vigorously and became audible. "Not you, Godmama V," she said. "Tell us about your super chum. What a dish!"

"*Prue*," expostulated Sybil, punctual as clockwork.

"Well, Mum, he is," said her daughter, relapsing into her whisper. "And you can't talk, darling," she added. "You gobbled him up like a turkey."

Mrs. Field-Innis said: "Really!" and spoilt the effect by bursting into a gruff laugh.

To Verity's relief this passage had the effect of putting a stop to further enquiries about Dr. Schramm. The ladies discussed local topics until they were joined by the gentlemen.

Verity had wondered whether anybody—their host or the Vicar or Dr. Field-Innis—had questioned Schramm, as she had been questioned, about their former acquaintanceship and if so, how he had answered and whether he would think it advisable to come and speak to her. After all, it would look strange if he did not.

He did come. Nikolas Markos, keeping up the deployment of his guests, so arranged it. Schramm sat beside her and the first thought that crossed her mind was that there was something unbecoming about not seeming, at first glance, to have grown old. If he had appeared to her, as she undoubtedly did to him, as a greatly changed person, she would have been able to get their confrontation into perspective. As it was he sat there like a hangover. His face at first glance was scarcely changed although when he turned it into a stronger light, a system of lines seemed to flicker under the skin. His eyes were more protuberant now, and slightly bloodshot. A man, she thought, of whom people would say he could hold his liquor. He used the stuff she remembered on hair that was only vestigially thinner at the temples.

As always he was, as people used to say twenty-five years ago, extremely well turned out. He carried himself like a soldier.

"How are you, Verity?" he said. "You look blooming."

"I'm very well, thank you."

"Writing plays, I hear."

"That's it."

"Absolutely splendid. I must go and see one. There is one, isn't there? In London?"

"At the Dolphin."

"Good houses?"

"Full," said Verity.

"Really! So they wouldn't let me in. Unless you told them to. Would you tell them to? Please?"

He bent his head toward her in the old way. "Why on earth," she thought, "does he bother?"

"I'm afraid they wouldn't pay much attention," she said.

"Were you surprised to see me?"

"I was, rather."

"Why?"

"Well—"

"Well?"

"The name, for one thing."

"Oh, that!" he said, waving his hand. "That's an old story. It's my mother's maiden name. Swiss. She always wanted me to use it. Put it in her Will if you'll believe it. She suggested that I make myself 'Smythe-Schramm' but that turned out to be such a wet mouthful I decided to get rid of Smythe."

"I see."

"So I qualified after all, Verity."

"Yes."

"From Lausanne, actually. My mother had settled there and I joined her. I got quite involved with that side of the family and decided to finish my course in Switzerland."

"I see."

"I practised there for some time—until she died, to be exact. Since then I've wandered about the world. One can always find something to do as a medico." He talked away, fluently. It seemed to Verity that he spoke in phrases that followed each other with the ease of frequent usage. He went on for some time, making, she thought, little sorties against her self-possession. She was surprised to find how ineffectual they proved to be. "Come," she thought, "I'm over the initial hurdle at least" and began to wonder what all the fuss was about.

"And now you're settling in Kent," she said, politely.

"Looks like it. A sort of hotel-cum-convalescent home. I've made rather a thing of dietetics—specialized, actually—and this place offers the right sort of scene. Greengages, it's called. Do you know it at all?"

"Sybil—Mrs. Foster—goes there quite often."

"Yes," he said. "So she tells me."

He looked at Sybil, who sat, discontentedly, beside the Vicar. Verity had realized that Sybil was observant of them. She now flashed a meaningful smile at Schramm as if she and he shared some exquisite joke.

Gideon Markos said: "Pop, may I show Prue your latest extravagance?"

"Do," said his father. "By all means."

When they had gone he said: "Schramm, I can't have you monopolizing Miss Preston like this. You've had a lovely session and must restrain your remembrance of things past. I'm going to move you on."

He moved him on to Mrs. Field-Innis and took his place by Verity.

"Gideon tells me," he said, "that when I have company to dine I'm bossy, old hat and a stuffed shirt or whatever the 'in' phrase is. But what should I do? Invite my guests to wriggle and jerk to one of his deafening records?"

"It might be fun to see the Vicar and Florence Field-Innis having a go."

"Yes," he said with a sidelong glance at her, "it might, indeed.

Would you like to hear about my 'latest extravagance'? You would? It's a picture. A Troy."

"From her show at the Arlington?"

"That's right."

"How lovely for you. Which one? Not by any chance *Several Pleasures?*"

"But you're brilliant!"

"It *is?*"

"Come and look."

He took her into the library, a large library it was, and still under renovation. Gideon and Prunella were nowhere to be seen. Open cases of books stood about the floors. The walls, including the backs of shelves, had been redone in a lacquer-red Chinese paper. The Troy painting stood on the chimney piece: a glowing flourish of exuberance, all swings and roundabouts.

"You *do* collect lovely pictures," she said.

"Oh, I'm a dedicated magpie. I even collect stamps."

"Seriously?"

"Passionately," he said. He half-closed his eyes and contemplated his picture.

Verity said: "You're going to hang it where it is, are you?"

"I think so. But whatever I do with it in this silly house is bound to be a compromise," he said.

"Does that matter very much?"

"Yes, it does. I lust," said Mr. Markos, "after Quintern Place."

He said this with such passion that Verity stared at him. "Do you?" she said. "It's a lovely house, of course. But just seeing it from the outside—"

"Ah, but I've seen it from inside, too."

Verity thought what a slyboots old Syb was not to have divulged this visit but he went on to say that on a house-hunting drive through Kent he saw Quintern Place from afar and had been so struck that he had himself driven up to it there and then.

"Mrs. Foster," he said, "was away but a domestic was persuaded to let me catch a glimpse of the ground floor. It was enough. I visited the nearest land agency only to be told that Quintern was not on their or anybody else's books and that former enquiries had led to the flattest of refusals. Mine suffered a like fate: there was no intention to sell. So, you may say that in a fit of pique, I bought this monster where I can sit down before my citadel in a state of fruitless siege."

"Does Sybil know about all this?"

"Not she. The approach has been discreet. Be a dear," said Mr. Markos, "and don't tell her."

"All right."

"How nice you are."

"But I'm afraid you haven't a hope."

"One can but try," he said and Verity thought if ever she saw fixity of purpose in a human face, she saw it now, in Mr. Markos's.

## V

As she drove home, Verity tried to sort out the events of the evening but had not got far with them, when at the bottom of the drive, her headlamps picked up a familiar trudging figure. She pulled up alongside.

"Hullo, Mrs. Jim," she said. "Nip in and I'll take you home."

"It's out of your way, Miss Preston."

"Doesn't matter. Come on."

"Very kind, I'm sure. I won't say no," said Mrs. Jim.

She got in neatly and quickly but settled in her seat with a kind of relinquishment of her body that suggested fatigue. Verity asked her if she'd had a long day and she said she had, a bit.

"But the money's good," said Mrs. Jim, "and with Jim on half-time you can't say no. There's always something," she added and Verity understood that she referred to the cost of living.

"Do they keep a big staff up there?" she asked.

"Five if you count the housekeeper. Like the old days," Mrs. Jim said, "when I was in regular service. You don't see much of them ways now, do you? Like I said to Jim: they're selling the big houses when they can, for institutions and that. Not trying all out to buy them, like Mr. Markos."

"Is Mr. Markos doing that?"

"He'd like to have Quintern," said Mrs. Jim. "He come to ask if it was for sale when Mrs. Foster was at Greengages a year ago. He was that taken with it, you could see. I was helping spring-clean at the time."

"Did Mrs. Foster know?"

"He never left 'is name. I told her a gentleman had called to enquire, of course. It give me quite a turn when I first seen him after he come to the Manor."

"Did you tell Mrs. Foster it was he who'd called?"

"I wasn't going out to Quintern Place at the time," said Mrs. Jim shortly and Verity remembered that there had been a rift.

"It come up this evening in conversation. Mr. Alfredo, that's the butler," Mrs. Jim continued, "reckons Mr. Markos is still dead set on Quintern. He says he's never known him not to get his way once he's made up his mind to it. You're suited with a gardener, then?"

Mrs. Jim had a habit of skipping without notice from one topic to another. Verity thought she detected a derogatory note but could not be sure. "He's beginning on Friday," she said. "Have you met him, Mrs. Jim?"

"Couldn't miss 'im, could I?" she said, rubbing her arthritic knee. "Annie Black's been taking him up and down the village like he was Exhibit A in the horse show."

"He'll be company for her."

"He's all of that," she said cryptically.

Verity turned into the narrow lane where the Jobbins had their cottage. When they arrived no light shone in any of the windows. Jim and the kids all fast asleep, no doubt. Mrs. Jim was slower leaving the car than she had been in entering it and Verity sensed her weariness. "Have you got an early start?" she asked.

"Quintern at eight. It was very kind of you to bring me home, Miss Preston. Ta, anyway. I'll say goodnight."

That's two of us going home to a dark house, Verity thought, as she turned the car.

But being used to living alone, she didn't mind letting herself into Keys House and feeling for the light switch.

When she was in bed she turned over the events of the evening and a wave of exhaustion came upon her together with a nervous condition she thought of as "restless legs." She realized that the encounter with Basil Schramm (as she supposed she should call him) had been more of an ordeal than she had acknowledged at the time. The past rushed upon her, almost with the injuriousness of her initial humiliation. She made herself relax, physically, muscle by muscle and then tried to think of nothing.

She did not think of nothing but she thought of thinking of nothing and almost, but not quite, lost the feeling of some kind of threat waiting offstage like the return of a baddie in one of the old moralities. And at last after sundry heart-stopping jerks she fell asleep.

# CHAPTER II

# Greengages (I)

## I

THERE WERE NO two ways about it, Gardener was a good gardener. He paid much more attention to his employers' quirks and fancies than McBride had ever done and he was a conscientious worker.

When he found his surname caused Verity some embarrassment, he laughed and said it wad be a' the same to him if she calt him by his first name, which was Brrruce. Verity herself was no Scot but she couldn't help thinking his dialect was laid on with a trowel. However, she availed herself of the offer and Bruce he became to all his employers. Praise of him rose high in Upper Quintern. The wee laddie he had found in the village was nearly six feet tall and not quite all there. One by one, as weeks and then months went by, Bruce's employers yielded to the addition of the laddie with the exception of Mr. Markos's head gardener, who was adamant against him.

Sybil Foster continued to rave about Bruce. Together they pored over nurserymen's catalogues. At the end of his day's work at Quintern he was given a pint of beer and Sybil often joined him in the staff sitting-room to talk over plans. When odd jobs were needed indoors he proved to be handy and willing.

"He's such a comfort," she said to Verity. "And, my dear, the energy of the man! He's made up his mind I'm to have home-grown asparagus and has dug two enormous deep, deep graves, beyond the tennis court of all places, and is going to fill them up with all sorts of stuff—seaweed, if you can believe me. The maids have fallen for him in a big way, thank God."

She alluded to her "outside help," a girl from the village and Beryl, Mrs. Jim's niece. Both, according to Sybil, doted on Bruce and she hinted that Beryl actually had designs. Mrs. Jim remained cryptic on the subject. Verity gathered that she thought Bruce "hated himself," which meant that he was conceited.

Dr. Basil Schramm had vanished from Upper Quintern as if he had never appeared there and Verity, after a time, was almost, but not quite, able to get rid of him.

The decorators had at last finished their work at Mardling and Mr. Markos was believed to have gone abroad. Gideon, however, came down from London on most week-ends, often bringing a house-party with him. Mrs. Jim reported that Prunella Foster was a regular attendant at these parties. Under this heading Sybil displayed a curiously ambivalent attitude. She seemed, on the one hand, to preen herself on what appeared, in her daughter's highly individual argot, to be a "grab." On the other hand she continued to drop dark, incomprehensible hints about Gideon: all based, as far as Verity could make out, on an infallible instinct. Verity wondered if, after all, Sybil merely entertained some form of maternal jealousy: it was O.K. for Prue to be all set about with ardent young men: but was it less gratifying if she took a fancy to one of them? Or was it, simply, that Sybil had set her sights on the undynamic Lord Swingletree for Prue?

"Of course, darling," she confided on the telephone one day, "there's lots of lovely lolly but you know me, that's not everything, and one doesn't know, does one, anything *at all* about the background. Crimpy hair and black eyes and large noses. Terribly good-looking, I grant you, like profiles on old pots, but what is one to think?" And sensing Verity's reaction to this observation she added hurriedly: "I don't mean what you mean, as you very well know."

Verity said: "Is Prue serious, do you suppose?"

"Don't ask me," said Sybil irritably. "She whispers away about him. Just when I was so pleased about John Swingletree. *Devoted*, my dear. All I can say is it's playing havoc with my health. Not a wink last night and I dread my back. She sees a lot of him in London. I prefer not to know what goes on there. I really can't take much more, Verry. I'm going to Greengages."

"When?" asked Verity, conscious of a jolt under her ribs.

"My dear, on Monday. I'm hoping your chum can do something for me."

"I hope so, too."

"What did you say? Your voice sounded funny."

"I hope it'll do the trick."

"I wrote to him, personally, and he answered at once. A charming letter, so understanding and informal."

"Good."

When Sybil prevaricated she always spoke rapidly and pitched her voice above its natural register. She did so now and Verity would have taken long odds that she fingered the hair at the back of her head.

"Darling," she gabbled, "you couldn't give me a boiled egg, could you? For lunch? Tomorrow?"

"Of course I could," said Verity.

She was surprised, when Sybil arrived, to find that she really did look unwell. She was a bad colour and clearly had lost weight. But apart from that there was a look—how to define it?—a kind of blankness, of a mask almost. It was a momentary impression and Verity wondered if she had only imagined she saw it. She asked Sybil if she'd seen a doctor and was given a fretful account of a visit to the clinic in Great Quintern, the nearest town. An unknown practitioner, she said, had "rushed over her" with his stethoscope, "pumped up her arm" and turned her on to a dim nurse for other indignities. Her impression had been one of complete professional detachment. "One might have been drafted, darling, into some yard, for all he cared. The deadliest of little men with a signet ring on the wrong finger. All right, I'm a snob," said Sybil crossly and jabbed at her cutlet.

Presently she reverted to her gardener. Bruce as usual had been "perfect," it emerged. He had noticed that Sybil looked done up and had brought her some early turnips as a present. "Mark my words," she said. "There's something *in* that man. You may look sceptical, but there is."

"If I look sceptical it's only because I don't understand. What sort of thing is there in Bruce?"

"You know *very* well what I mean. To be perfectly frank and straightforward—breeding. Remember," said Sybil surprisingly, "Ramsay MacDonald."

"Do you think Bruce is a blue-blooded bastard? Is that it?"

"Stranger things have happened," said Sybil darkly. She eyed Verity for a moment or two and then said airily: "He's not very comfortable with the dreary little Black sister—tiny dark room and nowhere to put his things."

"Oh?"

"Yes. I've been considering," said Sybil rapidly, "the possibility of housing him in the stable block—you know, the old coachman's quarters. They'd have to be done up, of course. It'd be a good idea to have somebody on the premises when we're away."

"You'd better watch it, old girl," Verity said, "or you'll find yourself doing a Queen Victoria to Bruce's Brown."

"Don't be ridiculous," said Sybil.

She tried without success to get Verity to fix a day when she would come to a weight-reducing luncheon at Greengages.

"I do think it's the least you can do," she said piteously. "I'll be segregated among a tribe of bores and dying for gossip. And besides you can bring me news of Prue."

"But I don't see Prue in the normal course of events."

"Ask her to lunch, darling. *Do.*"

"Syb, she'd be bored to sobs."

"She'd adore it. You *know* she thinks you're marvellous. It's odds-on she'll confide in you. After all, you're her godmother."

"It doesn't follow as the night the day. And if she should confide I wouldn't hear what she said."

"There *is* that difficulty, I know," Sybil conceded. "You must tell her to scream. After all, her friends seem to hear her. Gideon Markos does, presumably. And that's not all."

"Not all what?"

"All my woe. Guess who's turned up?"

"I can't imagine. *Not,*" Verity exclaimed on a note of real dismay. "*Not* Charmless Claude? Don't tell me!"

"I do tell you. He left Australia weeks ago and is working his way home on a ship called *Poseidon.* As a steward. I've had a letter."

The young man Sybil referred to was Claude Carter, her stepson: a left-over from her first marriage in whose favour not even Verity could find much to say.

"Oh, Syb," she said, "I *am* sorry."

"He wants me to forward a hundred pounds to Teneriffe."

"Is he coming to Quintern?"

"My dear, he doesn't say so but of course he will. Probably with the police in hot pursuit."

"Does Prue know?"

"I've told her. Horrified, of course. She's going to make a bolt to London when the time comes. This is why, on top of everything else, I'm hell-bent for Greengages."

"Will he want to stay?"

"I expect so. He usually does. I can't stop that."

"Of course not. After all—"

"Verry: he gets the very generous allowance his father left him and blows the lot. I'm always having to yank him out of trouble. And what's more—absolutely for your ears alone—when I pop off he gets everything his father left me for my lifetime. God knows what he'll do with it. He's been in gaol and I daresay he dopes. I'll go on paying up, I suppose."

"So he'll arrive and find—who?"

"Either Beryl, who's caretaking, or Mrs. Jim, who's relieving her and spring-cleaning, or Bruce, if it's one of his days. They're all under strict instruction to say I'm away ill and not seeing anybody. If he insists on being put up nobody can stop him. Of course he might—" There followed a long pause. Verity's mind misgave her.

"Might what?" she said.

"Darling, I wouldn't know but he *might* call on you. Just to enquire."

"What," said Verity, "do you want me to do?"

"Just not tell him where I am. And then let me know and come to Greengages. Don't just ring or write, Verry. Come. Verry, as my oldest friend, I ask you."

"I don't promise."

"No, but you will. You'll come to awful lunch with me at Greengages and tell me what Prue says and whether Charmless Claude has called. Think! You'll meet your gorgeous boy-friend again."

"I don't want to."

As soon as she had made this disclaimer, Verity realized it was a mistake. She visualized the glint of insatiable curiosity in Sybil's large blue eyes and knew she had aroused the passion that, second only to her absorption in gentlemen, consumed her friend: a devouring interest in other people's affairs.

"*Why* not?" Sybil said quickly. "I knew there was something. That night at Nikolas Markos's dinner-party. I sensed it. What was it?"

Verity pulled herself together. "Now, then," she said. "None of that. Don't you go making up nonsenses about me."

"There *was* something," Sybil repeated. "I'm never wrong. I sensed there was something. I know!" she sang out, "I'll ask Basil Schramm— Dr. Schramm, I mean—himself. He'll tell me."

"You'll do nothing of the sort," Verity said and tried not to sound panic-stricken. She added, too late, "He wouldn't know what on earth you were driving at. Syb—please don't go making a fool of me. And of yourself."

"*Tum-te-tiddily, tum-te-tee,*" sang Sybil idiotically. "See what a tizzy we've got into."

Verity kept her temper.

Wild horses, she decided, would not drag her to luncheon at Greengages. She saw Sybil off with the deepest misgivings.

## II

Gideon Markos and Prunella Foster lay on a magnificent hammock under a striped canopy beside the brand-new swimming pool at Mardling Manor. They were brown, wet and almost nude. Her white-gold hair fanned across his chest. He held her lightly as if some photographer had posed them for a glossy advertisement.

"Because," Prunella whispered, "I don't want to."

"I don't believe you. You do. Clearly, you want me. Why pretend?"

"All right, then. I do. But I'm not going to. I don't choose to."

"But why, for God's sake? Oh," said Gideon with a change of voice, "I suppose I know. I suppose, in a way, I understand. It's the 'too rash, too ill-advised, too sudden' bit. Is that it? What?" he asked, bending his head to hers. "What did you say? Speak up."

"I like you too much."

"Darling Prue, it's extremely nice of you to like me too much but it doesn't get us anywhere: now, does it?"

"It's not meant to."

Gideon put his foot to the ground and swung the hammock violently. Prunella's hair blew across his mouth.

"Don't," she said and giggled. "We'll capsize. Stop."

"No."

"I'll fall off. I'll be sick."

"Say you'll reconsider the matter."

"Gideon, *please.*"

"Say it."

"I'll reconsider the matter, damn you."

He checked the hammock but did not release her.

"But I'll come to the same conclusion," said Prunella. "No, darling. Not again! *Don't.* Honestly, I'll be sick. I promise you I'll be sick."

"You do the most dreadful things to me," Gideon muttered after an interval. "You beastly girl."

"I'm going in again before the sun's off the pool."

"Prunella, are you really fond of me? Do you think about me when we're not together?"

"Quite often."

"Very well, then, would you like—would you care to entertain the idea—I mean, couldn't we try it out? To see if we suit?"

"How do you mean?"

"Well—in my flat? Together. You like my flat, don't you? Give it, say, a month and then consider?"

She shook her head.

"I could beat you like a gong," said Gideon. "Oh, come *on*, Prunella, for Christ's sake. Give me a straight answer to a straight question. Are you fond of me?"

"I think you're fantastic. You know I do. Like I said: I'm too fond of you for a jolly affair. Too fond to face it all turning out to be a dead failure and us going back to square one and wishing we hadn't tried. We've seen it happen among the chums, haven't we? Everything super to begin with. And then the not-so-hot situation develops."

"Fair enough. One finds out and no bones broken, which is a damn sight better than having to plough through the divorce court. Well, isn't it?"

"It's logical and civilized and liberated but it's just not on for me. No way. I must be a throw-back or simply plain chicken. I'm sorry. Darling Gideon," said Prunella, suddenly kissing him. "Like the song said: 'I do, I do, I do, I do.'"

"What?"

"Love you," she mumbled in a hurry. "There. I've said it."

"*God!*" said Gideon with some violence. "It's not fair. Look here, Prue. Let's be engaged. Just nicely and chastely and frustratingly engaged to be married and you can break it off whenever you want to. And I'll swear, if you like, not to pester you with my ungentlemanly attentions. No. Don't answer. Think it over and in the meantime, like Donne says, 'for God's sake hold your tongue and let me love.'"

"He didn't say it to the lady. He said it to some irritating acquaintance."

"Come here."

The sun-baked landscape moved into late afternoon. Over at Quintern Place Bruce, having dug a further and deeper asparagus bed, caused the wee lad, whose name was Daft Artie, to fill it up with compost, fertilizer and soil while he himself set to work again with his long-handled shovel. Comprehensive drainage and nutrition were needed if his and his employer's plans were to be realized.

Twenty miles away at Greengages in the Weald of Kent, Dr. Basil Schramm completed yet another examination of Sybil Foster. She had introduced into her room a sort of overflow of her own surplus femininity: be-ribboned pillows, cushions, a negligee and a bed-cover both rose-coloured. Photographs. Slippers trimmed with marabou, a large box of petits-fours au massepain from the Marquise de Sevigné in Paris, which she had made but a feeble attempt to hide from the dietetic notice of her doctor. Above all, there was the pervasive scent of almond oil enclosed in a thin glass container that fitted over the light bulb of her table-lamp. Altogether the room, like Sybil herself, went much too far but, again like Sybil, contrived to get away with it.

"Splendid," said Dr. Schramm, withdrawing his stethoscope. He turned away and gazed out of the window with professional tact while she rearranged herself.

"There!" she said presently.

He returned and gazed down at her with the bossy, possessive air that she found so satisfactory.

"I begin to be pleased with you," he said.

"Truly?"

"Truly. You've quite a long way to go, of course, but your general condition is improved. You're responding."

"I feel better."

"Because you're not allowed to take it out of yourself. You're a highly strung instrument, you know, and mustn't be at the beck and call of people who impose upon you."

Sybil gave a deep sigh of concealed satisfaction.

"You do so understand," she said.

"Of course I do. It's what I'm here for. Isn't it?"

"Yes," said Sybil, luxuriating in it. "Yes, indeed."

He slid her bracelet up her arm and then laid his fingers on her pulse. She felt sure it was going like a train. When, after a final pressure, he released her she said as airily as she could manage: "I've just written a card to an old friend of yours."

"Really?"

"To ask her to lunch on Saturday. Verity Preston."

"Oh yes?"

"It must have been fun for you, meeting again after so long."

"Well, yes. It was," said Dr. Schramm, "very long ago. We used to run up against each other sometimes in my student days." He looked at his watch. "Time for your rest," he said.

"You must come and talk to her on Saturday."

"That would have been very pleasant."

But it turned out that he was obliged to go up to London on Saturday to see a fellow medico who had arrived unexpectedly from New York.

Verity, too, was genuinely unable to come to Greengages, having been engaged for luncheon elsewhere. She rang Sybil up and said she hadn't seen Prue but Mrs. Jim reported she was staying with friends in London.

"Does that mean Gideon Markos?"

"I've no idea."

"I'll bet it does. What about ghastly C.C.?"

"Not a sign of him as far as I know. I see by the shipping news that the *Poseidon* came into Southampton the day before yesterday."

"Keep your fingers crossed. Perhaps we'll escape after all."

"I think not," said Verity.

She was looking through her open window. An unmistakable figure shambled toward her up the avenue of limes.

"Your stepson," she said, "has arrived."

### III

Claude Carter was one of those beings whose appearance accurately reflects their character. He looked, and in fact was, damp. He seemed unable to face anything or anybody. He was almost forty but maintained a rich crop of post-adolescent pimples. He had very little chin, furtive eyes behind heavy spectacles, a vestigial beard and mouse-coloured hair that hung damply, of course, halfway down his neck.

Because he was physically so hopeless, Verity entertained a kind of horrified pity for him. This arose from a feeling that he couldn't be as awful as he looked and that anyway he had been treated unfairly: by his Maker in the first instance and probably in the second, by his masters (he had been sacked from three schools), his peers (he had been bullied at all of them) and life in general. His mother had died in childbirth and he was still a baby when Sybil married his father, who was killed in the blitz six months later and of whom Verity knew little beyond the fact that he collected stamps. Claude was brought up by his grandparents, who didn't care for him. These circumstances, when she thought of them, induced in Verity a muddled sense of guilt for which she could advance no justification and which was certainly not shared by Claude's stepmother.

When he became aware of Verity at her window he pretended, ineffectually, that he hadn't seen her and approached the front door with his head down. She went out to him. He did not speak but seemed to offer himself feebly for her inspection.

"Claude," said Verity.

"That's right."

She asked him in and he sat in her sunny drawing-room as if, she thought, he had been left till called for. He wore a T-shirt that had been made out of a self-rising-flour bag and bore the picture of a lady who thrust out a vast bosom garnished with the legend "Sure To Rise." His jeans so far exceeded in fashionable shrinkage as to cause him obvious discomfort.

He said he'd been up to Quintern Place where he'd found Mrs. Jim Jobbin, who told him Mrs. Foster was away and she couldn't say when she would return.

"Not much of a welcome," he said. "She made out she didn't know Prue's address, either. I asked who forwarded their letters." He blew three times down his nose which was his manner of laughing and gave Verity a knowing glance. "That made Mrs. Jim look pretty silly," he said.

"Sybil's taking a cure," Verity explained. "She's not seeing anybody."

"What, again! What is it this time?"

"She was run down and needs a complete rest."

"I thought you'd tell me where she was. That's why I came."

"I'm afraid not, Claude."

"That's awkward," he said fretfully. "I was counting on it."

"Where are you staying?"

"Oh, up there for the time being. At Quintern."

"Did you come by train?"

"I hitched."

Verity felt obliged to ask him if he'd had any lunch and he said: not really. He followed her into the kitchen where she gave him cold meat, chutney, bread, butter, cheese and beer. He ate a great deal and had a cigarette with his coffee. She asked him about Australia and he said it was no good, really, not unless you had capital. It was all right if you had capital.

He trailed back after her to the drawing-room and she began to feel desperate.

"As a matter of fact," he said, "I was depending on Syb. I happen to be in a bit of a patch. Nothing to worry about, really, but, you know."

"What sort of patch?" she asked against her will.

"I'm short."

"Of money?"

"What else is there to be short of?" he asked and gave his three inverted sniffs.

"How about the hundred pounds she sent to Teneriffe?"

He didn't hesitate or look any more hang-dog than he was already. "Did she send it?" he said. "Typical of the bloody Classic Line, that is. Typical inefficiency."

"Didn't it reach you?"

"Would I be cleaned out if it had?"

"Are you sure you haven't spent it?"

"I resent that, Miss Preston," he said, feebly bridling.

"I'm sorry if it was unfair. I can let you have twenty pounds. That should tide you over. And I'll let Sybil know about you."

"It's a bit off not telling where she is. But thanks, anyway, for helping out. I'll pay it back, of course, don't worry."

She went to her study to fetch it and again he trailed after her. Horrid to feel that it was not a good idea for him to see where she kept her housekeeping money.

In the hall she said: "I've a telephone call to make. I'll join you in the garden. And then I'm afraid we'll have to part: I've got work on hand."

"I quite understand," he said with an attempt at dignity.

When she rejoined him he was hanging about outside the front door. She gave him the money. "It's twenty-three pounds," she said. "Apart from loose change, it's all I've got in the house at the moment."

"I quite understand," he repeated grandly, and after giving her one of his furtive glances said: "Of course, if I had my own I wouldn't have to do this. Do you know that?"

"I don't think I understand."

"If I had The Stamp."

"The Stamp?"

"The one my father left me. The famous one."

"I'd forgotten about it."

"You wouldn't have if you were in my boots. The Black Alexander."

Then Verity remembered. The story had always sounded like something out of a boy's annual. Claude's father had inherited the stamp, which was one of an issue that had been withdrawn on the day of appearance because of an ominous fault: a black spot in the centre of the Czar Alexander's brow. It was reputed to be the only specimen known to be extant and worth a fabulous amount. Maurice Carter had been killed in the blitz while on leave. When his stamp collection was uplifted from his bank the Black Alexander was missing. It was never recovered.

"It was a strange business, that," Verity said.

"From what they've told me it was a very strange business indeed," he said, with his laugh.

She didn't answer. He shuffled his feet in the gravel and said he supposed he'd better take himself off.

"Goodbye, then," said Verity.

He gave her a damp and boneless handshake and had turned away when a thought seemed to strike him.

"By the way," he said. "If anyone asks for me I'd be grateful if you didn't know anything. Where I am and that. I don't suppose they will but, you know, if they do."

"Who would they be?"

"Oh—boring people. You wouldn't know them." He smiled and for a moment looked fully at her. "You're so good at not knowing where Syb is," he said. "The exercise ought to come easy to you, Miss Preston."

She knew her face was red. He had made her feel shabby.

"Look here. Are you in trouble?" she asked.

"Me? Trouble?"

"With the police?"

"Well, I must say! Thank you very much! What on earth could have given you that idea!" She didn't answer. He said, "Oh well, thanks for the loan anyway," and walked off. When he had got halfway to the gate he began, feebly, to whistle.

Verity went indoors meaning to settle down to work. She tried to concentrate for an hour, failed, started to write to Sybil, thought better of it, thought of taking a walk in the garden and was called back by the telephone.

It was Mrs. Jim, speaking from Quintern Place. She sounded unlike herself and said she was sure she begged pardon for giving the trouble but she was that worried. After a certain amount of preliminary explanation it emerged that it was about "that Mr. Claude Carter."

Sybil had told the staff it was remotely possible that he might appear and that if he did and wanted to stay they were to allow it. And then earlier this afternoon someone had rung up asking if he was there and Mrs. Jim had replied truthfully that he wasn't and wasn't expected and that she didn't know where he could be found. About half an hour later he arrived and said he wanted to stay.

"So I put him in the green bedroom, according," said Mrs. Jim, "and I told him about the person who'd rang and he says he don't want to take calls and I'm to say he's not there and I don't know nothing about him. Well, Miss Preston, I don't like it. I won't take the responsibility. There's something funny going on and I won't be mixed up. And I was wondering if you'd be kind enough to give me a word of advice."

"Poor Mrs. Jim," Verity said. "What a bore for you. But Mrs. Foster said you were to put him up and difficult as it may be, that's what you've done."

"I didn't know then what I know now, Miss Preston."

"What do you know now?"

"I didn't like to mention it before. It's not a nice thing to have to bring up. It's about the person who rang earlier. It was—somehow I knew it was, before he said—it was the police."

"O Lor', Mrs. Jim."

"Yes, Miss. And there's more. Bruce Gardener come in for his beer when he finished at five and he says he'd run into a gentleman in the garden, only he never realized it was Mr. Claude. On his way back from you, it must of been, and Mr. Claude told him he was a relation of Mrs. Foster's and they got talking and—"

"Bruce doesn't know—? Does he know?— Mrs. Jim, Bruce didn't tell him where Mrs. Foster can be found?"

"That's what I was coming to. She won't half be annoyed, will she? Yes, Miss Preston, that's just what he did."

"Oh *damn*," said Verity after a pause. "Well, it's not your fault, Mrs. Jim. Nor Bruce's if it comes to that. Don't worry about it."

"But what'll I say if the police rings again?"

Verity thought hard but any solution that occurred to her seemed to be unendurably shabby. At last she said: "Honestly, Mrs. Jim, I don't know. Speak the truth, I suppose I ought to say, and tell Mr. Claude about the call. Beastly though it sounds, at least it would probably get rid of him."

There was no answer. "Are you there, Mrs. Jim?" Verity asked. "Are you still there?"

Mrs. Jim had begun to whisper, "Excuse me, I'd better hang up." And in loud, artificial tones added: "That will be all, then, for today, thank you." And did hang up. Charmless Claude, thought Verity, was in the offing.

Verity was now deeply perturbed and at the same time couldn't help feeling rather cross. She was engaged in making extremely tricky alterations to the last act of a play that after a promising try-out in the provinces had attracted nibbles from a London management. To be interrupted at this stage was to become distraught.

She tried hard to readjust and settle to her job but it was no good. Sybil Foster and her ailments and problems, real or synthetic, weighed in against it. Should she, for instance, let Sybil know about the latest and really most disturbing news of her awful stepson? Had Verity any right to keep Sybil in the dark? She knew that Sybil would be only too pleased to be kept there but that equally some disaster might well develop for which she, Verity, would be held responsible. She would be told she had been secretive and had bottled up key information. It wouldn't be the first time that Sybil had shovelled responsibility all over her and then raised a martyred howl when the outcome was not to her liking.

It came to Verity that Prunella might reasonably be expected to take some kind of share in the proceedings but where, at the moment, was Prunella and would she become audible if rung up and asked to call? Verity read the same bit of dialogue three times without reading it at all, cast away her pen, swore and went for a walk in her garden. She loved her garden. There was no doubt that Bruce had done all the right things. There was no greenfly on the roses. Hollyhocks and delphiniums flourished against the lovely brick wall round her elderly orchard. He had not attempted to foist calceolarias upon her or indeed any objectionable annuals: only night-scented stocks. She had nothing but praise for him and wished he didn't irritate her so often.

She began to feel less badgered, picked a leaf of verbena, crushed and smelt it and turned back toward the house.

"I'll put the whole thing aside," she thought, "until tomorrow. I'll sleep on it."

But when she came through the lime trees she met Prunella Foster streaking hot-foot up the drive.

## IV

Prunella was breathless, a condition that did nothing to improve her audibility. She gazed at her godmother and flapped her hands in a manner that reminded Verity of her mother.

"Godma," she whispered, "are you alone?"

"Utterly," said Verity.

"Could I talk to you?"

"If you can contrive to make yourself heard, darling, of course you may."

"I'm sorry," said Prunella, who was accustomed to this admonishment. "I will try."

"Have you walked here?"

"Gideon dropped me. He's in the lane. Waiting."

"Come indoors. I wanted to see you."

Prunella opened her eyes very wide and they went indoors where without more ado she flung her arms round her godmother's neck, almost shouted the information that she was engaged to be married, and burst into excitable tears.

"My dear child!" said Verity, "what an odd way to announce it. Aren't you pleased to be engaged?"

A confused statement followed during which it emerged Prunella was very much in love with Gideon but was afraid he might not continue to be as much in love with her as now appeared because one saw that sort of thing happening all over the place, didn't one, and she knew if it happened to her she wouldn't be able to keep her cool and put it into perspective and she had only consented to an engagement because Gideon promised that for him it was for keeps but how could one be sure he knew what he was talking about?

She then blew her nose and said that she was fantastically happy.

Verity was fond of her goddaughter and pleased that she wanted to confide in her. She sensed that there was more to come.

And so there was.

"It's about Mummy," Prunella said. "She's going to be livid."

"But why?"

"Well, first of all she's a roaring snob and wants me to marry John Swingletree because he's a peer. Imagine!"

"I don't know John Swingletree."

"The more lucky, you. The bottom. And then, you see, she's got one of her things about Gideon and his papa. She thinks they've sprung from a mid-European ghetto."

"None the worse for that," said Verity.

"Exactly. But you know what she is. It's partly because Mr. Markos didn't exactly make a big play for her at that dinner-party when they first came to Mardling. You know," Prunella repeated, "what she is. Well, don't you, Godma?"

There being no way out of it, Verity said she supposed she did.

"Not," Prunella said, "that she's all that hooked on him. Not now. She's all for the doctor at Greengages—you remember? Wasn't he an ex-buddy of yours, or something?"

"Not really."

"Well, anyway, she's in at the deep end, boots and all. Potty about him. I do so wish," Prunella said as her large eyes refilled with tears, "I didn't have to have a mum like that. Not that I don't love her."

"Never mind."

"And now I've got to tell her. About Gideon and me."

"How do you think of managing that? Going to Greengages? Or writing?"

"Whatever I do she'll go ill at me and say I'll be sorry when she's gone. Gideon's offered to come too. He's all for taking bulls by the horns. But I don't want him to see what she can be like if she cuts up rough. You know, don't you? If anything upsets her apple-cart when she's nervy it can be a case of screaming hysterics. Can't it?"

"Well—"

"You know it can. I'd hate him to see her like that. Darling, darling Godma V, I was wondering—"

Verity thought: "She can't help being a bit like her mother," and was not surprised when Prunella said she had *just* wondered if Verity was going to visit her mother and if she did whether she'd kind of prepare the way.

"I hadn't thought of going. I've got a date. I really *am* busy, Prue."

"Oh," said Prunella, falling back on her whisper and looking desolate. "Yes. I see."

"In any case, shouldn't you and Gideon go together and Gideon— well—"

"Ask for my hand in marriage like Jack Worthing and Lady Bracknell?"

"Yes."

"That's what *he* says. Darling Godma V," said Prunella, once more hanging herself round Verity's neck, "if we took you with us and you just sort of—you know—first. Couldn't you? We've come all the way from London just this minute almost, to ask. She pays more attention to you than anybody. Couldn't you cancel your date? Please?"

"Oh, Prue."

"You *will?* I can see you're going to. And you can't possibly refuse when I tell you my other hideous news. Not that Gideon-and-me is hideous but just you wait."

"Charmless Claude?"

"You *knew!* I rang up Quintern from Mardling and Mrs. Jim told me. Isn't it *abysmal!* When we all thought he was safely stowed in Aussie."

"Are you staying tonight?"

"There? With Claudie-boy? Not on your Nelly. I'm going to Mardling. Mr. Markos is back and we'll tell him about us. He'll be super about it. I ought to go."

"Shall I come to the car and say hullo to Gideon?"

"Oh, you mustn't trouble to do that. He'll come," Prunella said. She put a thumb and finger between her teeth, leant out of the window and emitted a piercing whistle. A powerful engine started up in the lane, a rakish sports model shot through the drive in reverse and pulled up at the front door. Gideon Markos leapt out.

He really was an extremely good-looking boy, thought Verity, but she could see, without for a moment accepting the disparagement, what Sybil had meant by her central European remark. He was an exotic. He looked like a Latin member of the jet set dressed by an English tailor. But his manner was unaffected as well as assured and his face alive with a readiness to be amused.

"Miss Preston," he said, "I gather you're not only a godmother but expected to be a fairy one. Are you going to wave your wand and give us your blessing?"

He put his arm round Prunella and talked away cheerfully about how he'd bullied her into accepting him. Verity thought he was exalted by his conquest and that he would be quite able to manage not only his wife but if need be his mother-in-law as well.

"I expect Prue's confided her misgivings," he said, "about her mama being liable to cut up rough over us. I don't quite see why she should take against me in such a big way, but perhaps that's insufferable. Anyway I hope *you* don't feel I'm not a good idea?" He looked quickly at her and added, "But then, of course, you don't know me so that was a pretty gormless remark, wasn't it?"

"The early impression," said Verity, "is not unfavourable."

"Well, thank the Lord for that," said Gideon.

"Darling," breathed Prunella, "she's coming to Greengages with us. You are, Godma, you know you are. To temper the wind. Sort of."

"That's very kind of her," he said and bowed to Verity.

Verity knew she had been outmanoeuvred, but on the whole did not resent it. She saw them shoot off down the drive. It had been settled that they would visit Greengages on the coming Saturday but not, as Prunella put it, for a cabbage-water soup and minced grass luncheon. Gideon knew of a super restaurant en route.

Verity was left with the feeling of having spent a day during which unsought events converged upon her and brought with them a sense of mounting unease, of threats, even. She suspected that the major ingredient of this discomfort was an extreme reluctance to suffer another confrontation with Basil Schramm.

The following two days were uneventful but Thursday brought Mrs. Jim to Keys for her weekly attack upon floors and furniture. She reported that Claude Carter kept very much to his room up at Quintern, helped himself to the food left out for him and, she thought, didn't answer the telephone. Beryl, who was engaged to sleep in while Sybil Foster was away, had said she didn't fancy doing so with that Mr. Claude in residence. In the upshot the difficulty had been solved by Bruce, who offered to sleep in, using the coachman's room over the garage formerly occupied by a chauffeur-handyman.

"I knew Mrs. Foster wouldn't have any objections to *that*," said Mrs. Jim, with a stony glance out of the window.

"Perhaps, though, she ought just to be asked, don't you think?"

"He done it," said Mrs. Jim sparsely. "Bruce. He rung her up."

"At Greengages?"

"That's right, Miss. He's been over there to see her," she added. "Once a week. To take flowers and get orders. By bus. Of a Saturday. She pays."

Verity knew that she would be expected by her friends to snub Mrs. Jim for speaking in this cavalier manner of an employer but she preferred not to notice.

"Oh well," she generalized, "you've done everything you can, Mrs. Jim." She hesitated for a moment and then said: "I'm going over there on Saturday."

After a fractional pause Mrs. Jim said: "Are you, Miss? That's very kind of you, I'm sure," and switched on the vacuum cleaner. "You'll be able to see for yourself," she shouted above the din.

Verity nodded and returned to the study. "But what?" she wondered. "*What* shall I be able to see?"

## V

Gideon's super restaurant turned out to be within six miles of Greengages. It seemed to be some sort of club of which he was a member and was of an exalted character with every kind of discreet attention and very good food. Verity seldom lunched at this level and she enjoyed herself. For the first time she wondered what Gideon's occupation in life might be. She also remembered that Prunella was something of a *partie*.

At half-past two they arrived at Greengages. It was a converted Edwardian mansion approached by an avenue, sheltered by a stand of conifers and surrounded by ample lawns in which flower-beds had been cut like graves.

There were a number of residents strolling about with visitors or sitting under brilliant umbrellas on exterior furnishers' contraptions.

"She does know we're coming, doesn't she?" Verity asked. She had begun to feel apprehensive.

"You and me, she knows," said Prunella. "I didn't mention Gideon. Actually."

"Oh, Prue!"

"I thought you might sort of ease him in," Prue whispered.

"I really don't think—"

"Nor do I," said Gideon. "Darling, why can't we just—"

"There she is!" cried Verity. "Over there beyond the calceolarias and lobelia under an orange brolly. She's waving. She's seen us."

"Godma V, *please*. Gideon and I'll sit in the car and when you wave we'll come. Please."

Verity thought: "I've eaten their astronomical luncheon and drunk their champagne so now I turn plug-ugly and refuse?" "All right," she said, "but don't blame me if it goes hay-wire."

She set off across the lawn.

Nobody has invented a really satisfactory technique for the gradual approach of people who have already exchanged greetings from afar. Continue to grin while a grin dwindles into a grimace? Assume a sudden absorption in the surroundings? Make as if sunk in meditation? Break into a joyous canter? Shout? Whistle? Burst, even, into song?

Verity tried none of these methods. She walked fast and when she got within hailing distance cried: "There you are!"

Sybil had the advantage in so far as she wore enormous dark sunglasses. She waved and smiled and pointed, as if in mock astonishment or admiration at Verity and when she arrived extended her arms for an embrace.

"Darling Verry!" she cried. "You've come after all." She waved Verity into a canvas chair, seemed to gaze at her fixedly for an uneasy moment or two and then said with a change of voice: "Whose car's that? Don't tell me. It's Gideon Markos's. He's driven you both over. You needn't say anything. They're engaged!"

This, in a way, was a relief. Verity, for once, was pleased by Sybil's prescience. "Well, yes," she said, "they are. And honestly, Syb, there doesn't seem to me to be anything against it."

"In that case," said Sybil, all cordiality spent, "why are they going on like this? Skulking in the car and sending you to soften me up: If you call that the behaviour of a civilized young man! Prue would never be like that on her own initiative. He's persuaded her."

"The boot's on the other foot. He was all for tackling you himself."

"Cheek! Thick-skinned push. One knows where he got that from."

"Where?"

"God knows."

"You've just said you do."

"Don't quibble, darling," said Sybil.

"I can't make out what, apart from instinctive promptings, sets you against Gideon. He's intelligent, eminently presentable, obviously rich—"

"Yes, and where does it come from?"

"—and, which is the only basically important bit, he seems to be a young man of good character and in love with Prue."

"John Swingletree's devoted to her. Utterly devoted. And she was—"

Sybil boggled for a moment and then said loudly, "she was getting to be very fond of him."

"The Lord Swingletree, would that be?"

"Yes, it would and you needn't say it like that."

"I'm not saying it like anything. Syb, they're over there waiting to come to you. Do be kind. You won't get anywhere by being anything else."

"She's under age."

"I think she'll wait until she's not or else do a bunk. Really."

Sybil was silent for a moment and then said: "Do you know what I think? I think it's a put-up job between him and his father. They want to get their hands on Quintern."

"Oh, my *dear* old Syb!"

"All right. You wait. Just you wait."

This was said with all her old vigour and obstinacy and yet with a very slight drag, a kind of flatness in her utterance. Was it because of this that Verity had the impression that Sybil did not really mind all that much about her daughter's engagement? There was an extraordinary suggestion of hesitancy and yet of suppressed excitement—almost of jubilation.

The pampered little hand she raised to her sunglasses quivered. It removed the glasses and for Verity the afternoon turned cold.

Sybil's face was blankly smooth as if it had been ironed. It had no expression. Her great china-blue eyes really might have been those of a doll.

"All right," she said. "On your own head be it. Let them come. I won't make scenes. But I warn you I'll never come round. Never."

A sudden wave of compassion visited Verity.

"Would you rather wait a bit?" she asked. "How are you, Syb? You haven't told me. Are you better?"

"Much, much better. Basil Schramm is fantastic. I've never had a doctor like him. Truly. He so *understands*. I expect," Sybil's voice luxuriated, "he'll be livid when he hears about this visit. He won't let me be upset. I told him about Charmless Claude and he said I must on no account see him. He's given orders. Verry, he's quite fantastic," said Sybil. The warmth of these eulogies found no complementary expression in her face or voice. She wandered on, gossiping about Schramm and her treatment and his nurse, Sister Jackson, who, she said complacently, resented his taking so much trouble over her. "My dear," said Sybil, "jealous! Don't you worry, I've got that one buttoned up."

"Well," Verity said, swallowing her disquietude, "perhaps you'd better let me tell these two that you'll see Prue by herself for a moment. How would that be?"

"I'll see them both," said Sybil. "Now."

"Shall I fetch them, then?"

"Can't you just wave?" she asked fretfully.

As there seemed to be nothing else for it, Verity walked into the sunlight and waved. Prunella's hand answered from the car. She got out, followed by Gideon, and they came quickly across the lawn. Verity knew Sybil would be on the watch for any signs of a conference however brief and waited instead of going to meet them. When they came up with her she said under her breath: "It's tricky. Don't upset her."

Prunella broke into a run. She knelt by her mother and looked into her face. There was a moment's hesitation and then she kissed her.

"Darling Mummy," she said.

Verity turned to the car.

There she sat and watched the group of three under the orange canopy. They might have been placed there for a painter like Troy Alleyn. The afternoon light, broken and diffused, made nebulous figures of them so that they seemed to shimmer and swim a little. Sybil had put her sunglasses on again so perhaps, thought Verity, Prue won't notice anything.

Now Gideon had moved. He stood by Sybil's chair and raised her hand to his lips. "She ought to like that," Verity thought. "That ought to mean she's yielding but I don't think it does."

She found it intolerable to sit in the car and decided to stroll back toward the gates. She would be in full view. If she was wanted Gideon could come and get her.

A bus had drawn up outside the main gates. A number of people got out and began to walk up the drive. Among them were two men, one of whom carried a great basket of lilies. He wore a countrified tweed suit and hat and looked rather distinguished. It came as quite a shock to recognize him as Bruce Gardener in his best clothes. Sybil would have said he was "perfectly presentable."

And a greater and much more disquieting shock to realize that his shambling, ramshackle companion was Claude Carter.

## VI

When Verity was a girl there had been a brief craze for what were known as rhymes of impending disaster—facetious couplets usually on the lines of: "Auntie Maude's mislaid her glasses and thinks the burglar's making passes," accompanied by a childish drawing of a simpering lady being man-handled by a masked thug.

Why was she now reminded of this puerile squib? Why did she see her old friend in immediate jeopardy: threatened by something undefined but infinitely more disquieting than any nuisance Claude Carter could inflict upon her? Why should Verity feel as if the afternoon, now turned sultry, was closing about Sybil? Had she only imagined that there was an odd immobility in Sybil's face?

And what ought she to do about Bruce and Claude?

She pulled herself together and went to meet them.

Bruce was delighted to see her. He raised his tweed hat high in the air, beamed across the lilies and greeted her in his richest and most suspect Scots. He was, he said, paying his usual wee Saturday visit to his puir leddy and how had Miss Preston found her the noo? Would there be an improvement in her condeetion, then?

Verity said she didn't think Mrs. Foster seemed very well and that at the moment she had visitors to which Bruce predictably replied that he would bide a wee. And if she didna fancy any further visitors he'd leave the lilies at the desk to be put in her room. "She likes to know how her garden prospers," he said. Claude had listened to this exchange with a half-smile and a shifting eye.

"You found your way here, after all?" Verity said to him since she could scarcely say nothing.

"Oh, yes," he said. "Thanks to Bruce. He's sure she'll be glad to see me."

Bruce looked, Verity thought, as if he would like to disown this remark and indeed began to say he'd no' put it that way when Claude said: "That's her, over there, isn't it? Is that Prue with her?"

"Yes," said Verity shortly.

"Who's the jet-set type?"

"A friend."

"I think I'll just investigate," he said with a pallid show of effrontery and made as if to set out.

"Claude, please wait," Verity said and in her dismay turned to Bruce. He said at once: "Ou, now, Mr. Carter, would you no' consider it more advisable to bide a while?"

"No," said Claude over his shoulder, "thank you, I wouldn't," and continued on his way.

Verity thought: "I can't run after him and hang on his arm and make a scene. Prue and Gideon will have to cope."

Prue certainly did. The distance was too great for words to be distinguished and the scene came over like a mime. Sybil reached out a hand

and clutched her daughter's arm. Prue turned, saw Claude and rose. Gideon made a gesture of enquiry. Then Prue marched down upon Claude.

They faced each other, standing close together, Prue very upright, rather a dignified little figure, Claude with his back to Verity, his head lowered. And in the distance Sybil being helped to her feet by Gideon and walked toward the house.

"She'll be better indoors," said Bruce in a worried voice, "she will that."

Verity had almost forgotten him but there he stood gazing anxiously over the riot of lilies he carried. At that moment Verity actually liked him.

Prue evidently said something final to Claude. She walked quickly toward the house, joined her mother and Gideon on the steps, took Sybil's arm and led her indoors. Claude stared after them, turned toward Verity, changed his mind and sloped off in the direction of the trees.

"It wasna on any invitation of mine he came," said Bruce hotly. "He worrumed the information oot of me."

"I can well believe it," said Verity.

Gideon came to them.

"It's all right," he said to Verity. "Prue's taking Mrs. Foster up to her room." And to Bruce: "Perhaps you could wait in the entrance hall until Miss Prunella comes down."

"I'll do that, sir, thank you," Bruce said and went indoors.

Gideon smiled down at Verity. He had, she thought, an engaging smile. "What a very bumpy sort of a visit," he said.

"How was it shaping up? Before Charmless Claude intervened?"

"Might have been worse, I suppose. Not much worse, though. The reverse of open arms and cries of rapturous welcome. You must have done some wonderful softening-up, Miss Preston, for her to receive me at all. We couldn't be more grateful." He hesitated for a moment. "I hope you don't mind my asking but is there—is she—Prue's mother—I don't know how to say it. Is there something—?" He touched his face.

"I know what you mean. Yes. There is."

"I only wondered."

"It's new."

"I think Prue's seen it. Prue's upset. She managed awfully well but she *is* upset."

"Prue's explained Charmless Claude, has she?"

"Yes. Pretty ghastly specimen. She coped marvellously," said Gideon proudly.

"Here she comes."

When Prunella joined them she was white-faced but perfectly composed. "We can go now," she said and got into the car.

"Where's your bag?" asked Gideon.

"What? Oh, *damn*," said Prunella, "I've left it up there. Oh, *what* a fool! Now I'll have to go back."

"Shall I?"

"It's in her room. And she's been pretty beastly to you."

"Perhaps I could better myself by a blithe change of manner."

"*What* a good idea," cried Prunella. "Yes, do let's try it. Say she looks like Mrs. Onassis."

"She doesn't. Not remotely. Nobody less."

"She thinks she does."

"One can but try," Gideon said. "There's nothing to lose."

"No more there is."

He was gone for longer than they expected. When he returned with Prunella's bag he looked dubious. He started up the car and drove off.

"Any good?" Prunella ventured.

"She didn't actually throw anything at me."

"Oh," said Prunella. "Like that, was it."

She was very quiet on the homeward drive. Verity, in the back seat, saw her put her hand on Gideon's knee. He laid his own hand briefly over it and looked down at her. "He knows exactly how to handle her," Verity thought. "There's going to be no doubt about who's the boss."

When they arrived at Keys she asked them to come in for a drink but Gideon said his father would be expecting them.

"I'll see Godma V in," said Prue as Gideon prepared to do so.

She followed Verity indoors and kissed and thanked her very prettily. Then she said: "About Mummy. Has she had a stroke?"

"My dear child, why?"

"You noticed. I could see you did."

"I don't think it looked like that. In any case they—the doctor—would have let you know if anything serious was wrong."

"P'raps he didn't know. He may not be a good doctor. Sorry, I forgot he was a friend."

"He's not. Not to matter."

"I think I'll ring him up. I think there's something wrong. Honestly, don't you?"

"I did wonder. And yet—"

"What?"

"In a funny sort of way she seemed—well—excited, pleased."

"I thought so, too."

"It's very odd," said Prunella. "Everything was odd. Out of focus, kind of. Anyway I will ring up that doctor. I'll ring him up tomorrow. Do you think that's a good idea?"

Verity said: "Yes, darling. I do. It should put your mind at rest."

But it was going to be a long time before Prunella's mind would be in that enviable condition.

## VII

At five minutes past nine that evening, Sister Jackson, the resident nurse at Greengages, paused at Sybil Foster's door. She could hear the television. She tapped, opened and after a long pause approached the bed. Five minutes later she left the room and walked rather quickly down the passage.

At ten-thirty Dr. Schramm telephoned Prunella to tell her that her mother was dead.

# CHAPTER III

# Alleyn

*I*

BASIL LOOKED distinguished, Verity had to admit: exactly as he ought to look under the circumstances, and he behaved as one would wish him to behave, with dignity and propriety, with deference and with precisely the right shade of controlled emotion.

"I had no reason whatever to suspect that beyond symptoms of nervous exhaustion, which had markedly improved, there was anything the matter," he said. "I feel I must add that I am astonished that she should have taken this step. She was in the best of spirits when I last saw her."

"When was that, Dr. Schramm?" asked the coroner.

"On that same morning. About eight o'clock. I was going up to London and looked in on some of my patients before I left. I did not get back to Greengages until a few minutes after ten in the evening."

"To find?"

"To find that she had died."

"Can you describe the circumstances?"

"Yes. She had asked me to get a book for her in London: the autobiography of a Princess—somebody—I forget the name. I went to her room to deliver it. Our bedrooms are large and comfortable and are often used as sitting-rooms. I have been told that she went up to hers later that afternoon. Long before her actual bedtime. She had dinner there, watching television. I knocked and there was no reply but I could hear the television and presumed that because of it she had not heard me. I went in. She was in bed and lying on her back. Her bedside table-lamp was on and I saw at once that a bottle of tablets was overturned and several—five, in fact—were scattered over the surface of the table. Her drinking glass was empty but had been used and was lying on the floor. Subsequently a faint trace of alcohol—Scotch—was found in the glass. A small bottle of Scotch, empty, was on the table. She sometimes used to take a modest nightcap. Her jug of water was almost empty. I examined her and found that she was dead. It was then twenty minutes past ten."

"Can you give a time for when death occurred?"

"Not exactly, no. Not less than an hour before I found her."

"What steps did you take?"

"I made absolutely certain there was no possibility of recovery. I then called up our resident nurse. We employed a stomach pump. The results were subsequently analyzed and a quantity of barbiturates was found." He hesitated and then said: "I would like, Sir, if this is an appropriate moment to add a word about Greengages and its general character and management."

"By all means, Dr. Schramm."

"Thank you. Greengages is not a hospital. It is a hotel with a resident medical practitioner. Many, indeed most, of our guests are not ill. Some are tired and in need of a change and rest. Some come to us simply for a quiet holiday. Some for a weight-reducing course. Some are convalescents preparing to return to normal life. A number of them are elderly people who are reassured by the presence of a qualified practitioner and a registered nurse. Mrs. Foster had been in the habit of coming from time to time. She was a nervy subject and a chronic worrier. I must say at once that I had not prescribed the barbiturate tablets she had taken and have no idea how she had obtained them. When she first came I did, on request, prescribe phenobarbiturates at night to help her sleep but after her first week they were discontinued as she had no further need of them. I apologize for the digression but I felt it was perhaps indicated."

"Quite. Quite. Quite," chattered the complacent coroner.

"Well then, to continue. When we had done what had to be done, I got into touch with another doctor. The local practitioners were all engaged or out but finally I reached Dr. Field-Innis of Upper Quintern. He very kindly drove over and together we made further examination."

"Finding?"

"Finding that she had died of an overdose. There was no doubt of it, at all. We found three half-dissolved tablets at the back of the mouth and one on the tongue. She must have taken the tablets four or five at a time and lost consciousness before she could swallow the last ones."

"Dr. Field-Innis is present, is he not?"

"He is," Basil said with a little bow in the right direction. Dr. Field-Innis bobbed up and down in his seat.

"Thank you very much, Dr. Schramm," said the coroner with evident respect.

Dr. Field-Innis was called.

Verity watched him push his glasses up his nose and tip back his head to adjust his vision just as he always did after he had listened to one's chest. He was nice. Not in the least dynamic or lordly, but nice. And conscientious. And, Verity thought, at the moment very clearly ill at ease.

He confirmed everything that Basil Schramm had deposed as to the state of the room and the body and the conclusion they had drawn and added that he himself had been surprised and shocked by the tragedy.

"Was the deceased a patient of yours, Dr. Field-Innis?"

"She consulted me about four months ago."

"On what score?"

"She felt unwell and was nervy. She complained of migraine, sleeplessness and general anxiety. I prescribed a mild barbiturate. *Not* the proprietary tranquilizer she was found to have taken that evening, by the way." He hesitated for a moment. "I suggested that she should have a general overhaul," he said.

"Had you any reason to suspect there was something serious the matter?"

There was a longer pause. Dr. Field-Innis looked for a moment at Prunella. She sat between Gideon and Verity, who thought, irrelevantly, that like all blondes, especially when they were as pretty as Prunella, mourning greatly became her.

"That," said Dr. Field-Innis, "is not an easy question to answer. There were, I thought, certain possible indications: very slight indeed, that should be followed up."

"What were they?"

"A gross tremor in the hands. That does not necessarily imply a conspicuous tremor. And—this is difficult to define—a certain appearance in the face. I must emphasize that this was slight and possibly of no moment but I had seen something of the sort before and felt it should not be disregarded."

"What might these symptoms indicate, Dr. Field-Innis? A stroke?" hazarded the coroner.

"Not necessarily."

"Anything else?"

"I say this with every possible reservation. But yes. Just possibly—Parkinson's disease."

Prunella gave a strange little sound, half cry, half sigh. Gideon took her hand.

The coroner asked: "And did the deceased, in fact follow your advice?"

"No. She said she would think it over. She did not consult me again."

"Had she any idea you suspected—?"

"Certainly not," Dr. Field-Innis said loudly. "I gave no indication whatever. It would have been most improper to do so."

"Have you discussed the matter with Dr. Schramm?"

"It has been mentioned, yes."

"Had Dr. Schramm remarked these symptoms?" The coroner turned politely to Basil Schramm. "Perhaps," he said, "we may ask?"

He stood up. "I had noticed the tremor," he said. "On her case-history and on what she had told me, I attributed this to the general nervous condition."

"Quite," said the coroner. "So, gentlemen, we may take it, may we not, that fear of this tragic disease cannot have been a motive for suicide? We may rule that out?"

"Certainly," they said together and together they sat down. "Tweedledum and Tweedledee," Verity thought.

The resident nurse was now called: Sister Jackson, an opulent lady of good looks, a highish colour and an air of latent sexiness, damped down, Verity thought, to suit the occasion. She confirmed the doctors' evidence and said rather snootily that of course if Greengages had been a hospital there would have been no question of Mrs. Foster having a private supply of any medicaments.

And now Prunella was called. It was a clear day outside and a ray of sunlight slanted through a window in the parish hall. As if on cue from some zealous stage-director it found Prunella's white-gold head and made a saint of her.

"How lovely she is," Gideon said quite audibly. Verity thought he might have been sizing up one of his father's distinguished possessions. "And how obliging of the sun," he added and gave her a friendly smile. This young man, she thought, takes a bit of learning.

The coroner was considerate with Prunella. She was asked about the afternoon visit to Greengages. Had there been anything unusual in her mother's behaviour? The coroner was sorry to trouble her but would she mind raising her voice, the acoustics of the hall, no doubt, were at fault. Verity heard Gideon chuckle.

Prunella gulped and made a determined attempt to become fully vocal. "Not really," she said. "Not unusual. My mother was rather easily fussed and—well—you know. As Dr. Schramm said, she worried."

"About anything in particular, Miss Foster?"

"Well—about me, actually."

"I beg your pardon?"

"About *me*," Prunella shrilled and flinched at the sound of her own voice. "Sorry," she said.

"About you?"

"Yes. I'd just got engaged and she fussed about that, sort of. But it was all right. Routine, really."

"And you saw nothing particularly unusual?"

"Yes. I mean," said Prunella frowning distressfully and looking across at Dr. Field-Innis, "I did think I saw something—different—about her."

"In what way?"

"Well, she was—her hands—like Dr. Field-Innis said—were trembly. And her speech kind of, you know, dragged. And there was—or I thought there was—something about her face. As if it had kind of, you know, blanked out or sort of smoothed over, sort of—well—slowed up. I can't describe it. I wasn't even quite sure it was there."

"But it troubled you?"

"Yes. Sort of," whispered Prunella.

She described how she and Gideon took her mother back to the house and how she went up with her to her room.

"She said she thought she'd have a rest and go to bed early and have dinner brought up to her. There was something she wanted to see on television. I helped her undress. She asked me not to wait. So I turned the box on and left her. She truly seemed all right, apart from being tired and upset about—about me and my engagement." Prunella's voice wavered into inaudibility, and her eyes filled with tears.

"Miss Foster," asked the coroner, "just one more question. Was there a bottle of tablets on her bedside table?"

"Yes, there was," Prunella said quickly. "She asked me to take it out of her beauty-box: you know, a kind of face-box. It was on the table. She said they were sleeping-pills she'd got from a chemist ages ago and she thought if she couldn't go to sleep after her dinner she'd take one. I found them for her and put them out. And there was a lamp on the table, a book and an enormous box of petits-fours au massepain. She gets—she used to get them from that shop, the Marquise de Sevigné—in Paris. I ate some before I left."

Prunella knuckled her eyes like a small girl and then hunted for her handkerchief. The coroner said they would not trouble her anymore and she returned to Gideon and Verity.

Verity heard herself called and found she was nervous. She was taken over the earlier ground and confirmed all that Prunella had said. Nothing she was asked led to any mention of Bruce Gardener's and Claude Carter's arrivals at Greengages and as both of them had been fended off from meeting Sybil she did not think it incumbent on her to say anything about them. She saw that Bruce was in the hall, looking stiff and solemn as if the inquest was a funeral. He wore his Harris tweed suit and a black tie. Poor Syb would have liked that. She would have probably said there was "good blood there" and you could tell by the way he wore his clothes. Meaning blue blood. And suddenly and irrelevantly there came over Verity the realization that she could never believe ridiculous old Syb had killed herself.

She had found Dr. Field-Innis's remarks about Sybil's appearance deeply disturbing, not because she thought they bore the remotest relation to her death but because she herself had for so long paid so little attention to Sybil's ailments. Suppose, all the time, there had been ominous signs? Suppose she had felt as ill as she said she did? Was it a case of "wolf, wolf"? Verity was miserable.

She did not pay much attention when Gideon was called and said that he had returned briefly to Mrs. Foster's room to collect Prunella's bag and that she had seemed to be quite herself.

The proceedings now came to a close. The coroner made a short speech saying, in effect, that the jury might perhaps consider it was most unfortunate that nothing had emerged to show why the deceased had been moved to take this tragic and apparently motiveless step, so out of character according to all that her nearest and dearest felt about her. Nevertheless in face of what they had heard they might well feel that the circumstances all pointed in one direction. However—at this point Verity's attention was distracted by the sight of Claude Carter, whom she had not noticed before. He was sitting at the end of a bench against the wall, wearing a superfluous raincoat with the collar turned up and was feasting quietly upon his fingernails.

"—and so," the coroner was saying, "you may think that in view of the apparent absence of motive and not withstanding the entirely appropriate steps taken by Dr. Schramm, an autopsy should be carried out. If you so decide I shall, of course, adjourn the inquest *sine die.*"

The jury after a short withdrawal brought in a verdict along these lines and the inquest was accordingly adjourned until after the autopsy.

The small assembly emptied out into the summery quiet of the little village.

As she left the hall Verity found herself face to face with Young Mr. Rattisbon. Young Mr. Rattisbon was about sixty-five years of age and was the son of Old Mr. Rattisbon, who was ninety-two. They were London solicitors of eminent respectability and they had acted for Verity's family and for Sybil's unto the third and fourth generation. His father and Verity's were old friends. As the years passed the son grew more and more like the father, even to adopting his eccentricities. They both behaved as if they were character-actors playing themselves in some dated comedy. Both had an extraordinary mannerism: when about to pronounce upon some choice point of law they exposed the tips of their tongues and vibrated them as if they had taken sips of scalding tea. They prefaced many of their remarks with a slight whinny.

When Mr. Rattisbon saw Verity he raised his out-of-date city hat very high and said, "Good morning," three times and added, "Very sad, yes," as if she had enquired whether it was or was not so. She asked him if he was returning to London but he said no, he would find himself something to eat in the village and then go up to Quintern Place if Prunella Foster found it convenient to see him.

Verity rapidly surveyed her larder and then said: "You can't lunch in the village. There's only the Passcoigne Arms and it's awful. Come and have an omelette and cheese and a glass of reasonable hock with me."

He gave quite a performance of deprecating whinnies but was clearly delighted. He wanted, he said, to have a word with the coroner and would drive up to Keys when it was over.

Verity, given this start, was able to make her unpretentious preparations. She laid her table, took some cold sorrel soup with cream from the refrigerator, fetched herbs from the orchard, broke eggs into a basin and put butter in her omelette pan. Then she paid a visit to her cellar and chose one of the few remaining bottles of her father's sherry and one of the more than respectable hock.

When Mr. Rattisbon arrived she settled him in the drawing-room, joined him in a glass of sherry and left him with the bottle at his elbow while she went off to make the omelette.

They lunched successfully, finishing off with ripe Stilton and biscuits. Mr. Rattisbon had two and a half glasses of hock to Verity's one.

His face, normally the colour of one of his own parchments, became quite pink.

They withdrew into the garden and sat in weather-worn deck chairs under the lime trees.

"How very pleasant, my dear Verity," said Mr. Rattisbon. "Upon my word, how quite delightful! I suppose, alas, I must keep my eye upon the time. And if I may, I shall telephone Miss Prunella. I mustn't overstay my welcome."

"Oh, fiddle, Ratsy!" said Verity, who had called him by this Kenneth Grahamish nickname for some forty years, "what did you think about the inquest?"

The professional change came over him. He joined his fingertips, rattled his tongue and made his noise.

"M'nah," he said. "My dear Verity. While you were preparing our delicious luncheon I thought a great deal about the inquest and I may say that the more I thought the less I liked it. I will not disguise from you, I am uneasy."

"So am I. What exactly is *your* worry? Don't go all professionally rectitudinal like a diagram. Confide. Do, Ratsy, I'm the soul of discretion. My lips shall be sealed with red tape, I promise."

"My dear girl, I don't doubt it. I had, in any case, decided to ask you: you were, were you not, a close friend of Mrs. Foster?"

"A very *old* friend. I think perhaps the closeness was more on her side than mine if that makes sense."

"She confided in you?"

"She'd confide in the Town Crier if she felt the need but yes, she did quite a lot."

"Do you know if she has recently made a Will?"

"Oh," said Verity, "is that your trouble?"

"Part of it, at least. I must tell you that she did in fact execute a Will four years ago. I have reason to believe that she may have made a later one but have no positive knowledge of such being the case. She—yah—she wrote to me three weeks ago advising me of the terms of a new Will she wished me to prepare. I was—frankly appalled. I replied, as I hoped, temperately, asking her to take thought. *She* replied at once that I need concern myself no further in the matter, with additions of a—of an intemperate—I would go so far as to say a hostile, character. So much so that I concluded that I had been given the—not to put too fine a point upon it—sack."

"Preposterous!" cried Verity. "She couldn't!"

"As it turned out she didn't. On my writing a formal letter asking if she wished the return of Passcoigne documents which we hold, and I may add, have held since the barony was created, she merely replied by telegram."

"What did it say?"

"It said 'Don't be silly.' "

"How like Syb!"

"Upon which," said Mr. Rattisbon, throwing himself back in his chair, "I concluded that there was to be no severance of the connection. That is the last communication I had from her. I know not if she made a new Will. But the fact that I—yah—jibbed, might have led her to act on her own initiative. Provide herself," said Mr. Rattisbon, lowering his voice as one who speaks of blasphemy, "with A Form. From some stationer. Alas."

"Since she was in cool storage at Greengages, she'd have had to ask somebody to get the form for her. She didn't ask me."

"I think I hear your telephone, my dear," Mr. Rattisbon said.

It was Prunella. "Godma V," she said with unusual clarity, "I saw you talking to that fantastic old Mr. Rattisbon. Do you happen to know where he was going?"

"He's here. He's thinking of visiting you."

"Oh, good. Because I suppose he ought to know. Because, actually, I've found something he ought to see."

"What have you found, darling?"

"I'm afraid," Prunella's voice escalated to a plaintive squeak, "it's a Will."

When Mr. Rattisbon had taken his perturbed leave and departed, bolt upright, at the wheel of his car, Prunella rang again to say she felt that before he arrived she must tell her godmother more about her find.

"I can't get hold of Gideon," she said, "so I thought I'd tell you. Sorry, darling, but you know what I mean."

"Of course I do."

"Sweet of you. Well. It was in Mummy's desk in the boudoir top drawer. In a stuck-up envelope with 'Will' on it. It was signed and witnessed ten days ago. At Greengages, of course, and it's on a printed form thing."

"How did it get to Quintern?"

"Mrs. Jim says Mummy asked Bruce Gardener to take it and put it in the desk. He gave it to Mrs. Jim and she put it in the desk. Godma V, it's a stinker."

"Oh dear."

"It's—you'll never believe this—I can't myself. It starts off by saying she leaves half her estate to me. You do know, don't you, that darling Mummy was a Rich Bitch. Sorry, that's a fun-phrase. But true."

"I did suppose she was."

"I mean *really* rich. Rolling."

"Yes."

"Partly on account of grandpapa Passcoigne and partly because Daddy was a wizard with the lolly. Where was I?"

"Half the estate to you," Verity prompted.

"Yes. That's over and above what Daddy entailed on me if that's what it's called. And Quintern's entailed on me, too, of course."

"Nothing the matter with *that*, is there?"

"Wait for it. You'll never, never believe this—half to me *only* if I marry awful Swingles—John Swingletree. I wouldn't have thought it possible. Not even with Mummy, I wouldn't. It doesn't *matter*, of course. I mean, I've got more than is good for me with the entailment. Of course it's a lot less on account of inflation and all that but I've been thinking, actually, that I ought to give it away when I marry. Gideon doesn't agree."

"You astonish me."

"But he wouldn't stop me. Anyway *he's* rather more than O.K. for lolly." Prunella's voice trembled. "But, Godma V," she said, "how she *could!* How she could think it'd make me do it! Marry Swingles and cut Gideon just for the cash. It's repulsive."

"I wouldn't have believed it of her. Does Swingletree *want* you to marry him, by the way?"

"Oh, yes," said Prunella impatiently. "Never stops asking, the poor sap."

"It must have been when she was in a temper," said Verity. "She'd have torn it up when she came round."

"But she didn't, did she? And she'd had plenty of time to come round. And you haven't heard anything yet. Who do you suppose she's left the rest to?—well, all but twenty-five thousand pounds? She's left twenty-five thousand pounds to Bruce Gardener, as well as a super little house in the village that is part of the estate and provision for him to be kept on as long as he likes at Quintern. But the rest—including the half if I don't marry Swingles—to whom do you suppose—"

A wave of nausea came over Verity. She sat down by her telephone and saw with detachment that the receiver shook in her hand.

"Are you there?" Prunella was saying. "Hullo! Godma V?"

"I'm here."

"I give you three guesses. You'll never get it. Do you give up?"

"Yes."

"Your heart-throb, darling. Dr. Basil Schramm."

A long pause followed. Verity tried to speak but her mouth was dry.

"Godma, are you there? Is something the matter with your telephone? Did you hear me?"

"Yes, I heard. I—I simply don't know what to say."

"Isn't it awful?"

"It's appalling."

"I told you she was crackers about him, didn't I?"

"Yes, yes, you did and I saw it for myself. But to do this—!"

"I know. When I don't marry that ass Swingles, Schramm'll get the lot."

"Good God!" said Verity.

"Well, won't he? *I* don't know. Don't ask me. Perhaps it'll turn out to be not proper. The Will, I mean."

"Ratsy will pounce on that—Mr. Rattisbon—if it is so. Is it witnessed?"

"It seems to be. By G. M. Johnson and Marleena Briggs. Housemaids at Greengages, I should think, wouldn't you?"

"I daresay."

"Well, I thought I'd just tell you."

"Yes. Thank you."

"I'll let you know what Mr. Rats thinks."

"Thanks."

"Goodbye then, Godma darling."

"Goodbye, darling. I'm sorry. Especially," Verity managed, "about the Swingletree bit."

"I know. Bruce is chicken feed, compared," said Prunella. "And what a name!" she added. "Lady Swingletree! I ask you!" and hung up.

It was exactly a week after this conversation and in the morning of just such another halcyon day that Verity answered her front doorbell to find a very tall man standing in the porch.

He took off his hat. "Miss Preston?" he said. "I'm sorry to bother you. I'm a police officer. My name is Alleyn."

## II

Afterward, when he had gone away, Verity thought it strange that her first reaction had not been one of alarm. At the moment of encounter she had simply been struck by Alleyn himself: by his voice, his thin face and—there was only one word she could find—his distinction. There was a brief feeling of incredulity and then the thought that he might be on the track of Charmless Claude. He sat there in her drawing-room with his knees crossed, his thin hands clasped together and his eyes, which were bright, directed upon her. It came as a shock when he said: "It's about the late Mrs. Foster that I hoped to have a word with you."

Verity heard herself say: "Is there something wrong?"

"It's more a matter of making sure there isn't," he said. "This is a routine visit and I know that's what we're always supposed to say."

"Is it because something's turned up at the—examination: the—I can't remember the proper word."

"Autopsy?"

"Yes. Stupid of me."

"You might say it's arisen out of that, yes. Things have turned out a bit more complicated than was expected."

After a pause, Verity said: "I'm sure one's not meant to ask questions, is one?"

"Well," he said, and smiled at her, "I can always evade answering but the form is supposed to be for me to ask."

"I'm sorry."

"Not a bit. You shall ask me anything you like as the need arises. In the meantime shall I go ahead?"

"Please."

"My first one is about Mrs. Foster's room."

"At Greengages?"

"Yes."

"I was never in it."

"Do you know if she habitually used a sort of glass sleeve contraption filled with scented oil that fitted over a lamp bulb?"

"'Oasis'? Yes, she used it in the drawing-room at Quintern and sometimes, I think, in her bedroom. She adored what she called a really groovy smell."

"'Oasis,' if that's what it was, is all of that. They tell me the memory lingers on in the window curtains. Did she usually have a nightcap, do you know? Scotch?"

"I think she did, occasionally, but she wasn't much of a drinker. Far from it."

"Miss Preston, I've seen the notes of your evidence at the inquest but if you don't mind I'd like to go back to the talk you had with Mrs. Foster on the lawn that afternoon. It's simply to find out if by any chance, and on consideration, hindsight if you like, something was said that now seems to suggest she contemplated suicide."

"Nothing. I've thought and thought. Nothing." And as she said this Verity realized that with all her heart she wished there had been something and at the same time told herself how appalling it was that she could desire it. "I shall never get myself sorted out over this," she thought and became aware that Alleyn was speaking to her.

"If you could just run over the things you talked about. Never mind if they seem irrelevant or trivial."

"Well, she gossiped about the hotel. She talked a lot about—the doctor—and the wonders of his cure and about the nurse—Sister something —who she said resented her being a favourite. But most of all we talked about Prunella—her daughter's—engagement."

"Didn't she fancy the young man?"

"Well—she *was* upset," Verity said. "But—well, she was often upset. I suppose it would be fair to say she was inclined to get into tizzies at the drop of a hat."

"A fuss-pot?"

"Yes."

"Spoilt, would you say?" he asked, surprisingly.

"Rather indulged, perhaps."

"Keen on the chaps?"

He put this to her so quaintly that Verity was startled into saying: "You *are* sharp!"

"A happy guess, I promise you," said Alleyn.

"You must have heard about the Will," she exclaimed.

"Who's being sharp now?"

"I don't know," Verity said crossly, "why I'm laughing."

"When, really, you're very worried, aren't you? Why?"

"I don't *know*. Not really. It's all so muddling," she broke out. "And I *hate* being muddled."

She stared helplessly at Alleyn. He nodded and gave a small affirmative sound.

"You see," Verity began again, "when you asked if she said anything that suggested suicide I said 'nothing,' didn't I? And if you'd known Syb as well as I did, there *was* nothing. But if you ask me whether she's ever suggested anything of the sort—well, yes. If you count her being in a bit of a stink over some dust-up and throwing a temperament and saying life wasn't worth living and she might as well end it all. But that was just histrionics. I often thought Syb's true métier was the theatre."

"Well," said Alleyn, "you ought to know."

"Have you seen Prunella? Her daughter?" Verity asked.

"Not yet. I've read her evidence. I'm on my way there. Is she at home, do you know?"

"She has been, lately. She goes up to London quite a lot."

"Who'll be there if she's out?"

"Mrs. Jim Jobbin. General factotum. It's her morning at Quintern."

"Anyone else?"

"*Damn!*" thought Verity, "here we go." She said: "I haven't been in touch. Oh, it's the gardener's day up there."

"Ah yes. The gardener."

"Then you *do* know about the Will?"

"Mr. Rattisbon told me about it. He's an old acquaintance of mine. May we go back to the afternoon in question? Did you discuss Miss Foster's engagement with her mother?"

"Yes. I tried to reconcile her to the idea."

"Any success?"

"Not much. But she did agree to see them. Is it all right to ask—did they find—did the pathologist find—any signs of a disease?"

"He thinks, as Dr. Field-Innis did, that she might have had Parkinson's disease."

"If she had known that," Verity said, "it might have made a difference. If she was told—but Dr. Field-Innis didn't tell her."

"And Dr. Schramm apparently didn't spot it."

Sooner or later it had to come. They'd arrived at his name.

"Have you met Dr. Schramm?" Alleyn asked casually.

"Yes."

"Know him well?"

"No. I used to know him many years ago but we had entirely lost touch."

"Have you seen him lately?"

"I've only met him once at a dinner-party some months ago. At Mardling: Mardling Manor belonging to Mr. Nikolas Markos. It's his son who's engaged to Prunella."

"The millionaire Markos, would that be?"

"Not that I know. He certainly seems to be extremely affluent."

"The millionaire who buys pictures," said Alleyn, "if that's any guide."

"This one does that. He'd bought a Troy."

"That's the man," said Alleyn. "She called it *Several Pleasures*."

"But—how did you—? Oh, I see," said Verity, "you've been to Mardling."

"No. The painter is my wife."

"Curiouser," said Verity, after a long pause, "and curiouser."

"Do you find it so? I don't quite see why."

"I should have said, how lovely. To be married to Troy."

"Well, we like it," said Troy's husband. "Could I get back to the matter in hand, do you think?"

"Of course. Please," said Verity with a jolt of nausea under her diaphragm.

"Where were we?"

"You asked me if I'd met Basil Smythe."

*"Smythe?"*

"I should have said Schramm," Verity amended quickly. "I believe Schramm was his mother's maiden name. I think she wanted him to take it. He said something to that effect."

"When would that have happened, would you suppose?"

"Sometime after I knew him, which was in 1951, I think," Verity added and hoped it sounded casual.

"How long had Mrs. Foster known him, do you imagine?"

"Not—very long. She met him first at that same dinner-party. But," said Verity quickly, "she'd been in the habit of going to Greengages for several years."

"Whereas he only took over the practice last April," he said casually. "Do you like him? Nice sort of chap?"

"As I said I've only met him that once."

"But you knew him before?"

"It was—so very long ago."

"I don't think you liked him very much," he murmured as if to himself. "Or perhaps—but it doesn't matter."

"Mr. Alleyn," Verity said loudly and, to her chagrin, in an unsteady voice. "I know what was in the Will."

"Yes, I thought you must."

"And perhaps I'd better just say it—the Will—might have happened at any time in the past if Sybil had been thoroughly upset. On the rebound from a row, she could have left anything to anyone who was in favour at the time."

"But did she to your knowledge ever do this in the past?"

"Perhaps she never had the same provocation in the past."

"Or was not sufficiently attracted?"

"Oh," said Verity, "she took fancies. Look at this whacking great legacy to Bruce."

"Bruce? Oh, yes. The gardener. She thought a lot of him, I suppose? A faithful and tried old retainer? Was that it?"

"He'd been with her about six months and he's middle-aged and rather like a resurrection from the more dubious pages of J. M. Barrie but Syb thought him the answer to her prayers."

"As far as the garden was concerned?"

"Yes. He does my garden, too."

"It's enchanting. Do you dote on him, too?"

"No. But I must say I like him better than I did. He took trouble over Syb. He visited her once a week with flowers and I don't think he was sucking up. I just think he puts on a bit of an act like a guide doing his sob-stuff over Mary Queen of Scots in Edinburgh Castle."

"I've never heard a guide doing sob-stuff in Edinburgh Castle."

"They drool. When they're not having a go at William and Mary, they get closer and closer to you and the tears seem to come into their eyes and they drool about Mary Queen of Scots. I may have been un-lucky, of course. Bruce is positively taciturn in comparison. He overdoes the nature-lover bit but only perhaps because his employers encourage it. He *is*, in fact, a dedicated gardener."

"And he visited Mrs. Foster at Greengages?"

"He was there that afternoon."

"While you were there?"

Verity explained how Bruce and she had encountered in the grounds and how she'd told him Sybil wouldn't be able to see him then and how Prunella had suggested later on that he left his lilies at the desk.

"So he did just that?"

"I think so. I suppose they both went back by the next bus."

*"Both?"*

"I'd forgotten Charmless Claude."

"Did you say 'Charmless'?"

"He's Syb's ghastly stepson."

Verity explained Claude but avoided any reference to his more dubi-ous activities, merely presenting him as a spineless drifter. She kept tell-ing herself she ought to be on her guard with this atypical policeman in whose company she felt so inappropriately conversational. At the drop of a hat, she thought, she'd find herself actually talking about that epi-sode of the past that she had never confided to anyone and which still persisted so rawly in her memory.

She pulled herself together. He had asked her if Claude was the son of Sybil's second husband.

"No, of her first husband, Maurice Carter. She married him when she was seventeen. He was a very young widower. His first wife died in childbirth—leaving Claude, who was brought up by his grandparents. They didn't like him very much, I'm afraid. Perhaps he might have turned out better if they had, but there it is. And then Maurice married Syb, who was in the WRENS. She was on duty somewhere in Scot-land when he got an unexpected leave. He came down here to Quin-tern—Quintern Place is *her* house, you know—and tried to ring her up but couldn't get through so he wrote a note. While he was doing this he was recalled urgently to London. The troop-train he caught was bombed and he was killed. She found the note afterwards. That's a sad story, isn't it?"

"Yes. Was this stepson, Claude, provided for?"

"Very well provided for, really. His father wasn't an enormously rich man but he left a trust fund that paid for Claude's upbringing. It still would be a reasonable stand-by if he didn't contrive to lose it, as fast as it comes in. Of course," Verity said more to herself than to Alleyn, "it'd have been different if the stamp had turned up."

"Did you say 'stamp'?"

"The Black Alexander. Maurice Carter inherited it. It was a pre-revolution Russian stamp that was withdrawn on the day it was issued because of a rather horrid little black flaw that looked like a bullet-hole in the Czar's forehead. Apparently there was only the one specimen known to be in existence and so this one was worth some absolutely fabulous amount of money. Maurice's own collection was medium-valuable and it went to Claude, who sold it, but the Black Alexander couldn't be found. He was known to have taken it out of his bank the day before he died. They searched and searched but with no luck and it's generally thought he must have had it on him when he was killed. It was a direct hit. It was bad luck for Claude about the stamp."

"Where is Claude now?"

Verity said uncomfortably that he had been staying at Quintern but she didn't know if he was still there.

"I see. Tell me: when did Mrs. Foster remarry?"

"In—when was it? In 1955. A large expensive stockbroker who adored her. He had a heart condition and died of it in 1964. You know," Verity said suddenly, "when one tells the whole story, bit by bit, it turns almost into a classic tragedy, and yet, somehow one can't see poor old Syb as a tragic figure. Except when one remembers the *look*."

"The look that was spoken of at the inquest?"

"Yes. It would have been quite frightful if she, of all people, had suffered that disease."

After a longish pause Verity said: "When will the inquest be re-opened?"

"Quite soon. Probably early next week. I don't think you will be called again. You've been very helpful."

"In what way? No, don't tell me," said Verity. "I—I don't think I want to know. I don't think I want to be helpful."

"Nobody loves a policeman," he said cheerfully and stood up. So did Verity. She was a tall woman but he towered over her.

He said: "I think this business has upset you more than you realize. Will you mind if I give you what must sound like a professionally motivated word of advice? If it turns out that you're acquainted with some episode or some piece of behaviour, perhaps quite a long way back in time, that might throw a little light on—say on the character of one or the other of the people we have discussed—don't withhold it. You never know. By doing so you might be doing a disservice to a friend."

"We're back to the Will again. Aren't we?"

"Oh, that? Yes. In a sense we are."

"You think she may have been influenced? Or that in some way it might be a cheat? Is that it?"

"The possibility must be looked at when the terms of a Will are extravagant and totally unexpected and the Will itself is made so short a time before the death of the testator."

"But that's not all? Is it? You're not here just because Syb made a silly Will. You're here because she died. You think it wasn't suicide. Don't you?"

He waited so long and looked so kindly at her that she was answered before he spoke.

"I'm afraid that's it," he said at last. "I'm sorry."

Again he waited, expecting, perhaps, that she might ask more questions or break down but she contrived, as she put it to herself, to keep up appearances. She supposed she must have gone white because she found he had put her back in her chair. He went away and returned with a glass of water.

"I found your kitchen," he said. "Would you like brandy with this?"

"No—why? There's nothing the matter with me," said Verity and tried to steady her hand. She took a hurried gulp of water.

"Dizzy spell," she improvised. "'Age with stealing steps' and all that."

"I don't think he can be said to have 'clawed you with his clutch.'"

"Thank you."

"Anyway, I shan't bother you any longer. Unless there's something I can do?"

"I'm perfectly all right. Thank you very much, though."

"Sure? I'll be off then. Goodbye."

Through the drawing-room window she watched him go striding down the drive and heard a car start up in the lane.

"Time, of course, does heal, as people say in letters of condolence," she thought. "But they don't mention the scars and twinges that crop up when the old wound gets an unexpected jolt. And this is a bad jolt," thought Verity. "This is a snorter."

And Alleyn, being driven by Inspector Fox to Quintern Place, said: "That's a nice intelligent creature, Br'er Fox. She's got character and guts but she couldn't help herself going white when I talked about Schramm. She was much concerned to establish that they hadn't met for many years and then only once. Why? An old affair? On the whole, I can't wait to meet Dr. Schramm."

### III

But first they must visit Quintern Place. It came into view unmistakably as soon as they had passed through the village: a Georgian house halfway up a hill, set in front of a stand of oaks and overlooking a rose-garden, lawns, a ha-ha and a sloping field and woodlands. Facing this restrained and lovely house and separated from it by a shallow declivity, was a monstrous Victorian pile, a plethora of towers and pepper pots approached by a long avenue that opened, by way of grandiloquent gates, off the lane leading to Quintern. "That's Mardling Manor, that is," said Alleyn, "the residence of Mr. Nikolas Markos, who had the good sense and taste to buy Troy's *Several Pleasures.*"

"I wouldn't have thought the house was quite his style," said Mr. Fox.

"And you'd have been dead right. I can't imagine what possessed him to buy such a monumental piece of complacency unless it was to tease himself with an uninterrupted view of a perfect house," said Alleyn and little knew how close to the mark he had gone.

"Did you pay a call on the local Super?" he asked.

"Yes. He's looking forward to meeting you. I got a bit of info out of him," said Mr. Fox, "which came in handy seeing I've only just been brought in on the case. It seems they're interested in the deceased lady's stepson, a Mr. Carter. He's a bit of a ne'er-do-well. Worked his way home from Australia in the *Poseidon* as a ship's steward. He's done porridge for attempted blackmail and he's sussy for bringing the hard stuff ashore but they haven't got enough for a catch. He's staying up at Quintern Place."

"So Miss Preston thought. And here we go."

The approach was through a grove of rhododendrons from which they came out rather unexpectedly on a platform in front of the house. Looking up at the facade, Alleyn caught a fractional impression of someone withdrawing from a window at the far end of the first floor. Otherwise there was no sign of life.

The door was opened by a compact little person in an apron. She looked quickly at the car and its driver and then doubtfully at Alleyn, who took off his hat.

"You must be Mrs. Jim Jobbin," he said.

Mrs. Jim looked hard at him. "That's correct," she said.

"Do you think Miss Foster could give me a moment if she's in?"

"She's not."

"Oh."

Mrs. Jim gave a quick look across the little valley to where Mardling Manor shamelessly exhibited itself. "She's out," she said.

"I'm sorry about that. Would you mind if I came in and had a word with you? I'm a police officer but there's no need to let that bother you. It's only to tidy up some details about the inquest on Mrs. Foster."

He had the impression that Mrs. Jim listened for something to happen inside the house and not hearing it, waited for him to speak and not hearing that either, was relieved. She gave him another pretty hard look and then stood away from the door.

"I'll just ask my colleague to wait if I may?" Alleyn said and returned to the car.

"A certain amount of caginess appears," he murmured. "If anything emerges and looks like melting away ask it if it's Mr. Carter and keep it here. Same goes for the gardener." Aloud he said: "I won't be long," and returned to the house.

Mrs. Jim stood aside for him and he went into a large and beautifully proportioned hall. It was panelled in parchment-coloured linenfold oak with a painted ceiling and elegant stairway. "What a lovely house," Alleyn said. "Do you look after it?"

"I help out," said Mrs. Jim guardedly.

"Miss Preston told me about you. Mrs. Foster's death must have been a shock after knowing her for so long."

"It seemed a pity," Mrs. Jim conceded economically.

"Did you expect anything of the kind?"

"I didn't expect anything. I never thought she'd make away with herself if that's what's meant. She wasn't the sort."

"Everybody seems to think that," Alleyn agreed.

The hall went right through the house and at the far end looked across rose-gardens to the misty Weald of Kent. He moved to the windows and was in time to see a head and shoulders bob up and down behind a box hedge. The owner seemed to be crouched and running.

"You've got somebody behaving rather oddly in your garden," said Alleyn. "Come and look."

She moved behind him.

"He's doubled up," Alleyn said, "behind that tallish hedge. Could he be chasing some animal?"

"I don't know, I'm sure."

"Who could it be?"

"The gardener's working here today."

"Has he got long fair hair?"

"No," she said quickly and passed her working hand across her mouth.

"Would the gentleman in the garden, by any chance, be Mr. Claude Carter?"

"It might."

"Perhaps he's chasing butterflies."

"He might be doing anything," said Mrs. Jim woodenly.

Alleyn, standing back from the window and still watching the hedge, said: "There's only one point I need bother you with, Mrs. Jobbin. It's about the envelope that I believe you put in Mrs. Foster's desk after her death."

"She give it to the gardener about a week before she died and said he was to put it there. He give it to me and asked me to. Which I did."

"And you told Miss Foster it was there?"

"Correct. I remembered it after the inquest."

"Do you know what was in it?"

"It was none of my business, was it, sir?" said Mrs. Jim, settling for the courtesy title. "It had 'Will' written on the outside and Miss Prue said it was a stinker. She give it to the lawyer."

"Was it sealed, do you remember?"

"It was gummed up. Sort of."

"Sort of, Mrs. Jim?"

"Not what you'd call a proper job. More of a careless lick. She was like that with her letters. She'd think of something she'd meant to say and open them up and then stick them down with what was left of the gum. She was great on afterthoughts."

"Would you mind letting me see the desk?"

Mrs. Jim's face reddened and she stuck out her lower lip.

"Mrs. Jobbin," Alleyn said. "Don't think we're here for any other purpose than to try and sort matters out in order that there shall be no injustice done to anybody, including Miss Prunella Foster, or if it comes to that, to the memory of her mother. I'm not setting traps at the moment, which is not to say a copper never does. As I expect you very well know. But not here and not now. I would simply like to see the desk, if you'll show me where it is."

She looked fixedly at him for an appreciable interval and then broke out: "It's no business of mine, this isn't. I don't know anything about anything that goes on up here, sir, and if you'll excuse my speaking out, I don't want to. Miss Prue's all right. She's a nice young lady for all you can't hear half she says and anyone can see she's been upset. But she's got her young man and he's sharp enough for six and he'll look after her. So'll his old—his father," amended Mrs. Jim. "He's that pleased, anyway, with the match, seeing he's getting what he'd set his heart on."

"Really? What was that?" Alleyn asked still keeping an eye on the box hedge.

"This property. He wanted to buy it and they say he would have paid anything to get it. Well, in a sort of way he'll get his wish now, won't he? It's settled he's to have his own rooms; self-contained like. I'll show you the desk, then, if you'll come this way."

It was in a smallish room, known in her lifetime as Sybil's boudoir, which lay between the great drawing-room and the dining-room where, on the day of the old gardener's death, the Upper Quintern ladies had held their meeting. The desk, a nice piece of Chippendale, stood in the window. Mrs. Jim indicated the centre drawer and Alleyn opened it. Letter paper, stamps and a diary were revealed.

"The drawer wasn't locked?" he asked.

"Not before, it wasn't. I left the envelope on top of some papers and then I thought it best to turn the key in the lock and keep it. I handed the key to Miss Prue. She doesn't seem to have locked it." She waited for a moment and then, for the second time, broke out.

"If you want to know any more about it you can ask Bruce. He fetched it. Mrs. Foster give it to him."

"Do you think he knows what was in it? The details, I mean?"

"Ask him. I don't know. I don't discuss the business of the house and I don't ask questions: no more than I expect them to ask me."

"Mrs. Jobbin, I'm sure you don't and I won't bother you much further."

He was about to shut the drawer when he noticed a worn leather case. He opened it and disclosed a photograph, in faded sepia, of a group from a Scottish regiment. Among the officers was a second lieutenant, so emphatically handsome as to stand out from among his fellows.

"That's her first," said Mrs. Jim, at Alleyn's back. "Third from the left. Front row. First war. Name of Carter."

"He must have been a striking chap to look at."

"Like a Greek god," Mrs. Jim startled him by announcing, still in her wooden voice. "That's what they used to say: them in the village that remembered him."

Wondering which of the Upper Quintern worthies had employed this classy simile, Alleyn pushed the drawer shut and looked at the objects on the top of the desk. Prominent among them was a photograph of pretty Prunella Foster: one of the ultra-conservative kind, destined for glossy magazines and thought of by Alleyn as "Cabinet Pudding." Further off, and equally conventional, was that of a middle-aged man of full habit and slightly prominent eyes who had signed himself "John." That would be Foster: the second husband and Prunella's father. Alleyn looked down into the pink-shaded lamp on Sybil Foster's desk. The bulb was covered by a double-glass slipper. A faint rumour of sweet almonds still hung about it.

"Was there anything else you was wanting?" asked Mrs. Jim.

"Not from you, thank you, Mrs. Jobbin. I'd like a word with the gardener. I'll find him somewhere out there, I expect." He waited for a moment and then said cheerfully: "I gather you're not madly keen on him."

"Him," said Mrs. Jim. "I wouldn't rave and that's a fact. Too much of the Great I Am."

"The—?"

"Letting on what a treat he is to all and sundry."

"Including Mrs. Foster?"

"Including everybody. It's childish. One of these days he'll burst into poetry and stifle himself," said Mrs. Jim and then seemed to think better of it. "No harm in 'im, mind," she amended. "Just asking for attention. Like a child, pathetic, reely. And good at his work, he is. You've got to hand it to him. He's all right at bottom even if it is a long way down."

"Mrs. Jobbin," said Alleyn, "you are a very unexpected and observant lady. I will leave my card for Miss Foster and I wish you a grateful good morning."

He held out his hand. Mrs. Jobbin, surprised into a blush, put her corroded little paw into it and then into her apron pocket.

"Bid you good-day, then," she said. "Sir. You'll likely find him near the old stables. First right from the front door and right again. Growing mushrooms, for Gawd's sake."

Bruce was not near the old stables but in them. As Alleyn approached he heard the drag and slam of a door and when he "turned right again," found his man.

Bruce had evidently taken possession of what had originally been some kind of open-fronted lean-to abutting on the stables. He had removed part of the flooring and dug up the ground beneath. Bags of humus and a heap of compost awaited his attention.

In response to Alleyn's greeting he straightened up, squared his shoulders and came forward. "Guid day, sir," he said: "Were you looking for somebody?"

"For you," Alleyn said, "if your name's Gardener."

"It is that. Gardener's the name and gardener's the occupation," he said, evidently cracking a vintage quip. "What can I do for you, then?"

Alleyn made the usual announcement.

"Police?" said Bruce loudly and stared at him. "Is that a fact? Ou aye, who'd have thowt it?"

"Would you like me to flash a card at you?" Alleyn asked lightly. Bruce put his head on one side, gazed at him, waited for a moment and then became expansive.

"Och, na, na, na, na," he said. "Not at a', not at a'. There's no call for anything o' the sort. You didna strike me at first sight as a constabulary figure, just. What can I do for you?"

Members of the police force develop a sixth sense about the undeclared presence of offstage characters. Alleyn had taken the impression that Bruce was aware, but not anxiously, of a third person somewhere in the offing.

"I wanted to have a word with you, if I might," he said, "about the late Mrs. Foster. I expect you know about the adjourned inquest."

Bruce looked fixedly at him. "He's refocussing," thought Alleyn. "He was expecting something else."

"I do that," Bruce said. "Aye. I do that."

"You'll realize, of course, that the reason for the adjournment was to settle, beyond doubt, the question of suicide."

Bruce said slowly: "I wad never have believed it of her. Never. She was aye fu' of enthusiasm. She like fine to look ahead to the pleasures of her garden. Making plans! What for would we be planning for mushrooms last time I spoke with her if she was of a mind to make awa' wi' herself?"

"When was that?"

He pushed his gardener's fingers through his sandy hair and said it would have been when he visited her a week before it happened and that she had been in great good humour and they had drawn plans on the back of an envelope for a lily-pond and had discussed making a mushroom bed here in the old stables. He had promised to go into matters of plumbing and mulching and here he was, carrying on as if she'd be coming home to see it. Something, he said, must have happened during that last week to put sic' awfu' thoughts into her head.

"Was it on that visit," Alleyn asked, "that she gave you her Will to put in her desk here at Quintern?"

Bruce said aye, it was that and intimated that he hadn't fancied the commission but that her manner had been so light-hearted he had not entertained any real misgivings.

Alleyn said: "Did Mrs. Foster give you any idea of the terms of this Will?"

For the first time he seemed to be discomforted. He bent his blue unaligned gaze on Alleyn and muttered: she had mentioned that he wasn't forgotten.

"I let on," he said, "that I had no mind to pursue the matter."

He waited for a moment and then said Alleyn would consider maybe that this was an ungracious response but he'd not like it to be thought he looked for anything of the sort from her. He became incoherent, shuffled his boots and finally burst out: "To my way of thinking it isna just the decent thing."

"Did you say as much to Mrs. Foster?"

"I did that."

"How did she take it?"

"She fetched a laugh and said I'd no call to be sae squeamish."

"Did she tell you how much she'd left you?"

A pause.

"She didna," he said at last. "She fetched a bit laugh and asked me would I like to make a guess. I said I would not."

"And that was all?"

"Ou aye. I delivered the thing into the hand of Mrs. Jim, having no mind to tak' it further, and she told me she'd put it in the desk."

"Was the envelope sealed?"

"No' sealed in the literal sense but licked up. The mistress was na' going to close it but I said I'd greatly prefer that she should." He waited for a moment. "It's no' that I wouldna have relished the acquisition of a wee legacy," he said. "Not a great outlandish wallop, mind, but a wee, decent amount. I'd like that. I would so. I'd like it fine and put it by, remembering the bonny giver. But I wouldna have it thowt or said I took any part in the proceedings."

"I understand that," said Alleyn. "By the way, did Mrs. Foster ask you to get the form for her?"

"The forrum? What forrum would that be, sir?"

"The Will. From a stationer's shop?"

"Na, na," he said, "I ken naething o' that."

"And, while we're on the subject, did she ask you to bring things in for her? When you visited her?"

It appeared that he had from time to time fetched things from Quintern to Greengages. She would make a list and he would give it to Mrs. Jim. "Clamjampherie," mostly, he thought, things from her dressing-table. Sometimes, he believed, garments. Mrs. Jim would put them in a small case so that he wasn't embarrassed by impedimenta unbecoming to a man. Mrs. Foster would repack the case with things to be laundered. Alleyn gathered that the strictest decorum was observed. If he was present at these exercises he would withdraw to the window. He was at some pains to make this clear, arranging his mouth in a prim expression as he did so.

A picture emerged from these recollections of an odd, a rather cosy, relationship, enjoyable, one would think, for both parties. Plans had been laid, pontifications exchanged. There had been, probably, exclamatory speculation as to what the world was coming to, consultations over nurserymen's catalogues, strolls round the rose-garden and conservatory. Bruce sustained an air of rather stuffy condescension in letting fall an occasional reference to these observances and still he gave, as Mrs. Jim in her own fashion had given, an impression of listening for somebody or something.

Behind him in the side wall was a ramshackle closed door leading, evidently, into the main stables. Alleyn saw that it had gaps between the planks and had dragged its course through loose soil on what was left of the floor.

He made as if to go and then looking at Bruce's preparations asked if this was in fact to be the proposed mushroom bed. He said it was.

"It was the last request she made," he said. "And I prefer to carry it out." He expanded a little on the techniques of mushroom culture and then said, not too pointedly, if that was all he could do for Alleyn he'd better get on with it and reached for his long-handled shovel.

"There was one other thing," Alleyn said. "I almost forgot. You did actually go over to Greengages on the day of her death, didn't you?"

"I did so. But I never saw her," he said and described how he had waited in the hall with his lilies and how Prunella—"the wee lassie," he predictably called her—had come down and told him her mother was very tired and not seeing anybody that evening. He had left the lilies at the desk and the receptionist lady had said they would be attended to. So he had returned home by bus.

"With Mr. Claude Carter?" asked Alleyn.

Bruce became very still. His hands tightened on the shovel. He stared hard at Alleyn, made as if to speak and changed his mind. Alleyn waited.

"I wasna aware, just," Bruce said at last, "that you had spoken to that gentleman."

"Nor have I. Miss Preston mentioned that he arrived with you at Greengages."

He thought that over. "He arrived. That is so," said Bruce, "but he did not depart with me." He raised his voice. "I wish it to be clearly understood," he said. "I have no perrsonal relationship with that gentleman." And then very quietly and with an air of deep resentment: "He attached himself to me. He wurrumed the information out of me as to her whereabouts. It was an indecent performance and one that I cannot condone."

He turned his head fractionally toward the closed door. "And that is the total sum of what I have to say in the matter," he almost shouted.

"You've been very helpful. I don't think I need pester you any more: thank you for co-operating."

"There's no call for thanks: I'm a law-abiding man," Bruce said, "and I canna thole mysteries. Guid day to you, sir."

"This is a lovely old building," Alleyn said, "I'm interested in Georgian domestic architecture. Do you mind if I have a look round?"

Without waiting for an answer he passed between Bruce and the closed door, dragged it open and came face-to-face with Claude Carter.

"Oh, hullo," said Claude. "I thought I heard voices."

# CHAPTER IV

# Routine

## I

THE ROOM WAS EMPTY and smelt of rats with perhaps an undertone of long-vanished fodder. There was a tumbledown fireplace in one corner and in another a litter of objects that looked as if they had lain there for a century: empty tins, a sack that had rotted, letting out a trickle of cement, a bricklayer's trowel, rusted and handleless, a heap of empty manure bags. The only window was shuttered. Claude was a dim figure.

He said: "I was looking for Bruce. The gardener. I'm afraid I don't know—?"

The manner was almost convincing, almost easy, almost that of a son of the house. Alleyn thought the voice was probably pitched a little above its normal level but it sounded quite natural. For somebody who had been caught red-eared in the act of eavesdropping, Claude displayed considerable aplomb.

Alleyn shut the door behind him. Bruce Gardener, already plying his long-handled shovel, didn't look up.

"And I was hoping to see you," said Alleyn. "Mr. Carter, isn't it?"

"That's right. You have the advantage of me."

"Superintendent Alleyn."

After a considerable pause, Claude said: "Oh. What can I do for you, Superintendent?"

As soon as Alleyn told him he seemed to relax. He answered all the questions readily: yes, he had spoken to Miss Preston and Prue Foster but had not been allowed to visit his stepmother. He had gone for a stroll in the grounds, had missed the return bus and had walked into the village and picked up a later one there.

"A completely wasted afternoon," he complained. "And I must say I wasn't wildly enthusiastic about the reception I got. Particularly in the light of what happened. After all, she was my stepmother."

"When was the last time you saw her?"

"When? I don't know when. Three—four years ago."

"Before you went to Australia?"

He shot a sidelong look at Alleyn. "That's right," he said and after a pause: "You seem to be very well informed of my movements, Superintendent."

"I know you returned as a member of the ship's complement in the *Poseidon.*"

After a much longer pause, Claude said, "Oh, yes?"

"Shall we move outside and get a little more light and air on the subject?" Alleyn suggested.

Claude opened a door that gave directly on the yard. As they walked into the sunshine a clock in the stable turret told eleven very sweetly. The open front of the lean-to faced the yard. Bruce, shovelling vigorously, was in full view, an exemplar of ostentatious nonintervention. Claude stared resentfully at his stern and walked to the far end of the yard. Alleyn followed him.

"How long," he asked cheerfully, "had you been in that dark and rather smelly apartment?"

"How *long?* I don't know. No time at all really. Why?"

"I don't want to waste my breath and your time repeating myself, if you've already heard about the Will. And I think you must have heard it because, as I came up, the adjoining door in there was dragged shut."

Claude gave a rather shrill titter. "You *are* quick, aren't you?" he said. He lowered his voice. "As I said," he confided, "I was looking for that gardener-man in there. As a matter of fact I thought he might be in the other room and then when you came in and began talking it was jolly awkward. I didn't want to intrude so I—I mean I—you know—it's difficult to explain—"

"You're making a brave shot at it, though, aren't you? Your sense of delicacy prompted you to remove into the next room, shut that same openwork door and remain close by it throughout our conversation. Is that it?"

"Not at all. You haven't understood."

"You'd seen us arrive in a police car, perhaps, and you left the house in a hurry for the rose-garden and thence proceeded round the left wing to the stables?"

"I don't know," said Claude with a strange air of frightened effrontery, "why you're taking this line with me, Superintendent, but I must say I resent it."

"Yes, I thought you might be a bit put out by our appearance. Because of an irregularity in your departure from the *Poseidon*."

Claude began feverishly to maintain that there had been some mistake and the police had had to climb down and he was thinking of lodging a complaint only it didn't seem worth while.

Alleyn let him talk himself to a standstill and then said his visit had nothing to do with any of this and that he only wanted to be told if Claude did in fact know of a recent Will made by Mrs. Foster shortly before her death.

An elaborate shuffling process set in, hampered, it seemed, by the proximity of the ever-industrious Bruce. By means of furtive little nods and becks Claude indicated the desirability of a remove. Alleyn disregarded these hints and continued on a loudish, cheerful note.

"It's a perfectly simple question," he said. "Nothing private about it. Have you, in fact, known of such a Will?"

Claude made slight jabs with his forefinger, in the direction of Bruce's rear elevation.

"As it happens, yes," he mouthed.

"You have? Do you mind telling me how it came to your knowledge?"

"It's—I—it just so happened—"

"What did?"

"I mean to say—"

"*Havers!*" Bruce suddenly roared out. He became upright and faced them. "What ails you, man?" he demanded. "Can you no' give a straight answer when you're speired a straight question? Oot wi' it, for pity's sake. Tell him and ha' done. There's nothing wrong wi' the facts o' the matter."

"Yes, well, all right, all right," said the wretched Claude and added with a faint show of grandeur: "And you may as well keep a civil tongue in your head."

Bruce spat on his hands and returned to his shovelling.

"Well, Mr. Carter?" Alleyn asked.

By painful degrees it emerged that Claude had happened to be present when Bruce came into the house with the Will and had happened to see him hand it over to Mrs. Jim and had happened to notice what it was on account of the word "Will" being written in large letters on the envelope.

"And had happened," Bruce said without turning round but with a thwack of his shovel on the heap of earth he had raised, "to inquire with unco perrrsistence as to the cirrrcumstances."

"Look here, Gardener, I've had about as much of you as I can take," said Claude with a woeful show of spirit.

"You can tak' me or leave me, Mr. Carter, and my preference would be for the latter procedure."

"Do you know the terms of the Will?" Alleyn cut in.

"No, I don't. I'm not interested. Whatever they are they don't affect me."

"How do you mean?"

"My father provided for me. With a trust fund or whatever it's called. Syb couldn't touch that and she's not bloody likely to have added to it," said Claude with a little spurt of venom.

Upon this note Alleyn left them and returned deviously, by way of a brick-walled vegetable garden, to Fox. He noticed two newly made asparagus beds and a multitude of enormous cabbages and wondered where on earth they all went and who consumed them. Fox, patient as ever, awaited him in the car.

"Nothing to report," Fox said. "I took a walk round but no signs of anyone."

"The gardener's growing mushrooms in the stables and the stepson's growing butterflies in the stomach," said Alleyn and described the scene.

"Miss Preston," he said, "finds Bruce's Scots a bit hard to take."

"Phoney?"

"She didn't say that. More, 'laid on with a trowel.' She might have said with a long-handled shovel if she'd seen him this morning. But—I don't know. I'm no expert on dialects, Scots or otherwise, but it seemed to me he uses it more in the manner of someone who has lived with the genuine article long enough to acquire and display it inconsistently and inaccurately. His last job was in Scotland. He may think it adds to his charm or pawkiness or whatever."

"What about the stepson?"

"Oh, quite awful, poor devil. Capable of anything if he had the guts to carry it through."

"We move on?"

"We do. Hark forrard, hark forrard away to Greengages and the point marked X if there is one. Shall I drive and you follow the map?"

"Fair enough, if you say so, Mr. Alleyn. What do I look for?"

"Turn right after Maidstone and follow the road to the village of Greendale. Hence 'Greengages,' no doubt."

"Colicky sort of name for a hospital."

"It's not a hospital."

"Colicky sort of a name for whatever it is."

"There's no suggestion that the lady in question died of that, at least."

"Seeing I've only just come in could we re-cap on the way? What've we got for info?"

"We've got the lady who is dead. She was in affluent circumstances, stinking rich, in fact, and probably in the early stages of Parkinson's disease but unaware of it, and we've got the medical incumbent of an expensive establishment that is neither hospital nor nursing home but a hotel that caters for well-to-do invalids, whose patient the lady was, and who did not spot the disease. We've got a local doctor called Field-Innis and a police pathologist who did. We've got the lady's daughter who on the afternoon of her mother's death announced her engagement to a rich young man who did not meet with the lady's approval. We've got the rich young man's millionaire papa who coveted the lady's house, failed to buy it but will now live in it when his son marries the daughter."

"Hold on," said Fox, after a pause. "O.K. I'm with you."

"We've got an elderly Scottish gardener, possible pseudoish, to whom the lady has left twenty-five-thousand deflated quid in a recent Will. The rest of her fortune is divided between her daughter if she marries a peer called Swingletree and the medical incumbent who didn't diagnose Parkinson's disease. If the daughter doesn't marry Swingletree the incumbent gets the lot."

"That would be Dr. Schramm?"

"Certainly. The rest of the cast is made up of the lady's stepson by her first marriage who is the archetype of all remittance-men and has a police record. Finally we have a nice woman of considerable ability called Verity Preston."

"That's the lot?"

"Give and take a trained nurse and a splendid lady called Mrs. Jim who obliges in Upper Quintern, that's the lot."

"What's the score where we come in? Exactly, I mean?"

"The circumstances are the score really, Br'er Fox. The Will and the *mise-en-scène*. The inquest was really adjourned because everybody

says the lady was such an unlikely subject for suicide and had no motive. An extended autopsy seemed to be advisable. Sir James Curtis performed it. The undelicious results of Dr. Schramm's stomach pump had
been preserved and Sir James confirms that they disclosed a quantity of
the barbiturate found in the remaining tablets on the bedside table and
in the throat and at the back of the tongue. The assumption had been
that she stuffed down enough of the things to become so far doped as
to prevent her swallowing the last lot she put in her mouth."

"Plausible?"

"Dr. Schramm thought so. Sir James won't swallow it but says she
would have—if you'll excuse a joke in bad taste, Br'er Fox. He points
out that there's a delay of anything up to twenty minutes before the
barbiturate in question, which is soluble in alcohol, starts to work and
it's hard to imagine her waiting until she was too far under to swallow
before putting the final lot in her mouth."

"So what do we wonder about?"

"Whether somebody else put them there. By the way, Sr. James
looked for traces of cyanide."

"Why?" Mr. Fox asked economically.

"There'd been a smell of almonds in the room and in the contents of
the stomach but it turned out that she used sweet almond oil in one of
those glass-slipper things they put over lamp bulbs and that she'd
wolfed quantities of marzipan petits-fours from La Marquise de Sevigné in Paris. The half-empty box was on her bedside table along with
the vanity box and other litter."

"Like—the empty bottle of Scotch?"

"And the overturned glass. Exactly."

"Anybody know how much there'd been in the bottle? That day, for
instance?"

"Apparently not. She kept it in a cupboard above the hand-basin.
One gathers it lasted her a good long time."

"What about dabs?"

"The local chaps had a go before calling us in. Bailey and Thompson are coming down to give the full treatment."

"Funny sort of set-up though, isn't it?" Fox mused.

"The funniest bit is yet to come. Cast your mind back, however reluctantly, to the contents of the stomach as examined by Doctors Field-
Innis and Schramm."

"Oodles of barbiturate?"

"According to Schramm. But according to Sir James an appreciable
amount but not enough, necessarily, to have caused death. You know
how guarded he can be. Even allowing for what he calls 'a certain de-

gree of excretion' he would not take it as a matter of course that death would follow. He could find nothing to suggest any kind of suscep- tibility or allergy that might explain why it did."

"So now we begin to wonder about the beneficiaries in the recent and eccentric Will?"

"That's it. And who provided her with the printed form. Young Mr. Rattisbon allowed me to see it. It looks shop-new: fresh creases, sharp corners and edges."

"And all in order?"

"He's afraid so. Outrageous though the terms may be. I gather, by the way, that Miss Prunella Foster would sooner trip down the aisle with a gorilla than with the Lord Swingletree."

"So her share goes to this Dr. Schramm?"

"In addition to the princely dollop he would get in any case."

"It scarcely seems decent," said Fox primly.

"You should hear the Rattisbons, *père et fils*, on the subject."

"It's twenty to one," Fox said wistfully as they entered a village. "There's a nice-looking little pub ahead."

"So there is. Tell me your thoughts."

"They seem to dwell upon Scotch eggs, cheese and pickle sand- wiches and a pint of mild-and-bitter."

"So be it," said Alleyn and pulled in.

## II

Prunella Foster arrived from London at Quintern Place on her way to lunch with her fiancé and his father at Mardling. At Quintern Mrs. Jim informed her of Alleyn's visit earlier in the morning. As a *racon- teuse*, Mrs. Jim was strong on facts and short on atmosphere. She gave a list of events in order of occurrence, answered Prunella's questions with the greatest possible economy and expressed no opinion of any sort whatsoever. Prunella was flustered.

"And he was a *policeman*, Mrs. Jim?"

"That's what he said."

"Do you mean there was any doubt about it?"

"Not to say doubt. It's on his card."

"Well—what?"

Cornered, Mrs. Jim said Alleyn had seemed a bit on the posh side for it. "More after the style of one of your friends, like," she offered and added that he had a nice way with him.

Prunella got her once more to rehearse the items of the visit, which she did with accuracy.

"So he asked about—?" Prunella cast her eyes and jerked her head in the direction, vaguely, of that part of the house generally frequented by Claude Carter.

"That's right," Mrs. Jim conceded. She and Prunella understood each other pretty well on the subject of Claude. "But it was only to remark he'd noticed him dodging up and down in the rose-garden. He went out, after, to the stables. The gentleman did."

"To find Bruce?"

"That's right. Mr. Claude too, I reckon."

"Oh?"

"Mr. Claude come in after the gentleman had gone and went into the dining-room."

This, Prunella recognized, was an euphemism for "helped himself to a drink."

"Where is he now?" she asked.

Mrs. Jim said she'd no idea. They'd come to an arrangement about his meals, it emerged. She prepared a hot luncheon for one o'clock and laid the table in the small morning-room. She then beat an enormous gong and left for home. When she returned to Quintern in two days' time she would find the *disjecta membra* of this meal, together with those of any subsequent snacks, unpleasantly congealed upon the table.

"How difficult everything is," Prunella muttered. "Thank you, Mrs. Jim. I'm going to Mardling for lunch. We're making plans about Quintern: you know, arranging for Mr. Gideon's father to have his own quarters with us. He's selling Mardling, I think. After all that he'd done to it! Imagine! And keeping the house in London for his head-quarters."

"Is that right, Miss?" said Mrs. Jim and Prunella knew by the wooden tone she employed that she was deeply stimulated. "We'll be hearing wedding-bells one of these days, then?" she speculated.

"Well—not yet, of course."

"No," Mrs. Jim agreed. "That wouldn't be the thing. Not just yet."

"I'd really rather not have a 'wedding,' Mrs. Jim. I'd rather be just married early in the morning in Upper Quintern with hardly anyone there. But he—Gideon—wants it the other way so I suppose my aunt—Auntie Boo—" she whispered her way into inaudibility and her eyes filled with tears. She looked helplessly at Mrs. Jim and thought how much she liked her. For the first time since her mother died it occurred to Prunella that, apart, of course, from Gideon, she was very much alone in the world. She had never been deeply involved with her mother and had indeed found her deviousness and vanities irritating when not positively comical and even that degree of tolerance had been shaken by the preposterous terms of this wretched Will. And yet now, abruptly, when she realized that Sybil was not and never would be there to be laughed at or argued with: that where she had been there was—nothing, a flood of desolation poured over Prunella and she broke down and cried with her face in Mrs. Jim's cardigan, which smelt of floor polish.

Mrs. Jim said: "Never mind, then. It's been a right shock and all. We know that."

"I'm so sorry," Prunella sobbed. "I'm awfully sorry."

"You have your cry out, then."

This invitation had the opposite result to what had been intended. Prunella blew her nose and pulled herself together. She returned shakily to her wedding arrangements. "Somebody will have to give me away," she said.

"As long as it's not that Mr. Claude," said Mrs. Jim loudly.

"God forbid. I wondered—I don't know—can one be given away by a woman? I could ask the Vicar."

"Was you thinking of Miss Verity?"

"She *is* my godmother. Yes, I was."

"Couldn't do better," said Mrs. Jim.

"I must be off," said Prunella, who did not want to run into Claude. "You don't happen to know where those old plans of Quintern are? Mr. Markos wants to have a look at them. They're in a sort of portfolio thing."

"Library. Cupboard near the door. Bottom shelf."

"How clever of you, Mrs. Jim."

"Your mother had them out to show Bruce. Before she went to that place. She left them out and *he*"—the movement of the head they both used to indicate Claude—"was handling them and leaving them all over the place so I put them away."

"Good for you. Mrs. Jim—tell me. Does he—well—does he sort of peer and prowl? Do you know what I mean? Sort of?"

"Not my place to comment," said Mrs. Jim, "but as you've brought it up: yes, he do. I can tell by the way things have been interfered with—shifted like."

"Oh dear."

"Yes. Specially them plans. He seemed to fancy them, particular. I seen him looking at that one of the grounds through the magnifying glass in the study. He's a proper nosey parker if you ask me and don't mind my mentioning it," said Mrs. Jim rapidly. She brought herself up with a jerk. "Will I fetch them then? Put out your washing," said Mrs. Jim as an afterthought.

"Bless you. I'll just collect some things from my room."

Prunella ran up a lovely flight of stairs and across a first floor landing to her bedroom: a muslin and primrose affair with long windows opening over terraces, rose-gardens and uncluttered lawns that declined to a ha-ha, meadows, hayfields, spinnies and the tower of St. Crispin's-in-Quintern. A blue haze veiled the more distant valleys and hills and turned the chimneys of a paper-making town into minarets. Prunella was glad that after she had married she would still live in this house.

She bathed her eyes, repacked her suitcase and prepared to leave. On the landing she ran into Claude.

There was no reason why he should not be on the landing or that she should have been aware that he had arrived there but there was something intrinsically furtive about Claude that gave her a sensation of stealth.

He said: "Oh, hullo, Prue, I saw your car."

"Hullo, Claude. Yes. I just looked in to pick up some things."

"Not staying, then?"

"No."

"I hope I'm not keeping you away," he said and looked at his feet and smiled.

"Of course not. I'm mostly in London, these days."

He stole a glance at her left hand.

"Congratulations are in order, I see."

"Yes. Thank you."

"When's it to be?"

She said it hadn't been decided and began to move toward the stairs.

"Er—" said Claude, "I was wondering—"

"Yes?"

"Whether I'm to be handed the push."

Prunella made a panic decision to treat this as a joke.

"Oh," she said jauntily, "you'll be given plenty of notice."

"Too kind. Are you going to live here?"

"As a matter of fact, yes. After we've made some changes. You'll get fair warning, I promise."

"Syb said I could be here, you know."

"I know what she said, Claude. You're welcome to stay until the workmen come in."

"Too kind," he repeated, this time with an open sneer. "By the way you don't mind my asking, do you? I would like to know when the funeral is to be."

Prunella felt as if winter had come into the house and closed about her heart. She managed to say: "I don't—we won't know until after the inquest. Mr. Rattisbon is going to arrange everything. You'll be let know, Claude. I promise."

"Are you going to this new inquest?"

"I expect so. I mean: yes. Yes, I am."

"So am I. Not that it affects me, of course."

"I really must go. I'm running late."

"I never wrote to you. About Syb."

"There was no need. Goodbye."

"Shall I carry your case down?"

"No thanks. Really. It's quite light. Thank you very much, though."

"I see you've got the old plans out. Of Quintern."

"Goodbye," Prunella said desperately and made a business of getting herself downstairs.

She had reached the ground floor when his voice floated down to her. "Hi!"

She wanted to bolt but made herself stop and look up to the first landing. His face and hands hung over the balustrade.

"I suppose you realize we've had a visit from the police," said Claude. He kept his voice down and articulated pedantically.

"Yes, of course."

One of the dangling hands moved to cup the mouth. "They seem to be mightily interested in your mother's horticultural favorite," Claude mouthed. "I wonder why."

The teeth glinted in the moon-face.

Prunella bolted. She got herself, the immense portfolio and her baggage through the front door and into her car and drove, much too fast, to Mardling.

"Honestly," she said ten minutes later to Gideon and his father. "I almost feel we should get in an exorciser when Claude goes. I wonder if the Vicar's any good on the bell, book and candle lay."

"You enchanting child," said Mr. Markos in his florid way and raised his glass to her. "Is this unseemly person really upsetting you? Should Gideon and I advance upon him with threatening gestures? Can't he be dispensed with?"

"I must say," Gideon chimed in, "I really do think it's a bit much he should set himself up at Quintern. After all, darling, he's got no business there, has he? I mean no real family ties or anything. Face it."

"I suppose not," she agreed. "But my mama did feel she ought not to wash her hands of him completely, awful though he undoubtedly is. You see, she was very much in love with his father."

"Which doesn't, if one looks at it quite cold-bloodedly, give his son the right to impose upon her daughter," said Mr. Markos.

Prunella had noticed that this was a favourite phrase—"quite cold-bloodedly"—and was rather glad that Gideon had not inherited it. But she liked her father-in-law-to-be and became relaxed and expansive in the atmosphere (anything, she reflected, but "cold-blooded") that he created around himself and Gideon. She felt that she could say what she chose to him without being conscious of the difference in their ages and that she amused and pleased him.

They sat out of doors on swinging seats under canopies. Mr. Markos had decided that it was a day for preprandial champagne: "A sparkling, venturesome morning," he called it. Prunella, who had skipped breakfast and was unused to such extravagance, rapidly expanded. She downed her drink and accepted another. The horrors, and lately there really had been moments of horror, slipped into the background. She became perfectly audible and began to feel that this was the life for her and was meant for her and she for it, that she blossomed in the company of the exotic Markoses, the one so delightfully *mondain*, the other so enchantingly in love with her. Eddies of relief, floating on champagne, lapped over her and if they were vaguely disturbed by little undertows of guilt (for after all, she had a social conscience), that, however reprehensibly, seemed merely to add to her exhilaration. She took a vigorous pull at her champagne and Mr. Markos refilled her glass.

"Darling," said Gideon, "what *have* you got in that monstrous compendium or whatever it is, in your car?"

"A surprise," cried Prunella, waving her hand. "Not for you, love. For Pil." She raised her glass to Mr. Markos and drank to him.

"For *whom?*" asked the Markoses in unison.

"For my papa-in-law-to-be. I've been too shy to know what to call you," said Prunella. "Not for a moment, that you *are* a Pill. Far from it. *Pillicock sat on Pillicock-hill*," she sang before she could stop herself. She realized she had shaken her curls at Nikolas, like one of Dickens's more awful little heroines, and was momentarily ashamed of herself.

"You shall call me whatever you like," said Mr. Markos and kissed her hand. Another Dickens reference swam incontinently into Prunella's dizzy ken: "*Todgers were going it*." For a second or two she slid aside from herself and saw herself "going it" like mad in a swinging chair under a canopy and having her hand kissed. She was extravagantly pleased with life.

"Shall I fetch it?" Gideon asked.

"Fetch what?" Prunella shouted recklessly.

"Whatever you've brought for your papa-in-law-to-be."

"Oh, *that*. Yes, darling, do and I think perhaps no more champagne."

Gideon burst out laughing. "And I think perhaps you may be right," he said and kissed the top of her head. He went to her car and took out the portfolio.

Prunella said to Mr. Markos, "I'm tightish. How awful."

"Are you? Eat some olives. Stuff down lots of those cheese things. You're not really very tight."

"Promise? All right, I will," said Prunella and was as good as her word. A car came up the avenue.

"Here is Miss Verity Preston," said Mr. Markos. "Did we tell you she was lunching?"

"No!" she exclaimed and blew out a little shower of cheese straw. "How too frightful, she's my godmother."

"Don't you like her?"

"I adore her. But *she* won't like to see *me* flown with fizz so early in the day. Or ever. And as a matter of fact it's not my form at all, by and large," said Prunella, swallowing most of an enormous mouthful of cheese straw and helping herself to more. "I'm a sober girl."

"You're a divine girl. I doubt if Gideon deserves you."

"You're absolutely right. The cheese straws and olives are doing the trick. I shan't go on about being drunk. People who do that are such a bore, always, don't you feel? And anyway I'm rapidly becoming sober." As if to prove it she had begun to whisper again.

The Markoses went to meet Verity. Prunella thought of following them but compromised by getting up from her swinging seat, which she did in a quickly controlled flounder.

"Godma V," she said. And when they were close enough to each other she hung herself about Verity's neck and was glad to do so.

"Hullo, young party," said Verity, surprised by this effusion and not knowing what to do about it. Prunella sat down abruptly and inaccurately on the swinging chair.

The Markoses, father and son, stood one on each side of her smiling at Verity, who thought that her godchild looked like a briar rose between a couple of succulent exotics. "They will absorb her," Verity thought, "into their own world and one doesn't know what that may be. Was Syb by any chance right? And ought I to take a hand? What about her Aunt Boo?" Boo was Syb's flighty sister. "I'd better talk to Prue and I suppose write to Boo, who ought to have come back and taken some responsibility instead of sending vague cables from Acapulco." She realized that Nikolas Markos was talking to her.

"—hope you approve of champagne at this hour."

"Lovely," Verity said hastily, "but demoralizing."

"That's what I found, Godma V," whispered Prunella, lurching about in her swinging chair.

"For Heaven's sake," thought Verity, "the child's tipsy."

But when Mr. Markos had opened the portfolio, tenderly drawn out its contents and laid them on the garden table, which he dusted with his handkerchief, Prunella had so far recovered as to give a fairly informed comment on them.

"They're the original plans, I think. The house was built for my I don't know how many times great-grandfather. You can see the date is 1780. He was called Lord Rupert Passcoigne. My mama was the last Passcoigne of that family and inherited Quintern from her father. I hope I've got it right. The plans are rather pretty, aren't they, with the coat-of-arms and all the trimmings and nonsense?"

"My dear child," said Mr. Markos, poring over them, "they're exquisite. It's—I really can't tell you how excited I am to see them."

"There are some more underneath."

"We mustn't keep them too long in this strong light. Gideon, put this one back in the portfolio. Carefully. Gently. No, let me do it."

He looked up at Verity. "Have you seen them?" he asked. "Come and look. Share my gloat, do."

Verity had seen them, as it happened, many years ago when Sybil had first married her second husband, but she joined the party round the table. Mr. Markos had arrived at a plan for the gardens at Quintern and dwelt on it with greedy curiosity.

"But this has never been carried out," he said. "Has it? I mean, nicest possible daughter-in-law-to-be, the gardens today bear little resemblance in concept to this exquisite *schema*. Why?"

"Don't ask me," said Prunella. "Perhaps they ran out of cash or something. I rather think Mummy and Bruce were cooking up a grand idea about carrying out some of the scheme but decided we couldn't afford it. If only they hadn't lost the Black Alexander they could have done it."

"Yes indeed," said Verity.

Mr. Markos looked up quickly. "The Black Alexander!" he said. "What can you mean? You can't mean—"

"Oh, yes, of course. You're a collector."

"I am indeed. Tell me."

She told him and when she had done so he was unusually quiet for several seconds.

"But how immensely rewarding it would be—" he began at last and then pulled himself up. "Let us put the plans away," he said. "They arouse insatiable desires. I'm sure you understand, don't you, Miss Preston? I've allowed myself to build—not castles in Spain but gardens in Kent, which is much more reprehensible. Haven't I?"

How very intelligent, Verity thought, finding his black eyes focussed on hers, this Mr. Markos is. He seems to be making all sorts of assumptions and I seem to be liking it.

"I don't remember that I saw the garden plan before," she said. "It would have been a perfect marriage, wouldn't it?"

"Ah. And you have used the perfect phrase for it."

"Would you like to keep the plans here," asked Prunella, "to have another gloat?"

He thanked her exuberantly and luncheon having been announced, they went indoors.

Since that first dinner-party, which now seemed quite a long time ago, and the visit to Greengages on the day of Sybil's death, Verity had not seen much of the Markoses. She had been twice asked to Mardling for cocktail parties and on each occasion had been unable to go and one evening Markos Senior had paid an unheralded visit to Keys House, having spotted her, as he explained, in her garden and acted on the spur of the moment. They had got on well, having tastes in common and he showing a pretty acute appreciation of the contemporary theatre. Verity had been quite surprised to see the time when he finally took his stylish leave of her. The next thing that she had heard of him was that he had "gone abroad," a piece of information conveyed by village telegraph through Mrs. Jim. And "abroad," as far as Verity knew, he had remained until this present reappearance.

They had their coffee in the library, now completely finished. Verity wondered what would happen to all the books if, as Mrs. Jim had reported, Mr. Markos really intended to sell Mardling. This was by no means the sterile, unhandled assembly made by a monied person more interested in interior decoration than the written word.

As soon as she came in she saw above the fireplace the painting called *Several Pleasures* by Troy.

"So you did hang it there," she said. "How well it looks."

"Doesn't it?" Mr. Markos agreed. "I dote on it. Who would think it was painted by a policeman's Missus."

Verity said: "Well, I can't see why not. Although I suppose you'd say a rather exceptional policeman."

"So you know him?"

"I've met him, yes."

"I see. So have I. I met him when I bought the picture. I should have thought him an exotic in the Force but perhaps the higher you go at the Yard the rarer the atmosphere."

"He visited me this morning."

Prunella said: "You don't tell me!"

"But I do," said Verity.

"And me. According to Mrs. Jim," said Prue.

Gideon said: "Would it be about the egregious Claude?"

"No," said Verity. "It wouldn't. Not so far as I was concerned. Not specifically, anyway. It seemed to be—" she hesitated, "—as much about this new Will as anything."

And in the silence that followed the little party in the library quietly collapsed. Prunella began to look scared and Gideon put his arm round her.

Mr. Markos had moved in front of his fireplace. Verity thought she saw a change in him: the subtle change that comes over men when something has led a conversation into their professional field: a guarded attentiveness.

Prunella said: "I've been pushing things off. I've been pretending to myself nothing is really very much the matter. It's not true. Is it?" she insisted, appealing to Verity.

"Perhaps not quite, darling," Verity said and for a moment it seemed to her that she and Prunella were, in some inexplicable way, united against the two men.

### III

It was half past two when Alleyn and Fox arrived at Greengages. The afternoon being clement some of the guests were taking their postprandial ease in the garden. Others, presumably, had retired to their rooms. Alleyn gave his professional card in at the desk and asked if they might have a word with Dr. Schramm.

The receptionist stared briefly at Alleyn and hard at Mr. Fox. She tightened her mouth, said she would see, appeared to relax slightly and left them.

"Know us when she sees us again," said Fox placidly. He put on his spectacles and, tilting back his head, contemplated an emaciated water-colour of Canterbury Cathedral. "Airy-fairy," he said. "Not my notion of the place at all," and moved to a view of the Grand Canal.

The receptionist returned with an impeccably dressed man who had Alleyn's card in his hand and said he was the manager of the hotel. "I hope," he added, "that we're not in for any further disruption." Alleyn cheerfully assured him that he hoped so too and repeated that he would like to have a word or two with Dr. Schramm. The manager retired to an inner office.

Alleyn said to the receptionist: "May I bother you for a moment? Of course you're fussed we're here to ask tedious questions and generally make nuisances of ourselves about the death of Mrs. Foster."

"You said it," she returned, "not me." But she touched her hair and she didn't sound altogether antagonistic.

"It's only a sort of tidying-up job. But I wonder if you remember anything about flowers that her gardener left at the desk for her."

"I wasn't at the desk at the time."

"Alas!"

"Pardon? Oh, yes. Well, as a matter of fact I *do* happen to remember. The girl on duty mentioned that the electrical repairs man had taken them up when I was off for a minute or two."

"When would that be?"

"I really couldn't say."

"Is the repairs man a regular visitor?"

"Not that I know. He wasn't called in from the desk, that I can tell you."

"Could you by any merciful chance find out when, where and why he was here?"

"Well, I must say!"

"It would be *very* kind indeed. Really."

She said she would see what she could do and retired into her office. Alleyn heard the whirr of a telephone dial. After a considerable interlude a highly starched nurse of opulent proportions appeared.

"Dr. Schramm will see you now," she said in a clinical voice. Only the copies of *Punch*, Alleyn felt, were missing.

The nurse rustled them down a passage to a door bearing the legend: "Dr. Basil Schramm, M.B. Hours 3–5 P.M. and by appointment."

She ushered them into a little waiting-room and there, sure enough, were the copies of *Punch* and *The Tatler*. She knocked at an inner door, opened it and motioned them to go in.

Dr. Schramm swivelled round in his desk chair and rose to greet them.

A police officer of experience and sensibility may come to recognize mannerisms common to certain persons with whom he has to deal. If he is wise he will never place too much reliance on this simplification. When, for instance, he is asked by the curious layman if the police can identify certain criminal types by looking at them, he will probably say no. Perhaps he will qualify this denial by adding that he does find that certain characteristics tend to crop up—shabby stigmata—in sexual offenders. He is not referring to raincoats or to sidelong lurking but to a look in the eyes and about the mouth, a look he is unable to define.

To Alleyn it seemed that there were traits held in common by men who, in Victorian times, were called ladykillers: a display, covert or open, of sexual vainglory that sometimes, not always, made less heavily endowed acquaintances want, they scarcely knew why, to kick the possessors.

If ever he had recognized this element he did so now in Dr. Basil Schramm. It declared itself in the brief, perfectly correct but experienced glance that he gave his nurse. It was latent in the co-ordinated ease with which he rose to his feet and extended his hand, in the boldish glance of his widely separated eyes and in the folds that joined his nostrils to the corners of his mouth. Dr. Schramm was not unlike a better-looking version of King Charles II.

As a postscript to these observations Alleyn thought that Dr. Schramm looked like a heavy, if controlled, drinker.

The nurse left them.

"I'm so sorry to keep you waiting," said Dr. Schramm. "Do sit down." He glanced at Alleyn's card and then at him. "Should I say Superintendent or Mr. or just plain Alleyn?"

"It couldn't matter less," said Alleyn. "This is Inspector Fox."

"Sit, sit, sit, do."

They sat.

"Well, now, what's the trouble?" asked Dr. Schramm. "Don't tell me it's more about this unhappy business of Mrs. Foster?"

"I'm afraid I do tell you. It's just that, as I'm sure you realize, we have to tidy up rather exhaustively."

"Oh, yes. That—of course."

"The local Force has asked us to come in on the case. I'm sorry but this does entail a tramp over ground that I daresay you feel has already been explored ad nauseam."

"Well—" He raised his immaculately kept hands and let them fall. "Needs must," he said and laughed.

"That's about it," Alleyn agreed. "I believe her room has been kept as it was at the time of her death? Locked up and sealed."

"Certainly. Your local people asked for it. To be frank it's inconvenient but never mind."

"Won't be long now," said Alleyn cheerfully.

"I'm glad to hear it. I'll take you up to her room."

"If I could have a word before we go."

"Oh? Yes, of course."

"I really wanted to ask you if you were at all, however slightly, uneasy about Mrs. Foster's general health and spirits?"

Schramm started to make an instantly controlled gesture. "I've stated repeatedly: to her solicitors, to the coroner and to the police that Mrs. Foster was in improved health and in good spirits when I last saw her before I went up to London."

"And when you returned she was dead."

"Precisely."

"You didn't know, did you, that she had Parkinson's disease?"

"That is by no means certain."

"Dr. Field-Innis thought so."

"And is, of course, entitled to his opinion. In any case it is not a positive diagnosis. As I understand it, Dr. Field-Innis merely considers it a possibility."

"So does Sir James Curtis."

"Very possibly. As it happens I have no professional experience of Parkinson's disease and am perfectly ready to bow to their opinion. Of course, if Mrs. Foster had been given any inkling—"

"Dr. Field-Innis is emphatic that she had not—"

"—there would certainly have been cause for anxiety, depression—"

"Did she strike you as being anxious or depressed?"

"No."

"On the contrary?"

"On the contrary. Quite. She was—"

"Yes?"

"In particularly good form," said Dr. Schramm.

"And yet you are persuaded it was suicide?"

An ornate little clock on Dr. Schramm's desk ticked through some fifteen seconds before he spoke. He raised his clasped hands to his pursed lips and stared over them at Alleyn. Mr. Fox, disregarded, coughed slightly.

With a definitive gesture—abrupt and incisive, Dr. Schramm clapped his palms down on the desk and leant back in his chair.

"I had hoped," he said, "that it wouldn't come to this."

Alleyn waited.

"I have already told you she was in particularly good form. That was an understatement. She gave me every reason to believe she was happier than she had been for many years."

He got to his feet, looked fixedly at Alleyn and said loudly: "She had become engaged to be married."

The lines from nostril to mouth tightened into a smile of sorts.

"I had gone up to London," he said, "to buy the ring."

*IV*

"I knew, of course, that it would probably have to come out," said Dr. Schramm, "but I hoped to avoid that. She was so very anxious that we should keep our engagement secret for the time being. The thought of making a sort of—well, a posthumous announcement at the inquest— was indescribably distasteful. One knew how the press would set about it and the people in this place—I loathed the whole thought of it."

He took one or two steps about the room. He moved with short strides, holding his shoulders rigid like a soldier. "I don't offer this as an excuse. The thing has been a—an unspeakable shock to me. I can't believe it was suicide. Not when I remember— Not unless something that I can't even guess at happened between the time when I said good-bye to her and my return."

"You checked with the staff, of course?"

"Of course. She had dinner in bed and watched television. She was perfectly well. No doubt you've seen the report of the inquest and know all this. The waiter collected her tray round about eight-thirty. She was in her bathroom and he heard her singing to herself. After that—nothing. Nothing, until I came back. And found her."

"That must have been a terrible shock."

Schramm made the brief sound that usually indicates a sort of contempt. "You may say so," he said. And then, suddenly: "Why have you been called in? What's it mean? Look here, do you people suspect foul play?"

"Hasn't the idea occurred to you?" Alleyn asked.

"The *idea* has. Of course it has. Suicide being inconceivable, the *idea* occurred. But that's inconceivable, too. The circumstances. The evidence. Everything. She had no enemies. Who would want to do it? It's—" He broke off. A look of—what? Sulkiness? Derision?—appeared. It was as if he sneered at himself.

"It was *meant* to be a secret," he said.

"Are you wondering if Mrs. Foster did after all confide in somebody about your engagement?"

He stared at Alleyn. "That's right," he said. "And then: there were visitors that afternoon, as of course you know."

"Her daughter and the daughter's fiancé and Miss Preston."

"And the gardener."

"Didn't he leave his flowers with the receptionist and go away without seeing Mrs. Foster?" Alleyn asked.

"That's what he says, certainly."

"It's what your receptionist says too, Dr. Schramm."

"Yes. Very well, then. Nothing in that line of thinking. In any case the whole idea is unbelievable. Or ought to be."

"I gather you don't much fancy the gardener?"

"A complete humbug, in my opinion. I tried to warn her. Out to get all he could from her. *And* he has," said Dr. Schramm.

"Including the right to stay on at Quintern?"

"By God, he wouldn't have lasted there for long if things had gone differently. I'd have seen to that. *And* he knew it."

"You think, then, that he knew about the engagement?"

"I think, poor darling, she'd said something that gave him the idea. As a matter of fact, I ran into him going up to her room one afternoon without asking at the desk. I tore a strip off him and he came back at me with a bloody impertinent sneer. To the effect that I wasn't yet in a position to—to order her private affairs. I'm afraid I lost my temper and told him that when I was he'd be the first to know it."

Mr. Fox, using a technique that Alleyn was in the habit of alluding to as his disappearing act, had contrived to make his large person unobservable. He had moved as far away from Alleyn as possible and to a chair behind Dr. Schramm. Here he palmed a notebook and his palm was vast. He used a stub of pencil and kept his work on his knee and his eyes respectfully on nothing in particular. Alleyn and Fox made a point of not looking at each other but at this juncture he felt sure Fox contemplated him, probably with that air of bland approval that generally meant they were both thinking the same thing.

Alleyn said: "Are you still considering motive, Dr. Schramm?"

Schramm gave a short meaningless laugh. His manner, unexpected in a doctor, seemed to imply that nothing under discussion was of importance. Alleyn wondered if he treated his patients to this sort of display. "I don't want to put ideas in your head," Schramm said, "but to be quite, quite frank that did occur to me. Motive."

"I'm resistant to ideas," said Alleyn. "Could you explain?"

"It's probably a lot of bumph but it does seem to me that our engagement wouldn't have been madly popular in certain quarters. Gardener, for one. And her family, to make no bones about it."

"Are you thinking of Mrs. Foster's stepson?"

"You said it. I didn't."

"Motive?"

"I know of no motive but I do know he sponged on her and pestered her and has a pretty disgraceful record. She was very much upset at the thought of his turning up here and I gave orders that if he did he must not be allowed to see her. Or speak to her on the telephone. I tell you this," Dr. Schramm said, "as a fact. I don't for a moment pretend that it has any particular significance."

"But I think you have something more than this in mind, haven't you?"

"If I have, I wouldn't want too much weight to be given to it."

"I shall not give too much weight to it, I hope."

Dr. Schramm thumbed up the ends of his moustache. "It's just that it does occur to me that he might have expectations. I've no knowledge of any such thing. None."

"You know, do you, that Carter was on the premises that afternoon?"

"I do not!" he said sharply. "Where did you get that from?"

"From Miss Verity Preston," said Alleyn.

Again the shadow of a smile: not quite a sneer, not entirely complacent.

"Verity Preston?" he said. "Oh, yes? She and Syb were old friends."

"He arrived in the same bus as Bruce Gardener. I gather he was ordered off seeing Mrs. Foster."

"I should bloody well hope so," said Dr. Schramm. "Who by?"

"By Prunella Foster."

"Good for her."

"Tell me," said Alleyn, "speaking as a medical man, and supposing, however preposterously, that there was foul play, how would you think it could be accomplished?"

"There you are again! Nothing to indicate it! Everything points to the suicide I can't believe in. Everything. Unless," he said sharply, "something else has been found."

"Nothing, as I understand it."

"Well then—!" He made a dismissive, rather ineloquent, gesture.

"Dr. Schramm, there's one aspect of her death I wanted to ask you about. Knowing, now, the special relationship between you I am very sorry to have to put this to you: it can't be anything but distressing to go over the circumstances again."

"Christ Almighty!" he burst out, "do you suppose I don't 'go over' them day in, day out? What d'you think I'm made of!" He raised his hand. "I'm sorry!" he said. "You're doing your job. What is it you want to ask?"

"It's about the partly dissolved tablets found in the throat and on the tongue. Do you find any inconsistency there? I gather the tablets take some twenty minutes to dissolve in water but are readily soluble in alcohol. It was supposed, wasn't it, that the reason they were not swallowed was because she became unconscious after putting them in her mouth.

But—I suspect this is muddled thinking—would the tablets she had already taken have had time to induce insensibility? And anyway she couldn't have been insensible when she put these last ones in her mouth. I don't seem able to sort it out."

Dr. Schramm put his hand to his forehead, frowned and moved his head slowly from side to side.

"I'm sorry," he said. "Touch of migraine. Yes. The tablets. She took them with Scotch, you know. As you say, they dissolve readily in alcohol."

"Then wouldn't you think these would have dissolved in her mouth?"

"I would think that she didn't take any more Scotch with them. Obviously, or she would have swallowed them."

"You mean that she was conscious enough to put these four in her mouth but not conscious enough to drink or to swallow them? Yes," said Alleyn. "I see."

"Well," Dr. Schramm said loudly, "what else? What do you suppose?"

"I? I don't go in for supposing: we're not allowed. Oh, by the way, do you know if Mrs. Foster had made a Will—recently, I mean?"

"Of that," said Dr. Schramm, "I have no idea." And after a brief pause: "Is there anything else?"

"Do you know if there are members of the staff here called G. M. Johnson and Marleena Briggs?"

"I have not the faintest idea. I have nothing to do with the management of the hotel."

"Of course you haven't. Stupid of me. I'll ask elsewhere. If it's convenient could we look at the room?"

"I'll take you up." He pressed a buzzer on his desk.

"Please don't bother. Tell me the number and we'll find our way."

"No, no. Wouldn't dream of it."

These protestations were interrupted by the entrance of the nurse. She stood inside the door, her important bosom, garnished with its professional badge, well to the fore. A handsome, slightly florid lady, specifically plentiful.

"Oh, Sister," said Dr. Schramm, "would you be very kind and hold the fort? I'm just going to show our visitors upstairs. I'm expecting that call from New York."

"Certainly," she said woodenly.

Alleyn said: "You must be Sister Jackson, mustn't you? I'm very glad to see you. Would you be very kind and give us a moment or two?"

She looked fixedly at Dr. Schramm, who said grudgingly: "Chief Superintendent Alleyn."

"And Inspector Fox," said Alleyn. "Perhaps, as Dr. Schramm expects his long distance call, it won't be troubling you too much to ask you to show us the way to Mrs. Foster's room?"

She still looked at Dr. Schramm, who began: "No, that's all right, I'll—" when the telephone rang. Sister Jackson made a half-move as if to answer it but he picked up the receiver.

"Yes. Yes. Speaking. Yes, I accept the call."

Alleyn said: "Shall we?" to Sister Jackson and opened the door.

Schramm nodded to her and with the suggestion of a bridle she led the way back to the hall.

"Do we take the lift?" Alleyn asked. "I'd be very much obliged if you would come. There are one or two points about the room that I don't quite get from the reports. We've been asked by the local Force to take a look at the general picture. A formality, really, but the powers-that-be are always rather fussy in these sorts of cases."

"Oh yes?" said Sister Jackson.

In the lift it became apparent that she used scent.

For all her handsome looks, she was a pretty tough lady, Alleyn thought. Black, sharp eyes and a small hard mouth, set at the corners. It wouldn't be long before she settled into the battle-axe form.

The room, Number 20, was on the second floor at the end of a passage and at a corner of the building. The Quintern police had put a regulation seal on the door and had handed the key over to Alleyn. They had also taken the precaution of slipping an inconspicuous morsel of wool between door and jamb. Sister Jackson looked on in silence while Mr. Fox, who wore gloves, dealt with these obstructions.

The room was dark, the closed window curtains admitting only a sliver or two of daylight. It smelt thickly of material, carpet, stale scent, dust and of something indefinable and extremely unpleasant. Sister Jackson gave out a short hiss of distaste. Fox switched on the light. He and Alleyn moved into the centre of the room. Sister Jackson remained by the door.

The room had an air of suspended animation. The bed was unmade. Its occupant might have just left it to go into the bathroom. One of the pillows and the lower sheet were stained as if something had been spilt on them. Another pillow lay, face-down, at the foot of the bed. The bottle of Scotch, glass and tablets were all missing and were no doubt still in the custody of the local police, but an unwrapped parcel, obviously a book, together with a vanity box and the half-empty box of marzipan confections lay on the table alongside a lamp. Alleyn peered down the top of a rose-coloured shade and saw the glass slipper in place over the bulb. He took it off and examined it. There was no oil left but it retained a faint reek of sweet almonds. He put it aside.

The dressing-table carried, together with an array of bottles and pots, three framed photographs, all of which he had seen that morning on and in Sybil Foster's desk at Quintern: her pretty daughter; her second husband; the regimental group with her handsome young first husband prominent among the officers. This was a less faded print and Alleyn looked closely at it, marvelling that such an Adonis could have sired the undelicious Claude. He peered at an enormous corporal in the back row who squinted amicably back at him. Alleyn managed to make out the man's badge: antlers enclosed by something—what?—a heather wreath? Wasn't there some nickname? "The Spikes"? That was it. "The Duke of Montrose's" nicknamed "The Spikes." Alleyn wondered how soon after this photograph was taken Maurice Carter had died. Claude would have been a child of three or four, he supposed, and remembered Verity Preston's story of the lost Black Alexander stamp. What the hell is it, he thought, still contemplating the large corporal, that's nagging on the edge of my memory.

He went into the bathroom. A large bunch of dead lilies lay in the hand-basin. A dirty greenish stain showed where water had drained away. A new and offensive smell rose from the basin. " 'Lilies that fester,' " he reminded himself, " 'smell far worse than weeds.' "

He returned to the bedroom and found Fox, placid in attendance, and Sister Jackson looking resentful.

"And this," Alleyn said, "is how it was when you were called in?"

"The things on the table have been removed. And there's no body," she pointed out sourly.

"No more there is."

"It's disgusting," said Sister Jackson. "Being left like this."

"Horrid, isn't it? Could you just give us a picture of how things were when you arrived on the scene?"

She did so, eyeing him closely and with a certain air of appraisal. It emerged that she had been in her room and thinking of retiring when Dr. Schramm telephoned her, asking her to come at once to Number 20. There she found him stooping over the bed on which lay Mrs. Foster, dead and cooling. Dr. Schramm had drawn her attention to the table and its contents and told her to go to the surgery and fetch the equipment needed to empty the stomach. She was to do this without saying anything to anyone she met.

"We knew it was far too late to be of any use," she said, "but we did it. Dr. Schramm said the contents should be kept and they were. In a sealed jar. We had to move the table away from the bed but nothing else was disturbed. Dr. Schramm was very particular about that. Very."

"And then?"

"We informed Mr. Delaware, the manager. He was upset, of course. They don't like that sort of thing. Then we got Dr. Field-Innis to come over from Upper Quintern and he said the police should be informed. We couldn't see why but he said he thought they ought to be. So they were."

Alleyn noticed the increased usage of the first person plural in this narrative and wondered if he only imagined that it sounded possessive.

He thanked Sister Jackson warmly and handed her a glossy photograph of Mr. Fox's Aunt Elsie which was kept for this purpose. Aunt Elsie had become a kind of code-person between Alleyn and Fox and was sometimes used as a warning signal when one of them wished to alert the other without being seen to do so. Sister Jackson failed to identify Aunt Elsie and was predictably intrigued. He returned the photograph to its envelope and said they needn't trouble her any longer. Having dropped his handkerchief over his hand, he opened the door to her.

"Pay no attention," he said. "We do these things, hoping they give us the right image. Goodbye, Sister."

In passing between him and Fox her hand brushed his. She rustled off down the passage, one hundred and fifty pounds of active femininity if she was an ounce.

"Cripes," said Fox thoughtfully.

"Did she establish contact?"

"*En passant,*" he confessed in his careful French. "What about you, Mr. Alleyn?"

"*En passant, moi aussi.*"

"Do you reckon," Mr. Fox mused, "she knew about the engagement?"

"Do you?"

"If she did, I'd say she didn't much fancy it," said Fox.

"We'd better push on. You might pack up that glass slipper, Fox. We'll get Sir James to look at it."

"In case somebody put prussic acid in it?"

"Something like that. After all there was and *is* a strong smell of almonds. Only 'Oasis,' you'll tell me, and I'm afraid you'll be right."

On their way out the receptionist said she had made enquiries as to the electrical repairs man. Nobody knew anything about him except the girl who had given him Mrs. Foster's flowers. He told her he had been sent to repair a lamp in Number 20 and the lady had asked him to collect her flowers when he went down to his car to get a new bulb for the bedside lamp. She couldn't really describe him except that he was slight, short and well-spoken and didn't wear overalls but did wear spectacles.

"What d'you make of that?" said Alleyn when they got outside.

"Funny," said Fox. "Sussy. Whatever way you look at it, not convincing."

"There wasn't a new bulb in the bedside lamp. Old bulb, murky on top. Ready to conk out."

"Lilies in the basin, though."

"True."

"What now, then?"

Alleyn looked at his watch. "I've got a date with the coroner," he said. "In one hour. At Upper Quintern. In the meantime Bailey and Thompson had better give these premises the full treatment. Every inch of them."

"Looking for what?"

"All the usual stuff. Latent prints, including Sister J.'s on Aunt Elsie, of course. Schramm's will be on the book wrapping and Prunella Foster's and her mother's on the vanity box. We've got to remember the room was done over in the morning by the housemaids so anything that crops up will have been established during the day. We haven't finished with that sickening little room, Br'er Fox. Not by a long bloody chalk."

# CHAPTER V

# Greengages (II) Room 20

## I

"—IN VIEW OF WHICH circumstances, members of the jury," said the coroner, "you may consider that the appropriate decision would be again to adjourn these proceedings *sine die.*"

Not surprisingly the jury embraced this suggestion and out into the age-old quietude of Upper Quintern village walked the people who, in one way or another, were involved, or had been obliged to concern themselves in the death of Sybil Foster: her daughter, her solicitor, her oldest friend, her gardener, the doctor she had disregarded and the doctor who had become her fiancé. And her stepson, who by her death inherited the life interest left by her first husband. Her last and preposterous Will and testament could not upset this entailment nor, according to Mr. Rattisbon, could this Will itself be upset. G. M. Johnson and Marleena Briggs, chambermaids on the second floor of the hotel, confessed with uneasy giggles that they had witnessed Mrs. Foster's signature a week before she died.

This Will provided the only sensation of the inquest. Nobody seemed to be overwhelmingly surprised at Bruce Gardener's legacy of £25,000 but the Swingletree clause and the sumptuous inheritance of Dr. Schramm caused a sort of stupefaction in court. Three reporters from the provincial press were seen to be stimulated. Verity Preston, who was there because her goddaughter seemed to expect it, had a horrid foreboding of growing publicity.

The inquest had again been held in the parish hall. The spire of St. Crispin's-in-Quintern cast its shadow over an open space at the foot of steps that led up to the church. The local people referred to this area as the "green" but it was little more than a rough lateral bulge in the lane. Upper Quintern was really a village only by virtue of its church and was the smallest of its kind: hamlet would have seemed a more appropriate title.

Sunlight, diffused by autumnal haze, the absence of wind and, until car engines started up, of other than countrified sounds, all seemed to set at a remove any process other than the rooted habit of the Kentish soil. Somehow or another, Verity thought, whatever the encroachments, continuity survives. And then she thought that it had taken this particular encroachment to put the idea into her head.

She wondered if Young Mr. Rattisbon would expect a repetition of their former conviviality and decided to wait until he emerged. People came together in desultory groups and broke up again. They had the air of having been involved in some social contretemps.

Prunella came out between the two Markos men. Clearly she was shaken; Gideon held her hand and his father with his elegant head inclined, stooped over her. Again, Verity had the feeling that they absorbed Prunella.

Prunella saw her godmother, said something to the men and came to Verity.

"Godma V," she said. "Did you know? I meant to let you know. It's the day after the day after tomorrow—Thursday—they're going to—they say we can—"

"Well, darling," said Verity, "that's a good thing, isn't it? What time?"

"Three-thirty. Here. I'm telling hardly anyone: just very old friends like you. And bunches of flowers out of our gardens, don't you think?"

"I do indeed. Would you like me to bring you? Or—are you—?"

Prunella seemed to hesitate and then said: "That's sweet of you, Godma V. Gideon and Papa M are—coming with me but—could we sit together, please?"

"Of course we could," Verity said and kissed her.

The jury had come out. Some straggled away to the bus stop, some to a car. The landlord of the Passcoigne Arms was accompanied into the pub by three of his fellow jurors. The coroner appeared with Mr.

Rattisbon. They stood together in the porch, looking at their feet and conversing. They were joined by two others.

Prunella, who held Verity's hand, said: "Who's that, I wonder? Do you know? The tall one?"

"It's the one who called on me. Superintendent Alleyn."

"I can see what you mean about him," said Prunella.

The three representatives of the provincial press slid up to Alleyn and began to speak to him. Alleyn looked over their heads toward Verity and Prunella and as if he had signalled to her Verity moved to hide Prunella from the men. At the same instant Bruce Gardener came out of the hall and at once the three men closed round him.

Alleyn came over to Verity and Prunella.

"Good morning, Miss Preston," he said. "I wondered if you'd be here." And to Prunella. "Miss Foster? I expect your splendid Mrs. Jobbin told you I'd called. She was very kind and let me come into your house. *Did* she tell you?"

"Yes. I'm sorry I was out."

"There wasn't any need, at that juncture, to bother you. *I'm* sorry you're having such a horrid time. Actually," Alleyn said, "I may have to ask you to see me one of these days but only if it's really necessary. I promise."

"O.K.," Prunella said. "Whenever you like. O.K."

"My dear Alleyn!" said a voice behind Verity. "How very nice to meet you again."

Mr. Markos had come up, with Gideon, unnoticed by the others. The temper of the little scene changed with their appearance. He put his arm round Prunella and told Alleyn how well Troy's picture looked. He said Alleyn really ought to come and see it. He appealed to Verity for support and by a certain change in his manner seemed to attach a special importance to her answer. Verity was reminded of poor Syb's encomium before she took against the Markoses. She had said that Nikolas Markos was "ultra sophisticated" and "a complete man of the world." He's a man of a world I don't belong to, Verity thought, but we have things in common, nevertheless.

"Miss Preston will support me," Mr. Markos said, "won't you?"

Verity pulled herself together and said the picture was a triumph.

Alleyn said: "The painter will be delighted," and to all of them: "The gentlemen of the press look like heading this way. I suggest it might be as well if Miss Foster escaped."

"Yes, of course," said Gideon quickly. "Darling, let's go to the car. Quick."

But a stillness had fallen on the people who remained at the scene.

Verity turned and saw that Dr. Schramm had come out into the sunshine. The reporters fastened on him.

A handsome car was parked nearby. Verity thought: that's got to be his car. He'll have to come past us to get to it. We can't break up and bolt.

He said something—"No comment," Verity supposed—to the press and walked briskly toward the group. As he passed them he lifted his hat. "Good morning, Verity," he said. "Hullo, Markos, how are you? Morning, Superintendent." He paused, looked at Prunella, gave a little bow and continued on his way. It had been well done, Verity thought, if you had the nerve to do it, and she was filled with a kind of anger that he had included her in his performance.

Mr. Markos said: "We all of us make mistakes. Come along, children."

Verity, left with Alleyn, supposed Mr. Markos had referred to his dinner-party.

"I must be off," she said. She thought: Death creates social contretemps. One doesn't say: "See you on Thursday" when the meeting will be at a funeral.

Her car was next to Alleyn's and he walked beside her. Dr. Schramm drove past them and lifted a gloved hand as he did so.

"That child's surviving all this pretty well, isn't she?" Alleyn asked. "On the whole, wouldn't you say?"

"Yes. I think she is. She's sustained by her engagement."

"To young Markos? Yes. And by her godmama, too, one suspects?"

"Me! Not at all. Or anyway, not as much as I'd like."

He grunted companionably, opened her car door for her and stood by while she fastened her safety belt. She was about to say goodbye but changed her mind. "Mr. Alleyn," she said, "I gather that probate has been granted or passed or whatever it is? On the second Will?"

"It's not a *fait accompli* but it will be. Unless, of course, she made yet another and later one, which doesn't seem likely. Would it be safe to tell you something in confidence?"

Verity, surprised, said: "I don't break confidences but if it's anything that I would want to speak about to Prunella, you'd better not tell me."

"I don't think you would want to but I'd make an exception of Prunella. Dr. Schramm and Mrs. Foster were engaged to be married."

In the silence that she was unable to break Verity thought that it really was not so very surprising, this information. There was even a kind of logic about it. Given Syb. And given Basil Schramm.

Alleyn said: "Rather staggering news, perhaps?"

"No, no," she heard herself saying. "Not really. I'm just—trying to assimilate it. Why did you tell me?"

"Partly because I thought there was a chance that she might have confided it to you that afternoon but mostly because I had an idea it might be disagreeable for you to learn of it accidentally."

"Will it be made known, then? Will *he* make it known?"

"Well," said Alleyn, "I'm not sure. If it's anything to go by, he did tell *me*."

"I suppose it explains the Will?"

"That's the general idea, of course."

Verity heard herself say: "Poor Syb." And then: "I hope it doesn't come out. Because of Prue."

"Would she mind so much?"

"Oh, I think so. Don't you? The young mind terribly if they believe their parents have made asses of themselves."

"And would any woman engaging herself to Dr. Schramm make an ass of herself?"

"Yes," said Verity. "She would. I did."

## II

When Alleyn had gone Verity sat inert in her car and wondered what had possessed her to tell him something that for twenty-odd years she had told nobody. A policeman! More than that, a policeman who must, the way things had gone, take a keen professional interest in Basil Schramm, might even—no, almost certainly did—think of him as a "Suspect." And she turned cold when she forced herself to complete the sequence—a suspect in what might turn out to be a case of foul play: of—very well, then, use the terrible soft word—of murder.

He had not followed up her statement or pressed her with questions nor, indeed, did he seem to be greatly interested. He merely said: "Did you? Sickening for you," made one or two remarks of no particular significance and said goodbye. He drove off with a large companion who could not be anything that was not constabular. Mr. Rattisbon, too, looking gravely preoccupied, entered his own elderly car and quitted the scene.

Still Verity remained, miserably inert. One or two locals sauntered off. The Vicar and Jim Jobbin, who was part-time sexton, came out of the church and surveyed the weathered company of headstones. The Vicar pointed to the right and they made off in that direction, round the church. Verity knew, with a jolt, that they discussed the making of a grave. Sybil's remotest Passcoigne forebears lay in the vault but there was a family plot among the trees beyond the south transept.

Then she saw that Bruce Gardener, in his Harris tweed suit, had come out of the hall and was climbing up the steps to the church. He followed the Vicar and Jim Jobbin and disappeared. Verity had noticed him at the inquest. He had sat at the back, taller than his neighbours, upright, with his gardener's hands on his thighs, very decorous and solemn. She thought that perhaps he wanted to ask about the funeral, about flowers from Quintern Place, it might be. If so, that was nice of Bruce. She herself, she thought, must offer to do something about flowers. She would wait a little longer and speak to the Vicar.

"Good morning," said Claude Carter, leaning on the passenger's door.

Her heart seemed to leap into her throat. She had been looking out of the driver's window and he must have come up from behind the car on her blind side.

"Sorry," he said, and grinned. "Made you jump, did I?"

"Yes."

"My mistake. I just wondered if I might cadge a lift to the turn-off. If you're going home, that is."

There was nothing she wanted less but she said yes, if he didn't mind waiting while she went up to the church. He said he wasn't in a hurry and got in. He had removed his vestigial beard, she noticed, and had his hair cut to a conservative length. He was tidily dressed and looked less hang-dog than usual. There was even a hint of submerged jauntiness about him.

"Smoking allowed?" he asked.

She left him lighting his cigarette in a guarded manner as if he was afraid someone would snatch it out of his mouth.

At the head of the steps she met the Vicar returning with Bruce and Jim. To her surprise Jim, a bald man with a loud voice, was now bent double. He was hovered over by the Vicar.

"It's a fair bugger," he shouted. "Comes over you like a bloody thunderclap. Stooping down to pull up them bloody teazles and now look at me. Should of minded me own business."

"Yes, well: jolly bad luck," said the Vicar. "Oh. Hullo, Miss Preston. We're in trouble as you see. Jim's smitten with lumbago."

"Will he be able to negotiate the descent?" Bruce speculated anxiously. "That's what I ask myself. Awa' wi ye, man, and let us handle you doon the steps."

"No, you don't. I'll handle myself if left to myself, won't I?"

"Jim!" said Verity, "*what* a bore for you. I'll drive you home."

"No, ta all the same, Miss Preston. It's happened before and it'll happen again. I'm best left to manage myself and if you'll excuse me that's what I'll do. I'll use the handrail. Only," he added with a sudden shout of agony, "I'd be obliged if I wasn't watched."

"Perhaps," said the Vicar, "we'd better—?"

Jim, moving like a gaffer in a Victorian melodrama, achieved the handrail and clung to it. He shouted: "I won't be able to do the job now, will I?"

There was an awkward silence broken by Bruce. "Dinna fash yourself," he said. "No problem. With the Minister's kind permission I'll dig it mysel' and think it an honour. I will that."

"The full six foot, mind."

"Ou aye," Bruce agreed. "All of it. I'm a guid hand at digging," he added.

"Fair enough," said Jim and began to ease himself down the steps.

"This is a most fortunate solution, Bruce," said the Vicar. "Shall we just leave Jim as he wishes?" and he ushered them into the church.

St. Crispin's-in-Quintern was one of the great company of parish churches that stand as milestones in rural history: obstinate resisters to the ravages of time. It had a magnificent peal of bells, now unsafe to ring, one or two brasses, a fine east window and a surprising north window in which—strange conceit—a walrus-mustachioed Passcoigne, looking startlingly like Sir Arthur Conan Doyle, was depicted in full plate armour, an Edwardian St. Michael without a halo. The legend indicated that he had met his end on the African veld. The familiar ecclesiastical odour of damp held at bay by paraffin heaters greeted Verity and the two men.

Verity explained that she would like to do anything that would help about the flowers. The Vicar said that custody of all brass vases was inexorably parcelled out among the Ladies Guild, five in number. She gathered that any attempt to disrupt this procedure would trigger off a latent pecking order.

"But they would be grateful for flowers," he added.

Bruce said that there were late roses up at Quintern Place and he'd thought it would be nice to have her ain favourites to see her off. He muttered in an uneven voice that the name was appropriate: Peace. "They endure better than most oot o' watter," he added and blew his nose. Verity and the Vicar warmly supported this suggestion and Verity left the two men to complete, she understood, the arrangements for digging Sybil's grave.

When she returned to the top of the steps she found that Jim Jobbin had reached the bottom on his hands and knees and was being manipulated through the lych-gate by his wife. Verity joined them. Mrs. Jim explained that she was on her way to get dinner and had found Jim crawling backward down the last four steps. It was no distance, they both reminded Verity, along the lane to their cottage. Jim got to his feet by swarming up his wife as if she was a tree.

"It'll ease off once he straightens himself," she said. "It does him good to walk."

"That's what you think," her husband groaned but he straightened up and let out an oath as he did so. They made off in slow motion.

Verity returned to her car and to Claude, lounging in the passenger's seat. He made a token shuffle with his feet and leant over to open the door.

"That was as good as a play," he said. "Poor old Jobbin. Did you see him beetling down the steps? Fantastic!" He gave a neighing laugh.

"Lumbago's no joke to the person who's got it," Verity snapped.

"It's hysterical for the person who hasn't, though."

She drove as far as the corner where the lane up to Quintern Place branched off to the left.

"Will this suit you?" she asked, "or would you like me to run you up?"

He said he wouldn't take her out of her way but when she pulled up he didn't get out.

"What did you make of the inquest?" he asked. "I must say I thought it pretty off."

"Off?"

"Well—you know. I mean what does that extraordinary detective person think he's on about? And a further postponement. Obviously they suspect something."

Verity was silent.

"Which isn't exactly welcome news," he said. "Is it? Not for this medico, Schramm. Or for Mr. Folksy Gardener if it comes to that."

"I don't think you should make suggestions, Claude."

"Suggestions! I'm not suggesting anything, but people are sure to look sideways. I know I wouldn't feel comfortable if I were in those gentlemen's boots, that's all. Still, they're getting their lovely legacies, aren't they, which'll be a great consolation. I could put up with plenty of funny looks for twenty-five thousand of the best. Still more for Schramm's little lot."

"I must get home, Claude."

"Nothing can touch my bit, anyway. God, can I use it! Only thing: that old relic Rattisbon says it won't be available until probate is allowed or passed or whatever. Still, I suppose I can borrow on my prospects, wouldn't you think?"

"I'm running late."

"Nobody seems to think it's a bit off-colour her leaving twenty-five thousand of the best to a jobbing gardener she'd only hired a matter of months ago. It's pretty obvious he'd got round her in a big way: I could tell you one or two things about Mr. gardener-Gardener."

"I must go, Claude."

"Yes. O.K."

He climbed out of the car and slammed the door. "Thanks for the lift, anyway," he said. "See you at the funeral. Ain't we got fun?"

Glad to be rid of him but possessed by a languor she could not understand, Verity watched him turn up the lane. Even seen from behind there was a kind of furtive jauntiness in his walk, an air of complacency that was out of character. He turned a corner and was gone.

"I wonder," she thought, "what he'll do with himself."

She drove on up her own lane into her own little avenue and got her own modest luncheon. She found she hadn't much appetite for it.

The day was gently sunny but Verity found it oppressive. The sky was clear but she felt as if it would almost be a relief if bastions of cloud shouldered each other up from beyond the horizon. It occurred to her that writers like Ibsen and Dickens—unallied in any other respect—were right to make storms, snow, fog and fire the companions of human disorders. Shakespeare too, she thought. We deprive ourselves aesthetically when we forgo the advantages of symbolism.

She had finished the overhaul of her play and had posted it off to her agent. It was not unusual, when work-in-hand had been dealt with and she was cleaned out, for her to experience a nervous impulse to start off at once on something new. As now, when she found herself wondering if she could give a fresh look to an old, old theme: that of an intelligent woman enthralled by a second-rate charmer, a "bad lot," in Verity's dated jargon, for whom she had no respect but was drawn to by an obstinate attraction. If she could get such a play successfully off her chest, would she scotch the bogey that had returned to plague her?

When at that first Markos dinner-party, she found that Basil Schramm's pinchbeck magnetism had evaporated, the discovery had been a satisfaction to Verity. Now, when a shadow crept toward him, how did she feel? And why, oh why, had she bleated out her confession to Alleyn? He won't let it rest, she thought, her imagination bolting with her. He'll want to know more about Basil. He may ask if Basil ever got into trouble and what'll I say to that?

And Alleyn, returning with Fox to Greengages via Maidstone, said:

"This case is getting nasty. She let it out without any pushing or prob-
ing and I think she amazed herself by doing so. I wouldn't mind betting there was more to it than the predatory male jilt and the humili-
ated woman, though there was all of that, too, I daresay."

"If it throws any light on his past?"

"We may have to follow it up, of course. Do you know what I think
she'll do about it?"

"Refuse to talk?"

"That's it. There's not much of the hell-knows-no-fury in Verity
Preston's makeup."

"Well," said Fox reasonably, "seeing how pretty he stands we have
to make it thorough. What comes first?"

"Get the background. Check up on the medical side. Qualified at
Lausanne, or wherever it was. Find out the year and the degree. See if
there was any regular practice in this country. Or in the U.S.A. So
much waste of time, it may be, but it'll have to be done, Br'er Fox.
And, on a different lay: here comes Maidstone again. Call at stationers
and bookshops and see if anyone's bought any Will forms lately. If not,
do the same in villages and towns and in the neighbourhood of Greengages."

"Hoping we don't have to extend to London?"

"Fervently. And, by the by, Fox, we'd better ask Mr. Rattisbon to let
us fingerprint the Will. They should find the lady herself, Mr. R. and
Johnson and Briggs. And Lord knows how many shop-assistants. But
courage, comrade, we may find that in addition to witnessing the Will,
G. M. Johnson or Marleena Briggs or even that casket of carnal
delights, Sister Jackson, was detailed to pop into a stationer's shop on
her day off."

When they reached Greengages, this turned out to be the answer.
Johnson and Briggs had their days off together and a week before Mrs.
Foster died they had made the purchase at a stationer's in Greendale.
Mrs. Foster had given them a present and told them to treat themselves
to the cinema and tea.

"That's fine," said Alleyn. "We just wanted to know. Was it a good
film?"

They fell into an ecstasy of giggles.

"I see. One of those?"

"Aw!"

"Anybody else know about the shopping?"

"Aw, no," said G. M. Johnson.

"Yes they did, you're mad," said Marleena Briggs.

"They never."

"They did, too. The Doctor did. He come in while she told us."

"Dr. Schramm came in and heard all about it?" said Alleyn casually. They agreed and were suddenly uninterested.

He then asked each of them in turn if she recognized the writing on an envelope he had addressed to himself and their prints having been thus obtained he gave them a tip.

"There you are, both of you. Treat yourselves to another shocker and a blow-out of cream buns."

This interview concluded, Alleyn was approached by the manager of the hotel, who evidently viewed their visit with minimal enthusiasm. He hustled them into his office, offered drinks and looked apprehensive when these were declined.

"It's just about the room," he said. "How much longer do you people want it? We're expecting a full house by next week and it's extremely inconvenient, you know."

"I hope this will be positively our last appearance," said Alleyn cheerfully.

"Without being uncivil, so do I. Do you want someone to take you up?"

"We'll take ourselves, thank you all the same. Come along, Br'er Fox," said Alleyn. "*En avant.* You're having one of your dreamy spells."

He led the way quickly to the lifts.

The second floor seemed to be deserted. They walked soundlessly down the carpeted passage to Number 20. The fingerprint and photography men had called and gone and their seal was still on the door. Fox was about to break it when Alleyn said: "Half a jiffy. Look at this."

Opposite the bedroom door was a curtained alcove. He had lifted the curtain and disclosed a vacuum cleaner. "Handy little hidey-hole, isn't it?" he said. "Got your torch on you?"

"As it happens," Fox said and gave it to him. He went into the alcove and closed the curtain.

The lift at the far end of the long passage whined to a stop. Sister Jackson and another lady emerged. Fox, with a movement surprisingly nippy for one of his bulk, joined his superior in the alcove.

"Herself," he whispered. Alleyn switched off his torch.

"See you?"

"Not to recognize."

"Impossible. Once seen."

"She had somebody with her."

"No need for you to hide, you fathead. Why should you?"

"She flusters me."

"You're bulging the curtain."

But it was too late. The curtain was suddenly withdrawn and Sister Jackson discovered. She screamed.

"Good morning, Sister," Alleyn said and flashed his torchlight full in her face. "Do forgive us for startling you."

"What," she panted, her hand on her spectacular bosom, "are you doing in the broom cupboard?"

"Routine procedure. Don't give it another thought."

"And you, don't shine that thing in my face. Come out."

They emerged.

In a more conciliatory tone and with a sort of huffy come-to-ishness she said: "You gave me a shock."

"So did you us," said Mr. Fox. "A nice one," he roguishly added.

"I daresay."

She was between them. She flashed upward glances first at one, then the other. Her bosom slightly heaved.

"We really do apologize," he said.

"I should hope so." She laid her hand, which was plump, on his closed one. He was surprised to feel a marked tremor and to see that the colour had ebbed out of her face. She kept up the flirtatious note, however, though her voice was unsteady. "I suppose I'll have to forgive you," she said. "But only if you tell me why you were there."

"I caught sight of something."

He turned his hand over, opened it and exposed the crumpled head of a pink lily. It was very dead and its brown pollen had stained his palm.

"I think," he said, "it will team up with the ones in Mrs. Foster's last bouquet. I wondered what the electrician was doing in the broom cupboard."

She gaped at him. "Electrician?" she said. "What electrician?"

"Don't let it worry you. Excuse us, please. Come on, Fox. Goodbye, Sister."

When she had starched and bosomed herself away he said: "I'm going to take another look at that broom-hide. Don't spring any more confrontations this time. Stay here."

He went into the alcove, drew the curtains on himself and was away for some minutes. When he rejoined Fox he said: "They're not so fussy about housework in there. Quite a lot of dust on the floor. Plenty of prints—housemaid's, no doubt, but on the far end, in the corner away from the vacuum cleaner where nobody would go normally, there are prints, left and right, side by side, with the heels almost touching the wall. Men's crepe-soled shoes, and beside them—guess."

He opened his hand and disclosed another dead lily head. "Near the curtain I could just find the prints again but overlaid by the housemaid's and some regulation type extras. Whose, do you think?"

"All right, all right," said Fox. "Mine."

"When we go down we'll look like sleuths and ask the desk lady if she noticed the electrician's feet."

"That's a flight of fancy, if you like," said Fox. "And she won't have."

"In any case Bailey and Thompson will have to do their stuff. Come on."

When they were inside Number 20 he went to the bathroom where the fetid bouquet still mouldered in the basin. It was possible to see that the finds matched exactly and actually to distinguish the truss from which they had been lost.

"So I make a note: 'Find the electrician'?" asked Fox.

"You anticipate my every need."

"How do you fancy this gardener? Gardener?"

"Not much!" said Alleyn. "Do you?"

"You wouldn't fancy him sneaking back with the flowers when Miss Foster and party had gone?"

"Not unless he's had himself stretched: the reception girl said slight, short and bespectacled. Bruce Gardener's six foot three and big with it. He doesn't wear spectacles."

"He'd be that chap in the Harris tweed suit at the inquest?"

"He would. I meant to point him out to you."

"I guessed," said Fox heavily.

"Claude Carter, on the contrary, is short, slight, bespectacled and in common with the electrician and several million other males, doesn't wear overalls."

"Motive? No. Hang on. He gets Mrs. Foster's bit from her first husband."

"Yes."

"Ask if anyone knows about electricians? And nobody will," Fox prophesied.

"Ask about what bus he caught back to Quintern and get a dusty answer."

"Ask if anyone saw him any time, anywhere."

"With or without lilies. In the meantime, Fox, I seem to remember there's an empty cardboard box and a paper shopping bag in the wardrobe. Could you put those disgusting lilies in the box? Keep the ones from the broom cupboard separate. I want another look at her pillows."

They lay as they had lain before: three of them: luxuriant pillowcases in fine lawn with broiderie-anglaise threaded with ribbon. Brought them with her, Alleyn thought. Even Greengages wouldn't run to these lengths.

The smallest of them carried a hollow made by her dead or alive head. The largest lay at the foot of the bed and was smooth. Alleyn turned it over. The under surface was crumpled, particularly in the centre—crumpled and stained as if it had been wet and, in two places, faintly pink with small, more positive indentations, one of them so sharp that it actually had broken the delicate fabric. He bent down and caught a faint nauseating reek. He went to the dressing table and found three lipsticks, all of them, as was the fashion at that time, very pale. He took one of them to the pillow. It matched.

## III

During the remaining sixty hours before Sybil Foster's burial in the churchyard of St. Crispin's-in-Quintern the police investigations, largely carried out over the telephone, multiplied and accelerated. As is always the case, much of what was unearthed turned out to be of no relevance, much was of a doubtful or self-contradictory nature and only a scanty winnowing found to be of real significance. It was as if the components of several jig-saw puzzles had been thrown down on the table and before the one required picture could be assembled, the rest would have to be discarded.

The winnowings, Alleyn thought, were for the most part suggestive rather than definitive. A call to St. Luke's Hospital established that Basil Smythe, as he then was, had indeed been a first year medical student at the appropriate time and had not completed the course. A contact of Alleyn's in Swiss Police headquarters put through a call to a hospital in Lausanne confirming that a Dr. Basilé Schramm had graduated from a teaching hospital in that city. Basilé, Alleyn was prepared to accept, might well have been a Swiss shot at Basil. Schramm had accounted to Verity Preston for the change from Smythe. They would have to check if this was indeed his mother's maiden name.

So far nothing had been found in respect of his activities in the United States.

Mrs. Jim Jobbin had, at Mrs. Foster's request and a week before she died, handed a bottle of sleeping-pills over to Bruce Gardener. Mrs. Foster had told Bruce where they would be found: in her writing desk. They had been bought some time ago from a Maidstone chemist and were a proprietary brand of barbiturate. Mrs. Jim and Bruce had both noticed that the bottle was almost full. He had duly delivered it that same afternoon.

Claude Carter had what Mr. Fox called a sussy record. He had been mixed up, as a very minor figure, in the drug racket. In his youth he had served a short sentence for attempted blackmail. He was thought to have brought a small quantity of heroin ashore from S.S. *Poseidon.* If so he had got rid of it before he was searched at the customs.

Verity Preston had remembered the august name of Bruce Gardener's latest employer. Discreet enquiries had confirmed the authenticity of Bruce's references and his unblemished record. The head gardener, named McWhirter, was emphatic in his praise and very, very Scottish.

This, thought Alleyn, might tally with Verity Preston's theory about Bruce's dialectical vagaries.

Enquiries at appropriate quarters in the City elicited the opinion that Nikolas Markos was a millionaire with a great number of interests of which oil, predictably, was the chief. He was also the owner of a string of luxury hotels in Switzerland, the South Pacific, and the Costa Brava. His origin was Greek. Gideon had been educated at a celebrated public school and at the Sorbonne and was believed to be in training for a responsible part in his father's multiple business activities.

Nothing further could be discovered about the "electrician" who had taken Bruce's flowers up to Sybil Foster's room. The desk lady had not noticed his feet.

"We'll be having a chat with Mr. Claude Carter, then?" asked Fox, two nights before the funeral. He and Alleyn were at the Yard, having been separated during the day on their several occasions, Fox in and about Upper Quintern and Alleyn mostly on the telephone and in the City.

"Well, yes," he agreed. "Yes. We'll have to, of course. But we'd better walk gingerly over that particular patch, Br'er Fox. If he's in deep, he'll be fidgety. If he thinks we're getting too interested he may take off and we'll have to waste time and men on running him down."

"Or on keeping obbo to prevent it. Do you reckon he'll attend the funeral?"

"He may decide we'd think it odd if he didn't. After his being so assiduous about gracing the inquests. There you are! We'll need to go damn' carefully. After all, what have we got? He's short, thin, wears spectacles and doesn't wear overalls?"

"If you put it like that."

"How would you put it?"

"Well," said Fox, scraping his chin, "he'd been hanging about the premises for we don't know how long and, by the way, no joy from the bus scene. Nobody remembers him or Gardener. I talked to the conductors on every return trip that either of them might have taken but it was a Saturday and there was a motor rally in the district and they were crowded all the way. They laughed at me."

"Cads."

"There's the motive, of course," Fox continued moodily. "Not that you can do much with that on its own. How about the lilies in the broom cupboard?"

"How about them falling off in the passage and failing to get themselves sucked up by the vacuum cleaner?"

"You make everything so difficult," Fox sighed.

"Take heart. We have yet to see his feet. And him, if it comes to that. Bailey and Thompson may have come up with something dynamic. Where are they?"

"Like they say in theatrical circles. Below and awaiting your pleasure."

"Admit them."

Bailey and Thompson came in with their customary air of being incapable of surprise. Using the minimum quota of words they laid out for Alleyn's inspection an array of photographs: of the pillowcase *in toto*, of the stained area on the front in detail and of one particular, tiny indentation, blown up to the limit, which had actually left a cut in the material. Over this, Alleyn and Fox concentrated.

"Well, you two," Alleyn said at last, "what do you make of this lot?"

It was by virtue of such invitations that his relationship with his subordinates achieved its character. Bailey, slightly more communicative than his colleague, said: "Teeth. Like you thought, Governor. Biting the pillow."

"All right. How about it?"

Thompson laid another exhibit before him. It was a sort of macabre triptych: first a reproduction of the enlargement he had already shown and beside it, corresponding in scale, a photograph of all too unmistakably human teeth from which the lips had been retracted in a dead mouth.

"We dropped in at the morgue," said Bailey. "The bite could tally."

The third photograph, one of Thompson's montages, showed the first superimposed upon the second. Over this, Thompson had ruled vertical and horizontal lines.

"Tallies," Alleyn said.

"Can't fault it," said Bailey dispassionately.

He produced a further exhibit: the vital section of the pillowcase itself mounted between two polythene sheets, and set it up beside Thompson's display of photographs.

"Right," Alleyn said. "We send this to the laboratory, of course, and in the meantime, Fox, we trust our reluctant noses. People who are trying to kill themselves with an overdose of sleeping-pills may vomit but they don't bite holes in the pillowcase."

"It's nice to know we haven't been wasting our time," said Fox.

"You are," said Alleyn staring at him, "probably the most remorseless realist in the service."

"It was only a passing thought. Do we take it she was smothered, then?"

"If Sir James concurs, we do. He'll be cross about the pillowcase."

"You'd have expected the doctors to spot it. Well," Fox amended, "you'd have expected the Field-Innis one to, anyway."

"At that stage their minds were set on suicide. Presumably the great busty Jackson had got rid of the stomach-pumping impedimenta after she and Schramm, as they tell us, had seen to the bottling of the results. Field-Innis says that by the time he got there, this had been done. It was he, don't forget, who said the room should be left untouched and the police informed. The pillow was face-downwards at the foot of the bed but in any case only a very close examination reveals the mark of the tooth. The stains, which largely obscure it, could well have been the result of the overdose. What about dabs, Bailey?"

"What you'd expect. Dr. Schramm's, the nurse Jackson's. Deceased's, of course, all over the shop. The other doctor's—Field-Innis. I called at his surgery and asked for a take. He wasn't all that keen but he obliged. The girl Foster's on the vanity box and her mother's like you indicated."

"The tumbler?"

"Yeah," said Bailey with his look of mulish satisfaction. "That's right. That's the funny bit. Nothing. Clean. Same goes for the pill bottle and the Scotch bottle."

"Now, we're getting somewhere," said Fox.

"Where do we get to, Br'er Fox?"

"Gloves used but only after she lost consciousness."

"What I reckoned," said Bailey.

"Or after she'd passed away?" Fox speculated.

"No, Mr. Fox. Not if smothering's the story."

Alleyn said: "No dabs on the reverse side of the pillow?"

"That's correct," said Thompson.

"I tried for latents," said Bailey. "No joy."

He produced, finally, a polythene bag containing the back panel of the pretty lawn pillow, threaded with ribbon. "This," he said, "is kind of crushed on the part opposite to the tooth print and stains. Crumpled up, like. As if by hands. No dabs but crumpled. What I reckon— hands."

"Gloved. Like the Americans say: it figures. Anything else in the bedroom?"

"Not to signify."

They were silent for a moment or two and then Bailey said: "About the Will. Dabs."

"What? Oh, yes?"

"The lawyer's. Mr. Rattisbon's. Small female in holding position near edges: the daughter's, probably: Miss Foster."

"Probably. And—?"

"That's the lot."

"Well, blow me down flat," said Alleyn.

The telephone rang. It was a long distance call from Berne. Alleyn's contact came through loud and clear.

"Monsieur le Superintendant? I am calling immediately to make an amendment to our former conversations."

"An amendment, mon ami?"

"An addition, perhaps more accurately. In reference to the Doctor Schramm at the Sacré Coeur, you recollect?"

"Vividly."

"Monsieur le Superintendant, I regret. My contact at the bureau has made a further search. It is now evident that the Doctor Schramm in question is deceased. In effect, since 1952."

During the pause of the kind often described as pregnant Alleyn made a face at Fox and said: "Dead." Fox looked affronted.

"At the risk," Alleyn said into the telephone, "of making the most intolerable nuisance of myself, dare I ask if your source would have the very great kindness to find out if, over the same period, there is any record of an Englishman called Basil Smythe having qualified at Sacré Coeur? I should explain, my dear colleague, that there is now the possibility of a not unfamiliar form of false pretence."

"But of course. You have but to ask. And the name again?"

Alleyn spelt it out and was told he could expect a return call within the hour. It came through in twelve minutes. An Englishman called Basil Smythe had attended the courses at the time in question but had failed to complete them. Alleyn thanked his expeditious confrere profusely. There was a further interchange of compliments and he hung up.

## IV

"It's not only in the story-books," observed Fox on the following morning as they drove once more to Greengages, "that you get a surplus of suspects but I'll say this for it: it's unusual. The dates tally, don't they?"

"According to the records at St. Luke's, he was a medical student in London in 1950. It would seem he didn't qualify there."

"And now we begin to wonder if he qualified anywhere at all?"

"Does the doctor practise to deceive, in fact?" Alleyn suggested.

"Perhaps if he was at the hospital and knew the real Schramm he might have got hold of his diploma when he died. Or am I being fanciful?" asked Fox.

"You are being fanciful. And yet I don't know. It's possible."

"Funnier things have happened."

"True," said Alleyn and they fell silent for the rest of the drive.

They arrived at Greengages under the unenthusiastic scrutiny of the receptionist. They went directly to Number 20 and found it in an advanced stage of unloveliness.

"It's not the type of case I like," Fox complained. "Instead of knowing who the villain is and getting on quietly with routine until you've collected enough to make a charge, you have to go dodging about from one character to another like the chap in the corner of a band."

"Bang, tinkle, crash?"

"Exactly. Motive," Fox indignantly continued. "Take motive. There's Bruce Gardener who gets twenty-five thousand out of it and the stepson who gets however much his father entailed on him after his mother's death and there's a sussy-looking quack who gets a fortune. Not to mention Mr. Markos who fancied her house and Sister Jackson who fancies the quack. You can call them fringe characters. I don't know! Which of the lot can we wipe? Tell me that, Mr. Alleyn."

"I'm sorry too many suspects makes you so cross, Br'er Fox, but I can't oblige. Let's take a look at an old enemy, *modus operandi*, shall we? Now that Bailey and Thompson have done their stuff what do we take out of it? *You* tell *me* that, my Foxkin."

"Ah!" said Fox. "Well now, what? What happened, eh? I reckon— and you'll have to give me time, Mr. Alleyn—I reckon something after this fashion. After deceased had been bedded down for the night by her daughter and taken her early dinner, a character we can call the electrician, though he was nothing of the kind, collected the lilies from the reception desk and came up to Number 20. While he was still in the passage he heard or saw someone approaching and stepped into the curtained alcove."

"As you did, we don't exactly know why."

"With me it was what is known as a reflex action," said Fox modestly. "While in the alcove two of the lilies' heads got knocked off. The electrician (*soi disant*) came out and entered Number 20. He now —don't bustle me—"

"I wouldn't dream of it. He now?"

"Went into the bedroom and bathroom," said Fox and himself suited the action to the word, raising his voice as he did so, "and put the lilies in the basin. They don't half stink now. He returned to the bedroom and kidded to the deceased?"

"Kidded?"

"Chatted her up," Fox explained. He leant over the bed in a beguiling manner. "She tells him she's not feeling quite the thing and he says why not have a nice drink and a sleeping-pill. And, by the way, didn't the young lady say something about putting the pill bottle out for her mother? She did? Right! So this chap gets her the drink—Scotch and water. Now comes the nitty-gritty bit."

"It did, for her at any rate."

"He returns to the bathroom which I shan't bother to do. Ostensibly," said Fox, looking his superior officer hard in the eye, "*ostensibly* to mix the Scotch and water but he slips in a couple, maybe three, maybe four pills. Soluble in alcohol, remember."

"There's a water jug on her table."

"I thought you'd bring that up. He says it'll be stale. The water. Just picks up the Scotch and takes it into the bathroom."

"Casual-like?"

"That's it."

"Yes. I'll swallow that, Br'er Fox. Just."

"So does she. She swallows the drink knowing nothing of the tablets and he gives her one or maybe two more which she takes herself thinking they're the first, with the Scotch and water."

"How about the taste, if they do taste?"

"It's a *strong* Scotch. And," Fox said quickly, "she attributes the taste, if noticed, to the one or maybe two tablets she's given herself. She has now taken, say, six tablets."

"Go on. If you've got the nerve."

"He waits. He may even persuade her to have another drink. With him. And puts more tablets in it."

"What's he drink out of? The bottle?"

"Let that be as it may. He waits, I say, until she's dopey."

"Well?"

"And he puts on his gloves and smothers her," said Fox suddenly. "With the pillow."

"I see."

"You don't buy it, Mr. Alleyn?"

"On the contrary, I find it extremely plausible."

"You do? I forgot to say," Fox added, greatly cheered, "that he put the extra tablets in her mouth after she was out. Gave them a push to the back of the tongue. That's where he overdid it. One of those fancy touches you're so often on about. Yerse. To make suicide look convincing he got rid of a lot more down the loo."

"Was the television going all this time?"

"Yes. Because Dr. Schramm found it going when he got there. Blast," said Fox vexedly. "Of course if *he's* our man—"

"He got home much earlier than he makes out. The girl at reception would hardly mistake him for an itinerant electrician. So someone else does that bit and hides with the vacuum cleaner and puts the lilies in the basin and goes home as clean as a whistle."

"Yerse," said Fox.

"There's no call for you to be crestfallen. It's a damn' good bit of barefaced conjecture and may well be right if Schramm's not our boy."

"But if this Claude Carter is?"

"It would fit."

"Ah! And Gardener? Well," said Fox, "I know he's all wrong if the receptionist girl's right. I know that. Great hulking cross-eyed lump of a chap," said Fox crossly.

There followed a discontented pause at the end of which Fox said, with a touch of diffidence: "Of course, there is another fringe character, isn't there? Perhaps two. I mean to say, by all accounts the deceased *was* dead set against the engagement, wasn't she?"

Alleyn made no reply. He had wandered over to the dressing-table and was gazing at its array of Sybil Foster's aids to beauty and at the regimental photograph in a silver frame. Bailey had dealt delicately with them all and scarcely disturbed the dust that had settled on them or upon the looking-glass that had reflected her altered face.

After another long silence Alleyn said: "Do you know, Fox, you have, in the course of your homily, proved me, to my own face and full in my own silly teeth, to be a copybook example of the unobservant investigating officer."

"You don't say!"

"But I do say. Grinding the said teeth and whipping my cat, I do say."

"It would be nice," said Fox mildly, "to know why."

"Let's pack up and get out of this and I'll tell you on the way."

"On the way to where?" Fox reasonably inquired.

"To the scene where I was struck down with sand-blindness or whatever. To the source of all our troubles, my poor Foxkin."

"Upper Quintern, would that be?"

"Upper Quintern it is. And I think, Fox, we'd better find ourselves rooms at a pub. Better to be there than here. Come on."

# CHAPTER VI

# Point Marked X

*I*

PRUNELLA WAS AT HOME at Quintern Place. Her car was in the drive and she herself answered the door, explaining that she was staying at Mardling and had merely called in to pick up her mail. She took Alleyn and Fox into the drawing-room. It was a room of just proportions with appointments that had occurred quietly over many years rather than by any immediate process of collective assembly. The panelling and ceiling were graceful. It was a room that seemed to be full of gentle light.

Alleyn exclaimed with pleasure.

"Do you like it?" Prunella said. "Most people seem to like it."

"I'm sure you do, don't you?"

"I expect so. It always feels quite nice to come back to. It's not exactly riveting, of course. Too predictable. I mean it doesn't *send* one, does it? I don't know though. It sends my father-in-law-to-be up like a rocket. Do sit down."

She herself sat between them. She arranged her pretty face in a pout almost as if she parodied some Victorian girl. She was pale and, Alleyn thought, very tense.

"We won't be long about this," he said. "There are one or two bits and pieces we're supposed to tidy up. Nothing troublesome, I hope."

"Oh," said Prunella. "I see. I thought that probably you'd come to tell me my mother was murdered. Officially tell me, I mean. I know, of course, that you thought so."

Until now she had spoken in her customary whisper but this was brought out rapidly and loudly. She stared straight in front of her and her hands were clenched in her lap.

"No," Alleyn said. "That's not it."

"But you think she was, don't you?"

"I'm afraid we do think it's possible. Do you?"

Prunella darted a look at him and waited a moment before she said: "I don't know. The more I wonder the less I can make up my mind. But then, of course, there are all sorts of things the police dig up that other people know nothing about. Aren't there?"

"That's bound to happen," he agreed. "It's our job to dig, isn't it?"

"I suppose so."

"My first reason for coming is to make sure you have been properly consulted about the arrangements for tomorrow and to ask if there is anything we can do to help. The service is at half-past three, isn't it? The present suggestion is that your mother will be brought from Maidstone to the church arriving about two o'clock but it has occurred to me that you might like her to rest there tonight. If so, that can easily be arranged."

Prunella for the first time looked directly at him. "That's kind," she said. "I'd like that, I think. Please."

"Good. I'll check with our chaps in Maidstone and have a word with your Vicar. I expect he'll let you know."

"Thank you."

"All right, then?"

"Super," said Prunella with shaking lips. Tears trickled down her cheeks. "I'm sorry," she said. "I thought I'd got over all this. I thought I was O.K." She knuckled her eyes and fished a handkerchief out of her pocket. Mr. Fox rose and walked away to the farthest windows through which he contemplated the prospect.

"Never mind," Alleyn said. "That's the way delayed shock works. Catches you on the hop when you least expect it."

"Sickening of it," Prunella mumbled into her handkerchief. "You'd better say what you wanted to ask."

"It can wait a bit."

"No!" said Prunella and stamped like an angry child. "Now."

"All right. I'd better say first what we always say. Don't jump to conclusions and read all sorts of sinister interpretations into routine questions. You must realize that in a case of this sort everyone who saw anything at all of your mother or had contact, however trivial, with her during the time she was at Greengages, and especially on the last day, has to be crossed off."

"All except one."

"Perhaps not excepting even one and then we *do* look silly."

Prunella sniffed. "Go ahead," she said.

"Do you know a great deal about your mother's first husband?"

Prunella stared at him.

"*Know?* Me? Only what everyone knows. Do you mean about how he was killed and about the Black Alexander stamp?"

"Yes. We've heard about the stamp. And about the unfinished letter to your mother."

"Well then—. There's nothing else that I can think of."

"Do you know if she kept that letter? And any other of his letters?"

Prunella began: "If I did I wouldn't—" and pulled herself up. "Sorry," she said, "yes, she did. I found them at the back of a drawer in her dressing-table. It's a converted sofa-table and it's got a not terribly secret, secret drawer."

"And you have them still?"

She waited for a second or two and then nodded. "I've read them," she said. "They're fantastic, lovely letters. They can't possibly have anything at all to do with any of this. Not possibly."

"I've seen the regimental group photograph."

"Mrs. Jim told me."

"He was very good-looking, wasn't he?"

"Yes. They used to call him Beau Carter. It's hard to believe when you see Claude, isn't it? He was only twenty-one when his first wife died. Producing Claude. Such an awful waste, I've always thought. Much better if it'd been the other way round though of course in that case I would have been—just not. Or would I? How muddling."

She glanced down the long room to where Mr. Fox, at its furthest extreme, having put on his spectacles, was bent over a glass-topped curio table. "What's he doing?" she whispered.

"Being tactful."

"Oh. I see."

"About your mother—did she often speak of her first husband?"

"Not often. I think she got out of the way of it when my papa was alive. I think he must have been jealous, poor love. He wasn't exactly a heart-throb to look at, himself. You know—pink and portly. So I think she kept things like pre-papa photographs and letters discreetly out of circulation. Sort of. But she did tell me about Maurice—that was his name."

"About his soldiering days? During the war when I suppose that photograph was taken?"

"Yes. A bit about him. Why?"

"About his brother officers, for instance? Or the men under him?"

"*Why?*" Prunella insisted. "Don't be like those awful pressmen who keep bawling out rude questions that haven't got anything to do with the case. Not," she added hastily, "that you'd really do that because you're not at all that kind. But, I mean what on *earth* can my mum's first husband's brother officers and men have to do with his wife's murder when most of them are dead, I daresay, themselves?"

"His soldier-servant, for instance? Was there anything in the letters about *him?* The officer-batman relationship can be, in its way, quite a close one."

"Now you mention it," said Prunella on a note of impatience, "there were jokey bits about somebody he called The Corp, who I suppose might have been his servant but they weren't anything out of the way. In the last letter, for instance. It was written here. He'd got an unexpected leave and come home but Mummy was with her WRENS in Scotland. It says he's trying to get a call through to her but will leave the letter in case he doesn't. It breaks off abruptly saying he's been recalled urgently to London and has just time to get to the station. I expect you know about the train being bombed."

"Yes. I know."

"Well," said Prunella shortly, "it was a direct hit. On his carriage. So that's all."

"And what about The Corp? In the letter?"

"What? Oh. There's a very effing bit about—sorry," said Prunella. "'Effing' is family slang for 'affecting' or kind of 'terribly touching.' This bit is about what she's to do if he's killed and how much—how he feels about her and she's not to worry and anyway The Corp looks after him like a nanny. He must have been rather a super chap, Maurice, I always think."

"Anything about the Black Alexander?"

"Oh, that! Well—actually, yes, there is something. He says he supposes she'll think him a fuss-pot but, after all, his London bank's in the hottest blitz area and he's taken the stamp out and will store it elsewhere. There's something about it being in a waterproof case or something. It was at that point he got the urgent recall to London. So he breaks off—and—says goodbye. Sort of."

"And the stamp was never found."

"That's right. Not for want of looking. But obviously he had it on him."

"Miss Foster, I wouldn't ask you this if it wasn't important and I hope you won't mind very much that I do ask. Will you let me see those letters?"

Prunella looked at her own hands. They were clenched tightly on her handkerchief and she hurriedly relaxed them. The handkerchief lay in a small damply crumpled heap in her lap. Alleyn saw where a fingernail had bitten into it.

"I simply can't imagine *why*," she said. "I mean, it's fantastic. Love letters, pure and simple, written almost forty years ago and concerning nothing and nobody but the writer. And Mummy, of course."

"I know. It seems preposterous, doesn't it? But I can't tell you how 'professional' and detached I shall be about it. Rather like a doctor. Please let me see them."

She glanced at the distant Fox, still absorbed in the contents of the curio table. "I don't want to make a fuss about nothing," she said. "I'll get them."

"Are they still in the not-so-secret, secret drawer of the converted sofa-table?"

"Yes."

"I should like to see it."

They had both risen.

"Secret drawers," said Alleyn lightly, "are my speciality. At the Yard they call me Peeping Tom Alleyn." Prunella compressed her lips. "Fox," Alleyn said loudly, "may I tear you away?"

"I beg your pardon, Mr. Alleyn," Fox said, removing his spectacles but staying where he was. "I beg *your* pardon, Miss Foster. My attention was caught by this—should I call it specimen table? My aunt, Miss Elsie Smith, has just such another in her shop in Brighton."

"Really?" said Prunella and stared at him.

Alleyn strolled down to the other end of the room and bent over the table. It contained a heterogeneous collection of medals, a vinaigrette, two miniatures, several little boxes in silver or cloisonné and one musical box, all set out on a blue velvet base.

"I'm always drawn to these assemblies," Alleyn said. "They are family history in hieroglyphics. I see you've rearranged them lately."

"No, I haven't. Why?" asked Prunella, suddenly alerted. She joined them. It was indeed clear from indentations in the velvet that a rearrangement had taken place. "Damn!" she said. "At it again! No, it's too much."

"At it?" Alleyn ventured. "Again? Who?"

"Claude Carter. I suppose you know he's staying here. He—does so fiddle and pry."

"What does he pry into?"

"All over the place. He's always like that. The old plans of this house and garden. Drawers in tables. He turns over other people's letters when they come. I wouldn't put him past reading them. I'm not living here at the moment so I daresay he's having field days. I don't know why I'm talking about it."

"Is he in the house at this moment?"

"I don't know. I've only just come in, myself. Never mind. Forget it. Do you want to see the letters?"

She walked out of the room, Alleyn opening the door for her. He followed her into the hall and up the staircase.

"How happy Mr. Markos will be," he remarked, "climbing up the golden stairs. They *are* almost golden, aren't they? Where the sun catches them?"

"I haven't noticed."

"Oh, but you should. You mustn't allow ownership to dull the edge of appetite. One should always know how lucky one is."

Prunella turned on the upper landing and stared at him.

"Is it your habit," she asked, "to go on like this? When you're on duty?"

"Only if I dare hope for a sympathetic reception. What happens now? Turn right, proceed in a westerly direction and effect an entrance?"

Since this was in fact what had to be done, Prunella said nothing and led the way into her mother's bedroom.

A sumptuous room. There was a canopied bed and a silken counterpane with a lacy nightgown case topped up by an enormous artificial rose. A largesse of white bearskin rugs. But for all its luxury the room had a depleted air as if the heart had gone out of it. One of the wardrobe doors was open and disclosed complete emptiness.

Prunella said rapidly: "I sent everything, all the clothes, away to the nearest professional theatre. They can sell the things they don't use: fur hats and coats and things."

There were no photographs or feminine toys of any kind on the tables and chimney-piece, and Sybil's sofa-cum-dressing-table, with its cupid-encircled looking-glass, had been bereft of all the pots, bottles and jars that Alleyn supposed had adorned it.

Prunella said, following his look, "I got rid of everything. Everything." She was defiant.

"I expect it was the best thing to do."

"We're going to change the room. Completely. My father-in-law-to-be's fantastic about houses—an expert. He'll advise us."

"Ah, yes," said Alleyn politely.

She almost shouted at him: "I suppose you think I'm hard and modern and over-reacting to everything. Well, so I may be. But I'll thank you to remember that Will. How she tried to bribe me, because that's what it was, into marrying a monster, because that's what he is, and punish me if I didn't. I never thought she had it in her to be so mean and despicable and I'm not going to bloody cry again and I don't in the least know why I'm talking to you like this. The letters are in the dressing-table and I bet you can't find the hidden bit."

She turned her back on Alleyn and blew her nose.

He went to the table, opened the central drawer, slid his finger round inside the frame and found a neat little knob that released a false wall at the back. It opened and there in the "secret" recess was the classic bundle of letters tied with the inevitable faded ribbon.

There was also an open envelope with some half-dozen sepia snapshots inside.

"I think," he said, "the best way will be for me to look at once through the letters and if they are irrelevant return them to you. Perhaps there's somewhere downstairs where Fox and I could make ourselves scarce and get it settled."

Without saying anything further Prunella led the way downstairs to the "boudoir" he had visited on his earlier call. They paused at the drawing-room to collect Mr. Fox, who was discovered in contemplation of a portrait in pastel of Sybil as a young girl.

"If," said Prunella, "you don't take the letters away perhaps you'd be kind enough to leave them in the desk."

"Yes, of course," Alleyn rejoined with equal formality. "We mustn't use up any more of your time. Thank you so much for being helpful."

He made her a little bow and was about to turn away when she suddenly thrust out her hand.

"Sorry I was idiotic. No bones broken?" Prunella asked.

"Not even a green fracture."

"Goodbye, then."

They shook hands.

"That child," said Alleyn when they were alone, "turned on four entirely separate moods, if that's what they should be called, in scarcely more than as many minutes. Not counting the drawing-room comedy which was not a comedy. You and your Aunt Elsie!"

"Perhaps the young lady's put about by recent experience," Fox hazarded.

"It's the obvious conclusion, I suppose."

In the boudoir Alleyn divided the letters—there were eight—between them. Fox put on his spectacles and read with the catarrhal breathing that always afflicted him when engaged in that exercise.

Prunella had been right. They were indeed love letters, "pure and simple" within the literal meaning of the phrase, and most touching. The young husband had been deeply in love and able to say so.

As his regiment moved from the Western Desert to Italy, the reader became accustomed to the nicknames of fellow officers and regimental jokes. The Corp, who was indeed Captain Carter's servant, featured more often as time went on. Some of the letters were illustrated with lively little drawings. There was one of the enormous Corp being harassed by bees in Tuscany. They were represented as swarming inside his kilt and he was depicted with a violent squint and his mouth wide open. A balloon issued from it with a legend that said: "It's no sae much the ticklin', it's the imperrtinence, ye ken."

The last letter was as Prunella had described it. The final sentences read: "So my darling love, I shan't see you this time. If I don't stop I'll miss the bloody train. About the stamp—sorry, no time left. Your totally besotted husband, Maurice."

Alleyn assembled the letters, tied the ribbon and put the little packet in the desk. He emptied out the snapshots: a desolate, faded company well on its slow way to oblivion. Maurice Carter appeared in all of them and in all of them looked like a near relation of Rupert Brooke. In one, he held by the hand a very small nondescript child: Claude, no doubt. In another, he and a ravishingly pretty young Sybil appeared together. A third was yet another replica of the regimental group still in her desk drawer. The fourth and last showed Maurice kilted and a captain now, with his enormous "Corp" stood-to-attention in the background.

Alleyn took it to the window, brought out his pocket lens and examined it. Fox folded his arms and watched him.

Presently he looked up and nodded.

"We'll borrow these four," he said. "I'll leave a receipt."

He wrote it out, left it in the desk and put the snapshots in his pocket. "Come on," he said.

They met nobody on their way out. Prunella's car was gone. Fox followed Alleyn past the long windows of a library and the lower west flank of the house. They turned right and came at last to the stables.

"As likely as not, he'll still be growing mushrooms," Alleyn said.

And so he was. Stripped to the waist, bronzed, golden-bearded and looking like a much younger man, Bruce was hard at work in the converted lean-to. When he saw Alleyn he grounded his shovel and arched his earthy hand over his eyes to shield them from the sun.

"Ou aye," he said, "so it's you again, Chief Superintendent. What can I do for you, the noo?"

"You can tell us, if you will, Corporal Gardener, the name of your regiment, and of its captain," said Alleyn.

## II

"I canna credit it," Bruce muttered and gazed out of his nonaligned blue eyes at Alleyn. "It doesna seem within the bounds of possibility. It's dealt me a wee shock. I'll say that for it."

"You hadn't an inkling?"

"Don't be sae daft, man," Bruce said crossly. "Sir, I should say. How would I have an inkling, will you tell me that? I doubt if her first husband was ever mentioned in my hearing and why would he be?"

"There was this stepson," Fox said to nobody in particular. "Name of Carter."

"Be damned to that," Bruce shouted. "Carrrter! Carrrter! Why would he not be Carrrter? Would I be sae daft as to say: my Captain, dead nigh on forty years, was a man o' the name of Carrrter so you must be his son and he the bonniest lad you'd ever set eyes on and you, not to dra' it mild, a puir, sickly, ill-put-taegither apology for a man? Here, sir, can I have anither keek at them photies?"

Alleyn gave them to him.

"Ah," he said, "I mind it fine, the day that group was taken. I'd forgotten all about it but I mind it fine the noo."

"But didn't you notice the replica of this one in her bedroom at the hotel?"

Bruce stared at him. His expression became prudish. He half-closed his eyes and pursed his enormous mouth. He said, in a scandalized voice: "Sir, I never set fut in her bedroom. It would have not been the thing at a'. Not at a'."

"Indeed?"

"She received me in her wee private parlour upstairs or in the garden."

"I see. I beg your pardon."

"As for these ither ones: I never see them before."

He gazed at them in silence for some moments. "My God," he said quietly, "look at the bairn, just. That'll be the bairn by the first wife. My God, it'll be this Claude! Who'd've thought it. And here's anither wi' me in the background. It's a strange coincidence, this, it is indeed."

"You never came to Quintern or heard him speak of it?"

"If I did, the name didna stick in my mind. I never came here.

What for would I? When we had leave and we only had but one before he was kilt, he let me gang awa' home. Aye, he was a considerate
officer. *Christ!*"

"What's the matter?" Alleyn asked. Bruce had dealt his knees a
devastating smack with his ginger-haired earthy hands.

"When I think of it," he said. "When I mind how me and her
would have our bit crack of an evening when I came in for my dram.
Making plans for the planting season and a' that. When I remember
how she'd talk sae free and friendly and there, all unbeknownst, was
my captain's wife that he'd let on to me was the sonsiest lass in the
land. He had her picture in his wallet and liked fine to look at it. I took
a wee keek mysel' one morning when I was brushing his tunic. She
was bonny, aye she was that. Fair as a flooer. She seems to have
changed and why wouldn't she over the passage of the years? Ou aye,"
he said heavily. "She changed."

"We all do," said Alleyn. "You've changed, yourself. I didn't recognize you at first, in the photographs."

"That'd be the beard," he said seriously and looked over his lightly
sweating torso with the naive self-approval of the physically fit male.
"I'm no' so bad in other respects," he said.

"You got to know Captain Carter quite well, I suppose?"

"Not to say well, just. And yet you could put it like that. What's
that speil to the effect that no man's a hero to his valet? He can be so to
his soldier-servant and the Captain came near enough to it with me."

"Did you get in touch with his wife after he was killed? Perhaps
write to her?"

"Na, na. I wadna tak' the liberty. And foreby I was back wi' the regiment that same night and awa' to the front. We didna get the news
until after we landed."

"When did you return to England?"

"After the war. I was taken at Cassino and spent the rest of the dura-
tion in a prison camp."

"And Mrs. Carter never got in touch? I mean: Captain Carter wrote
quite a lot about you in his letters. He always referred to you as The
Corp. I would have thought she would have liked to get in touch."

"Did he? Did he mention me, now?" said Bruce eagerly. "To think
o' that."

"Look here, Gardener, you realize by this time, don't you, that we
are considering the possibility of foul play in this business?"

Bruce arranged the photographs carefully like playing cards, in his
left fist and contemplated them as if they were all aces.

"I'm aware of that," he said absently. "It's a horrid conclusion but

I'm aware of it. To think he made mention of me in his corre-spondence. Well, now!"

"Are you prepared to help us if you can? Do," begged Alleyn, "stop looking at those damn' photographs. Here—give them to me and attend to what I say."

Bruce with every sign of reluctance yielded up the photographs.

"I hear you," he said. "Ou aye. I am prepared."

"Good. Now. First question. Did Captain Carter ever mention to you or in your hearing, a valuable stamp in his possession?"

"He did not. Wait!" said Bruce dramatically. "Aye. I mind it now. It was before he went on his last leave. He said it was in his bank in the City but he was no' just easy in his mind on account of the blitz and intended to uplift it."

"Did he say what he meant to do with it?"

"Na, na. Not a wurrred to that effect."

"Sure?"

"Aye, I'm sure," said Bruce, indifferently.

"Oh, well," Alleyn said after a pause and looked at Fox.

"You can't win all the time," said Fox.

Bruce shook himself like a wet dog. "I'll not deny this has been a shock to me," he said. "It's given me an unco awkward feeling. As if," he added opening his eyes very wide and producing a flight of fancy that seemed to surprise him, "as if time, in a manner of speaking, had got itself mixed. That's a gey weird notion, to be sure."

"Tell me, Gardener. Are you a Scot by birth?"

"Me? Na, na, I'm naething of the sort, sir. Naething of the sort. But I've worked since I was a laddie, in Scotland and under Scots instruc-tion. I enlisted in Scotland. I served in a Scots regiment and I daresay you've noticed I've picked up a trick or two of the speech."

"Yes," said Alleyn. "I had noticed."

"Aye," said Bruce complacently. "I daresay I'd pass for one in a crowd and proud to do it." As if to put a signature to his affirmation he gave Alleyn a look that he would have undoubtedly described as "canny." "I ken weel enough," he said, "that I must feature on your short list if it's with homicide that you're concerning yourself, Superin-tendent. For the simple reason the deceased left me twenty-five thou-sand pounds, et cetera. That's correct, is it not?"

"Yes," Alleyn said. "That's correct."

"I didna reckon to be contradicted and I can only hope it won't be long before you eliminate me from the file. In the meantime I can do what any guiltless man can do under the circumstances: tell the truth and hope I'm believed. For I have told you the truth, Chief Superintendent. I have indeed."

"By and large, Bruce," said Alleyn, "I believe you have."

"There's no 'by' and there's no 'large' in it," he said seriously, "and I don't doubt you'll come to acknowledge the fact."

"I hope to," Alleyn said cheerfully. "With that end in view tell me what you think of Dr. Schramm. You've met him, haven't you?"

Bruce stared at him. He turned red and looked wary. "I canna see what my opinion of the doctor would have to do wi' the matter in hand," he said.

"You prefer not to give it?"

"I didna say so. I make no secret of what I think of the doctor. I think he's not to be trusted."

"Really? Why?"

"Leave it at that. Call it instinct. I canna thole the man and that's the long and the short of it."

He looked at his wrist-watch, a Big Ben of its species, glanced at the sun and said he ought to be getting down to the churchyard.

"At St. Crispin's?"

"Aye. Did ye no' hear? Jim Jobbin has the lumbago on him and I'm digging the grave. It's entirely appropriate that I should do so."

"Yes?"

"Aye, 'tis. I've done her digging up here and she'd have been well content I'd do it down there in the finish. The difference being we canna have our bit crack over the matter. So if you've no further requirements of me, sir, I'll bid you good-day and get on with it."

"Can we give you a lift?"

"I'm much obliged, sir, but I have my ain auld car. Mrs. Jim has left a piece and a bottle ready and I'll take them with me. If it's a long job and it may be that, I'll get a bite of supper at my sister's. She has a wee piece up Stile Lane, overlooking the kirk. When would the deceased be brought for burying, can you tell me that?"

"This evening. After dark, very likely."

"And rest in the kirk overnight?"

"Yes."

"Ou aye," said Bruce on an indrawn breath. "That's a very decent arrangement. Aweel, I've a long job ahead of me."

"Thank you for your help."

Alleyn went to the yard door of the empty room. He opened it and looked in. Nothing had changed.

"Is this part of the flat that was to be built for you?" he called out.

"Aye, that was the idea," said Bruce.

"Does Mr. Carter take an interest in it?"

"Ach, he's always peering and prying. You'd think," said Bruce distastefully, "it was him that's the lawful heir."

"Would you so," said Alleyn absently. "Come along, Fox."

They left Bruce pulling his shirt over his head in an easy workmanlike manner. He threw his jacket across his shoulder, took up his shovel and marched off.

"In his way," said Fox, "a remarkable chap."

## III

Verity, to her surprise, was entertaining Nikolas Markos to luncheon. He had rung her up the day before and asked her to "take pity" on him.

"If you would prefer it," he had said, "I will drive you somewhere else, all the way to the Ritz if you like, and you shall be my guest. But I did wonder, rather wistfully, if we might have an egg under your lime trees. Our enchanting Prue is staying with us and I suddenly discover myself to be elderly. Worse, she, dear child, is taking pains with me."

"You mean?"

"She laughs a little too kindly at my dated jokes. She remembers not to forget I'm there. She includes me, with scarcely an effort, in their conversations. She's even taken to bestowing the odd butterfly kiss on the top of my head. I might as well be bald," said Mr. Markos bitterly.

"I'll undertake not to do that, at least. But I'm not much of a cook."

"My dear, my adorable lady, I said Egg and I meant Egg. I am," said Mr. Markos, "your slave forever and if you will allow me will endorse the declaration with what used to be called a bottle of The Widow. Perhaps, at this juncture I should warn you that I shall also present you with a problem. A *demain* and a thousand thanks."

"He gets away with it," Verity thought, "but only just. And if he says eggs, eggs he shall have. On creamed spinach. And my standby: iced sorrel soup first and the Stilton afterwards."

And as it was a lovely day they did have lunch under the limes. Mr. Markos, good as his word, had brought a bottle of champagne in an ice bucket and the slightly elevated atmosphere that Verity associated with him was quickly established. She could believe that he enjoyed himself as fully as he professed to do but he was as much of an exotic in her not very tidy English garden as frangipani. His hair luxuriant but disciplined, his richly curved, clever mouth and large, black eyes, his clothes that, while they avoided extravagance were inescapably very, very expensive—all these factors reminded Verity of Sybil Foster's strictures.

"The difference is," she thought, "that I don't mind him being like this. What's more I don't think Syb would have minded either if he'd taken a bit more notice of her."

When they had arrived at the coffee stage and he at his Turkish cigarette, he said: "I would choose, of course, to hear you talk about your work and this house and lovely garden. I should like you to confide in me and perhaps a little to confide in you myself." He spread his hands. "What am I saying! How ridiculous! Of course I am about to confide in you: that is my whole intention, after all. I think you are accustomed to confidences: they are poured into your lap and you are discreet and never pass them on. Am I right?"

"Well," said Verity, who was not much of a hand at talking about herself and didn't enjoy it, "I don't know so much about that." And she thought how Alleyn, though without any Markosian floridity, had also introduced confidences. "Ratsy too," she remembered, and thought irrelevantly that she had become quite a one for gentlemen callers over the last fortnight.

Mr. Markos fetched from his car two large sheets of cardboard tied together. "Do you remember," he asked, "when we examined Prunella's original plans of Quintern Place there was a smaller plan of the grounds that you said you had not seen before?"

"Yes, of course."

"This is it."

He put the cardboards on the table and opened them out. There was the plan.

"I think it is later than the others," he said, "and by a different hand. It is drawn on the scale of a quarter of an inch to the foot and is very detailed. Now. Have a close, a *very* close look. Can you find a minute extra touch that doesn't explain itself? Take your time," Mr. Markos invited, with an air of extraordinary relish. He took her arm and led her close to the table.

Verity felt that he was making a great build-up and that the climax had better be good but she obediently pored over the map.

Since it was a scheme for laying out the grounds, the house was shown simply as an outline. The stable block was indicated in the same manner. Verity, not madly engaged, plodded conscientiously over elaborate indications of water-gardens, pavilions, fountains, terraces and spinnies but although they suggested a prospect that Evelyn himself would have treasured, she could find nothing untoward. She was about to say so when she noticed that within the empty outline of the stables there was an interior line suggesting a division into two rooms, a line that seemed to be drawn free-hand in pencil rather than ruled in the brownish ink of the rest of the plan. She bent down to examine it more closely and found, in one corner of the indicated stableroom a tiny X, also, she was sure, pencilled.

Mr. Markos, who had been watching her intently, gave a triumphant little crow. "Aha!" he cried. "You see! You've spotted it."

"Well, yes," said Verity. "If you mean—" and she pointed to the pencilled additions.

"Of course, of course. And what, my dear Miss Preston-Watson, do you deduce? You know my methods. Don't bustle."

"Only, I'm afraid, that someone at some time has thought of making some alteration in the old stable buildings."

"A strictly Watsonian conclusion: I must tell you that at the moment a workman is converting the outer half of the amended portion— now an open-fronted broken-down lean-to, into a mushroom bed."

"That will be Bruce, the gardener. Perhaps he and Sybil, in talking over the project, got out this plan and marked the place where it was to go."

"But why 'the point marked X'? It does not indicate the mushroom bed. It is in a deserted room that opens off the mushroom shed."

"They might have changed their minds."

"It is crammed into a corner where there are the remains of an open fireplace. I must tell you that after making this discovery I strolled round the stable yard and examined the premises."

"I can't think of anything else," said Verity.

"I have cheated. I have withheld evidence. You must know, as Scheherazade would have said, meaning that you are to learn, that a few evenings after Prunella brought the plans to Mardling she found me poring over this one in the library. She remarked that it was strange that I should be so fascinated by it and then, with one of her nervous little spurts of confidence (she *is*, you will have noticed, unusually but, Heaven knows, understandably nervous just now), she told me that the egregious Claude Carter exhibited a similar interest in the plans and had been discovered examining this one through a magnifying glass. And I should like to know," cried Mr. Markos, sparkling at Verity, "what you make of all that!"

Verity did not make a great deal of it. She knew he expected her to enter into zestful speculation but, truth to tell, she found herself out of humour with the situation. There was something unbecoming in Nikolas Markos's glee over his discovery and if, as she suspected, he was going to link it in some way with Sybil Foster's death, she herself

wanted no part in the proceedings. At the same time she felt apologetic
—guilty, even—about her withdrawal, particularly as she was sure he
was very well aware of it. "He really is," she thought, "so remarkably
sharp."

"To look at the situation quite cold-bloodedly," he was saying, "and
of course that is the only sensible way to look at it, the police clearly
are treating Mrs. Foster's death as a case of homicide. This being so,
anything untoward that has occurred at Quintern either before or after
the event should be brought to their notice. You agree?"

Verity pulled herself together. "I suppose so. I mean, yes, of course.
Unless they've already found it out for themselves. What's the matter?"

"If they have not, we have, little as I welcome the intrusion, an opportunity to inform them. Alas, you have a visitor, dear Verity," said
Mr. Markos and quickly kissed her hand.

Alleyn, in fact, was walking up the drive.

## IV

"I'm sorry," he said, "to come at such an unlikely time of day but I'm
on my way back from Quintern Place and I thought perhaps you might
like to know about the arrangements for this evening and tomorrow."

He told them. "I daresay the Vicar will let you know," he added,
"but in case he doesn't, that's what will happen."

"Thank you," Verity said. "We were to do flowers first thing in the
morning. It had better be this afternoon, hadn't it? Nice of you to
think of it."

She told herself she knew precisely why she was glad Alleyn had arrived: idiotically it was because of Mr. Markos's manner, which had
become inappropriately warm. Old hand though she was, this had flustered Verity. He had made assumptions. He had been too adroit. Quite
a long time had gone by since assumptions had been made about Verity
and still longer since she had been ruffled by them. Mr. Markos made
her feel clumsy and foolish.

Alleyn had spotted the plan. He said Prunella had mentioned the
collection. He bent over it, made interested noises, looked closer and
finally took out a pocket lens. Mr. Markos crowed delightedly: "At
last!" he cried, "we can believe you are the genuine article." He put his
arm round Verity and gave her a quick little squeeze. "What is he
going to look at?" he said. "What do you think?"

And when Alleyn used his lens over the stable buildings, Mr.
Markos was enraptured.

"There's an extra bit pencilled in," Alleyn said. "Indicating the room next the mushroom bed."

"So, my dear Alleyn, what do you make of *that?*"

"Nothing very much, do you?"

"Not of the 'point marked X'? No buried treasure, for instance? Come!"

"Well," Alleyn said, "you can always dig for it, can't you? Actually it marks the position of a dilapidated fireplace. Perhaps there was some thought of renovating the rooms. A flat for the gardener, for instance."

"Do you know," Verity exclaimed, "I believe I remember Sybil said something about doing just that. Setting him up on the premises because his room at his sister's house was tiny and he'd nowhere to put his things and they didn't hit it off, anyway."

"No doubt you are right, both of you," admitted Mr. Markos, "but what a dreary solution. I am desolate."

"Perhaps I can cheer you up with news of an unexpected development," said Alleyn. "It emerges that Bruce Gardener was Captain Maurice Carter's soldier-servant during the war."

After a considerable interval Mr. Markos said: "The *gardener.* You mean the local man? Are you saying that this was known to Sybil Foster? And to Prunella? No. No, certainly not to Prunella."

"Not, it seems, even to Gardener himself."

Verity sat down abruptly. "What *can* you mean?" she said.

Alleyn told her.

"I have always," Mr. Markos said, "regarded stories of coincidence in a dubious light. My invariable instinct is to discredit them."

"Is it?" said Verity. "I always believe them and find them boring. I am prepared to acknowledge, since everyone tells me so, that life is littered with coincidences. I don't much mind. But this," she said to Alleyn, "is something else, again. This takes a hell of a lot of acceptance."

"Is that perhaps because of what has happened? If Mrs. Foster hadn't died and if one day in the course of conversation it had emerged that her Maurice Carter had been Bruce Gardener's Captain Carter, what would have been the reaction?"

"I can tell you what Syb's reaction would have been. She'd have made a big tra-la about it and said she'd always sensed there was 'something.'"

"And you?"

Verity thought it over. "Yes," she said. "You're right. I'd have said: fancy! Extraordinary coincidence, but wouldn't have thought much more about it."

"If one may ask?" said Mr. Markos, already asking. "How did you find out? You or whoever it was?"

"I recognized him in an old photograph of the regiment. Not at first. I was shamefully slow. He hadn't got a beard in those days but he had got his squint."

"Was he embarrassed?" Verity asked. "When you mentioned it, I mean?"

"I wouldn't have said so. Flabbergasted is the word that springs to mind. From there he passed quickly to the 'what a coincidence' bit and then into the realms of misty Scottish sentiment on 'who would have thought it' and 'had I but known' lines."

"I can imagine."

"Your Edinburgh Castle guide would have been brassy in comparison."

"Castle?" asked Mr. Markos. "Edinburgh?"

Verity explained.

"What's he doing now?" Mr. Markos sharply demanded. "Still cultivating mushrooms? Next door, by yet another coincidence"—he tapped the plan—"to the point marked X."

"When we left him he was going to the church."

"To the *church!* Why?"

Verity said: "I know why."

"You do?"

"Yes. Oh," said Verity, "this is all getting too much. Like a Jacobean play. He's digging Sybil's grave."

"Why?" asked Mr. Markos.

"Because Jim Jobbin has got lumbago."

"Who is—no," Mr. Markos corrected himself, "it doesn't matter. My dear Alleyn, forgive me if I'm tiresome, but doesn't all this throw a very dubious light upon the jobbing Gardener?"

"If it does he's not the only one."

"No? No, of course. I am forgetting the egregious Claude. By the way—I'm sorry, but you may slap me back if I'm insufferable—where does all this information come from?"

"In no small part," said Alleyn, "from Mrs. Jim Jobbin."

Mr. Markos flung up his hands. "These Jobbins!" he lamented and turned to Verity. "Come to my rescue. Who *are* the Jobbins?"

"Mrs. Jim helps you out once a week at Mardling. Her husband digs drains and graves and mows lawns. I daresay he mows yours if the truth were known."

"Odd job Jobbins, in fact," said Alleyn and Verity giggled.

"Gideon would know," his father said. "He looks after that sort of thing. In any case, it doesn't matter. Unless—I suppose she's—to be perfectly cold-blooded about it—trustworthy?"

"She's a long-standing friend," said Verity, "and the salt of the earth. I'd sooner suspect the Vicar's wife of hanky-panky than Mrs. Jim."

"Well, of course, my very dear Verity" (damn', thought Verity, I wish he wouldn't) "that disposes of her, no doubt." He turned to Alleyn. "So the field is, after all, not extensive. Far too few suspects for a good read."

"Oh, I don't know," Alleyn rejoined. "You may have overlooked a candidate."

In the pause that followed a blackbird somewhere in Verity's garden made a brief statement and traffic on the London motorway four miles distant established itself as a vague rumour.

Mr. Markos said: "Ah, yes. Of course. But I hadn't overlooked him. You're talking about my acquaintance, Dr. Basil Schramm."

"Only because I was going to ring up and ask if I might have a word with you about him. I think you introduced him to the Upper Quintern scene, didn't you?"

"Well—fleetingly, I suppose I did."

Verity said: "Would you excuse me? I've got a telephone call I must make and I *must* see about the flowers."

"Are you being diplomatic?" Mr. Markos asked archly.

"I don't even know how," she said and left them not, she hoped, too hurriedly. The two men sat down.

"I'll come straight to the point, shall I?" Alleyn said. "Can you and if so, will you, tell me anything of Dr. Schramm's history? Where he qualified, for instance? Why he changed his name? Anything?"

"Are you checking his own account of himself? Or hasn't he given a satisfactory one? You won't answer that, of course, and very properly not."

"I don't in the least mind answering. I haven't asked him."

"As yet?"

"That's right. As yet."

"Well," said Mr. Markos, airily waving his hand, "I'm afraid I'm not much use to you. I know next to nothing of his background except that he took his degree somewhere in Switzerland. I had no idea he'd changed his name, still less why. We met when crossing the Atlantic in the Q.E. Two and subsequently in New York at a cocktail party given at the St. Regis by fellow passengers. Later on that same evening at his suggestion we dined together and afterwards visited some remarkable clubs to which he had the entrée. The entertainment was curious. That was the last time I saw him until he rang me up at Mardling on his way to Greengages. On the spur of the moment I asked him to dinner. I have not seen him since then."

"Did he ever talk about his professional activities—I mean whether he had a practice in New York or was attached to a hospital or clinic or what have you?"

"Not in any detail. In the ship going over he was the life and soul of a party that revolved round an acquaintance of mine—the Princess Palevsky. I rather gathered that he acquired her and two American ladies of considerable renown as—patients. I imagine," said Mr. Markos smoothly, "that he is the happy possessor of a certain expertise in that direction. And, really, my dear Alleyn, that is the full extent of my acquaintance with Basil Schramm."

"What do you think of him?" said Alleyn abruptly.

"*Think* of him? What can I say? And what exactly do you mean?"

"Did you form an opinion of his character, for instance? Nice chap? Lightweight? Man of integrity?"

"He is quite entertaining. A lightweight, certainly, but good value as a mixer and with considerable charm. I would trust him," said Mr. Markos, "no further than I could toss a grand piano. A concert grand."

"Where women are concerned?"

"Particularly where women are concerned."

"I see," said Alleyn cheerfully and got up. "I must go," he said, "I'm running late. By the way, is Miss Foster at Quintern Place now, do you happen to know?"

"Prunella? No. She and Gideon went up to London this morning. They'll be back for dinner. She's staying with us."

"Ah yes. I must go. Would you apologize for me to Miss Preston?"

"I'll do that. Sorry not to have been more informative."

"Oh," Alleyn said, "the visit has not been unproductive. Goodbye to you."

Fox was in the car in the lane. When he saw Alleyn he started up his engine.

"To the nearest telephone," Alleyn said. "We'll use the one at Quintern Place. We've got to lay on surveillance and be quick about it. The local branch'll have to spare a copper. Send him up to Quintern as a labourer. He's to dig up the fireplace and hearth and dig deep and anything he finds that's not rubble, keep it. And when he's finished tell him to board up the room and seal it. If anyone asks what he's up to he'll have to say he's under police orders. But I hope no one will ask."

"What about Gardener?"

"Gardener's digging the grave."

"Fair enough," said Fox.

"Claude Carter may be there though."

"Oh," said Fox. "Aha. Him."

But before they reached Quintern they met Mrs. Jim on her way to do flowers in the church. She said Claude Carter had gone out that morning. "To see a man about a car," he had told her and he said he would be away all day.

"Mrs. Jim," Alleyn said. "We want a telephone and we want to take a look inside the house. Miss Foster's out. Could you help us? Do you have a key?"

She looked fixedly at him. Her workaday hands moved uneasily.

"I don't know as I have the right," she said. "It's not my business."

"I know. But it is, I promise you, very important. An urgent call. Look, come with us, let us in, follow us about if you like or we'll drive you back to the church at once. Will you do that? Please?"

There was another and a longer pause. "All right," said Mrs. Jim and got into the car.

They arrived at Quintern and were admitted by Mrs. Jim's key, which she kept under a stone in the coal house.

While Fox rang the Upper Quintern police station from the staff sitting-room telephone, Alleyn went out to the stable yard. Bruce's mushroom beds were of course in the same shape as they had been earlier in the afternoon when he left them, taking his shovel with him. The ramshackle door into the deserted room was shut. Alleyn dragged it open and stood on the threshold. At first glance it looked and smelt as it had on his earlier visit. The westering sun shone through the dirty window and showed traces of his own and Carter's footprints on the dusty floorboards. Nobody else's, he thought, but more of Carter's than his own. The litter of rubbish lay undisturbed in the corner. With a dry-mouthed sensation of foreboding he turned to the fireplace.

Alleyn began to swear softly and prolifically, an exercise in which he did not often indulge.

He was squatting over the fireplace when Fox appeared at the window, saw him and looked in at the yard door.

"They're sending up a chap at once," he said.

"Like hell, they are," said Alleyn. "Look here."

"Had I better walk in?"

"The point's academic."

Fox took four giant strides on tiptoe and stooped over the hearth. "Broken up, eh?" he said. "Fancy that, eh?"

"As you say. But look at this." He pointed a long finger. "Do you see what I see?"

"Remains of a square hole. Something regular in shape like a box or tin's been dug out. Right?"

"I think so. And take a look here. And here. And in the rubble."

"Crepe soles, by gum."

"So what do you say now to the point marked bloody X?"

"I'd say the name of the game is Carter. But why? What's he up to?"

"I'll tell you this, Br'er Fox. When I looked in here before this hearth was as it had been for Lord knows how long."

"Gardener left when we left," Fox mused.

"And is digging a grave and should continue to do so for some considerable time."

"Anybody up here since then?"

"Not Mrs. Jim, at all events."

"So we're left—" Fox said.

"—with the elusive Claude. We'll have to put Bailey and Thompson in but I bet you that's going to be the story."

"Yes. And he's seeing a man about a car," said Fox bitterly. "It might as well be a dog."

"And we might as well continue in our futile ways by seeing if there's a pick and shovel on the premises. After all, he couldn't have rootled up the hearth with his fingernails. Where's the gardener's shed?"

It was near at hand, hard by the asparagus beds. They stood in the doorway and if they had entered would have fallen over a pick that lay on the floor, an untidy note in an impeccably tidy interior. Bruce kept his tools as they should be kept, polished, sharpened and in racks. Beside the pick, leaning against a bench was a lightweight shovel and, nearby, a crowbar.

They all bore signs of recent and hard usage.

Alleyn stooped down and without touching, examined them.

"Scratches," he said. "Blunted. Chucked in here in a hurry. And take a look—crepe-soled prints on the path."

"Is Bob your uncle, then?" said Fox.

"If you're asking whether Claude Carter came down to the stable yard as soon as Bruce Gardener and you and I left it, dug up the hearth and returned the tools to this shed, I suppose he is. But if you're asking whether this means that Claude Carter murdered his stepmother I can't say it follows as the night the day."

Alleyn reached inside the door and took a key from a nail. He shut and locked the door and put the key in his pocket.

"Bailey and Thompson can pick it up from the nick," he said. "They'd better get here as soon as possible."

He led the way back to the car. Halfway there he stopped. "I tell you what, Br'er Fox," he said. "I've got a strong feeling of being just a couple of lengths behind and in danger of being beaten to the post."

"What," said Fox, pursuing his own line of thought, "would it be? What was it? That's what I ask myself."

"And how do you answer?"

"I don't. I can't. Can you?"

"One can always make wild guesses, of course. Mr. Markos was facetious about buried treasure. He might turn out to be right."

"Buried treasure," Fox echoed disgustedly. "What sort of buried treasure?"

"How do you fancy a Black Alexander stamp?" said Alleyn.

# CHAPTER VII

# Graveyard (I)

## I

MR. MARKOS HAD STAYED at Keys for only a short time after Alleyn had gone. He had quietened down quite a lot and Verity wondered if she had turned into one of those dreadful spinsters of an all too certain age who imagine that any man who shows them the smallest civility is making a pass.

He had said goodbye with a preoccupied air. His black liquid gaze was turned upon her as if in speculation. He seemed to be on the edge of asking her something but, instead, thanked her for "suffering" him to invite himself, took her hand, kissed his own thumb and left her.

Verity cut roses and stood them in scalding water for half an hour. Then she tidied herself up and drove down to St. Crispin's.

It was quite late in the afternoon when she got there. Lengthening shadows stretched out toward gravestones lolling this way and that, in and out of the sunshine. A smell, humid yet earthy, hung on the air and so did the sound of bees.

As Verity, carrying roses, climbed the steps, she heard the rhythmic, purposeful squelch of a shovel at work. It came from beyond the church and of course she knew what it was: Bruce at his task. Suddenly she was filled with a liking for Bruce: for the direct way he thought about Sybil's death and his wish to perform the only service he could provide. It no longer seemed to matter that he so readily took to sentimental manifestations and she was sorry she had made mock of them. She thought that of all Sybil's associates, even including Prunella, he was probably the only one who honestly mourned her. I won't shy off, she thought. When I've done the flowers, little as I like graves, I'll go and talk to him.

The Vicar's wife and Mrs. Field-Innis and the Ladies Guild, including Mrs. Jim, were in the church and well advanced with their flowers and brass vases. Verity joined Mrs. Jim, who was in charge of Bruce's lilies from Quintern and was being bossily advised by Mrs. Field-Innis what to do with them.

An unoccupied black trestle stood in the transept: waiting for Sybil. The Ladies Guild, going to and fro with jugs of water, gave it a wide berth as if, thought Verity, they were cutting it dead. They greeted Verity and spoke in special voices.

"Come on, Mrs. Jim," said Verity cheerfully, "let's do ours together." So they put their lilies and red roses in two big jars on either side of the chancel steps, flanking the trestle. "They'll be gay and hopeful there," said Verity. Some of the ladies looked as if they thought she had chosen the wrong adjectives.

When Mrs. Jim had fixed the final lily in its vase, she and Verity replaced the water jugs in their cupboard.

"Police again," Mrs. Jim muttered with characteristic abruptness. "Same two, twice today. Give me a lift up there. Got me to let them in, and the big one drove me back. I'll have to tell Miss Prunella, won't I?"

"Yes, I expect you must."

They went out into the westering sunlight, golden now and shining full in their faces.

"I'm going round to have a word with Bruce," said Verity. "Are you coming?"

"I seen him before. I'm not overly keen on graves. Give me the creeps," said Mrs. Jim. "He's making a nice job of it, though. Jim'll be pleased. He's still doubled up and crabby with it. We don't reckon he'll make it to the funeral but you never know with lumbago. I'll be getting along, then."

The Passcoigne plot was a sunny clearing in the trees. There was quite a company of headstones there, some so old that the inscriptions were hard to make out. They stood in grass that was kept scythed but were not formally tended. Verity preferred them like that. One day the last of them would crumble and fall. Earth to earth.

Bruce had got some way with Sybil's grave and now sat on the edge of it with his red handkerchief on his knee and his bread and cheese and bottle of beer beside him. To Verity he looked a timeless figure and the gravedigger's half-forgotten doggerel came into her head.

> *In youth when I did love, did love,*
> *Methought 'twas very sweet—*

His shovel was stuck in the heap of earth he had built up and behind him was a neat pile of small sticky pine branches, sharpened at the ends. Their resinous scent hung on the air.

"You've been hard at work, Bruce."

"I have so. There's a vein of clay runs through the soil here and that makes heavy going of it. I've broken off to eat my piece and wet my whistle and then I'll set to again. It'll tak' me all my time to get done before nightfall and there's the pine branches foreby to line it."

"That's a nice thing to do. How good they smell."

"They do that. She'd be well enough pleased, I daresay."

"I'm sure of it," said Verity. She hesitated for a moment and then said: "I've just heard about your link with Captain Carter. It must have been quite a shock for you—finding out after all these years."

"You may weel ca' it that," he said heavily. "And to tell you the truth, it gets to be more of a shock, the more I think aboot it. Ou aye, it does so. It's unco queer news for a body to absorb. I don't seem," said Bruce, scratching his head, "to be able to sort it out. He was a fine man and a fine officer, was the Captain."

"I'm sure he was."

"Aweel," he said, "I'd best get on for I've a long way to go."

He stood up, spat on his hands and pulled his shovel out of the heap of soil.

She left him hard at work and drove herself home.

Bruce dug through sunset and twilight and when it grew dark lit an acetylene lamp. His wildly distorted shadow leapt and gesticulated among the trees. He had almost completed his task when the east window, representing the Last Supper, came to life and glowed like a miraculous apparition, above his head. He heard the sound of a motor drawing up. The Vicar came round the corner of the church using a torch.

"They've arrived, Gardener," he said. "I thought you would like to know."

Bruce put on his coat. Together they walked round to the front of the church.

Sybil, in her coffin, was being carried up the steps. The doors were open and light from the interior flooded the entrances. Even outside, the scent of roses and lilies was heavily noticeable. The Vicar in his cassock welcomed his guest for the night and walked before her into her hostelry. When he came away, locking the door behind him, he left the light on in the sanctuary. From outside the church glowed faintly.

Bruce went back to her grave.

A general police search for Claude Carter had been set up.

In his room up at Quintern, Alleyn and Fox had completed an extremely professional exploration. The room, slapped up twice a week by Mrs. Jim, was drearily disordered and smelt of cigarette smoke and of an indefinable and more personal staleness. They had come at last upon a japanned tin box at the bottom of a rucksack shoved away at the top of the wardrobe. It was wrapped in a sweater and submerged in a shirt, three pairs of unwashed socks and a wind-jacket. The lock presented no difficulties to Mr. Fox.

Inside the box was a notebook and several papers.

And among these a rough copy of the plan of the room in the stable yard, the mushroom shed and the point marked X.

## II

"Earth to earth," said the Vicar, "ashes to ashes, dust to dust. In sure and certain hope . . ."

To Alleyn, standing a little apart from them, the people around the grave composed themselves into a group that might well have been chosen by the Douanier Rousseau: simplified persons of whom the most prominent were clothed in black. Almost, they looked as if they had been cut out of cardboard, painted and then endowed with a precarious animation. One expected their movements, involving the lowering of the coffin and the ritual handful of earth, to be jerky.

There they all were and he wondered how many of them had Sybil Foster in their thoughts. Her daughter, supported on either side by the two men now become her guardians-in-chief? Verity Preston, who stood nearby and to whom Prunella had turned when the commitment began? Bruce Gardener, in his Harris tweed suit, black arm-band and tie, decently performing his job as stand-in sexton with his gigantic wee laddie in support? Young Mr. Rattisbon, decorous and perhaps a little tired from standing for so long? Mrs. Jim Jobbin among the representatives of the Ladies Guild, bright-eyed and wooden-faced? Sundry friends in the county. And finally, taller than the rest, a little apart from them, impeccably turned out and so handsome that he looked as if he had been type-cast for the role of distinguished medico—Dr. Basil

Schramm, the presumably stricken but undisclosed fiancé of the deceased and her principal heir.

Claude Carter, however, was missing.

Alleyn had looked for him in church. At both sittings of the inquest Claude had contrived to get himself into an inconspicuous place and might have been supposed to lurk behind a pillar or in a sort of no-man's-land near the organ but out here in the sunny graveyard he was nowhere to be seen. There was one large Victorian angel, slightly lopsided on its massive base but pointing, like Agnes in *David Copperfield*, upward. Alleyn trifled with the notion that Claude might be behind it and would come sidling out when all was over, but no, there was no sign of him. This was not consistent. One would have expected him to put in a token appearance. Alleyn wondered if by any chance something further had cropped up about Claude's suspected drug-smuggling activities and he was making himself scarce accordingly. But if anything of that sort had occurred Alleyn would have been informed.

It was all over. Bruce Gardener began to fill in the grave. He was assisted by the wee lad, the six-foot adolescent known to the village as Daft Artie, he being, as was widely acknowledged, no more than fifty p. in the pound.

Alleyn, who had kept in the background, withdrew still further and waited.

People now came up to Prunella, said what they could find to say and walked away, not too fast but with the sense of release and buoyancy that follows the final disposal of (however deeply loved) the dead. Prunella shook hands, kissed, thanked. The Markos pair stood behind her and Verity a little farther off.

The last to come was Dr. Schramm. Alleyn saw the fractional pause before Prunella touched his offered hand. He heard her say: "Thank you for the beautiful flowers," loudly and quickly and Schramm murmur something inaudible. It was to Verity that Prunella turned when he had gone.

Alleyn had moved further along the pathway from the grave to the church. It was flanked by flowers lying in rows on the grass, some in cellophane wrappings, some picked in local gardens and one enormous professional bouquet of red roses and carnations. Alleyn read the card.

"From B.S. with love."

"Mr. Alleyn?" said Prunella, coming up behind him. He turned quickly. "It was kind of you to come," she said. "Thank you."

"What nice manners you have," Alleyn said gently. "Your mama must have brought you up beautifully."

She gave him a surprised look and a smile.

"Did you hear that, Godma V?" she said and she and her three supporters went down the steps and drove away.

When the Vicar had gone into the vestry to take his surplice off and there was nobody left in the churchyard, Alleyn went to the grave. Bruce said: "She's laid to her rest, then, Superintendent, and whatever brought her to it, there's no disturbing her in the latter end."

He spat on his hands. "Come on, lad," he said. "What are you gawping at?"

Impossible to say how old Daft Artie was—somewhere between puberty and manhood—with an incipient beard and a feral look as if he would have little difficulty in melting into the landscape and was prepared to do so at a moment's alarm.

He set to, with excessive, almost frantic energy. With a slurp and a flump, shovelfuls of dark, friable soil fell rhythmically into Sybil Foster's grave.

"Do you happen," Alleyn asked Bruce, "to have seen Mr. Claude Carter this morning?"

Bruce shot a brief glance at him. "Na, na," he said, plying his shovel, "I have not but there's nothing out of the ordinary in that circumstance. Him and me don't hit it off. And foreby I don't fancy he's been just all that comfortable within himself. Nevertheless it's a disgrace on his head not to pay his last respects. Aye, I'll say that for him: a black disgrace," said Bruce, with relish.

"When *did* you last see him?"

"Ou now—when? I couldna say with any precision. My engagements take me round the district, ye ken. I'm sleeping up at Quintern but I'm up and awa' before eight o'clock. I take my dinner with my widowed sister, Mrs. Black, puir soul up in yon cottage on the hill there, and return to Quintern in time for supper and my bed, which is in the chauffeur's old room above the garage. Not all that far," said Bruce, pointedly, "from where you unearthed him, so to speak."

"Ah yes, by the way," said Alleyn, "we're keeping observation on those premises. For the time being."

"You are! For what purpose? Och!" said Bruce irritably. "The Lord knows and you, no doubt, won't let on."

"Oh," said Alleyn airily. "It's a formality, really. Pure routine. I fancy Miss Foster hasn't forgotten that her mother was thinking of turning part of the buildings into a flat for you?"

"Has she not? I wouldna mind and that's a fact. I wouldna say no for I'm crampit up like a hen in a wee coopie where I am and God forgive me, I'm sick and tired of listening to the praises of the recently deceased."

"The recently deceased!" Alleyn exclaimed. "Do you mean Mrs. Foster?"

Bruce grounded his shovel and glared at him. "I am shocked," he said at last, pursing up his mouth to show how shocked he was and using his primmest tones, "that you should entertain such a notion. It comes little short of an insult. I referred to the fact that my sister, Mrs. Black, is recently widowed."

"I beg your pardon."

"Och, well. It was an excusable misunderstanding. So there's some idea still of fixing the flat?" He paused and stared at Alleyn. "That's not what you'd call a reason for having the premises policed, however," he said dryly.

"Bruce," Alleyn said. "Do you know what Mr. Carter was doing in that room on the morning I first visited you?"

Bruce gave a ringing sniff. "That's an easy one," he said. "I told you yesterday. Peering and prying. Spying. Trying to catch what you were spiering. To me. Aye, aye, that's what *he* was up to. He'd been hanging about the premises, feckless-like, making oot he was interested in mushrooms and letting on the police were in the hoose. When he heard you coming he was through the door like a rabbit and dragging it to, behind him. You needna suppose I'm not acquainted with Mr. Carter's ways, Superintendent. My lady telt me aboot him and Mrs. Jim's no' been backward in coming forward on the subject. When persons of his class turn aside they make a terrible bad job of themsel's. Aye, they're worse by a long march than the working-class chap with some call to slip from the paths of rectitude."

"I agree with you."

"You can depend on it."

"And you can't think when you last saw him?"

Bruce dragged his hand over his beard. "When would it have been, now?" he mused. "Not today. I left the premises before eight and I was hame for dinner and after that I washed myself and changed to a decent suit for the burying. I'll tell you when it was," he said, brightening up. "It was yesterday morning. I ran into him in the stable yard and he asked me if I knew how the trains run to Dover. He let on he has an acquaintance there and might pay him a visit some time."

"Did he say anything about going to the funeral?"

"Did he, now? Wait, now. I canna say for certain but I carry the impression he passed a remark that led me to suppose he'd be attending the obsequies. That," said Bruce, summing up, "is the length and breadth of my total recollection." He took up his shovel.

The wee laddie, who had not uttered nor ceased with frantic zeal to cast earth on earth, suddenly gave tongue.

"I seen 'im," he said loudly.

Bruce contemplated him. "You seen who, you puir daftie?" he asked kindly.

"Him. What you're talking about."

Bruce slightly shook his head at Alleyn, indicating the dubious value of anything the gangling creature had to offer. "Did ye noo?" he said tolerantly.

"In the village. It weren't 'alf dark, 'cept up here where you was digging the grave, Mr. Gardener, and had your 'ceterlene lamp."

"Where'd you been, then, young Artie, stravaging abroad in the night?"

"I dunno," said Artie, showing the whites of his eyes.

"Never mind," Alleyn intervened. "Where were you when you saw Mr. Carter?"

"Corner of Stile Lane, under the yedge, weren't I? And him coming down into Long Lane." He began to laugh again: the age-old gaffaw of the rustic oaf. "I give him a proper scare, din' I?" He let out an eldritch screech. "Like that. I was in the yedge and he never knew where it come from. Reckon he was dead scared."

"What did he do, Artie?" Alleyn asked.

"I dunno," Artie muttered, suddenly uninterested.

"Where did he go, then?"

"I dunno."

"You must know," Bruce roared out. "Oot we' it. Where did he go?"

"I never see. I was under the yedge, wasn' I? Up the steps, then, he must of, because I yeard the gate squeak. When I come out 'e'd gone."

Bruce cast his eyes up and shook his head hopelessly at Alleyn. "What are you trying to tell us, Artie?" he asked patiently. "Gone *wheer*? I never saw the man and there I was, was I no'? He never came my way. Would he enter the church and keep company wi' the dead?"

This produced a strange reaction. Artie seemed to shrink into himself. He made a movement with his right hand, almost as if to bless himself with the sign of the cross, an age-old self-defensive gesture.

"Did you know," Alleyn asked quietly, "that Mrs. Foster lay in the church last night?"

Artie looked into the half-filled grave and nodded. "I seen it. I seen them carry it up the steps," he whispered.

"That was before you saw Mr. Carter come down the lane?"

He nodded.

Bruce said: "Come awa', laddie. Nobody's going to find fault with you. Where did Mr. Carter go? Just tell us that now."

Artie began to whimper. "I dunno," he whined. "I looked out of the yedge, din' I? And I never saw 'im again."

"Where did *you* go?" Alleyn asked.

"Nowhere."

Bruce said: "Yah!" and with an air of hardly controlled exasperation returned to his work.

"You must have gone somewhere," Alleyn said. "I bet you're quite a one for getting about the countryside on your own. A night bird, aren't you, Artie?"

A look of complacency appeared. "I might be," he said and then with a sly glance at Bruce, "I sleep out," he said, "of a night. Often."

"Did you sleep out last night? It was a warm night, wasn't it?"

"Yeah," Artie conceded off-handedly, "it was warm. I slep' out."

"Where? Under the hedge?"

"In the yedge. I got a place."

"Where you stayed hid when you saw Mr. Carter?"

"That's right." Stimulated by the recollection he repeated his screech and raucous laugh.

Bruce seemed about to issue a scandalized reproof but Alleyn checked him. "And after that," he said, "you settled down and went to sleep? Is that it?"

"'Course," said Artie haughtily and attacked his shovelling with renewed energy.

"When you caught sight of him," Alleyn asked, "did you happen to notice how he was dressed?"

"I never see nothing to notice."

"Was he carrying anything? A bag or suitcase?" Alleyn persisted.

"I never see nothing," Artie repeated morosely.

Alleyn jerked his head at Artie's back. "Is he to be relied on?" he said quietly.

"Hard to say. Weak in the head but truthful as far as he goes and that's not far." Bruce lowered his voice. "There's a London train goes through at five past eleven: a slow train with a passenger carriage. Stops at Great Quintern. You can walk it in an hour," said Bruce with a steady look at Alleyn.

"Is there, indeed?" said Alleyn. "Thank you, Bruce. I won't keep you any longer but I'm very much obliged to you."

As he turned away Artie said in a sulky voice and to nobody in particular: "He were carrying a pack. On his back." Pleased with the rhyme he improvised: "Pack on 'is back and down the track," and, as an inspired addition: "E'd got the sack."

"Alas, alack," Alleyn said and Artie giggled. "Pack on 'is back and got the sack," he shouted.

"Och, *havers!*" said Bruce disgustedly. "You're nowt but a silly, wanting kind of crittur. Haud your whist and get on with your work."

"Wait a moment," said Alleyn, and to Artie. "Did you sleep out all night? When did you wake up?"

"When 'e went 'ome," said Artie, indicating the indignant Bruce. "You woke me up, Mr. Gardener, you passed that close. Whistling. I could of put the wind up you, proper, couldn't I? I could of frown a brick at you, Mr. Gardener. But I never," said Artie virtuously.

Bruce made a sound of extreme exasperation.

"When was this, Artie? You wouldn't know, would you?" said Alleyn.

"Yes, I would, then. Twelve. Church clock sounded twelve, din' it?"

"Is that right?" Alleyn asked Bruce.

"He can't count beyond ten. It was nine when I knocked off."

"Long job, you had of it."

"I did that. There's a vein of solid clay runs through, three foot depth of it. And after that the pine boughs to push in. It was an unco weird experience. Everybody in the village asleep by then and an owl overhead and bats flying in and out of the lamplight. And inside the kirk, the leddy herself, cold in her coffin and me digging her grave. Aye, it was, you may say, an awfu', uneasy situation, yon. In literature," said Bruce, lecturing them, "it's an effect known as Gothic. I was pleased enough to have done it."

Alleyn lowered his voice. "Do you think he's got it right?"

"That he slept under the hedge and woke as I passed? I daresay. It might well be, puir daftie."

"And that he saw Carter, earlier?"

"I'd be inclined to credit it. I didna see anything of the man mysel' but then I wouldn't, where I was."

"No, of course not. Well, thanks again," Alleyn said. He returned to the front of the church, ran down the steps and found Fox waiting in the car.

"Back to Quintern," he said. "The quest for Charmless Claude sets in with a vengeance."

"Skiddadled?"

"Too soon to say. Bruce indicates as much."

"Ah, to hell with it," said Fox in a disgusted voice. "What's the story?"

Alleyn told him.

"There you are!" Fox complained when he had finished. "Scared him off, I daresay, putting our chap in. Here's a pretty kettle of fish."

"We'll have to take up the Dover possibility, of course, but I don't like it much. If he'd considered it as a get-away port he wouldn't have been silly enough to ask Bruce about trains. Still, we'll check. He's thought to have some link with a stationer's shop in Southampton."

"Suppose we do run him down, what's the charge?"

"You may well ask. We've got nothing to warrant an arrest unless we can hold him for a day or two on the drug business and that seems to have petered out. We can't run him in for grubbing up an old fire-place in a disused room in his stepmother's stable yard. Our chap's found nothing to signify, I suppose?"

"Nothing, really. You've had a better haul, Mr. Alleyn."

"I don't know, Foxkin, I don't know. In one respect I think perhaps I have."

## III

When Verity drove home from the funeral it was with the expectation of what she called "putting her boots up" and relaxing for an hour or so. She found herself to be suddenly used up and supposed that the events of the past days must have been more exhausting, emotionally, than she had realized. And after further consideration an inborn honesty prompted her to conclude that the years were catching up on her.

"Selfishly considered," she told herself, "this condition has its advantages. Less is expected of one." And then she pulled herself together. Anyone would think she was involved up to her ears in this wretched business whereas, of course, apart from being on tap whenever her goddaughter seemed to want her, she was on the perimeter.

She had arrived at this reassuring conclusion when she turned in at her own gate and saw Basil Schramm's car drawn up in front of her house.

Schramm himself was sitting at the iron table under the lime trees. His back was toward her but at the sound of her car, he swung round and saw her. The movement was familiar.

When she stopped he was there, opening the door for her.

"You didn't expect to see me," he said.

"No."

"I'm sorry to be a bore. I'd like a word or two if you'll let me."

"I can't very well stop you," said Verity lightly. She walked quickly to the nearest chair and was glad to sit on it. Her mouth was dry and there was a commotion going on under her ribs.

He took the other chair. She saw him through a kind of mental double focus: as he had been when, twenty-five years ago, she made a fool of herself, and as he was now, not so much changed or aged as exposed.

"I'm going to ask you to be terribly, terribly kind," he said and waited.

"Are you?"

"Of course you'll think it bloody cool. It *is* bloody cool but you've always been a generous creature, Verity, haven't you?"

"I shouldn't depend on it, if I were you."

"Well—I can but try." He took out his cigarette case. It was silver with a sliding action. "Remember?" he said. He slid it open and offered it to her. She had given it to him.

Verity said, "No, thank you, I don't."

"You used to. How strong-minded you are. I shouldn't, of course, but I do." He gave his rather empty social laugh and lit a cigarette. His hands were unsteady.

Verity thought: I know the line I ought to take if he says what I think he's come here to say. But can I take it? Can I avoid saying things that will make him suppose I still mind? I know this situation. After it's all over you think of how dignified and quiet and unmoved you should have been and remember how you gave yourself away at every turn. As I did when he degraded me.

He was preparing his armory. She had often, even when she had been most attracted, thought how transparent and silly and predictable were his ploys.

"I'm afraid," he was saying, "I'm going to talk about old times. Will you mind very much?"

"I can't say I see much point in the exercise," she said cheerfully. "But I don't *mind*, really."

"I hoped you wouldn't."

He waited, thinking perhaps that she would invite him to go on. When she said nothing he began again.

"It's nothing, really. I didn't mean to give it a great build-up. It's just an invitation for you to preserve what they call 'a masterly inactivity.'" He laughed again.

"Yes?"

"About—well, Verity, I expect you've guessed what about, haven't you?"

"I haven't tried."

"Well, to be quite, quite honest and straightforward—" He boggled for a moment.

"Quite honest and straightforward?" Verity couldn't help repeating but she managed to avoid a note of incredulity. She was reminded of another stock phrase-maker—Mr. Markos and his "quite cold-bloodedly."

"It's about that silly business a thousand years ago, at St. Luke's," Schramm was saying, "I daresay you've forgotten all about it."

"I could hardly do that."

"I know it looked bad. I know I ought to have—well—asked to see you and explain. Instead of—all right, then—"

"Bolting?" Verity suggested.

"Yes. All right. But you know there were extenuating circumstances. I was in a bloody bad jam for money and I would have paid it back."

"But you never got it. The bank questioned the signature on the cheque, didn't they? And my father didn't make a charge."

"Very big of him! He only gave me the sack and shattered my career."

Verity stood up. "It would be ridiculous and embarrassing to discuss it. I think I know what you're going to ask. You want me to say I won't tell the police. Is that it?"

"To be perfectly honest—"

"Oh, *don't*," Verity said, and closed her eyes.

"I'm sorry. Yes, that's it. It's just that they're making nuisances of themselves and one doesn't want to present them with ammunition."

Verity was painfully careful and slow over her answer. She said: "If you are asking me not to go to Mr. Alleyn and tell him that when you were one of my father's students I had an affair with you and that you used this as a stepping-stone to forging my father's signature on a cheque—no, I don't propose to do that."

She felt nothing more than a reflected embarrassment when she saw the red flood into his face but she did turn away.

She heard him say: "Thank you for that, at least. I don't deserve it and I didn't deserve you. God, what a fool I was!"

She thought: I mustn't say, "In more ways than one." She made herself look at him and said: "I think I should tell you that I know you were engaged to Sybil. It's obvious that the police believe there was foul play and I imagine that as a principal legatee under the Will—"

He shouted her down: "You can't— Verity, you would never think I—I—? Verity?"

"Killed her?"

"My God!"

"No. I don't think you did that. But I must tell you that if Mr. Alleyn finds out about St. Luke's and the cheque episode and asks me if it was all true, I shan't lie to him. I shan't elaborate or make any statements. On the contrary I shall probably say I prefer not to answer. But I shan't lie."

"By God," he repeated, staring at her. "So you haven't forgiven me, have you?"

"Forgiven? It doesn't arise." Verity looked squarely at him. "That's true, Basil. It's the wrong sort of word. It upsets me to look back at what happened, of course it does. After all, one has one's pride. But otherwise the question's academic. Forgiven you? I suppose I must have but—no, it doesn't arise."

"And if you 'prefer not to answer,'" he said, sneering, it seemed, at himself as much as at her, "what's Alleyn going to think? Not much doubt about that one, is there? Look here: has he been at you already?"

"He came to see me."

"What for? Why? Was it about—that other nonsense? On Capri?"

"On the long vacation? When you practised as a qualified doctor? No, he said nothing about that."

"It was a joke. A ridiculous old hypochondriac, dripping with jewels and crying out for it. What did it matter?"

"It mattered when they found out at St. Luke's."

"Bloody pompous lot of stuffed shirts. I knew a damn' sight more medics than most of their qualified teacher's pets."

"Have you *ever* qualified? No, don't tell me," said Verity quickly.

"Has Nick Markos talked about me? To you?"

"No."

"Really?"

"Yes, Basil, really," she said and tried to keep the patient sound out of her voice.

"I only wondered. Not that he'd have anything to say that mattered. It's just that you seemed to be rather thick with him, I thought."

There was only one thing now that Verity wanted and she wanted it urgently. It was for him to go away. She had no respect left for him and had had none for many years but it was awful to have him there, pussyfooting about in the ashes of their past and making such a shabby job of it. She felt ashamed and painfully sorry for him, too.

"Was that all you wanted to know?" she asked.

"I think so. No, there's one other thing. You won't believe this but it happens to be true. Ever since that dinner-party at Mardling—months ago when we met again—I've had—I mean I've not been able to get you out of my head. You haven't changed all that much, Verry. Whatever you may say, it was very pleasant. Us. Well, wasn't it? What? Come on, be honest. Wasn't it quite fun?"

He actually put his hand over hers. She was aghast. Something of her incredulity and enormous distaste must have appeared in her face. He withdrew his hand as if it had been scalded.

"I'd better get on my tin tray and slide off," he said. "Thank you for seeing me."

He got into his car. Verity went indoors and gave herself a strong drink. The room felt cold.

IV

Claude Carter had gone. His rucksack and its contents had disappeared and some of his undelicious garments. His room was in disorder. It had not been Mrs. Jim's day at Quintern Place. She had told Alleyn to use her key hidden under the stone in the coal house, and they had let themselves in with it.

There was a note scrawled on a shopping pad in the kitchen. "Away for an indefinite time. Will let you know if and when I return. C.C." No date. No time.

And now, in his room, they searched again and found nothing of interest until Alleyn retrieved a copy of last week's local newspaper from the floor behind the unmade bed.

He looked through it. On the advertisement page under "Cars for Sale" he found, halfway down the column, a ring round an insertion that offered a 1964 Heron for £500 or nearest offer. The telephone number had been underlined.

"He gave it out," Alleyn reminded Fox, "that he was seeing a man about a car."

"Will I ring them?"

"If you please, Br'er Fox."

But before Fox could do so a distant telephone began to ring. Alleyn opened the door and listened. He motioned to Fox to follow him and walked down the passage toward the stairhead.

The telephone in the hall below could now be heard. He ran down the stairs and answered it, giving the Quintern number.

"Er, yes," said a very loud man's voice. "Would this be the gentleman who undertook to buy a sixty-four Heron off of me and was to collect it yesterday evening? Name of Carter?"

"He's out at the moment, I'm afraid. Can I take a message?"

"Yes, you can. I'll be obliged if he'll ring up and inform me one way or the other. If he don't, I'll take it the sale's off and dispose of the vehicle elsewhere. He can collect his deposit when it bloody suits him. Thank *you*."

The receiver was jammed back before Alleyn could reply.

"Hear that?" he asked Fox.

"Very put about, wasn't he? Funny, that. Deposit paid down and all. Looks like something urgent cropped up to make him have it on the toes," said Fox, meaning "bolt." "Or it might be he couldn't raise the principal. What do you reckon, Mr. Alleyn? He's only recently returned from abroad so his passport ought to be in order."

"Presumably."

"Or he may be tucked away somewhere handy or gone to try and raise the cash for the car. Have we got anything on his associates?"

"Nothing to write home about. His contact in the suspected drug business is thought to be a squalid little stationer's shop in Southampton: one of the sort that provides an accommodation address. It's called The Good Read and is in Port Lane."

"Sussy on drugs," Fox mused, "and done for blackmail."

"Attempted blackmail. The victim didn't play ball. He charged him and Claude did three months. Blackmail tends to be a chronic condition. He may have operated at other times with success."

"What's our move, then?"

"Complete this search and then get down to the village again and see if we can find anything to bear out Artie's tale of Claude's nocturnal on-goings."

When they arrived back at the village and inspected the hedgerow near the corner of Stile Lane and Long Lane they soon found what they sought, a hole in the tangle of saplings, blackthorn and weeds that could be crept into from the field beyond and was masked from the sunken lane below by grasses and wild parsnip. Footprints from a hurdle-gate into the field led to the hole and a flattened depression within it where they found five cigarette butts and as many burnt matches. Clear of the hedge was an embryo fireplace constructed of a few old bricks and a crossbar of wood supported by two cleft sticks.

"Snug," said Fox. "And here's where sonny-boy plays Indian."

"That's about the form."

"And kips with the bunnies and tiggywinkles."

"And down the lane comes Claude with his pack on his back."

"All of a summer's night."

"All right, all right. He must have passed more or less under Artie's nose."

"Within spitting range," Fox agreed.

"Come on."

Alleyn led the way back into Long Lane and to the lych-gate at the foot of the church steps. He pushed it open and it squeaked.

"I wonder," Alleyn said, "how many people have walked up those steps since nine o'clock last night. The whole funeral procession."

"That's right," said Fox gloomily.

"Coffin bearers, mourners. Me. After that, tidy-uppers, and the Vicar, one supposes."

He stooped down, knelt, peered. "Yes, I think so," he said. "On the damp earth the near side of the gate and well to the left. In the shelter of the lych, if that's the way to put it. Very faint but I fancy they're our old friends the crepe-soled shoes. Take a look."

Fox did so. "Yes," he said. "By gum, I think so."

"More work for Bill Bailey and until he gets here the local copper can undisguise himself and take another turn at masterly inactivity. So far it's one up to Artie."

"Not a chance of anything on the steps."

"I'm afraid, not a chance. Still—up we go."

They climbed the steps, slowly and searchingly. Inside the church the organ suddenly blared and infant voices shrilled.

*Through the night of doubt and sorrow—*

"Choir practice," said Alleyn. "Damn. Not an inappropriate choice, though, when you come to think of it."

The steps into the porch showed signs of the afternoon's traffic. Alleyn took a look inside. The Vicar's wife was seated at the organ with five little girls and two little boys clustered round her. When she saw Alleyn her jaw dropped in the middle of "Onward." He made a pacifying signal and withdrew. He and Fox walked round the church to Sybil Foster's grave.

Bruce and Artie had taken trouble over finishing their job. The flowers—Bruce would certainly call them "floral tributes"—no longer lined the path but had been laid in meticulous order on the mound which they completely covered, stalks down, blossoms pointing up, in receding size. The cellophane covers on the professional offerings glistened in the sun and looked, Alleyn thought, awful. On the top, as a sort of baleful *bon-bouche,* was the great sheaf of red roses and carnations "From B.S."

"It's quite hopeless," Alleyn said. "There must have been thirty or more people tramping round the place. If ever his prints were here they've been trodden out. We'd better take a look but we won't find."

Nor did they.

"Not to be fanciful," Fox said. "As far as the footsteps go it's like coming to the end of a trail. Room with the point marked X, gardener's shed, broom recess, lych-gate and—nothing. It would have been appropriate, you might say, if they'd finished up for keeps at the graveside."

Alleyn didn't answer for a second or two.

"You do," he then said, "get the oddest flights of fancy. It *would*, in a macabre sort of way, have been dramatically satisfactory."

"If he did her, that is."

"Ah. If."

"Well," said Fox, "it looks pretty good to me. How else do you explain the ruddy prints? He lets on he's an electrician, he takes up the lilies, he hides in the recess and when the coast's clear he slips in and does her. Motive: the cash: a lot of it. You *can't* explain it any other way."

"Can't you?"

"Well, can you?"

"We mentioned his record, didn't we? Blackmail. Shouldn't we perhaps bestow a passing thought on that?"

"Here! Wait a bit—wait a bit," said Fox, startled. He became broody and remained so all the way to Greater Quintern.

They drove to the police station where Alleyn had established his headquarters and been given a sort of mini-office next door to the charge room. It had a table, three chairs, writing material and a telephone, which was all he expected to be given, and suited him very well.

The sergeant behind the counter in the front office was on the telephone when they came in. When he saw Alleyn he raised his hand.

"Just a minute, Madam," he said. "The Chief Superintendent has come in. Will you hold on, please?" He put his enormous hand over the receiver. "It's a lady asking for you, sir. She seems to be upset. Shall I take the name?"

"Do."

"What name was it, Madam? Yes, Madam, he *is* here. What name shall I say? Thank you. Hold the line please," said the sergeant, restopping the receiver. "It's a Sister Jackson, sir. She says it's very urgent."

Alleyn gave a long whistle, pulled a face at Fox and said he'd take the call in his room.

Sister Jackson's voice, when it came through, was an extraordinary mixture of refinement and what sounded like sheer terror. She whispered, and her whisper was of the piercing kind. She gasped, she faded out altogether and came back with a rush. She apologized for being silly and said she didn't know what he would think of her. Finally she breathed heavily into the receiver, said she was "in shock" and wanted to see him. She could not elaborate over the telephone.

Alleyn, thoughtfully contemplating Mr. Fox, said he would come to Greengages, upon which she gave an instantly muffled shriek and said no, no that would never do and that she had the evening off and would meet him in the bar-parlour of the Iron Duke on the outskirts of Maidstone. "It's quite nice, really," she quavered.

"Certainly," Alleyn said. "What time?"

"About nayne?"

"Nine let it be. Cheer up, Sister. You don't feel like giving me an inkling as to what it's all about?"

When she answered she had evidently put her mouth inside the receiver.

"Blackmail," she articulated and his eardrum tingled.

Approaching voices were to be heard. Sister Jackson came through from a normal distance. "O.K." she cried. "That'll be fantastic, cheery-bye" and hung up.

"Blackmail," Alleyn said to Fox. "We've only got to mention it and up it rises."

"Well!" said Fox, "fancy that! Would it be going too far to mention Claude?"

"Who can tell? But at least it's suggestive. I'll leave you to get things laid on up in the village. Where are Bailey and Thompson, by the way?"

"Doing the fireplace and the toolshed. They're to ring back here before leaving."

"Right. Get the local copper to keep an eye on the lych-gate until B and T arrive. Having dealt with that and just to show zealous they may then go over the churchyard area and see if they can find a trace we've missed. And having turned them on, Fox, check the progress, if any, of the search for Claude Carter. Oh, and see if you can get a check on the London train from Great Quintern at eleven-five last night. I think that's the lot."

"You don't require me?"

"No. *La belle Jackson* is clearly not in the mood. Sickening for you."

"We'll meet at our pub, then?"

"Yes."

"I shan't wait up," said Fox.

"Don't dream of it."

"In the meantime I'll stroll down to the station hoping for better luck than I had with the Greengages bus."

"Do. I'll bring my file up to date."

"Were you thinking of taking dinner?"

"I was thinking of taking worm-coloured fish in pink sauce and athletic fowl at our own pub. Do join me."

"Thanks. That's all settled, then," said Fox comfortably and took himself off.

## V

There were only seven customers in the bar-parlour of the Iron Duke when Alleyn walked in at a quarter to nine: an amorous couple at a corner table and five city-dressed men playing poker.

Alleyn took a glass of a respectable port to a banquette at the farthest remove from the other tables and opened the evening paper. A distant roar of voices from the two bars bore witness to the Duke's popularity. At five to nine Sister Jackson walked in. He received the slight shock caused by an encounter with a nurse seen for the first time out of uniform. Sister Jackson was sheathed in clinging blue with a fairly reckless cleavage. She wore a velvet beret that rakishly shaded her face, and insistent gloves. He saw that her makeup was more emphatic than usual, especially about the eyes. She had been crying.

"How punctual we both are," he said. He turned a chair to the table with its back to the room and facing the banquette. She sat in it without looking at him and with a movement of her shoulders that held a faint suggestion of what might have passed as provocation under happier circumstances. He asked her what she would have to drink and when she hesitated and bridled a little, proposed brandy.

"Well—thank you," she said. He ordered a double one. When it came she took a sudden pull at it, shuddered and said she had been under a severe strain. It was the first remark of more than three words that she had offered.

"This seems quite a pleasant pub," he said. "Do you often come here?"

"No. Never. They—we—all use the Crown at Greendale. That's why I suggested it. To be sure."

"I'm glad," Alleyn said, "that whatever it's all about you decided to tell me."

"It's very difficult to begin."

"Never mind. Try. You said something about blackmail, didn't you? Shall we begin there?"

She stared at him for an awkwardly long time and then suddenly opened her handbag, pulled out a folded paper and thrust it across the table. She then took another pull at her brandy.

Alleyn unfolded the paper, using his pen and a fingernail to do so. "Were you by any chance wearing gloves when you handled this?" he asked.

"As it happened. I was going out. I picked it up at the desk."

"Where's the envelope?"

"I don't know. Yes, I do. I think. On the floor of my car. I opened it in the car."

The paper was now spread out on the table. It was of a kind as well-known to the police as a hand-bill: a piece of off-white commercial paper, long and narrow, that might have been torn from a domestic *aide-mémoire*. The message was composed of words and letters that had been cut from newsprint and gummed in two irregular lines.

"Post £500 fives and singles to C. Morris 11 Port Lane Southampton otherwise will inform police your visit to room 20 Genuine"

Alleyn looked at Sister Jackson and Sister Jackson looked like a mesmerized rabbit at him.

"When did it come?"

"Yesterday morning."

"To Greengages?"

"Yes."

"Is the envelope addressed in this fashion?"

"Yes. My name's all in one. I recognized it—it's from an advertisement in the local rag for Jackson's Drapery and it's the same with Greengages Hotel. Cut out of an advertisement."

"You didn't comply, of course?"

"No. I didn't know what to do. I—nothing like that's ever happened to me—I—I was dreadfully upset."

"You didn't ask anyone to advise you?"

She shook her head.

"Dr. Schramm, for instance?"

He could have sworn that her opulent flesh did a little hop and that for the briefest moment an extremely vindictive look flicked on and off. She wetted her mouth. "Oh, no," she whispered. "No, *thank* you!"

"This is the only message you've received?"

"There's been something else. Something much worse. Last evening. Soon after eight. They fetched me from the dining-room."

"What was it? A telephone call?"

"You knew!"

"I guessed. Go on, please."

"When the waiter told me, I knew. I don't know why but I did. I knew. I took it in one of the telephone boxes in the hall. I think he must have had something over his mouth. His voice was muffled and peculiar. It said: 'You got the message.' I couldn't speak and then it said: 'You did or you'd answer. Have you followed instructions?' I—didn't know what to say so I said: 'I will' and it said 'you better.' It said something else, I don't remember exactly, something about the only warning, I think. That's all," said Sister Jackson, and finished her cognac. She held the unsteady glass between her white-gloved paws and put it down awkwardly.

Alleyn said: "Do you mind if I keep this? And would you be kind enough to refold it and put it in here for me?" He took an envelope from his pocket and laid it beside the paper.

She complied and made a shaky business of doing so. He put the envelope in his breast pocket.

"What will he do to me?" asked Sister Jackson.

"The odds are: nothing effective. The police may get something from him but you've anticipated that, haven't you? Or you will do so."

"I don't understand."

"Sister Jackson," Alleyn said. "Don't you think you had better tell me about your visit to Room Twenty?"

She tried to speak. Her lips moved. She fingered them and then looked at the smudge of red on her glove.

"Come along," he said.

"You won't understand."

"Try me."

"I can't."

"Then why have you asked to see me? Surely it was to anticipate whatever the concocter of this message might have to say to us. You've got in first."

"I haven't done anything awful. I'm a fully qualified nurse."

"Of course you are. Now then, when did you pay this visit?"

She focussed her gaze on the couple in the far corner, stiffened her neck and rattled off her account in a series of disjointed phrases.

It had been at about nine o'clock on the night of Mrs. Foster's death (Sister Jackson called it her "passing"). She herself walked down the passage on her way to her own quarters. She heard the television bawling away in Number 20. Pop music. She knew Mrs. Foster didn't appreciate pop and she thought she might have fallen asleep and the noise would disturb the occupants of neighbouring rooms. So she tapped and went in.

Here Sister Jackson paused. A movement of her chin and throat indicated a dry swallow. When she began again her voice was pitched higher but not by any means louder than before.

"The patient—" she said, "Mrs. Foster, I mean—was, as I thought she would be. Asleep. I looked at her and made sure she was—asleep. So I came away. *I came away.* I wasn't there for more than three minutes. That's all. All there is to tell you."

"How was she lying?"

"On her side, with her face to the wall."

"When Dr. Schramm found her she was on her back."

"I know. That proves it. Doesn't it? *Doesn't it!*"

"Did you turn off the television?"

"No. Yes! I don't remember. I think I must have. I don't know."

"It was still going when Dr. Schramm found her."

"Well, I didn't, then, did I? I didn't turn it off."

"Why, I wonder?"

"It's no good asking me things like that. I've been shocked. I don't remember details."

She beat on the table. The amorous couple unclinched and one of the card players looked over his shoulder. Sister Jackson had split her glove.

Alleyn said: "Should we continue this conversation somewhere else?"

"No. I'm sorry."

With a most uncomfortable parody of coquettishness she leant across the table and actually smiled or seemed to smile at him.

"I'll be all right," she said.

Their waiter came back and looked enquiringly at her empty glass.

"Would you like another?" Alleyn asked.

"I don't think so. No. Well, a small one, then."

The waiter was quick bringing it.

"Right. Now—how was the room? The bedside table? Did you notice the bottle of barbiturates?"

"I didn't notice. I've said so. I just saw she was asleep and I went away."

"Was the light on in the bathroom?"

This seemed to terrify her. She said: "Do you mean—? Was he *there?* Whoever it was? Hiding? Watching? No, the door was shut, I mean— I think it was shut."

"Did you see anybody in the passage? Before you went into the room or when you left it?"

"No."

"Sure?"

"Yes."

"There's that alcove, isn't there? Where the brooms and vacuum cleaner are kept?"

She nodded. The amorous couple were leaving. The man helped the girl into her coat. They both looked at Alleyn and Sister Jackson. She fumbled in her bag and produced a packet of cigarettes.

Alleyn said: "I'm sorry. I've given up and forget to keep any on me. At least I can offer you a light." He did so and she made a clumsy business of using it. The door swung to behind the couple. The card players had finished their game and decided, noisily, to move into the bar. When they had gone Alleyn said: "You realize, don't you—well of course you do—that the concocter of this threat must have seen you?"

She stared at him. "Naturally," she said, attempting, he thought, a sneer.

"Yes," he said. "It's a glimpse of the obvious, isn't it? And you'll remember that I showed you a lily head that Inspector Fox and I found in the alcove?"

"Of course."

"And that there were similar lilies in the hand-basin in Mrs. Foster's bathroom?"

"Naturally. I mean—yes, I saw them afterwards. When we used the stomach pump. We scrubbed up under the bath taps. It was quicker than clearing away the mess in the basin."

"So it follows as the night the day that the person who dropped the lily head in the alcove was the person who put the flowers in the hand-basin. Does it also follow that this same person was your blackmailer?"

"I—yes. I suppose it might."

"And does it also follow, do you think, that the blackmailer was the murderer of Mrs. Foster?"

"But you don't know. You don't know that she was—*that*."

"We believe we do."

She ought, he thought, to be romping about like a Rubens lady in an Arcadian setting: all sumptuous flesh, no brains and as happy as Larry, instead of quivering like an overdressed jelly in a bar-parlour.

"Sister Jackson," he said. "Why didn't you tell the coroner or the police or anyone at all that you went into Room Twenty at about nine o'clock that night and found Mrs. Foster asleep in her bed?"

She opened and shut her smudged lips two or three times, gaping like a fish.

"Nobody asked me," she said. "Why should I?"

"Are you sure Mrs. Foster was asleep?"

Her lips formed the words but she had no voice. "Of course I am."

"She wasn't asleep, was she? She was dead."

The swing door opened and Basil Schramm walked in. "I thought I'd find you," he said. "Good evening."

# CHAPTER VIII

# Graveyard (II)

## I

"MAY I JOIN YOU?" asked Dr. Schramm. The folds from his nostrils to the corners of his mouth lifted and intensified. It was almost a Mephistophelian grin.

"Do," said Alleyn and turned to Sister Jackson. "If Sister Jackson approves," he said.

She looked at nothing, said nothing and compressed her mouth.

"Silence," Dr. Schramm joked, "gives consent, I hope." And he sat down.

"What are you drinking?" he invited.

"Not another for me, thank you," said Alleyn.

"On duty?"

"That's my story."

"Dot?"

Sister Jackson stood up. "I'm afraid I must go," she said to Alleyn and with tolerable success achieved a social manner. "I hadn't realized it was so late."

"It isn't late," said Schramm. "Sit down."

She sat down. "First round to the doctor," thought Alleyn.

"The bell's by you, Alleyn," said Schramm. "Do you mind?"

Alleyn pressed the wall-bell above his head. Schramm had leant forward. Alleyn caught a great wave of whiskey and saw that his eyes were bloodshot and not quite in focus.

"I happened to be passing," he chatted. He inclined his head toward Sister Jackson, "I noticed your car. And yours, Superintendent."

"Sister Jackson has been kind enough to clear up a detail for us."

"That's what's known as 'helping the police in their investigation,' isn't it? With grim connotations as a rule."

"You've been reading the popular press," said Alleyn.

The waiter came in. Schramm ordered a large Scotch. "Sure?" he asked them and then, to the waiter. "Correction. Make that two large Scotches."

Alleyn said: "Not for me. Really."

"Two large Scotches," Schramm repeated on a high note. The waiter glanced doubtfully at Alleyn.

"You heard what I said," Schramm insisted. "Two large Scotches."

Alleyn thought: "This is the sort of situation where one could do with the odd drop of omnipotence. One wrong move from me and it'll be a balls-up."

Complete silence set in. The waiter came and went. Dr. Schramm downed one of the two double whiskeys very quickly. The bar-parlour clock ticked. He continued to smile and began on the second whiskey slowly with concentration: absorbing it and cradling the glass. Sister Jackson remained perfectly still.

"What's she been telling you?" Schramm suddenly demanded. "She's an inventive lady. You ought to realize that. To be quite, quite frank and honest she's a liar of the first water. Aren't you, sweetie?"

"You followed me."

"It's some considerable time since I left off doing that, darling."

Alleyn had the passing thought that it would be nice to hit Dr. Schramm.

"I really must insist," Schramm said. "I'm sorry, but you have seen for yourself how things are, here. I realize, perf'ly well, that you will think I had a motive for this crime, if crime it was. Because I am a legatee I'm a suspect. So of course it's no good my saying that I asked Sybil Foster to marry me. *Not*," he said wagging his finger at Alleyn, "*not* because I'd got my sights set on her money but because I loved her. Which I did, and that," he added, staring at Sister Jackson, "is precisely where the trouble lies." His speech was now all over the place like an actor's in a comic drunken scene. "You wouldn't have minded if it had been like that. You wouldn't have minded all that much if you believed I'd come back earlier and killed her for her money. You really are a bitch, aren't you, Dotty? My God, you even threatened to take to her yourself. Didn't you? Well, didn't you? Where's the bloody waiter?"

He got to his feet, lurched across the table and fetched up with the palms of his hands on the wall, the left supporting him and the right clamped down over the bell-push which could be heard distantly to operate. His face was within three inches of Alleyn's. Sister Jackson shrank back in her chair.

"Disgusting!" she said.

Alleyn detached Dr. Schramm from the wall and replaced him in his chair. He then moved over to the door, anticipating the return of the waiter. When the man arrived Alleyn showed his credentials.

"The gentleman's had as much as is good for him," he said. "Let me handle it. There's a side door, isn't there?"

"Well, yes," said the waiter, looking dubious. "Sir," he added.

"He's going to order another Scotch. Can you cook up a poor single to look like a double? Here—this'll settle the lot and forget the change. Right?"

"Well, thank you very much, sir," said the waiter, suddenly avid with curiosity and gratification. "I'll do what I can."

"Waiter!" shouted Dr. Schramm. "Same 'gain."

"There's your cue," said Alleyn.

"What'll I say to him?"

"'Anon, anon, sir' would do."

"Would that be Shakespeare?" hazarded the waiter.

"It would, indeed."

"*Waiter!*"

"*Anon, anon*, sir," said the waiter self-consciously. He collected the empty glasses and hurried away.

"'Strordinary waiter," said Dr. Schramm. "As I was saying. I insist on being informed for reasons that I shall make 'bundantly clear. What's she said? 'Bout me?"

"You didn't feature in our conversation," said Alleyn.

"That's what you say."

Sister Jackson, with a groggy and terrified return to something like her habitual manner, said, "I wouldn't demean myself." She turned on Alleyn. "You're mad," she said, exactly as if there had been no break in their exchange. "You don't know what you're talking about. She was asleep."

"Why didn't you report your visit, then?" Alleyn said.

"It didn't matter."

"Oh, nonsense. It would have established, if true, that she was alive at that time."

With one of those baffling returns to apparent sobriety by which drunken persons sometimes bewilder us, Dr. Schramm said: "Do I understand, Sister, that you visited her in her room?"

Sister Jackson ignored him. Alleyn said: "At about nine o'clock."

"And didn't report it? Why? *Why?*" He appealed to Alleyn.

"I don't know. Perhaps because she was afraid. Perhaps because—"

Sister Jackson gave a strangulated cry. "No! No, for God's sake! He'll get it all wrong. He'll jump to conclusions. It wasn't like that. She was asleep. Natural sleep. There was nothing the matter with her."

The waiter came back with a single glass, half full.

"Take that away," Schramm ordered. "I've got to have a clear head. Bring some ice. Bring me a lot of ice."

The waiter looked at Alleyn, who nodded. He went out.

"I'm going," said Sister Jackson.

"You'll stay where you are unless you want a clip over the ear."

"And you," said Alleyn, "will stay where you are unless you want to be run in. Behave yourself."

Schramm stared at him for a moment. He said something that sounded like: "Look who's talking" and took an immaculate handkerchief from his breast coat-pocket, laid it on the table and began to fold it diagonally. The waiter reappeared with a jug full of ice.

"I really ought to mention this to the manager, sir," he murmured.

"If he gets noisy again, I'll have to."

"I'll answer for you. Tell the manager it's an urgent police matter. Give him my card. Here you are."

"It—it wouldn't be about that business over at Greengages, would it?"

"Yes, it would. Give me the ice and vanish, there's a good chap."

Alleyn put the jug on the table. Schramm with shaking hands began to lay ice on his folded handkerchief.

"Sister," he said impatiently. "Make a pack, if you please."

To Alleyn's utter astonishment she did so in a very professional manner. Schramm loosened his tie and opened his shirt. It was as if they both responded like Pavlovian dogs to some behaviouristic prompting. He rested his forehead on the table and she placed the pack of ice on the back of his neck. He gasped. A trickle of water ran down his jawline. "Keep it up," he ordered and shivered.

Alleyn, watching this performance, thought how unpredictable the behaviour of drunken persons could be. Sister Jackson had been in the condition so inaccurately known as "nicely, thank you." Basil Schramm had been in an advanced stage of intoxication but able to assess his own condition and after a fashion deal with it. And there they were, both of them, behaving like automata and, he felt sure, frightened out of what wits they still, however precariously, commanded.

She continued to operate the ice packs. A pool of water enlarged itself on the table and began to drip to the carpet.

"That's enough," Schramm said presently. Sister Jackson squeezed his handkerchief into the jug. Alleyn offered his own and Schramm mopped himself up with it. He fastened his shirt and reknotted his tie. As if by common consent he and Sister Jackson sat down simultaneously, facing each other across the table with Alleyn between them on the banquette: like a referee, he thought. This effect was enhanced when he took out his notebook. They paid not the smallest attention to him. They glared at each other, he with distaste and she with hatred. He produced a comb and used it.

"Now, then," he said. "What's the story? You went to her room at nine. You say she was asleep. And *you*," he jabbed a finger at Alleyn, "say she was dead. Right?"

"I don't say so, positively. I suggested it."

"Why?"

"For several reasons. If Mrs. Foster was sleeping, peacefully and naturally, it's difficult to see why Sister Jackson did not report her visit."

"If there'd been anything wrong, I would have," she said.

Schramm said: "Did you think it was suicide?"

"She was asleep."

"Did you see the tablets—spilled on the table?"

"No. *No*."

"Did you think she'd been drugged?"

"She was asleep. Peacefully and naturally. Asleep."

"You're lying, aren't you? Aren't you? Come on!"

She began to gabble at Alleyn: "It was the shock, you know. When he rang through and told me, I came and we did everything—such a shock—I couldn't remember anything about how the room had looked before. Naturally not."

"It was no shock to you," Dr. Schramm said profoundly. "You're an old hand. An experienced nurse. And you didn't regret her death, my dear. You gloated. You could hardly keep a straight face."

"Don't listen to this," Sister Jackson gabbled at Alleyn, "it's all lies. Monstrous lies. Don't listen."

"You'd better," said Schramm. "This is the hell-knows-no-fury bit, Superintendent, and you may as well recognize it. Oh, yes. She actually said when she heard about Sybil and me that she bloody well wished Syb was dead and she meant it. Fact, I assure you. And I don't mind telling you she felt the same about me. Still does. Look at her."

Sister Jackson was hardly a classical figure of panic but she certainly presented a strange picture. The velvet beret had flopped forward over her left eye so that she was obliged to tilt her head back at an extravagant angle in order to see from under it. Oddly enough and deeply unpleasant as the situation undoubtedly was, she reminded Alleyn momentarily of a grotesque lady on a comic postcard.

They began to exchange charge and countercharge, often speaking simultaneously. It was the kind of row that is welcome as manna from Heaven to an investigating officer. Alleyn noted it all down, almost under their noses, and was conscious, as often before, of a strong feeling of distaste for the job.

They repeated themselves ad nauseam. She used the stock phrases of the discarded mistress. He, as he became articulate, also grew reckless and made more specific his accusations as to her having threatened to do harm to Sybil Foster and even hinted that on her visit to Room 20 she might well have abetted Sybil in taking an overdose.

At that point they stopped dead, stared aghast at each other and then, for the first time since the slanging match had set in, at Alleyn.

He finished his notes and shut the book.

"I could," he said, "and perhaps I should, ask you both to come to the police station and make statements. You would then refuse to utter or to write another word until you had seen your respective solicitors. A great deal of time would be wasted. Later on you would both state that you had been dead drunk and that I had brought about this pitiable condition and made false reports about your statements and taken them down in writing. All this would be very boring and unproductive. Instead, I propose that you go back to Greengages, think things over and then concoct your statements. You've been too preoccupied to notice, I fancy, but I've made pretty extensive notes and I shall make a report of the conversation and in due course, invite you to sign it. And now, I expect you will like to go. If, that is, you are in a fit state to drive. If not you'd better go to the lavatories and put your fingers down your throats. I'll be in touch. Good evening."

He left them gaping and went out to his car where he waited about five minutes before they appeared severally, walking with unnatural precision. They entered their cars and drove, very slowly, away.

## II

Fox had not gone to bed at their pub. He and Alleyn took a nightcap together in Alleyn's room.

"Well, now," said Fox rubbing his hands on his knees. "That was a turn-up for the books, wasn't it? I'd've liked to be there. How do you read it, then, Mr. Alleyn? As regards the lady, now? Dropped in on the deceased round about nine P.M. and was watched by crepe-soles from the alcove and is being blackmailed by him. Which gives us one more reason, if we'd needed it, for saying crepe-soles is Claude?"

"Go on."

"*But*," said Fox opening his eyes wide, "*but* when the Doctor (which is what he isn't, properly speaking, but never mind) when the Doctor rings through an hour or thereabouts later and tells her to come to Room Twenty and she does come and the lady's passed away, does she say—" and here Mr. Fox gave a sketchy impersonation of a female voice: "'Oh, Doctor, I looked in at nine and she was as right as Christmas'? No. She does not. She keeps her tongue behind her teeth and gets cracking with the stomach pump. Now why? Why not mention it?"

"Schramm seemed to suggest that at some earlier stage, in a fit of jealous rage, the Jackson had threatened she'd do some mischief to Mrs. Foster. And was now afraid he'd think that on this unmentioned visit she'd taken a hand in overdosing her with barbiturates."

"Ah," said Fox. "But the catch in that is: Mrs. Foster, according to our reading of the evidence, was first drugged and then smothered. So it looks as if he didn't realize she was smothered, which if true puts him in the clear. Any good?"

"I think so, Br'er Fox. I think it's quite a lot of good."

"Would you say, now, that Sister J. would be capable of doing the job herself—pillow and all?"

"Ah, there you have me. I think she's a jealous, slighted woman with a ferocious temper. Jealous, slighted women have murdered their supplanters before now but generally speaking they're more inclined to take to the man. And by George, judging by the way she shaped up to Schramm tonight I wouldn't put it past her."

"By and large, then, these two are a bit of a nuisance. We'd got things more or less settled—well, *I* had," said Mr. Fox with a hard look at Alleyn, "and it was just a matter of running Claude to earth. And now this silly lot crops up."

"Very inconsiderate."

"Yerse. And there's no joy from the Claude front, by the way. The Yard rang through. The search is what the press likes to call nation-wide but not a squeak."

"Southampton?"

"They'd sent a copper they don't reckon looks like it, into The Good Read, in Port Lane. It's an accommodation-address shop all right but there was nothing for 'Morris.' Very cagey the chap was: sussy for drugs but they've never collected enough to knock him off. The D.I. I talked to thinks it's possible Claude Carter off-loaded the stuff he brought ashore there. If he's thinking of slipping out by Southampton he could have fixed it to collect Sister J.'s blackmail delivery on the way."

"Suppose she'd posted it today, first-class mail, it wouldn't arrive at the earliest until tomorrow," said Alleyn.

"They've got the shop under obbo non-stop. If he shows, they'll feel his collar, all right," said Fox.

"If. It's an odd development, isn't it?" Alleyn said. "There he is, large as life, mousing about up at Quintern Place and in and around the district until (according to Daft Artie) twelve o'clock or (according to Bruce) nine, last night. He comes down the lane with his pack on his back. He opens the squeaky lych-gate and leaves his prints there. And vanishes."

"Now you see him, now you don't. Lost his nerve, d'you reckon?"

"We mustn't forget he left that note for Mrs. Jim."

"P'raps that's all there is to it. P'raps," said Fox bitterly, "he'll come waltzing back with a silly grin on his face having been to stay with his auntie. P'raps it was somebody else blackmailing Sister J., and we'll get egg all over our faces."

"It's an occupational hazard," Alleyn said vaguely and then to him-self: " 'Into thin air' and but for the footprints at the lych-gate, leaving 'not a rack behind.' *Why?* And then—where to, for pity's sake?"

"Not by the late train to London," said Fox. "They said at the sta-tion, nobody entered or left it at Great Quintern."

"Hitched a lift?"

"Nice job for our boys, that'll be. Ads in the papers and what a hope."

"You're in a despondent mood, my poor Foxkin."

Mr. Fox, who, although an occasional grumbler, was never known to succumb to the mildest hint of depression, placidly ignored this obser-vation.

"I shall cheer you up," Alleyn continued. "You need a change of scene. What do you say to a moonlight picnic?"

"Now then!" said Fox guardedly.

"Well, not perhaps a picnic but a stroll in a graveyard? Bruce Gardener would call it a Gothic stroll, no doubt."

"You don't mean this, I suppose, Mr. Alleyn?"

"I do, though. I can *not* get Daft Artie's story out of my head, Fox. It isn't all moonshine, presumably, because there *are* those prints, Carter *has* disappeared and there *is* the lay-by in the hedge. I suggest we return to the scene and step it out. What's the time?"

"Eleven-ten."

"The village ought to be asleep."

"So ought we," sighed Fox.

"We'd better give the 'factory' a shout and ask if they can raise an acetylene lamp or its equivalent."

"A reconstruction, then?"

"You find it a fanciful notion? A trifle *vieux-jeu*, perhaps?"

"I daresay it makes sense," said Fox resignedly and went off to telephone.

Sergeant McGuiness on night duty at the station did produce an acetylene lamp, kept in reserve against power failures. He had it ready for them and handed it over rather wistfully. "I'd've liked to be in on this," he confided to Fox. "It sounds interesting."

Alleyn overheard him. "Can you raise a copper to hold the desk for an hour?" he asked. "We could do with a third man."

Sergeant McGuiness brightened. He said: "Our P.C. Dance was competing in the darts semi-finals at the local tonight. He'll be on his way home but if he's won he'll be looking in to tell me. I daresay if it's agreeable to you, sir—"

"I'll condone it," said Alleyn.

A scraping sound and a bobbing light on the window-blind announced the arrival of a bicycle. The sergeant excused himself and hurried to the door. A voice outside shouted: "Done it, Sarge."

"You never!"

"Out on the double seven."

"That's the stuff."

"Very near thing, though. Wait till I tell you."

"Hold on." The sergeant's voice dropped to a mumble. There was a brief inaudible exchange. He returned followed by a ginger-headed simpering colossus.

"P.C. Dance, sir," said Sergeant McGuiness.

Alleyn congratulated P.C. Dance on his prowess and said he would be obliged if they could "borrow" him. "Borrow" is a synonym for "arrest" in the Force and the disreputable pun, if pun it was, had an undeserved success. They left Dance telephoning in triumph to his wife.

On their way to the village Alleyn outlined the object of the exercise for the gratified McGuiness. "We're trying to make sense of an apparently senseless situation," he said. "Item: could a walker coming down Stile Lane into Long Lane see much or anything of the light from Bruce Gardener's lamp? Item: can someone hidden in the hedge see the walker? Item: can the walker, supposing he climbs the steps to the church and goes into the church—"

"Which," said the sergeant, "excuse me, he can't. The church is locked at night, sir. By our advice. Possibility of vandals."

"See how right we were to bring you in. Who locks it? The Vicar?"

"That's correct, Mr. Alleyn. And once the deceased lady was brought in that's what he'd do. Lock up the premises for the night."

"Leaving the church in darkness?" Fox asked.

"I think not, Fox. I think he'd leave the sanctuary lamp alight. We can ask."

"So it's after the arrival of the deceased that Artie's story begins?"

"And our performance too for what it's worth. Do they keep early hours in the village, Sergeant?"

"Half an hour after the local closes they're all in bed."

"Good."

"Suppose," Fox said on a note of consternation, "Daft Artie's sleeping out?"

"It'll be a bloody nuisance," Alleyn grunted. "If he is we'll have to play it by ear. I don't know, though. We might pull him in to demonstrate."

"Would he co-operate?"

"God knows. Here we are. We make as little noise as possible. Don't bang the doors. Keep your voices down."

They turned a sharp corner through a stand of beech trees and entered the village: a double row of some dozen cottages on either side of Long Lane, all fast asleep: the church, high above, its tower silhouetted against the stars, the rest almost disappearing into its background of trees. The moon had not yet risen so that Long Lane and the bank and hedge above it and the hillside beyond were all deep in shadow.

Alleyn drove the car on to the green near the steps and they got out.

"Hullo," he said. "There's somebody still awake up Stile Lane."

"That's the widow Black's cottage," said the sergeant. "There'll be someone looking after her—the brother, no doubt."

"Looking after her? Why?"

"Did you not hear? She was knocked over by a truck on the way back from the funeral this afternoon. The blind corner up the lane.

I've been saying for years it'd happen. The chap was driving dead slow for the turning and she fell clear. He helped her in and reported it to us."

"Would that be Bruce Gardener's sister?" asked Fox.

"That's right, Mr. Fox. We're not likely to disturb them."

"I don't know so much about that," Alleyn murmured. "If it's Bruce up there and he looks out of the window and sees light coming from where he dug the grave and had his own lamp last night, he may come down to investigate. Damn!" He thought for a moment. "Oh, well," he said, "we tell him. Why not? Let's get moving. I'd like you, Sergeant, to act as the boy says he did. Get into the lay-by in the hedge when the time comes. Not yet. We'll set you up. I'll do the Carter bit. Mr. Fox is Bruce. All you have to do is to keep your eyes and ears open and report exactly what you see. Got the lamp? And the shovel? Come on, and quietly does it."

He opened the lych-gate very cautiously, checking it at the first sign of the squeak. They slid through, one by one and moved quietly up the steps.

"Don't use your torches unless you have to," Alleyn said and as their eyes adjusted to the dark it thinned and gravestones stood about them. They reached the top. Alleyn led the way round the church: the nave, the north transept, the chancel, until they came to the Passcoigne plot and Sybil Foster's grave. The flowers on the mound smelt heavy on the night air and the plastic covers glinted in the starlight as if phospho-rescent.

Fox and McGuiness crouched over the lamp. Presently it flared. The area became explicit in a white glare. The sergeant spent some time regulating the flame. Fox stood up and his gigantic shadow rose against the trees. The lamp hissed. Fox lifted it and put it by the grave. They waited to make sure it was in good order.

"Right," said Alleyn at last. "Give us eight minutes to get down, Fox, and then start. Don't look into the light, Sergeant, it'll blind you. Come on."

The shadow of the church was intensified by the light beyond it and the steps took longer to descend than to climb. When they were back at the car Alleyn murmured: "Now, I'll show you the lay-by. It's in the hedge across the lane and a little to our right. About four yards further on there's a gap at the top of the bank with a hurdle-gate. You can ease round the post, go through into the field and turn back to the lay-by. If by any chance somebody comes down the lane and gets nosey we're looking for a missing child thought to be asleep near the hedge. Here

we are. Make sure you'll recognize it from the other side. There's that
hazel plant sticking up above the level of the hedge."

They moved along the hedge until they came to the gap.

"Through you go," Alleyn whispered, "turn left and then back six
paces. You'll have to crawl in, helmet and all. Give one low whistle
when you're set and I'll go on into Stile Lane. That's when your obbo
begins."

He watched the shadowy sergeant climb the bank and edge his bulk
between the gate-post and the hedge. Then he turned about and looked
up at the church. It was transformed. A nimbus of light rose behind it.
Treetops beyond the Passcoigne plot started up, uncannily defined, like
stage scenery and as he watched, a gargantuan shadow rose, moved
enormously over the trees, threw up arms, and the sweeping image of a
shovel, sank and rose again. Mr. Fox had embarked on his pantomime.

The sergeant was taking his time. No whistle. The silence, which is
never really silence, of a countryside, breathed out its nocturnal preoc-
cupations: stirrings in the hedgerow, far-distant traffic, the movements
of small creatures going about their business in the night.

"Sst!"

It was the sergeant, back in the gap up the hill. His helmet showed
against Mrs. Black's lighted window in Stile Lane. Alleyn climbed the
bank and leant over the hurdle.

"Artie is there," breathed Sergeant McGuiness. "In his hidey-hole.
Curled up. My Gawd, I nearly crawled in on top of him."

"Asleep?"

"Sound."

"It doesn't matter. Come back into the lane and lean into the hollow
in the bank below the lay-by. Your head will be pretty much on a level
with his. I simply want to check that he could have seen what he said
he saw and heard what he said he heard. Back you come."

The sergeant had gone. Alleyn slipped into the lane and walked up
it, treading on the soft margin. Fox's shadow still performed its gigantic
ritual against the treetops.

Alleyn turned left into Stile Lane and walked a little way up it. He
was now quite close to Mrs. Black's cottage. The light behind the window was out. He waited for a moment or two and then retraced his
steps, walking, now, in the middle of the road. He wondered if Claude
Carter had worn his crepe-soled shoes last night. He wondered, supposing Daft Artie woke and saw him, if he would repeat his eldritch
shriek.

Now he was almost opposite the lay-by. Not a hint of the sergeant,
in blackest shadow under the hedge.

Alleyn paused.

It was as if an ironclad fist struck him on the jaw.

### III

He lay in the lane and felt grit against his face and pain and he heard a confusion of sounds. Disembodied voices shouted angrily.

"Mr. Fox! Come down here. Mr. Fox."

He had been lifted and rested against a massive thigh. "I'm all right," somebody said. He said it. "Where's Fox? What happened?"

"The bloody kid. He chucked a brick at you. Over my head. Gawd, I thought he'd done you, Mr. Alleyn," said Sergeant McGuiness.

"Where's Fox?"

"Here," said Fox. His large concerned face blotted out the stars. He was breathing hard. "Here I am," he said. "You'll be all right."

A furious voice was roaring somewhere out on the hillside beyond the hedge. "Come back. You damned, bloody young murderer. Come back, till I have the hide off of you." Footsteps thudded and retreated.

"That's Bruce," said Alleyn, feeling his jaw. "Where did he spring from? The cottage?"

"That's right," somebody said.

Fox was saying: "Get cracking, Sarge. Sort it out. I'll look after this!" More retreating footsteps at the run.

"Here, get me up. What hit me?"

"Take it easy, Mr. Alleyn. Let me have a look. Caught you on the jaw. Might have broken it."

"You're telling me. What did?" He struggled to his knees and then with Fox's help to his feet. "Damn and blast!" he said. "Let me get to that bank while my head clears. What hit me?"

"Half a brick. The boy must have woken up. Bruce and the sarge are chasing him."

Fox had propped him against the bank and was playing a torch on his face and dabbing it very gently with his handkerchief. "It's bleeding," he said.

"Never mind that. Tell me what happened."

"It seems that when you got as far as here—almost in touching distance of the sarge—the boy must have woken up, seen you, dark and all though it is, picked up a half-brick from his fireplace and heaved it. It must have passed over the sarge's head. Then he lit off."

"But, Bruce?"

"Yes. Bruce. Bruce noticed the light in the graveyard and thought it might be vandals. There's been trouble with them lately. Anyway, he came roaring down the hill and saw the boy in the act. How's it feel now?"

"Damn' sore but I don't think it's broken. And the sergeant's chasing Daft Artie?"

"Him and Bruce."

"No good making a song and dance over it: the boy's not responsible."

"It's my bet they won't catch him. For a start, they can't see where they're going."

"I wonder where his home is," said Alleyn.

"Bruce'll know. It must," said Fox, still examining Alleyn's jaw, "have caught you on the flat. There's a raw patch but no cut. We'll have to get you to a doctor."

"No, we won't," Alleyn mumbled. "I'll do all right. Fox, how much could he see from the lay-by? Enough to recognize me? Go and stand where I was, will you?"

"Are you sure—?"

"Yes. Go on."

Fox moved away. The light still glowed beyond the church. It was refracted faintly into the centre of the lane. Fox was an identifiable figure. Just.

Alleyn said: "So we know Artie could have recognized Carter and I suppose, me. Damnation, look at this."

A window in the parsonage on the far side of the green shone out. Somebody opened it and was revealed as a silhouette. "Hullo!" said a cultivated voice. "Is anything the mattah?"

The Vicar.

"Nothing at all," Alleyn managed. "A bit of skylarking in the lane. Some young chaps. We've sorted it out."

"Is that the police?" asked the Vicar plaintively.

"That's us," Fox shouted. "Sorry you've been disturbed, sir."

"Nevah mind. Is there something going on behind the church? What's that light?"

"We're just making sure there's been no vandalism," Alleyn improvised. It hurt abominably to raise his voice. "Everything's in order."

By this time several more windows along the lane had been opened.

"It's quite all right, sir," Fox said. "No trouble. A bunch of young chaps with too much on board."

"Get that bloody light out," Alleyn muttered.

Fox, using his own torch, crossed the lane. The lych-gate shrieked. He hurried up the steps and round the church.

"You don't think perhaps I should just pop down?" the Vicar asked doubtfully, after a considerable pause.

"Not the slightest need. It's all over," Alleyn assured him. "They've bolted."

Windows began to close. The light behind the church went out.

"Are you sure? Was it those lads from Great Quintern? I didn't hear motor bikes."

"They hadn't got bikes. Go back to bed, Vicar," Alleyn urged him. "You'll catch your death."

"No mattah. Goodnight then."

The window was closed. Alleyn watched Fox's torchlight come bobbing round the church and down the steps. Voices sounded in the field beyond the hedge. Bruce and the sergeant. They came through the hurdle and down the bank.

"I'm here," Alleyn said. "Don't walk into me." The sergeant's torchlight found him.

"Are you all right, sir? 'E's got clean away, I'm afraid. It was that bloody dark and there's all them trees."

Bruce said: "I'll have the hide off my fine laddie for this. What's possessed the fule? He's never showed violent before. By God, I'll teach him a lesson he won't forget."

"I suppose it *was* Artie?"

"Nae doubt about it, sir."

"Where did you come from, Bruce?"

It was as they had thought. Bruce had been keeping company with his shaken sister. She had gone to bed and he was about to return to Quintern Place. He looked out of the window and saw the glare of the lamp in the churchyard.

"It gied me a shock," he said, and with one of his occasional vivid remarks: "It was oncanny: as if I mysel' was in two places at once. And then I thought it might be they vandals and up to no good. And I saw the shadow on the trees like mine had been. Digging. Like me. It fair turrned my stomach, that."

"I can imagine."

"So I came the short cut down the brae to the lane as fast as I could in the dark. I arrived at the hedge and his figure rose up clear against the glow behind the kirk. It was him all right. He stood there for a second and then he hurrled something and let out a bit screech as he did so. I shouted and he bolted along the hedge. The sergeant was in the lane, sir, with you in the light of his torch and flat on your back and him saying by God, the bugger's got him and yelling for Mr. Fox. So I went roaring after the lad and not a hope in hell of catching him. He's a wild crittur. You'd say he could see in the dark. Who's to tell where he's hiding?"

"In his bed, most likely," said the sergeant. "By this time."

"Aye, you may say so. His mother's cottage is a wee piece further down the lane. Are you greatly injured, Superintendent? What was it he hurrled at you?"

"Half a brick. No, I'm all right."

Bruce clicked his tongue busily. "He might have kilt you," he said.

"Leave it alone, Bruce. Don't pitch into him when you see him. It wouldn't do any good. I mean that."

"Well," said Bruce dourly, "if you say so."

"I do say so."

Fox joined them, carrying his doused lamp and the shovel.

Bruce, who wasted no ceremony with Fox, whom he seemed to regard as a sort of warrant-officer, asked him in scandalized tones what he thought he'd been doing up yon. "If you've been tampering with the grave," he said furiously, "it's tantamount to sacrilege and there's no doubt in my mind there's a law to deal with it. Now then, what was it? What where you doing with yon shovel?"

"It was dumb show, Bruce," Alleyn said wearily. "We were testing the boy's story. Nothing's been disturbed."

"I've a mind to look for mysel'."

"Go ahead, by all means if you want to. Have you got a torch?"

"I'll leave it," Bruce said morosely. "I dinna like it but I'll leave it."

"Goodnight to you, then. I think, Br'er Fox," said Alleyn, "I'll get in the car."

His face throbbed enormously and the ground seemed to shift under his feet. Fox piloted him to the car. The sergeant hovered.

When they were under way Fox said he proposed to drive to the out-patients' department at the nearest hospital. Alleyn said he would see Dr. Field-Innis in the morning, that he'd had routine tetanus injections and that if he couldn't cope with a chuck under the chin the sooner he put in for retirement the better. He then fainted.

He was out only for a short time, he thought, as they seemed not to have noticed. He said in as natural a manner as he could contrive that he felt sleepy, managed to fold his arms and lower his head, and did, in fact, drift into a sort of doze. He was vaguely aware of Fox giving what is known as "a shout" over the blower.

Now they were at the station and so, surprisingly, was the district police surgeon.

"There's no concussion," said the police surgeon, "and no breakage and your teeth are O.K. We'll just clean you up and make you comfortable and send you home to bed, um?"

"Too kind," said Alleyn.

"You'll be reasonably comfortable tomorrow."

"Thank you."

"Don't push it too far, though. Go easy."

"That," said Mr. Fox in the background, "will be the day."

Alleyn grinned, which hurt. So did the cleaning up and dressing.

"There we are!" said the police surgeon, jollily. "It'll be a bit colourful for a day or two and there's some swelling. You won't have a permanent scar."

"Most reassuring. I'm sorry they knocked you up."

"What I'm there for, isn't it? Quite an honour in this case. Good morning."

When he had gone Alleyn said: "Fox, you're to get on to the Home Secretary."

"*Me!*" exclaimed the startled Fox. "Him? Not *me!*"

"Not directly you, but get the Yard and the A.C. and ask for it to be laid on."

"What for, though, Mr. Alleyn? Lay on what?"

"What do you think? The usual permit."

"You're *not*," said Fox, "—you can't be—you're not thinking of digging her up?"

"Aren't I? Can't I? I am, do you know. Not," said Alleyn, holding his pulsing jaw, "in quite the sense you mean but—digging her up, Br'er Fox. Yes."

# CHAPTER IX

# Graveyard (III)

*I*

WHEN ALLEYN LOOKED in the glass the following morning his face did not appear as awful as it felt. No doubt the full panoply of bruises was yet to develop. He shaved painfully round the dressing, took a bath and decided he was in more or less reasonable form to face the day.

Fox came in to say their Assistant Commissioner was on the telephone. "If you can speak, that is."

Alleyn said: "Of course I can speak," and found that it was best to do so with the minimum demand upon his lower jaw. He stifled the explosive grunt of pain that the effort cost him.

The telephone was in the passage outside his room.

"Rory?" said their A.C. "Yes. I want a word with you. What's all this about an exhumation?"

"It's not precisely that, sir."

"What? I can't catch what you say. You sound as if you were talking to your dentist."

Alleyn thought: "I daresay I shall be when there's time for it," but he merely replied that he was sorry and would try to do better.

"I suppose it's the clip on the jaw Fox talked about. Does it hurt?"

"Not much," Alleyn lied angrily.

"Good. Who did it?"

"The general idea is a naughty boy with a brick."

"About this exhumation that is not an exhumation. What am I to say to the H.S.? Confide in me, for Heaven's sake."

Alleyn confided.

"Sounds devilish far-fetched to me," grumbled the A.C. "I hope you know what you're about."

"So do I."

"You know what I think about hunches."

"If I may say so, you don't mistrust them any more than I do, sir."

"All right, all right. We'll go ahead, then. Tomorrow night, you suggest? Sorry you've had a knock. Take care of yourself."

*"There is none that can compare,"* Alleyn hummed in great discomfort. *"With a tow, row bloody row to / Our A. Commissionaire.* It's on, Br'er Fox."

"This'll set the village by the ears. What time?"

"Late tomorrow night. We'll be turning into tombstones ourselves if we keep up these capers."

"What's our line with the populace?"

"God knows. We hope they won't notice. But what a hope!"

"How about someone accidentally dropped a valuable in the open grave? Such as—er—"

"What?"

"I don't know," said Fox crossly. "A gold watch?"

"When?" Alleyn asked. "And whose gold watch?"

"Er. Well. Bruce's? Anytime before the interment. I appreciate," Fox confessed, "that it doesn't sound too hot."

"Go on."

"I'm trying to picture it," said Fox after a longish pause.

"And how are you getting on?"

"It'd be ludicrous."

"Perhaps the best way will be to keep quiet and if they do notice tell them nothing. 'The police declined to comment.'"

"The usual tarpaulin, et cetera, I suppose? I'll lay it on, will I?"

"Do. My face, by the way, had better be the result of a turn-up with a gang outside the village. Where's the sergeant?"

"Down at the 'factory.' He's going to take a look at Daft Artie."

Alleyn began to walk about the room, found this jolted his jaw and sat on his bed. "Br'er Fox," he said, "there's that child. Prunella. We can't possibly risk her hearing of it by accident."

"The whole story?"

"Upon my soul," Alleyn said after a long pause, "I'm not at all sure I won't have recourse to your preposterous golden watch, or its equivalent. Look, I'll drop you in the village and get you to call on the Vicar and tell him."

"Some tarradiddle? Or what?" Fox asked.

"The truth but not the whole truth about what we hope to find. *Hope!*" said Alleyn distastefully. "What a word!"

"I see what you mean. Without wishing to pester—" Fox began. To his surprise and gratification Alleyn gave him a smack on the shoulder.

"All right, fuss-pot," he said, "fat-faced but fit as a flea, that's me. Come on."

So he drove Fox to the parsonage and continued up Long Lane, passing the gap in the hedge. He looked up at the church and saw three small boys and two women come round from behind the chancel end. There was something self-conscious about the manner of the women's gait and their unconvincing way of pointing out a slanting headstone to each other.

"There they go," Alleyn thought. "It's all round the village by now. Police up to something round the grave! We'll have a queue for early doors tomorrow night."

He drove past the turning into Stile Lane and on toward the road that led uphill to Mardling Manor on the left and Quintern Place on the right. Keys Lane, where Verity Preston lived, branched off to the left. Alleyn turned in at her gate and found her sitting under her lime trees doing *The Times* crossword.

"I came on an impulse," he said. "I want some advice and I think you're the one to give it to me. I don't apologize because, after all, in its shabby way it's a compliment. You may not think so, of course."

"I can't say until I've heard it, can I?" she said. "Come and sit down."

When they were settled she said: "It's no good being heavily tactful and not noticing your face, is it? What's happened?"

"A boy and a brick, is my story."

"Not a local boy, I hope."

"Your gardener's assistant."

"Daft Artie!" Verity exclaimed. "I can't believe it."

"Why can't you?"

"He doesn't do things like that. He's not violent: only silly."

"That's what Bruce said. This may have been mere silliness. I may have just happened to be in the path of the trajectory. But I didn't come for advice about Daft Artie. It's about your goddaughter. Is she still staying at Mardling?"

"She went back there after the funeral. Now I come to think of it, she said that tomorrow she's going up to London for a week."

"Good."

"Why good?"

"This is not going to be pleasant for you, I know. I think you must have felt—you'd be very unusual if you hadn't—relieved when it was all over, yesterday afternoon. Tidily put away and mercifully done with. There's always that sense of release, isn't there, however deep the grief? Prunella must have felt it, don't you think?"

"I expect she did, poor child. And then there's her youth and her engagement and her natural ebullience. She'll be happy again. If it's about her you want to ask, you're not going to—" Verity exclaimed and stopped short.

"Bother her again? Perhaps. I would like to know what you think. But first of all," Alleyn broke off. "This is in confidence. Very strict confidence. I'm sure you'll have no objections at all to keeping it so for forty-eight hours."

"Very well," she said uneasily. "If you say so."

"It's this. It looks as if we shall be obliged to remove the coffin from Mrs. Foster's grave for a very short time. It will be replaced within an hour at the most and no indignity will be done it. I can't tell you any more than that. The question is: should Prunella be told? If she's away in London there may be a fair chance she need never know, but villages being what they are and certain people, the Vicar for one, having to be informed, there's always the possibility that it might come out. What do you think?"

Verity looked at him with a sort of incredulous dismay. "I can't think," she said. "It's incomprehensible and grotesque and I wish you hadn't told me."

"I'm sorry."

"One keeps forgetting—or I do—that this is a matter of somebody killing somebody whom one had known all one's life. And that's a monstrous thought."

"Yes, of course it's monstrous. But to us, I'm afraid, it's all in the day's work. But I *am* concerned about the young Prunella."

"So of course am I. I am indeed," said Verity, "and I do take your point. Do you think, perhaps, that Gideon Markos should be consulted? Or Nikolas? Or both?"

"Do you?"

"They've—well, they've kind of taken over, you see. Naturally. She's been absorbed into their sort of life and will belong to it."

"But she's still looking to you, isn't she? I noticed it yesterday at the funeral."

"Is there anything," Verity found herself saying, "that you don't notice?" Alleyn did not answer.

"Look," Verity said. "Suppose you—or I, if you like—should tell Nikolas Markos and suggest that they take Prue away? He's bought a yacht, he informs me. Not the messing-about-in-boats sort but the jet-set, Riviera job. They could waft her away on an extended cruise."

"Even plutocratic yachts are not necessarily steamed up and ready to sail at the drop of a hat."

"This one is."

"Really?"

"He happened to mention it," said Verity, turning pink. "He's planning a cruise in four weeks' time. He could put it forward."

"Are you invited?"

"I can't go," she said shortly. "I've got a first night coming up."

"You know, your suggestion has its points. Even if someone does talk about it, long after it's all over and done with, that's not going to be as bad as knowing it is going to be done *now* and that it's actually happening. Or is it?"

"Not nearly so bad."

"And in any case," Alleyn said, more to himself than to her, "she's going to find out—ultimately. Unless I'm all to blazes." He stood up. "I'll leave it to you," he said. "The decision. Is that unfair?"

"No. It's good of you to concern yourself. So I talk to Nikolas. Is that it?"

To Verity's surprise he hesitated for a moment.

"Could you, perhaps, suggest he put forward the cruise because Prunella's had about as much as she can take and would be all the better for a complete change of scene: now?"

"I suppose so. I don't much fancy asking a favour."

"No? Because he'll be a little too delighted to oblige?"

"Something like that," said Verity.

## II

The next day dawned overcast with the promise of rain. By late afternoon it was coming down inexorably.

"Set in solid," Fox said, staring out of the station window.

"In one way a hellish bore and in another an advantage."

"You mean people will be kept indoors?"

"That's right."

"It'll be heavy going, though," sighed Fox. "For our lot."

"All of that."

The telephone rang. Alleyn answered it quickly. It was the Yard. The duty squad with men and equipment was about to leave in a "nondescript" vehicle and wanted to know if there were any final orders. The sergeant in charge checked over details.

"Just a moment," Alleyn said. And to Fox. "What time does the village take its evening meal, would you say?"

"I'll ask McGuiness." He went into the front office and returned. "Between five-thirty and six-thirty. And after that they'll be at their tellies."

"Yes. Hullo," Alleyn said into the receiver. "I want you to time it so that you arrive at six o'clock with the least possible amount of fuss. Come to the vicarage. Make it all look like a repair job. No uniform copper. There's a downpour going on here, you'll need to dress for it. I'll be there. You'll go through the church and out by an exit on the far side, which is out of sight from the village. If by any unlikely chance somebody gets curious, you're looking for a leak in the roof. Got it? Good. Put me through to Missing Persons and stay where you are for ten minutes in case there's a change of procedure. Then leave."

Alleyn waited. He felt the pulse in the bruise on his jaw and knew it beat a little faster. "If they give a positive answer," he thought, "it's all up. Call off the exercise and back we go to square one."

A voice on the line. "Hullo? Superintendent Alleyn? You were calling us, sir?"

"Yes. Any reports come in?"

"Nothing, sir. No joy anywhere."

"Southampton? The stationer's shop?"

"Nothing."

"Thank God."

"I beg pardon, Mr. Alleyn?"

"Never mind. It's, to coin a phrase, a case of no news being good news. Keep going, though. Until you get orders to the contrary and if any sign or sniff of Carter comes up let me know at once. At once. This is of great importance. Understood?"

"Understood, Mr. Alleyn."

Alleyn hung up and looked at his watch. Four-thirty.

"We give it an hour and then go over," he said.

The hour passed slowly. Rain streamed down the blinded window pane. Small occupational noises could be heard in the front office and the intermittent sounds of passing vehicles.

At twenty past five the constable on duty brought in that panacea against anxiety that the Force has unfailingly on tap: strong tea in heavy cups and two recalcitrant biscuits.

Alleyn, with difficulty, swallowed the tea. He carried his cup into the front office where Sergeant McGuiness, with an affectation of nonchalance, said it wouldn't be long now, would it?

"No," said Alleyn, "you can gird up your loins, such as they are," and returned to his own room. He and Fox exchanged a nod and put on heavy mackintoshes, sou'westers and gum boots. He looked at his watch. Half-past five.

"Give it three minutes," he said. They waited.

The telephone rang in the front office but not for them. They went through. Sergeant McGuiness was attired in oilskin and sou'wester.

Alleyn said to P.C. Dance: "If there's a call for me from Missing Persons, ring Upper Quintern Rectory. Have the number under your nose."

He and Fox and McGuiness went out into the rain and drove to Upper Quintern village. The interior of the car smelt of stale smoke, rubber and petrol. The wind-screen wipers jerked to and fro, surface water fanned up from under their wheels and sloshed against the windows. The sky was so blackened with rainclouds that a premature dusk seemed to have fallen on the village. Not a soul was abroad in Long Lane. The red window curtains in the bar of the Passcoigne Arms glowed dimly.

"This is not going to let up," said Fox.

Alleyn led the way up a steep and slippery path to the vicarage. They were expected and the door was opened before they reached it.

The Vicar, white-faced and anxious, welcomed them and took them to his study, which was like all parsonic studies with its framed photographs of ordinands and steel engravings of classic monuments, its high fender, its worn chairs and its rows of predictable literature.

"This is a shocking business," said the Vicar. "I can't tell you how distressing I find it. Is it—I mean I suppose it must be—absolutely necessary?"

"I'm afraid it is," said Alleyn.

"Inspector Fox," said the Vicar, looking wistfully at him, "was very discreet."

Fox modestly contemplated the far wall of the study.

"He said he thought he should leave it to you to explain."

"Indeed," Alleyn rejoined with a long hard stare at his subordinate.

"And I do hope you will. I think I should know. You see, it is consecrated ground."

"Yes."

"So—may I, if you please, be told?" asked the Vicar with what Alleyn thought, rather touching simplicity.

"Of course," he said. "I'll tell you why we are doing it and what we think we may find. In honesty I should add that we may find nothing and the operation therefore may prove to have been quite fruitless. But this is the theory."

The Vicar listened.

"I think," he said when Alleyn had finished, "that I've never heard anything more dreadful. And I have heard some very dreadful things. We do, you know."

"I'm sure."

"Even in quiet little parishes like this. You'd be surprised, wouldn't he, Sergeant McGuiness?" asked the Vicar. He waited for a moment and then said: "I must ask you to allow me to be present. I would rather not, of course, because I am a squeamish man. But—I don't want to sound pompous—I think it's my duty."

Alleyn said: "We'll be glad to have you there. As far as possible we'll try to avoid attracting notice. I've been wondering if by any chance there's a less public way of going to the church than up those steps."

"There is *our* path. Through the shrubbery and thicket. It will be rather damp but it's short and inconspicuous. I would have to guide you."

"If you will. I think," Alleyn said, "our men have arrived. They're coming here first, I hope you don't mind?"

He went to the window and the others followed. Down below on the "green" a small delivery van had pulled up. Three men in mackintoshes and wet hats got out. They opened the rear door and took out a large carpenter's kit-bag and a corded bundle of considerable size that required two men to carry it.

"In the eye of a beholder," Alleyn grunted, "this would look like sheer lunacy."

"Not to the village," said the Vicar. "If they notice. They'll only think it's the boiler again."

"The boiler?"

"Yes. It has become unsafe and is always threatening to explode. Just look at those poor fellows," said the Vicar. "Should I ask my wife to make tea? Or coffee?"

Alleyn declined this offer. "Perhaps later," he said.

The men climbed the path in single file, carrying their gear. Rain bounced off their shoulders and streamed from their hat brims. Alleyn opened the door to them.

"We're in no shape to come into the house, sir," one of them said. He removed his hat and Bailey was revealed. Thompson stood behind him hung about with well-protected cameras.

"No, no, no. Not a bit of it," bustled the Vicar. "We've people in and out all day. Haven't we, McGuiness? Come in. Come in."

They waited, dripping, in the little hall. The Vicar kilted up his cassock, found himself a waterproof cape and pulled on a pair of galoshes. "I'll just get my brolly," he said and sought it in the porch.

Alleyn asked the men: "Is that a tent or an enclosure?" A framed tent, they said. It wouldn't take long to erect: there was no wind.

"We go out by the back," said the Vicar. "Shall I lead the way?"

The passage reeked of wetness and of its own house-smell: something suggestive of economy and floor polish. From behind one door came the sound of children's voices and from the kitchen the whirr of an egg-beater. They arrived at a side door that opened on to the all-pervading sound and sight of rain.

"I'm afraid," said the Vicar, "it will be rather heavy going. Especially with—" he paused and glanced unhappily at their gear, "—your burden," he said.

It was indeed heavy going. The shrubbery, a dense untended thicket, came to within a yard of the house and the path plunged directly into it. Water-laden branches slurred across their shoulders and slapped their faces, runnels of water gushed about their feet. They slithered, manoeuvred, fell about and shambled on again. The Vicar's umbrella came in for a deal of punishment.

"Not far now," he said at last and sure enough they were out of the wood and within a few yards of the church door.

The Vicar went first. It was already twilight in the church and he switched on lights, one in the nave and one in the south transept, which was furnished as a lady chapel. The men followed him self-consciously down the aisle and Bailey only just fetched up in time to avoid falling over the Vicar when he abruptly genuflected before turning right. The margin between tragedy and hysteria is a narrow one and Alleyn suppressed an impulse, as actors say, to "corpse": an only too apposite synonym in this context.

The Vicar continued into the lady chapel. "There's a door here," he said to Alleyn. "Rather unusual. It opens directly on the Passcoigne plot. Perhaps—?"

"It will suit admirably," Alleyn said. "May we open up our stuff in the church? It will make things a good deal easier."

"Yes. Very well."

So the men, helped by Sergeant McGuiness, unfolded their waterproof-covered bundle and soon two shovels, two hurricane lamps, three high-powered torches, a screwdriver and four coils of rope were set out neatly on the lady chapel floor. A folded mass of heavy plastic and a jointed steel frame were laid across the pews.

Bailey and Thompson chose a separate site in the transept for the assembling of their gear.

Alleyn said: "Right. We can go. Would you open the door, Vicar?"

It was down a flight of three steps in the corner of the lady chapel by the south wall. The Vicar produced a key that might have hung from the girdle of a Georgian jailer. "We hardly ever use it," he said. "I've oiled the key and brought the lubricant with me."

"Splendid."

Presently, with a clocking sound and a formidable screech, the door opened on a downpour so dense that it looked like a multiple sequence of beaded curtains closely hung one behind the other. The church filled with the insistent drumming of rain and with the smell of wet earth and trees.

Sybil Foster's grave was a dismal sight: the mound of earth, so carefully embellished by Bruce, looked as if it had been washed ashore with its panoply of dead flowers clinging to it: disordered and bespattered with mud.

They got the tent up with some trouble and great inconvenience. It was large enough to allow a wide margin round the grave. On one part of this they spread a ground-sheet. This added to an impression of something disreputable that was about to be put on show. The effect was emphasized by the fairground smell of the tent itself. The rain sounded more insistent inside than out.

The men fetched their gear from the church.

Until now, the Vicar, at Alleyn's suggestion, had remained in the church. Now, when they were assembled and ready—Fox, Bailey, Thompson, Sergeant McGuiness and the three Yard men, Alleyn went to fetch him.

He was at prayer. He had put off his mackintosh and he knelt there in his well-worn cassock with his hands folded before his lips. So, Alleyn thought, had centuries of parsons, for this reason and that, knelt in St. Crispin's-in-Quintern. He waited.

The Vicar crossed himself, opened his eyes, saw Alleyn and got up. "We're ready, sir," Alleyn said.

He found the Vicar's cape and held it out. "No, thanks," said the Vicar. "But I'd better take my brolly."

So with some ado he was brought into the tent where he shut his umbrella and stood quietly in the background, giving no trouble.

They made a pile of sodden flowers in a corner of the tent and then set about the earth mound, heaping it up into a wet repetition of itself. The tent fabric was green and this, in the premature twilight, gave the interior an underwater appearance.

The shovels crunched and slurped. The men, having cleared away the mound, dug deep and presently there was the hard sound of steel on wood. The Vicar came nearer. Thompson brought the coils of rope.

The men were expeditious and skillful and what they had to do was soon accomplished. As if in a reverse playback the coffin rose from its bed and was lifted on to the wet earth beside it.

One of the men went to a corner of the tent and fetched the screwdriver.

"You won't need that," Fox said quickly.

"No, sir?" The man looked at Alleyn.

"No," Alleyn said. "What you do now is dig deeper. But very cautiously. One man only. Bailey, will you do it? Clear away the green flooring and then explore with your hands. If the soil is easily moved, then go on—remove it. But with the greatest possible care. Stand as far to the side as you can manage."

Bailey lowered himself into the grave. Alleyn knelt on the ground-sheet, looking down, and the others in their glistening mackintoshes grouped round him. The Vicar stood at the foot of the grave, removed from the rest. They might have been actors in a modern production of the churchyard scene in *Hamlet*.

Bailey's voice, muffled, said: "It's dark down here: could I have a torch?" They shone their torches into the grave and the beams moved over pine branches. Bailey gathered together armfuls of them and handed them up. "Did we bring a trowel?" he asked.

The Vicar said there was one on the premises, kept for the churchyard guild. Sergeant McGuiness fetched it. While they waited Bailey could be heard scuffling. He dumped handfuls of soil on the lip of the grave. Alleyn examined them. The earth was loamy, friable and quite dry. McGuiness returned with a trowel and the mound at the lip of the grave grew bigger.

"The soil's packed down, like," Bailey said presently, "but it's not hard to move. I—I reckon—" his voice wavered, "I reckon it's been dug over—or filled in—or—hold on."

"Go steady, now," Fox said.

"There's something."

Bailey began to push earth aside with the edge of his hands and brush it away with his palms.

"A bit more light," he said.

Alleyn shone his own torch in and the light found Bailey's hands, palms down and fingers spread, held in suspended motion over the earth they had disturbed.

"Go on," Alleyn said. "Go on."

The hands came together, parted and swept aside the last of the earth.

Claude Carter's face had been turned into a gargoyle by the pressure of earth, and earth lay in streaks across its eyeballs.

### III

Before they moved it Thompson photographed the body where it lay. Then with great care and difficulty, it was lifted and stretched out on the ground-sheet. Where it had lain they found Claude's rucksack, tightly packed.

"He'd meant to pick up his car," Fox said, "and drive to Southampton."

"I think so."

Sybil Foster was returned to her grave and covered.

The Vicar said: "I'll go now. May God rest their souls."

Alleyn saw him into the church. He paused on the steps. "It's stopped raining," he said. "I hadn't noticed. How strange."

"Are you all right?" Alleyn asked him. "Will you go back to the vicarage?"

"What? Oh. Oh no. Not just yet. I'm quite all right, thank you. I must pray now, for the living, mustn't I?"

"The living?"

"Oh, yes," said the Vicar shakily. "Yes indeed. That's my job. I have to pray for my brother man. The murderer, you know." He went into the church.

Alleyn returned to the tent.

"It's clearing," he said. "I think you'd better stand guard outside." The Yard men went out.

Bailey and Thompson were at their accustomed tasks. The camera flashed for Claude as assiduously as a pressman's for a celebrity. When they turned him over and his awful face was hidden they disclosed a huge red grin at the nape of the neck.

"Bloody near decapitated," Thompson whispered and photographed it in close-up.

"Don't exaggerate," Fox automatically chided. He was searching the rucksack.

"It's not far wrong, Mr. Fox," said Bailey.

"If you've finished," Alleyn said. "Search him."

Bailey found a wallet containing twenty pounds, loose change, cigarettes, matches, his pocket-book, a passport and three dirty postcards.

And in the inside breast pocket, a tiny but extremely solid steel box such as a jeweller might use to house a ring. The key was in Claude's wallet.

Alleyn opened the box and disclosed a neatly folded miniature envelope wrapped in a waterproof silk and inside the envelope, between two watch-glasses, a stamp: the Emperor Alexander with a hole in his head.

"Look here, Fox," he said.

Fox restrapped the rucksack and came over. He placed his great palms on his knees and regarded the stamp.

"That was a good bit of speculative thinking on your part," he said. "It looks to me as if that large box we found in his room could have contained this one and left the trace in the rubble, all right. Funny, you know, there it's lain all these years. I suppose Captain Carter stowed it there that evening. Before he was killed."

"And may well have used some of the cement in the bag that's still rotting quietly away in the corner. And marked the place on the plan in which this poor scoundrel showed such an interest."

"He wouldn't have tried to sell it in England, surely?"

"We've got to remember it was his by right. Being what he was he might have settled for a devious approach to a fanatic millionaire collector somewhere abroad whose zeal would get the better of his integrity."

"Funny," Fox mused. "A bit of paper not much bigger than your thumbnail. Not very pretty and flawed at that. And could be worth as much as its own size in a diamond. I don't get it."

"Collector's passion? Nor I. But it comes high in the list as an incentive to crime."

"Where'll we put it?"

"Lock the box and give it to me. If I'm knocked on the head again take charge of it yourself. I can't wait till I get it safely stowed at the Yard. In the meantime—"

"We go in for the kill?" said Fox.

"That's it. Unless it comes in of its own accord."

"Now?"

"When we've cleared up, here." He turned to Bailey and Thompson. They had finished with what was left of Claude Carter and were folding the ground-sheet neatly round him and tying him up with rope. They threaded the two shovels inside the rope to make hand-holds.

And everything else being ready they struck the tent, folded it and

laid it with its frame across the body. Bailey, Thompson, McGuiness
and the Yard man stood on either side. "Looks a bit less like a corpse,"
said Thompson.

"You'll have to go down the steps this time," Alleyn told them. "Mr.
Fox and I will bring the rest of the gear and light the way."

They took their torches from their pockets. Twilight had closed in
now. The after-smell of rain and the pleasant reek of a wood fire hung
on the air. Somewhere down in the village a door banged and then the
only sound was of water dripping from branches. Sybil's grave looked
as if it had never been disturbed.

"Quiet," said one of the men. "Isn't it?"

"Shall we move off, then?" Fox asked.

He stooped to pick up his load and the other four men groped for
their hand-holds under the tent.

"Right?" said Bailey.

But Alleyn had lifted a hand. "No," he whispered. "Not yet. Keep
still. Listen."

Fox was beside him. "Where?"

"Straight ahead. In the trees."

He turned his light on the thicket. A cluster of autumnal leaves
sprang up and quivered. One after another the torch-beams joined his.
This time all the men heard the hidden sound.

They spread out to the left and right of Alleyn and moved forward.
The light on the thicket was intensified and details of foliage appeared
in uncanny precision, as if they carried some significance and must
never be forgotten. A twig snapped and the head of a sapling jerked.

"Bloody Daft Artie, by God!" said Sergeant McGuiness.

"Shall we go in?" asked Fox.

"No," said Alleyn and then, loudly: "Show yourself. You can't run
away from it this time. Call it a day and come out."

The leaves parted but the face that shone whitely between them,
blinking in the torchlight, was not Daft Artie's.

"This is it, Bruce," said Alleyn. "Come out."

## IV

Bruce Gardener sat bolt upright at the table with his arms folded.
He still bore the insecure *persona* of his chosen role: red-gold beard,
fresh mouth, fine torso, loud voice, pawky turn of speech: the
straightforward Scottish soldier-man with a heart of gold. At first sight
the pallor, the bloodshot eyes and the great earthy hands clenched hard
on the upper arms were not conspicuous. To Alleyn, sitting opposite

him, to Fox, impassive in the background and to the constable with a notebook in the corner, however, these were unmistakable signs.

Alleyn said: "Shorn of all other matters: motive, opportunity and all the rest of it, what do you say about this one circumstance? Who but you could have dug Sybil Foster's grave four feet deeper than was necessary, killed Carter, buried his body there, covered it, trampled it down and placed the evergreen flooring? On your own statement and that of other witnesses you were there, digging the grave all that afternoon and well into the night. Why were you so long about it?"

Alleyn waited. Gardener stared at the opposite wall. Once or twice his beard twitched and the red mouth moved as if he was about to speak. But nothing came of it.

"Well?" Alleyn said at last and Bruce gave a parody of clearing his throat. "Clay," he said loudly.

The constable wrote: "*Ans. Clay,*" and waited.

"So you told me. But there was no sign of clay in that mound of earth. The spoil is loamy and easy to shift. So that's no good," Alleyn said. "Is it?"

"I'll no' answer any questions till I have my solicitor present."

"He's on his way. You might, however, like to consider this. On that night after the funeral when we had an acetylene lamp like yours up there by the grave, you, from your sister's window, saw the light and it worried you. You told us so. And it wasn't Daft Artie who lay in the cubbyhole in the hedge, it was you. It wasn't Daft Artie who heaved half a brick at me, it was you. You were so shaken by the thought of us opening the grave that you lost your head, came down the hill, hid in the hedge, chucked the brick and then set up a phoney hunt for an Artie who wasn't there. Right?"

"No comment."

"You'll have to find some sort of comment, sooner or later, won't you? However, your solicitor will advise you. But suppose Artie was in bed with a cold that evening, how would you feel about that?"

"*Ans. No comment,*" wrote the constable.

"Well," Alleyn said, "there's no point in plugging away at it. The case against you hangs on this one point. If you didn't kill and bury Claude Carter, who did? I shall put it to you again when your solicitor comes and he no doubt will advise you to keep quiet. In the meantime I must tell you that not one piece of information about your actions can be raised to contradict the contention that you killed Mrs. Foster; that Carter, a man with a record of blackmail, knew it and exercised his knowledge on you and that you, having arranged with him to pay the blackmail if he came to the churchyard that night, had the grave ready, killed him with the shovel you used to dig the grave and buried him there. Two victims in one grave. Is there still no comment?"

In the silence that followed, Alleyn saw, with extreme distaste, tears well up in Bruce's china-blue, slightly squinting eyes and trickle into his beard.

"We were close taegither, her and me," he said and his voice trembled. "From the worrrd go we understood each ither. She was more than an employer to me, she was a true friend. Aye. When I think of the plans we made for the beautifying of the property—" his voice broke convincingly.

"Did you plan those superfluous asparagus beds together and were the excavations in the mushroom shed your idea or hers?"

Bruce half-rose from his chair. Fox made a slight move and he sank back again.

"Or," said Alleyn, "did Captain Carter, who, as you informed us, used to confide in you, tell you before he came down to Quintern on the last afternoon of his life that he proposed to bury the Black Alexander stamp somewhere on the premises? And forty years later when you found yourself there did you not think it a good idea to have a look round on your own accord?"

"You can't prove it on me," he shouted without a trace of Scots. "And what about it if you could?"

"Nothing much, I confess. We've got more than enough without that. I merely wondered if you knew when you killed him that Claude Carter had the Black Alexander in his breast pocket. You gave it its second burial."

Purple-red flooded up into Bruce's face. He clenched his fists and beat them on the table.

"The bastard!" he shouted. "The bloody bastard. By Christ, he earned what he got."

The station sergeant tapped on the door. Fox opened it.

"It's his solicitor," he said.

"Show him in," said Fox.

## V

Verity Preston weeded her long border and wondered where to look for a gardener. She chided herself for taking so personal a view. She remembered that there had been times when she and Bruce had seemed to understand each other over garden matters. It was monstrous to contemplate what they said he had done but she did not think it was untrue.

A shadow fell across the long border. She swivelled round on her knees and there was Alleyn.

"I hope I'm not making a nuisance of myself," he said, "but I expect I am. There's something I wanted to ask you."

He squatted down beside her. "Have you got beastly couch-grass in your border?" he asked.

"That can hardly be what you wanted to ask but no, I haven't. Only fat-hen, dandelions and wandering-willy."

He picked up her handfork and began to use it. "I wanted to know whether the plan of Quintern Place with the spot marked X is still in Markos's care or whether it's been returned."

"The former, I should imagine. Do you need it?"

"Counsel for the prosecution may."

"Mrs. Jim might know. She's here today, would you like to ask her?"

"In a minute or two, if I may," he said shaking the soil off a root of fat-hen and throwing it into the wheelbarrow.

"I suppose," he said, "you'll be looking for a replacement."

"Just what I was thinking. Oh," Verity exclaimed, "it's all so flattening and awful. I suppose one will understand it when the trial's over but to me, at present, it's a muddle."

"Which bits of it?"

"Well, first of all, I suppose what happened at Greengages."

"After you left?"

"Good Heavens, not before, I do trust."

"I'll tell you what we believe happened. Some of it we can prove: the rest follows from it. The prosecution will say it's pure conjecture. In a way that doesn't matter. Gardener will be charged with the murder of Claude Carter, not Sybil Foster. However, the one is consequent upon the other. We believe, then, that Gardener and Carter, severally, stayed behind at Greengages, each hoping to get access to Mrs. Foster's room, Carter probably to sponge on her, Gardener, if the opportunity presented itself, to do away with her. It all begins from the time when young Markos went to Mrs. Foster's room to retrieve his fiancée's bag."

"I hope," Verity said indignantly, "you don't attach—"

"Don't jump the gun like that or we shall never finish. He reported Mrs. Foster alive and, it would be improper but I gather, appropriate, to add, kicking."

"Against the engagement. Yes."

"At some time before nine o'clock Claude appeared at the reception desk and, representing himself to be an electrician come to mend Mrs. Foster's lamp, collected the lilies left at the desk by Bruce and took them upstairs. When he was in the passage something moved him to hide in an alcove opposite her door leaving footprints and a lily head behind him. We believe he had seen Bruce approaching and that when Bruce left the room after a considerable time, Carter tapped on the door and walked in. He found her dead.

"He dumped the lilies in the bathroom basin. While he was in there, probably with the door ajar, Sister Jackson paid a very brief visit to the room."

"That large lady who gave evidence? But she didn't say—"

"She did, later on. We'll stick to the main line. Well. Claude took thought. It suited him very well that she was dead: he now collected a much bigger inheritance. He also had, ready-made, an instrument for blackmail and Gardener would have the wherewithal to stump up. Luckily for us he also decided by means of an anonymous letter and a telephone call to have a go at Sister Jackson, who had enough sense to report it to us."

"I suppose you know he went to prison for blackmail?"

"Yes. So much for Greengages. Now for Claude, the Black Alexander and the famous plan."

Verity listened with her head between her hands, making no further interruptions and with the strangest sense of hearing an account of events that had taken place a very, very long time ago.

"—so Claude's plan matured," Alleyn was saying. "He decided to go abroad until things had settled down. Having come to this decision, we think, he set about blackmailing Gardener. Gardener appeared to fall for it. No doubt he told Claude he needed time to raise the money and put him off until the day before the funeral. He then said he would have it by that evening and Claude could collect it in the churchyard. And I think," said Alleyn, "you can guess the rest."

"As far as Claude is concerned—yes, I suppose I can. But—Bruce Gardener and Sybil—that's much the worst. That's so—disgusting. All those professions of attachment, all that slop and sorrow act—no, it's beyond everything."

"You did have your reservations about him, didn't you?"

"They didn't run along homicidal lines," Verity snapped.

"Not an unusual reaction. You'd be surprised how it crops up after quite appalling cases. Heath, for instance. Some of his acquaintances couldn't believe such a nice chap would behave like that."

"With Bruce, though, it was simply for cash and comfort?"

"Just that. Twenty-five thousand and a very nice little house which he could let until he retired."

"But he'd have got them anyway in the long run."

"They were about the same age. She might well have outlived him."

"Even so—. Yes, all right. So he knew the terms of the Will?"

"Oh, yes. He handed it over to Mrs. Jim, who noticed that the envelope was groggily gummed up. Mrs. Jim knew Mrs. Foster was given to afterthoughts: reopening and inefficiently resealing her correspondence and thought nothing of it. And there were only the Rattisbon and Prunella prints on the Will. Who do you think had removed Mrs. Foster's and Johnson's and Marleena Briggs's? And his own."

"Still," Verity said. "He'd have been sitting pretty at Quintern if Sybil had lived."

"Not if Dr. Schramm knew anything about it. They had a row and he intimated to Gardener, almost in so many words, that he'd get the sack."

After a long pause, Verity said: "What about the stamp?"

"The Black Alexander? He knew about it. Captain Carter had talked about it. Bruce Gardener," said Alleyn, "is in some ways the most accomplished villain I've come across. He's never told me a lie when it wasn't necessary. Over a long, long span, probably from his boyhood, he's developed the *persona* that has served him best: the honest, downright chap; winning, plausible, a bit of a character with the added slightly phoney touch of the pawky Scot. By and large," said Alleyn, "a loss to the Stage. I can see him stealing the show in superior soap."

"The stamp?"

"Ah, yes. He hasn't admitted it but I've no doubt he knew perfectly well that his sister lived in his captain's village and that the stamp had never been found. Hence the multiplicity of asparagus and mushroom beds."

"And then—Claude?"

"Yes. And along comes Claude and Claude's found a map with a point marked X and while heart-stricken Bruce is digging his kind and generous lady's grave Claude has a go in the fireplace and strikes it rich."

"Oh, well!" said Verity and gave it up. And then, with great difficulty, she said: "I would be glad to know—Basil Smythe wasn't in any way involved, was he? I mean—as her doctor he couldn't be held to have been irresponsible or anything?"

"Nothing like that."

"But—there's something, isn't there?"

"Well, yes. It appears that the Dr. Schramm who qualified at Lausanne was never Mr. Smythe, and I'm afraid Schramm was *not* a family name of Mr. Smythe's mama. But it appears he will inherit his fortune. He evidently suggested—no doubt with great tact—that as the change had not been confirmed by deed poll, Smythe was still his legal name. And Smythe, to Mr. Rattisbon's extreme chagrin, it is in the Will."

"That," said Verity, "is I'm afraid all too believable."

Alleyn waited for a moment and then said: "You'll see, won't you, why I was so anxious that Prunella should be taken away before we went to work in the churchyard?"

"What? Oh, that. Yes. Yes, of course I do."

"If she was on the high seas she couldn't be asked as next of kin to identify."

"That would have been—too horrible."

Alleyn got to his feet. "Whereas she is now, no doubt, contemplating the flesh-pots of the Côte d'Azure and running herself in as the future daughter-in-law of the Markos millions."

"Yes," Verity said, catching her breath in a half-sigh, "I expect so."

"You sound as if you regret it."

"Not really. She's a level-headed child and it's the height of elderly arrogance to condemn the young for having different tastes from one's own. It's not my scene," said Verity, "but I think she'll be very happy in it."

And at the moment, Prunella was very happy indeed. She was stretched out in a chaise-longue looking at the harbour of Antibes, drinking iced lemonade and half-listening to Nikolas and Gideon, who were talking about the post from London that had just been brought aboard.

Mr. Markos had opened up a newspaper. He gave an instantly stifled exclamation and made a quick movement to refold the paper.

But he was too late. Prunella and Gideon had both looked up as an errant breeze caught at the front page.

### "BLACK ALEXANDER
Famous Stamp Found on Murdered Man"

"It's no good, darlings," Prunella said after a pause, "trying to hide it all up. I'm bound to hear, you know, sooner or later."

Gideon kissed her. Mr. Markos, after making a deeply sympathetic noise, said: "Well—perhaps."

"Go on," said Prunella. "You know you're dying to read it."

So he read it and as he did so the circumspection of the man of affairs and the avid, dotty desire of the collector were strangely combined in Mr. Markos. He folded the paper.

"Darling child," said Mr. Markos. "You now possess a fortune."

"I suppose I must."

He picked up her hands and beat them gently together. "You will, of course, take advice. It will be a momentous decision. But *if*," said Mr. Markos, kissing first one hand and then the other, "*if* after due deliberation you decide to sell, may your father-in-law have the first refusal? Speaking quite cold-bloodedly, of course," said Mr. Markos.

The well-dressed, expensively gloved and strikingly handsome passenger settled into his seat and fastened his belt.

Heathrow had passed off quietly.

He wondered when it would be advisable to return. Not, he fancied, for some considerable time. As they moved off the label attached to an elegant suitcase in the luggage rack slipped down and dangled over his head.

> "Dr. Basil Schramm
> Passenger to New York
> Concorde
> Flight 123"

# SPINSTERS

# IN

# JEOPARDY

# Contents

|  | Prologue | 219 |
| Chapter I | Journey to the South | 225 |
| Chapter II | Operation Truebody | 243 |
| Chapter III | Morning with Mr. Oberon | 255 |
| Chapter IV | The Elusiveness of Mr. Garbel | 268 |
| Chapter V | Ricky in Roqueville | 287 |
| Chapter VI | Consultation | 303 |
| Chapter VII | Sound of Ricky | 321 |
| Chapter VIII | Ricky Regained | 339 |
| Chapter IX | Dinner at Roqueville | 357 |
| Chapter X | Thunder in the Air | 374 |
| Chapter XI | P. E. Garbel | 390 |
| Chapter XII | Eclipse of the Sun | 411 |

# Cast of Characters

| | |
|---|---|
| Roderick Alleyn | Chief Detective-Inspector, Criminal Investigation Department, New Scotland Yard |
| Agatha Troy Alleyn | his wife |
| Ricky | their son |
| Miss Truebody | their fellow-passenger |
| Dr. Claudel | a French physician |
| Raoul Milano | of Roqueville. Owner-driver |
| Dr. Ali Baradi | a surgeon |
| Mahomet | his servant |
| Mr. Oberon | of the Château de la Chèvre d'Argent |
| Ginny Taylor Robin Herrington Carbury Glande Annabella Wells | his guests |
| Teresa | the fiancée of Raoul |
| M. Dupont | of the Sûreté. Acting Commissaire at the Préfecture, Roqueville |
| M. Callard | Managing Director of the Compagnie Chimique des Alpes Maritimes |
| M. and Madame Milano | the parents of Raoul |
| Marie | a maker of figurines |
| M. Malaquin | proprietor of the Hôtel Royal |
| P. E. Garbel | a chemist |

# Prologue

## I

WITHOUT moving his head, Ricky slewed his eyes round until he was able to look slantways at the back of his mother's easel.

"I'm getting pretty bored, however," he announced.

"Stick it a bit longer, darling, I implore you, and look at Daddy."

"Well, because it's just about as boring a thing as a person can have to do. Isn't it, Daddy?"

"When I did it," said his father, "I was allowed to look at your mama, so I wasn't bored. But as there are degrees of boredom," he continued, "so there are different kind of bores. You might almost say there are recognizable schools."

"To which school," said his wife, stepping back from her easel, "would you say Mr. Garbel belonged? Ricky, look at Daddy for five minutes more and then I promise we'll stop."

Ricky sighed ostentatiously and contemplated his father.

"Well, as far as we know him," Alleyn said, "to the espistolatory school. There, he's a classic. In person he's undoubtedly the sort of bore that shows you things you don't want to see. Snapshots in envelopes. Barren conservatories. Newspaper cuttings. He's relentless in this. I think he carries things on his person and puts them in front of you without giving you the smallest clue about what you're meant to say. You're moving, Ricky."

"Isn't it five minutes yet?"

"No, and it never will be if you fidget. How long is it, Troy, since you first heard from Mr. Garbel?"

"About eighteen months. He wrote for Christmas. All told I've had six letters and five postcards from Mr. Garbel. This last arrived this morning. That's what put him into my head."

"Daddy, who is Mr. Garbel?"

"One of Mummy's admirers. He lives in the Maritime Alps and writes love letters to her."

"Why?"

"He says it's because he's her third cousin once removed, but I know better."

"What do you know better?"

With a spare paintbrush clenched between her teeth, Troy said indistinctly: "Keep like that, Ricky darling, I *implore* you."

"O.K. Tell me properly, Daddy, about Mr. Garbel."

"Well, he suddenly wrote to Mummy and said Mummy's great-aunt's daughter was his second cousin, and that he thought Mummy would like to know that he lived at a place called Roqueville in the Maritime Alps. He sent a map of Roqueville, marking the place where the road he lived on ought to be shown, but wasn't, and he told Mummy how he didn't go out much or meet many people."

"Pretty dull, however."

"He told her about all the food you can buy there that you can't buy here, and he sent her copies of newspapers with bus timetables marked and messages at the side saying: 'I find this bus convenient and often take it. It leaves the corner by the principal hotel every half-hour.' Do you still want to hear about Mr. Garbel?"

"Unless it's time to stop, I might as well."

"Mummy wrote to Mr. Garbel and said how interesting she found his letter."

"Did you, Mummy?"

"One has to be polite," Troy muttered and laid a thin stroke of rose on the mouth of Ricky's portrait.

"And he wrote back sending her three used bus tickets and a used train ticket."

"Does she collect them?"

"Mr. Garbel thought she would like to know that they were his tickets punched by guards and conductors all for him. He also sends her beautifully coloured postcards of the Maritime Alps."

"What's that? May I have them?"

". . . with arrows pointing to where his house would be if you could see it and to where the road goes to a house he sometimes visits only the house is off the postcard."

"Like a picture puzzle, sort of?"

"Sort of. And he tells Mummy how, when he was young and doing chemistry at Cambridge, he almost met her great-aunt who was his second cousin once removed."

"Did he have a shop?"

"No, he's a special kind of chemist without a shop. When he sends Mummy presents of used tickets and old newspapers he writes on them: 'Sent by P. E. Garbel, 16 Rue des Violettes, Roqueville, to Mrs. Agatha Alleyn (née Troy) daughter of Stephen and Harriet Troy (née Baynton).'"

"That's you, isn't it, Mummy? What else?"

"Is it possible, Ricky," asked his wondering father, "that you find this interesting?"

"Yes," said Ricky. "I like it. Does he mention me?"

"I don't think so."

"Or you?"

"He suggests that Mummy might care to read parts of his letter to me."

"May we go and see him?"

"Yes," said Alleyn. "As a matter of fact I think we may."

Troy turned from her work and gaped at her husband. "What can you mean?" she exclaimed.

"Is it time, Mummy? Because it must be, so may I get down?"

"Yes, thank you, my sweet. You have been terribly good and I must think of some exciting reward."

"Going to see Mr. Garbel frinstance?"

"I'm afraid," Troy said, "that Daddy, poor thing, was being rather silly."

"Well then—ride to Babylon?" Ricky suggested, and looked out of the corners of his eyes at his father.

"All right," Alleyn groaned, parodying despair. "O.K. *All right*. Here we go!"

He swung the excitedly squealing Ricky up to his shoulders and grasped his ankles.

"Good old horse," Ricky shouted and patted his father's cheek. "Non-stop to Babylon. Good old horse."

Troy looked dotingly at him. "Say to Nanny that I said you could ask for an extra high tea."

"Top highest with strawberry jam?"

"If there is any."

"Lavish!" said Ricky and gave a cry of primitive food-lust. "Giddy-up horse," he shouted. The family of Alleyn broke into a chant:

"How many miles to Babylon?
Five score and ten.
Can I get there by candle-light?"

*"Yes! And back again!"* Ricky yelled, and was carried at a canter from the room.

Troy listened to the diminishing rumpus on the stairs and looked at her work.

"How happy we are!" she thought, and then, foolishly, "Touch wood!" And she picked up a brush and dragged a touch of colour from the hair across the brow. "How lucky I am," she thought, more soberly, and her mood persisted when Alleyn came back with his hair tousled like Ricky's and his tie under his ear.

He said: "May I look?"

"All right," Troy agreed, wiping her brushes, "but don't say anything."

He grinned and walked round to the front of the easel. Troy had painted a head that seemed to have light as its substance. Even the locks of dark hair might have been spun from sunshine. It was a work in line rather than in mass, but the line flowed and turned with a subtlety that made any further elaboration unnecessary. "It needs another hour," Troy muttered.

"In that case," Alleyn said, "I can at least touch wood."

She gave him a quick grateful look and said, "What is all this about Mr. Garbel?"

"I saw the A.C. this morning. He was particularly nice, which generally means he's got you pricked down for a particularly nasty job. On the face of it this one doesn't sound so bad. It seems M.I.5. and the Sûreté are having a bit of a party with the Narcotics Bureau, and our people want somebody with fairly fluent French to go over for talks and a bit of field-work. As it *is* M.I.5. we'd better observe the usual rule of airy tact on your part and phony inscrutability on mine. But it turns out that the field-work lies, to coin a coy phrase, not a hundred miles from Roqueville."

"Never!" Troy ejaculated. "In the Garbel country?"

"Precisely. Now it occurs to me that what with war, Ricky and the atrocious nature of my job, we've never had a holiday abroad together.

Nanny is due for a fortnight at Reading. Why shouldn't you and Ricky come with me to Roqueville and call on Mr. Garbel?"

Troy looked delighted, but she said: "You can't go round doing top-secret jobs for M.I.5. trailing your wife and child. It would look so amateurish. Besides, we agreed never to mix business with pleasure, Rory."

"In this case the more amateurish I look, the better. And I should only be based on Roqueville. The job lies outside it, so we wouldn't really be mixing business with pleasure."

He looked at her for a moment. "Do come," he said, "you know you're dying to meet Mr. Garbel."

Troy scraped her palette. "I'm dying to come," she amended, "but not to meet Mr. Garbel. And yet: I don't know. There's a sort of itch, I confess it, to find out just how deadly dull he is. Like a suicidal tendency."

"You must yield to it. Write to him and tell him you're coming. You might enclose a bus ticket from Putney to the Fulham Road. How do you address him: 'Dear Cousin—' But what is his Christian name?"

"I've no idea. He's just P. E. Garbel. To his intimates, he tells me, he is known as Peg. He adds, inevitably, a quip about being square in a round hole."

"Roqueville being the hole?"

"Presumably."

"Has he a job, do you think?"

"For all I know he may be writing a monograph on bicarbonate-of-soda. If he is he'll probably ask us to read the manuscript."

"At all events we must meet him. Put down that damn palette and tell me you're coming."

Troy wiped her hands on her smock. "We're coming," she said.

## II

In the château outside Roqueville, Mr. Oberon looked across the nighted Mediterranean towards North Africa and then smiled gently upon his assembled guests.

"How fortunate we are," he said. "Not a jarring note. All gathered together with one pure object in mind." He ran over their names as if they composed a sort of celestial roll-call. "Our youngest disciple," he said, beaming on Ginny Taylor. "A wonderful field of experience awaits her. She stands on the threshold of ecstasy. It is not too much to say, of ecstasy. And Robin too." Robin Herrington, who had been watching Ginny Taylor, looked up sharply. "Ah, youth, youth," sighed

Mr. Oberon, ambiguously, and turned to the remaining guests, two men and a woman. "Do we envy them?" he asked, and answered himself. "No! No, for ours is the richer tilth. We are the husbandmen, are we not?"

Dr. Baradi lifted his dark, fleshy and intelligent head. He looked at his host. "Yes, indeed," he said. "We are precisely that. And when Annabella arrives—I think you said she was coming?"

"Dear Annabella!" Mr. Oberon exclaimed. "Yes. On Tuesday. Unexpectedly."

"Ah!" said Carbury Glande, looking at his paint-stained fingernails. "On Tuesday. Then she will be rested and ready for our Thursday rites."

"Dear Annabella!" Dr. Baradi echoed sumptuously.

The sixth guest turned her ravaged face and short-sighted eyes towards Ginny Taylor.

"Is this your first visit?" she asked.

Ginny was looking at Mr. Oberon. She wore an expression that was unbecoming to her youth, a look of uncertainty, excitement and perhaps fear.

"Yes," she said. "My first."

"A neophyte," Baradi murmured richly.

"Soon to be so young a priestess," Mr. Oberon added. "It is very touching." He smiled at Ginny with parted lips.

A tinkling crash broke across the conversation. Robin Herrington had dropped his glass on the tessellated floor. The remains of his cocktail ran into a little pool near Mr. Oberon's feet.

Mr. Oberon cut across his apologies. "No, no," he said. "It is a happy symbol. Perhaps a promise. Let us call it a libation," he said. "Shall we dine?"

# CHAPTER I

# Journey to the South

## I

ALLEYN lifted himself on his elbow and turned his watch to the blue light above his pillow. Twenty minutes past five. In another hour they would be in Roqueville.

The abrupt fall of silence when the train stopped must have woken him. He listened intently but, apart from the hiss of escaping steam and the slam of a door in a distant carriage, everything was quiet and still.

He heard the men in the double sleeper next his own exchange desultory remarks. One of them yawned loudly.

Alleyn thought the station must be Douceville. Sure enough, some-one walked past the window and a lonely voice announced to the night: *"Douce-v-i-ll-e."*

The engine hissed again. The same voice, apparently continuing a broken conversation, called out: *"Pas ce soir, par exemple!"* Someone else laughed distantly. The voices receded to be followed by the most characteristic of all stationary train noises, the tap of steel on steel. The taps tinkered away into the distance.

Alleyn manoeuvred to the bottom of his bunk, dangled his long legs in space for a moment, and then slithered to the floor. The window was not completely shuttered. He peered through the gap and was confronted by the bottom of a poster for Dubonnet and the lower half of a porter carrying a lamp. The lamp swung to and fro, a bell rang, and the train clanked discreetly. The lamp and poster were replaced by the lower halves of two discharged passengers, a pile of luggage, a stretch of empty platform, and a succession of swiftly moving pools of light. Then there was only the night hurrying past with blurred suggestions of rocks and olive trees.

The train gathered speed and settled down to its perpetual choriambic statement: "What a to-*do*. What a to-*do*."

Alleyn cautiously lowered the window-blind. The train was crossing the seaward end of a valley and the moon in its third quarter was riding the western heavens. Its radiance emphasized the natural pallor of hills and trees and dramatized the shapes of rocks and mountains. With the immediate gesture of a shutter, a high bank obliterated this landscape. The train passed through a village and for two seconds Alleyn looked into a lamplit room where a woman watched a man intent over an early breakfast. What occupation got them up so soon? They were there, sharp in his vision, and were gone.

He turned from the window wondering if Troy, who shared his pleasure in train journeys, was awake in her single berth next door. In twenty minutes he would go and see. In the meantime he hoped that, in the almost complete darkness, he could dress himself without making a disturbance. He began to do so, steadying himself against the lurch and swing of this small, noisy and unstable world.

"Hullo." A treble voice ventured from the blackness of the lower bunk. "Are we getting out soon?"

"Hullo," Alleyn rejoined. "No, go to sleep."

"I couldn't be wakier. Matter of fac' I've been awake pretty well all night."

Alleyn groped for his shirt, staggered, barked his shin on the edge of his suitcase and swore under his breath.

"Because," the treble voice continued, "if we aren't getting out why are you dressing yourself?"

"To be ready for when we are."

"I see," said the voice. "Is Mummy getting ready for getting out, too?"

"Not yet."

"Why?"

"It's not time."

"Is she asleep?"

"I don't know, old boy."

"Then how do you know she's not getting ready?"

"I don't know, really. I just hope she's not."

"Why?"

"I want her to rest, and if you say why again I won't answer."

"I see." There was a pause. The voice chuckled. "Why?" it asked.

Alleyn had found his shirt. He now discovered that he had put it on inside out. He took it off.

"If," the voice pursued, "I said a sensible why, would you answer, Daddy?"

"It would have to be entirely sensible."

"Why are you getting up in the dark?"

"I had hoped," Alleyn said bitterly, "that all little boys were fast asleep and I didn't want to wake them."

"Because now you know they aren't asleep so why—?"

"You're perfectly right," Alleyn said. The train rounded a curve and he ran with some violence against the door. He switched on the light and contemplated his son.

Ricky had the newly made look peculiar to little boys in bed. His dark hair hung sweetly over his forehead, his eyes shone and his cheeks and lips were brilliant. One would have said he was so new that his colours had not yet dried.

"I like being in a train," he said, "more lavishly than anything that's ever happened so far. Do you like being in a train, Daddy?" "Yes," said Alleyn. He opened the door of the washing-cabinet, which lit itself up. Ricky watched his father shave.

"Where are we now?" he said presently.

"By a sea. It's called the Mediterranean and it's just out there on the other side of the train. We shall see it when it's daytime."

"Are we in the middle of the night?"

"Not quite. We're in the very early morning. Out there everybody is fast asleep," Alleyn suggested, not very hopefully.

"Everybody?"

"Almost everybody. Fast asleep and snoring."

"All except us," Ricky said with rich satisfaction, "because we are lavishly wide awake in the very early morning in a train. Aren't we, Daddy?"

"That's it. Soon we'll pass the house where I'm going tomorrow. The train doesn't stop there, so I have to go on with you to Roqueville and drive back. You and Mummy will stay in Roqueville."

"Where will you be most of the time?"

"Sometimes with you and sometimes at this house. It's called the

Château de la Chèvre d'Argent. That means the House of the Silver Goat."

"Pretty funny name, however," said Ricky.

A stream of sparks ran past the window. The light from the carriage flew across the surface of a stone wall. The train had begun to climb steeply. It gradually slowed down until there was time to see nearby objects lamplit, in the world outside: a giant cactus, a flight of steps, part of an olive grove. The engine laboured almost to a standstill. Outside their window, perhaps a hundred yards away, there was a vast house that seemed to grow out of the cliff. It stood full in the moonlight, and shadows, black as ink, were thrown by buttresses across its recessed face. A solitary window, veiled by a patterned blind, glowed dully yellow.

"*Somebody* is awake out there," Ricky observed. " 'Out,' 'in'?" he speculated. "Daddy, what are those people? 'Out' or 'in'?"

"Outside for us, I suppose, and inside for them."

"Outside the train and inside the house," Ricky agreed. "Suppose the train ran through the house, would they be 'in' for us?"

"I hope," his father observed glumly, "that you don't grow up a metaphysician."

"What's that? Look, there they are in their house. We've stopped, haven't we?"

The carriage window was exactly opposite the lighted one in the cliff-like wall of the house. A blurred shape moved in the room on the other side of the blind. It swelled and became a black body pressed against the window.

Alleyn made a sharp ejaculation and a swift movement.

"Because you're standing right in front of the window," Ricky said politely, "and it would be rather nice to see out."

The train jerked galvanically and with a compound racketing noise, slowly entered a tunnel, emerged, and gathering pace, began a descent to sea-level.

The door of the compartment opened and Troy stood there, in a woollen dressing-gown. Her short hair was rumpled and hung over her forehead like her son's. Her face was white and her eyes dark with perturbation. Alleyn turned quickly. Troy looked from him to Ricky. "Have you seen out of the window?" she asked.

"*I* have," said Alleyn. "And so, by the look of you, have you."

Troy said, "Can you help me with my suitcase?" and to Ricky: "I'll come back and get you up soon, darling."

"Are you both going?"

"We'll be just next door. We shan't be long," Alleyn said.

"It's only because it's in a train."

"We know," Troy reassured him. "But it's all right. Honestly. O.K.?"

"O.K.," Ricky said in a small voice, and Troy touched his cheek.

Alleyn followed into her own compartment. She sat down on her bunk and stared at him. "I can't believe that was true," she said.

"I'm sorry you saw it."

"Then it was true. Ought we to do anything? Rory, ought you to do anything? Oh *dear*, how tiresome."

"Well, I can't do much while moving away at sixty miles an hour. I suppose I'd better ring up the Préfecture when we get to Roqueville."

He sat down beside her. "Never mind, darling," he said, "there may be another explanation."

"I don't see how there can be, unless—Do you mind telling me what you saw?"

Alleyn said carefully, "A lighted window, masked by a spring blind. A woman falling against the blind and releasing it. Beyond the woman, but out of sight to us, there must have been a brilliant lamp and in its light, farther back in the room and on our right, stood a man in a white garment. His face, oddly enough, was in shadow. There was something that looked like a wheel, beyond his right shoulder. His right arm was raised."

"And in his hand—?"

"Yes," Alleyn said, "that's the tricky bit, isn't it?"

"And then the tunnel. It was like one of those sudden breaks in an old-fashioned film, too abrupt to be really dramatic. It was there and then it didn't exist. No," said Troy, "I won't believe it was true. I won't believe something is still going on inside that house. And what a house too! It looked like a Gustave Doré, really bad romantic."

Alleyn said: "Are you all right to get dressed? I'll just have a word with the car attendant. He may have seen it, too. After all, we may not be the only people awake and looking out, though I fancy mine was the only compartment with the light on. Yours was in darkness, by the way?"

"I had the window shutter down, though. I'd been thinking how strange it is to see into other people's lives through a train window."

"I know," Alleyn said. "There's a touch of magic in it."

"And then—to see that! Not so magical."

"Never mind. I'll talk to the attendant and then I'll come back and get Ricky up. He'll be getting train-fever. We should reach Roqueville in about twenty minutes. All right?"

"Oh, I'm right as a bank," said Troy.

"Nothing like the Golden South for a carefree holiday," Alleyn said.
He grinned at her, went out into the corridor and opened the door of
his own sleeper.

Ricky was still sitting up in his bunk. His hands were clenched and
his eyes wide open. "You're being a pretty long time, however," he said.

"Mummy's coming in a minute. I'm just going to have a word with
the chap outside. Stick it out, old boy."

"O.K.," said Ricky.

The attendant, a pale man with a dimple in his chin, was dozing on
his stool at the forward end of the carriage. Alleyn, who had already
discovered that he spoke very little English, addressed him in diplomatic French that had become only slightly hesitant through disuse.
Had the attendant, he asked, happened to be awake when the train
paused outside a tunnel a few minutes ago? The man seemed to be
in some doubt as to whether Alleyn was about to complain because he
was asleep or because the train had halted. It took a minute or two
to clear up this difficulty and to discover that the attendant had, in point
of fact, been asleep for some time.

"I'm sorry to trouble you," Alleyn said, "but can you, by any chance,
tell me the name of the large building near the entrance to the
tunnel?"

"Ah, yes, yes," the attendant said. "Certainly, Monsieur, since I am a
native of these parts. It is known to everybody, this house, on account
of its great antiquity. It is the Château de la Chèvre d'Argent."

"I thought it might be," said Alleyn.

## II

Alleyn reminded the sleepy attendant that they were leaving the
train at Roqueville and tipped him generously. The man thanked him
with that peculiarly Gallic effusiveness that is at once too logical and
too adroit to be offensive.

"Do you know," Alleyn said, as if on an afterthought, "who lives in
the Château de la Chèvre d'Argent?"

The attendant believed it was leased to an extremely wealthy gentleman, possibly an American, possibly an Englishman, who entertained
very exclusively. He believed the ménage to be an excessively distinguished one.

Alleyn waited for a moment and then said, "I think there was a little
trouble there tonight. One saw a scene through a lighted window when
the train halted."

The attendant's shoulders suggested that all things are possible and that speculation is vain. His eyes were as blank as boot buttons in his pallid face. Should he not perhaps fetch the baggage of Monsieur and Madame and the little one, in readiness for their descent at Roqueville? He had his hand on the door of Alleyn's compartment when from somewhere towards the rear of the carriage, a woman screamed twice.

They were short screams, ejaculatory in character, as if they had been wrenched out of her, and very shrill. The attendant wagged his head from side to side in exasperation, begged Alleyn to excuse him and went off down the corridor to the rear-most compartment. He tapped. Alleyn guessed at an agitated response. The attendant went in and Troy put her head out of her own door.

"What now, for pity's sake?" she asked.

"Somebody having a nightmare or something. Are you ready?"

"Yes. But what a rum journey we're having!"

The attendant came back at a jog-trot. Was Alleyn perhaps a doctor? An English lady had been taken ill. She was in great pain: the abdomen, the attendant elaborated, clutching his own in pantomime. It was evidently a formidable seizure. If Monsieur, by any chance—

Alleyn said he was not a doctor. Troy said, "I'll go and see the poor thing, shall I? Perhaps there's a doctor somewhere in the train. You get Ricky up, darling."

She made off down the swaying corridor. The attendant began to tap on doors and to enquire fruitlessly of his passengers if they were doctors. "I shall see my comrades of the other *voitures*," he said importantly. "Evidently one must organize."

Alleyn found Ricky sketchily half-dressed and in a child's panic.

"Where have you been, however?" he demanded. "Because I didn't know where everyone was. We're going to be late for getting out. I can't find my pants. Where's Mummy?"

Alleyn calmed him, got him ready and packed their luggage. Ricky, white-faced, sat on the lower bunk with his gaze turned on the door. He liked, when travelling, to have his family under his eye. Alleyn, remembering his own childhood, knew his little son was racked with an illogical and bottomless anxiety, an anxiety that vanished when the door opened and Troy came in.

"Oh golly, Mum!" Ricky said and his lip trembled.

"Hullo, there," Troy said in the especially calm voice she kept for Ricky's panics. She sat down beside him, putting her arm where he could lean back against it, and looked at her husband.

"I think that woman's very ill," she said. "She looks frightful. She had what she thought was some kind of food poisoning this morning and dosed herself with castor-oil. And then, just now she had a violent pain, really awful, she says, in the appendix place and now she hasn't any pain at all and looks ghastly. Wouldn't that be a perforation, perhaps?"

"Your guess is as good as mine, my love."

"Rory, she's about fifty and she comes from the Bermudas and has no relations in the world and wears a string bag on her head and she's never been abroad and we can't just let her be whisked on into the Italian Riviera with a perforated appendix, if that's what it is."

"Oh, damn!"

"Well, can we? I said—" Troy went on, looking sideways at her husband—"that you'd come and talk to her."

"Darling, what the hell can I do?"

"You're calming in a panic, isn't he, Rick?"

"Yes," said Ricky, again turning white. "I don't suppose you're both going away, are you, Mummy?"

"You can come with us. You could look through the corridor window at the sea. It's shiny with moonlight and Daddy and I will be just on the other side of the poor thing's door. Her name's Miss Truebody and she knows Daddy's a policeman."

"Well, I must say . . ." Alleyn began indignantly.

"We'd better hurry, hadn't we?" Troy stood up, holding Ricky's hand. He clung to her like a limpet.

At the far end of the corridor their own car attendant stood with two of his colleagues outside Miss Truebody's door. They made dubious grimaces at one another and spoke in voices that were drowned by the racket of the train. When they saw Troy, they all took off their silver-braided caps and bowed to her. A doctor, they said, had been discovered in the *troisième voiture* and was now with the unfortunate lady. Perhaps Madame would join him. Their own attendant tapped on the door and with an ineffable smirk at Troy, opened it. "Madame!" he invited.

Troy went in, and Ricky feverishly transferred his hold to Alleyn's hand. Together, they looked out of the corridor window.

The railway, in this part of the coast, followed an embankment a few feet above sea level and as Troy had said, the moon shone on the Mediterranean. A long cape ran out over the glossy water and near its tip a few points of yellow light showed in early-rising households. The stars were beginning to pale.

"That's Cap St. Gilles," Alleyn said. "Lovely, isn't it, Rick?"

Ricky nodded. He had one ear tuned to his mother's voice which could just be heard beyond Miss Truebody's door.

"Yes," he said, "it is lovely." Alleyn wondered if Ricky was really as pedantically mannered a child as some of their friends seemed to think.

"Aren't we getting a bit near?" Ricky asked. "Bettern't Mummy come now?"

"It's all right. We've ten minutes yet and the train people know we're getting off. I promise it's all right. Here's Mummy now."

She came out followed by a small bald gentleman with waxed moustaches, wearing striped professional trousers, patent-leather boots and a frogged dressing-gown.

"Your French is badly needed. This is the doctor," Troy said, and haltingly introduced her husband.

The doctor was formally enchanted. He said crisply that he had examined the patient, who almost certainly suffered from a perforated appendix and should undoubtedly be operated upon as soon as possible. He regretted extremely that he himself had an urgent professional appointment in St. Céleste and could not, therefore, accept responsibility. Perhaps the best thing to do would be to discharge Miss Truebody at Roqueville and send her back by the evening train to St. Christophe where she could go to a hospital. Of course, if there was a surgeon in Roqueville the operation might be performed there. In any case he would give Miss Truebody an injection of morphine. His shoulders rose. It was a position of extreme difficulty. They must hope, must they not, that there would be a medical man and suitable accommodation available at Roqueville? He believed he had understood Madame to say that she and Monsieur l'Inspecteur-en-Chef would be good enough to assist their compatriot.

Monsieur l'Inspecteur-en-Chef glared at his wife and said they would, of course, be enchanted. Troy said in English that it had obviously comforted Miss Truebody and impressed the doctor to learn of her husband's rank. The doctor bowed, delivered a few definitive compliments and, lurching in a still dignified manner down the swinging corridor, made for his own carriage, followed by his own attendant.

Troy said: "Come and speak to her, Rory. It'll help."

"Daddy?" Ricky said in a small voice.

"We won't be a minute," Troy and Alleyn answered together, and Alleyn added, "We know how it feels, Rick, but one has to get used to these things." Ricky nodded and swallowed.

Alleyn followed Troy into Miss Truebody's compartment. "This is my husband, Miss Truebody," Troy said. "He's had a word with the doctor and he'll tell you all about it."

Miss Truebody lay on her back with her knees a little drawn up and her sick hands closed vise-like over the sheet. She had a rather blunt face that in health probably was rosy, but now was ominously blotched and looked as if it had shrunk away from her nose. This effect was heightened by the circumstance of her having removed her teeth. There were beads of sweat along the margin of her grey hair and her upper lip and the ridges where her eyebrows would have been if she had possessed any; the face was singularly smooth and showed none of the minor blemishes characteristic of her age. Over her head, she wore, as Troy had noticed, a sort of net bag made of pink string. She looked terrified. Something in her eyes reminded Alleyn of Ricky in one of his travel-panics.

He told her, as reassuringly as might be, of the doctor's pronouncement. Her expression did not change and he wondered if she had understood him. When he had finished she gave a little gasp and whispered indistinctly: "Too awkward, so inconvenient. Disappointing." And her mottled hands clutched at the sheet.

"Don't worry," Alleyn said, "don't worry about anything. We'll look after you."

Like a sick animal, she gave him a heart-rending look of gratitude and shut her eyes. For a moment Troy and Alleyn watched her being slightly but inexorably jolted by the train, and then stole uneasily from the compartment. They found their son dithering with agitation in the corridor and the attendant bringing out the last of their luggage.

Troy said hurriedly: "This is frightful. We can't take the responsibility. Or must we?"

"I'm afraid we must. There's no time to do anything else. I've got a card of sorts up my sleeve in Roqueville. If it's no good we'll get her back to St. Christophe."

"What's your card? Not," Troy ejaculated, "Mr. Garbel?"

"No, no, it's—hi—look! We're there."

The little town of Roqueville, wan in the first thin wash of dawn-light, slid past the windows, and the train drew into the station.

Fortified by a further tip from Troy and in evident relief at the prospect of losing Miss Truebody, the attendant enthusiastically piled the Alleyns' luggage on the platform while the guard plunged into earnest conversation with Alleyn and the Roqueville station-master. The doctor reappeared fully clad and gave Miss Truebody a shot of morphine. He and Troy, in incredible association, got her into a magenta dressing-gown in which she looked like death itself. Troy hurriedly packed Miss Truebody's possessions, uttered a few words of encouragement, and with Ricky and the doctor joined Alleyn on the platform.

Ricky, his parents once deposited on firm ground and fully accessible, forgot his terrors and contemplated the train with the hard-boiled air of an experienced traveller.

The station-master with the guard and three attendants in support was saying to the doctor: "One is perfectly conscious, Monsieur le Docteur, of the extraordinary circumstances. Nevertheless, the schedule of the Chemin de Fer des Alpes Maritimes cannot be indefinitely protracted."

The doctor said: "One may, however, in the few moments that are being squandered in this unproductive conversation, M. le Chef de Gare, consult the telephone directory and ascertain if there is a doctor in Roqueville."

"One may do so undoubtedly, but I can assure M. le Docteur that such a search will de fruitless. Our only doctor is at a conference in St. Christophe. Therefore, since the train is already delayed one minute and forty seconds . . ."

He glanced superbly at the guard, who began to survey the train like a sergeant-major. A whistle was produced. The attendants walked towards their several cars.

"Rory!" Troy cried out. "We can't . . ."

Alleyn said: "All right," and spoke to the station-master. "Perhaps," he said, "M. le Chef de Gare, you are aware of the presence of a surgeon—I believe his name is Dr. Baradi—among the guests of M. Oberon some twenty kilometres back at the Château de la Chèvre d'Argent. He is an Egyptian gentleman. I understand he arrived two weeks ago."

"*Alors*, M. l'Inspecteur-en-Chef . . ." the doctor began but the station-master, after a sharp glance at Alleyn, became alert and neatly deferential. He remembered the arrival of the Egyptian gentleman for whom he had caused a taxi to be produced. If the gentleman should be —he bowed—as M. l'Inspecteur-en-Chef evidently was informed, a surgeon, all their problems were solved, were they not? He began to order the sleeping-car attendants about and was briskly supported by the guard. Troy, to the renewed agitation of her son, and with the assistance of their attendant, returned to the sleeping-car and supported Miss Truebody out of it, down to the platform and into the waiting-room, where she was laid out, horribly corpse-like, on a bench. Her luggage followed. Troy, on an afterthought, darted back and retrieved from a tumbler in the washing cabinet, Miss Truebody's false teeth, dropping them with a shudder into a tartan spongebag. On the platform the doctor held a private conversation with Alleyn. He wrote in his notebook, tore out the page and gave it to Alleyn with his card. Alleyn, in the interests of Franco-British relationships, insisted on paying the doctor's fee and the train finally drew out of Roqueville in an atmosphere of the liveliest cordiality. On the strangely quiet platform Alleyn and Troy looked at each other.

"This," Alleyn said, "is not your holiday as I had planned it."

"What do we do now?"

"Ring up the Chèvre d'Argent and ask for Dr. Baradi, who, I have reason to suppose, is an admirable surgeon and an unmitigated blackguard."

They could hear the dawn cocks crowing in the hills above Roqueville.

### III

In the waiting-room Ricky fell fast asleep on his mother's lap. Troy was glad of this as Miss Truebody had begun to look quite dreadful. She too had drifted into a kind of sleep. She breathed unevenly, puffing out her unsupported lips, and made unearthly noises in her throat. Troy could hear her husband and the station-master talking in the office next door and then Alleyn's voice only, speaking on the telephone and in French! There were longish pauses during which Alleyn said: "'Allo! 'Allo!" and "Ne coupez pas, je vous en prie, mademoiselle," which Troy felt rather proud of understanding. A grey light filtered into the waiting-room; Ricky made a touching little sound, rearranged his lips, sighed, and turned his face against her breast in an abandonment of relaxation. Alleyn began to speak at length, first in French, and then in English. Troy heard fragments of sentences.

". . . I wouldn't have roused you up like this if it hadn't been so urgent. . . . Dr. Claudel said definitely that it was really a matter of the most extreme urgency. . . . He will telephone from St. Céleste. I am merely a fellow-passenger . . . yes, yes, I have a car here. . . . Good. . . . Very well. . . . Yes, I understand. Thank you." A bell tinkled.

There was a further conversation and then Alleyn came into the waiting-room. Troy, with her chin on the top of Ricky's silken head, gave him a nod and an intimate family look: her comment on Ricky's sleep. He said: "It's not fair."

"What?"

"Your talent for turning my heart over."

"I thought," Troy said, "you meant about our holiday. What's happened?"

"Baradi says he'll operate if it's necessary." Alleyn looked at Miss Truebody. "Asleep?"

"Yes. So, what are we to do?"

"We've got a car. The Sûreté rang up the local commissioner yesterday and told him I was on my way. He's actually one of their experts

who's been sent down here on a special job, superseding the local chap
for the time being. He's turned on an elderly Mercedes and a driver.
Damn civil of him. I've just been talking to him. Full of apologies for
not coming down himself but he thought, very wisely, that we'd better
not be seen together. He says our chauffeur is a reliable chap with an
admirable record. He and the car are on tap outside the station now
and our luggage will be collected by the hotel waggon. Baradi suggests
I take Miss Truebody straight to the Chèvre d'Argent. While we're on
the way he will make what preparations he can. Luckily he's got his instruments, and Claudel has given me some pipkins of anaesthetic.
Baradi asked if I could give the anaesthetic."

"Can you?"

"I did once, in a ship. As long as nothing goes very wrong, it's fairly
simple. If Baradi thinks it is safe to wait he'll try to get an anaesthetist
from Douceville or somewhere. But it seems there's some sort of doctor's
jamboree on today at St. Christophe and they've all cleared off to it. It's
only ten kilometres from here to the Chèvre d'Argent by the inland
road. I'll drop you and Ricky at the hotel here, darling, and take Miss
Truebody on."

"Are there any women in the house?"

"I don't know." Alleyn stopped short and then said: "Yes. Yes, I do.
There are women."

Troy watched him for a moment and then said: "All right. Let's get
her aboard. You take Ricky."

Alleyn lifted him from her lap and she went to Miss Truebody.
"She's tiny," Troy said under her breath. "Could she be carried?"

"I think so. Wait a moment."

He took Ricky out and was back in a few seconds with the station-
master and a man wearing a chauffeur's cap over a mop of glossy curls.

He was a handsome little fellow with an air of readiness. He saluted
Troy gallantly, taking off his peaked cap and smiling at her. Then he
saw Miss Truebody and made a clucking sound. Troy had put a travelling rug on the bench and they made a sort of stretcher of it and
carried Miss Truebody out to a large car in the station yard. Ricky was
curled up on the front seat. They managed to fit Miss Truebody into
the back one. The driver pulled down a tip-up seat and Troy sat on
that. Miss Truebody had opened her eyes. She said in a quiet, clear
voice: "Too kind," and Troy took her hand. Alleyn, in the front, held
Ricky on his lap and they started off up a steep little street through
Roqueville. The thin dawnlight gave promise of a glaring day. It was
already very warm.

"To the Hôtel Royal, Monsieur?" asked the driver.

"No," said Troy with Miss Truebody's little claw clutching at her fingers. "No, please, Rory. I'll come with her. Ricky won't wake for hours. We can wait in the car or he can drive us back. I might be some use."

"To the Château de la Chèvre d'Argent," Alleyn said, "and gently."

"Perfectly, Monsieur," said the driver. "Always, always gently."

Roqueville was a very small town. It climbed briefly up the hill and petered out in a string of bleached villas. The road mounted between groves of olive trees and the air was like a benison, soft and clean. The sea extended itself beneath them and enriched itself with a blueness of incredible intensity.

Alleyn turned to look at Troy. They were quite close to each other and spoke over their shoulders like people in a Victorian "Conversation" chair. It was clear that Miss Truebody, even if she could hear them, was not able to concentrate or indeed to listen. "Dr. Claudel," Alleyn said, "thought it was the least risky thing to do. I half expected Baradi would refuse, but he was surprisingly co-operative. He's supposed to be a good man at his job." He made a movement of his head to indicate the driver. "This chap doesn't speak English," he said. "And, by the way, darling, no more chat about my being a policeman."

Troy said: "Have I been a nuisance?"

"It's all right. I asked Claudel to forget it and I don't suppose Miss Truebody will say anything or that anybody will pay much attention if she does. It's just that I don't want to brandish my job at the Chèvre d'Argent." He turned and looked into her troubled face. "Never mind, my darling. We'll buy false beards and hammers in Roqueville and let on we're archeologists. Or load ourselves down with your painting-gear." He paused for a moment. "That, by the way, is not a bad idea at all. Distinguished painter visits Côte d'Azur with obscure husband and child. We'll keep it in reserve."

"But honestly, Rory. How's this débâcle going to affect your job at the Chèvre d'Argent?"

"In a way it's useful entrée. The Sûreté suggested that I call there representing myself either to be an antiquarian captivated by the place itself—it's an old Saracen stronghold—or else I was to be a seeker after esoteric knowledge and offer myself as a disciple. If both failed I could use my own judgment about being a heroin addict in search of fuel. Thanks to Miss Truebody, however, I shall turn up as a reluctant Good Samaritan. All the same," Alleyn said, rubbing his nose, "I wish Dr. Claudel could have risked taking her on to St. Céleste or else waiting for the evening train back to St. Christophe. I don't much like this party, and that's a fact. This'll larn the Alleyn family to try combining business with pleasure, won't it?"

"Ah, well," said Troy, looking compassionately at Miss Truebody, "we're doing our blasted best and no fool can do more."

They were silent for some time. The driver sang to himself in a light tenor voice. The road climbed the Maritime Alps into early sunlight. They traversed a tilted landscape compounded of earth and heat, of opaque clay colours—ochres and pinks—splashed with magenta, tempered with olive-grey and severed horizontally at its base by the ultramarine blade of the Mediterranean. They turned inland. Villages emerged as logical growths out of rock and earth. A monastery safely folded among protective hills spoke of some tranquil adjustment of man's spirit to the quiet rhythm of soil and sky.

"It's impossible," Troy said, "to think that anything could go very much amiss in these hills."

A distant valley came into view. Far up it, a strange anachronism in that landscape, was a long modern building with glittering roofs and a great display of plate glass.

"The factory," the driver told them, "of the Compagnie Chimique des Alpes Maritimes."

Alleyn made a little affirmative sound as if he saw something that he had expected and for as long as it remained in sight he looked at the glittering building.

They drove on in silence. Miss Truebody turned her head from side to side and Troy bent over her. "Hot," she whispered, "such an oppressive climate. Oh, dear!"

"One approaches the objective," the driver announced, and changed gears. The road tipped downwards and turned the flank of a hill. They had crossed the headland and were high above the sea again. Immediately below them the railroad emerged from a tunnel. On their right was a cliff that mounted into a stone face pierced irregularly with windows. This in its turn broke against the skyline into fabulous turrets and parapets. Troy gave a sharp ejaculation. "Oh, *no!*" she said. "It's not that! No, it's too much!"

"Well, darling," Alleyn said, "I'm afraid that's what it is."

"La Chèvre d'Argent," said the driver, and turned up a steep and exceedingly narrow way that ended in a walled platform from which one looked down at the railway and beyond it sheer down again to the sea. "Here one stops, Monsieur," said the driver. "That is the entrance."

He pointed to a dark passage between two masses of rock from which walls emerged as if by some process of evolution. He got out and opened the doors of the car. "It appears," he said, "that Mademoiselle is unable to walk."

"Yes," Alleyn said. "I shall go and fetch the doctor. Madame will remain with Mademoiselle and the little boy." He settled the sleeping Ricky into the front seat and got out. "You stay here, Troy," he said. "I shan't be long."

"Rory, we shouldn't have brought her to this place."

"There was no alternative that we could honestly take."

"Look!" said Troy.

A man in white was coming through the passage. He wore a Panama hat. His hands and face were so much the colour of the shadows that he looked like a white suit walking of its own accord towards them. He moved out into the sunlight and they saw that he was olive-coloured with a large nose, full lips and a black moustache. He wore dark glasses. The white suit was made of sharkskin and beautifully cut. His sandals were white suède. His shirt was pink and his tie green. When he saw Troy he took off his hat and the corrugations of his oiled hair shone in the sunlight.

"Dr. Baradi?" Alleyn said.

Dr. Baradi smiled brilliantly, swept off his Panama hat and held out a long dark hand. "So you bring my patient?" he said. "Mr. Allen, is it not?" He turned to Troy. "My wife," Alleyn said, and saw Troy's hand lifted to the full lips. "Here is your patient," he added. "Miss Truebody."

"Ah, yes." Dr. Baradi went to the car and bent over Miss Truebody. Troy, rather pink in the face, moved to the other side. "Miss Truebody," she said, "here is the doctor."

Miss Truebody opened her eyes, looked into the dark face and cried out: "Oh! No! No!"

Dr. Baradi smiled at her. "You must not trouble yourself about anything," they heard him say. He had a padded voice. "We are going to make everything much more comfortable for you, isn't it? You must not be frightened of my dark face. I assure you I am quite a good doctor."

Miss Truebody said: "Please excuse me. Not at all. Thank you."

"Now, without moving you, if I may just—that will do very nicely. You must tell me if I hurt you." A pause. Cicadas had broken out in a chittering so high-pitched that it shrilled almost above the limit of human hearing. The driver moved away tactfully. Miss Truebody moaned a little. Dr. Baradi straightened up, walked to the edge of the platform, and waited there for Troy and Alleyn. "It is a perforated appendix undoubtedly," he said. "She is very ill. I should tell you that I am the guest of Mr. Oberon, who places a room at our disposal. We

have an improvised stretcher in readiness." He turned towards the passage-way: "And here it comes!" he said, looking at Troy with an air of
joyousness which she felt to be entirely out of place.

Two men walked out of the shadowed way onto the platform carrying between them a gaily striped object, evidently part of a garden seat.
Both the men wore aprons. "The gardener," Dr. Baradi explained,
"and one of the indoor servants, strong fellows both and accustomed to
the exigencies of our entrance. She has been given morphine, I think."

"Yes," Alleyn said. "Dr. Claudel gave it. He has sent you an adequate amount of something called, I think, Pentothal. He was taking a
supply of it to a brother-medico, an anaesthetist, in St. Céleste and said
that you would probably need some and that the local chemist would
not be likely to have it."

"I am obliged to him. I have already telephoned to the pharmacist in
Roqueville who can supply ether. Fortunately he lives above his establishment. He is sending it up here by car. It is fortunate also that I
have my instruments with me." He beamed and glittered at Troy.
"And now, I think . . ."

He spoke in French to the two men, directing them to stand near the
car. For the first time apparently he noticed the sleeping Ricky and
leaned over the door to look at him.

"Enchanting," he murmured, and his teeth flashed at Troy. "Our
household is also still asleep," he said, "but I have Mr. Oberon's
warmest invitation that you, Madame, and the small one join us for
*petit déjeuner*. As you know, your husband is to assist me. There will
be a little delay before we are ready and coffee is prepared."

He stood over Troy. He was really extremely large: his size and his
padded voice and his smell, which was compounded of hair-lotion,
scent and something that reminded her of the impure land-breeze from
an eastern port, all flowed over her.

She moved back and said quickly: "It's very nice of you, but I think
Ricky and I must find our hotel."

Alleyn said: "Thank you so much, Dr. Baradi. It's extremely kind of
Mr. Oberon and I hope I shall have a chance to thank him for all of
us. What with one thing and another, we've had an exhausting journey
and I think my wife and Ricky are in rather desperate need of a bath
and a rest. The man will drive them down to the hotel and come back
for me."

Dr. Baradi bowed, took off his hat, and would have possibly kissed
Troy's hand again if Alleyn had not somehow been in the way.

"In that case," Dr. Baradi said, "we must not insist."

He opened the door of the car. "And now, dear lady," he said to

Miss Truebody, "we make a little journey, isn't it? Don't move. There is no need."

With great dexterity and no apparent expenditure of energy, he lifted her from the car and laid her on the improvised stretcher. The sun beat down on her glistening face. Her eyes were open, her lips drawn back a little from her gums. She said: "But where is—? You're not taking me away from—? I don't know her name."

Troy went to her. "Here I am, Miss Truebody," she said. "I'll come and see you quite soon. I promise."

"But I don't know where I'm going. It's so unsuitable. . . . Unseemly really. . . . Somehow with another lady . . . English . . . I don't know what they'll do to me. . . . I'm afraid I'm nervous. . . . I had hoped . . ."

Her jaw trembled. She made a thin shrill sound, shocking in its nakedness. "No," she stammered, "no . . . no . . . no." Her arm shot out and her hand closed on Troy's skirt. The two bearers staggered a little and looked agitatedly at Dr. Baradi.

"She should not be upset," he murmured to Troy. "It is most undesirable. Perhaps, for a little while, you'll be so kind . . ."

"But of course," Troy said, and in answer to a look from her husband, "of course, Rory, I must."

And she bent over Miss Truebody and told her she wouldn't go away. She felt as though she herself was trapped in the kind of dream that, without being a positive nightmare, threatens to become one. Baradi released Miss Truebody's hand and as he did so, his own brushed against Troy's skirt.

"You're so kind," he said. "Perhaps Mr. Allen will bring the little boy. It is not well for such tender ones to sleep overlong in the sun on the Côte d'Azur."

Without a word Alleyn lifted Ricky out of the car. Ricky made a small questioning sound, stirred, and slept again.

The men walked off with the stretcher, Dr. Baradi followed them. Troy, Alleyn and Ricky brought up the rear.

In this order the odd little procession moved out of the glare into the shadowed passage that was the entrance to the Château de la Chèvre d'Argent.

The driver watched them go, his lips pursed in a soundless whistle and an expression of concern darkening his eyes. Then he drove the car into the shade of the hill and composed himself for a long wait.

# CHAPTER II

# Operation Truebody

## I

AT FIRST their eyes were sun-dazzled so that they could scarcely see their way. Dr. Baradi paused to guide them. Alleyn, encumbered with Ricky and groping up a number of wide, shallow and irregular steps, was aware of Baradi's hand piloting Troy by the elbow. The blotches of non-existent light that danced across their vision faded and they saw that they were in a sort of hewn passage-way between walls that were incorporated in rock, separated by outcrops of stone and pierced by stairways, windows and occasional doors. At intervals they went through double archways supporting buildings that straddled the passage and darkened it. They passed an open doorway and saw into a cave-like room where an old woman sat among shelves filled with small gaily painted figures. As Troy passed, the woman smiled at her and gestured invitingly, holding up a little clay goat.

Dr. Baradi was telling them about the Chèvre d'Argent.

"It is a fortress built originally by the Saracens. One might almost say it was sculptured out of the mountain, isn't it? The Normans stormed it on several occasions. There are legends of atrocities and so on. The fortress is, in effect, a village since the many caves beneath and around it have been shaped into dwellings and house a number of peas-

ants, some dependent on the château and some, like the woman you
have noticed, upon their own industry. The château itself is most interesting, indeed unique. But not inconvenient. Mr. Oberon has, with
perfect tact, introduced the amenities. We are civilized, as you shall
see."

They arrived at a double gate of wrought iron let into the wall on
their left. An iron bell hung beside it. A butler appeared beyond the
doors and opened them. They passed through a courtyard into a wide
hall with deep-set windows through which a cool ineffectual light was
admitted.

Without at first taking any details of this shadowed interior, Troy received an impression of that particular kind of suavity that is associated
with costliness. The rug under her feet, the texture and colour of the
curtains, the shape of cabinets and chairs and, above all, a smell which
she thought must arise from the burning sweet-scented oils, all united
to give this immediate reaction. "Mr. Oberon," she thought, "must be
immensely rich." Almost at the same time she saw above the great fireplace a famous Brueghel which, she remembered, had been sold privately some years ago. It was called: "Consultation of Sorceresses." An
open door showed a stone stairway built inside the thickness of the
wall.

"The stairs," Dr. Baradi said, "are a little difficult. Therefore we
have prepared rooms on this floor."

He pulled back a leather curtain. The men carried Miss Truebody
into a heavily carpeted stone passage hung at intervals with rugs and lit
with electric lights fitted into ancient hanging lamps, witnesses, Troy
supposed, of Mr. Oberon's tact in modernization. She heard Miss
Truebody raise her piping cry of distress.

Dr. Baradi said: "Perhaps you would be so kind as to assist her into
bed?"

Troy hurried after the stretcher and followed it into a small bedroom
charmingly furnished and provided, she noticed, with an adjoining
bathroom. The two bearers waited with an obliging air for further instructions. As Baradi had not accompanied them, Troy supposed that
she herself was for the moment in command. She got Miss Truebody
off the stretcher and onto the bed. The bearers hovered solicitously. She
thanked them in her school-girl French and managed to get them out
of the room, but not before they had persuaded her into the passage,
opened a further door, and exhibited with evident pride a bare freshly
scrubbed room with a bare freshly scrubbed table near its window. A
woman rose from her knees as the door opened, a scrubbing brush in
her hand and a pail beside her. The room reeked of disinfectant. The

indoor servant said something about it being *"convenable,"* and the gardener said something about somebody, she thought himself, being
*"bien fatigué, infiniment fatigué."* It dawned upon her that they
wanted a tip. Poor Troy scuffled in her bag, produced a 500 franc note
and gave it to the indoor servant, indicating that they were to share it.
They thanked her and, effulgent with smiles, went back to get the luggage. She hurried to Miss Truebody and found her crying feverishly.

Remembering what she could of hospital routine, Troy washed the
patient, found a clean nightdress (Miss Truebody wore white locknit
nightdresses, sprigged with posies), and got her into bed. It was difficult
to make out how much she understood of her situation. Troy wondered
if it was the injection of morphine or her condition or her normal habit
of mind or all three, that made her so confused and vague. When she
settled in bed she began to talk with hectic fluency about herself. It was
difficult to understand her as she had frantically waved away the offer
of her false teeth. Her father, it seemed, had been a doctor, a widower,
living in the Bermudas. She was his only child and had spent her life
with him until, a year ago, he had died, leaving her, as she put it, quite
comfortably though not well off. She had decided that she could just
afford a trip to England and the continent. Her father, she muttered
distractedly, had "not kept up," had "lost touch." There had been an
unhappy break in the past, she believed, and their relations were never
mentioned. Of course there were friends in the Bermudas but not, it
appeared, very many or very intimate friends. She rambled on for a
little while, continually losing the thread of her narrative and frowning
incomprehensibly at nothing. The pupils of her eyes were contracted
and her vision seemed to be confused. Presently her voice died away
and she dozed uneasily.

Troy stole out and returned to the hall. Alleyn, Ricky and Baradi
had gone, but the butler was waiting for her and showed her up the
steep flight of stairs in the wall. It seemed to turn about a tower and
they passed two landings with doors leading off them. Finally the man
opened a larger and heavier door and Troy was out in the glare of full
morning on a canopied roof-garden hung, as it seemed, in blue space
where sky and sea met in a wide crescent. Not till she advanced some
way towards the balustrade did Cap St. Gilles appear, a sliver of earth
pointing south.

Alleyn and Baradi rose from a breakfast-table near the balustrade.
Ricky lay, fast asleep, on a suspended seat under a gay canopy. The
smell of freshly ground coffee and of *brioches* and *croissants* reminded
Troy that she was hungry.

They sat at the table. It was long, spread with a white cloth and set for a number of places. Troy was foolishly reminded of the Mad Hatter's Tea-party. She looked over the parapet and saw the railroad about eighty feet below her and perhaps a hundred feet from the base of the Chèvre d'Argent. The walls, buttressed and pierced with windows, fell away beneath her in a sickening perspective. Troy had a hatred of heights and drew back quickly. "Last night," she thought, "I looked into one of those windows."

Dr. Baradi was assiduous in his attentions and plied her with coffee. He gazed upon her remorselessly and she sensed Alleyn's annoyance rising with her own embarrassment. For a moment she felt weakly inclined to giggle.

Alleyn said: "See here, darling, Dr. Baradi thinks that Miss Truebody is extremely ill, dangerously so. He thinks we should let her people know at once."

"She has no people. She's only got acquaintances in the Bermudas; I asked. There seems to be nobody at all."

Baradi said: "In that case . . ." and moved his head from side to side. He turned to Troy and parodied helplessness with his hands. "So, in that direction, we can do nothing."

"The next thing," Alleyn said, speaking directly to his wife, "is the business of giving an anaesthetic. We could telephone to a hospital in St. Christophe and try to get someone, but there's this medical jamboree and in any case it'll mean a delay of some hours. Or Dr. Baradi can try to get his own anaesthetist to fly from Paris to the nearest airport. More delay and considerable expense. The other way is for me to have a shot at it. Should we take the risk?"

"What," Troy asked, making herself look at him, "do you think, Dr. Baradi?"

He sat near and a little behind her on the balustrade. His thighs bulged in their sharkskin trousers. "I think it will be less risky if your husband, who is not unfamiliar with the procedure, gives the anaesthetic. Her condition is not good."

His voice flowed over her shoulder. It was really extraordinary, she thought, how he could invest information about peritonitis and ruptured abscesses with such a gross suggestion of flattery. He might have been paying her the most objectionable compliments imaginable.

"Very well," Alleyn said, "that's decided, then. But you'll need other help, won't you?"

"If possible, two persons. And here we encounter a difficulty." He moved round behind Troy but spoke to Alleyn. His manner was now authoritative. "I doubt," he said, "if there is anyone in the house-party who could assist me. It is not every layman who enjoys a visit to an op-

erating theatre. Surgery is not everybody's cup of tea." The collo-
quialism came oddly from him. "I have spoken to our host, of course.
He is not yet stirring. He offers every possible assistance and all the
amenities of the château with the reservation that he himself shall not
be asked to perform an active part. He is," said Baradi—putting on
his sun-glasses—"allergic to blood."

"Indeed," said Alleyn politely.

"The rest of our household—we are seven—" Dr. Baradi explained
playfully to Troy, "is not yet awake. Mr. Oberon gave a party here last
night. Some friends with a yacht in port. We were immeasurably gay
and kept going till five o'clock. Mr. Oberon has a genius for parties and
a passion for charades. They were quite wonderful, our charades." Troy
was about to give a little ejaculation, which she immediately checked.
He beamed at her. "I was cast for one of King Solomon's concubines.
And we had the Queen of Sheba, you know. She stabbed Solomon's
favourite wife. It was all a little strenuous. I don't think any of my
friends will be in good enough form to help us. Indeed, I doubt if any
of them, even at the top of his or her form, would care to offer for
the role. I don't know if you have met any of them. Grizel Locke, perhaps? The Honourable Grizel Locke?"

The Alleyns said they did not know Miss Locke.

"What about the servants?" Alleyn suggested. Troy was all too easily
envisaging Dr. Baradi as one of King Solomon's concubines.

"One of the men is a possibility. He is my personal attendant and
valet and is not quite unfamiliar with surgical routine. He will not lose
his head. Any of the others would almost certainly be worse than useless. So we need one other, you see."

A silence fell upon them, broken at last by Troy.

"I know," she said, "what Dr. Baradi is going to suggest." Alleyn
looked fixedly at her and raised his left eyebrow.

"It's quite out of the question. You well know that you're punctually
sick at the sight of blood, my darling."

Troy, who was nothing of the sort, said: "In that case I've no suggestions. Unless you'd like to appeal to cousin Garbel."

There was a moment of silence.

"To whom?" said Baradi softly.

"I'm afraid I was being facetious," Troy mumbled.

Alleyn said: "What about our driver? He seems a hardy, intelligent
sort of chap. What would he have to do?"

"Fetch and carry," Dr. Baradi said. He was looking thoughtfully at
Troy. "Count sponges. Hand instruments. Clean up. Possibly, in an
emergency, play a minor role as unqualified assistant."

"I'll speak to him. If he seems at all possible I'll bring him in to see you. Would you like to stroll back to the car with me, darling?"

"Please don't disturb yourselves," Dr. Baradi begged them. "One of the servants will fetch your man."

Troy knew that her husband was in two minds about this suggestion and also about leaving her to cope with Dr. Baradi. She said: "You go, Rory, will you? I'm longing for my sun-glasses and they're locked away in my dressing-case."

She gave him her keys and a ferocious smile. "I think, perhaps, I'll have a look at Miss Truebody," she added.

He grimaced at her and walked out quickly.

Troy went to Ricky. She touched his forehead and found it moist. His sleep was profound and when she opened the front of his shirt he did not stir. She stayed, lightly swinging the seat, and watched him, and she thought with tenderness that he was her defense in a stupid situation which fatigue and a confusion of spirit, brought about by many untoward events, had perhaps created in her imagination. It was ridiculous, she thought, to feel anything but amused by her embarrassment. She knew that Baradi watched her and she turned and faced him.

"If there is anything I can do before I go," she said and kept her voice down because of Ricky, "I hope you'll tell me."

It was a mistake to speak softly. He at once moved towards her and, with an assumption of intimacy, lowered his own voice. "But how helpful!" he said. "So we shall have you with us for a little longer? That is good: though it should not be to perform these unlovely tasks."

"I hope I'm equal to them." She moved away from Ricky and raised her voice. "What are they?"

"She must be prepared for the operation."

He told her what should be done and explained that she would find everything she needed for her purpose in Miss Truebody's bathroom. In giving these specifically clinical instructions, he reverted to his professional manner, but with an air of amusement that she found distasteful. When he had finished she said: "Then I'll get her fixed up now, shall I?"

"Yes," he agreed, more to himself than to her. "Yes, certainly, we shouldn't delay too long." And seeing a look of preoccupation and responsibility on his face, she left him, disliking him less in that one moment than at any time since they had met. As she went down the stone stairway she thought: "Thank heaven, at least, for the Queen of Sheba."

*II*

Alleyn found their driver in his vest and trousers on the running-board of the car. A medallion of St. Christopher dangled from a steel chain above the mat of hair on his chest. He was exchanging improper jokes with a young woman and two small boys, who, when he rose to salute his employer, drifted away without embarrassment. He gave Alleyn a look that implied a common understanding of women, and opened the car door.

Alleyn said: "We're not going yet. What is your name?"

"Raoul, Monsieur. Raoul Milano."

"You've been a soldier, perhaps?"

"Yes, Monsieur. I am thirty-three and therefore I have seen some service."

"So your stomach is not easily outraged, then; by a show of blood, for instance? By a formidable wound, shall we say?"

"I was a medical orderly, Monsieur. My stomach also is an old campaigner."

"Excellent! I have a job for you, Raoul. It is to assist Dr. Baradi, the gentleman you have already seen. He is about to remove Mademoiselle's appendix and since we cannot find a second doctor, we must provide unqualified assistants. If you will help us there may be a little reward and certainly there will be much grace in performing this service. What do you say?"

Raoul looked down at his blunt hands and then up at Alleyn:

"I say yes, M'sieur. As you suggested, it is an act of grace and in any case one may as well do something."

"Good. Come along, then." Alleyn had found Troy's sun-glasses. He and Raoul turned towards the passage, Raoul slinging his coat across his shoulders with the grace of a ballet dancer.

"So you live down in Roqueville?" Alleyn asked.

"In Roqueville, M'sieur. My parents have a little café, not at all smart, but the food is good and I also hire myself out in my car, as you see."

"You've been up to the château before, of course?"

"Certainly. For little expeditions and also to drive guests and sometimes tourists. As a rule Mr. Oberon sends a car for his guests." He waved a hand at a row of garage-doors, incongruously set in a rocky face at the back of the platform. "His cars are magnificent."

Alleyn said: "The Commissaire at the Préfecture sent you to meet us, I think?"

"That is so, M'sieur."

"Did he give you my name?"

"Yes, M'sieur l'Inspecteur-en-Chef. It is Ahrr-lin. But he said that M'sieur l'Inspecteur-en-Chef would prefer, perhaps, that I did not use his rank."

"I would greatly prefer it, Raoul."

"It is already forgotten, M'sieur."

"Again, good."

They passed the cave-like room, where the woman sat among her figurines. Raoul hailed her in a cheerful manner and she returned his greeting. "You must bring your gentleman in to see my statues," she shouted. He called back over his shoulder: "All in good time, Marie," and added, "She is an artist, that one. Her saints are pretty and of assistance in one's devotions; but then she overcharges ridiculously, which is not so amusing."

He sang a stylish little cadence and tilted up his head. They were walking beneath a part of the Château de la Chèvre d'Argent that straddled the passage-way. "It goes everywhere, this house," he remarked. "One would need a map to find one's way from the kitchen to the best bedroom. Anything might happen."

When they reached the entrance he stood aside and took off his chauffeur's cap. They found Dr. Baradi in the hall. Alleyn told him that Raoul had been a medical orderly and Baradi at once described the duties he would be expected to perform. His manner was cold and uncompromising. Raoul gave him his full attention. He stood easily, his thumbs crooked in his belt. He retained at once his courtesy, his natural grace of posture, and his air of independence.

"Well," Baradi said sharply when he had finished: "Are you capable of this work?"

"I believe so, M'sieur le Docteur."

"If you prove to be satisfactory, you will be given 500 francs. That is extremely generous payment for unskilled work."

"As to payment, M'sieur le Docteur," Raoul said, "I am already employed by this gentleman and consider myself entirely at his disposal. It is at his request that I engage myself in this task."

Baradi raised his eyebrows and looked at Alleyn. "Evidently an original," he said in English. "He seems tolerably intelligent but one never knows. Let us hope that he is at least not too stupid. My man will give him suitable clothes and see that he is clean."

He went to the fireplace and pulled a tapestry bell-rope. "Mrs. Allen," he said, "is most kindly preparing our patient. There is a room at your disposal and I venture to lend you one of my gowns. It will, I'm afraid, be terribly voluminous but perhaps some adjustment can be made. We are involved in compromise, isn't it?"

A man wearing the dress of an Egyptian house-servant came in. Baradi spoke to him in his own language, and then to Raoul in French: "Go with Mahomet and prepare yourself in accordance with his instructions. He speaks French." Raoul acknowledged this direction with something between a bow and a nod. He said to Alleyn: "Monsieur will perhaps excuse me?" and followed the servant, looking about the room with interest as he left it.

Baradi said: "Italian blood there, I think. One comes across these hybrids along the coast. May I show you to my room?"

It was in the same passage as Miss Truebody's, but a little further along it. In Alleyn the trick of quick observation was a professional habit. He saw not only the general sumptuousness of the room but the details also: the Chinese wallpaper, a Wu Tao-tzu scroll, a Ming vase.

"This," Dr. Baradi needlessly explained, "is known as the Chinese room but, as you will observe, Mr. Oberon does not hesitate to introduce modulation. The bureau is by Vernis-Martin."

"A modulation, as you say, but an enchanting one. The cabinet there is a bolder departure. It looks like a Mussonier."

"One of his pupils, I understand. You have a discerning eye. Mr. Oberon will be delighted."

A gown was laid out on the bed. Baradi took it up. "Will you try this? There is an unoccupied room next door with access to a bathroom. You have time for a bath and will, no doubt, be glad to take one. Since morphine has been given there is no immediate urgency, but I should prefer all the same to operate as soon as possible. When you are ready, my own preparations will be complete and we can discuss final arrangements."

Alleyn said: "Dr. Baradi, we haven't said anything about your fee for the operation: indeed, it is neither my business nor my wife's, but I do feel some concern about it. I imagine Miss Truebody will at least be able . . ."

Baradi held up his hand. "Let us not discuss it," he said. "Let us assume that it is of no great moment."

"If you prefer to do so." Alleyn hesitated and then added: "This is an extraordinary situation. You will, I'm sure, realize that we are reluctant to take such a grave responsibility. Miss Truebody is a complete stranger to us. You yourself must feel it would be much more satisfactory if there was a relation or friend from whom we could get some kind of authority. Especially as her illness is so serious."

"I agree. However, she would undoubtedly die if the operation was not performed and, in my opinion, would be in the gravest danger if it was unduly postponed. As it is, I'm afraid there is a risk, a great risk, that she will not recover. We can," Baradi added, with what Alleyn felt was a genuine, if controlled, anxiety, "only do our best and hope that all may be well."

And on this note Alleyn turned to go. As he was in the doorway Baradi, with a complete change of manner, said: "Your enchanting wife is with her. Third door on the left. Quite enchanting. Delicious, if you will permit me."

Alleyn looked at him and found what he saw offensive.

"Under these unfortunate circumstances," he said politely, "I can't do anything else."

Evidently Dr. Baradi chose to regard this observation as a pleasantry. He laughed richly. "Delicious!" he repeated, but whether in reference to Alleyn's comment or as a reiterated observation upon Troy it was impossible to determine. Alleyn, who had every reason and no inclination for keeping his temper, walked into the next room.

### III

Troy had carried out her instructions and Miss Truebody had slipped again into sleep. The sound of her breathing cut the silence into irregular intervals. Her eyes were not quite closed. Segments of the eyeballs appeared under the pathetic insufficiency of her lashes. Troy was at once unwilling to leave her and anxious to return to Ricky. She heard Alleyn and Dr. Baradi in the passage. Their voices were broken off by a door slam and again there was only Miss Truebody's breathing. Troy waited, hoping that Alleyn knew where she was and would come to her. After what seemed an interminable interval there was a tap at the door. She opened it and he was there in a white gown looking tall, elegant and angry. Troy shut the door behind her and they whispered together in the passage.

"Rum go," he said, "isn't it?"

"Not 'alf. When do you begin?"

"Soon. He's trying to make himself aseptic. A losing battle, I should think."

"Frightful, isn't he?"

"The bottom. I'm sorry, darling, you have to suffer his atrocious gallantries."

"Well, I daresay they're just elaborate Oriental courtesy, or something."

"Elaborate bloody impertinence."

"Never mind, Rory. I'll skip out of his way."

"I shouldn't have brought you to this damn place."

"Fiddle! In any case he's going to be too busy."

"Is she asleep?"

"Sort of. I don't like to leave her, but suppose Ricky should wake?"

"Go up to him. I'll stay with her. Baradi's going to give her an injection before I get going with the ether. And, Troy—"

"Yes?"

"It's important these people don't get a line on who I am."

"I know."

"I haven't told you anything about them, but I think I'll have to come moderately clean when there's a chance. It's a rum setup. I'll get you out of it as soon as possible."

"I'm not worrying now we know about the charades. Funny! You said there might be an explanation, but we never thought of charades, did we?"

"No," Alleyn said, "we didn't, did we?" and suddenly kissed her. "Now, I suppose I'll have to wash again," he added.

Raoul came down the passage with Baradi's servant. They were carrying the improvised stretcher and were dressed in white overalls.

Raoul said: "Madame!" to Troy, and to Alleyn, "It appears, Monsieur, that M. le Docteur orders Mademoiselle to be taken to the operating room. Is that convenient for Monsieur?"

"Of course. We are under Dr. Baradi's orders."

"Authority," Raoul observed, "comes to roost on strange perches, Monsieur."

"That," Alleyn said, "will do."

Raoul grinned and opened the door. They took the stretcher in and laid it on the floor by the bed. When they lifted her down to it, Miss Truebody opened her eyes and said distinctly: "But I would prefer to stay in bed." Raoul deftly tucked blankets under her. She began to wail dismally.

Troy said: "It's all right, dear. You'll be all right," and thought: "But I never call people dear!"

They carried Miss Truebody into the room across the passage and put her on the table by the window. Troy went with them, holding her hand. The window coverings had been removed and a hard glare beat down on the table. The room still reeked of disinfectant. There was a second table on which a number of objects were now laid out. Troy, after one glance, did not look at them again. She held Miss Truebody's hand and stood between her and the instrument table. A door in the wall facing her opened and Baradi appeared against a background of bathroom. He wore his gown and a white cap. Their austerity of design emphasized the opulence of his nose and eyes and teeth. He had a hypodermic syringe in his left hand.

"So, after all, you are to assist me?" he murmured to Troy. But it was obvious that he didn't entertain any such notion.

Still holding the flaccid hand, she said: "I thought perhaps I should stay with her until . . ."

"But of course! Please remain a little longer." He began to give instructions to Alleyn and the two men. He spoke in French presumably, Troy thought, to spare Miss Truebody's feelings. "I am left-handed," he said. "If I should ask for anything to be handed to me you will please remember that. Now, Mr. Allen, we will show you your equipment, isn't it? Milano!" Raoul brought a china dish from the instrument table. It had a bottle and a hand towel on it. Alleyn looked at it and nodded. "*Parfaitement*," he said.

Baradi took Miss Truebody's other hand and pushed up the long sleeve of her nightgown. She stared at him and her mouth worked soundlessly.

Troy saw the needle slide in. The hand she held flickered momentarily and relaxed.

"It is fortunate," Baradi said as he withdrew the needle, "that this little Dr. Claudel had Pentothal. A happy coincidence."

He raised Miss Truebody's eyelid. The pupil was out of sight. "Admirable," he said. "Now, Mr. Allen, we will, in a moment or two, induce a more profound anaesthesia which you will continue. I shall scrub up and in a few minutes more we begin operations." He smiled at Troy, who was already on the way to the door. "One of our party will join you presently on the roof-garden. Miss Locke; the Honourable Grizel Locke. I believe she has a vogue in England. Quite mad, but utterly charming."

Troy's last impression of the room, a vivid one, was of Baradi, enormous in his white gown and cap, of Alleyn standing near the table and smiling at her, of Raoul and the Egyptian servant waiting near the instruments, and of Miss Truebody's wide-open mouth and of the sound of her breathing. Then the door shut off the picture as abruptly as the tunnel had shut off her earlier glimpse into a room in the Chèvre d'Argent.

"Only *that* time—" Troy told herself, as she made her way back to the roof-garden—"it was only a charade."

# CHAPTER III

# Morning with Mr. Oberon

## I

THE SUN shone full on the roof-garden now, but Ricky was shielded from it by the canopy of his swinging couch. He was, as he himself might have said, lavishly asleep. Troy knew he would stay so for a long time.

The breakfast-table had been cleared and moved to one side and several more seats like Ricky's had been set out. Troy took the one nearest to his. When she lifted her feet it swayed gently. Her head sank back into a heap of cushions. She had slept very little in the train.

It was quiet on the roof-garden. A few cicadas chittered far below and once, somewhere a long way away, a car hooted. The sky, as she looked into it, intensified itself in blueness and bemused her drowsy senses. Her eyes closed and she felt again the movement of the train. The sound of the cicadas became a dismal chattering from Miss True-body and soared up into nothingness. Presently, Troy, too, was fast asleep.

When she awoke, it was to see a strange lady perched, like some fantastic fowl, on the balustrade near Ricky's seat. Her legs, clad in scarlet pedal-pushers, were drawn up to her chin which was sunk between her knees. Her hands, jewelled and claw-like, with vermillion talons, clasped her shins, and her toes protruded from her sandals like branched corals. A scarf was wound around her skull and her eyes were hidden by sun-glasses in an enormous frame below which a formidable nose jutted over a mouth whose natural shape could only be conjectured. When she saw Troy was awake and on her feet she unfolded herself, dropped to the floor, and advanced with a hand extended. She was six feet tall and about forty-five to fifty years old.

"How do you do?" she whispered. "I'm Grizel Locke. I like to be called Sati, though. The Queen of Heaven, you will remember. Please call me Sati. Had a good nap, I hope? I've been looking at your son and wondering if I'd like to have one for myself."

"How do you do?" Troy said without whispering and greatly taken aback. "Do you think you would?"

"Won't he awake? I've got *such* a voice as you can hear when I speak up." Her voice was indeed deep and uncertain like an adolescent boy's. "It's hard to say," she went on. "One might go all possessive and peculiar and, on the other hand, one might get bored and off-load him on repressed governesses. I was off-loaded as a child which, I am told, accounts for almost everything. Do lie down again. You must feel like a boiled owl. So do I. Would you like a drink?"

"No, thank you," Troy said, running her fingers through her short hair.

"Nor would I. What a poor way to begin your holiday. Do you know anyone here?"

"Not really. I've got a distant relation somewhere in the offing but we've never met."

"Perhaps we know them. What name?"

"Garbel. Something to do with a rather rarefied kind of chemistry. I don't suppose you—"

"I'm afraid not," she said quickly. "Has Baradi started on your friend?"

"She's not a friend or even an acquaintance. She's a fellow-traveller."

"How sickening for you," said the lady earnestly.

"I mean, literally," Troy explained. She was indeed feeling like a boiled owl and longed for nothing as much as a bath and solitude.

"Lie down," the lady urged. "Put your boots up. Go to sleep again if you like. I was just going to push ahead with my tanning, only your son distracted my attention."

Troy sat down and as her companion was so insistent she did put her feet up.

"That's right," the lady observed. "I'll blow up my li-low. The servants, alas, have lost the puffer."

She dragged forward a flat rubber mattress. Sitting on the floor she applied her painted mouth to the valve and began to blow. "Uphill work," she gasped a little later, "still, it's an exercise in itself and I daresay will count as such."

When the li-low was inflated she lay face down upon it and untied the painted scarf that was her sole garment. It fell away from a back so thin that it presented, Troy thought, an anatomical subject of considerable interest. The margins of the scapulae shone like ploughshares and the spinal vertebrae looked like those of a flayed snake.

"I've given up oil," the submerged voice explained, "since I became a Child of the Sun. Is there any particular bit that seems underdone, do you consider?"

Troy, looking down upon a uniformly dun-coloured expanse, could make no suggestions and said so.

"I'll give it ten minutes for luck and then toss over the bod," said the voice. "I must say I feel ghastly."

"You had a late night, Dr. Baradi tells us," said Troy, who was making a desperate effort to pull herself together.

"Did we?" The voice became more indistinct, and added something like: "I forget."

"Charades and everything, he said."

"Did he? Oh. Was I in them?"

"He didn't say particularly," Troy answered.

"I passed," the voice muttered, "utterly and definitely out." Troy had just thought how unattractive such statements always were when she noticed with astonishment that the shoulderblades were quivering as if their owner was convulsed. "I suppose you might call it charades," the lady was heard to say.

Troy was conscious of a rising sense of uneasiness.

"How do you mean?" she asked.

Her companion rolled over. She had taken off her sun-glasses. Her eyes were green with pale irises and small pupils. They were singularly blank in expression. Clad only in her scarlet sans-culotte and head-scarf, she was an uncomfortable spectacle.

"The whole thing is," she said rapidly, "I wasn't at the party. I began one of my headaches after luncheon, which was a party in itself, and I passed, as I mentioned a moment ago, out. That must have been at about four o'clock, I should think, which is why I am up so early, you know." She yawned suddenly and with gross exaggeration as if her jaws would crack.

"Oh, God," she said, "here I go again!"

Troy's jaws quivered in imitation. "I hope your headache is better," she said.

"Sweet of you. In point of fact it's hideous."

"I'm so sorry."

"I'll have to find Baradi if it goes on. And it will, of course. How long will he be over your fellow-traveller's appendix? Have you seen Ra?"

"I don't think so. I've only seen Dr. Baradi."

"Yes, yes," she said restlessly, and added, "You wouldn't know, of course. I mean Oberon, our Teacher, you know. That's our name for him—Ra. Are you interested in The Truth?"

Troy was too addled with unseasonable sleep and a surfeit of anxiety to hear the capital letters. "I really don't know," she stammered. "In the truth—?"

"Poor sweet, I'm muddling you." She sat up. Troy had a painter's attitude towards the nude but the aspect of this lady, so wildly and so unpleasantly displayed, was distressing and doubly so because Troy couldn't escape the impression that the lady herself was far from unselfconscious. Indeed she kept making tentative clutches at her scarf and looking at Troy as if she felt she ought to apologize for herself. In her embarrassment Troy turned away and looked vaguely at the tower wall which rose above the roof-garden not far from where she sat. It was pierced at ascending intervals by narrow slits. Troy's eyes, glazed with fatigue, stared in aimless fixation at the third slit from the floor level. She listened to a strange exposition on The Truth as understood and venerated by the guests of Mr. Oberon.

". . . just a tiny group of Seekers . . . Children of the Sun in the Outer . . . Evil exists only in the minds of the earthbound . . . goodness is oneness . . . the great Dark co-exists with the great Light. . . ." The phrases disjointed and eked out by ineloquent and unco-ordinated gestures, tripped each other up by the heels. Clichés and aphorisms were tumbled together from the most unlikely sources. One must live dangerously, it appeared, in order to attain merit. Only by encompassing the gamut of earthly experience could one return to the oneness of universal good. One ascended through countless ages by something which the disciple, corkscrewing an unsteady finger in illustrations, called the mystic navel spiral. It all sounded the most dreadful nonsense to poor Troy but she listened politely and, because her companion so clearly expected them, tried to ask one or two intelligent questions. This was a mistake. The lady, squinting earnestly up at her, said abruptly: "You're fey, of course. But you know that, don't you?"

"Indeed, I don't."

"Yes, yes," she persisted, nodding like a mandarin. "Unawakened perhaps, but it's there, oh! so richly. Fey as fey can be."

She yawned again with the same unnatural exaggeration and twisted round to look at the door into the tower.

"He won't be long appearing," she whispered. "It isn't as if he ever touched anything and he's always up for the rites of Ushas. What's the time?"

"Just after ten," said Troy, astonished that it was no later. Ricky, she thought, would sleep for at least another hour, perhaps for two hours. She tried to remember if she had ever heard how long an appendectomy took to perform. She tried to console herself with the thought that there must be a limit to this vigil, that she would not have to listen forever to Grizel Locke's esoteric small-talk, that somewhere down at the Hôtel Royal in Roqueville there was a tiled bathroom and a cool bed, that perhaps Miss Locke would go in search of whatever it was she seemed to await with such impatience, and finally that she herself might, if left alone, sleep away the remainder of this muddled and distressing interlude.

It was at this juncture that something moved behind the slit in the tower wall. Something that tweaked at her attention. She had an impression of hair or fur and thought at first that it was an animal, perhaps a cat. It moved again and was gone, but not before she recognized a human head. She came to the disagreeable conclusion that someone had stood at the slit and listened to their conversation. At that moment she heard steps inside the tower. The door moved.

"Someone's coming!" she cried out in warning. Her companion gave an ejaculation of relief, but made no attempt to resume her garment. "Miss Locke! Do look out!"

"What? Oh! Oh, all right. Only, do call me Sati." She picked up the square of printed silk. Perhaps, Troy thought, there was something in her own face that awakened in Miss Locke a dormant regard for the conventions. Miss Locke blushed and began clumsily to knot the scarf behind her.

But Troy's gaze was upon the man who had come through the tower door onto the roof-garden and was walking towards them. The confusion of spirit that had irked her throughout the morning clarified into one recognizable emotion.

She was frightened.

## II

Troy would have been unable to say at that moment why she was afraid of Mr. Oberon. There was nothing in his appearance, one would have thought, to inspire fear. Rather, he had, at first sight, a look of mildness.

Beards, in general, are not rare nowadays though beards like his are perhaps unusual. It was blonde, sparse and silky and divided at the chin which was almost bare. The moustache was a mere shadow at the corners of his mouth, which was fresh in colour. The nose was straight and delicate and the light eyes abnormally large. His hair was parted in the middle and so long that it overhung the collar of his gown. This, and a sort of fragility in the general structure of his head, gave him an air of effeminacy. What was startling and to Troy quite shocking, was the resemblance to Roman Catholic devotional prints such as the "Sacred Heart." She was to learn that this resemblance was deliberately cultivated. He wore a white dressing gown to which his extraordinary appearance gave the air of a ceremonial robe.

It seemed incredible that such a being could make normal conversation. Troy would not have been surprised if he had acknowledged the introduction in Sanskrit. However, he gave her his hand, which was small and well-formed, and a conventional greeting. He had a singularly musical voice and spoke without any marked accent, though Troy fancied she heard a faint American inflection. She said something about his kindness in offering harbourage to Miss Truebody. He smiled gently, sank on to an Algerian leather seat, drew his feet up under his gown and placed them, apparently, against his thighs. His hands fell softly to his lap.

"You have brought," he said, "a gift of great price. We are grateful."

From the time that they had confronted each other he had looked fully into Troy's eyes and he continued to do so. It was not the half-unseeing attention of ordinary courtesy but an unswerving fixed regard. He seemed to blink less than most people.

His disciple said: "Dearest Ra, I've got the most monstrous headache."

"It will pass," he said, still looking at Troy. "You know what you should do, dear Sati."

"Yes, I do, don't I! But it's so hard sometimes to feel the light. One gropes and gropes."

"Patience, dear Sati. It will come."

She sat up on her li-low, seized her ankles and with a grunt of discomfort adjusted the soles of her feet to the inside surface of her thighs. "Om," she said discontentedly.

Mr. Oberon said to Troy: "We speak of things that are a little strange to you. Or perhaps they are not altogether strange?"

"Just what I thought," the lady began eagerly. "Isn't she *fey?*"

He disregarded her.

"Should I explain that we—my guests here and I—follow what we believe to be the true Way of Life? Perhaps, up here, in this ancient house, we have created an atmosphere that to a visitor is a little overwhelming. Do you feel it so?"

Troy said: "I'm afraid I'm just rather addled with a long journey, not much sleep, and an anxious time with Miss Truebody."

"I have been helping her. And, I hope, our friend Baradi."

"Have you?" Troy exclaimed in great surprise. "I thought . . . ? But how kind of you. . . . Is . . . is the operation going well?"

He smiled, showing his perfect teeth. "Again, I do not make myself clear. I have been with them, not in the body but in the spirit."

"Oh," mumbled Troy. "I'm sorry."

"Particularly with your friend. This was easy because when by the will, or, as with her, by the agency of an anaesthetic, the soul is set free of the body, it may be greatly helped. Hers is a pure soul. She should be called Miss Truesoul instead of Truebody." He laughed, a light breathy sound, and showed the pink interior of his mouth. "But we must not despise the body," he said, apparently as an afterthought.

His disciple whispered: "Oh, no! No, indeed! No," and started to breathe deeply, stopping one nostril with a finger and expelling her breath with a hissing sound. Troy began to wonder if Miss Locke was, perhaps, a little mad.

Oberon had shifted his gaze from Troy. His eyes were still very wide open and quite without expression. He had seen the sleeping Ricky.

It was with the greatest difficulty that Troy gave her movement towards Ricky a semblance of casualness. Her instinct, she afterwards told Alleyn, was entirely that of a mother cat. She leaned over her small son and made a pretence of adjusting the cushion behind him. She heard Oberon say: "A beautiful child," and thought that no matter how odd it might look, she would stand between Ricky and his eyes until something else diverted their gaze. But Ricky himself stirred a little, flinging out his arm. She moved him over with his face away from Oberon. He murmured: "Mummy?" and she answered: "Yes," and kept her hand on him until he had fallen back into sleep.

She turned and looked past the ridiculous back of the deep-breathing disciple to the figure seated in the glare of the sun, and, being a painter, she recognized, in the midst of her alarm, a remarkable subject. At the same time it seemed to her that Oberon and she acknowledged each other as enemies.

This engagement, if it was one, was broken off by the appearance of two more of Mr. Oberon's guests: a tall girl and a lame young man who were introduced as Ginny Taylor and Robin Herrington. Both their names were familiar to Troy, the girl's as that of a regular sacrifice on the altars of the glossy weeklies, and the man's as that of the reputably wildish son of a famous brewer who was also an indefatigable patron of the fine arts. To Troy their comparative normality was as a freshening breeze and she was ready to overlook the shadows under their eyes and their air of unease. They greeted her politely, lowered their voices when they saw Ricky and sat together on one seat, screening him from Mr. Oberon. Troy returned to her former place.

Mr. Oberon was talking. It seemed that he had bought a book in Paris, a newly discovered manuscript, one of those assembled by Roger de Gaignières. Troy knew that he must have paid a fabulous sum for it and, in spite of herself, listened eagerly to a description of the illuminations. He went on to speak of other works: of the calendar of Charles d'Angoulême, of Indian art, and finally of the moderns—Rouault, Picasso and André Derain. "But, of course, André is not a modern. He derives quite blatantly from Rubens. Ask Carbury, when he comes, if I am not right."

Troy's nerves jumped. Could he mean Carbury Glande, a painter whom she knew perfectly well and who would certainly, if he appeared, greet her with feverish effusiveness? Mr. Oberon no longer looked at her or at anyone in particular, yet she had the feeling that he talked at her and he was talking very well. Yes, here was a description of one of Glande's works. "He painted it yesterday from the Saracens' Watchtower: the favourite interplay of lemon and lacquer-red with a single note of magenta, and everything arranged about a central point. The esoteric significance was eloquent and the whole thing quite beautiful." It was undoubtedly Carbury Glande. Surely, surely, the operation must be over and if so, why didn't Alleyn come and take them away? She tried to remember if Carbury Glande knew she was married to a policeman.

Ginny Taylor said: "I wish I knew about Carbury. I can't get anything from his works. I can only say awful Philistinish things such as they look as if they were too easy to do." She glanced in a friendly manner at Troy.

"Do *you* know about modern art?" she asked.

"I'm always ready to learn," Troy hedged with a dexterity born of fright.

"I shall never learn however much I try," sighed Ginny Taylor and suddenly yawned.

The jaws of everyone except Mr. Oberon quivered responsively.

"Lord, I'm sorry," said Ginny, and for some unaccountable reason looked frightened. Robin Herrington touched her hand with the tip of his fingers. "I wonder why they're so infectious," he said. "Sneezes, coughs and yawns. Yawns worst of all. To read about them's enough to set one going."

"Perhaps," Mr. Oberon suggested, "it's another piece of evidence, if a homely one, that separateness is an illusion. Our bodies as well as our souls have reflex actions." And while Troy was still wondering what on earth this might mean his Sati gave a little yelp of agreement.

"True! True!" she cried. She dived, stretched out with her right arm and grasped her toes. At the same time she wound her left arm behind her head and seized her right ear. Having achieved this unlikely posture, she gazed devotedly upon Mr. Oberon. "Is it all right, dearest Ra," she asked, "for me to press quietly on with my Prana and Prana-yama?"

"It is well at all times, dear Sati, if the spirit also is attuned."

Troy couldn't resist stealing a glance at Ginny Taylor and Robin Herrington. Was it possible that they found nothing to marvel at in these antics? Ginny was looking doubtfully at Sati, and young Herrington was looking at Ginny as if, Troy thought with relief, he invited her to be amused with him.

"Ginny?" Mr. Oberon said quietly.

The beginning of a smile died on Ginny's lips. "I'm sorry," she said quickly. "Yes, Ra?"

"Have you formed a design for today?"

"No. At least . . . this afternoon . . ."

"I thought, if it suited general arrangements," Robin Herrington said, "that I might ask Ginny to come into Douceville this afternoon. I want her to tell me what colour I should have for new awnings on the afterdeck."

But Ginny had got up and walked past Troy to Mr. Oberon. She stood before him white-faced with the dark marks showing under her eyes.

"Are you going, then, to Douceville?" he asked. "You look a little pale, my child. We were so late with our gaieties last night. Should you rest this afternoon?"

He was looking at her as he had looked at Troy.

"I think perhaps I should," she said in a flat voice.

"I, too. The colour of the awnings can wait until the colour of the cheeks is restored. Perhaps Annabella would enjoy a drive to Douceville. Annabella Wells," he explained to Troy, "is with us. Her latest picture is completed and she is to make a film for Durant Frères in the spring."

Troy was not much interested in the presence of a notoriously erratic if brilliant actress. She had been watching young Herrington, whose brows were drawn together in a scowl. He got up and stood behind Ginny, looking at Oberon over the top of her head. His hands closed and he thrust them into his pockets.

"I thought a drive might be a good idea for Ginny," he said.

But Ginny had sunk down on the end of the li-low at Mr. Oberon's feet. She settled herself there quietly, with an air of obedience. Mr. Oberon said to Troy: "Robin has a most wonderful yacht. You must ask him to show it to you." He put his hand on Ginny's head.

"I should be delighted," said Robin and sounded furious. He had turned aside and now added in a loud voice: "Why not this afternoon? I still think Ginny should come to Douceville."

Troy knew that something had happened that was unusual between Mr. Oberon and his guests and that Robin Herrington was frightened as well as angry. She wanted to give him courage. Her heart thumped against her ribs.

In the dead silence they all heard someone come quickly up the stone stairway. When Alleyn opened the door their heads were already turned towards him.

## III

He waited for a moment to accustom his eyes to the glare and during that moment he and the five people whose faces were turned toward him were motionless.

One grows scarcely to see one's lifelong companions and it is more difficult to call up the face of one's beloved than that of a mere acquaintance. Troy had never been able to make a memory-drawing of her husband. Yet, at that moment, it was as if a veil of familiarity was withdrawn and she looked at him with fresh perception.

She thought: "I've never been gladder to see him."

"This is my husband," she said.

Mr. Oberon had risen and come forward. He was five inches shorter than Alleyn. For the first time Troy thought him ridiculous as well as disgusting.

He held out his hand. "We're so glad to meet you at last. The news is good?"

"Dr. Baradi will be able to tell you better than I," Alleyn said. "Her condition was pretty bad. He says she will be very ill."

"We shall all help her," Mr. Oberon said, indicating the antic Sati, the bemused Ginny Taylor and the angry-looking Robin Herrington. "We can do so much."

He put his hand on Alleyn's arm and led him forward. The reek of ether accompanied them. Alleyn was introduced to the guests and offered a seat but he said: "If we may, I think perhaps I should see my wife and Ricky on their way back to Roqueville. Our driver is free now and can take them. He will come back for me. We're expecting a rather urgent telephone call at our hotel."

Troy, who dreaded the appearance of Carbury Glande, knew Alleyn had said "my wife" because he didn't want Oberon to learn her name. He had an air of authority that was in itself, she thought, almost a betrayal. She got up quickly and went to Ricky.

"Perhaps," Alleyn said, "I should stay a little longer in case there's any change in her condition. Baradi is going to telephone to St. Christophe for a nurse and, in the meantime, two of your maids will take turns sitting in the room. I'm sure, sir, that if she were able, Miss Truebody would tell you how grateful she is for your hospitality."

"There is no need. She is with us in a very special sense. She is in safe hands. We must send a car for the nurse. There is no train until the evening."

"I'll go," Robin Herrington said. "I'll be there in an hour."

"Robin," Oberon explained lightly, "has driven in the Monte Carlo rally. We must hope that the nurse has iron nerves."

Alleyn said to Robin: "It sounds an admirable idea. Will you suggest it to Dr. Baradi?"

He went to Ricky and lifted him in his arms. Troy gave her hand to Mr. Oberon. His own wrapped itself round hers, tightened, and was suddenly withdrawn. "You must visit us again," he said. "If you are a voyager of the spirit, and I think you are, it might interest you to come to one of our meditations."

"Yes, do come," urged his Sati, who had abandoned her exercises on Alleyn's entrance. "It's madly wonderful. You must. Where are you staying?"

"At the Royal."

"Couldn't be easier. No need to hire a car. The Douceville bus leaves from the corner. Every half-hour. You'll find it perfectly convenient."

Troy was reminded vividly of Mr. Garbel's letters. She murmured something non-committal, said goodbye and went to the door.

"I'll see you out," Robin Herrington offered and took up his heavy walking stick.

As she groped down the darkened stairway she heard their voices rumbling above her. They came slowly; Alleyn because of Ricky and Herrington because of his stiff leg. The sensation of nightmare that threatened without declaring itself mounted in intensity. The stairs seemed endless, yet when she reached the door into the hall she was half-scared of opening it because Carbury Glande might be on the other side. But the hall was untenanted. She hurried through it and out to the courtyard. The iron gates had an elaborate fastening. Troy fumbled with it, dazzled by the glare of sunlight beyond. She pulled at the heavy latch, bruising her fingers. A voice behind her and at her feet said: "Do let me help you."

Carbury Glande must have come up the stairs from beneath the courtyard. His face, on a level with her knees, peered through the interstices of the wrought-iron banister. Recognition dawned on it.

"Can it be Troy?" he exclaimed hoarsely. "But it is! Dear heart, how magical and how peculiar. Where *have* you sprung from? And why are you scrabbling away at doors? Has Oberon alarmed you? I may say he petrifies me. What are you up to?"

He had arrived at her level, a short gnarled man whose hair and beard were red and whose face, at the moment, was a dreadful grey. He blinked up at Troy as if he couldn't get her into focus. He was wearing a pair of floral shorts and a magenta shirt.

"I'm not up to anything," said Troy. "In fact, I'm scarcely here at all. We've brought your host a middle-aged spinster with a perforated appendix and now we're on our way."

"Ah, yes. I heard about the spinster. Ali Baradi woke me at cockcrow, full of professional zeal, and asked me if I'd like to thread needles and count sponges. How he dared! Are you going?"

"I must," Troy said. "Do open this damned door for me."

She could hear Alleyn's and Herrington's voice in the hall and the thump of Herrington's stick.

Glande reached for the latch. His hand, stained round the nails with paint, was tremulous. "I am, as you can see, a wreck," he said. "A Homeric party and only four hours' sottish insensitivity in which to recover. Imagine it! There you are."

He opened the doors and winced at the glare outside. "Oberon will be thrilled you're here," he said. "Did you know he bought a thing of yours at the Rond-Point show? It's in the library. 'Boy with a Kite.' He adores it."

"Look here," Troy said hurriedly, "be a good chap and don't tell him I'm me. I've come here for a holiday and I'd so much rather . . ."

"Well, if you like. Yes, of course. Yes, I understand. And on mature consideration I fancy this ménage is not entirely your cup of tea. You're almost pathologically normal, aren't you? Forgive me if I bolt back to my burrow, the glare is really more than I can endure. God, somebody's coming!"

He stumbled away from the door. Alleyn, with Ricky in his arms came out of the hall followed by Robin Herrington. Glande ejaculated: "Oh, sorry!" and bolted down the stairs. Herrington scowled after him and said: "That's our tame genius. I'll come to the car, if I may."

As they walked in single file down the steps and past the maker of figurines, Troy had the feeling that Robin wanted to say something to them and didn't know how to begin. They had reached the open platform where Raoul waited by the car before he blurted out:

"I do hope you will let me drive you down to see the yacht. Both of you, I mean. I mean . . ." he stopped short. Alleyn said: "That's very nice of you. I hadn't heard about a yacht."

"She's quite fun." He stood there, still with an air of hesitancy. Alleyn shifted Ricky and looked at Troy, who held out her hand to Robin.

"Don't come any further," she said. "Goodbye and thank you."

"Goodbye. If we may, Ginny and I will call at the hotel. It's the Royal, I suppose. I mean, it might amuse you to come for a drive. I mean, if you don't know anybody here . . ."

"It'd be lovely," Troy temporized, wondering if Alleyn wanted her to accept.

"As a matter of fact," Alleyn said, "we *have* got someone we ought to look up in Roqueville. Do you know anybody about here with the unlikely name of Garbel?"

Robin's jaw dropped. He stared at them with an expression of extraordinary consternation. "I . . . no. We haven't really met any of the local people. No. Well, I mustn't keep you standing in the sun. Goodbye."

And with a precipitancy as marked as his former hesitation, he turned and limped off down the passage-way.

"Now what," Troy asked her husband, "in a crazy world, is the significance of that particular bit of lunacy?"

"I've not the beginning of a notion," he said. "But I suggest that when we've got time to think, we call on Mr. Garbel."

# CHAPTER IV

# The Elusiveness of Mr. Garbel

## I

RICKY woke up before they could get him to the car and was bewildered to find himself transported. He was hot, hungry, thirsty and uncomfortable, and he required immediate attention.

While Troy and Alleyn looked helplessly about the open platform Raoul advanced from the car, his face brilliant with understanding. He squatted on his heels beside the flushed and urgent Ricky and addressed him in very simple French which he appeared to understand and to which he readily responded. Marie, of the figurines, Raoul explained to the parents, would offer suitable hospitality and he and Ricky went off together, Ricky glancing up at him with admiration.

"It appears," Alleyn said, "that a French nanny and those bi-weekly conversational tramps with Mademoiselle to the Round Pond have not been unproductive. Our child has the rudiments of the language."

"Mademoiselle," Troy rejoined, "says he's prodigiously quick for his age. An amazing child, she thinks." And she added hotly: "Well, all right, I don't say so to anyone else, do I?"

"My darling, you do not and you shall never say so too often to me. But for the moment let us take our infant phenomenon for granted and look at the situation Chèvre d'Argent. Tell me as quickly as you can, what happened before I cropped up among those cups of tea on the roof-top."

They sat together on the running-board of the car and Troy did her best. "Admirable," he said when she had finished. "I fell in love with you in the first instance because you made such beautiful statements. Now, what do you suppose goes on in that house?"

"Something quite beastly," she said vigorously. "I'm sure of it. Oberon's obviously dishing out to his chums some fantastic hodgepodge of mysticism-cum-religion-cum, I'm very much afraid, eroticism. Grizel Locke attempted a sort of résumé. You never heard such a rigmarole . . . yoga, Nietzsche, black-magic. Voodoo, I wouldn't be surprised. With Lord knows what fancy touches of their own thrown in. It ought to be merely silly but it's not, it's frightening. Grizel Locke, I should say, is potty but the two young ones in any other setting would have struck me as being pleasant children. The boy's obviously in a state about the girl, who seems to be completely in Oberon's toils. It's so fantastic, it isn't true."

"Have you ever heard of the case of Horus and the Swami Vivi Ananda?"

"No."

"They appeared before Curtis Bennett with Edward Carson prosecuting and got swinging sentences for their pains. There's no time to tell you about them now, but you've more or less described their setup and I assure you there's nothing so very unusual about the religio-erotic racket. Oberon's name, by the way, is Albert George Clarkson. He's a millionaire and undoubtedly one of the drug barons. The cult of the Children of the Sun in the Outer is merely a useful sideline and a means, I suspect, of gratifying a particularly nasty personal taste. They suggested as much at the Sûreté though they don't know exactly what goes on among the Sun's Babies. The Sûreté is interested solely in the narcotics side of the show and the Yard's watching it from our end."

"And you?"

"I'm supposed to be the perishing link or something. What about the red-headed gentleman with painty hands and a carryover who was letting you out?"

"He might be serious, Rory. He's Carbury Glande. He paints those post-surrealist things . . . witches' sabbaths and mystic unions. You must remember. Rather pretty colour and good design, but a bit nasty in feeling. The thing is, he knows me and although I asked him not to, he'll probably talk."

"Does he know about us?"

"I can't tell. He might."

"Damn!"

"I shouldn't have come, should I? If Glande knows who you are, he won't be able to resist telling them and bang goes your job."

"They didn't give me Glande's name at the Sûreté. He must be a later arrival. Never mind, we'll gamble on his not knowing you made a *mésalliance* with a policeman. Now, listen, my darling, I don't know how long I'll be up here. It may be an hour and it may be twenty-four. Will you settle yourself and Ricky at the Royal and forget about the Chèvre d'Argent? If there's any goat on the premises it will probably be your devoted husband. I'll make what hay I can while the sun shines in the Outer and I'll turn up as soon as may be. One thing more. Will you try, when you've come to your poor senses, to ring up Mr. Garbel? He may not be on the telephone, of course, but if he is . . ."

"Lord, yes! Mr. Garbel! Now why, for pity's sake, did Robin Herrington run like a rabbit at the mention of P. E. Garbel? Can cousin Garbel be a drug baron? Or an addict, if it comes to that? It might account for his quaint literary style."

"Have you by any chance, brought his letters?"

"Only the last, for the sake of his address."

"Hang on to it, I implore you. If he is on the telephone and answers, ask him to luncheon tomorrow and I'll be there. If, by any chance, he turns up before then, find out if he knows any of Oberon's chums and is prepared to talk about them. Here come Raoul and Ricky. Forget about this blasted business, my own true love, and enjoy yourself if you can."

"What about Miss Truebody?"

"Baradi is pretty worried, he says. I'm quite certain he's doing all that can be done for her. He's a kingpin at his job, you know, however much he may stink to high heaven as a chap."

"Shouldn't I wait with her?"

"*No.* Any more of that and I'll begin to think you like having your hand kissed by luscious Oriental gentlemen. Hullo, Rick, ready for your drive?"

Ricky advanced with his hands behind his back and with strides designed to match those of his companion. "Is Raoul driving us?" he asked.

"He is. You and Mummy."

"Good. Daddy, look! Look, Mummy!"

He produced from behind his back a little goat, painted silver grey with one foot upraised and mounted on a base that roughly traced the outlines of the Château de la Chèvre d'Argent. "The old lady made it and Raoul gave it to me," Ricky said. "It's a silver goat and when it's nighttime it makes itself shine. Doesn't it, Raoul? *N'est ce pas, Raoul?*"

"*Oui, oui. Une chèvre d'argent qui s'illumine.*"

"Daddy, isn't Raoul kind?"

Alleyn, a little embarrassed, told Raoul how kind he was and Troy, haltingly, attempted to say that he shouldn't.

Raoul said: "But it is nothing, Madame. If it pleases this young gallant and does not offend Madame, all is well. What are my orders, Monsieur?"

"Will you drive Madame and Ricky to their hotel? Then go to M. le Commissaire at the Préfecture and give him this letter. Tell him that I will call on him as soon as possible. Tell him also about the operation and of course reply to any questions he may ask. Then return here. There is no immediate hurry and you will have time for *déjeuner*. Do not report at the Château but wait here for me. If I haven't turned up by 3:30 you may ask for me at the Château. You will remember that?"

Raoul repeated his instructions. Alleyn looked steadily at him. "Should you be told I am not there, drive to the nearest telephone, ring up the Préfecture and tell M. le Commissaire precisely what has happened. Understood?"

"Well understood, Monsieur."

"Good. One thing more, Raoul. Do you know anyone in Roqueville called Garbel?"

"Garr-bel? No, Monsieur. It will be an English person for whom Monsieur enquires?"

"Yes. The address is 16 Rue des Violettes."

Raoul repeated the address. "It is an apartment house, that one. It is true one finds a few English there, for the most part ladies no longer young and with small incomes who do not often engage taxis."

"Ah well," Alleyn said. "No matter."

He took off his hat and kissed his wife. "Have a nice holiday," he said, "and give my love to Mr. Garbel."

"What were you telling Raoul?"

"Wouldn't you like to know! Goodbye, Rick. Take care of your mama, she's a good kind creature and means well."

Ricky grinned. He was quick, when he didn't understand his father's remarks, to catch their intention from the colour of his voice. "*Entendu*," he said, imitating Raoul, and climbed into the car beside him.

"I suppose I may sit here?" he said airily.

"He *is* a precocious little perisher and no mistake," Alleyn muttered. "Do you suppose it'll all peter out and he'll be a dullard by the time he's eight?"

"A lot of it's purely imitative. It sounds classier than it is. Move up, Ricky, I'm coming in front, too."

Alleyn watched the car drive down the steep lane to the main road. Then he turned back to the Château de la Chèvre d'Argent.

## II

On the way back to Roqueville Raoul talked nursery French to Ricky and Troy, pointing out the places of interest: the Alpine monastery where, in the cloisters, one might see many lively pictures executed by the persons of the district whose relations had been saved from abrupt destruction by the intervention of Our Lady of Paysdoux; villages that looked as if they had been thrown against the rocks and had stuck to them; distant prospects of little towns. On a lonely stretch of road, Troy offered him a cigarette and while he lit it he allowed Ricky to steer the scarcely moving car. Ricky's dotage on Raoul intensified with every kilometre they travelled together and Troy's understanding of French improved with astonishing rapidity. Altogether they enjoyed each other's company immensely and the journey seemed a short one. They could scarcely believe that the cluster of yellow and pink buildings that presently appeared beneath them was Roqueville.

Raoul turned aside from the steeply descending road and drove down a narrow side-street past an open market where bunches of dyed immortelles hung shrilly above the stalls and the smells of tuberoses was mingled with the pungency of fruit and vegetables. All the world, Raoul said, was abroad at this hour in the market and he flung loud unembarrassed greetings to many persons of his acquaintance. Troy felt her spirits rising and Ricky dropped into the stillness that with him was a sign of extreme pleasure. He sighed deeply and laid one hand on Raoul's knee and one, clasping his silver goat, on Troy's.

They were in a shadowed street where the houses were washed over with faint candy-pink, lemon and powder-blue. Strings of washing hung from one iron balcony to another.

"Rue des Violettes," Raoul said, pointing to the street-sign and presently halted. "*Numéro seize.*"

Troy gathered that he offered her an opportunity to call on Mr. Garbel or, if she was not so inclined, to note the whereabouts of his lodging. She could see through the open door into a dim and undistinguished interior. A number of raffish children clustered about the car. They chattered in an incomprehensible patois and stared with an air of hardihood at Ricky, who instantly became stony.

Troy thought Raoul was offering to accompany her into the house, but sensing panic in the breast of her son, she managed to say that she would go in by herself. "I can leave a note," she thought, and said to Ricky: "I won't be a moment. You stay with Raoul, darling."

"O.K.," he agreed, still fully occupied with disregarding the children. He was like a dog who, when addressed by his master, wags his tail but does not lower his hackles. Raoul shouted at the children and made a shooing noise driving them from the car. They retreated a little, skittishly twitting him. He got out and opened the door for Troy, removing his cap as if she were a minor royalty. Impressed by this evidence of prestige, most of the children fell back, though two of the hardier raised a beggar's plaint and were silenced by Raoul.

The door of Number 16 was ajar. Troy pushed it open and crossed a dingy tessellated floor to a lift-well beside which hung a slotted board holding cards, some with printed and some with written names on them. She had begun hunting up and down the board when a voice behind her said: "Madame?"

Troy turned as if she'd been struck. The door of a sort of cubby-hole opposite the lift was held partly open by a grimy and heavily ringed hand. Beyond the hand Troy could see folds of a black satin dress, an iridescence of bead-work and three quarters of a heavy face and piled-up coiffure.

She felt as if she'd been caught doing something shady. Her nursery French deserted her.

"Pardon," she stammered. "*Je désire—je cherche—Monsieur—Garbel —le nom de Garbel.*"

The woman said something incomprehensible to Troy, who replied, "*Je ne parle pas français. Malheureusement,*" she added on an after-thought. The woman made a resigned noise and waddled out of her cubby-hole. She was enormously fat and used a walking stick. Her eyes were like black currants sunk in uncooked dough. She prodded with her stick at the top of the board and, strangely familiar in that alien place, a spidery signature in faded ink was exhibited: "P. E. Garbel."

"*Ah, merci,*" Troy cried, but the fat woman shook her head contemptuously and appeared to repeat her former remark. This time Troy caught something like . . . "*Pas chez elle . . . il y a vingt-quatre heures.*"

"Not at home?" shouted Troy in English. The woman shrugged heavily and began to walk away. "May I leave a note?" Troy called to her enormous back. "*Puis-je vous donner un billet pour Monsieur?*"

The woman stared at her as if she were mad. Troy scrambled in her bag and produced a notebook and the stub of a BB pencil. Sketches she had made of Ricky in the train fell to the floor. The woman glanced at them with some appearance of interest. Troy wrote: "Called at 11:15. Sorry to have missed you. Hope you can lunch with us at the Royal tomorrow." She signed the note, folded it over and wrote: "M. P. E. Garbel" on the flap. She gave it to the woman (was she a concierge?) and stooped to recover her sketches, aware as she did so, of a dusty skirt, dubious petticoats and broken shoes. When she straightened up it was to find her note displayed with a grey-rimmed sunken finger-nail jabbing at the inscription. "She can't read my writing," Troy thought and pointed first to the card and then to the note, nodding like a mandarin and smiling constrainedly. "Garbel," said Troy, "Gar-r-bel." She remembered about tipping and pressed a 100 franc note into the padded hand. This had an instantaneous effect. The woman coruscated with black unlovely smiles. "Mademoiselle," she said, gaily waving the note. "Madame," Troy responded. *"Non, non, non, non, Mademoiselle,"* insisted the woman with an ingratiating leer.

Troy supposed this to be a compliment. She tried to look deprecating, made an ungraphic gesture and beat a retreat.

Ricky and Raoul were in close conversation in the car when she rejoined them. Three of the hard-boiled children were seated on the running-board while the others played leap-frog in an exhibitionist manner up and down the street.

"Darling," Troy said as they drove away, "you speak French much better than I do."

Ricky slewed his eyes round at her. They were a brilliant blue and his lashes, like his hair, were black. *"Naturellement!"* he said.

"Don't be a prig, Ricky," said his mother crossly. "You're much too uppity. I think I must be bringing you up very badly."

"Why?"

"Now then!" Troy warned him.

"Did you see Mr. Garbel, Mummy?"

"No, I left a note."

"Is he coming to see us?"

"I hope so," said Troy and after a moment's thought added: "If he's true."

"If he writes letters to you he must be true," Ricky pointed out. *"Naturellement!"*

Raoul drove them into a little square and pulled up in front of the hotel.

At that moment the concierge at 16 Rue des Violettes, after having sat for ten minutes in morose cogitation, dialled the telephone number of the Chèvre d'Argent.

### III

Alleyn and Baradi stood on either side of the bed. The maid, an eld-erly pinched-looking woman, had withdrawn to the window. The beads of her rosary clicked discreetly through her fingers.

Miss Truebody's face, still without its teeth, seemed to have collapsed about her nose and forehead and to be less than human-sized. Her mouth was a round hole with puckered edges. She was snoring. Each expulsion of her breath blew the margin of the hole outwards and each intake sucked it in so that in a dreadful way her face was busy. Her eyes were incompletely closed and her almost hairless brows drawn to-gether in a meaningless scowl.

"She will be like this for some hours," Baradi said. He drew Miss Truebody's wrist from under the sheet: "I expect no change. She is very ill, but I expect no change for some hours."

"Which sounds," Alleyn said absently, "like a rough sketch for a villanelle."

"You are a poet?"

Alleyn waved a hand: "Shall we say, an undistinguished amateur."

"You underrate yourself, I feel sure," Baradi said, still holding the flaccid wrist. "You publish?"

Alleyn was suddenly tempted to say: "The odd slim vol," but he con-trolled himself and made a slight modest gesture that was entirely non-committal. Dr. Baradi followed this up with his now familiar comment. "Mr. Oberon," he said, "will be delighted," and added: "He is already greatly moved by your personality and that of your enchanting wife."

"For my part," Alleyn said, "I was enormously impressed with his."

He looked with an air of ardent expectancy into that fleshy mask and could find in it no line or fold that was either stupid or credulous. What was Baradi? Part Egyptian, part French? Wholly Egyptian? Wholly Arab? "Which is the kingpin," Alleyn speculated, "Baradi or Oberon?" Baradi, taking out his watch, looked impassively into Alleyn's face. Then he snapped open his watch and a minute went past, clicked out by the servant's beads.

"Ah, well," Baradi muttered, putting up his watch, "it is as one would expect. Nothing can be done for the time being. This woman will report any change. She is capable and, in the village, has had some experience of sickbed attendance. My man will be able to relieve her. We may have difficulty in securing a trained nurse for tonight, but we shall manage."

He nodded at the woman, who came forward and listened passively to his instructions. They left her, nun-like and watchful, seated by the bed.

"It is eleven o'clock, the hour of meditation," Baradi said as they walked down the passage, "so we must not disturb. There will be something to drink in my room. Will you join me? Your car has not yet returned."

He led the way into the Chinese room where his servant waited behind a table set with Venetian goblets, dishes of olives and sandwiches and something that looked like Turkish Delight. There was also champagne in a silver ice-bucket. Alleyn was almost impervious to irregular hours but the last twenty-four had been exacting, the heat was excessive, and the reek of ether had made him feel squeamish. Lager was his normal choice but champagne would have done very nicely indeed. It was an arid concession to his job that obliged him to say with what he hoped was the right degree of pale complacency: "Will you forgive me if I have water? You see, I've lately become rather interested in a way of life that excludes alcohol."

"But how remarkable. Mr. Oberon will be most interested. Mr. Oberon," Baradi said—signing to the servant that the champagne was to be opened—"is perhaps the greatest living authority on such matters. His design for living transcends many of the ancient cults, drawing from each its purest essence. A remarkable synthesis. But while he himself achieves a perfect balance between austerity and, shall we say, selective enjoyment, he teaches that there is no merit in abstention for the sake of abstention. His disciples are encouraged to experience many pleasures, to choose them with the most exquisite discrimination: 'arrange' them, indeed, as a painter arranges his pictures or a composer traces out the design for a fugue. Only thus, he tells us, may the Ultimate Goal be reached. Only thus may one experience Life to the Full. Believe me, Mr. Allen, he would smile at your rejection of this admirable vintage, thinking it as gross an error, if you will forgive me, as overindulgence. Let me persuade you to change your mind. Besides, you have had a trying experience. You are a little nauseated, I think, by the fumes of ether. Let me, as a doctor," he ended playfully, "insist on a glass of champagne."

Alleyn had taken up a ruby goblet and was looking into it with admiration. "I must say," he said, "this is all most awfully interesting: what you've been saying about Mr. Oberon's teaching, I mean. You make my own fumbling ideas seem pitifully naïve." He smiled. "I should adore some champagne from this quite lovely goblet."

He held it out and watched the champagne mount and cream. Baradi was looking at him across the rim of his own glass. One could scarcely, Alleyn thought, imagine a more opulent picture: the corrugations of hair glistened, the eyes were lustrous, the nose overhung a bubbling field of amber stained with ruby, one could guess at the wide expectant lips.

"To the fullness of life," said Dr. Baradi.

"Yes, indeed," Alleyn rejoined, and they drank.

The champagne was, in fact, admirable.

Alleyn's head was as strong as the next man's but he had had a light breakfast and therefore helped himself freely to the sandwiches, which were delicious. Baradi, always prepared, Alleyn supposed, to experience life to the full, gobbled up the sweetmeats, popping them one after another into his red mouth and abominably washing them down with champagne.

The atmosphere took on a spurious air of unbuttoning, which Alleyn was careful to encourage. So far, he felt tolerably certain, Baradi knew nothing about him, but was nevertheless concerned to place him accurately. The situation was a delicate one. If Alleyn could establish himself as an eager neophyte to the synthetic mysteries preached by Mr. Oberon, he would have taken a useful step towards the performance of his job. At least he would be able to give an inside report on the domestic setup in the Château de la Chèvre d'Argent. Officers on loan to the Special Branch preserve a strict anonymity and it was unlikely that his name would be known in the drug-racket as an M.I.5. investigator. It might be recognized, however, as that of a detective-officer of the C.I.D. Carbury Glande might respect Troy's request, but if he didn't, it was more than likely that he or one of the others would remember she had married a policeman. Alleyn himself remembered the exuberances of the gossip columnists at the time of their marriage and later, when Troy had held one-man shows or when he had appeared for the police in some much-publicized case. It looked as if he should indeed make what hay he could while the sun shone on the Chèvre d'Argent.

"If Miss Truebody and I get through this party," he thought, "blow me down if I don't take her out and we'll break a bottle of fizz on our own account."

Greatly cheered by this thought, he began to talk about poetry and esoteric writing, speaking of Rabindranath Tagore and the Indian "Tantras," of the "Amanga Ranga" and parts of the Cabala. Baradi listened with every appearance of delight, but Alleyn felt a little as if he were prodding at a particularly resilient mattress. There seemed to be no vulnerable spot and, what was worse, his companion began to exhibit signs of controlled restlessness. It was clear that the champagne was intended for a stirrup cup and that he waited for Alleyn to take his departure. Yet, somewhere, there must be a point of penetration. And remembering with extreme distaste Dr. Baradi's attentions to Troy, Alleyn drivelled hopefully onward, speaking of the secret rites of Eleusis and the cult of Osiris. Something less impersonal at last appeared in Baradi as he listened to these confidences. The folds of flesh running from the corners of his nostrils to those of his mouth became more apparent and he began to look like an Eastern and more fleshy version of Charles II. He went to the bureau by Vernis-Martin, unlocked it, and presently laid before Alleyn a book bound in grey silk on which a design had been painted in violet, green and repellent pink.

"A rare and early edition," he said. "Carbury Glande designed and executed the cover. Do admire it!"

Alleyn opened the book at the title page. It was a copy of *The Memoirs of Donatien Alphonse François, Marquis de Sade.*

"A present," said Baradi, "from Mr. Oberon."

It was unnecessary, Alleyn decided, to look any further for the chink in Dr. Baradi's armour.

From this moment, when he set down his empty goblet on the table in Dr. Baradi's room, his visit to the Chèvre d'Argent developed into a covert battle between himself and the doctor. The matter under dispute was Alleyn's departure. He was determined to stay for as long as the semblance of ordinary manners could be preserved. Baradi obviously wanted to get rid of him, but for reasons about which Alleyn could only conjecture, avoided any suggestion of precipitancy. Alleyn felt that his safest line was to continue in the manner of a would-be disciple to the cult of the Children of the Sun. Only thus, he thought, could he avoid planting in Baradi a rising suspicion of his own motives. He must be a bore, a persistent bore, but no more than a bore. And he went gassing on, racking his memory for remnants of esoteric gossip. Baradi spoke of a telephone call. Alleyn talked of telepathic communication. Baradi said that Troy would doubtless be anxious to hear about Miss Truebody; Alleyn asked if Miss Truebody would not be greatly helped by the banishment of anxiety from everybody's mind. Baradi mentioned luncheon. Alleyn prattled of the lotus posture. Baradi said he must not waste any more of Alleyn's time; Alleyn took his stand on the postulate that time, in the commonly accepted sense of the word, did not exist. A final skirmish during which an offer to enquire for Alleyn's car was countered by Rosicrucianism and the fiery cross of the Gnostics, ended with Baradi saying that he would have another look at Miss Truebody and must then report to Mr. Oberon. He said he would be some time and begged Alleyn not to feel he must wait for his return. At this point Baradi's servant reappeared to say a telephone call had come through for him. Baradi at once remarked that no doubt Alleyn's car would arrive before he returned. He regretted that Mr. Oberon's meditation class would still be in progress and must not be interrupted, and he suggested that Alleyn might care to wait for his car in the hall or in the library. Alleyn said that he would very much like to stay where he was and to examine the de Sade. With a flush of exasperation mounting on his heavy cheeks, Baradi consented, and went out, followed by his man.

They had turned to the right and gone down the passage to the hall. The rings on an embossed leather curtain in the entrance clashed as they went through.

Alleyn was already squatting at the Vernis-Martin bureau.

He had the reputation in his department of uncanny accuracy when a quick search was in question. It's doubtful if he ever acted more swiftly than now. Baradi had left the bottom drawer of the bureau open.

It contained half a dozen books, each less notorious if more infamous than the de Sade, and all on the proscribed list at Scotland Yard. He lifted them one by one and replaced them.

The next drawer was locked but yielded to the application of a skeleton-key Alleyn had gleaned from a housebreaker of virtuosity. It contained three office ledgers and two note-books. The entries in the first ledger were written in a script that Alleyn took to be Egyptian, but occasionally there appeared proper names in English characters. Enormous sums of money were shown in several currencies: piastres, francs, pounds and lire neatly flanked each other in separate columns. He turned the pages rapidly, his hearing fixed on the passage outside, his mind behind his eyes.

Between the first ledger and the second lay a thin quarto volume in violet leather, heavily embossed. The design was tortuous, but Alleyn recognized a pentagram, a triskelion, winged serpents, bulls and a broken cross. Superimposed over the whole was a double-edged sword with formalized flames rising from it in the shape of a raised hand. The covers were mounted with a hasp and lock which he had very little trouble in opening.

Between the covers was a single page of vellum, elaborately illuminated and embellished with a further number of symbolic ornaments. Baradi had been gone three minutes when Alleyn began to read the text:

Here in the names of Ra and the Sons of Ra and the Daughters of Ra who are also, in the Mystery of the Sun, The Sacred

Spouses of Ra, I, about to enter into the Secret Fellowship of Ra, swear before Horus and Osiris, before Annum and Apsis, before the Good and the Evil that are One God, who is both Good and Evil, that I will set a seal upon my lips and eyes and ears and keep forever secret the mysteries and the Sacred Rites of Ra.

I swear that all that passes in this place shall be as if it had never been. If I break this oath in the least degree may my lips be burnt away with the fire that is now set before them. May my eyes be put out with the knife that is now set before them. May my ears be stopped with molten lead. May my entrails rot and my body perish with the disease of the crab. May I desire death before I die and suffer torment for evermore. If I break silence may these things be unto me. I swear by the fire of Ra and the Blade of Ra. So be it.

Alleyn uttered a single violent expletive, relocked the covers and opened the second ledger.

It was inscribed: "Compagnie Chimique des Alpes Maritimes," and contained names, dates and figures in what appeared to be a balance of expenditure and income. Alleyn's attention sharpened. The company seemed to be showing astronomical profits. His fingers, nervous and delicate, leafed through the pages, moving rhythmically.

Then abruptly they were still. Near the bottom of a page, starting out of the unintelligible script and written in a small, rather elaborate handwriting, was a name—P. E. Garbel.

The curtain rings clashed in the passage. He had locked the drawer and with every appearance of avid attention was hanging over the de Sade, when Baradi returned.

IV

Baradi had brought Carbury Glande with him and Alleyn thought he knew why. Glande was introduced and after giving Alleyn a damp runaway handshake, retired into the darker part of the room fingering his beard, and eyed him with an air, half curious, half defensive. Baradi said smoothly that Alleyn had greatly admired the de Sade book-wrapper and would no doubt be delighted to meet the distinguished artist. Alleyn responded with an enthusiasm which he was careful to keep on an amateurish level. He said he wished so much he knew more about the technique of painting. This would do nicely, he thought, if Glande, knowing he was Troy's husband, was still unaware of his job. If, on the other hand, Glande knew he was a detective, Alleyn would have said nothing to suggest that he tried to conceal his occupation. He thought it extremely unlikely that Glande had respected Troy's request for anonymity. No. Almost certainly he had reported that their visitor was Agatha Troy, the distinguished painter of Mr. Oberon's "Boy with a Kite." And then? Either Glande had also told them that her husband was a C.I.D. officer, in which case they would be anxious to find out if his visit was pure coincidence; or else Glande had been able to give little or no information about Alleyn and they merely wondered if he was as ready a subject for skulduggery as he had tried to suggest. A third possibility and one that he couldn't see at all clearly, involved the now highly debatable integrity of P. E. Garbel.

Baradi said that Alleyn's car had not arrived, and with no hint of his former impatience suggested that they show him the library.

It was on the far side of the courtyard. On entering it he was confronted with Troy's "Boy with a Kite." Its vigour and cleanliness struck like a sword-thrust across the airlessness of Mr. Oberon's library. For a second the "Boy" looked with Ricky's eyes at Alleyn.

A sumptuous company of books lined the walls with the emphasis, as was to be expected, upon mysticism, the occult and Orientalism. Alleyn recognized a number of works that a bookseller's catalogue would have described as rare, curious, and collector's items. Of far greater interest to Alleyn, however, was a large framed drawing that hung in a dark corner of that dark room. It was, he saw, a representation, probably medieval, of the Château de la Chèvre d'Argent and it was part elevation and part plan. After one desirous glance he avoided it. He professed himself fascinated with the books and took them down with ejaculations of interest and delight. Baradi and Glande watched him and listened.

"You are a collector, perhaps, Mr. Allen?" Baradi conjectured.

"Only in a very humble way. I'm afraid my job doesn't provide for the more expensive hobbies."

There was a moment's pause. "Indeed?" Baradi said. "One cannot, alas, choose one's profession. I hope yours is at least congenial."

Alleyn thought: "He's fishing. He doesn't know or he isn't sure." And he said absently, as he turned the pages of a superb Book of the Dead, "I suppose everyone becomes a little bored with his job at times. What a wonderful thing this is, this book. Tell me, Dr. Baradi, as a scientific man—"

Baradi answered his questions. Glande glowered and shuffled impatiently. Alleyn reflected that by this time it was possible that Baradi and Robin Herrington had told Oberon of the Alleyns' enquiries for Mr.

Garbel. Did this account for the change in Baradi's attitude? Alleyn was now unable to bore Dr. Baradi.

"It would be interesting," Carbury Glande said in his harsh voice, "to hear what Mr. Alleyn's profession might be. I am passionately interested in the employment of other people."

"Ah, yes," Baradi agreed. "Do you ever play the game of guessing at the occupation of strangers and then proving yourself right or wrong by getting to know them? Come!" he cried with a great show of frankness. "Let us confess, Carbury, we are filled with unseemly curiosity about Mr. Allen. Will he allow us to play our game? Indulge us, my dear Allen. Carbury, what is your guess?"

Glande muttered: "Oh, I plump for one of the colder branches of learning. Philosophy."

"Do you think so? A don, perhaps? And yet there is something that to me suggests that Mr. Allen was born under Mars. A soldier. Or, no. I take that back. A diplomat."

"How very perceptive of you," Alleyn exclaimed, looking at him over the Book of the Dead.

"Then I am right?"

"In part, at least. I started in the Diplomatic," said Alleyn truthfully, "but left it at the file-and-corridor stage."

"Really? Then, perhaps, I am allowed another guess. No!" he cried after a pause. "I give up. Carbury, what do you say?"

"I? God knows! Perhaps he left the Diplomatic Service under a cloud and went big-game hunting."

"I begin to think you are all psychic in this house," Alleyn said delightedly. "How on earth do you do it?"

"A mighty hunter!" Baradi ejaculated, clapping his hands softly.

"Not at all mighty, I'm afraid, only pathetically persevering."

"Wonderful," Carbury Glande said, drawing his hand across his eyes and suppressing a yawn. "You live in South Kensington, I feel sure, in some magnificently dark apartment from the walls of which glower the glass eyes of monstrous beasts. Horns, snouts, tusks. Coarse hair. Lolling tongues made of a suitable plastic. Quite wonderful."

"But Mr. Allen is a poet and a hunter of rare books as well as of rare beasts. Perhaps," Baradi speculated, "it was during your travels that you became interested in the esoteric?"

Alleyn suppressed a certain weariness of spirit and renewed his raptures. You saw some rum things, he said with an air of simple credulity, in native countries. He had been told and told on good authority— He rambled on, saying that he greatly desired to learn more about the primitive beliefs of ancient races.

"Does your wife accompany you on safari?" Glande asked. "I should have thought—" He stopped short. Alleyn saw a flash of exasperation in Baradi's eyes.

"My wife," Alleyn said lightly, "couldn't approve less of blood sports. She is a painter."

"I am released," Glande cried, "from bondage!" He pointed to the "Boy with a Kite." "*Ecce!*"

"No!" Really, Alleyn thought, Baradi was a considerable actor. Delight and astonishment were admirably suggested. "Not—? Not Agatha Troy? But, my dear Mr. Allen, this is quite remarkable. Mr. Oberon will be enchanted."

"I can't wait," Carbury Glande said, "to tell him." He showed his teeth through his moustache. "I'm afraid you're in for a scolding, Alleyn. Troy swore me to secrecy. I may say," he added, "that I knew in a vague way, that she was a wedded woman but she has kept the Mighty Hunter from us." His tongue touched his upper lip. "Understandably, perhaps," he added.

Alleyn thought that nothing would give him more pleasure than to seize Dr. Baradi and Mr. Carbury Glande by the scruffs of their respective necks and crash their heads together.

He said apologetically: "Well, you see, we're on holiday."

"Quite," said Baradi and the conversation languished.

"I think you told us," Baradi said casually, "that you have friends in Roqueville and asked if we knew them. I'm afraid that I've forgotten the name."

"Only one. Garbel."

Baradi's smile looked as if it had been left on his face by an oversight. The red hairs of Glande's beard quivered very slightly as if his jaw was clenched.

"A retired chemist of sorts," Alleyn said.

"Ah, yes! Possibly attached to the monstrous establishment which defaces our lovely olive groves. Monstrous," Baradi added, "aesthetically speaking."

"Quite abominable!" said Glande. His voice cracked and he wetted his lips.

"No doubt admirable from an utilitarian point-of-view. I believe they produce artificial manure in great quantities."

"The place," Glande said, "undoubtedly stinks," and he laughed unevenly.

"Aesthetically?" Alleyn asked.

"Always, aesthetically," said Baradi.

"I noticed the factory on our way up. Perhaps we'd better ask there for our friend."

There was a dead silence.

"I can't think what has become of that man of mine," Alleyn said lightly.

Baradi was suddenly effusive. "But how inconsiderate we are! You, of course, are longing to rejoin your wife. And who can blame you? No woman has the right to be at once so talented and so beautiful. But your car? No doubt, a puncture or perhaps merely our Mediterranean *dolce far niente*. You must allow us to send you down. Robin would, I am sure, be enchanted. Or, if he is engaged in meditation, Mr. Oberon would be delighted to provide a car. How thoughtless we have been!"

This, Alleyn realized, was final. "I wouldn't dream of it," he said. "But I do apologize for being such a pestilent visitor. I've let my ruling passion run away with me and kept you hovering interminably. The car will arrive any moment now, I feel sure, and I particularly want to see the man. If I might just wait here among these superb books I shan't feel I'm making a nuisance of myself."

It was a toss-up whether this would work. They wanted, he supposed, to consult together. After a fractional hesitation, Baradi said something about their arrangements for the afternoon. Perhaps, if Mr. Allen would excuse them, they should have a word with Mr. Oberon. There was the business of the nurse—Glande, less adroit, muttered unintelligibly and they went out together.

Alleyn was in front of the plan two seconds after the door had shut behind them.

It was embellished with typical medieval ornaments—a coat of arms, a stylized goat and a great deal of scroll-work. The drawing itself was in two main parts, an elevation, treated as if the entire face of the building had been removed and a multiple plan of great intricacy. It would have taken an hour to follow out the plan in detail. With a refinement of concentration that Mr. Oberon himself might have envied, Alleyn fastened his attention upon the main outlines of the structural design. The great rooms and principal bedrooms were all, more or less, on the library level. Above this level the Château rose irregularly in a system of connected turrets to the battlements. Below it, the main stairway led down by stages through a maze of rooms that grew progressively smaller until, at a level which must have been below that of the railway, they were no bigger than prison cells and had probably served as such for hundreds of years. A vast incoherent maze that had followed, rather than overcome the contour of the mountain; an architectural compromise, Alleyn murmured, and sharpened his attention upon one room and its relation to the rest.

It was below the library and next to a room that had no outside windows. He marked its position and cast back in his mind to the silhouette of the Château as he had seen it, moonlit, in the early hours of that morning. He noticed that it had a window much longer than it was high and he remembered the shape of the window they had seen.

If it was true that Mr. Oberon and his guests were now occupied, as Baradi had represented, with some kind of esoteric keep-fit exercises on the roof-garden, it might be worth taking a risk. He thought of two or three plausible excuses, took a final look at the plan, slipped out of the library and ran lightly down a continuation of the winding stair that, in its upper reaches, led to the roof-garden.

He passed a landing, a closed door and three narrow windows. The stairs corkscrewed down to a wider landing from which a thickly carpeted passage ran off to the right. Opposite the stairway was a door and, a few steps away, another—the door he sought.

He went up to it and knocked.

There was no answer. He turned the handle delicately. The door opened inwards until there was a wide enough gap for him to look through. He found himself squinting along a wall hung with silk rugs and garnished about midway along with a big prayer wheel. At the far end there was an alcove occupied by an extremely exotic-looking divan. He opened the door fully and walked into the room.

From inside the door his view of Mr. Oberon's room was in part blocked by the back of an enormous looking-glass screwed to the floor at an angle of about 45 degrees to the outside wall. For the moment he didn't move beyond this barrier, but from where he stood, looked at the left-hand end of the room. It was occupied by a sort of altar hung with a stiffly embroidered cloth and garnished with a number of objects: a pentacle in silver, a triskelion in bronze and a large crystal affair resembling a sunburst. Beside the altar was a door, leading, he decided, into the windowless room he had noted on the plan.

He moved forward with the intention of walking round the looking-glass into the far part of the room.

"Bring me the prayer wheel," said a voice beyond the glass.

It fetched Alleyn up with the jolt of a punch over the heart. He looked at the door. If the glass had hidden him on his entrance it would mask his exit. He moved towards the door.

"I am at the Third Portal of the Outer and must not uncover my eyes. Do not speak. Bring me the prayer wheel. Put it before me."

Alleyn walked forward.

There, on the other side of the looking-glass facing it and seated on the floor, was Mr. Oberon, stark naked, with the palms of his hands pressed to his eyes. Beyond him was a long window masked by a dyed silk blind, almost transparent, with the design of the sun upon it.

Alleyn took the prayer wheel from the wall. It was an elaborate affair, heavily carved, with many cylinders. He set it before Oberon.

He turned and had reached the door when somebody knocked peremptorily on it. Alleyn stepped back as it was flung open. It actually struck his shoulder. He heard someone go swiftly past and into the room.

Baradi's voice said: "Where are you? Oh. Oh, there you are! See here, I've got to talk to you."

He must be behind the glass. Alleyn slipped round the door and darted out. As he ran lightly up the stairs he heard Baradi shut the door.

There was nobody on the top landing. He walked back into the library, having been away from it for five and a half minutes.

He took out his notebook and made a very rough sketch of Mr. Oberon's room, taking particular pains to mark the position of the prayer wheel on the wall. Then he set about memorizing as much of its detail as he had been able to take in. He was still at this employment when the latch turned in the door.

Alleyn pulled out from the nearest shelf a copy of Mr. Montague Summer's major work on witchcraft. He was apparently absorbed in it when a woman came into the library.

He looked up from the book and knew that as far as preserving his anonymity was concerned, he was irrevocably sunk.

"If it's not Roderick Alleyn!" said Annabella Wells.

# CHAPTER V

# Ricky in Roqueville

*I*

IT WAS some years ago, in a transatlantic steamer, that Alleyn had met Annabella Wells: the focal point of shipboard gossip to which she had seemed to be perfectly indifferent. She had watched him with undisguised concentration for four hours and had then sent her secretary with an invitation for drinks. She herself drank pretty heavily and, he thought, was probably a drug addict. He had found her an embarrassment and was glad when she suddenly dropped him. Since then she had turned up from time to time as an onlooker at criminal trials where he appeared for the police. She was, she told him, passionately interested in criminology.

In the English theatre her brilliance had been dimmed by her outrageous eccentricities, but in Paris, particularly in the motion-picture studios, she was still one of the great ones. She retained a ravaged sort of beauty and an individuality which would be arresting when the last of her good looks had been rasped away. A formidable woman, and an enchantress still.

She gave him her hand and the inverted and agonized smile for which she was famous. "They said you were a big-game hunter," she said. "I couldn't wait."

"It was nice of them to get that impression."

"An accurate one, after all. Are you on the prowl down here? After some master-felon?"

"I'm on a holiday with my wife and small boy."

"Ah, yes! The beautiful woman who paints famous pictures. I am told by Baradi and Glande that she is beautiful. There is no need to look angry, is there?"

"Did I look angry?"

"You looked as if you were trying not to show a certain uxorious irritation."

"Did I, indeed?" said Alleyn.

"Baradi *is* a bit lush. I will allow and must admit that he's a bit lush. Have you seen Oberon?"

"For a few moments."

"What did you think of *him?*"

"Isn't he your host?"

"Honestly," she said, "you're not true. Much more fabulous, in your way, than Oberon."

"I'm interested in what I have been told of his philosophy."

"So they said. What sort of interest?"

"Personal and academic."

"My interest is personal and unacademic." She opened her cigarette case. Alleyn glanced at the contents. "I see," he said, "that it would be useless to offer you a Capstan."

"Will you have one of these? They're Egyptian. The red won't come off on your lips."

"Thank you. They would be wasted on me." He lit her cigarette. "I wonder," he said, "if I could persuade you to say nothing about my job."

"Darling," she rejoined—she called everyone "darling"—"you could persuade me to to do anything. My trouble was, you wouldn't try. Why do you look at me like that?"

"I was wondering if any dependence could be placed on a heroin addict. Is it heroin?"

"It is. I get it," said Miss Wells, "from America."

"How very tragic."

"Tragic?"

"You weren't taking heroin when you played Hedda Gabler at the Unicorn in '42. Could you give a performance like that now?"

"*Yes,*" she said vehemently.

"But what a pity you don't!"

"My last film is the best thing I've ever done. Everyone says so." She looked at him with hatred. "I can still do it," she said.

"On your good days, perhaps. The studio is less exacting than the theatre. Will the cameras wait when the gallery would boo? I couldn't know less about it."

She walked up to him and struck him across the face with the back of her hand.

"You have deteriorated," said Alleyn.

"Are you mad? What are you up to? Why are you here?"

"I brought a woman who may be dying to your Dr. Baradi. All I want is to go away as I came in—a complete nonentity."

"And you think that by insulting me you'll persuade me to oblige you."

"I think you've already talked to your friends about me and that they've sent you here to find out if you were right."

"You're a very conceited man. Why should I talk about you?"

"Because," Alleyn said, "you're afraid."

"Of you?"

"Specifically. Of me."

"You idiot," she said. "Coming here with a dying spinster and an arty-crafty wife and a dreary little boy! For God's sake, get out and get on with your holiday."

"I should like it above all things."

"Why don't you want them to know who you are?"

"It would quite spoil my holiday."

"Which might mean anything."

"It might."

"Why do you say I'm afraid?"

"You're shaking. That may be a carry-over from alcohol or heroin, or both, but I don't think it is. You're behaving like a frightened woman. You were in a blue funk when you hit me."

"You're saying detestable, unforgivable things to me."

"Have I said anything that is untrue?"

"My life's my own. I've a right to do what I like with it."

"What's happened to your intelligence? You should know perfectly well that this sort of responsibility doesn't end with yourself. What about those two young creatures? The girl?"

"I didn't bring them here."

"No, really," Alleyn said, going to the door, "you're saying such very stupid things. I'll go down to the front and see if my car's come. Good-bye to you."

She followed him and put her hand on his arm. "Look!" she said.

"Look at me. I'm terrifying, aren't I? A wreck? But I've still got more than my share of what it takes. Haven't I?"

"For Baradi and his friends?"

"Baradi!" she said contemptuously.

"I really didn't want to insult you with Oberon."

"What do you know about Oberon?"

"I've seen him."

She left her hand on him, but with an air of forgetfulness. A tremor communicated itself to his arm. "You don't know," she said. "You don't know what he's like. It's no good thinking about him in the way you think about other men. There are *hommes fatals,* too, you know. He's terrifying and he's marvellous. You can't understand that, can you?"

"No. To me, if he wasn't disgusting, he'd be ludicrous. A slug of a man."

"Do you believe in hypnotism?"

"Certainly. If the subject is willing."

"Oh," she said hopelessly, "I'm willing enough. Not that it's as simple as hypnotism." She hung her head, looking, with that gesture, like the travesty of a shamed girl. He couldn't hear all she said but caught one phrase: ". . . wonderful degradation. . . ."

"For God's sake," Alleyn said, "what nonsense is this?"

She frowned and looked at him out of her disastrous eyes. "Could you help me?" she said.

"I have no idea. Probably not."

"I'm in a bad way."

"Yes."

"If I were to keep faith? I don't know what you're up to, but if I were to keep faith and not tell them who you are? Even if it ruined me? Would you think you could help me then?"

"Are you asking me if I could help you to cure yourself of drugging? I couldn't. Only an expert could do that. If you've still got enough character and sense of purpose to keep faith, as you put it, perhaps you should have enough guts to go through with a cure. I don't know."

"I suppose you think I'm trying to bribe you?"

"In a sense—yes."

"Do you know," she said discontentedly, "you're the only man I've ever met—" She stopped and seemed to hesitate. "I can't get this right," she said. "With you it's not an act, is it?"

Alleyn smiled for the first time. "I'm not attempting the well-known gambit of rudeness introduced with a view to amorous occasions," he said. "Is that what you mean?"

"I suppose it is."

"You should stick to classical drama. Shakespeare's women don't fall for the insult-and-angry-seduction stuff. Sorry. I'm forgetting Richard III."

"Beatrice and Benedick? Petruchio and Katharina?"

"I was excluding comedy."

"How right you were. There's nothing very funny about my situation."

"No, it seems appalling."

"What can I do? Tell me, what I can do?"

"Leave the Chèvre d'Argent today. Now, if you like. I've got a car outside. Go to a doctor in Paris and offer yourself for a cure. Recognize your responsibility and, before further harm can come of this place, tell me or the local commissary or anyone else in a position of authority everything you know about the people here."

"Betray my friends?"

"A meaningless phrase. In protecting them you betray decency itself. Can you think of that child Ginny Taylor and still question what you should do?"

She stepped back from him as if he was a physical menace.

"You're not here by accident," she said. "You've planned this visit."

"I could hardly plan a perforated appendix in an unknown maiden lady. The place and all of you speak for yourselves. Yawning your heads off because you want your heroin. Pinpoint pupils and leathery faces."

She caught her breath in what sounded like a sigh of relief. "Is that all?" she said.

"I really must go. Goodbye."

"I can't do it. I can't do what you ask."

"I'm sorry."

He opened the door. She said: "I won't tell them what you are. But don't come back. Don't come back here. I'm warning you. Don't come back."

"Goodbye," Alleyn said, and without encountering anyone walked out of the house and down the passage-way to the open platform.

Raoul was waiting there with the car.

## II

When she returned to the roof-garden, Annabella Wells found the men of the house party waiting for her. Dr. Baradi closed his hand softly round her arm, leading her forward.

"Don't," she said, "you smell of hospitals."

Carbury Glande said: "Annabella, who is he? I mean we all know he's Agatha Troy's husband but, for God's sake, *who* is he?"

"You know as much as I do."

"But you said you'd crossed the Atlantic with him. You said it was a shipboard affair and one knows they don't leave many stones unturned, especially in your hands, my angel."

"He was one of my rare failures. He talked of nothing but his wife. He spread her over the Atlantic like an overflow from the Gulf Stream. I gave him up as a bad job. A dull chap, I decided."

"I rather liked him," young Herrington said defiantly.

Mr. Oberon spoke for the first time. "A dangerous man," he said. "Whoever he is and whatever he may be. Under the circumstances, a dangerous man."

Baradi said: "I agree. The enquiry for Garbel is inexplicable."

"Unless they are initiates," Glande said, "and have been given the name."

"They are not initiates," Oberon said.

"No," Baradi agreed.

Young Herrington said explosively: "My God, is there no other way out?"

"Ask yourself," said Glande.

Mr. Oberon rose. "There is no other way," he said tranquilly. "And they must not return. That at least is clear. They must not return."

### III

As they drove back to Roqueville, Alleyn said: "You did your job well this morning, Raoul. You are, evidently, a man upon whom one may depend."

"It pleases Monsieur to say so," said Raoul cheerfully. "The Egyptian gentleman is also, it appears, good at his job. In wartime a medical orderly learns to recognize talent, Monsieur. Very often one saw the patients zipped up like a placket-hole. *Paf!* and he's open. *Pan!* and he's shut. But this was different."

"Dr. Baradi is afraid that she may not recover."

"She had not the look of death upon her."

"Can you recognize it?"

"I fancy that I can, Monsieur."

"Did Madame and the small one get safely to their hotel?"

"Safely, Monsieur. On the way we stopped in the Rue des Violettes. Madame inquired for Mr. Garbel."

Alleyn said sharply: "Did she see him?"

"I understand he was not at home, Monsieur."

"Did she leave a message?"

"I believe so, Monsieur. I saw Madame give a note to the concierge."

"I see."

"She is a type, that one," Raoul said thoughtfully.

"The concierge? Do you know her?"

"Yes, Monsieur. In Roqueville all the world knows all the world. She's an original, is old Blanche."

"In what way?"

"*Un article défrâichi*. One imagines she has other interests besides the door-keeping. To be fat is not always to be idle. But the apartments," Raoul added politely, "are perfectly correct." Evidently he felt it would be in bad taste to disparage the address of any friend of the Alleyns.

Alleyn said, choosing his French very carefully: "I am minded to place a great deal of confidence in you, Raoul."

"If Monsieur pleases."

"I think you were more impressed with Dr. Baradi's skill than with his personality."

"That is a fact, Monsieur."

"I also. Have you seen Mr. Oberon?"

"On several occasions."

"What do you think about him?"

"I have no absolute knowledge of his skill, Monsieur, but I think even less of his personality than of the Egyptian's."

"Do you know how he entertains his guests?"

"One hears a little gossip from time to time. Not much, Monsieur. The servants at the Château are for the most part imported and extremely reticent. But there is an under-chambermaid from the Paysdoux, who is not unapproachable. A blonde, which is unusual in the Paysdoux."

"What has the unusual blonde to say about it?"

Raoul did not answer at once and Alleyn turned his head to look at him. He was scowling magnificently.

"I do not approve of what Teresa has to say. Her name, Monsieur, is Teresa. I find what she has to say immensely unpleasing. You see, it's like this, Monsieur. The time has come when I should marry and for one reason or another—one cannot rationalize about these things—my preference is for Teresa. She has got what it takes," Raoul said, using a phrase—*elle a du fond*—which reminded Alleyn of Annabella Wells's desperate claim. "But in a wife," Raoul continued, "one expects certain reticences where other men are in question. I dislike what Teresa tells me of her employer, Monsieur. I particularly dislike her account of a certain incident."

"Am I to hear it?"

"I shall be glad to recount it. It appears, Monsieur, that Teresa's duties are confined to the sweeping of carpets and polishing of floors and that it is not required of her to take *petit déjeuner* to guests or to perform any personal services for them. She is young and inexperienced. And so, one morning, this Egyptian surgeon witnesses Teresa from the rear when she is on her knees polishing. Teresa is as good from behind as she is from in front, Monsieur. And the doctor passes her and pauses to look. Presently he returns with Mr. Oberon and they pause and speak to each other in a foreign language. Next, the *femme de charge* sends for Teresa and she is instructed that she is to serve *petit déjeuner* to this animal Oberon, if Monsieur will overlook the description, in his bedroom and that her wage is to be raised. So Teresa performs this service. On the first morning there is no conversation. On the second he enquires her name. On the third this *vilain coco* asks her if she is not a fine strong girl. On the fourth he talks a lot of *blague* about the spirituality of the body and the non-existence of evil, and on the fifth, when Teresa enters, he is displayed, immodestly clad, before a full-length glass in his salon. I must tell you, Monsieur, that to reach the bedroom, Teresa must first pass through the salon. She is obliged to approach this unseemly animal. He looks at her fixedly and speaks to her in a manner that is irreligious and blasphemous and anathema. Monsieur, Teresa is a good girl. She is frightened, not so much of this animal, she tells me, as of herself because she feels herself to be like a bird when it is held in terror by a snake. I have told her she must leave, but she says that the wages are good and they are a large family with sickness and much in debt. Monsieur, I repeat, she is a good girl and it is true she needs the money, but I cannot escape the thought that she is in a kind of bondage from which she cannot summon enough character to escape. And on some mornings, when she goes in, there is nothing to which one could object, but on others he talks and talks and stares and stares at Teresa. So that when I last saw her we quarrelled and I have told her that unless she leaves her job before she is no longer respectable she may look elsewhere for a husband. So she wept and I was discomforted. She is not unique but, there it is, I have a preference for Teresa."

Alleyn thought: "This is the first bit of luck I've had since we got here." He looked up the valley at the glittering works of the Maritime Alps Chemical Company and said: "I think it well to tell you that I am interested professionally in the ménage at the Chèvre d'Argent. If it had not been for the accident of Mademoiselle's illness I should have tried to gain admittance there. M. le Commissaire is also interested. We are colleagues in this affair. You and I agreed to forget my rank, Raoul, but for the purposes of this discussion perhaps we should recall it."

"Good, M. l'Inspecteur-en-Chef."

"There's no reason on earth why you should put yourself out for an English policeman in an affair which, however much it may also concern the French police, hasn't very much to do with you. Apart from Teresa, for whom you have a preference."

"There is always Teresa."

"Are you a discreet man?"

"I don't chatter like a one-eyed magpie, Monsieur."

"I believe you. It is known to the police here and in London that the Chèvre d'Argent is used as a place of distribution in a particularly ugly trade."

"Women, Monsieur?"

"Drugs. Women, it seems, are a purely personal interest. A side-line. I believe neither Dr. Baradi nor Mr. Oberon is a drug addict. They are engaged in the traffic from a business point-of-view. I think that they have cultivated the habit of drug-taking among their guests and are probably using at least one of them as a distributor. Mr. Oberon has also established a cult."

"A cult, Monsieur?"

"A synthetic religion concocted from scraps of mysticism, witchcraft, mythology, Hindooism, Egyptology, what-have-you, with, I very much suspect, a number of particularly revolting fancy touches invented by Mr. Oberon."

"Anathema," Raoul said, "all this is anathema. What do they do?" he added with undisguised interest.

"I don't know exactly but I must, I'm afraid, find out. There have been other cases of this sort. No doubt there are rites. No doubt the women are willing to be drugged."

Raoul said: "It appears that I must be firm with Teresa."

"I should be very firm, Raoul."

"This morning she is in Roqueville at the market. I am to meet her at my parents' restaurant, where I shall introduce a firm note. I am disturbed for her. All this, Monsieur, that you have related is borne out by Teresa. On Thursday nights the local servants and some of the other permanent staff are dismissed. It is on Thursday, therefore, that I escort Teresa to her home up in the Paysdoux where she sleeps the night. She has heard a little gossip, not much, because the servants are discreet, but a little. It appears that there is a ceremony in a room which is kept locked at other times. And on Fridays nobody appears until late in the afternoon and then with an air of having a formidable *gueule de bois*. The ladies are strangely behaved on Fridays. It is as if they are half-asleep, Teresa says. And last Friday a young English lady, who has recently arrived, seemed as if she was completely *bouleversée*; dazed, Monsieur," Raoul said, making a graphic gesture with one hand. "In a trance. And also as if she had wept."

"Isn't Teresa frightened by what she sees on Fridays?"

"That is what I find strange, Monsieur. Yes: she says she is frightened, but it is clear to me that she is also excited. That is what troubles me in Teresa."

"Did she tell you where the room is? The room that is unlocked on Thursday nights?"

"It is in the lower part of the Château, Monsieur. Beneath the library, Teresa thinks. Two flights beneath."

"And today is Wednesday."

"Well, Monsieur?"

"I am in need of an assistant."

"Yes, Monsieur?"

"If I asked at the Préfecture they would give me the local gendarme, who is doubtless well-known. Or they would send me a clever man from Paris who as a stranger would be conspicuous. But a man of Roqueville who is well-known and yet is accepted as the friend of one of the maids at the Chèvre d'Argent is not conspicuous if he calls. Do you in fact call often to see Teresa?"

"Often, Monsieur."

"Well, Raoul?"

"Well, Monsieur?"

"Do you care, with M. le Commissaire's permission, to come adventuring with me on Thursday night?"

"Enchanted," said Raoul, gracefully.

"It may not be uneventful, you know. They are a formidable lot, up there."

"That is understood, Monsieur. Again, it will be an act of grace."

"Good. Here is Roqueville. Drive to the hotel, if you please. I shall see Madame and have some luncheon and at three o'clock I shall call on M. le Commissaire. You will be free until then, but leave me a telephone number and your address."

"My parents' restaurant is in the street above that of the hotel. L'Escargot Bienvenu, 20 Rue des Sarrasins. Here is a card, Monsieur, with the telephone number."

"Right."

"My father is a good cook. He has not a great repertoire, but his judgment is sound. Such dishes as he makes he makes well. His *filets mignons* are a speciality of the house, Monsieur, and his sauces are inspired."

"You interest me profoundly. In the days when there was steak in England, one used to dream of *filet mignon* but even then one came to France to eat it."

"Perhaps if Monsieur and Madame find themselves a little weary of the table d'hôte at the Royal they may care to eat cheaply but with satisfaction at L'Escargot Bienvenu."

"An admirable suggestion."

"Of course, we are not at all smart. But good breeding," Raoul said simply, "creates its own background and Monsieur and Madame would not feel out of place. Here is your hotel, Monsieur, and—" His voice changed. "Here is Madame."

Alleyn was out of the car before it stopped. Troy stood in the hotel courtyard with her clasped hands at her lips and a look on her face that he had never seen there before. When he took her arms in his hands he felt her whole body trembling. She tried to speak to him but at first was unable to find her voice. He saw her mouth frame the word "Ricky."

"What is it, darling?" he said. "What's the matter with him?"

"He's gone," she said. "They've taken him. They've taken Ricky."

## IV

For the rest of their lives they would remember too vividly the seconds in which they stood on the tessellated courtyard of the hotel, plastered by the mid-day sun. Raoul on the footpath watched them and the blank street glared behind him. The air smelt of petrol. There was a smear of magenta bougainvillea on the opposite wall, and in the centre of the street a neat pile of horse-droppings. It was already siesta time and so quiet that they might have been the only people awake in Roqueville.

"I'll keep my head and be sensible," Troy whispered. "Won't I, Rory?"

"Of course. We'll go indoors and you'll tell me about it."

"I want to get into the car and look somewhere for him, but I know that won't do."

"I'll ask Raoul to wait."

He did so. Raoul listened, motionless. When Alleyn had spoken Raoul said, "Tell Madame it will be all right, Monsieur. Things will come right." As they turned away he called his reassurance after them and the sound of his words followed them: *"Les affaires s'arrangeront. Tout ira bien, Madame."*

Inside the hotel it seemed very dark. A porter sat behind a reception desk and an elegantly dressed man stood in the hall wringing his hands.

Troy said: "This is my husband. This is the manager, Rory. He speaks English. I'm sorry, Monsieur, I don't know your name."

"Malaquin, Madame. Mr. Alleyn, I am sure there is some simple explanation— There have been other cases—"

"I'll come and see you, if I may, when I've heard what has happened."

"But of course. *Garçon—*"

The porter, looking ineffably compassionate, took them up in the lift. The stifling journey was interminable.

Troy faced her husband in a large bedroom made less impersonal by the slight but characteristic litter that accompanied her wherever she went. Beyond her was an iron-railed balcony and beyond that the arrogant laundry-blue of the Mediterranean. He pushed a chair up and she took it obediently. He sat on his heels before her and put his hands on the arms of the chair.

"Now tell me, darling," he said. "I can't do anything until you've told me."

"You were such a lifetime coming."

"I'm here now. Tell me."

"Yes."

She did tell him. She made a great effort to be lucid, frowning when she hesitated or when her voice shook, and always keeping her gaze on him. He had said she was a good witness and now she stuck to the bare bones of her story, but every word was shadowed by a multitude of unspoken terrors.

She said that when they arrived at the hotel Ricky was fretful and white after his interrupted sleep and the excitement of the drive. The manager was attentive and suggested that Ricky could have a tray in their rooms. Troy gave him a bath and put him into pyjamas and dressing-gown and he had his luncheon, falling asleep almost before it was finished. She put him to bed in a dressing-room opening off her own bedroom. She darkened the windows, and seeing him comfortably asleep with his silver goat clutched in his hand, had her bath, changed and lunched in the dining-room of the hotel. When she returned to their rooms Ricky had gone.

At first she thought that he must have wakened and gone in search of a lavatory or that perhaps he had had one of his panics and was looking for her. It was only after a search of their bathroom and the passages, stairs and such rooms as were open that with mounting anxiety she rang for the chambermaid, and then, as the woman didn't understand English, spoke on the telephone to the manager. M. Malaquin was helpful and expeditious. He said he would at once speak to the servants on duty and report to her. As she put down the receiver Troy looked at the chair across which she had laid Ricky's day clothes ready for his awakening—a yellow shirt and brown linen shorts—and she saw that they were gone.

From that moment she had fought against a surge of terror so imperative that it was accompanied by a physical pain. She ran downstairs and told the manager. The porter and two of the waiters and Troy herself had gone out into the deserted and sweltering streets, Troy running uphill and breathlessly calling Ricky's name. She stopped the few people she met, asking them for a *"petit garçon, mon fils."* The men shrugged, one woman said something that sounded sympathetic. They all shook their heads or made negative gestures with their fingers. Troy found herself in a maze of back streets and stone stairways. She thought she was lost, but looking down a steep alleyway, saw one of the waiters walk across at the lower end and she ran down after him. When she reached the cross-alley she was just in time to see his coattails disappear round a further corner. Finally she caught him up. They were back in the little square, and there was the hotel. Her heart rammed against her ribs and she suffered a disgusting sense of constriction in her throat. Sweat poured between her shoulder blades and ran down her forehead into her eyes. She was in a nightmare.

The waiter grimaced. He was idiotically polite and deprecating and he couldn't understand a word that she said. He pursed his lips, bowed and went indoors. She remembered the Commissary of Police and was about to ask the manager to telephone the Préfecture when she heard Raoul's car turn into the street.

Alleyn said: "Right. I'll talk to the Préfecture. But before I do, my dearest dear, will you believe one thing?"

"All right. I'll try."

"Ricky isn't in danger. I'm sure of it."

"But it's true. He's been—it's those people up there—they've kidnapped him, haven't they?"

"It's possible that they've taken a hand. If they have it's because they want to keep me busy. It's also possible, isn't it, that something entered into his head and he got himself up and trotted out."

"He'd never do it, Rory. Never. You know he wouldn't."

"All right. Now, I'll ring the Préfecture. Come on."

He sat her beside him on the bed and kept his arm about her. While he waited for the number he said: "Did you lock the door?"

"No. I didn't like the idea of locking him in. The manager's spoken to the servants. They didn't see anybody. Nobody asked for our room numbers."

"The heavy trunk is still in the hall downstairs and the room number's chalked on it. What colour are his clothes?"

"Pale yellow shirt and brown shorts."

"Right. We may as well— 'Allo! 'Allo! . . .'"

He began to talk into the telephone, keeping his free hand on her shoulder. Troy turned her cheek to it for a moment and then freed herself and went out on the balcony.

The little square—it was called the Place des Sarrasins—was at the top of a hilly street and the greater part of Roqueville lay between it and the sea. The maze of alleys where Troy had lost herself was out of sight behind and above the hotel. As if from a high tower, she looked down into the streets and prayed incoherently that in one of them she would see a tiny figure: Ricky, in his lemon-coloured shirt and brown linen shorts. But all Troy could see was a pattern of stucco and stone, a distant row of carriages whose drivers and horses were snoozing, no doubt, in the shadows, a system of tiled roofs and the paint-like blue of the sea. She looked nearer at hand and there, beneath her, was Raoul Milano's car, seeming like a toy, and Raoul himself, rolling a cigarette. The hotel porter, at that moment, came out and she heard the sound of his voice. Raoul got up and they disappeared beneath her into the hotel.

The tone of Alleyn's voice suggested that he was near the end of his telephone call. She had turned away from her fruitless search of the map-like town and was about to go indoors when out of the tail of her eye she caught a flicker of colour.

It was a flicker of lemon-yellow and brown.

The hot iron of the balcony rail scorched the palms of her hands. She leant far out and stared at a tall building on a higher level than herself, a building that was just in view round the corner of the hotel. It was perhaps a quarter of a mile away and from behind a huddle of intervening roofs, rose up in a series of balconies. It was on the highest of these, behind a blur of iron railings, that she saw her two specks of colour.

"Rory," she cried. "Rory!"

It took several seconds that seemed like as many minutes for Alleyn to find the balcony. "It's Ricky," she said, "isn't it? It must be Ricky."

And she ran back into the room, snatched the thin cover from her bed and waved it frantically from the balcony.

"Wait a moment," Alleyn said.

His police case had been brought up to their room and contained a pair of very powerful field glasses. While he focussed them on the distant balcony he said: "Don't be too certain, darling, there may be other small boys in yellow and—no—no, it's Ricky. He's all right. Look."

Troy's eyes were masked with tears of relief. Her hands shook and her fingers were too precipitant with the focussing governors. "I can't do it—I can't see."

"Steady. Wipe your eyes. Here, I will. He's still there. He may have spotted us. Try this way. Kneel down and rest the glasses on the rail. Get each eye right in turn. Quietly does it."

Circles of blurred colour mingled and danced in the two fields of vision. They swam together and clarified. The glasses were in focus now but were trained on some strange blue door, startling in its closeness. She moved them and an ornate gilded steeple was before her with a cross and a clock telling a quarter to two. "I don't know where I am. It's a church. I can't find him."

"You're nearly there. Keep at that level and come round gently."

And suddenly Ricky looked through iron rails with vague, not quite frightened eyes whose gaze, while it was directed at her, yet passed beyond her.

"Wave," she said. "Go on waving."

Ricky's strangely impersonal and puzzled face moved a little so that an iron standard partly hid it. His right arm was raised and his hand moved to and fro above the railing.

"He's seen!" she said. "He's waving back."

The glasses slipped a little. The wall of their hotel, out-of-focus and stupid, blotted out her vision. Someone was tapping on the bedroom door behind them.

"*Entrez!*" Alleyn called, and then sharply, "Hullo! Who's that?"

"What? I've lost him."

"A woman came out and led him away. They've gone indoors."

"A woman?"

"Fat and dressed in black."

"Please let's go quickly."

Raoul had come through the bedroom and stood behind them. Alleyn said in French, "Do you see that tall building, just to the left of our wall and to the right of the church? It's pinkish with blue shutters and there's something red on one of the balconies."

"I see it, Monsieur."

"Do you know what building it is?"

"I think so, Monsieur. It will be Number 16 in the Rue des Violettes where Madame enquired this morning."

"Troy," Alleyn said. "The Lord knows why, but Ricky's gone to call on Mr. Garbel."

Troy stopped short on her way to the door. "Do you mean . . . ?"

"Raoul says that's the house."

"But—. No," Troy said vigorously. "No, I don't believe it. He wouldn't just get up and go there. Not of his own accord. Not like that. He wouldn't. Come on, Rory."

They were following her when Alleyn said: "When did these flowers come?"

"What flowers? Oh, that. I hadn't noticed it. I don't know. Dr. Baradi, I should think. Please don't let's wait."

An enormous florist's box garnished with a great bow of ribbon lay on the top of a pile of suitcases.

Watched in an agony of impatience by his wife, Alleyn slid a card from under the ribbon and looked at it.

"So sorry," he read, "that I shall be away during your visit. Welcome to Roqueville. P. E. Garbel."

# CHAPTER VI

# Consultation

### I

Troy wouldn't wait for the lift. She ran downstairs with Alleyn and Raoul at her heels. Only the porter was there, sitting at the desk in the hall.

Alleyn said: "This will take thirty seconds, darling. I'm in as much of a hurry as you. Please believe it's important. You can get into the car. Raoul can start the engine." And to the porter he said: "Please telephone this number and give the message I have written on the paper to the person who answers. It is the number of the Préfecture and the message is urgent. It is expected. Were you on duty here when flowers came for Madame?"

"I was on duty when the flowers arrived, Monsieur. It was about an hour ago. I did not know they were for Madame. The woman went straight upstairs without enquiry, as one who knows the way."

"And returned?"

The porter lifted his shoulders. "I did not see her return, Monsieur. No doubt she used the service stairs."

"No doubt," Alleyn said and ran out to the car.

On the way to the Rue des Violettes he said: "I'm going to stop the car a little way from the house, Troy, and I'm going to ask you to wait in it while I go indoors."

"Are you? But why? Ricky's there, isn't he? We saw him."

"Yes, we saw him. But I'm not too keen for other people to see us. Cousin Garbel seems to be known, up at the Chèvre d'Argent."

"But Robin Herrington said he didn't know him and anyway, according to the card on the flowers, Cousin Garbel's gone away. That must be what the concierge was trying to tell me. She said he was *'pas chez elle.'* "

" *'Pas chez soi'* surely?"

"All right. Yes, of course. I couldn't really understand her. I don't understand anything," Troy said desperately. "I just want to get Ricky."

"I know, darling. Not more than I do."

"He didn't look as if he was in one of his panics. Did he?"

"No."

"I expect we'll have a reaction and be furiously snappish with him for frightening us, don't you?"

"We must learn to master our ugly tempers," he said, smiling at her.

"Rory, he will be there still? He won't have gone?"

"It's only ten minutes ago that we saw him on a sixth floor balcony."

"Was she a fat shiny woman who led him in?"

"I hadn't got the glasses. I couldn't spot the shine with the naked eye."

"I didn't like the concierge. Ricky would hate her."

"That is the street, Monsieur," said Raoul. "At the intersection."

"Good. Draw up here by the kerb. I don't want to frighten Madame, but I think all may not be well with the small one whom we have seen on the balcony at Number 16. If anyone were to leave by the back or side of the house, Raoul, would they have to come this way from that narrow side-street and pass this way to get out of Roqueville?"

"This way, Monsieur, either to go east or west out of Roqueville. For the rest there are only other alleyways with flights of steps that lead nowhere."

"Then if a car should emerge from behind Number 16 perhaps it may come about that you start your car and your engine stalls and you block the way. In apologizing you would no doubt go up to the other car and look inside. And if the small one were in the car you would not be able to start your own though you would make a great disturbance by leaning on your horn. And by that time, Raoul, it is possible that M. le Commissaire will have arrived in his car. Or that I have come out of Number 16."

"Aren't you going, Rory?"

"At once, darling. All right, Raoul?"

"Perfectly, Monsieur."

Alleyn got out of the car, crossed the intersection, turned right and entered Number 16.

The hall was dark and deserted. He went at once to the lift-well, glanced at the index of names and pressed the call-button.

"Monsieur?" said the concierge, partly opening the door of her cubby-hole.

Alleyn looked beyond the ringed and grimy hand at one beady eye, the flange of a flattened nose and half a grape-coloured mouth.

"Madame," he said politely and turned back to the lift.

"Monsieur desires?"

"The lift, Madame."

"To ascend where, Monsieur?"

"To the sixth floor, Madame."

"To which apartment on the sixth floor?"

"To the principal apartment. With a balcony."

The lift was wheezing its way down.

"Unfortunately," said the concierge, "the tenant is absent on vacation. Monsieur would care to leave a message?"

"It is the small boy for whom I have called. The small boy whom Madame has been kind enough to admit to the apartment."

"Monsieur is mistaken. I have admitted no children. The apartment is locked."

"Can Nature have been so munificent as to lavish upon us a twin-sister of Madame? If so she has undoubtedly admitted a small boy to the principal apartment on the sixth floor."

The lift came into sight and stopped. Alleyn opened the door.

"One moment," said the concierge. He paused. Her hand was withdrawn from the cubby-hole door. She came out, waddling like a duck and bringing a bunch of keys.

"It is not amusing," she said, "to take a fool's trip. However, Monsieur shall see for himself."

They went up in the lift. The concierge quivered slightly and gave out the combined odours of uncleanliness, frangipani, garlic and hot satin. On the sixth floor she opened a door opposite the lift, waddled through it and sat down panting and massively triumphant on a high chair in the middle of a neat and ordered room whose French windows gave on to a balcony.

Alleyn completely disregarded the concierge. He stopped short in the entrance of the room and looked swiftly round it: at the dressing-table, the shelf above the wash-basin, the gown hanging on the bed-rail and at the three pairs of shoes set out against the wall. He moved to the wardrobe and pulled open the door. Inside it were three sober dresses and a couple of modestly trimmed straw hats. An envelope was lying on the floor of the wardrobe. He stooped down to look at it. It was a business envelope and bore the legend "Compagnie Chimique des Alpes Maritimes." He read the superscription:

A Mlle. Penelope E. Garbel,
16 Rue des Violettes,
Roqueville-de-Sud,
Côte d'Azur

He straightened up, shut the wardrobe door with extreme deliberation and contemplated the concierge, still seated like some obscene goddess, in the middle of the room.

"You disgusting old bag of tripes," Alleyn said thoughtfully in English, "you little know what a fool I've been making of myself."

And he went out to the balcony.

## II

He stood where so short a time ago he had seen Ricky stand and looked across the intervening rooftops to one that bore a large sign: HÔTEL ROYAL. Troy had left the bed-cover hanging over the rail of their balcony.

"A few minutes ago," Alleyn said, returning to the immovable concierge, "from the Hôtel Royal over there I saw my son who was here, Madame, on this balcony."

"It would require the eyes of a hawk to recognize a little boy at that distance. Monsieur is mistaken."

"It required the aid of binoculars and those I had."

"Possibly the son of the laundress who was on the premises and has now gone."

"I saw you, Madame, take the hand of my son, who like yourself was clearly recognizable, and lead him indoors."

"Monsieur is mistaken. I have not left my office since this morning. Monsieur will be good enough to take his departure. I do not insist," the concierge said magnificently, "upon an apology."

"Perhaps," Alleyn said, taking a mille franc note from his pocket-book, "you will accept this instead."

He stood well away from her, holding it out. The eyes glistened and the painted lips moved, but she did not rise. For perhaps four seconds they confronted each other. Then she said, "If Monsieur will wait downstairs I shall be pleased to join him. I have another room to visit."

Alleyn bowed, stooped and pounced. His hand shot along the floor and under the hem of the heavy skirt. She made a short angry noise and tried to trample on the hand. One of her heels caught his wrist.

"Calm yourself, Madame. My intentions are entirely honourable."

He stepped back neatly and extended his arm, keeping the hand closed.

"A strange egg, Madame Blanche," Alleyn said, "for a respectable hen to lay."

He opened his hand. Across the palm lay a little clay goat, painted silver.

### III

From that moment the proceedings in Number 16 Rue des Violettes were remarkable for their unorthodoxy.

Alleyn said: "You have one chance. Where is the boy?"

She closed her eyes and hitched her colossal shoulders up to her ear-rings.

"Very good," Alleyn said and walked out of the room. She had left the key in the lock. He turned it and withdrew the bunch.

It did not take long to go through the rest of the building. For the rooms that were unoccupied he found a master-key. As he crossed each threshold he called once: "Ricky?" and then made a rapid search. In the occupied rooms his visits bore the character of a series of disconnected shots on a cinema screen. He exposed in rapid succession persons of different ages taking their siestas in varying degrees of *désha-billé*. On being told that there was no small boy within, he uttered a word of apology and under the dumbfounded gaze of spinsters, elderly gentlemen, married or romantic couples and, in one instance, an outraged Negress of uncertain years, walked in, opened cupboards, looked under and into beds and, with a further apology, walked out again.

The concierge had begun to thump on the door of the principal apartment of the sixth floor.

On the ground floor he found a crisp bright-eyed man with a neat moustache, powerful shoulders and an impressive uniform.

"M. l'Inspecteur-en-Chef, Alleyn? Allow me to introduce myself. Dupont of the Sûreté, at present acting as Commissary at the Préfecture, Roqueville." He spoke fluent English with a marked accent. "So we are already in trouble," he said as they shook hands. "I have spoken to Madame Alleyn and to Milano. And the boy is not yet found?"

Alleyn quickly related what had happened.

"And the woman Blanche? Where is she, my dear Inspecteur-en-Chef?"

"She is locked in the apartment of Miss P. E. Garbel on the sixth floor. The distant thumping which perhaps you can hear is produced by the woman Blanche."

The Commissary smiled all over his face. "And we are reminded how correct is the deportment of Scotland Yard. Let us leave her to her activities and complete the search. As we do so will you perhaps be good enough to continue your report."

Alleyn complied and they embarked on an exploration of the unsavoury private apartments of Madame Blanche. Alleyn checked at a list of telephone numbers and pointed to the third. "The Château Chèvre d'Argent," he said.

"Indeed? Very suggestive," said M. Dupont; and with a startling and incredible echo from Baker Street added, "Pray continue your most interesting narrative while we explore the basement."

But Ricky was not in any room on the ground floor nor in the cellars under the house. "Undoubtedly they have removed him," said Dupont, "when they saw you wave from your balcony. I shall at once warn my confrères in the surrounding districts. There are not many roads out of Roqueville and all cars can be checked. We then proceed with a tactful but thorough investigation of the town. This affair is not without precedent. Have no fear for your small son. He will come to no harm. Excuse me. I shall telephone from the office of the woman Blanche. Will you remain or would you prefer to rejoin Madame?"

"Thank you. I will have a word with her if I may."

"Implore her," M. Dupont said briskly, "to remain calm. The affair will arrange itself. The small one is in no danger." He bowed and went into the cubby-hole. As he went out Alleyn heard the click of a telephone dial.

A police-car was drawn up by the kerb outside Number 16. Alleyn crossed the road to Raoul's car.

There was no need to calm Troy: she was very quiet indeed, and perfectly collected. She looked ill with anxiety but she smiled at him and said: "Bad luck, darling. No sign?"

"Some signs," he said, resting his arms on the door beside her. "Dupont agrees with me that it's an attempt to keep me occupied. He's sure Ricky's all right."

"He *was* there, wasn't he? We did see him?"

Alleyn said: "We did see him," and after a moment's hesitation he took the little silver goat from his pocket. "He left it behind him."

Raoul ejaculated: *"La petite chèvre d'argent."*

Troy's lips quivered. She took the goat in her hands and folded it between them. "What do we do now?"

"Dupont is stopping all cars driving out of Roqueville and will order a house-to-house search in the town. He's a good man."

"I'm sure he is," Troy said politely. She looked terrified. "You're not going back to the Chèvre d'Argent, are you? You're not going to call their bluff?"

"We're going to take stock." Alleyn closed his hand over hers. "I know one wants to drive off madly in all directions, yelling for Ricky but honestly, darling, that's not the form for this kind of thing. We've *got* to take stock. So far we've scarcely had time to think, much less reason."

"It's just—when he knows he's lost—it's his nightmare—mislaying us."

Two gendarmes, smart in their uniforms and sun-helmets, rode past on bicycles, turned into the Rue des Violettes, dismounted and went into Number 16.

"Dupont's chaps," said Alleyn. "Now we shan't be long. And I have got one bit of news for you. Cousin Garbel is a spinster."

"What on earth do you mean?"

"His name is Penelope and he wears a straw hat trimmed with parma violets."

Troy said: "Don't muddle me, darling. I'm so desperately addled already."

"I'm terribly sorry. It's true. Your correspondent is a woman who has some connection with the chemical works we saw this morning. For reasons I can only guess at, she's let you address her letters as if to a man. How *did* you address them?"

"To M. P. E. Garbel."

"Perhaps she thought you imagined 'M.' to be the correct abbreviation of Mademoiselle?"

Troy shook her head: "It doesn't seem to matter much now, but it's quite incredible. Look: something's beginning to happen."

The little town was waking up. Shop doors opened and proprietors came out in their shirt sleeves scratching their elbows. At the far end of the Rue des Violettes there was an eruption of children's voices and a clatter of shoes on stone. The driver of the police-car outside Number 16 started up his engine and the Commissary came briskly down the steps. He made a crisp signal to the driver, who turned his car, crossed the intersection and finally pulled up in front of Raoul. M. Dupont walked across, saluted Troy and addressed himself to Alleyn.

"We commence our search of houses in Roqueville, my dear Inspecteur-en-Chef. The road patrols are installed and a general warning is being issued to my colleagues in the surrounding territory. Between 2:15 by the church clock when you saw your son until the moment when you arrived at these apartments, there was an interval of about ten minutes. If he was removed in an auto it was during those minutes. The patrols were instructed at five minutes to three. Again if he was removed in an auto it has had half an hour's advance and can in that time have gone at the most no further on our roads than fifty kilometres. Outside every town beyond that radius we have posted a patrol and if they have nothing to report we shall search exhaustively within the radius. Madame, it is most fortunate that you saw the small one from your hotel. Thus have you hurled a screwdriver in the factory."

The distracted Troy puzzled over the Commissary's free use of English idiom, but Alleyn gave a sharp exclamation. "*The factory!*" he said. "By the Lord, I wonder."

"Monsieur?"

"My dear Dupont, you have acted with the greatest expedition and judgment. What do you suggest we do now?"

"I am entirely at your disposal, M. l'Inspecteur-en-Chef. May I suggest that perhaps a fuller understanding of the situation—"

"Yes, indeed. Shall we go to our hotel?"

"Enchanted, Monsieur."

"I think," Alleyn said, "that our driver here is very willing to take an active part. He's been extremely helpful already."

"He is a good fellow, this Milano," said Dupont and addressed Raoul in his own language: "See here, my lad, we are making enquiries for the missing boy in Roqueville. If he is anywhere in the town it will be at the house of some associate of the woman Blanche at Number 16. Are you prepared to take a hand?"

Raoul, it appeared, was prepared. "If he is in the town, M. le Commissaire, I shall know it inside an hour."

"Oh, *là-là!*" M. Dupont remarked, "what a song our cock sings."

He scowled playfully at Raoul and opened the doors of the car. Troy and Alleyn were ushered ceremoniously into the police-car and the driver took them back to the hotel.

In their bedroom, which had begun to take on a look of half-real familiarity, Troy and Alleyn filled in the details of their adventures from the time of the first incident in the train until Ricky's disappearance. M. Dupont listened with an air of deference tempered by professional detachment. When they had finished he clapped his knees lightly and made a neat gesture with his thumb and forefinger pressed together.

"Admirable!" he said. "So we are in possession of our facts and now we act in concert, but first I must tell you one little fact that I have in my sleeve. There has been, four weeks ago, a case of child-stealing in the Paysdoux. It was the familiar story. A wealthy family from Lyons. A small one. A flightish nurse. During the afternoon promenade a young man draws the attention of this sexy nurse. The small one gambols in the gardens by our casino. The nurse and the young man are tête-à-tête upon a seat. Automobiles pass to and fro, sometimes stopping. In one are the confederates of the young man. Presently the nurse remembers her duty. The small one is vanished and remains so. Also vanished is the young man. A message is thrown through the hotel window. The small one is to be recovered with five hundred mille francs at a certain time and at a place outside St. Céleste. There are the customary threats in the matter of informing the police. Monsieur Papa, under pressure from Madame Maman, obeys. He is driven to within a short distance of the place. He continues on foot. A car appears. Stops. A man with a handkerchief over his face and a weapon in his hand gets out. Monsieur Papa, again following instructions, places the money under a stone by the road and retires with his hands above his head. The man collects and examines the money and returns to the car. The small one gets out. The car drives away. The small one," said M. Dupont, opening his eyes very wide at Troy, "is not pleased. He wishes to remain with his new acquaintances."

"Oh, no!" Troy cried out.

"But yes. He has found them enchanting. Nevertheless he rejoins his family. And now, having facilitated the escape of the cat, Monsieur Papa attempts to close the bag. He informs the police." M. Dupont spread his hands in the classic gesture and waited for his audience-reaction.

"The usual story," Alleyn said.

"M. Dupont," Troy said, "do you think the same men have taken Ricky?"

"No, Madame. I think we are intended to believe it is the same men."

"But why? Why should it not be these people?"

"Because," M. Dupont rejoined, touching his small moustache, "this morning at 7:30 these people were apprehended and are now locked up in the *poste de police* at St. Céleste. Monsieur Papa had the forethought to mark the notes. It was tactfully done. A slight addition to the décor. And the small one gave useful information. The news of the arrest would have appeared in the evening papers but I have forbidden it. The affair was already greatly publicized."

"So our friends," Alleyn suggested, "unaware of the arrest, imitate the performance and hope our reactions will be those of Monsieur Papa and Madame Maman and that you will turn our attention to St. Céleste."

"But can you be so sure—" Troy began desperately. M. Dupont bent at the waist and gazed respectfully at her. "Ah, Madame," he said, "consider. Consider the facts. At the Château de la Chèvre d'Argent there is a group of persons very highly involved in the drug 'raquette.' By a strange accident your husband, already officially interested in these persons, is precipitated into their midst. One, perhaps two of the guests, know who he is. The actress Wells, who is an addict, is sent to make sure. She returns and tells them: 'We entertain, let me inform you, the most distinguished and talented officer of The Scotland Yard. If we do not take some quick steps he will return to enquire for his invalid. It is possible he already suspects.' And it is agreed he must not return. How can he be prevented from doing so? By the apparent kidnapping of his son. This is effected very adroitly. The woman with the bouquet tells the small Ricketts that his mother awaits him at the house she visited this morning. In the meantime a car is on its way from the Château to take them to St. Céleste. He is to be kept in the apartment of Garbel until it comes. The old Blanche takes him there. She omits to lock the doors on to the balcony. He goes out. You see him. He sees you. Blanche observes. He is removed and before you can reach him there the car arrives and he is removed still further."

"Where?"

"If, following the precedent, they go to St. Céleste, they will be halted by our patrols, but I think perhaps they will have thought of that and changed their plans and if so it will not be to St. Céleste."

"I agree," Alleyn said.

"We shall be wiser when their message arrives, as arrive it assuredly will. There is also the matter of this Mademoiselle Garbel whose name is in the books and who has some communication with the Compagnie Chimique des Alpes Maritimes, which may very well be better named the Compagnie pour l'Elaboration de Diacetylmorphine. She is of the 'raquette,' no doubt, and you have enquired for her."

"For him. We thought: 'him.'"

"Darling," Alleyn said, "can you remember the letters pretty clearly?"

"No," said poor Troy, "how should I? I only know they were full of dreary information about buses and roads and houses."

"Have you ever checked the relationship?"

"No. He—she—talked about distant cousins who I knew had existed but were nearly all dead."

"Did she ever write about my job?"

"I don't think, directly. I don't think she ever wrote things like 'how awful' or 'how lovely' to be married to a chief detective-inspector. She said things about my showing her letters to my distinguished husband, who would no doubt be interested in their contents."

"And, unmitigated clod that I am, I wasn't. My dear Dupont," Alleyn said, "I've been remarkably stupid. I think this lady has been trying to warn me about the activities of the drug racket in the Paysdoux."

"But I thought," Troy said, "I thought it was beginning to look as if it was she who had taken Ricky. Weren't the flowers a means of getting into our rooms while I was at luncheon? Wasn't the message about being away a blind? Doesn't it look as if she's one of the gang? She knew we were coming here. If she wanted to tell you about the drug racket why did she go away?"

"Why indeed? We don't know why she went away."

"Rory, I don't want to be a horror, but— No," said Troy, "I won't say it."

"I'll say it for you. Why in Heaven's name can't we do something about Ricky instead of sitting here gossiping about Miss Garbel?"

"But, dear Madame," cried M. Dupont, "we *are* doing things about Ricketts. Only—" M. Dupont continued, fortunately mistaking for an agonized sob the snort of hysteria that had escaped Troy—"only by an assemblage of the known facts can we arrive at a rational solution. Moreover, if the former case is to be imitated we shall certainly receive a message and it is important that we are here when it arrives. In the meantime all precautions have been taken. But all!"

"I know," Troy said, "I'm terribly sorry. I know."

"You brought Miss Garbel's last letter, darling. Let's have a look at it."

"I'll get it."

Troy was not very good at keeping things tidy. She had a complicated rummage in her travelling case and handbag before she unearthed the final Garbel letter, which she handed with an anxious look to Alleyn. It was in a crumpled condition and he spread it out on the arm of his chair.

"Here it is," he said, and read aloud.

My dear Agatha Troy,

I wrote to you on December 17th of last year and hope that you received my letter and that I may have the pleasure of hearing from you in the not *too* distant future! I pursue my usual round of activities. Most of my jaunts take me into the district lying *west* of Roqueville, a district known as the Paysdoux (Paysdoux, literally translated, but allowing for the reversed position of the adjective, means Sweet Country) though a close acquaintance with some of the inhabitants might suggest that Pays *Dopes* would be a better title ! ! ! (Forgive the parenthesis and the indifferent and slangy *pun*. I have never been able to resist an opportunity to play on words.)

"Hell's boots!" Alleyn said. "Under our very noses! *Pays Dopes* indeed, District of Dopes and Dope pays." He read on:

As the acquaintances I visit most frequently live some thirty kilometres (about seventeen miles) away on the western reaches of the Route Maritime I make use of the omnibus, No. *16,* leaving the Place des Sarrasins at five minutes past the hour. The fare at the present rate of exchange is about 1/– English, single, and 1/9 return. I enclose a ticket which will no doubt be of interest. It is a pleasant drive and commands a pretty prospect of the Mediterranean on one's left and on one's right a number of ancient buildings as well as some evidence of progress, if progress it can be called, in the presence of a large *chemical* works, in which, owing to my chosen profession, I have come to take some interest.

"Oh Lord!" Alleyn lamented. "Why didn't I read this before we left? We have been so bloody superior over this undoubtedly admirable spinster."

"Please?" said M. Dupont.

"Listen to this, Dupont. Suppose this lady, who is a qualified chemist, was in the hands of the drug racket. Suppose she worked for them. Suppose she wanted to let someone in authority in England know what goes on inside the racket. Now. Do you imagine that there is any reason why she shouldn't write what she knows to this person and put the letter in the post?"

"There is good reason to suppose she might fear to do so, Mr. Chief," rejoined Dupont, who no doubt considered that the time had come for a more familiar mode of address. "As an Englishwoman she is perhaps not quite trusted in the 'raquette.' Her correspondence may be watched. Someone who can read English at the *bureau-de-poste* may be bribed. Perhaps she merely suspects that this may be so. They are thorough, these blackguards. Their net is fine in the mesh."

"So she writes her boring letters and every time she writes, she drops a veiled hint, hoping I may see the letter. The Chèvre d'Argent is about thirty kilometres west on the Route Maritime. She tells us by means of tedious phrases, ferocious puns, and used bus tickets that she is a visitor there. How did she address her letters, Troy?"

"To 'Agatha Troy.' She said in her first letter that she understood that I would prefer to be addressed by my professional name. Like an actress, she added, though not in other respects. With the usual row of ejaculation marks. I don't think she ever used your name. You were always my brilliant and distinguished husband!"

"And is my face red!" said Alleyn. M. Dupont's was puzzled. Alleyn continued reading the letter.

If ever you and your distinguished husband should visit "these parts"! you may care to take this drive which is full of interesting topographic features that often escape the notice of the *ordinary Tourist*. I fear my own humble account of our local background is a somewhat *Garbelled* (! ! !) version and suggest that first-hand observation would be much more rewarding! With kindest regards . . .

"Really—" Alleyn said, handing the letter back to Troy—"short of cabling: 'Drug barons at work come and catch them' she could scarcely have put it more clearly."

"You didn't read the letters. I only told you about bits of them. I ought to have guessed."

"Well, it's no good blackguarding ourselves. Look here, both of you. Suppose we're on the right track about Miss Garbel. Suppose, for some reason, she's in the racket yet wants to put me wise about it and has hoped to lure me over here. Why, when Troy writes and tells her we're coming, does she go away without explanation?"

"And why," Troy interjected, "does she send flowers by someone who used them as a means of kidnapping Ricky and taking him to her flat?"

"The card on the flowers isn't in her writing."

"She might have telephoned the florist."

"Which can be checked," said M. Dupont, "of course. Will you allow me? This, I assume is the bouquet."

He inspected the box of tuberoses. "Ah, yes. Le Pot des Fleurs. May I telephone, Madame?"

While he did so, Troy went out to the balcony and Alleyn, seeing her there, her fingers against her lips in the classic gesture of the anxious woman, joined her and put his arm about her shoulders.

"I'm looking at that other balcony," she said. "It's silly, isn't it? Suppose he came out again. It's like one of those dreams of frustration."

He touched her cheek and she said: "You mustn't be too nice to me."

"Little perisher," Alleyn muttered, "you may depend upon it he's airing his French and saying 'why' with every second breath he draws. Did you know W. S. Gilbert was pinched by bandits when he was a kid?"

"I think I did. Might they have taken him to the Chèvre d'Argent? As a sort of double bluff?"

"I don't think so, my darling. My bet is he's somewhere nearer than that."

"Nearer to Roqueville? Where, Rory, where?"

"It's a guess and an unblushing guess, but—"

M. Dupont came bustling out to the balcony.

"Alors!" he began and checked himself. "My dear Monsieur and Madame, we progress a little. Le Pot des Fleurs tells me the flowers were bought and removed by a woman of the servant class, not of the district, who copied the writing on the card from a piece of paper. They do not remember seeing the woman before. We may find she is a maid of the Château, may we not?"

"May we?" said Troy a little desperately.

"But there are better news than these, Madame. The good Raoul Milano has reported to the hotel. It appears that an acquaintance of his, an idle fellow living in the western suburb, has seen a car, a light blue Citroën, at 2:30 P.M. driving out of Roqueville by the western route. In the car were the driver, a young woman and a small boy dressed in yellow and brown. The man wears a red beret and the woman is bareheaded. The car was impeded for a moment by an omnibus and the acquaintance of Milano heard the small one talking. He spoke in French but childishly and with a little difficulty, using foreign words. He appeared to be making an enquiry. The acquaintance heard him say 'pourquoi' several times."

"Conclusive," Alleyn said, watching Troy.

She cried out: "Did he seem frightened?"

"Madame, no. It appears that Milano made the same enquiry. The acquaintance said the small one seemed exigent. The actual phrase,"

M. Dupont said, turning to Alleyn, "was: *'Il semblait être impatient de comprendre quelque chose'l*"

"He was impatient to understand something," Troy ejaculated, "is that it?"

"*Mais oui, Madame,*" said Dupont and added a playful compliment in French to the effect that Troy evidently spoke the language as if she were born to it. Troy failed to understand a word of this and gazed anxiously at him. He continued in English. "Now, between Roqueville and the point where the nearest patrol on the western route is posted there are three deviations: all turning inland. Two are merely rural lanes. The third is a road that leads to a monastery and also—" Here M. Dupont raised his forefinger and looked roguish.

"And also," Alleyn said, "to the Factory of the Maritime Alps Chemical Company."

"*Parfaitement!*" said M. Dupont.

## IV

"And you think he's there!" Troy cried out. "But why? Why take him there?"

Alleyn said: "As I see it, and I don't pretend, Lord knows, to see at all clearly, this might be the story. Oberon & Co. have a strong interest in the factory but they don't realize we know it. Baradi and your painting chum Glande were at great pains to deplore the factory: to repudiate the factory as an excrescence in the landscape. But we suspect it probably houses the most impudent manufactory of hyoscine in Europe and we know Oberon's concerned in the traffic. All right. They realize we've seen Ricky on the balcony of Number 16 and have called in the police. If Blanche has succeeded in getting herself out of durance vile she's told them all about it. They've lost their start. They daren't risk taking Ricky to St. Céleste, as they originally planned. What are they to do with him? It would be easy and safe to house him in one of the offices at the factory and have him looked after. You must remember that nobody up at the Château knows that he understands a certain amount of French."

"The people who've got him will have found that out by now."

"And also that his French doesn't go beyond the nursery stage. They may have told him that we've gone back to look after Miss Truebody and have arranged for him to be minded until we are free. I think they may have meant to keep him at Number 16 while we went haring off to St. Céleste. *La Belle Blanche* (damn her eyes) probably rang up and said we'd spotted him on the balcony and they thought up the factory in a hurry."

"Could they depend on our going to St. Céleste? Just on the strength of our probably getting to hear about the other kidnapping?"

"No," said Alleyn and Dupont together.

"Then—I don't understand."

"Madame," said Dupont, "there is no doubt that you shall be directed, if not to a place near St. Céleste, at least to some other place along the eastern route. To some place as far as possible from the true whereabouts of Ricketts."

"Directed?"

"There will be a little note or a little telephone message. Always remember they fashion themselves on the pattern of the former affair, being in ignorance of this morning's arrest."

"It all sounds so terribly like guesswork," Troy said after a moment. "Please, what do we do?"

Alleyn looked at Dupont, whose eyebrows rose portentously. "It is a little difficult," he said. "From the point-of-view of my department, it is a delicate situation. We are not yet ready to bring an accusation against the organization behind the factory. When we are ready, Madame, it will be a very big matter, a matter not only for the department but for the police forces of several nations, for the International Police and for the United Nations Organization itself."

Troy suddenly had a nightmarish vision of Ricky in his lemon shirt and brown shorts abandoned to a labyrinth of departmental corridors.

Watching her, Alleyn said: "So that we mustn't suggest, you see, that we are interested in anything but Ricky."

"Which, God knows, I'm not," said Troy.

"Ah, Madame," Dupont said, "I too am a parent." And to Troy's intense embarrassment he kissed her hand.

"It seems to me," Alleyn said, "that the best way would be for your department, my dear Dupont, to make a great show of watching the eastern route and the country round St. Céleste and for us to make an equally great show of driving in a panic-stricken manner about the countryside. Indeed, it occurs to me that I might very well help matters by ringing up the Château and *registering* panic. What do you think?"

Dupont made a tight purse of his mouth, drew his brows together, looked pretty sharply at Alleyn and then lightly clapped his hands together.

"In effect," he said, "why not?"

Alleyn went to the telephone. "Baradi, I fancy," he said thoughtfully, and after a moment's consideration: "Yes, I think it had better be Baradi."

He dialled the hotel office and gave the number. While he waited he grimaced at Troy: "Celebrated imitation about to begin. You will notice that I have nothing in my mouth."

They could hear the bell ringing, up at the Chèvre d'Argent.

"'Allo, 'allo!" Alleyn began in a high voice and broke into a spate of indifferent French. Was that the Chèvre d'Argent? Could he speak to Dr. Baradi? It was extremely urgent. He gave his name. They heard the telephone quack: "Un moment, Monsieur." He grinned at Troy and covered the receiver with his hand. "Let's hope they have to wake him up," he said. "Give me a cigarette, darling."

But before he could light it Baradi had come to the telephone. Alleyn's deep voice was pitched six tones above its normal range and sounded as if it was only just under control. He began speaking in French, corrected himself, apologized and started again in English. "Do forgive me," he said, "for bothering you again. The truth is, we are in trouble here. I know it sounds ridiculous but has my small boy by any chance turned up at the Château? Yes. Yes, we've lost him. We thought there might be the chance—there are buses, they say—and we're at our wits' end. No, I was afraid not. It's just that my wife is quite frantic. Yes. Yes, I know. Yes, so we've been told. Yes, I've seen the police but you know what they're like." Alleyn turned towards M. Dupont, who immediately put on a heroic look. "They're the same wherever you go, red-tape and inactivity. Most unsatisfactory." M. Dupont bowed. "Yes, if it's the same blackguards we shall be told what we have to do. No, no, I refuse to take any risks of that sort. Somehow or another I'll raise the money but it won't be easy with the restrictions." Alleyn pressed his lips together. His long fingers blanched as they tightened round the receiver. "Would you really?" he said and the colour of his voice, its diffidence and its hesitancy, so much at variance with the look in his eyes, gave him the uncanny air of a ventriloquist. "Would you really? I say, that's most awfully kind of you both. I'll tell my wife. It'll be a great relief to her to know—yes, well I ought to have said something about that, only I'm so damnably worried—I'm afraid we shan't be able to do anything about Miss Truebody until we've found Ricky. I am taking my wife to St. Céleste, if that's where—yes, probably this afternoon if I—I don't think we'll feel very like coming back after what's happened, but of course— Is she? Oh, dear! I'm very sorry. That's very good of him. I am sorry. Well, if you really don't mind. I'm afraid I'm not much use. Thank you. Yes. Well, goodbye."

He hung up the receiver. His face was white.

"He offers every possible help," he said, "financial and otherwise, and is sure Mr. Oberon will be immeasurably distressed. He has now, no doubt, gone away to enjoy a belly laugh at our expense. It is going to be difficult to keep one's self-control over Messrs. Oberon and Baradi."

"I believe you," said M. Dupont.

"Rory, you're certain now, in your own mind, aren't you?"

"Yes. He didn't utter a word that was inconsistent with genuine concern and helpfulness, but I'm certain in my own mind."

"Why?"

"One gets a sixth sense about that sort of bluff. And I think he made a slip. He said: 'Of course you can do nothing definite until these scoundrels ring you up.'"

M. Dupont cried, "Ahah!"

"But you said to him," Troy objected, "that we would be told what to do."

"'Would be *told* what to do!' Exactly. In the other case the kidnappers' instructions came by letter. Why should Baradi think that this time they would telephone?"

As if in answer, the bedroom telephone buzzed twice.

"This will be it," said Alleyn and took up the receiver.

# CHAPTER VII

# Sound of Ricky

## I

ALLEYN was used to anonymous calls on the telephone. There was a quality of voice that he had learned to recognize as common to them all. Though this new voice spoke in French it held the familiar tang of artifice. He nodded to Dupont, who at once darted out of the room.

The voice said: "M. Allen?"

"C'est Allen qui parle."

"Bien. Écoutez. A sept heures demain soir, presentez-vous à pied et tout seul, vis-à-vis du pavillon de chasse en ruines, il y a sept kilomètres vers le midi du village St. Céleste-des-Alpes. Apportez avec vous cent mille francs en billets de cent. N'avertissez-pas la police, ou le petit apprendra bien les consequences. Compris?"

Alleyn repeated it in stumbling French, as slowly as possible and with as many mistakes as he dared to introduce. He wanted to give Dupont time. The voice grew impatient in correction. Alleyn, however, repeated his instructions for the third time and began to expostulate in English. "Plus rien à dire," said the voice and rang off.

Alleyn turned to Troy. "Did you understand?" he asked.

"I don't know. I think so."

"Well, it's all right, my dearest. It's as we thought. Tomorrow evening outside a village called St. Céleste-des-Alpes with a hundred quid in my hand. The village, no doubt, will be somewhere above St. Céleste."

"You didn't recognize the voice?"

"It wasn't Baradi or Oberon. It wasn't young Herrington. I wouldn't swear it wasn't Carbury Glande, who was croaking with hangover this morning and might have recovered by now. And I would by no means swear that it wasn't Baradi's servant, whom I've only heard utter about six phrases in Egyptian but who certainly understands French. There was a bit of an accent and I didn't think it sounded local."

Dupont tapped and entered. "Any luck?" Alleyn said.

"Of a kind. I rang the *centrale* and was answered by an imbecile but the call has been traced. And to where do you suppose?"

"Number 16, Rue des Violettes?"

"Precisely!"

"Fair enough," Alleyn said. "It must be their town office."

"I also rang the Préfecture. No reports have come in from the patrols. What was the exact telephone message, if you please?"

Alleyn told him in French, wrapping up the threats to Ricky in words that were outside Troy's vocabulary.

"The same formula," Dupont said, "as in the reported version of the former affair. My dear Mr. Chief and Madame, it seems that we should now pursue our hunch."

"To the chemical works?"

"Certainly."

"Thank God!" Troy ejaculated.

"All the same," Alleyn said, "it's tricky. As soon as we get there the gaff is blown. The Château, having been informed that the telephone message went through, will wait for us to go to St. Céleste. When we turn up at the factory, the factory will ring the Château. Tricky! How far away is St. Céleste?"

"About seventy kilometres."

"Is it possible to start off on the eastern route and come round to the factory by a detour? Behind Roqueville?"

M. Dupont frowned. "There are some mountain lanes," he said. "Little more than passages for goats and cattle but of a width that is possible."

"Possible for Raoul who is, I have noticed, a good driver."

"He will tell us, at least. He is beneath."

"Good." Alleyn turned to his wife. "See here, darling. Will you go down and ask Raoul to fill up his tank—*faire plein d'essence* will be all right—and ask him to come back as soon as he's done it. Will you then ask for the manager and tell him we're going to St. Céleste, but would like to leave our heavy luggage here and keep our rooms. Perhaps you should offer to pay a week in advance. Here's some money. I'll bring down a couple of suitcases and join you in the hall. All right?"

"All right. *Voulez-vous*," Troy said anxiously, "*faire plein d'essence et revenez ici.* O.K.?"

"O.K."

When she had gone Alleyn said, "Dupont, I wanted a word with you. You can see what a hellish business this is for me, can't you? I know damn well how important it is not to let our investigation go off like a damp squib. I realize, nobody better, that a premature inquiry at the factory might prejudice a very big coup. I'm here on a job and my job is with the police of your country and my own. In a way it's the most critical assignment I've ever had."

"And for me, also."

"But the boy's my boy and his mother's my wife. It looked perfectly safe to bring them here and they gave me admirable cover, but as things have turned out, I shouldn't have brought them. But for the unfortunate Miss Truebody, of course, it *would* have been all right."

"And she, too, provided admirable cover. An unquestioned entrée."

"Not for long, however. What I'm trying to say is this: I've fogged out a scheme of approach. I realize that in suggesting it I'm influenced by an almost overwhelming anxiety about Ricky. I'll be glad if you tell me at once if you think it impracticable and, from the police angle, unwise."

Dupont said: "M. l'Inspecteur-en-Chef, I understand the difficulty and respect, very much, your delicacy. I shall be honoured to advise."

"Thank you. Here goes, then. It's essential that we arouse no suspicion of our professional interest in the factory. It's highly probable that the key men up there have already been informed from the Château of my real identity. There's a chance, I suppose, that Annabella Wells has kept her promise, but it's a poor chance. After all, if these people don't know who I am why should they kidnap Ricky? All right. We make a show of leaving this hotel and taking the eastern route for St. Céleste. That will satisfy anybody who may be watching us at this end. We take to the hills and double back to the factory. By this time, you, with a suitable complement of officers, are on your way there. I go in and ask for Ricky. I am excitable and agitated. They say he's not there. I insist that I've unimpeachable evidence that he is there. I demand to see the manager. I produce Raoul, who says he took his girl for a drive and saw a car with Ricky in it turn in at the factory gates. They stick to

their guns. I make a hell of a row. I tell them I've applied to you. You
arrive with a carload of men. You take the manager aside and tell him
I am a V.I.P. on holiday."

"Comment? V.I.P.?"

"A very important person. You see it's extremely awkward. That you
think the boy's been kidnapped and that it's just possible one of their
workmen has been bribed to hide him. You'll say I'll make things very
hot for you at the Sûreté if you don't put on a show of searching for
Ricky. You produce a *mandat de perquisition*. You are terribly apologetic and very bored with me, but you say that unfortunately you have
no alternative. As a matter of form you must search the factory. Now,
what does the manager do?"

Dupont's sharp eyebrows were raised to the limit. Beneath them his
round eyes stared with glazed impartiality at nothing in particular. His
arms were folded. Alleyn waited.

"In effect," Dupont said at last, "he sends his secretary to investigate.
The secretary returns with Ricketts and there are a great many apologies. The manager assures me that there will be an exhaustive enquiry
and appropriate dismissals."

"What do you say to this?"

"Ah," said Dupont, suddenly lowering his eyebrows and unfolding
his arms. "That is more difficult."

"Do I perhaps intervene? Having clasped my son to my bosom and
taken him out with his mother to the car, thus giving the manager an
opportunity to attempt bribery at a high level, do I not return and take
it as matter of course that you consider this an admirable opportunity to
pursue your search for the kidnappers?"

Dupont's smile irradiated his face. "It is possible," he said. "It is conceivable."

"Finally, my dear Dupont, can we act along these lines or any other
that suggest themselves without arousing the smallest suspicion that we
are interested in anything but the recovery of the child?"

"The word of operation is indeed 'act.' From your performance on
the telephone, Mr. Chief, I can have no misgivings about your own
performance. And for myself"—here Dupont tapped his chest, touched
his moustache and gave Alleyn an indescribably roguish glance—"I believe I shall do well enough."

They stood up. Alleyn put his police bag inside a large suitcase.
After looking at the chaos within Troy's partly unpacked luggage, he
decided on two cases. He also collected their overcoats and Ricky's.

"Shall we about it?" he asked.

"*En avant, alors!*" said Dupont.

## II

Mr. Oberon looked down at the figure on the bed. "Quite peaceful," he said. "Isn't it strange?"

"The teeth," Baradi pointed out, "make a great difference."

"There is a certain amount of discolouration."

"Hypostatic staining. The climate."

"Then there is every reason," Mr. Oberon observed with satisfaction, "for an immediate funeral."

"Certainly."

"If they have in fact gone off to St. Céleste they cannot return until the day after tomorrow."

"If, on the other hand, this new man at the Préfecture is intelligent, which Allen says is not the case, they may pick up some information."

"Let us—" Mr. Oberon suggested as he absent-mindedly rearranged the sprigged locknit nightgown which was pinned down by crossed hands to the rigid bosom—"let us suppose the worst. They recover the child," he raised his hand. "Yes, yes, it is unlikely, but suppose it happens. They call to enquire. They ask to see her."

The two men were silent for a time. "Very well," Baradi said. "So they see her. She will not be a pretty sight, but they see her."

Mr. Oberon was suddenly inspired. "There must be flowers," he ejaculated. "Masses and masses of flowers. A nest. A coverlet of flowers, smelling like incense. Tuberoses," he cried softly clapping his hands together. "They will be entirely appropriate. I shall order them. Tuberoses! And orchids."

## III

The eastern route followed the seaboard for three miles out of Roqueville and then turned slightly inland. At this point a country road branched off it to the left. Raoul took the road which mounted into the hills by a series of hairpin bends. They climbed out of soft coastal air and entered a region of mountain freshness. A light breeze passed like a hand through the olive groves and sent spirals of ruddy dust across the road. The seaboard with its fringe of meretricious architecture had dwindled into an incident, while the sea and sky and warm earth widely enlarged themselves.

The road, turning about the contour of the hills, was littered with rock and scarred by wheel tracks. Sometimes it became a ledge traversing the face of sheer cliffs, and in normal times Troy, who disliked heights, would have feared these passages. Now she dreaded them merely because they had to be taken slowly.

"How long," she asked, "will it be, do you suppose?"

"Roqueville's down there a little ahead of us. We'll pass above it in a few minutes. I gather we now cast back into the mountains for about the same distance as we've travelled already and then work round to a junction with the main road to the factory. Sorry about these corners, darling," Alleyn said as they edged round a bend that looked like a take-off into space. "Are you minding it very much?"

"Only because it's slow. Raoul's a good driver, isn't he?"

"Very good indeed. Could you bear it if I told you about this job? I think perhaps I ought to, but it'll be a bit dreary."

"Yes," Troy said. "I'd like that. The drearier the better because I'll have to concentrate."

"Well, you know it's to do with the illicit drug trade, but I don't suppose you know much about the trade itself. By and large it's probably the worst thing apart from war that's happened to human beings in modern times. Before the 1914 war the nations most troubled by the opium racket had begun to do something about it. There was a Shanghai conference and a Hague Convention. Both were cautious tentative shows. None of the nations came to them with a clean record and all the delegates were embarrassed by murky backgrounds in which production, manufacture and distribution involved the revenue both of states and of highly placed individuals. Dost thou attend me?"

"Sir," said Troy, "most heedfully."

They exchanged the complacent glance of persons who recognize each other's quotations.

"At the Hague Convention they did get round to making one or two conservative decisions but before they were ratified the war came along and the whole thing lapsed. After the peace the traffic was stepped up most murderously. It's really impossible to exaggerate the scandal of those years. At the top end were nations getting a fat revenue out of the sale of opium and its derivatives. An investigator said at one stage that half Europe was being poisoned to bolster up the domestic policy of Bulgaria. The goings-on were fantastic. Chargés d'affaires smuggled heroin in their diplomatic baggage. Drug barons built works all over Europe. Diacetylmorphine, which is heroin to you, was brewed on the Champs Élysées. Highly qualified chemists were offered princely salaries to work in drug factories and a great number of them fell for it. Many of the smartest and most fashionable people in European society lived on the trade: murderers, if the word has any meaning. At the other end of the stick were the street pedlars, at the foot of Nurse

Cavell's statue among other places, and the addicts. The addicts were killing themselves in studies, studios, dressing-rooms, brothels, boudoirs and garrets; young intellectuals and young misfits were ruining themselves by the score. Girls were kept going by their *souteneurs* with shots of the stuff. And so on. Thou attendest not."

"Oh, good sir, I do."

"I pray thee, mark me. At the Peace Conference this revolting baby was handed over to the League of Nations, who appointed an Advisory Committee who began the first determined assault on the thing. The international police came in, various bodies were set up and a bit of real progress was made. Only a bit. Factories pulled down in Turkey were rebuilt in Bulgaria. Big centralized industries were busted only to reappear like crops of small ulcers in other places. But something was attempted and a certain amount was achieved by 1939."

"Oh, dear! History at it again?"

"More or less. The difference lies in the fact that this time the preliminary work had been done and the machinery for investigation partly set up. But the Second World War did its stuff and everything lapsed. U.N.O. doesn't start from scratch in the way that the League did. But it faces the old situation and it's still up against the Big Boys. The police still catch the sprats at the customs counter and miss the mackerels in high places. The factories have again moved: from Bulgaria into post-war Italy and from post-war Italy, it appears, into the Paysdoux of Southern France. And the Big Boys have moved with them. Particularly Dr. Baradi and Mr. Oberon."

"Are they really big?"

"Not among the tops, perhaps. There we climb into very rarefied altitudes and by as hazardous a road as this one. But Oberon and Baradi are certainly in the mackerel class. Oberon, I regret to tell you, is a British subject at the moment although he began in the Middle East where he ran a quack religion of a dubious sort and got six months for his pains. He came to us by way of Portugal and Egypt. In Portugal he practiced the same game during the war and made his first connection with the dope trade. In Egypt he was stepped up in the racket and made the acquaintance of his chum Baradi. By that time he'd acquired large sums of money. Two fortunes fell into his lap from rich disciples in Lisbon—middle-aged women, who became Daughters of the Sun or something, remade their wills and died shortly afterwards."

"Oh, Lord!"

"You may well say so. Baradi's a different story. Baradi was a really brilliant medical student who trained in Paris and has become one of the leading surgeons of his time. He had some sort of entrée to court circles in Cairo and, thanks to his skill and charms, any number of useful connections in France. *You* may not think him very delicious but it appears that a great many women do. He got in with the Boys in Paris and Egypt and is known to be a trafficker in a big way. It's his money and Oberon's that's behind the Chemical Company of the Maritime Alps. That's as much as the combined efforts of the international police, the Sûreté and the Yard have gleaned about Baradi and Oberon, and it's on that information I'm meant to act."

"And is Ricky a spanner in the works?"

"He may be a spanner in their works, my pretty. He gives us an excuse for getting into the factory. They may have played into our hands when they took Ricky into the factory."

"*If* they took him there," Troy said under her breath.

"If they drove beyond the turn-off to the factory the patrols would have got them. Of course he may be maddening the monks in the monastery further up."

"Mightn't the car have pushed on and come round by this appalling route?"

"The patrols on the eastern route will get it if it did and there are no fresh tyre tracks."

"It's so strange," Troy said, "to hear you doing your stuff."

Raoul humoured the car down a steep incline and past a pink-washed hovel overhanging the cliff. A peasant stood in the doorway. At Alleyn's suggestion Raoul called to him.

"*Hé* friend! Any other driver comes this way today?"

"*Pas un de si bête!*"

"That was: 'no such fool,' wasn't it?" Troy asked.

"It was."

"I couldn't agree more."

They bumped and sidled on for some time without further conversation. Raoul sang. The sky was a deeper blue and the Mediterranean, now almost purple, made unexpected gestures between the tops of hills. Troy and Alleyn each thought privately how much, in spite of the road, they would have enjoyed themselves if Ricky had been with them.

Presently Raoul, speaking slowly out of politeness to Troy, pointed to a valley they were about to enter.

"The Monastery Road. M'sieur—Madame. We descend."

They did so, precipitately. The roofs of the Monastery of Our Lady of Paysdoux appeared, tranquil and modest, folded in a confluence of olive groves. As they came into the lower valley they looked down on an open place where a few cars were parked and where visitors to the cloisters moved in and out of long shadows. The car dived down behind the monastery, turned and ran out into the head of a good sealed road. "The factory," Raoul said, "is round the next bend. Beyond, Monsieur can see the main road and away to the right is the headland with the tunnel that comes out by the Château de la Chèvre d'Argent."

"Is there a place lower down and out of sight of the factory where we can watch the main road on the Roqueville side?"

"Yes, Monsieur. As one approaches the bend."

"Let us stop there for a moment."

"Good, Monsieur."

Raoul's point of observation turned out to be a pleasant one overlooking the sea and commanding a full view of the main road as it came through the hills from Roqueville. He ran the car to the outer margin of their road and stopped. Alleyn looked at his watch. "A quarter past four. The works shut down at five. I hope Dupont's punctual. We'll have a final check. Raoul first, darling, if you don't mind. See how much you can follow and keep your eye on the main road for the police car. *Alors*, Raoul."

Raoul turned to listen. He had taken off his chauffeur's cap, and his head, seen in profile against the Homeric blue of the Mediterranean, took on classic air. Its colour was a modulation of the tawny earth. Grape-like curls clustered behind his small ears, his mouth was fresh, reflected light bloomed on his cheekbones and his eyes held a look of untroubled acceptance. It was a beautiful head, and Troy thought: "When we're out of this nightmare I shall want to paint it."

Alleyn was saying: ". . . so you will remain at first in the car. After a time I may fetch or send for you. If I do you will come into the office and tell a fairy story. It will be to this effect . . ."

Raoul listened impassively, his eyes on the distant road. When Alleyn had done, Raoul made a squaring movement with his shoulders, blew out his cheeks into a mock-truculent grimace and intimated that he was ready for anything.

"Now, darling," Alleyn said, "do you think you can come in with me and keep all thought of our inside information out of your mind? You know only this: Ricky has been kidnapped and Raoul has seen him being driven into the factory. I'm going to have a shot at the general manager, who is called Callard. We don't know much about him. He's a Parisian who worked in the States for a firm that was probably implicated in the racket and he speaks English. Any of the others we may run into may also speak English. We'll assume, whatever we find, that they understand it. So don't say anything to me that they shouldn't hear. On the other hand, you can with advantage keep up an agitated chorus. I shall speak bad French. We don't know what may develop so we'll have to keep our heads and ride the skids as we meet them. How do you feel about it?"

"Should I be a brave little woman biting on the bullet or should I go in, boots and all, and rave?"

"Rave if you feel like it, my treasure. They'll probably expect it."

"I daresay a Spartan mother would seem more British in their eyes or is that a contradiction in terms? Oh, Rory!" Troy said in a low voice. "It's so grotesque. Here we are half-crazy with anxiety and we have to put on a sort of anxiety act. It's—it's a cruel thing, isn't it?"

"It'll be all right," Alleyn said. "It *is* cruel but it'll be all right. I promise. You'll be as right as a bank whatever you do. Hallo, there's Dupont."

A car had appeared on the main road from Roqueville.

"M. le Commissaire," said Raoul, and flicked his headlamps on and off. The police car, tiny in the distance, winked briefly in response.

"We're off," said Alleyn.

## IV

The entrance hall of the factory was impressive. The décor was carried out in obscured glass, chromium and plastic and was beautifully lit. In the centre was a sculptured figure, modern in treatment, suggestive of some beneficent though pin-headed being, who drew strength from the earth itself. Two flights of curved stairs led airily to remote galleries. There was an imposing office on the left. Double doors at the centre back and a series of single doors in the right wall all bore legends in chromium letters. The front wall was plate glass and commanded a fine view of the valley and the sea.

Beyond a curved counter in the outer office a girl sat over a ledger. When she saw Alleyn and Troy she rose and stationed herself behind a chromium notice on the counter: *Renseignements*.

"Monsieur?" asked the girl. "Madame?"

Alleyn, without checking his stride, said: "Don't disarrange yourself, Mademoiselle," and made for the central doors.

The girl raised her voice: "One moment, Monsieur, whom does Monsieur wish to see?"

"M. Callard, le Controleur."

The girl pushed a bell on her desk. Before Alleyn could reach the double doors they opened and a commissionaire came through. Alleyn turned to the desk.

"Monsieur has an appointment?" asked the girl.

"No," Alleyn said, "but it is a matter of extreme urgency. I must see M. Callard, Mademoiselle."

The girl was afraid that M. Callard saw nobody without an appointment. Troy observed that her husband was making his usual impression on the girl, who touched her hair, settled her shoulders and gave him a look.

Troy said in a high voice: "Darling, what's she saying? Has she seen him?"

The girl just glanced at Troy and then opened her eyes at Alleyn. "Perhaps I can be of assistance to Monsieur?" she suggested.

Alleyn leaned over the counter and haltingly asked her if by any chance she had seen a little boy in brown shorts and a yellow shirt. The question seemed to astonish her. She made an incredulous sound and repeated it to the commissionaire, who merely hitched up his shoulders. They had not seen any little boys, she said. Little boys were not permitted on the premises.

Alleyn stumbled about with his French and asked the girl if she spoke English. She said that unfortunately she did not.

"Mademoiselle," Alleyn said to Troy, "doesn't speak English. I think she says M. Callard won't see us. And she says she doesn't know anything about Ricky."

Troy said: "But we know he's here. We must see the manager. Tell her we must."

This time the girl didn't so much as glance at Troy. With a petunia-tipped finger and thumb she removed a particle of mascara from her lashes and discreetly rearranged her figure for Alleyn to admire. She said it was too bad that she couldn't do anything for him. She thought he had better understand this and said that at any other time she might do a lot. She reacted with a facial expression which corresponded, Troy thought, with the "haughty little *moue*" so much admired by Edwardian novelists.

He said: "Mademoiselle, will you have the kindness of an angel? Will you take a little message to M. Callard?" She hesitated and he added in English: "And do you know that there is a large and I believe poisonous spider on your neck?"

She flashed a smile at him. "Monsieur makes a *grivoiserie* at my expense. He says naughty things in English, I believe, 'to pull a carrot at me.'"

"Doesn't speak English," Alleyn said to Troy without moving his eyes from the girl. He took out his pocket-book, wrote a brief message and slid it across the counter with a five hundred franc note underneath. He playfully lifted the girl's hand and closed it over both.

"Well, I must say!" said Troy, and she thought how strange it was that she could be civilized and amused and perhaps a little annoyed at this incident.

With an air that contrived to suggest that Alleyn as well as being a shameless flirt was also a gentleman, the girl moved back from the counter, glanced through the plate-glass windows of the main office where a number of typists and two clerks looked on with undisguised curiosity, seemed to change her mind, and came out by way of a gate at the top of the counter and walked with short steps to the double doors. The commissionaire opened them for her. They looked impassively at each other. She passed through and he followed her.

Alleyn said: "She's taking my note to the boss. It ought to surprise him. By all the rules he should have been rung up and told we're on the road to St. Céleste."

"Will he see us?"

"I don't see how he can refuse."

While they waited, Troy looked at the spidery stairs, the blind doors and the distant galleries. "If he should appear!" she thought. "If there could be another flash of yellow and brown." She began to imagine how it would be when they found Ricky. Would his face be white with smudges under the eyes? Would he cry in the stifled inarticulate fashion that always gripped her heart in a stricture? Would he shout and run to her? Or, by a merciful chance, would he behave like the other boy and want to stay with his terrible new friends? She thought: "It's unlucky to anticipate. He may not be here at all. It may be a false scent. If we don't find him before tonight I think I shall crack up."

She knew Alleyn's mind followed hers as closely as one mind can follow another, and she knew that as far as one human being can find solace in another she found solace in him, but she suffered, nevertheless, a great loneliness of spirit. She turned to him and saw compassion and anger in his eyes.

"If anything could make me want more to get these gentlemen," he said, "it would be this. We'll get them, Troy."

"Oh, yes," she said. "I expect you will."

"Ricky's here. I know it in my bones. I promise you."

The girl came back through the double doors. She was very formal. "Monsieur Callard will see Monsieur and Madame," she said. The commissionaire waited on the far side, holding one door open. As Alleyn stood aside for Troy to go through, the girl moved nearer to him. Her back was turned to the commissionaire. Her eyes made a sign of assent.

He murmured: "And I may understand—what, Mademoiselle?"

"What Monsieur pleases," she said, and minced back to the desk.

Alleyn caught Troy up and took her arm in his hand. The commissionaire was several paces ahead. "Either that girl's given me the tip that Ricky's here," Alleyn muttered, "or she's the smartest job off the skids in the Maritime Alps."

"What did she say?"

"Nothing. Just gave the go-ahead signal."

"Good Lord! Or did it mean Ricky?"

"It'd better mean Ricky," Alleyn said grimly.

They were in an inner hall, heavily carpeted and furnished with modern wall-tables and chairs. They passed two doors and were led to a third in the end wall. The commissionaire opened it and went in. They heard a murmur of voices. He returned and asked them to enter.

A woman with blue hair and magnificent poise rose from a typewriter. "Bon jour, Monsieur et Madame," she said. "Entrez, s'il vous plaît." She opened another door. "Monsieur et Madame Allen," she announced.

"Come right in!" invited a voice in hearty American. "C'm on! Come right in."

V

M. Callard was a fat man with black eyebrows and bluish chops. He was not a particularly evil-looking man: rather one would have said that there was something meretricious about him. His mouth looked as if it had been disciplined by meaningless smiles and his eyes seemed to assume rather than possess an air of concentration. He was handsomely dressed and smelt of expensive cigars. His English was fluent and falsely Americanized with occasional phrases and inflections that made it clear he wasn't speaking his native tongue.

"Well, well, well," he said, pulling himself up from his chair and extending his hand. The other held Alleyn's note. "Very pleased to meet you, Mr.—— I just can't quite get the signature."

"Alleyn."

"Mr. Allen."

"This is my wife."

"Mrs. Allen," said M. Callard, bowing. "Now, let's sit down, shall we, and get acquainted. What's all this I hear about Junior?"

Alleyn said: "I wouldn't have bothered you if we hadn't by chance heard that our small boy who went missing early this afternoon, had, Heaven knows how, turned up at your works. In your office they didn't seem to know anything about him and our French doesn't go very far. It's a great help that your English is so good. Isn't it, darling?" he said to Troy.

"Indeed, yes. M. Callard, I can't tell you how anxious we are. He just disappeared from our hotel. He's only six and it's so dreadful—"

To her horror Troy heard her voice tremble. She was silent.

"Now, that's just too bad," M. Callard said. "And what makes you think he's turned up in this part of the world?"

"By an extraordinary chance," Alleyn said, "the man we've engaged to drive us took his car up this road earlier this afternoon and he saw Ricky in another car with a man and woman. They turned in at the entrance to your works. We don't pretend to understand all this, but you can imagine how relieved we are to know he's all right."

M. Callard sat with a half smile on his mouth, looking at Alleyn's left ear. "Well," he said, "I don't pretend to understand it either. Nobody's told me anything. But we'll soon find out."

He bore down with a pale thumb on his desk bell. The blue-haired secretary came in and he spoke to her in French.

"It appears," he said, "that Monsieur and Madame have been given information by their chauffeur that their little boy who has disappeared was seen in an auto somewhere on our premises. Please make full enquiries, Mademoiselle, in all departments."

"At once, Monsieur le Directeur," said the secretary and went out.

M. Callard offered Troy a cigarette and Alleyn a cigar, both of which were refused. He seemed mysteriously to expand. "Maybe," he said, "you folks are not aware there's a gang of kidnappers at work along this territory. Child-kidnappers."

Alleyn at once broke into a not too coherent and angry dissertation on child-kidnappers and the inefficiency of the police. M. Callard listened with an air of indulgence. He had taken a cigar and he rolled it continuously between his thumb and fingers, which were flattish and backed with an unusual amount of hair. This movement was curiously disturbing. But he listened with perfect courtesy to Alleyn and every now and then made sympathetic noises. There was, however, a certain quality in his stillness which Alleyn recognized. M. Callard was listening to him with only part of his attention. With far closer concentration he listened for something outside the room: and for this, Alleyn thought, he listened so far in vain.

The secretary came back alone.

She told M. Callard that in no department of the works nor among the gardens outside had anyone seen a small boy. Troy only understood the tenor of this speech. Alleyn, who had perfectly understood the whole of it, asked to have it translated. M. Callard obliged, the secretary withdrew, and the temper of the interview hardened. Alleyn got up and moved to the desk. His hand rested on the top of a sound system apparatus. Troy found herself looking at the row of switches and the loud-speaker and at the good hand above them.

Alleyn said he was not satisfied with the secretary's report. M. Callard said he was sorry but evidently there had been some mistake. Alleyn said he was certain there was no mistake. Troy, taking her cue from him, let something of her anxiety and anger escape. M. Callard received her outburst with odious compassion and said it was quite understandable that she was not just 100 per cent reasonable. He rose, but before his thumb could reach the bell-push Alleyn said that he must ask him to listen to the account given by their chauffeur.

"I'm sure that when you hear the man you will understand why we are so insistent," Alleyn said. And before Callard could do anything to stop him he went out leaving Troy to hold, as it were, the gate open for his return.

Callard made a fat, wholly Latin gesture, and flopped back into his chair. "My dear lady," he said, "this good man of yours is just a little difficult. Certainly I'll listen to your chauffeur who is, no doubt, one of the local peasants. I know how they are around here. They say what they figure you want them to say and they don't worry about facts: it's not conscious lying, it's just that they come that way. They're just naturally obliging. Now, your husband's French isn't so hot and my guess is, he's got this guy a little bit wrong. We'll soon find out if I'm correct. Pardon me if I make a call. This is a busy time with us and right now I'm snowed under."

Having done his best to make Troy thoroughly uncomfortable he put through a call on his telephone, speaking such rapid French that she scarcely understood a word of what he said. He had just hung up the receiver when something clicked. This sound was followed by a sense of movement and space beyond the office. M. Callard glanced at the switchboard on his desk and said: *"Ah?"* A disembodied voice spoke in mid-air.

*"Monsieur le Directeur? Le service de transport avise qu'il est incapable d'expédier la marchandise."*

*"Qu'est ce qu'il se passe?"*

*"Rue barrée!"*

*"Bien. Prenez garde. Remettez la marchandise à sa place."*

"*Bien, Monsieur,*" said the voice. The box clicked and the outside world was shut off.

"My, oh my," sighed M. Callard, "the troubles I have!" He opened a ledger on his desk and ran his flattened forefinger down the page.

Troy thought distractedly that perhaps he was right about Raoul and then, catching herself up, remembered that Raoul had in fact never seen the car drive in at the factory gates with Ricky and a man and woman in it, that they were bluffing and that perhaps all Alleyn's and Dupont's theories were awry. Perhaps this inhuman building had never contained her little son. Perhaps it was idle to torture herself by thinking of him: near at hand yet hopelessly withheld.

M. Callard looked at a platinum mounted wristwatch and then at Troy, and sighed again. "He's trying to shame me out of his office," she thought and she said boldly: "Please don't let me interrupt your work." He glanced at her with a smile from which he seemed to make no effort to exclude the venom.

"My work requires the closest concentration, Madame," said M. Callard.

"Sickening for you," said Troy.

Alleyn came back with Raoul at his heels. Through the door Troy caught a glimpse of the blue-haired secretary, half-risen from her desk, expostulation frozen on her face. Raoul shut the door.

"This is Milano, M. Callard," Alleyn said. "He will tell you what he saw. If I have misunderstood him you will be able to correct me. He doesn't speak English."

Raoul stood before the desk and looked about him with the same air of interest and ease that had irritated Dr. Baradi. His gaze fell for a moment on the sound system apparatus and then moved to M. Callard's face.

"Well, my friend," said M. Callard in rapid French. "What's the tarradiddle Monsieur thinks you've told him?"

"I think Monsieur understood what I told him," Raoul said cheerfully and even more rapidly. "I spoke slowly and what I said, with all respect, was no tarradiddle. With Monsieur's permission I will repeat it. Early this afternoon, I do not know the exact time, I drove my young lady along the road to the factory. I parked my car and we climbed a little way up the hillside opposite the gates. From here we observed a car come up from the main road. In it were a man and a woman and the small son of Madame and Monsieur who is called Riki. This little Monsieur Riki was removed from the car and taken into the factory. That is all, Monsieur le Directeur."

M. Callard's eyelids were half-closed. His cigar rolled to and fro between his fingers and thumb.

"So. You see a little boy and a man and a woman. Let me tell you that early this afternoon a friend of my works-superintendent visited the factory with his wife and boy and that undoubtedly it was this boy whom you saw."

"With respect, what is the make of the car of the friend of Monsieur's works-superintendent?"

"I do not concern myself with the cars of my employees' acquaintances."

"Or with the age and appearance of their children, Monsieur?"

"Precisely."

"This was a light blue Citroën, 1946, Monsieur, and the boy was Riki, the son of Monsieur and Madame, a young gentleman whom I know well. He was not two hundred yards away and was speaking his bizarre French, the French of an English child. His face was as unmistakable," said Raoul, looking full into M. Callard's face, "as Monsieur's own. It was Riki."

M. Callard turned to Alleyn: "How much of all that did you get?" he asked.

Alleyn said: "Not a great deal. When he talks to us he talks slowly. But I'm sure—"

"Pardon me," M. Callard said, and turned smilingly to Raoul.

"My friend," he said, "you are undoubtedly a conscientious man. But I assure you that you are making a mistake. Mistakes can cost a lot of money. On the other hand, they sometimes yield a profit. As much, for the sake of argument, as five thousand francs. Do you follow me?"

"No, Monsieur."

"Are you sure? Perhaps—" suggested M. Callard thrusting his unoccupied hand casually into his breast pocket—"when we are alone I may have an opportunity to make my meaning plainer and more acceptable."

"I regret. I shall still be unable to follow it," Raoul said.

M. Callard drew a large handkerchief from his breast pocket and dabbed his lips with it. "*Sacré nigaud*," he said pleasantly and shot a venomous glance at Raoul before turning to Troy and Alleyn.

"My dear good people," he said expansively, "I'm afraid this boy has kidded you along quite a bit. He admits that he did not get a good look at the child. He was up on the hillside with a dame and his attention was—well, now," said M. Callard smirking at Troy, "shall we say, kind of semi-detached. It's what I thought. He's told you what he figures you'd like to be told and if you ask him again he'll roll out the same tale all over."

"I'm afraid I don't believe that," said Alleyn.

"I'm afraid you don't have an alternative," said M. Callard. He turned on Raoul. *"Fichez-moi le camp,"* he said toughly.

"What's that?" Alleyn demanded.

"I've told him to get out."

*"Vous permettez, Madame, Monsieur?"* Raoul asked and placed himself between the two men with his back to M. Callard.

"What?" Alleyn said. He winked at Raoul. Raoul responded with an ineffable grimace. "What? Oh, all right. *All right. Oui. Allez.*"

With a bow to Troy and another that was rather less respectful than a nod to M. Callard, Raoul went out. Alleyn walked up to the desk and took up his former position.

"I'm not satisfied," he said.

"That's too bad."

"I must ask you to let me search this building."

"You!" said M. Callard and laughed. "Pardon my mirth but I guess there'd be two of you gone missing if you tried that one. This is quite a building, Mr.—" he glanced again at Alleyn's note—"Mr. Allen."

"If it's as big as all that your secretary's enquiries were too brief to be effective. I don't believe any enquiries have been made."

*"Look!"* M. Callard said, and smacked the top of his desk with a flat palm. "This sound system operates throughout these works. I can speak to every department or all departments together. We don't have to go round on a hiking trip when we make general enquiries. Now!"

"Thank you," Alleyn said and his hand darted over the switchboard. There was a click. *"Ricky!"* he shouted, and Troy cried out: *"Ricky! Are you there? Ricky!"*

And as if they had conjured it from the outer reaches of space a small voice said excitedly: "They've come! *Mummy!*"

A protesting outcry was cut off as M. Callard struck at Alleyn's hand with a heavy paper knife. At the same moment M. Dupont walked into the room.

# CHAPTER VIII

# Ricky Regained

*I*

TROY could scarcely endure the scene that followed and very nearly lost control of herself. She couldn't understand a word of what was said. Alleyn held her by the arm and kept saying: "In a minute, darling. He'll be here in a minute. He's all right. Hold on. He's all right."

Dupont and Callard were behaving like Frenchmen in English farces. Callard, especially, kept giving shrugs that began in his middle and surged up to his ears. His synthetic Americanisms fell away and when he threw a sentence in English at Troy or at Alleyn he spoke it like a Frenchman. He shouted to Alleyn: "If I lose my temper it is natural. I apologize. I knew nothing. It was the fault of my staff. There will be extensive dismissals. I am the victim of circumstances. I regret that I struck you."

He pounded his desk bell and shouted orders into the sound system. Voices from the other places said in mid-air: *"Immédiatement, M. le Directeur." "Tout de suite, Monsieur." "Parfaitement, M. le Directeur."* The secretary ran in at a high-heeled double and set up a gabble of protest which was cut short by Dupont. She teetered out again and could be heard yelping down her own sound system.

With one part of her mind Troy thought of the door and how it

must soon open for Ricky and with another part she thought it was unlucky to anticipate this event and that the door would open for the secretary or a stranger and, so complicated were her thoughts, she also
wondered if, when she saw Ricky, he would have a blank look of panic
in his eyes, or if he would cry or be casually pleased, or if these specula-
tions too were unlucky and he wouldn't come at all.

Stifled and terrified, she turned on Dupont and Callard and cried
out: "Please speak English. You both can. Where is he? Why doesn't
he come?"

"Madame," said Dupont gently, "he is here."

He had come in as she turned away from the door.

The secretary was behind him. She gave his shoulder a little push
and he made a fastidious movement away from her and into the room.
Troy knew that if she spoke her voice would shake. She held out her
hand.

"Hallo, Rick," Alleyn said. "Sorry we've muddled you about."

"You have, rather," Ricky said. He saw Dupont and Callard. "How
do you do," he said. He looked at Troy and his lip trembled. He ran
savagely into her arms and fastened himself upon her. His fierce hard
little body was rammed against hers, his arms gripped her neck and his
face burrowed into it. His heart thumped pistonlike at her breast.

"We'll take him out to the car," Alleyn said.

Troy rose, holding Ricky with his legs locked about her waist. Alleyn
steadied her and they went out through the secretary's room and the
lobby and the entrance hall to where Raoul waited in the sunshine.

## II

When they approached the car Ricky released his hold on his mother
as abruptly as he had imposed it. She put him down and he walked a
little distance from her. He acknowledged Raoul's greeting with an uncertain nod and stood with his back turned to them, apparently looking
at M. Dupont's car which was occupied by three policemen.

Alleyn murmured: "He'll get over it all right. Don't worry."

"He thinks we've let him down. He's lost his sense of security."

"We can do something about that. He's puzzled. Give him a moment and then I'll try."

He went over to the police car.

"I suppose," Ricky said to nobody in particular, "Daddy's not going
away again."

Troy moved close to him. "No, darling, I don't think so. Not far anyway. He's on a job, though, helping the French police."

"Are those French policemen?"

"Yes. And the man you saw in that place is a French detective."

"As good as Daddy?"

"I don't expect quite as good but good all the same. He helped us find you."

Ricky said: "Why did you let me be got lost?"

"Because," Troy explained with a dryness in her throat, "Daddy didn't know about it. As soon as he knew, it was all right, and you weren't lost any more. We came straight up here and got you."

The three policemen were out of the car and listening ceremoniously to Alleyn. Ricky watched them. Raoul, standing by his own car, whistled a lively air and rolled a cigarette.

"Let's go and sit with Raoul, shall we," Troy suggested, "until Daddy's ready to come home with us?"

Ricky looked miserably at Raoul and away again. "He might be cross of me," he muttered.

"*Raoul* cross with you, darling? *No*. Why?"

"Because—because—I—lost—I lost—"

"No, you didn't!" Troy cried. "We found it. Wait a moment." She rootled in her bag. "Look."

She held out the little silver goat. Ricky's face was transfused with a flush of relief. He took the goat carefully into his square hands. "He's the nicest thing I've ever had," he said. "He shines in the night. *Il s'illume*. Raoul and the lady said he does."

"Has he got a name?"

"His name's Goat," Ricky said.

He walked over to the car. Raoul opened the door and Ricky got into the front seat, casually displaying the goat.

"*C'est ça,*" Raoul said comfortably. He glanced down at Ricky, nodded three times with an air of sagacity, and lit his cigarette. Ricky shoved one hand in the pocket of his shorts and leaned back. "Coming, Mum?" he asked.

Troy got in beside him. Alleyn called Raoul, who swept off his chauffeur's cap to Troy and excused himself.

"What's going to happen?" Ricky asked.

"I think Daddy's got a job for them. He'll come and tell us in a minute."

"Could we keep Raoul?"

"While we are here I think we can."

"I daresay he wouldn't like to live with us always."

"Well, his family lives here. I expect he likes being with them."

"I do think he's nice, however. Do you?"

"Very," Troy said warmly. "Look, there he goes with the police-men."

M. Dupont had appeared in the factory entrance. He made a crisp signal. Raoul and the three policemen walked across and followed him into the factory. Alleyn came to the car and leaned over the door. He pulled Ricky's forelock and said: "How's the new policeman?" Ricky blinked at him.

"Why?" he asked.

"I think you've helped us to catch up with some bad lots."

"Why?"

"Well, because they thought we'd be so busy looking for you we wouldn't have time for them. But, sucks to them, we didn't lose you and do you know why?"

"Why?"

"Because you waved from the balcony and dropped your silver goat and that was a clue and because you called out to us and we knew you were there. Pretty good."

Ricky was silent.

Troy said: "Jolly good, helping Daddy like that."

Ricky was turned away from her. She could see the charming back of his neck and the curve of his cheek. He hunched his shoulders and tucked in his chin.

"Was the fat, black smelly lady a bad lot?" he asked in a casual tone.

"Not much good," Alleyn said.

"Where is she?"

"Oh, I shut her up. She's a silly old thing, really. Better, shut up."

"Was the other one a bad lot?"

"Which one?"

"The Nanny."

Alleyn and Troy looked at each other over his head.

"The one who fetched you from the hotel?" Alleyn asked.

"Yes, the new Nanny."

"Oh, *that* one. Hadn't she got a red hat or something?"

"She hadn't got a hat. She'd got a moustache."

"Really? Was her dress red perhaps?"

"No. Black with kind of whitey blobs."

"Did you like her?"

"Not extra much. Quite, though. She wasn't bad. I didn't think I had to have a Nan over here."

"Well, you needn't. She was a mistake. We won't have her."

"Anyway, she shouldn't have left me there with the fat lady, should she, Daddy?"

"No." Alleyn reached over the door and took the goat. He held it up admiring it. "Nice, isn't it?" he said. "Did she speak English, that Nanny?"

"Not properly. A bit. The man didn't."

"The driver?"

" 'M."

"Was he a chauffeur like Raoul?"

"No. He had funny teeth. Sort of black. Funny sort of driver for a person to have. He didn't have a cap like Raoul or anything. Just a red beret and no coat and he wasn't very clean either. He's Mr. Garbel's driver, only Mr. Garbel's a *Mademoiselle* and not a Mr."

"*Is* he? How d'you know?"

"May I have Goat again, please? Because the Nanny said you were waiting for me in Mademoiselle Garbel's room. Only you weren't. And because Mademoiselle Garbel rang up. The lady in the goat shop has got other people that light themselves at night too. Saints and shepherds and angels and Jesus. Pretty decent."

"I'll have a look next time I'm there. When did Miss Garbel ring up, Rick?"

"When I was in her room. The fat lady told the Nanny. They didn't know about me understanding which was sucks to them."

"What did the fat lady say?"

" '*Mademoiselle Garbel a téléphoné.*' Easy!"

"What did she telephone about, do you know?"

"Me. She said they were to take me away and they told me you would be up here. Only—"

Ricky stopped short and looked wooden. He had turned rather white.

"Only—?" Alleyn said and then after a moment: "Never mind. I think I know. They went away to talk on the telephone and you went out on the balcony. And you saw Mummy and me waving on our balcony and you didn't know quite what was up with everybody. Was it like that?"

"A bit."

"Muddly?"

"A bit," Ricky said tremulously.

"I know. We were muddled too. Then that fat old thing came out and took you away, didn't she?"

Ricky leaned back against his mother. Troy slipped her arm round him and her hand protected his two hands and the silver goat. He looked at his father and his lip trembled.

"It was beastly," he said. "She was beastly." And then in a most desolate voice: "They took me away. I was all by myself for ages in there. They said you'd be up here and you weren't. You weren't here at all." And he burst into a passion of sobs, his tear-drenched face turned in bewilderment to Alleyn. His precocity fell away from him: he was a child who had not long ago been a baby.

"It's all right, old boy," Alleyn said, "it was only a sort of have. They're silly bad lots and we're going to stop their nonsense. We wouldn't have been able to if you hadn't helped."

Troy said: "Daddy *did* come, darling. He'll always come. We both will."

"Well, anyway," Ricky sobbed, "another time you'd jolly well better be a bit quicker."

A whistle at the back of the factory gave three short shrieks. Ricky shuddered, covered his ears and flung himself at Troy.

"I'll have to go in," Alleyn said. He closed his hand on Ricky's shoulder and held it for a moment. "You're safe, Rick," he said, "you're safe as houses."

"O.K.," Ricky said in a stifled voice. He slewed his head round and looked at his father out of the corner of his eyes.

"Do you think in a minute or two you could help us again? Do you think you could come in with me to the hall in there and tell me if you can see that old Nanny and Mr. Garbel's driver?"

"Oh, *no*, Rory," Troy murmured. "Not now!"

"Well, of course, Rick needn't if he'd hate it, but it'd be helping the police quite a lot."

Ricky had stopped crying. A dry sob shook him but he said: "Would you be there? And Mummy?"

"We'll be there."

Alleyn reached over, picked up Troy's gloves from the floor of the car and put them in his pocket.

"Hi!" Troy said. "What's that for?"

"'To be worn in my beaver and borne in the van,'" he quoted, "or something like that. If Raoul or Dupont or I come out and wave will you and Ricky come in? There'll be a lot of people there, Rick, and I just want you to look at 'em and tell me if you can see that Nanny and the driver. O.K.?"

"O.K.," Ricky said in a small voice.

"Good for you, old boy."

He saw the anxious tenderness in Troy's eyes and added: "Be kind enough, both of you, to look upon me as a tower of dubious strength."

Troy managed to grin at him. "We have every confidence," she said, "in our wonderful police."

"Like hell!" Alleyn said and went back to the factory.

## III

He found a sort of comic-opera scene in full swing in the central hall. Employees of all conditions were swarming down the curved stairs and through the doors: men in working overalls, in the white coat of the laboratory, in the black jacket of bureaucracy; women equally varied in attire and age: all of them looking in veiled annoyance at their watches. A loudspeaker bellowed continually:

"'Allo, 'allo, Messieurs et Dames, faites attention, s'il vous plaît. Tous les employés, ayez la bonté de vous rendre immédiatement au grand vestibule. 'Allo, 'allo."

M. Dupont stood in a commanding position on the base of the statue and M. Callard, looking sulky, stood at a little distance below him. A few paces distant, Raoul, composed and god-like in his simplicity, surveyed the milling chorus. The gendarmes were nowhere to be seen.

Alleyn made his way to Dupont, who was obviously in high fettle and, as actors say, well inside the skin of his part. He addressed Alleyn in English with exactly the right mixture of deference and veiled irritability. Callard listened moodily.

"Ah, Monsieur! You see we make great efforts to clear up this little affair. The entire staff is summoned by Monsieur le Directeur. We question everybody. This fellow of yours is invited to examine the persons. You are invited to bring the little boy, also to examine. Monsieur le Directeur is most anxious to assist. He is immeasurably distressed, is it not, Monsieur le Directeur?"

"That's right," said M. Callard without enthusiasm.

Alleyn said with a show of huffiness that he was glad to hear that they recognized their responsibilities. M. Dupont bent down as if to soothe him and he murmured: "Keep going as long as you can. Spin it out."

"To the last thread."

Alleyn made his way to Raoul and was able to mutter: "Ricky describes the driver as a man with black teeth, a red beret, as your friend observed, and no jacket. The woman has a moustache, is bareheaded and wears a black dress with a whitish pattern. If you see a man and woman answering to that description you may announce that they resemble the persons in the car."

Raoul was silent. Alleyn was surprised to see that his face, usually a ready mirror of his emotions, had gone blank. The loud-speaker kept up its persistent demands. The hall was filling rapidly.

"Well, Raoul?"

"Would Monsieur describe again the young woman and the man?"

Alleyn did so. "If there are any such persons present you may pretend to recognize them, but not with positive determination. The general appearance, you may say, is similar. Then we may be obliged to bring Ricky in to see if he identifies them."

Raoul made a singular little noise in his throat. His lips moved. Alleyn saw rather than heard his response.

"*Bien, Monsieur,*" he said.

"M. Dupont will address the staff when they are assembled. He will speak at some length. I shall not be present. He will continue proceedings until I return. Your *soi-disant* identification will then take place. *Au 'voir, Raoul.*"

" '*Voir, Monsieur.*"

Alleyn edged through the crowd and round the wall of the room to the double doors. The commissionaire stood near them and eyed him dubiously. Alleyn looked across the sea of heads and caught the notice of M. Dupont, who at once held up his hand. "*Attention!*" he shouted. "*Approchez-vous davantage, je vous en prie.*" The crowd closed in on him, and Alleyn, left on the margin, slipped through the doors.

He had at the most fifteen minutes in which to work. The secretary's office was open, but the door into M. Callard's room was, as he had anticipated, locked. It responded to his manipulation and he relocked it behind him. He went to the desk and turned on the general intercommunication switch in the sound system releasing the vague rumour of a not quite silent crowd and the voice of M. Dupont embarked on an elaborate exposé of child-kidnapping on the Mediterranean coast.

Perhaps, Alleyn thought, at this rate he would have a little longer than he had hoped. If he could find a single piece of evidence, enough to ensure the success of a surprise investigation by the French police, he would be satisfied. He looked at the filing cabinet against the walls. The drawers had independent key-holes but the first fifteen were unlocked. He tried them and shoved them back without looking inside. The sixteenth, marked with the letter P, was locked. He got it open. Inside he found a number of the usual folders each headed with its appropriate legend: *Produits chimiques en commande; Peron et Cie; Plastiques,* and so on. He went through the first of these, memorizing one or two names of drugs he had been told to look out for. Peron et

Cie was on the suspect list at the Sûreté and a glance at the corre-
spondence showed a close business relationship between the two firms.
He flipped over the next six folders and came to the last which was
headed: *Particulier à M. Callard. Secret et confidentiel.*

It contained rough notes, memoranda and a number of letters, and
Alleyn would have given years of routine plodding for the right to put
the least of them into his pocket. He found letters from distributors in
New York, Cairo, London, Paris and Istanbul, letters that set out modes
of conveyance, suggested suitable contacts, gave details of the methods
used by other illicit traders and warnings of leakage. He found a list of
the guests at the Chèvre d'Argent with Robin Herrington's name
scored under and a query beside it.

"*Cette pratique abominable,*" boomed the voice of M. Dupont,
warming to its subject, "*cette tache indéracinable sur l'honneur de
notre communauté—*"

"Boy," Alleyn muttered in the manner of M. Callard, "you said
it."

He laid on the desk a letter from a wholesale firm dealing in cos-
metics in Chicago. It suggested quite blandly that *Crème Veloutée* in
tubes might be a suitable mode of conveyance for diacetylmorphine and
complained that the last consignment of calamine lotion had been tam-
pered with in transit and had proved on opening to contain nothing
but lotion. It suggested that a certain customs official had set up in business on his own account and had better be dealt with pretty smartly.

Alleyn unshipped from his breast pocket a minute and immensely expensive camera. Groaning to himself he switched on M. Callard's
fluorescent lights.

"*—et, Messieurs, Dames,*" thundered the voice of M. Dupont, "*parmi
vous, ici, ici, dans cette usine, ce crime dégoûtant a élevé sa tête
hideuse.*"

Alleyn took four photographs of the letter, replaced it in the folder
and the folder in its file, relocked the drawer and stowed away his
Lilliputian camera. Then, with an ear to M. Dupont, who had evidently arrived at the point where he could not prolong the cackle, but
must come to the 'osses, Alleyn made notes, lest he should forget them,
of points from the other documents. He returned his notebook to his
pocket, switched off the loud-speaker and turned to the door.

He found himself face-to-face with M. Callard.

"And what the hell," M. Callard asked rawly, "do you think you are
doing?"

Alleyn took Troy's gloves from his pocket. "My wife left these in
your office. I hope you don't mind."

"She did not and I do. I locked this office."

"If you did someone obviously unlocked it. Perhaps your secretary came back for something."

"She did not," said M. Callard punctually. He advanced a step. "Who the hell are you?"

"You know very well who I am. My boy was kidnapped and brought into your premises. You denied it until you were forced to give him up. Your behavior is extremely suspicious, M. Callard, and I shall take the matter up with the appropriate authorities in Paris. I have never," continued Alleyn, who had decided to lose his temper, "heard such damned impudence in my life! I was prepared to give you the benefit of the doubt but in view of your extraordinary behavior I am forced to suspect that you are implicated personally in this business. And in the former affair of child-stealing. Undoubtedly in the former affair."

M. Callard began to shout in French, but Alleyn shouted him down. "You are a child-kidnapper, M. Callard. You speak English like an American. No doubt you have been to America where child-kidnapping is a common racket."

"Sacré nom d'un chien—"

"It's no use talking jargon to me, I don't understand a bloody word of it. Stand aside and let me out."

M. Callard's face was not an expressive one, but Alleyn thought he read incredulity and perhaps relief in it.

"You broke into my office," M. Callard insisted.

"I did nothing of the sort. Why the hell should I? And pray what have you got in your office," Alleyn asked as if on a sudden inspiration, "to make you so damned touchy about it? Ransom money?"

"Imbécile! Sale cochon!"

"Oh, get to hell!" Alleyn said, and advanced upon him. He stood, irresolute, and Alleyn with an expert movement neatly shouldered him aside and went back to the hall.

## IV

Dupont saw him come in. Dupont, Alleyn considered, was magnificent. He must have had an appalling job spinning out a short announcement into a fifteen-minute harangue, but he wore the air of an orator in the first flush of his eloquence.

His gaze swept over Alleyn and round his audience.

"Eh bien, Messieurs, Dames, chacun à sa tâche. Defilez, s'il vous plaît, devant cette statue. . . . Rappelez-vous de mes instructions. Milano!"

He signalled magnificently to Raoul, who stationed himself below him, at the base of the statue. Raoul was pale and stood rigid like a man who faces an ordeal. M. Callard appeared through the double doors and watched with a leaden face.

The gendarmes, who had also reappeared, set about the crowd in a business-like manner, herding it to one side and then sending it across in single file in front of Raoul. Alleyn adopted a consequential air and bustled over to Dupont.

"What's all this, Monsieur?" he asked querulously. "Is it an identification parade? Why haven't I been informed of the procedure?"

Dupont bent in a placatory manner towards him and Alleyn muttered: "Enough to justify a search," and then shouted: "I have a right to know what steps are being taken in this affair."

Dupont spread his blunt hands over Alleyn as if he were blessing him.

"Calm yourself, Monsieur. Everything arranges itself," he said magnificently and added in French for the benefit of the crowd: "The gentleman is naturally overwrought. Proceed, if you please."

Black-coated senior executive officers and white-coated chemists advanced, turned and straggled past with dead-pan faces. They were followed by clerks, assistant chemists, stenographers and laboratory assistants. One or two looked at Raoul, but by far the greater number kept on without turning their heads. When they had gone past, the gendarmes directed them to the top of the hall where they formed up into lines.

Alleyn watched the thinning ranks of those who were yet to come. At the back, sticking together, were a number of what he supposed to be the lesser fry: cleaners, van-drivers, workers from the canteen and porters. In a group of women he caught sight of one a little taller than the rest. She stood with her back towards the statue and at first he could see only a mass of bronze hair with straggling tendrils against the opulent curve of a full neck. Presently her neighbor gave her a nudge and for a moment she turned. Alleyn saw the satin skin and liquid eyes of a Murillo peasant. She had a brilliant mouth and had caught her under-lip between her teeth. Above her upper lip was a pencilling of hair.

Her face flashed into sight and was at once turned away again with a movement that thrust up her shoulder. It was clad in a black material spattered with a whitish-grey pattern.

Behind the girls was a group of four or five men in labourer's clothes: boiler-men, perhaps, or outside hands. As the girls hung back, the gendarme in charge of this group sent the men forward. They edged self-consciously past the girls and slouched towards Raoul. The third was a thick-set fellow wearing a tight-fitting short-sleeved vest and carrying a red beret. He walked hard on the heels of the men in front of him and kept his eyes on the ground. He had two long red scratches on the cheek nearest to Raoul. As he passed by, Alleyn looked at Raoul, who swallowed painfully and muttered: *"Voici le type."*

Dupont raised an eyebrow. The gendarme at the top of the room moved out quietly and stationed himself near the men. The girls came forward one by one and Alleyn still watched Raoul. The girl in the black dress with the whitish-grey pattern advanced, turned and went past with averted head. Raoul was silent.

Alleyn moved close to Dupont. "Keep your eye on that girl, Dupont. I think she's our bird."

"Indeed? Milano has not identified her."

"I think Ricky will."

Watched by the completely silent crowd, Alleyn went out of the hall and, standing in the sunshine, waved to Troy. She and Ricky got out of the car and, hand-in-hand, came towards him.

"Come on, Rick," he said, "let's see if you can find the driver and the Nanny. If you do we'll go and call on the goat-shop lady again. What do you say?"

He hoisted his little son across his shoulders and, holding his ankles in either hand, turned him towards the steps.

"Coming, Mum?" Ricky asked.

"Rather! Try and stop me."

"Strike up the band," Alleyn said. "Here comes the Alleyn family on parade."

He heard his son give a doubtful chuckle. A small hand was laid against his cheek. "Good old horse," Ricky said courageously and in an uncertain falsetto: "How many miles to Babylon?"

"Five score and ten," Alleyn and Troy chanted and she linked her arm through his.

They marched up the steps and into the hall.

The crowd was still herded at one end of the great room and had broken into a subdued chattering. One of the gendarmes stood near the man Raoul had identified. Another had moved round behind the crowd to a group of girls. Alleyn saw the back of that startlingly bronze head of hair and the curve of the opulent neck. M. Callard had not moved. M. Dupont had come down from his eminence and Raoul stood by himself behind the statue, looking at his own feet.

"Ah-ha!" cried M. Dupont, advancing with an air of camaraderie, "so here is Ricketts."

He reached up his hand. Ricky stooped uncertainly from his father's shoulders to put his own in it.

"This is Ricky," Alleyn said, "M. Dupont, Ricky, Superintendent of Police in Roqueville. M. Dupont speaks English."

"How do you do, sir," said Ricky in his company voice.

M. Dupont threw a complimentary glance at Troy.

"So we have an assistant," he said. "This is splendid. I leave the formalities to you, M. Alleyn."

"Just have a look at all these people, Rick," Alleyn said, "and tell us if you can find the driver and the Nanny who brought you up here."

Troy and Dupont looked at Ricky. Raoul, behind the statue, continued to look at his boots. Ricky, wearing the blank expression he reserved for strangers, surveyed the crowd. His attention came to halt on the thick-set fellow in the short-sleeved jersey. Dupont and Troy watched him.

"Mum?" said Ricky.

"Hallo?"

Ricky whispered something inaudible and nodded violently.

"Tell Daddy."

Rick stooped his head and breathed noisily into his father's ear.

"O.K.," Alleyn said. "Sure?"

"'M."

"Tell M. Dupont."

*"Monsieur, voici le chauffeur."*

*"Montrez avec le doigt, mon brave,"* said M. Dupont.

"Point him out, Rick," said Alleyn.

Ricky had been instructed by his French Nanny that it was rude to point. He turned pink in the face and made a rapid gesture, shooting out his finger at the man. The man drew back his upper lip and bared a row of blackened teeth. The first gendarme shoved in beside him. The crowd stirred and shifted.

"Bravo," said M. Dupont.

"Now the Nanny," Alleyn said. "Can you see her?"

There was a long pause. Ricky, looking at the group of girls at the back, said: "There's someone that hasn't turned round."

M. Dupont shouted: *"Présentez-vous de face, tout le monde!"*

The second gendarme pushed through the group of girls. They melted away to either side as if an invisible wedge had been driven through them. The impulse communicated itself to their neighbours: the gap widened and stretched, opening out as Alleyn carried Ricky towards it. Finally Ricky, on his father's shoulders, looked up an exaggerated perspective to where the girl stood with her back to them, her hands clasped across the nape of her neck as if to protect it from a blow. The gendarme took her by the arm, turned her, and held down the hands that now struggled to reach her face. She and Ricky looked at each other.

"Hallo, Teresa," said Ricky.

## V

Two cars drove down the Roqueville road. In the first was M. Callard and two policemen and in the second, a blue Citroën, were its owner and a third policeman. The staff of the factory had gone. M. Dupont was busy in M. Callard's office and a fourth gendarme stood, lonely and important, in the empty hall. Troy had taken Ricky, who had begun to be very pleased with himself, to Raoul's car. Alleyn, Raoul and Teresa sat on an ornamental garden seat in the factory grounds. Teresa wept and Raoul gave her cause to do so.

"Infamous girl," Raoul said, "to what sink of depravity have you retired? I think of your perfidy," he went on, "and I spit."

He rose, retired a few paces, spat and returned. "I compare your behaviour," he continued, "to its disadvantage with that of Herod, the Anti-Christ who slit the throats of first-born innocents. Ricky is an innocent and also, Monsieur will correct me if I speak in error, a first-born. He is, moreover, the son of Monsieur, my employer, who, as you observe, can find no words to express his loathing of the fallen woman with whom he finds himself in occupation of this contaminated piece of garden furniture."

"Spare me," Teresa sobbed. "I can explain myself."

Raoul bent down in order to place his exquisite but distorted face close to hers. "Female ravisher of infants," he apostrophized. "Trafficker in unmentionable vices. Associate of perverts."

"You insult me," Teresa sobbed. She rallied slightly. "You also lie like a brigand. The Holy Virgin is my witness."

"She blushes to hear you. Answer me," Raoul shouted and made a complicated gesture a few inches from her eyes. "Did you not steal the child? Answer!"

"Where there is no intention, there is no sin," Teresa bawled, taking her stand on dogma. "I am as pure as the child himself. If anything, purer. They told me his papa wished me to call for him."

"Who told you?"

"Monsieur," said Teresa, changing colour.

"Monsieur Goat! Monsieur Filth! In a word, Monsieur Oberon."

"It is a lie," Teresa repeated but rather vaguely. She turned her sumptuous and tear-blubbered face to Alleyn. "I appeal to Monsieur who is an English nobleman and will not spit upon the good name of a virtuous girl. I throw myself at his feet and implore him to hear me."

Raoul also turned to Alleyn and spread his hands out in a gesture of ineffable poignancy.

"If Monsieur pleases," he said, making Alleyn a present of the whole situation.

"Yes," Alleyn said. "Yes. Well now—"

He looked from one grand-opera countenance to the other. Teresa gazed at him with nerveless compliance, Raoul with grandeur and a sort of gloomy sympathy. Alleyn got up and stood over the girl.

"Now, see here, Teresa," he began. Raoul took a respectful step backwards. "It appears that you have behaved very foolishly for a long time and you are a fortunate girl to have come out of it without involving yourself in disaster."

"Undoubtedly," Teresa said with a hint of complacency, "I am under the protection of Our Lady of Paysdoux for whom I have a special devotion."

"Which you atrociously abuse," Raoul remarked to the landscape.

"Be that as it may," Alleyn hurriedly intervened. "It's time you pulled yourself together and tried to make amends for all the harm you have done. I think you must know very well that your employer at the Château is a bad man. In your heart you know it, don't you, Teresa?"

Teresa placed her hand on her classic bosom. "In my heart, Monsieur, I am troubled to suffocation in his presence. It is in my soul that I find him impure."

"Well, wherever it is, you are perfectly correct. He is a criminal who is wanted by the police of several countries. He has made fools of many silly girls before you. You're lucky not to be in gaol, Teresa. M. le Commissaire would undoubtedly have locked you up if I had not asked him to give you a chance to redeem yourself."

Teresa opened her mouth and let out an appropriate wail.

"To such deplorable depths have you reduced yourself," said Raoul, who had apparently assumed the maddening role of chorus. "And me!" he pointed out.

"However," Alleyn went on, "we have decided to give you this chance. On condition, Teresa, that you answer truthfully any questions I ask you."

"The Holy Virgin is my witness—" Teresa began.

"There are also other less distinguished witnesses," said Raoul. "In effect, there is the child-thief Georges Martel with whom you conspired and who is probably your paramour."

"It is a lie."

"How," Alleyn asked, "did it come about that you took Ricky from the hotel?"

"I was in Roqueville. I go to the market for the *femme de charge*. At one o'clock following my custom I visited the restaurant of the parents of Raoul, who is killing me with cruelty," Teresa explained, throwing a poignant glance at her fiancé. "There is a message for me to telephone the Château. I do so. I am told to wait as Monsieur wishes to speak to me. I do so. My heart churns in my bosom because that unfortunately is the effect Monsieur has upon it: it is not a pleasurable sensation."

"Tell that one in another place," Raoul advised.

"I swear it. Monsieur instructs me: there is a little boy at the Hôtel Royal who is the son of his dear friends, Monsieur and Madame All*aine*. He plans with Monsieur All*aine* a little trick upon Madame, a drollery, a *blague*. They have *nounou* for the child and while they are here I am to be presented by Monsieur as a *nounou* and I am to receive extra salary."

"More atrocity," said Raoul. "How much?"

"Monsieur did not specify. He said an increase. And he instructs me to go to Le Pot des Fleurs and purchase tuberoses. He tells me, spelling it out, the message I am to write. I have learned a little English from the servants of English guests at the Château so I understand. The flowers are from Mademoiselle Garbel who is at present at the Château."

"Is she, by Heaven!" Alleyn ejaculated. "Have you seen her?"

"Often, Monsieur. She is often there."

"What does she look like?"

"Like an Englishwoman. All Englishwomen with the exception, no doubt, of Madame, the wife of Monsieur, have teeth like mares and no *poitrine*. So, also, Mademoiselle Garbel."

"Go on, Teresa."

"In order that the drollery shall succeed, I am to go to the hotel while Madame is at *déjeuner*. I shall have the tuberoses and if without enquiry I can ascertain the apartments of Monsieur and Madame I am to go there. If I am questioned I am to say I am the new *nounou* and go up to the *appartements*. I am to remove the little one by the service stairs. Outside Georges Martel, who is nothing to me, waits in his auto. And from that point Georges will command the proceedings!"

"And that's what you did? No doubt you saw the number of the *appartement* on the luggage in the hall."

"Yes, Monsieur."

"And then?"

"Georges drives us to 16 Rue des Violettes where the concierge tells me she will take the little boy to the *appartement* of Mademoiselle Garbel where his father awaits him. I am to stay in the auto in the backstreet with Georges. Presently the concierge returns with the little boy. She says to Georges that the affair is in the water as the parents have seen the boy. She says that the orders are to drive at once to the factory. Georges protests: 'Is it not to St. Céleste?' She says: 'No, at once, quickly to the factory.' The little boy is angry and perhaps frightened and he shouts in French and in English that his papa and mama are not in a factory but in their hotel. But Georges uses blasphemous language and drives quickly away. And Monsieur will, I entreat, believe me when I tell him I regretted then very much everything that had happened. I was afraid. Georges would tell me nothing except to keep my mouth sewn up. So I see that I am involved in wickedness and I say several decades of the rosary and try to make amusements for the little boy who is angry and frightened and weeps for the loss of a statue bought from Marie of the Chèvre d'Argent. I think also of Raoul," said Teresa.

"It's easy to see," Raoul observed, "that in the matter of intelligence you have not invented the explosive." But he was visibly affected, nevertheless. "You should have known at once that it was a lot of *blague* about the *nounou*."

"And when you got to the factory?" Alleyn asked.

"Georges took the little boy inside. He then returned alone and we drove round to the garages at the back. I tried to run away and when he grasped my arms I inflicted some formidable scratches on his face. But he threw me a smack on the ear and told me Monsieur Oberon would put me under a malediction."

"When he emerges from gaol," Raoul said thoughtfully, "I shall make a meat *pâté* of Georges. He is already fried."

"And then, Teresa?"

"I was frightened again, Monsieur, not of Georges but of what Monsieur Oberon might do to me. And presently the whistle blew and a loud-speaker summoned everybody to the hall. And Goerges said we should clear out. He walked a little way and peeped round the corner and came back saying there were gendarmes at the gates and we must conceal ourselves. But one of the gendarmes came into the garage and said we must go into the hall. And when we arrived Georges left me saying: 'Get out, don't hang round my heels.' So I went to some of the girls I knew and when I heard the announcement of Monsieur le

Commissaire and saw Raoul and they said Raoul had seen me: Oh, Monsieur, judge of my feelings! Because, say what you will, Raoul is the friend of my heart and if he no longer loves me I am desolate."

"You are as silly as a foot," said Raoul, greatly moved, "but it is true that I love you."

"Ah!" said Teresa simply. *"Quelle extase!"*

"And upon that note," said Alleyn, "we may return to Roqueville and make our plans."

# CHAPTER IX

# Dinner at Roqueville

## I

On the return journey Alleyn and Troy sat in the back seat with Ricky between them. Teresa, who was to be given a lift to the nearest bus stop, sat in the front by Raoul. She leaned against him in a luxury of reconciliation, every now and then twisting herself sideways in order to gaze into his face. Ricky, who suffered from an emotional hangover and was, therefore, inclined to be querulous and in any case considered Raoul his especial property, looked at these manifestations with distaste.

"Why does she do that?" he asked fretfully. "Isn't she silly? Does Raoul like her?"

"Yes," said Troy, hugging him.

"I bet he doesn't really."

"They are engaged to be married," said Troy, "I think."

"You and Mummy are married, aren't you, Daddy?"

"Yes."

"Well, Mummy doesn't do it."

"True," said Alleyn, who was in good spirits, "but I should like it if she did."

"Ooh, Daddy, you would *not*."

Teresa wound her arm round Raoul's neck.

*"Je t'adore!"* she crooned.

"Oh, gosh!" said Ricky and shut his eyes.

"All the same," Alleyn said, "we'll have to call a halt to her raptures." He leaned forward. "Raoul, shall we stop for a moment? If Teresa misses her bus you may drive her back from Roqueville."

"Monsieur, may I suggest that we drive direct to Roqueville where, if Monsieur and Madame please, my parents will be enchanted to invite them to an *apéritif* or, if preferred, a glass of good wine, and perhaps an early but well-considered dinner. The afternoon has been fatiguing. Monsieur has not eaten, I think, since morning and Madame and Monsieur Ricky may be glad to dine early. Teresa is, no doubt, not expected at the house of infamy, being, as they will suppose, engaged in the abduction of Ricky and in any case I do not permit her to return."

Teresa made a complicated noise, partly protesting but mostly acquiescent. She essayed to tuck one of Raoul's curls under his cap.

Ricky, with his eyes still shut, said: "Is Raoul asking us to tea, Daddy? May we go? Just us however," he added pointedly.

"We shall all go," Alleyn said, "including Teresa. Unless, Troy darling, you'd rather take Ricky straight to the hotel."

Ricky opened his eyes. "Please not, Mummy. Please let's go with Raoul."

"All right, my mammet. How kind of Raoul."

So Alleyn thanked Raoul and accepted his invitation, and as they had arrived at the only stretch of straight road on their journey Raoul passed his right arm round Teresa and broke into song.

They drove on through an evening drenched in a sunset that dyed their faces and hands crimson and closely resembled the coloured postcards that are sold on the Mediterranean coast. Two police-cars passed them with a great sounding of horns and Alleyn told Troy that M. Dupont had sent for extra men to effect a search of the factory. "It was too good an opening to miss," he said. "He'll certainly find enough evidence to throw a spanner through the plate glass and thanks for the greater part, let's face it, to young Rick."

"What have I done, Daddy?"

"Well, you mustn't buck too much about it but by being a good boy and not making a fuss when you were a bit frightened you've helped us to shut up that factory back there and stop everybody's nonsense."

"Lavish!" said Ricky.

"Not bad. And now you can pipe down for a bit while I talk to Mummy."

Ricky looked thoughtfully at his father, got down from his seat and placed himself between Alleyn's knees. He then aimed a blow with his fist at Alleyn's chest and followed it up with a tackle. Alleyn picked him up. "Pipe down, now," he said, and Ricky, suddenly quiescent, lay against his father and tried to hide his goat from the light in the hope that it would illuminate itself.

"The next thing," Alleyn said to Troy, "is to tackle our acquaintance of this morning. And from this point onwards, my girl, you fade, graciously but inexorably, *out*. You succour your young, reside in your classy pub, and if your muse grows exigent you go out with Raoul and your young and paint pretty peeps of the bay, glimpsed between sprays of bougainvillea."

"And do we get any pretty peeps of you?"

"I expect to be busyish. Would you rather move on to St. Céleste or back to St. Christophe? Does this place stink for you, after today?"

"I don't think so. We know the real kidnappers are in jug, don't we? And I imagine the last thing Oberon and Co. will try on is another shot at the same game."

"The very last. After tomorrow night," Alleyn said, "I hope they will have no chance of trying anything on except the fruitless contemplation of their past infamies and whatever garments they are allowed to wear in the local lock-up."

"Really? A coup in the offing?"

"With any luck. But see here, Troy, if you're going to feel at all jumpy we'll pack you both off to—well, home, if necessary."

"I don't want to go home," Ricky said from inside Alleyn's jacket. "I think Goat's beginning to illumine himself, Daddy."

"Good. What about Troy?"

"I'd rather stay, Rory. Indeed, if it wasn't for the young, and yet I suppose because of him, I'd rather muck in on the job. I'm getting a first-hand look at the criminal classes and it's surprising how uncivilized it makes one feel."

Alleyn glanced at the now hazardously entwined couple in the front seat. He adjusted Ricky and flung an arm round Troy.

"A fat lot they know about it," he muttered.

As the car slipped down the familiar entry into Roqueville he said: "And how would you muck in, may I ask?"

"I might say I wanted to do a portrait of Oberon in the lotus bud position and thus by easy degrees become a Daughter of the Sun."

"Like hell, you might."

"Anyway, let's stay if only to meet Cousin Garbel."

She felt Alleyn's arm harden. Like Teresa, she turned to look at her man.

"Rory," she said, "did you believe Baradi's story about the charades?"

"Did you?"

"I thought I did. I wanted to. Now, I don't think I do."

"Nor do I," Alleyn said.

"*On arrive,*" said Raoul, turning into a narrow street. "*Voici L'Escargot Bienvenu.*"

## II

It was, as Raoul had said, an unpretentious restaurant. They entered through a *portière* of wooden beads into a white-washed room with fresh window curtains and nine tables. A serving counter ran along one side and on it stood baskets of fresh fruit, of bread and of *langoustes* bedded in water-cress. Bottles of wine and polished glasses filled the shelves behind the counter and an open door led into an inner room where a voice was announcing the weather forecast in French. There were no customers in the restaurant, and Raoul, having drawn out three chairs and seated his guests, placed his arm about Teresa's waist and led her into the inner room.

"Maman! Papa!" he shouted.

An excited babble broke out in the background.

"Come to think of it," Alleyn said, "I'm damned hungry. Raoul told me his papa was particularly good with steak. *Filet mignon?* What do you think?"

"Are we going to be allowed to pay?"

"No. Which means that good or bad we'll have to come back for more. But my bet is, it'll be good."

The hubbub in the background came closer, and Raoul reappeared accompanied by a magnificent Italian father and a plump French mother, both of whom he introduced with ceremony. Everybody was very polite, Ricky was made much of and a bottle of extremely good sherry was opened. Ricky was given grenadine. Healths were drunk, Teresa giggled modestly in the background. M. Milano made a short but succinct speech in which he said he understood that Monsieur and Madame Ah-laine had been instrumental in saving Teresa from a fate that was worse than death and had thus preserved the honour of both families and made possible an alliance that was the dearest wish of their hearts. It was also, other things being equal, a desirable match from the practical point of view. Teresa and Raoul listened without embarrassment and with the detachment of connoisseurs. M. Milano then begged that he and Madame might be excused as they believed they were to have the great pleasure of serving an early dinner and must therefore make a little preparation with which Teresa would no doubt be pleased to assist. They withdrew. Teresa embraced Raoul with passionate enthusiasm and followed them.

Alleyn said: "Bring a chair, Raoul. We have much to say to each other."

"Monsieur," Raoul said without moving, "no mention has been made of my neglect of duty this afternoon. I mean, Monsieur, my failure, which was deliberate, to identify Teresa."

"I have decided to overlook it. The circumstances were extraordinary."

"That is true, Monsieur. Nevertheless, the incident had the effect of incensing me against Teresa who, foolish as she is, has yet got something which caused me to betray my duty. That is why I spoke a little sharply to Teresa. With results," he added, "that are, as Monsieur may have noticed, not undesirable."

"I have noticed. Sit down, Raoul."

Raoul bowed and sat down. Madame Milano, beaming and businesslike, returned with a book in her hands. It was a shabby large book with a carefully mended binding. She laid it on the table in front of Ricky.

"When my son was no larger than this little Monsieur," she said, "it afforded him much amusement."

"*Merci*, Madame," Ricky said, eyeing it.

Troy and Alleyn also thanked her. She made a deprecating face and bustled away. Ricky opened the book. It was a tale of heroic and fabulous adventures enchantingly illustrated with coloured lithographs. Ricky honoured it with the silence he reserved for special occasions. He removed himself and the book to another table. "Coming, Mum?" he said and Troy joined him. Alleyn looked at the two dark heads bent together over the book and for a moment or two he was lost in abstraction. He heard Raoul catch his breath in a vocal sigh, a sound partly affirmative, partly envious. Alleyn looked at him.

"Monsieur is fortunate," Raoul said simply.

"I believe you," Alleyn muttered. "And now, Raoul, we make a plan. Earlier today, and I must say it feels more like last week, you said you were willing to join in an enterprise that may be a little hazardous: an enterprise that involves an unsolicited visit to the Chèvre d'Argent on Thursday night."

"I remember, Monsieur."

"Are you still of the same mind?"

"If possible, I feel an increase of enthusiasm."

"Good, now, listen. It is evident that there is a close liaison between the persons at the Château and those at the factory. Tonight the commissary will conduct an official search of the factory and he will find documentary evidence of the collaboration. It is also probable that he will find quantities of illicitly manufactured heroin. It is not certain whether he will find direct and conclusive evidence of sufficient weight to warrant an arrest of Mr. Oberon and Dr. Baradi and their associates. Therefore, it would be of great assistance if they could be arrested for some other offense and could be held while further investigations were made."

"There is no doubt, Monsieur, that their sins are not confined to contraband."

"I agree."

"They are capable of all."

"Not only capable but culpable! I think," Alleyn said, "that one of them is a murderer."

Raoul narrowed his eyes. His stained mechanic's hands lying on the table, flexed and then stretched.

"Monsieur speaks with confidence," he said.

"I ought to," Alleyn said drily, "considering that I saw the crime."

"You—"

"Through a train window." And Alleyn described the circumstances.

"Bizarre," Raoul commented, summing up the incident. "And the criminal, Monsieur?"

"Impossible to say. I had the impression of a man or woman in a white gown with a cowl or hood. The right arm was raised and held a weapon. The face was undistinguishable although there was a strong light thrown from the side. The weapon was a knife of some sort."

"The animal," said Raoul, who had settled upon this form of reference for M. Oberon, "displays himself in a white robe."

"Yes."

"And the victim was a woman, Monsieur?"

"A woman. Also, I should say, wearing some loose-fitting garment. One saw only a shape against a window blind and then for a second, against the window itself. The man, if it was a man, had already struck and had withdrawn the weapon which he held aloft. The impression was melodramatic," he added, almost to himself. "Over-dramatic. One might have believed it was a charade."

"A charade, Monsieur?"

"Dr. Baradi offered the information that there were charades last night. It appears that someone played the part of the Queen of Sheba stabbing King Solomon's principal wife. He himself enacted a concubine."

"Obviously he is not merely a satyr but also a perverted being—a distortion of nature. Only such a being could invent such a disgusting lie."

While he grinned at Raoul's scandalized sophistry Alleyn wondered at the ease with which they talked to each other. And, being a modest man, he found himself ashamed. Why, in Heaven's name, he thought, should he not find it good to talk to Raoul, who had an admirable mind and a simple approach? He thought: "We understand so little of our fellow creatures. Somewhere in Raoul there is a limitation but when it comes to the Oberons and Baradis he, probably by virtue of his limitation, is likely to be a much more useful judge than . . ."

"The Queen of Sheba," Raoul fumed, "is a Biblical personage. She was the *chère amie* of the Lord's anointed. To murder he adds a blasphemy which has not even the merit of being true. Unfortunately he is left-handed," he added in a tone of acute disappointment.

"Exactly! Moreover he offered this information," Alleyn pointed out. "One must remember the circumstances. The scene, real or simulated, reached its climax as the train drew up and stopped. The blind was released as the woman fell against it. And the man, not necessarily Oberon or Baradi, you know, saw other windows—those of the train."

"So knowing Monsieur must have been in the train and awake, since he was to alight at Roqueville, this blasphemer produces his lies."

"It might well be so. M. Dupont and I both incline to think so. Now, you see, don't you, that if murder *was* done in that room in the early hours of this morning, we have great cause to revisit the Château. Not only to arrest a killer but to discover why he killed. Not only to arrest a purveyor of drugs who has caused many deaths but to discover his associates. And not only for these reasons but also to learn, if we can, what happens in the locked room on Thursday nights. For all these reasons, Raoul, it seems imperative that we visit the Château."

"Well, Monsieur."

"Two courses suggest themselves. I may return openly to enquire after the health of Mademoiselle Truebody. If I do this I shall have to admit that Ricky has been found."

"They will have learned as much from the man Callard, Monsieur."

"I am not so sure. This afternoon M. Dupont ordered that all outward calls from the factory should be blocked at central and that the Château should be cut off. At the Château they will be extremely anxious to avoid any sign that they are in touch with the factory. They will, of course, question Teresa, to whom we must give instructions. If I pursue our first course I shall tell the story of the finding of Ricky to Mr. Oberon and his guests and I shall utter many maledictions against Callard as a child-kidnapper. And, having seen Miss Truebody, I must appear to go away and somehow or another remain. I've no idea how this can be done. Perhaps, if one had a colleague within the place one might manage it. The alternative is for me, and you, Raoul, to go secretly to the Château. To do this we would again need a colleague who would admit and conceal us."

Raoul put his head on one side with the air of a collector examining a doubtful treasure. "Monsieur refers, of course, to Teresa," he said.

"I do."

"Teresa," Raoul continued anxiously, "has not displayed herself to advantage this afternoon. She was *bouleversée* and therefore behaved foolishly. Nevertheless, she is normally a girl of spirit. She is also at the present time desirous of re-establishing herself in my heart. Possibly I have been too lenient with her but one inclines to leniency where one's affections are engaged. I have, as Monsieur knows, forbidden her return to this temple of shame. Nevertheless, where the cause is just and with the protection of Our Lady of Paysdoux (about whose patronage Teresa is so unbecomingly cocksure), there can be no sin."

"I take it," Alleyn said, "that you withdraw your objection?"

"Yes, Monsieur. Not without misgivings because Teresa is dear to me and, say what you like, it is no place for one's girl."

"Judging by the lacerations on Georges Martel's face, Teresa is able to defend herself on occasion."

"True," Raoul agreed, cheering up. "She has enterprise."

"Suppose we talk to her about it?"

"I will produce her."

Raoul went out to the kitchen.

"Hallo, you two," Alleyn said.

"Hallo, yourself," Troy said.

"Daddy, this is a lavish book. I can read it better than Mummy."

"Don't buck," Alleyn said automatically.

"Have you sent Raoul to get that nanny-person? Teresa?"

"Yes."

"Why?"

"We've got a job for her."

"*Not* minding me?"

"No, no. Nothing to do with you, old boy."

"Well, good, anyway," said Ricky returning to his book.

Raoul came back with Teresa, who now wore an apron and seemed to be in remarkably high spirits. On Alleyn's invitation she sat down using, however, the very edge of her chair. Alleyn told her briefly what he wanted her to do. Raoul folded his arms and scowled thoughtfully at the tablecloth.

"You see, Teresa," Alleyn said, "these are bad men and also unfortunately extremely clever men. They think they've made a fool of you as they have of a great many other silly girls. The thing is—are you ready to help Raoul and me and the police of your own country to put a stop to their wickedness?"

"Ah, yes, Monsieur," said Teresa cheerfully. "I now perceive my duty and with the help of Raoul and the holy saints, dedicate myself to the cause."

"Good. Do you think you can keep your head and behave sensibly and with address if an emergency should arise?"

Teresa gazed at him and said that she thought she could.

"Very well. Now, tell me: were you on duty last evening?"

"Yes, Monsieur. During the dinner I helped the housemaids go round the bedrooms and then I worked in the kitchen."

"Was there a party?"

"A party? Well, Monsieur, there was the new guest, Mlle. Wells, who is an actress. And after dinner there was a gathering of all the guests in the private apartments of M. Oberon. I know this because I heard the butler say that Monsieur wished it made ready for a special welcome for Mlle. Wells. And this morning," said Teresa, looking prim, "Jeanne Barre, who is an under-housemaid, said that Mlle. Locke, the English noblewoman, must have taken too much wine because her door was locked with a notice not to disturb and this is always a sign she has been indiscreet."

"I see. Tell me, Teresa: have you ever seen into the room that is only opened on Thursday night?"

"Yes, Monsieur. On Thursday morning I dust this room and on Fridays it is my duty to clean it."

"Where is it exactly?"

"It is down the stairs, three flights, from the vestibule, and beneath the library. It is next to the private apartments of M. Oberon."

"Has it many windows?"

"It has no windows, Monsieur. It is in a very old part of the Château."

"And M. Oberon's rooms?"

"Oh, yes, Monsieur. The salon has a window which is covered always by a white blind with a painting of the sun because Monsieur dislikes brilliant light, so it is always closed. But Monsieur has nevertheless a great lamp fashioned like the sun and many strange ornaments and a strange wheel which Monsieur treasures and a magnificent bed and in the salon a rich divan," said Teresa, warming to her subject, "and an enormous mirror where—" There she stopped short and blushed.

"Continue," Raoul ordered, with a face of thunder.

"Where once when I took in *petit déjeuner* I saw Monsieur contemplating himself in a state of nature."

Alleyn, with an eye on Raoul, said hurriedly, "Will you describe the room that you clean?"

Raoul reached across the table and moved his forefinger to and fro in front of his beloved's nose. "Choose your words, my treasure," he urged. "Invent nothing. Accuracy is all."

"Yes, indeed it is," said Alleyn heartily.

Thus warned, Teresa looked self-consciously at her folded hands and with a slightly sanctimonious air began her recital.

"If you please, Monsieur, it is a large room and at first I thought perhaps it was a chapel."

"*A chapel?*" Alleyn exclaimed. Raoul made a composite noise suggestive of angry incredulity.

"Yes, Monsieur. I thought perhaps it was reserved for the private devotions of M. Oberon and his friends. Because at one side is a raised place with a table like the holy altar, covered in a cloth which is woven in a rich pattern with gold and silver and jewels. But although one saw the holy cross, there were other things in the pattern that one does not see in altar cloths."

"The hoof prints of anathema!" Raoul ejaculated.

"Go on, Teresa," said Alleyn.

"And on the table there was something that was also covered with an embroidered cloth."

"What was that, do you suppose?"

Teresa's white eyelids were raised. She gave Alleyn the glance of a cunning child.

"Monsieur must not think badly of me if I tell him I raised the cloth and looked. Because I wanted to see if it was a holy relic."

"And was it?"

"No, Monsieur. At first I thought it was a big monstrance made of glass. Only it was not a monstrance although in shape it resembled a great sun and inside the sun a holy cross broken and a figure like this."

With a sort of disgusted incredulity Alleyn watched her trace with her finger on the table, a pentagram. Raoul groaned heavily.

"And it was, as I saw when I looked more closely, Monsieur, a great lamp because there were many, many electric bulbs behind it and behind the sun at the back was a bigger electric bulb than I have ever seen before. So I dropped the heavy cloth over it and wondered."

"What else did you see?"

"There was nothing else in the room, Monsieur. No chairs or any furniture or anything. The walls were covered with black velvet and there were no pictures."

"Any doors, other than the one leading from Mr. Oberon's room?"

"Yes, Monsieur. There was a door in the wall opposite the table. I didn't notice it the first time I cleaned the room because it is covered like the walls and had no handle. But the second time it was open and I was told to clean the little room beyond."

"What was it like, this room?"

"On the floor there were many black velvet cushions and one large one like the mattress for a divan. And the walls here also were covered in black velvet and there was a black velvet curtain behind which were hanging a great number of white robes such as the robe Monsieur wears and one black velvet robe. And on the table there were many candles in black candlesticks which I had to clean. There was also a door from the passage into this little room."

"Nastier and nastier," Alleyn muttered in English.

"I beg Monsieur's pardon?"

"Nothing. And this was the only other door into the big room?"

"No, Monsieur, there was another, very small like a trapdoor behind the table, painted with signs like the signs on the sunlamp and on the floor."

"There were signs on the floor?"

"Yes, Monsieur. I had been told to clean the floor, Monsieur. It is a beautiful floor with a pattern made of many pieces of stone and the pattern is the same as the other." Her finger traced the pentagram again. "And when I came to clean it, Monsieur, I knew the room was not a chapel."

"Why?"

"Because the floor in front of the table was as dirty as a farmyard," said Teresa. "It was like our yard at my home in the Paysdoux. There had been an animal in the room."

"An animal!" Raoul ejaculated. "I believe you! And what sort of animal?"

"That was easy to see," said Teresa simply. "It was a goat."

### III

Alleyn decided finally that the following evening he and Raoul would call at the Chèvre d'Argent. He would arrive after the hour of six when, according to Teresa, the entire household would have retired for something known as private meditation, but which was supposed by Teresa to be a sound sleep. It was unusual at this time for anyone to appear, and indeed again, according to Teresa, a rule of silence and solitude was imposed from six until nine by Mr. Oberon. On Thursdays there was no dinner, but Teresa understood that there was a very late supper at which the guests were served by the Egyptian servant only. Teresa herself was dismissed with the other servants as soon as their late afternoon and early evening tasks were executed. If they didn't encounter any member of the household on their way through the tunnel Alleyn and Raoul were to go past the main entrance and down a flight of steps to a little-used door through which Teresa would admit them. No attention would be paid to Raoul if he was seen by any other servants who might still be about, and if Alleyn kept in the background it might be possible to suggest that he was a relative from Marseilles. "A distinguished relative," Raoul amended, "seeing that in appearance and in speech Monsieur is clearly of a superior class."

Teresa would then conceal Alleyn and Raoul in her own room where, with any luck, she would have already secreted two of the white robes. She was pretty certain there were many more in the little anteroom than would be needed by M. Oberon's guests. It would be tolerably easy when she cleaned this room to remove them under cover of the laundry it was her duty to collect from the bedrooms.

"Is it not as I have said, Monsieur?" Raoul remarked, indicating his fiancée. "She is not without enterprise, is Teresa?" Teresa looked modestly at Alleyn and passionately at Raoul.

If all went well, up to this point, Teresa would have done as much as could be expected of her. She would take her departure as usual and could either wait in Raoul's car or catch the evening bus to her home in Paysdoux. It should be possible for Alleyn and Raoul to pass through the house without attracting attention. The cowls of their robes would be drawn over their heads and it might be supposed if they were seen that they were belated guests or even early arrivals for the ceremony. Teresa had heard that occasionally there were extra people on Thursday nights, people staying in Roqueville or in St. Christophe.

And then? "Then," Alleyn said, "it will be up to us, Raoul."

The alternative to this plan was tricky. If he was spotted on his way into the Chèvre d'Argent, Alleyn would put a bold face on it and say that he had come to see Miss Truebody. No doubt Baradi would be summoned from his private meditation and Alleyn would have to act upon the situations as they arose. Raoul would still call on Teresa and hide in her room.

"All right," Alleyn said. "That's as far as we need go. Now Teresa, this evening you will return to the Château and Mr. Oberon will no doubt question you about today's proceedings. You will tell him exactly what happened at the factory, up to and after the identification parade. You will tell him that Ricky identified you. Then, you will say, the police made you come back to Roqueville and asked you many questions, accusing you of complicity in the former kidnapping affair and asking who were your colleagues in that business. You will say that you told the police you know nothing: that Georges Martel offered you a little money to fetch the boy and beyond that you know nothing at all. This is important, Teresa. Repeat it, please."

Teresa folded her hands and repeated it, prompted without necessity by Raoul.

"Excellent," Alleyn said. "And you will, of course, have had no conversation with me. Perhaps it will be well to say, if you are asked, that you returned to Roqueville in Raoul's car. You may have been seen doing so. But you will say that Madame and I were so overjoyed on recovering our son that we had nothing to say except that no doubt the police would deal with you."

"Yes, Monsieur."

"Have courage, my little one," Raoul admonished her. "Lie no more than is necessary, you understand, but when you do lie, lie like a brigand. It is in the cause of the angels."

"Upon whose protection and of that of Our Lady of Paysdoux," Teresa neatly interpolated, "I hurl myself."

"Do so."

Teresa rose and made a convent-child's bob. Raoul also asked to be excused. As they went together to the door, Alleyn said: "By the way, did you hear tomorrow's weather forecast for the district?"

"Yes, Monsieur. It is for thunderstorms. There are electrical disturbances."

"Indeed? How very apropos. Thank you, Raoul."

"Monsieur," said Raoul obligingly and withdrew his beloved into the inner room.

Alleyn rejoined his family. "Did you get much of that?" he asked.

"I've reached exhaustion point for French," Troy said. "I can't even try to listen. And Ricky, as you see, is otherwise engaged."

Ricky looked up from a brilliant picture of two knights engaged in single combat. "I bet there'll be a wallop when they crash," he said. "Whang! I daresay I'd be able to read this pretty soon if we stayed here. I can read a bit, can't I, Mummy?"

"English, you can."

"I know. So don't you daresay I could, French, Daddy?"

"I wouldn't put it past you. Did you know what we were talking about, just now?"

"I wasn't listening much." Ricky lowered his voice to a polite whisper. "If it isn't a rude question," he said, "when's dinner?"

"Soon. Pipe down, now. I want to talk to Mummy."

"O.K. What are you going to do in Teresa's bedroom tomorrow night, Daddy?"

"I must say I should like to be associated with that enquiry," said Troy warmly.

"I am changing there for a party."

"Who's having a party?" Ricky demanded.

"A silver goat. I rather think he lights himself up."

The door opened. Teresa came in with a tray.

## IV

The dinner was superb, the *filets mignons* particularly being inspired. When it was finished the Alleyns invited the Milanos to join them for *fines* and M. Milano produced a bottle of distinguished cognac. The atmosphere was gay and *comme il faut*. Presently the regular clientele of the house began to come in: quiet middle-class people who greeted Madame Milano and took down their own table-napkins from hooks above their special places. A game of draughts was begun at the corner table. Troy, who had enjoyed herself enormously but was in a trance of fatigue, said she thought that they should go. Elaborate leave-takings were begun. Ricky, full of vegetables and rich gravy and sticky with grenadine, yawned happily and bestowed a smile of enchanting sweetness upon Madame Milano.

"*Mille remerciements, chère Madame,*" he said, stumbling a little over the long word, "*de mon beau repas,*" and held out his hand. Madame made a complicated, motherly, bustling movement and ejaculated, "*Ah, mon Dieu, quel amour d'enfant!*" There followed a great shaking of hands and interchange of compliments and the Alleyns took their departure on the crest of the wave.

Raoul drove them back to their hotel where, regrettably, a great fuss was again made over Ricky, who began to show infantile signs of vainglory and struck an attitude before M. Malaquin, the proprietor, shouting: "Kidnappers! Huh! Easy!" and was applauded by the hall porter.

Alleyn said: "That's more than enough from you, my friend," picked his son up and bore him into the lift. Troy followed wearily, saying: "Don't be an ass, Ricky darling." When they got upstairs Ricky, who had been making tentative sounds of defiance, became quiet. When he was ready for bed he turned white and said he wouldn't sleep in "that room." His parents exchanged the look that recognizes a dilemma. Troy muttered: "It *is* trying him a bit high, isn't it?" Alleyn locked the outer door of Ricky's room and took him into the passage to show him that it couldn't be opened. They returned, leaving the door between the two rooms open. Ricky hung back. He had shadows under his eyes and looked exhausted and miserable. "Why can't Daddy go in there?" he asked angrily.

Alleyn thought a moment and then said: "I can of course, and you can be with Mummy."

"Please," Ricky said. "Please."

"Well, I must say that's a bit more civil. Look here, old boy, will you lend me your goat to keep me company? I want to see if it really does light itself up."

"Yes, of course he will," said Troy with an attempt at maternal prompting, "which," she thought, "I should find perfectly maddening if I were Ricky."

Ricky said: "I want to be in here with Mummy and I want Goat to be here too. Please," he added.

"All right," Alleyn said. "You won't see him light himself up, of course, because Mummy will want her lamp on for some time, won't you, darling?"

"For ages and ages," Troy, who desired nothing less, agreed.

Ricky said: "Please take him in there and tell me if he illumines." He fished his silver goat out of the bosom of his yellow shirt. Alleyn took it into the next room, put it on the bedside table, shut the door and turned out the lights.

He sat on the bed staring into the dark and thinking of the events of the long day and of Troy and Ricky, and presently a familiar experience revisited him. He seemed to see himself for the first time, a stranger, a being divorced from experience, a chrysalis from which his spirit had escaped and which it now looked upon, he thought, with astonishment as a soul might look after death at its late housing. He thought: "I suppose Oberon imagines he's got all this sort of thing taped. Raoul and Teresa too, after *their* fashion and belief. But I have never found an answer." The illusion, if it were an illusion and he was never certain about this, could be dismissed, but he held to it still and in a little while he found he was looking at a fluorescence, a glimmer of something, no more than a bat-light. It grew into a shape. It was Ricky's little figurine faithfully illuminating itself in the dark. And Ricky's voice, still rather fretful, brought Alleyn back to himself.

"Daddy!" he was shouting. "Is he doing it? *Daddy!*"

"Yes," Alleyn called, rousing himself, "he's doing it. Come and see. But shut the door after you or you'll spoil it."

There was a pause. A blade of light appeared and widened. He saw Ricky come in, a tiny figure in pyjamas. "Shut the door, Ricky," Alleyn repeated, "and wait a moment. If you come to me, you'll see."

The room was dark again.

"If you'd go on talking, however," Ricky's voice said, very small and polite, "I'd find you."

Alleyn went on talking and Ricky found him. He stood between his father's knees and watched the goat shining. "He honestly is silver," he said. "It's all true." He leaned back against his father, smelling of soap, and laid his relaxed hand on Alleyn's. Alleyn lifted him on to his knee. "I'm fizzily and 'motionly zausted," Ricky said in a drawling voice.

"What in the world does that mean?"

"It's what Mademoiselle says I am when I'm overtired." He yawned cosily. "I'll look at Goat a bit more and then I daresay . . ." His voice trailed into silence.

Alleyn could hear Troy moving about quietly in the next room. He waited until Ricky was breathing deeply and then put him to bed. The door opened and Troy stood there listening. Alleyn joined her. "He's off," he said and watched while she went to see for herself. They left the door open.

"I don't know whether that was sound child-psychiatry or a bare-faced cheat," Alleyn said, "but it's settled his troubles. I don't think he'll be frightened of his bedroom now."

"Suppose he wakes and gets a panic, poor sweet."

"He won't. He'll see his precious goat and go to sleep again. What about you?"

"I'm practically snoring on my feet."

"Fizzily and 'motionly zausted?"

"Did he say that?"

"Queer little bloke that he is, he did. Shall I stay with you, too, until you go to sleep?"

"But—what about you?"

"I'm going up to the factory. Dupont's still there and Raoul's hiring me his car."

"Rory, you can't. You must be dead."

"Not a bit of it. The night's young and it'll be tactful to show up. Besides I've got to make arrangements for tomorrow."

"I don't know how you do it."

"Of course you don't, my darling. You're not a cop."

She tried to protest but was so bemused with sleepiness that her voice trailed away as Ricky's had done. By the time Alleyn had washed and found himself an overcoat, Troy too was in bed and fast asleep. He turned off the lights and slipped out of the room.

Left to itself, the little silver goat glowed steadfastly through the night.

# CHAPTER X

# Thunder in the Air

*I*

ALLEYN left word at the office that he might be late coming in and said that unless he himself rang up no telephone calls were to be put through to Troy. Anybody who rang was to be asked to leave a message. It was nine o'clock.

The porter opened the doors and Alleyn ran down the steps to Raoul's car. There was another car drawn up beside it, a long and stylish racing model with a G.B. plate. The driver leaned out and said cautiously: "Hallo, sir."

It was Robin Herrington.

"Hullo," Alleyn said.

"I'm on my way back actually, from Douceville. As a matter of fact I was just coming in on the chance of having a word with you," Herrington said rapidly, and in a muted voice. "I'm sorry you're going out. I mean, I don't suppose you could give me five minutes. Sorry not to get out, but as a matter of fact I sort of thought— It wouldn't take long. Perhaps I could drive you to wherever you're going and then I wouldn't waste your time. Sort of."

"Thank you, I've got a car but I'll give you five minutes with pleasure. Shall I join you?"

"Frightfully nice of you, sir. Yes, please do."

Alleyn walked round and climbed in.

"It won't take five minutes," Herrington said nervously and was then silent.

"How," Alleyn asked after waiting for some moments, "is Miss Truebody?"

Robin shuffled his feet. "Pretty bad," he said. "She was when I left. Pretty bad, actually."

Alleyn waited again and was suddenly offered a drink. His companion opened a door and a miniature cocktail cabinet lit itself up.

"No, thank you," Alleyn said. "What's up?"

"I will, if you don't mind. A very small one." He gave himself a tot of neat brandy and swallowed half of it. "It's about Ginny," he said.

"Oh!"

"As a matter of fact, I'm rather worried about her, which may sound a bit funny."

"Not very."

"Oh. Well, you see, she's so terrifyingly young, Ginny. She's only nineteen. And, as a matter of fact, I don't think this is a madly appropriate setting for her." Alleyn was silent and after a further pause Robin went on, "I don't know if you've any idea what sort of background Ginny's got. Her people were killed when she was a kid. In the blitz. She was trapped with them and hauled out somehow, which rocked her a good deal at the time and actually hasn't exactly worn off even now. She's rather been nobody's baby. Her guardian's a pretty odd old number. More interested in marmosets and miniatures than children, really. He's her great uncle."

"You don't mean Mr. Penderby Locke?" Alleyn said, recognizing this unusual combination of hobbies.

"Yes, that's right. He's quite famous on his own pitch, I understand, but he couldn't have been less interested in Ginny."

"Then—Miss Taylor is related to Miss Grizel Locke who, I think, is Penderby Locke's sister, isn't she?"

"Is she? I don't know. Yes, I think she must be," Robin said, shooting out the words quickly and hurrying on. "The thing is, Ginny just sort of grew up rather much under her own steam. She was sent to a French family and they weren't much cop, I gather, and then she came back to England and somebody brought her out and she got in with a pretty vivid set and had a miserable love affair with a poor type of chap and felt life wasn't as gay as it's cracked up to be. And this affair busted up when they were staying with some of his chums at Cannes and Ginny felt what was the good of anything anyway, and I must say I know what that's like."

"She arrived at this philosophy in Cannes?"

"Yes. And she met Baradi and Oberon there. And I was there too, as it happened," said Robin with a change of voice. "So we were both asked to come on here. About a fortnight ago."

"I see. And then?"

"Well, it's a dimmish sort of thing to talk about one's hosts, but I don't think it was a particularly good thing, her coming. I mean it's all right for oneself."

"Is it?"

"Well, I don't know. Just to do once and—and perhaps not do again. Quite amusing, really," said Robin miserably. "I mean, I'm not madly zealous about being a Child of the Sun. I just thought it might be fun. Of a sort. I mean, one knows one's way about."

"One would, I should think, need to."

"Ginny doesn't," Robin said.

"No?"

"She thinks she does, poor sweet, but actually she hasn't a clue when it comes to—well, to this sort of party, you know."

"What sort of party?"

Robin pushed his glass back and shut the cupboard with a bang. "You saw, didn't you, sir?"

"I believe Dr. Baradi is a very good surgeon. I only met the others for a few moments, you know."

"Yes, but—well, you know Annabella Wells, don't you? She said so."

"We crossed the Atlantic in the same ship. There were some five hundred other passengers."

"I'd have thought she'd have shown up if there'd been five million," Robin said with feeling. Alleyn glanced at his watch. "I'm sorry, I'm not exactly pressing ahead with this," Robin said.

"Don't you think you'd better tell me what you want me to do?"

"It sounds so odd. Mrs. Allen will think it such cheek."

"Troy? How can it concern her?"

"I—well, I was wondering if Mrs. Allen would ask Ginny to dinner tomorrow night."

"Why tomorrow night, particularly?"

Robin muttered: "There's going to be a sort of party up there. I'd rather Ginny was out of it."

"Would she rather be out of it?"

"Hell!" Robin shouted. "She would if she were herself. My God, she would!"

"And what exactly," Alleyn asked, "do you mean by that?"

Robin hit the wheel of his car with his clenched fist and said almost inaudibly: "He's got hold of her. Oberon. She thinks he's the bottom when she's not—it's just one of those bloody things."

"Well," Alleyn said, "we'd be delighted if Miss Taylor would dine with us but don't you think she'll find the invitation rather odd? After all, we've scarcely met her. She'll probably refuse."

"I'd thought of that," Robin said eagerly. "I know. But I thought if I could get her to come for a run in the car, I'd suggest we call on Mrs. Allen. Ginny liked Mrs. Allen awfully. And you, sir, if I may say so. Ginny's interested in art and all that and she was quite thrilled when she knew Mrs. Allen was Agatha Troy. So I thought if we might we could call about cocktail time and I'd say I'd got to go somewhere to see about something for the yacht or something and then I could ring up from somewhere and say I'd broken down."

"She would then take a taxi back to the Chèvre d'Argent."

Robin gulped. "Yes, I know," he said. "But—well, I thought perhaps by that time Mrs. Allen might have sort of talked to her and got her to see. Sort of."

"But why doesn't Miss Locke talk to her? Surely, as her aunt— What's the matter?"

Robin had made a violent ejaculation. He mumbled incoherently: "Not that sort. I've told you. They didn't care about Ginny."

Alleyn was silent for a minute.

"I know it's a hell of a lot to ask," Robin said desperately.

"I think it is," Alleyn said, "when you are so obviously leaving most of the facts out of your story."

"I don't know what you mean."

"You are asking us to behave in a difficult and extremely odd manner. You want us, in effect, to kidnap Miss Taylor. We have had," Alleyn said, "our bellyful of kidnapping, this afternoon. I suppose you heard about Ricky."

Robin made an inarticulate noise that sounded rather like a groan. "I know. Yes. We did hear. I'm awfully sorry. It must be terribly worrying."

"And how," Alleyn asked, "did you hear about it?" and would have given a good deal to have had a clear view of Robin's face.

"Well, I—well, we rang up the hotel this afternoon."

"I thought you said you had been to Douceville all the afternoon."

"Hell!"

"I think you must have known much earlier that Ricky was kidnapped, didn't you?"

"Look here, sir, I don't know what to say."

"I'll tell you. If you want me to help you with this child, Ginny, and

I believe you do, you will answer, fully and truthfully, specific questions that I shall put to you. If you don't want to answer, we'll say goodnight and forget we had this conversation. But don't lie. I shall know," Alleyn said mildly, "if you lie."

Robin waited for a moment and then said: "Please go ahead."

"Right. What precisely do you expect to happen at this party?"

A car came down the square. Its headlights shone momentarily on Robin's face. It looked very young and frightened, like the face of a sixth-form boy in serious trouble with his tutor. The car turned and they were in the dark again.

Robin said: "It's a regular thing. They have it on Thursday nights. It's a sort of cult. They call it the Rites of the Children of the Sun in the Outer and Oberon's the sort of high priest. You have to swear not to talk about it. I've sworn. I can't talk. But it ends pretty hectically. And tomorrow Ginny—I've heard them—Ginny's cast for—the leading part."

"And beforehand?"

"Well—it's different from ordinary nights. There's no dinner. We go to our rooms until the Rites begin at eleven. We're meant not to speak to each other or anything."

"Do you not eat or drink?"

"Oh, there are drinks. And so on."

"What does 'so on' mean?" Robin was silent. "Do you take drugs? Reefers? Snow?"

"What makes you think that?"

"Come on. Which is it?"

"Reefers mostly. There's food when we smoke. There has to be. I don't know if they are the usual kind. Oberon doesn't smoke. I don't think Baradi does."

"Are they traffickers?"

"I don't know much about them."

"Do you know that much?"

"I should think they might be."

"Have they asked you to take a hand?"

"Look," Robin said, "I'm sorry but I've got to say it. I don't know much about you either, sir. I mean, I don't know that you won't—" He had turned his head and Alleyn knew he was peering at him.

"Inform the police?" Alleyn suggested.

"Well—you might."

"Come: you don't, as you say, know me. Yet you've elected to ask me to rescue this wretched child from the clutches of your friends. You can't have it both ways."

"You don't know," Robin said. "You don't know how tricky it all is. If they thought I'd talked to you!"

"What would they do?"

"Nothing!" Robin cried in a hurry. "Nothing! Only I've accepted, as one says, their hospitality."

"You *have* got your values muddled, haven't you?"

"Have I? I daresay I have."

"Tell me this. Has anything happened recently—I mean within the last twenty-four hours—to precipitate the situation?"

Robin said: "Who are you?"

"My dear chap, I don't need to be a thought-reader to see there's a certain urgency behind all this preamble."

"I suppose not. I'm sorry. I'm afraid I can't answer any more questions. Only—only, for God's sake, sir, will you do something about Ginny?"

"I'll make a bargain with you. I gather that you want to remove the child without giving a previous warning to the house party."

"That's it, sir. Yes."

"All right. *Can* you persuade her, in fact, to drive into Roqueville at six o'clock?"

"I don't know. I was gambling on it. If *he's* not about, I might. She— I think she is quite fond of me," Robin said humbly, "when he's not there to bitch it all up."

"Failing a drive, could you get her to walk down to the car park?"

"I might do that. She wants to buy one of old Marie's silver goats."

"Would it help to tell her we had rung up and asked if she would choose a set of the figures for Ricky? Aren't there groups of them for Christmas? Cribs?"

"That might work. She'd like to do that."

"All right. Have your car waiting and get her to walk on to the park. Suggest you drive down to our hotel with the figures."

"You know, sir, I believe that'd do it."

"Good. Having got her in the car it's up to you to keep her away from the Château. Take her to see Troy by all means. But I doubt if you'll get her to stay to dinner. You may have to stage a breakdown on a lonely road. I don't know. Use your initiative. Block up the air vent in your petrol cap. One thing more. Baradi, or someone, said something about a uniform of sorts that you all wear on occasion."

"That's right. It's called the mantle of the sun. We wear them about the house and—and always on Thursday nights."

"Is it the white thing Oberon had on this morning?"

"Yes. A sort of glorified monk's affair with a hood."

"Could you bring two of them with you?"

Robin turned his head and peered at Alleyn in astonishment. "I suppose I could."

"Put them in your car during the day."

"I don't see—"

"I'm sure you don't. Two of your own will do, if you have two. You needn't worry about bringing Miss Taylor's gown specifically."

"Hers!" Robin cried out. "Bring hers! But that's the whole thing! Tomorrow night they'll make Ginny wear the Black Robe."

"Then you must bring a black robe," Alleyn said.

## II

On Thursday evening the Côte d'Azur, inclined always to the theatrical, became melodramatic and, true to the weather report, staged a thunderstorm.

"It's going to rain," a voice croaked from the balustrade of the Chèvre d'Argent. "Listen! Thunder!"

Far to southward the heavens muttered an affirmative.

Carbury Glande looked at the brilliantly-clad figure perched, knees to chin, on the balustrade. It mingled with a hanging swag of bougainvillea. "One sees a voice rather than a person. You look like some fabulous bird, dear Sati," he said. "If I didn't feel so ghastly I'd like to paint you."

"Rumble, mumble, jumble and clatter," said the other, absorbed in delighted anticipation. "And then the rains. That's the way it goes." She pursed her lips out and, drawing in air with the smoke, took a long puff at an attenuated cigarette.

Baradi walked over to her and removed the cigarette. "Against the rules," he said. "Everything in its appointed time. You're over-excited." He threw the cigarette away and returned to his chair.

A whiteness flickered above the horizon and was followed after a pause by a tinny rattle.

"We do this sort of thing much better at the Comédie Française," Annabella Wells paraphrased, twisting her mouth in self-contempt.

Baradi leaned forward until his nose was placed in surrealistic association with her ear. Beneath the nose his moustache shifted as if it had a life of its own and beneath the moustache his lips pouted and writhed in almost soundless articulation. Annabella Wells's expression did not change. She nodded slightly. His face hung for a moment above her neck and then he leaned back in his chair.

Above the blacked Mediterranean the sky splintered with forked lightning.

"One. Two. Three. Four," the hoarse voice counted to an accompaniment of clapping hands. The other guests ejaculated under a canopy of thunder.

"You always have to count," the voice explained when it could be heard again.

"The thing I really hate," Ginny Taylor said rapidly, "is not the thunder or lightning but the pauses between bouts. Like this one."

"Come indoors," Robin Herrington said. "You don't have to stay out here."

"It's a kind of dare I have with myself."

"Learning to be brave?" Annabella Wells asked with a curious inflexion in her voice.

"Ginny will have the courage of a lioness," said Baradi, "and the fire of a phoenix."

Annabella got up with an abrupt expert movement and walked over to the balustrade. Baradi followed her. Ginny pushed her hair back from her forehead and looked quickly at Robin and away again. He moved nearer to her. She turned away to the far end of the roof-garden. Robin hovered uncertainly. The other four guests had drawn closer together. Carbury Glande half-closed his eyes and peered at the cloud-blocked sky and dismal sea. "Gloriously ominous," he said, "and quite unpaintable. Which is such a good thing."

The pause was not really one of silence. It was dramatized by minor noises, themselves uncannily portentous. Mr. Oberon's canary, for instance, hopped scratchily from cage-floor to perch and back again. A cicada had forgotten to stop chirruping in the motionless cactus slopes that Mr. Oberon called his *jardin exotique*. Down in the servants' quarters a woman laughed, and many kilometres away, towards Douceville, a train shrieked effeminately. Still, beside the threat of thunder, these desultory sounds added up to silence.

Glande, with an eye on Ginny, muttered: "I damned well think we need something. After all—" He swallowed. "After everything. It's nervy work waiting." His voice shot up into falsetto. "I don't pretend to be phlegmatic. I'm a bloody artist, I am."

Baradi said: "Keep your voice down. You certainly have a flair for the appropriate adjective," and laughed softly.

Glande fingered his lips and stared at Baradi. "How you can!" he whispered.

Annabella, looking out to sea, said: "Keep your hand to the plough, Carbury dear. You've put it there. No looking back."

"*I'm* on your side," announced the voice from the balustrade. "Look what I am doing for you all."

From her remote station Ginny said: "I can't stand this."

"Well, don't," Robin said quietly. "Old Marie asked me to tell you there's only one of the big silver goats left. Why not dodge down before the rain and get it? In the passage you won't see if there's lightning. Come on."

Ginny looked at Baradi. He caught her glance and walked across to her. "What is it?" he said.

"I thought I might go to old Marie's shop," Ginny said. "It's away from the storm."

"Why not?" he said. "What a good idea."

"I thought I might," Ginny repeated doubtfully.

For a split second lightning wrote itself across the sky in livid calligraphy. The voice on the balustrade had counted two when the heavens crashed together in a monstrous report. Ginny's mouth was wide open. She ran into the tower and Robin followed her.

The initial clap was succeeded by a prolonged rattle and an ambiguous omnipotent muttering. Above this rumpus Glande could be heard saying: "What I mean to say: do we know we can trust them? After all, they're comparative strangers and I must say I don't like the boy's manner."

Baradi, who was watching Annabella Wells, said: "There's no need to disturb yourself on their account. Robin is much too heavily involved and as for Ginny, can we not leave her safely to Ra? In any case, she knows nothing."

"The boy does. He might blurt out something to those other two—Troy and her bloody high-hat husband."

"If Mr. and Mrs. Allen should arrive there need be no meeting."

"How do you know they don't suspect something already?"

"I have told you. The girl Teresa reports that having recovered the boy, they have retired to their hotel in high glee."

"There was a bungle over the kid. There might be another bungle. Suppose Allen hangs about like he did last time asking damn-fool esoteric questions?"

"They were not as silly as you think, my dear Carbury. The man is an intelligent man. He behaved intelligently during the operation. He would make a good anaesthetist."

"Well—there you are!"

"Please don't panic. He is both intelligent and inquisitive. That is why we thought it better to remove him, if possible, to St. Céleste, until the Truebody has been disposed of." Baradi's teeth gleamed under his moustache.

"I can see no cause for amusement."

"Can you not? You must cultivate a taste for irony. Annabella," Baradi continued, looking at her motionless figure against the steel-dark sky, "Annabella tells us that Mr. Allen, as far as she knows, is the person he appears to be: a dilettante with a taste for mysticism, curious literature and big-game hunting. The latter, I may add, in the generally accepted sense of the expression."

"Oh, for God's sake!" Glande cried out. The voice from the balustrade broke into undisciplined laughter. "Shut up!" he shouted. "Shut up, Sati! You of all people to laugh. It's so damned undignified. Remember who you are!"

"Yes, Grizel dear," Annabella Wells said, "pray do remember that."

It had grown so dark that the lightning darted white on their faces. They saw one another momentarily as if by a flash-lamp, each wearing a look of fixity. The thunder-clap followed at once. One might have imagined the heavens had burst outward like a gas-filled cylinder.

Mr. Oberon, wearing his hooded gown, stepped out of the tower door and contemplated his followers.

"*Cher maître*," shouted Baradi, waving his hand, "you come most carefully upon your hour. What an entrance! Superb!"

The volley rolled away into silence. Mr. Oberon moved forward and, really as if he had induced it, rain struck down in an abrupt deluge.

"You will get wet, dear Sati," said Mr. Oberon.

Glande said: "What's happened?"

They all drew near to Mr. Oberon. The rain made a frightful din, pelting like bullets on water and earth and stone and on the canvas awning above their heads. Landscape and seascape were alive with its noise. The four guests, with the anxious air of people who are hard-of-hearing, inclined their heads towards their host.

"What's happened?" Glande repeated, but with a subdued and more deferential manner.

"All is well. It is arranged for tomorrow afternoon. An Anglican ceremony," said Oberon, smiling slightly. "I have spoken to the—should I call him priest? I was obliged to call on him. The telephone is still out of order. He is a dull man but very obliging. A private funeral, of course."

"But the other business—the permit or whatever it is?"

"I've already explained," Baradi cut in irritably, "that my authority as a medical man is perfectly adequate. The appropriate official will be happy to receive me tomorrow when the necessary formalities will be completed."

"Poor old Truebody," said Annabella Wells.

"The name is, by the way, to be Halebory. Pronounced Harber. So English."

"They'll want to see the passport," Glande said instantly.

"They shall see it. It has received expert attention."

"Sati," said Mr. Oberon gently, "you have been smoking, I think."

"Dearest Ra, only the least puff."

"Yet, there is our rule. Not until tonight."

"I was upset. It's so difficult. Please forgive me. Please."

Mr. Oberon looked blankly at her. "You will go to your room and make an exercise. The exercise of the Name. You will light your candle and looking at the flame without blinking you will repeat one hundred times: 'I am Sati who am Grizel Locke!' Then you will remain without moving until it is time for the Rites. So."

She touched her forehead and lips and chest with a jerky movement of her hand and went at once.

"Where is Ginny?" Mr. Oberon asked.

"She was nervous," said Baradi. "The storm upset her. She went down to the stop where one buys those rather vulgar figurines."

"And Robin?"

"He went with her," said Annabella loudly.

Mr. Oberon's mouth parted to show his teeth. "She must rest," he said. "You are, of course, all very careful to say nothing of an agitating nature in front of her. She knows the lady has died as the result of a perforated appendix. Unfortunately it was unavoidable that she should be told so much. There must be no further disturbance. When she returns send her to her room. It is the time of meditation. She is to remain in her room until it is time for the Rites. There she will find the gift of enlightenment."

He moved to the tower door. The rain drummed on the awning above their heads but they heard him repeat: "She must rest," before he went indoors.

### III

Old Marie's shop was a cave sunk in the face of the hill and protected at its open end by the Chèvre d'Argent, which at this point straddled the passage. Ginny and Robin were thus hidden from the lightning and even the thunder sounded less formidable in there. The walls of the cave had been hewn out in shelves and on these stood Marie's figurines. She herself sat at a table over an oil lamp and wheezed out praises of her wares.

"She's got lots of goats," Ginny pointed out, speaking English.

"Cunning old cup-of-tea," Robin said. "Thought you needed gingering up, I suppose. By the way," he added, "Miss Troy or Mrs. Allen or whatever she should be called, wanted a set of nativity figures—don't you call it a crib?—for the little boy. Marie wasn't here when they left yesterday. I promised I'd get one and take it down this afternoon. How awful! I entirely forgot."

"Robin! How could you! And they'll want it more than ever after losing him like that."

"She thought perhaps you wouldn't mind choosing one."

"Of course I will," Ginny said, and began to inspect the groups of naïve little figures. Old Marie shouted: "Look, Mademoiselle, the Holy Child illuminates himself. And the beasts! One would say the she-ass almost burst herself with good milk. And the lamb is infinitely touching. And the ridiculous price! I cannot bring myself to charge more. It is an act of piety on my part."

Robin bought a large silver goat and Ginny bought the grandest of the cribs. "Let's take it down now," he said. "The storm's nearly over, I'm sure, and the car's out. It'd save my conscience. Do come, Ginny."

She raised her troubled face and looked at him. "I don't know," she said, "I suppose—I don't know."

"We shan't be half-an-hour. Come on."

He took her by the arm and hurried her into the passage-way. They ran into a world of rain, Ginny protesting and Robin shouting encouragement. With the help of his stick he broke into quite a lively sort of canter. "Do be careful!" Ginny cried. "Your dot-and-go-one leg!"

"Dot-and-go-run, you mean. Come on."

Their faces streamed with cool water and they laughed without cause.

"It's better out here," Robin said. "Isn't it, Ginny?"

The car stood out on the platform like a rock in a waterfall. He bundled her into it. "You look like—you look as you're meant to look," he said. "It's better outside. Say it's better, Ginny."

"I don't know what's come over you," Ginny said, pressing her hands to her rain-blinded face.

"I've got out. We've both got out." He scrambled in beside her and peered into the trough behind the driver's seat. "What are you doing?" Ginny asked hysterically. "What's happened? We've gone mad. What are you looking for?"

"Nothing. A parcel for my tailor. It's gone. Who cares! Away we go."

He started up his engine. Water splashed up like wings on either side and cascaded across the windscreen. They roared down the steep incline and turned left above the tunnel and over the high headland, on the road to Roqueville.

High up in the hills on their vantage point in the factory road, Alleyn and Raoul waited in Raoul's car.

"In five minutes," Alleyn said, "it will be dark."

"I shall still know the car, Monsieur."

"And I. The rain's lifting a little."

"It will stop before the light goes, I think."

"How tall are you, Raoul?"

"One mètre, sixty, Monsieur."

"About five foot eight," Alleyn muttered, "and the girl's tall. It ought to be all right. Where was the car exactly?"

"Standing out on the platform, Monsieur. The parcel was in the trough behind the driver's seat."

"He's stuck to his word so far, at least. Where did you put the note?"

"On the driver's seat, Monsieur. He could not fail to see it."

But Robin, driving in a state of strange exhilaration towards Roqueville, sat on the disregarded note and wondered if it was by accident or intention that Ginny leaned a little towards him.

"It will be fine on the other side of the hill," he shouted. "What do you bet?"

"It couldn't be."

"You'll see. You'll see. You'll jolly well see."

"Robin, what *has* come over you?"

"I'll tell you when we get to Roqueville. There you are! What did I say?"

They drove down the mountain-side into a translucent dusk, rain-washed and fragrant.

"There they go," Alleyn said and turned his field glasses on the tiny car. "She's with him. He's brought it off. So far."

"And now, Monsieur?"

Alleyn watched the car diminish. Just before it turned the point of a distant headland, Robin switched on his lamps. Alleyn lowered the glasses. "It is almost lighting-up time, Raoul. We wait a little longer." They turned as if by a shared consent and looked to the west where, above and beyond the tunnelled hill, the turrets of the Chèvre d'Argent stood black against a darkling sky.

Presently, out on Cap St. Gilles pricks of yellow began to appear. The window of a cottage in the valley showed red. Behind them the factory presented a dark front to the dusk, but higher up in its folded hills the monastery of Our Lady of Paysdoux was alive with glowing lights.

"They are late with their lamps at the Chèvre d'Argent," said Raoul.

"Which is not surprising," Alleyn rejoined. "Seeing that Monsieur le Commissaire has arranged that their electrical service is disconnected. The thunderstorm will have lent a happy note of credibility to the occurrence. The telephone also is still disconnected." He used his field glasses. "Yes," he said, "they are lighting candles. Start up your engine, Raoul. It is time to be off."

## IV

"You disturb yourself without cause," Baradi said, "she is buying herself a silver goat. Why not? It is a good omen."

"Already she's been away half-an-hour."

"She has gone for a walk, no doubt."

"With him."

"Again, why not? The infatuation is entirely on one side. Let it alone."

"I am unusually interested and therefore nervous," said Mr. Oberon. "It means more to me, this time, than ever before and besides the whole circumstance is extraordinary. The mystic association. The blood-sacrifice and then, while the victim is still here, the other, the living sacrifice. It is unique."

Baradi looked at him with curiosity. "Tell me," he said, "how much of all this"—he made a comprehensive gesture—"means anything to you? I mean I can understand the, what shall I call it, the factual pleasure. That is a great deal. I envy you your flair. But the esoteric window-dressing—is it possible that for you—?" He paused. Mr. Oberon's face was as empty as a mask. He touched his lips with the tip of his tongue.

He said: "Wherein, if not in my belief, do you suppose the secret of my flair is to be found? I am what I am and I go back to beyond the dawn. I was the King of the Wood."

Baradi examined his own shapely hands. "Ah, yes?" he said politely. "A fascinating theory."

"You think me a poseur?"

"No, no. On the contrary. It is only as a practical man I am concerned with the hazards of the situation. You, I gather, though you have every cause, are not at all anxious on that account? The Truebody situation, I mean?"

"I find it immeasurably stimulating."

"Indeed," said Baradi drily.

"Only the absence of the girl disturbs me. It is almost dark. Turn on the light."

Baradi reached out his hand to the switch. There was a click.

"No lights, it seems," he said and opened the door. "No lights anywhere. There must be a fuse."

"How can she be walking in the dark? And with a cripple like Robin? It is preposterous."

"The British do these things."

"I am British. I have my passport. Telephone the bureau in Roqueville."

"The telephone is still out of order."

"We must have light."

"It may be a fault in the house. The servants will attend to it. One moment."

He lifted the receiver from Mr. Oberon's telephone. A voice answered.

"What is the matter with the lights?" Baradi asked.

"We cannot make out, Monsieur. There is no fault here. Perhaps the storm has brought down the lines."

"Nothing but trouble. And the telephone? Can one telephone yet to Roqueville?"

"No, Monsieur. The centrale sent up a man. The fault is not in the Château. They are investigating. They will ring through when the line is clear."

"Since yesterday afternoon we have been without the telephone. Unparalleled incompetence!" Baradi ejaculated. "Have Mr. Herrington and Mlle. Taylor returned?"

"I will enquire, Monsieur."

"Do so, and ring Mr. Oberon's apartments if they are in."

He clapped down the receiver. "I am uneasy," he said. "It has happened at a most tiresome moment. We have only the girl Teresa's account of the affair at the factory. No doubt she is speaking the truth. Having found the boy, they are satisfied. All the same it is not too amusing, having had the police in the factory."

"Callard will have handled them with discretion."

"No doubt. The driver, Georges Martel, however, will be examined by the police."

"Can he be trusted?"

"He has too much at stake to be anything but dependable. We pay him very highly. Also he has his story. He was rung up by an unknown client purporting to be the boy's father. He took the job in good faith and merely asked the girl Teresa to accompany him. They know nothing. The police will at once suspect the former kidnappers. Nevertheless, I wish we had not attempted the affair with the boy."

"One wanted to rid oneself of the parents."

"Exactly. Of the father. If circumstances were different," Baradi said softly, "I should not be nearly so interested in ridding myself of Mama. Women!" he ejaculated sententiously.

"Women!" Mr. Oberon echoed with an inexplicable laugh and added immediately: "All the same I am getting abominably anxious. I don't trust him. And then, the light! Suppose it doesn't come on again before the Rites. How shall we manage?"

"Something can be done with car batteries, I think, and a soldering iron. Mahomet is ingenious in such matters. I shall speak to him in a moment."

Baradi walked over to the window and pulled back the silk blind. "It is quite dark." The blind shot up with a whirr and click.

"It really is much too quick on the trigger," he observed.

Mr. Oberon said loudly: "Don't do that! You exacerbate my nerves. Pull it down. Tie it down."

And while Baradi busied himself with the blind he added: "I shall send out. My temper is rising and that is dangerous. I must not become angry. If his car has gone I shall send after it."

"I strongly suggest you do nothing of the sort. It would be an unnecessary and foolish move. She will return. Surely you have not lost your flair."

Mr. Oberon, in the darkness, said: "You are right. She will return. She must."

"As for your rising temper," said Baradi, "you had better subdue it. It is dangerous."

# CHAPTER XI

# P. E. Garbel

## I

RAOUL slowed down at a point above the entrance to the tunnel.

"Where should we leave the car, Monsieur?"

"There's a recess off the road, on the far side, near the tunnel and well under the lee of the hill. Pull in there."

The silhouette of the Chèvre d'Argent showed black above the hills against a clearing but still stormy sky. A wind had risen and cloud-rack scurried across a brilliant display of stars.

"Gothic in spirit," Alleyn muttered, "if not in design."

The road turned the headland. Raoul dropped to a crawl and switched off his lights. Alleyn used a pocket torch. When they came down to the level of the tunnel exit he got out and guided Raoul into a recess hard by the stone facing.

Raoul dragged out a marketing basket from which the intermingled smells of cabbage, garlic and flowers rose incongruously on the rain-sweetened air.

"Have you hidden the cloaks underneath?" Alleyn asked him.

"Yes, Monsieur. It was an excellent notion. It is not unusual for me to present myself with such gear. The aunt of Teresa is a market-gardener."

"Good. We'll smell like two helpings of a particularly exotic soup."

"Monsieur?"

"No matter. Now, Raoul, to make certain we understand each other will you repeat the instructions?"

"Very well, Monsieur. We go together to the servants' entrance. If, by mischance, we encounter anybody on the way who recognizes Monsieur, Monsieur will at once say he has come to enquire for the sick Mademoiselle. I will continue on and will wait for Monsieur at the servants' entrance. If Monsieur, on arriving there, is recognized by one of the servants who may not yet have left, he will say he has been waiting for me and is angry. He will say he wishes to speak to Teresa about the stealing of Riki. If, on the other hand, all goes well and we reach the servants' quarters together and unchallenged, we go at once to Teresa's room. Monsieur is seen but not recognized, he is introduced as the intellectual cousin of Teresa who has been to England, working in a bank, and has greatly improved his social status, and again we retire quickly to Teresa's room before the Egyptian valet or the butler can encounter Monsieur. In either case, Teresa is to give a message saying it has come by a peasant on a bicycle. It is to say that Mr. Herrington's car has broken down but that Miss Taylor and he will arrive in time for the party. Finally, if Monsieur does not come at all, I wait an hour then go to seek for him."

"And if something we have not in the least anticipated turns up?"

Raoul laughed softly in the dark: "One must then use one's wits, Monsieur."

"Good, shall we start?"

They walked together up the steep incline to the platform.

A goods train came puffing up from Douceville. The glow from the engine slid across the lower walls and bastions of the Chèvre d'Argent. Behind the silk blind a dim light burned: a much fainter light than the one they had seen from the window of their own train. Higher up, at odd intervals in that vast façade, other windows glowed or flickered where candles had been placed or were carried from one room to another.

The train tooted and clanked into the tunnel.

It was quite cold on the platform. A mountain breeze cut across it and lent credibility to the turned-up collar of Alleyn's raincoat and the scarf across his mouth. The passage was almost pitch dark but they thought it better not to use a torch. They slipped and stumbled on wet and uneven steps. The glow from old Marie's door was a guide. As they passed by she shouted from behind the oil-lamp: "Hola, there! Is it still raining?"

Raoul said quietly: "The stars are out. Good night, Marie," and they hurried into the shadows. They heard her shouting jovially after them: "Give her something to keep out the cold."

"She speaks of Teresa," Raoul whispered primly. "There is a hint of vulgarity in Marie."

Alleyn stifled a laugh. They groped their way round a bend in the passage, brushing their hands against damp stone. Presently an elegant design of interlaced rosettes appeared against a background of reflected warmth. It was the wrought-iron gate of the Chèvre d'Argent.

"As quick as we dare," Alleyn whispered.

The passage glinted wet before the doorway. The soles of his shoes were like glass. He poised himself and moved lightly forward. As he entered the patch of light he heard a slither and an oath. Raoul hurtled against him, throwing him off his balance. He clung to the gate while Raoul, in a wild attempt to recover himself, clutched at the nearest object.

It was the iron bell-pull.

The bell gave tongue with a violence that was refracted intolerably by the stone walls.

Three cabbages rolled down the steps. Raoul by some desperate effort still clung to the basket with one hand and to the bell-pull with the other.

"Monsieur! Monsieur!" he stammered.

"Go on," Alleyn said. "*Go on!*"

Raoul let go the bell-pull and a single note fell inconsequently across the still-echoing clangour. He plunged forward and was lost in shadow.

Alleyn turned to face the door.

"Why, if it's not Mr. Allen!" said Mr. Oberon.

## II

He stood on the far side of the door with his back to a lighted candelabrum that had been set down on a chest in the entry. Little could be seen of him but his shape, enveloped in his white gown with the hood drawn over his head. He moved towards the door and his hands emerged and grasped two of the iron bars.

Alleyn said: "I'm afraid we made an appalling din. My chauffeur slipped and grabbed your bell-pull."

"Your chauffeur?"

"He's taken himself off. I fancy he knows one of your maids. He had some message for her, it seems."

Mr. Oberon said, as if to explain his presence at the door: "I am waiting for someone. Have you seen—" He paused and shifted his hands on the bars. His voice sounded out of focus. "Perhaps you met Ginny. Ginny Taylor? And Robin Herrington? We are a little anxious about them."

"No," Alleyn said. "I didn't see them. I came to ask about Miss Truebody."

Mr. Oberon didn't move. Alleyn peered at him. "How is she?" he asked.

Mr. Oberon said abruptly: "Our telephone has been out of order since yesterday afternoon. Do forgive me. I am a little anxious, you know."

"How is Miss Truebody?"

"Alas, she is dead," said Mr. Oberon.

They faced each other like actors in some medieval prison scene. The shadow of twisted iron was thrown across Alleyn's face and chest.

"Perhaps," Alleyn said, "I may come in for a moment."

"But, of course. How dreadful of me! We are all so distressed. Mahomet!"

Evidently the Egyptian servant had been waiting in the main hall. He unlocked the door, opened and stood aside. When Alleyn had come in he relocked the door.

With the air of having arrived at a decision, Mr. Oberon led the way into the great hall. Mahomet came behind them bringing the candelabrum, which he set down on a distant table. In that vast interior it served rather to emphasize the dark than relieve it.

"Monsieur," said Mahomet in French, "may I speak?"

"Well?"

"There is a message brought by a peasant from Mr. Herrington. He has had trouble with his auto. He is getting a taxi. He and Mlle. Taylor will arrive in time for the ceremony."

"Ah!" It was a long-drawn-out sigh. "Who took the message?"

"The girl Teresa, who was on her way to catch the omnibus. The peasant would not wait so the girl returned with the message. Miss Taylor also sent a message. It was that Monsieur must not trouble himself. She will not fail the ceremony. She will go immediately to her room."

"Is all prepared?"

"All is prepared, Monsieur."

Mr. Oberon raised his hand in dismissal. Mahomet moved away into the shadows. Alleyn listened for the rattle of curtain rings but there was no other sound than that of Mr. Oberon's uneven breathing. "Forgive me again," he said, coming closer to Alleyn. "As you heard it was news of our young people."

"I'm afraid my French is too rudimentary for anything but the most childish phrases."

"Indeed? It appears they have had a breakdown but all is now well." Alleyn said: "When did Miss Truebody die?"

"Ah, yes. We are so sorry. Yesterday afternoon. We tried to get you at the hotel, of course, but were told that you had gone to St. Céleste for a few days."

"We changed our plans," Alleyn said. "May I speak to Dr. Baradi?"

"To Ali? I am not sure—I will enquire—Mahomet!"

"Monsieur?" said a voice in the shadows.

"Tell your master that the English visitor is here. Tell him the visitor knows that his compatriot has left us."

"Monsieur."

The curtain rings jangled together.

"He will see if our friend is at home."

"I feel," Alleyn said, "that I should do everything that can be done. In a way she is our responsibility."

"That is quite wonderful of you, Mr. Allen," said Mr. Oberon, who seemed to have made a return to his normal form. "But I already sensed in you a rare and beautiful spirit. Still, you need not distress yourself. We felt it our privilege to speed this soul to its new life. The interment is tomorrow at three o'clock. Anglican. I shall, however, conduct a little valedictory ceremony here."

The curtain rings clashed again. Alleyn saw a large whiteness move towards them.

"Mr. Allen?" said Baradi, looming up on the far side of the candelabrum. He wore a white robe and his face was a blackness within the hood. "I am so glad you've come. We were puzzled what to do when we heard you had gone to St. Céleste."

"Fortunately there was no occasion. We ran Ricky to earth, I'm glad to say."

They both made enthusiastic noises. They were rejoiced. An atrocious affair. Where had he been found?

"In the chemical factory, of all places," Alleyn said. "The police think the kidnappers must have got cold feet and dumped him there." He allowed their ejaculations a decent margin and then said: "About poor Miss Truebody—"

"Yes, about her," Baradi began crisply. "I'm sorry it happened as it did. I can assure you that it would have made no difference if there had been a hospital with an entire corps of trained nurses and surgeons.

And certainly, may I add, she could not have had a more efficient anaesthetist. But, as you know, peritonitis was greatly advanced. Her condition steadily deteriorated. The heart, by the way, was not in good trim. Valvular trouble. She died at 4:28 yesterday afternoon without recovering consciousness. We found her address in her passport. I have made a report which I shall send to the suitable authorities in the Bermudas. Her effects, of course, will be returned to her home there. I understand there are no near relatives. I have completed the necessary formalities here. I should have preferred, under the circumstances, to have asked a brother medico to look at her, but it appears they are all in conclave at St. Christophe."

"I expect I should write to—well, to somebody."

"By all means. Enclose a letter with my report. The authorities in the Bermudas will see that it reaches the lawyer or whoever is in charge of her affairs."

"I think perhaps—one has a feeling of responsibility—I think perhaps I should see her."

There was an infinitesimal pause.

"Of course," Baradi said. "If you wish, of course, I must warn you that the climatic conditions and those of her illness and death have considerably accelerated the usual post-mortem changes."

"We have done what we could," Mr. Oberon said. "Tuberoses and orchids."

"How very kind. If it's not troubling you too much."

There was a further slight pause. Baradi said: "Of course," again and clapped his hands. "No electricity," he explained. "So provoking." The servant reappeared, carrying a single candle. Baradi spoke to him in their own language and took the candle from him. "I'll go with you," he said. "We have moved her into a room outside the main part of the Château. It is quite suitable and cooler."

With this grisly little announcement he led Alleyn down the now familiar corridor past the operating room and into a much narrower side-passage that ended in a flight of descending steps and a door. This, in turn, opened on a further reach of the outside passage-way. The night air smelled freshly after the incense-tainted house. They turned left and walked a short distance down the uneven steps. Alleyn thought that they could not be far from the servants' entrance.

Baradi stopped at a deeply recessed doorway and asked Alleyn to hold the candle. Alleyn produced his torch and switched it on. It shone into Baradi's face.

"Ah!" he said blinking, "that will be better. Thank you." He set down the candle. It flickered and guttered in the draught. He thrust his hand under his gown and produced a heavily furnished key-ring that might have hung from the girdle of a medieval gaoler. Alleyn turned his light on it and Baradi selected a great key with a wrought-iron loop. He stooped to fit it in a key-hole placed low in the door. His wide sleeves drooped from his arms, his hood fell over his face, and his shadow, grotesque and distorted, sprawled down the steps beyond him.

"If you would lend me your torch," he said. "It is a little awkward, this lock."

Alleyn gave him his torch. The shadow darted across the passage and reared itself up the opposite wall. After some fumbling, the key was engaged and noisily turned. Baradi shoved at the door and with a grind of its hinges it opened suddenly inwards and he fell forward with it, dropping the torch, nose first, on the stone threshold. There was a tinkle of glass and they were left with the guttering candle.

"*Ah, sacré nom d'un chien!*" Baradi ejaculated. "My dear Mr. Allen, what have I done!"

Alleyn said: "Be careful of the broken glass."

"I am wearing sandals. But how careless! I am so sorry."

"Never mind. The passage seems to be unlucky for us this evening. Let's hope there's not a third mishap. Don't give it another thought. Shall we go in?" Alleyn laid down his walking-stick and took up the candle and the broken torch. They went in, Baradi shutting the door with a heave and a weighty slam.

It seemed to be a small room with whitewashed stone walls and a shuttered window. Candlelight wavered over a bank of flowers. A coffin stood in the middle on trestles. The mingled odours of death and tuberoses were horrible.

"I hope you are not over-sensitive," Baradi said. "We have done our best, Mr. Oberon was most particular, but—well—as you see—"

Alleyn saw. The lid of the coffin had been left far enough withdrawn to expose the head of its inhabitant, which was literally bedded in orchids. A white veil of coarse net lay over the face, but it did little to soften the inexorable indignities of death.

"The teeth," said Baradi, "make a difference, don't they?"

Looking at them Alleyn was reminded of Teresa's generality to the effect that all English spinsters have teeth like mares. This lonely spinster's dentist had evidently subscribed to Teresa's opinion and Alleyn saw the other stigmata of her kind: the small mole, the lines and pouches, the pathetic tufts of grey hair from which the skin had receded.

He backed away. "I thought it better to see her," he said, and his voice was constrained and thin. "In case there should be any question of identification."

"Much better. Are you all right? For the layman it is not a pleasant experience."

Alleyn said: "I find it quite appalling. Shall we go? I'm afraid I—" His voice faded. He turned away with a violent movement and at the same time jerked his handkerchief. It flapped across the candle flame and extinguished it.

In the malodorous dark Baradi cursed unintelligibly. Alleyn gabbled: "The door, for God's sake, where is the door? I'm going to be sick." He lurched against Baradi and sent him staggering to the far end of the room. He drop-kicked the candlestick in the opposite direction. His hands were on the coffin. His left hand discovered the edge of the lid, slid under it, explored a soft material, a tight band and the surface beneath. His fingers, inquisitive and thrusting, found what they sought.

"I can't stand this!" he choked out. "The door!"

Baradi was now swearing in French. "*Idiot!*" he was saying. "*Maladroit, imbécile!*"

Alleyn made retching noises. He found his way unerringly to the door and dragged it open. A pale lessening of the dark was admitted. He staggered out into the passage-way and rested against the stone wall. Baradi came after him and and dragged the door shut. Alleyn heard him turn the key in the lock.

"That was not an amusing interlude," Baradi said. "I warned you it would not be pleasant."

Alleyn had his handkerchief pressed to his mouth. He said indistinctly: "I'm sorry. I didn't realize—I'll be all right."

"Of course you will," Baradi snapped at him. "So shall I when my bruises wear off."

"Please don't let me keep you. Fresh air. I'll go back to the car. Thank you: I'm sorry."

Apparently Baradi had regained his temper. He said: "It is undoubtedly the best thing you can do. I recommend a hot bath, a stiff drink, two aspirins and bed. If you're sure you're all right and can find your way back—"

"Yes, yes. It's passing off."

"Then if you will excuse me. I am already late. Good night, Mr. Allen."

Alleyn, over his handkerchief, watched Baradi return up the steps, open the side-door and disappear into the house. He waited for some minutes, accustoming his eyes to the night.

"Somehow," he thought, "I must get a wash," and he wiped his left hand vigorously on his handkerchief which he then threw into the shadows.

But he did not wipe away the memory of a not very large cavity under the left breast of a sprigged locknit nightgown.

### III

He had been right about the nearness of the servants' entrance. The stone passage-way dipped, turned and came to an end by a sort of open pent-house. Alleyn had to grope his way down steps, but the non-darkness that is starlight had filtered into the purlieus of the Chèvre d'Argent and glistened faintly on ledges and wet stone. He paused for a moment and looked back and upwards. The great mass of stone and rock made a black hole in the spangled heavens. The passage-way had emerged from beneath a bridge-like extension of the house. This linked the seaward portion with what he imagined must be the original for-tress, deep inside the cliff-face. Alleyn moved into an inky-dark recess. A light had appeared on the bridge.

It was carried by the Egyptian servant, who appeared to have some-thing else, possibly a tray, in his hand. He was followed by Baradi. Un-mistakably it was Baradi. The servant turned and his torchlight flick-ered across the dark face. The doctor no longer wore his robe. Something that looked like a smooth cord hung round his neck. They moved on and were lost inside the house. Alleyn gave a little grunt of satisfaction and continued on his way.

A lantern with a stub of candle in it hung by a half-open door and threw a yellow pool on the flat surface beneath.

"Monsieur?" a voice whispered.

"Raoul?"

"*Oui, Monsieur. Tout va bien. Allons.*"

Raoul slid out of the pent-house. Alleyn's wrist was grasped. He moved into the pool of light. Raoul pushed the door open with his foot. They entered a stone corridor, passed two closed doors and turned right. Raoul tapped with his finger-tips on a third door. Teresa opened it and admitted them.

It was a small neat bedroom, smelling a little fusty. One of old Marie's Madonnas, neatly inscribed: "Notre Dame de Paysdoux" stood on a corner shelf with a stool before it. Dusty paper flowers, candles and a photograph of Teresa in her confirmation dress, with folded hands and upturned eyes, completed the décor. A sacred print, looking dreadfully like Mr. Oberon, hung nearby. Across the bed were disposed two white gowns. A washstand with a jug and basin stood in a further corner.

Teresa, looking both nervous and complacent, pushed forward her only chair.

Alleyn said: "It is possible to wash one's hands, Teresa? A little water and some soap?"

"I will slip out for some warm water, Monsieur. It is quite safe to do so. Monsieur will forgive me. I had forgotten. The English always wish to wash themselves."

Alleyn did not correct this aphorism. When she had gone he said: "Well, Raoul?"

"The servants have gone out, Monsieur, with the exception of the Egyptian, who is occupied downstairs. The guests are in their rooms. It is unlikely that they will emerge before the ceremony." He extended his hands, palms upwards. "Monsieur, how much mischief have I made by my imbecility?"

Alleyn said: "Well, Raoul, you certainly rang the bell," and then seeing his companion's bewilderment and distress, added: "It was not so bad after all. It worked out rather well. Dr. Baradi and I have visited the body of a murdered woman."

"Indeed, Monsieur?"

"It lies among orchids in a handsome coffin in a room across the passage of entrance. The coffin, as M. le Commissaire had already ascertained, arrived this morning from an undertaker in Roqueville."

"But Monsieur—"

"There is a wound, covered by a surgical dressing, under the left breast."

"Teresa has told me that the English lady died."

"Here *is* Teresa," Alleyn said and held up his hand.

While he washed he questioned Teresa about Miss Truebody.

"Teresa, in what room of the house did the English lady die? Was it where we put her after the operation?"

"No, Monsieur. She was moved at once from there. The Egyptian and the porter carried her to a room upstairs in the Saracen's watchtower. It is not often used. She was taken there because it would be quieter, Monsieur."

"I'll be bound she was," Alleyn muttered. He dried his hands and began to outline a further plan of action. "Last night," he said, "I learned from Mr. Herrington a little more than Teresa perhaps may know, of the normal procedure on Thursday nights. At eleven o'clock a bell is rung. The guests then emerge from their rooms wearing their robes which have been laid out for them. They go in silence to the ceremony known as the Rites of the Children of the Sun. First they enter the small ante-room where each takes up a lighted candle. They then go into the main room and stay there until after midnight. Supper is served in Mr. Oberon's salon. The whole affair may go on, after a fashion, until five o'clock in the morning."

Teresa drew in her breath with an excited hiss.

"Now it is my intention to witness this affair. To that end I propose that you, Raoul, and I replace Miss Taylor and Mr. Herrington, who will not be there. Electricity will not be restored in the Château tonight and by candlelight we have at least a chance of remaining unrecognized."

Teresa made a little gesture. "If Monsieur pleases," she said.

"Well, Teresa?"

"The Egyptian has brought in iron boxes from Mr. Oberon's auto and a great deal of electrical cord and a soldering iron; he has arranged that the sun lamp in the room of ceremonies shall be lighted."

"Indeed? How very ingenious of him."

"Monsieur," Raoul said, eyeing the gowns on the bed, "is it your intention that I make myself to pass for a lady?"

Teresa cackled and clapped her hand over her mouth.

"Exactly so," said Alleyn. "You are about the same height as Miss Taylor. In the black gown with the hood drawn over your face and your hands—by the way, you too must wash your hands—hidden in the sleeves, you should, with luck, pass muster. You have small feet. Perhaps you may be able to wear Miss Taylor's slippers."

"*Ah, mon Dieu, quelle blague!*"

"Comport yourself with propriety, Teresa, Monsieur is speaking."

"If you cannot manage this I have bought a pair of black slippers which will have to do instead."

"And my costume, Monsieur?" Raoul asked, indicating with an expressive gesture his stained singlet, his greenish black trousers and his mackintosh hitched over his shoulders.

"I understand that, apart from the gown and slippers there is no costume at all."

"*Ah, mon Dieu, en voilà une affaire!*"

"*Teresa! Attention!*"

"However, the gown is voluminous. For propriety's sake, Raoul, you may retain your vest and underpants. In any case you must be careful to conceal your legs which, no doubt, are unmistakably masculine."

"They are superb," said Teresa. "But undoubtedly masculine."

"It seems to me," continued Alleyn, who had become quite used to the peculiarities of conversation with Raoul and Teresa, "that our first difficulty is the problem of getting from here to the respective rooms of Mr. Herrington and Miss Taylor. Teresa, I see, has brought two white gowns. Mr. Herrington has provided us with a white and a black one. Miss Taylor would have appeared in black tonight. Therefore, you must put on the black, Raoul, and I shall wear the longest of the white. Teresa must tell us where these rooms are. If the Egyptian or any of the guests should see us on our way to them we must hope they will observe the rule of silence which is enforced before the ceremony and pay no attention. It will be best if we can find our way without candles. Once inside our rooms we remain there until we hear the bell. How close, Teresa, are these rooms to the room where the ceremony is held? The room you described to me yesterday."

"The young lady's is nearby, Monsieur. It is therefore close also to the apartment of Mr. Oberon."

"In that case, Raoul, when you hear the bell, go at once to the anteroom. Take a candle and, by the communicating door, go into the ceremonial room. There will be five or six black cushions on the floor and a large black divan. If there are six cushions, yours will be apart from the others. If there are five, your position will be on the divan. I am only guessing at this. One thing I do know—the rule of silence will be observed until the actual ceremony begins. If you are in the wrong position it will be attributed, with luck, to stage-fright and somebody will put you right. Where is Mr. Herrington's room, Teresa?"

"It is off the landing, Monsieur, going down to the lower storey where the ceremonies are held."

"And the other guests?"

"They are in the higher parts of the Château, Monsieur. Across the outside passage and beyond it."

"Do you know the room of Miss Grizel Locke?"

"Yes, Monsieur."

"Have you seen her today?"

"Not since two days ago, Monsieur, but that is not unusual. As I have informed Monsieur, it is the lady's habit to keep to her room and leave a notice that she must not be disturbed."

"I see. Now, if I leave Mr. Herrington's room on the first stroke of the bell, I should arrive hard on your heels, Raoul, and in advance of the others. I may even go in a little earlier." He looked at his watch. "It is half-past-seven. Let us put on our gowns. Then, Teresa, you must go out and, if possible, discover the whereabouts of the Egyptian."

"Monsieur, he was summoned by M. Baradi before you came in. I heard him speaking on the house telephone."

"Let us hope the doctor keeps his man with him for some time. Now then, Raoul. On with the motley!"

The gowns proved to be amply made, wrapping across under their girdles. The hoods would come well forward and, when the head was bent, completely exclude any normal lighting from the face. "But it will be a different story if one holds a lighted candle," Alleyn said. "We must not be seen with our candles in our hands."

He had bought for Raoul a pair of feminine sandals, black and elegant with highish heels. Raoul said he thought they would fit admirably. With a grimace of humorous resignation he washed his small, beautiful and very dirty feet and then fitted them into the sandals. "*Oh, là, là!*" he said, "one must be an acrobat, it appears." And for the diversion of Teresa he minced to and fro, wagging his hips and making unseemly gestures. Teresa crammed her fists in her mouth and was consumed with merriment. "*Ah, mon Dieu,*" she gasped punctually, "*quel drôle de type!*"

Alleyn wondered rather desperately if he was dealing with children or merely with the celebrated Latin *joie de vivre*. He called them to order and they were at once as solemn as owls.

"Teresa," he said, "you will go a little ahead of us with your candle. Go straight through the house and down the stairs to the landing beneath the library. If you see anybody, blow your nose loudly."

"Have you a handkerchief, my jewel?"

"No."

"Accept mine," said Raoul, offering her a dubious rag.

"If anybody speaks to you and, perhaps, asks you why you are still on the premises, say that you missed your bus because of the message about Miss Taylor. If it is necessary, you must say you are going to her room to do some little act of service that you had forgotten and that you will leave to catch the later bus. If it is possible, in this event, Raoul and I will conceal ourselves until the coast is clear. If this is not possible, we will behave as Mr. Herrington and Miss Taylor would behave under the rule of silence. You will continue to Miss Taylor's room, open the door for Raoul and go in for a moment, but only for a moment. Then, Teresa, I have another task for you," continued Alleyn, feeling for the second time in two days that he had become as big a bore as Prospero. Teresa, however, was a complacent Ariel and merely gazed submissively upon him.

"You will find Mr. Oberon and will tell him that Miss Taylor has returned and asks to be allowed her private meditation alone in her room until the ceremony. That is very important."

"Ah, Monsieur, if he were not so troubling to my soul!"

"If you value my esteem, Teresa—" Raoul began.

"Yes, yes, Monsieur," said Teresa in a hurry, "I am resolved! I will face it."

"Good. Having given this message, come and report to me. After that your tasks for the night are finished. You will catch the late bus for your home in the Paysdoux. Heaven will reward you and I shall not forget you. Is all that clear, Teresa?"

Teresa repeated it all.

"Good. Now, Raoul, we may not have a chance to speak to each other again. Do as I have said. You are enacting the role of a frightened yet fascinated girl who is under the rule of silence. What will happen during the ceremony I cannot tell you. Mr. Herrington could not be persuaded to confide more than you already know. You can only try to behave as the others do. If there is a crisis I shall deal with it. You will probably see and hear much that will shock and anger you. However beastly the behaviour of these people, you must control yourself. Have you ever heard of the Augean Stables?"

"No, Monsieur."

"They were filthy and were cleansed. It was a heroic task. Now, when you get to Miss Taylor's room you will find a robe, like the one you are wearing, laid out for her. If there is no difference you need not change. I don't think you need try to wear her shoes but if there is anything else set out for her—gloves perhaps—you must wear whatever it may be. One thing more. There may be cigarettes in Miss Taylor's room. Don't smoke them. If cigarettes are given to us during the ceremony we must pretend to smoke. Like this."

Alleyn pouted his lips as if to whistle, held a cigarette in the gap between them and drew in audibly. "They will be drugged cigarettes. Air and smoke will be inhaled together. Keep your thumb over the end like this and you will be safe. That's all. A great deal depends upon us, Raoul. There have been many girls before Miss Taylor who have become the guests of Mr. Oberon. I think perhaps of all evil-doers, his kind are the worst. Monsieur le Commissaire and I are asking much of you."

Raoul, perched on his high heels and peering out of the black hood, said: "Monsieur l'Inspecteur-en-Chef, in the army one learns to recognize authority. I recognize it in you, Monsieur, and I shall serve it to the best of my ability."

Alleyn was acutely embarrassed and more than a little touched by this speech. He said: "Thank you. Then we must all do our best. Shall we set about it? Now, Teresa, as quietly as you can unless you meet anybody, and then—boldly. Off you go."

"Courage, my beloved. Courage and good sense."

Teresa bestowed a melting glance upon Raoul, opened the door and, after a preliminary look down the passage, took up her candle and went out. Alleyn followed with his walking-stick in his hand and Raoul, clicking his high heels and taking small steps, brought up the rear.

Down in Roqueville Troy absent-mindedly arranged little figures round a crib and pondered on the failure of her session with Ginny and Robin. She heard again Ginny's desperate protest: "I don't want to, I don't want to but I must. I've taken the oath. Dreadful things will happen if I don't go back."

"You don't really believe that," Robin had said and she had cried out: "You've sworn and you won't tell. If we don't believe why don't we tell?"

Suddenly, with something of Ricky's abandon, she had flung her arms round Troy. "If you could help," she had stammered, "but you can't; you can't!" And she had run out of the room like a frightened animal. Robin, limping after her, had turned at the door.

"It's all right," he had said. "Mrs. Allen, it's all right. She won't go back."

There was a tidily arranged pile of illustrated papers in the private sitting-room where they had had their drinks. Troy found herself idly turning the pages of the top one. Photographs of sunbathers and racegoers flipped over under her abstracted gaze. Dresses by Dior and dresses by Fath, Prince Aly Khan leading in his father's horse, the new ballet at the Marigny—"Les invités réunis pour quelques jours au Château de la Chèvre d'Argent. De gauche à droite: l'Hôte, M. Oberon; Mlle. Imogen Taylor, M. Carbury Glande, Dr. Baradi, M. Robin Herrington et la Hon. Grizel Locke—" Troy's attention was arrested and then transfixed. It was a clear photograph taken on the roof-garden. There they were, perfectly recognizable, all except Grizel Locke.

The photograph of Grizel Locke was that of a short, lean woman with the face of a complete stranger.

## IV

Robin was driving up a rough lane into the hills with Ginny beside him saying feverishly: "You're sure this is a shorter way? It's a quarter to eight, Robin! Robin, you're sure?"

He thought: "The tank was half-full. How long will it take for half a tank of air to be exhausted?"

"There's tons of time," he said, "and I'm quite sure." As he turned the next corner the engine missed and then stopped. Robin crammed on his brakes.

Looking at Ginny's blank face he thought: "Now, we're for it. It's tonight or nevermore for Ginny and me."

Dupont, waiting under the stars on the platform outside the Chèvre d'Argent, looked at his watch. It was a quarter to eight. He sighed and settled himself inside his coat. He expected a long vigil.

## V

Teresa's candle bobbed ahead. Sometimes it vanished round corners, sometimes dipped or ascended as she arrived at steps and sometimes it was stationary for a moment as she stopped and listened. Presently they were on familiar ground. Forward, on their left, was the operating room: opposite this, the room where Miss Truebody had waited. Nearer, on their right, a thin blade of light across the carpet indicated the door into Baradi's room. Teresa's hand, dramatized by candlelight, shielded the flame. Beyond her, the curtain at the end of the passage was faintly defined against some further diffusion of light.

She passed Baradi's room. Alleyn and Raoul approached it. Alleyn held up a warning hand. He halted and then crept forward. His ear was at the door. Beyond it, like erring souls, Baradi and his servant were talking together in their own language.

Alleyn and Raoul moved on. Teresa had come to the curtain. They saw her lift it and a triangle of warmth appeared. Her candle sank to the floor. The foot of the curtain was raised and the candle, followed by the doubled-up shape of Teresa, disappeared beneath it.

"Good girl," Alleyn thought, "she's remembered the rings."

He followed quickly. He was tall enough to reach the rings and hold the top of the curtain to the rail while he raised the skirt for Raoul to pass through.

Now Raoul was in the great hall where the candelabrum still burned on the central table. Teresa had already passed into the entrance lobby. Alleyn still held the curtain in his hand when Teresa blew her nose.

He slipped back behind the curtain, leaving a peephole for himself. He saw Raoul hesitate and then move forward until his back was to the light and he saw a white-robed figure that might have been himself come in from the lobby. Looking beyond the six burning candles he watched the two figures confront each other. The white hood was thrust back and Carbury Glande's red beard jutted out. Alleyn heard him mutter:

"Well, thank God for you, anyway. You *have* put him in a tizzy! What happened?"

The black cowl moved slightly from side to side. The head was bent.

"Oh, *all* right!" Glande said pettishly. "What a stickler you are, to be sure!"

The white figure crossed the end of the hall and disappeared up the stairway.

Raoul moved on into the lobby and Alleyn came out of cover and followed him. When he entered the lobby, Alleyn went to the carved chest that stood against the back wall. It was there that the Egyptian servant had put the key of the wrought-iron door. Alleyn found the key and through the grill tossed it out of reach into the outside passageway.

From the lobby, the staircase wound downstairs. Teresa's candle, out of sight and sinking, threw up her own travelling shadow and that of Raoul. Alleyn followed them, but they moved faster than he and he was left to grope his way down in a kind of twilight. He had completed three descending spirals when he arrived at the landing. The door he had noticed on his previous visit was now open and beyond it was a bedroom with a light burning before a looking-glass. This, evidently, was Robin Herrington's room. Alleyn went in. On the inside door-handle hung a notice: *"Heure de Méditation. Ne dérangez pas."* He hung it outside and shut the door.

The room had the smell and sensation of luxury that were characteristic of the Chèvre d'Argent. A white robe, like his own, was laid out together with silk shorts and shirt and a pair of white sandals. Alleyn changed quickly. On a table near the bed was a silver box, an ashtray, an elaborate lighter and, incongruously, a large covered dish which, on examination, proved to contain a sumptuous assortment of hors d'oeuvres and savouries. In the box were three cigarettes: long, thin and straw-coloured. He took one up, smelt it, broke it across and put the two halves in his case. He held a second to his candle, kept it going by returning it continuously to the flame and, as it was consumed, broke the ash into the tray.

"Three of those," he thought, "and young Herrington's values would be as cockeyed as one of Carbury Glande's abstracts."

There was the lightest of taps on the door. It opened slightly. "Monsieur?" whispered Teresa.

He let her in.

"Monsieur, it is to tell you that I have executed your order. I have spoken to Mr. Oberon. Tonight he was not as formerly he has been. He was not interested in me, but all the same he was excited. One would have thought he was intoxicated, Monsieur, but he does not take wine."

"You gave the message?"

"Yes, Monsieur. He listened eagerly and questioned me, saying: 'Have you seen her?' and I thought best, with the permission of the saints, to say 'yes.'"

"Quite so, Teresa."

"He then asked me if Mademoiselle Taylor was quite well and I said she was and then if she seemed happy and I said: 'Yes, she seemed pleased and excited,' because that is how one is, Monsieur, when one keeps an appointment. And I repeated that Mademoiselle had asked to be alone and he said: 'Of course, of course. It is essential,' as if to himself. And he was staring in a strange manner as if I was not there and so I left him. And although I was frightened, Monsieur, I was not troubled as formerly by M. Oberon because Raoul is the friend of my bosom and to him I will be constant."

"I should certainly stick to that, if I were you. You are a good girl, Teresa, and now you must catch your bus. Tomorrow you shall choose a fine present against your wedding-day."

"Ah, Monsieur!" Teresa exclaimed and neatly sketching ineffable astonishment and delight, she slipped out of the room.

It was now eight o'clock. Alleyn settled down to his vigil. He thought of poor Miss Truebody and of the four remaining guests and Mr. Oberon, each in his or her room, and each, he believed, oppressed by an almost intolerable sense of approaching climax. He wondered if Robin Herrington had followed his advice about blocking the vent in the cap on his petrol tank and he wondered if Troy had had any success in breaking down Ginny's enthralment.

He turned over in his mind all he had read of that curious expression of human credulity called magic. As it happened he had been obliged on a former case to dig up evidence of esoteric ritual and had become fascinated by its witness to man's industry in the pursuit of a chimera. Hundreds and hundreds of otherwise intelligent men, he found, had subjected themselves throughout the centuries to the boredom of memorizing and reciting senseless formulae, to the indignity of unspeakable practices and to the threat of the most ghastly reprisals. Through age after age men and women had starved, frightened and exhausted themselves, had got themselves racked, broken and burned, had delivered themselves up to what they believed to be the threat of eternal damnation and all without any firsthand evidence of the smallest success. Age after age the Oberons and Baradis had battened on this unquenchable credulity, had traced their pentagrams, muttered their interminable spells, performed their gruelling ceremonies and taken their toll. And at the same time, he reflected, the Oberons (never the Baradis) had ended by falling into their own traps. The hysteria they induced was refracted upon themselves. Beyond the reek of ceremonial smoke they too began to look for the terrifying reward.

He wondered to what class of adept Oberon belonged. There was a definite hierarchy. There had always been practitioners who, however misguided, could not be accused of charlatanism. To this day, he believed, such beings existed, continuing their barren search for a talisman, for a philosopher's stone, for power and for easy money.

Magical rituals from the dawn of time had taken on the imprint of their several ages. From the scope and dignity of the Atkadian Inscriptions to the magnificence of the Graeco-Egyptian Papyri, from the pious Jewish mysteries to the squalors, brutalities and sheer silliness of the German pseudo-Faustian cults. From the Necromancer of the Coliseum to the surprisingly fresh folklorishness of the English genre: each had its peculiar character and its own formula of frustration. And alongside the direct line like a bastard brother ran the cult of Satanism, the imbecile horrors of the Black Mass, the Amatory Mass and the Mortuary Mass.

If Oberon had read all the books in his own library he had a pretty sound knowledge of these rituals together with a generous helping of Hindooism, Voodoo and Polynesian mythology: a wide field from which to concoct a ceremony for the downfall of Ginny Taylor and her predecessors. Alleyn fancied that the orthodox forms would not be followed. The oath of silence he had read in Baradi's room was certainly original. "If it's the Amatory Mass as practised by Madame de Montespan," he thought, "poor old Raoul's sunk from the word go." And he began to wonder what he should do if this particular crisis arose.

He spent the rest of his vigil eating the savouries that had no doubt been provided to satisfy the hunger of the reefer addict and smoking his own cigarettes. He checked over the possibilities of disaster and found them many and formidable. "All the same," he thought, "it's worth it. And if the worst comes to the worst we can always—"

Somebody was scratching at his door.

He ground out his cigarette, extinguished his candle and seated himself on the floor with his back to the door and his legs folded Oberonwise under his gown. He was facing the dressing-table with its large tilted looking-glass. The scratching persisted and turned into a featherlight tattoo of finger-tips. He kept his gaze on that part of the darkness where he knew the looking-glass must be. He heard a fumbling and a slight rap and guessed that the notice had been moved from the door-handle. A vertical sliver of light appeared. He watched the reflexion of the opening door and of the white-robed candle-bearer. He caught a glimpse, under the hood, of a long face with a beaked nose. Robed like that she seemed incredibly tall: no longer the figure of fantasy that she had presented yesterday in pedal-pushers and scarf and yet, unmistakably, the same woman. The door was shut. He bent his head and looked from under his brows at the reflexion of the woman, who advanced so close that he could hear her breathing behind him.

"I know it's against the Rule," she whispered. "I've got to speak to you."

He made no sign.

"I don't know what they'll do to me if they find out but I'm actually past caring!" In the glass he saw her put the candle on the table. "Have you smoked?" she said. "If you have I suppose it's no good. I haven't." He heard her sit heavily in the chair. "Well," she whispered almost cosily, "it's about Ginny. You've never seen an initiation, have you? I mean of that sort. You might at least nod or shake your head."

Alleyn shook his head.

"I thought not. You've got to stop her doing it. She's fond of you, you may depend upon it. If it was not for *him* she'd be in love, like any other nice girl, with you. And you're fond of her. I know. I've watched. Well, you've got to stop it. She's a thoroughly nice girl," the prim whisper insisted, "and you're still a splendid young fellow. Tell her she mustn't."

Alleyn's shoulders rose in an exaggerated shrug.

"Oh, *don't!*" The whisper broke into a vocal protest. "If you only knew how I've been watching you both. If you only knew what I'm risking. Why, if you tell on me I don't know what they won't do. Murder me, as likely as not. It wouldn't be the first time unless you believe she killed herself, and I certainly don't."

The voice stopped. Alleyn waited.

"One way or another," the voice said quite loudly, "you've got to give me a sign."

He raised his hand and made the Italian negative sign with his finger.

"You won't! You mean you'll let it happen. To Ginny? In front of everybody? Oh, dear me!" The voice sighed out most lamentably. "Oh, dear, dear me, it's enough to break one's heart!" There was a further silence. Alleyn thought: "The time's going by: we haven't much longer. If she'd just say one thing!"

The voice said strongly, as if its owner had taken fresh courage:

"Very well. I shall speak to her. It won't do any good. I look at you and I ask myself what sort of creature you are. I look—"

She broke off. She had moved her candle so that its reflexion in the glass was thrown back upon Alleyn. He sat frozen.

"*Who are you?*" the voice demanded strongly. "You're not Robin Herrington."

She was behind him. She jerked the hood back from his head and they stared at each other in the looking-glass.

"And you're not Grizel Locke," Alleyn said. He got up, faced her and held out his hand. "Miss P. E. Garbel, I presume," he said gently.

# CHAPTER XII

# Eclipse of the Sun

## I

"THEN you guessed!" said Miss Garbel, clinging to his hand and shaking it up and down as if it were a sort of talisman. "How did you guess? How did you get here? What's happening?"

Alleyn said: "We've got twenty-five minutes before that damn bell goes. Don't let's squander them. I wasn't sure. Yesterday morning, when you talked like one of your letters, I wondered."

"I couldn't let either of you know who I was. Oberon was watching. They all were. I thought the remark about the Douceville bus might catch your attention."

"I didn't dare ask outright, of course. Now, tell me. Grizel Locke's dead, isn't she?"

"Yes; small hours of yesterday morning. We were told an overdose of self-administered heroin. *I* think—murdered."

"Why was she murdered?"

"*I* think, because she protested about Ginny. Ginny's her niece. *I* think she may have threatened them with exposure."

"Who killed her?"

"I haven't an idea. Oh, not a notion!"

"What exactly were you told?"

"That if it was found out we'd all be in trouble. That the whole thing would be discovered: the trade in diacetylmorphine, the connection with the factory—have you discovered about the factory?—everything, they said, would come out and we'd all be arrested and the British subjects would be extradited and tried and imprisoned. Then, it appears, you rang up about Miss Truebody. Baradi saw it as a chance to dispose of poor Grizel Locke. She would be buried, you see, and you would be told it was Miss Truebody. Then later on when you were out of the way and Miss Truebody was well, a made-up name would be put over the grave. Baradi said that if anybody could save Miss Truebody's life, he could. I'm guessing at how much you know. Stop me if I'm not clear. And then you or your wife asked about 'Cousin Garbel.' You can imagine how that shocked them! I was there, you see. I'm their liaison with the factory. I work at the factory. I'll tell you why and how if we've time. Of course I guessed who you were, but I told them I hadn't a notion. I said I supposed you must be some unknown people with an introduction or something. They were terribly suspicious. They said I must see you both and find out what you were doing, and why you'd asked about me. Then Baradi said it would be better if I didn't present myself as me. And then they said I must pretend to be Grizel Locke so that if there was ever an enquiry or trouble, you and Cousin Aggie—"

"*Who!*" Alleyn ejaculated.

"Your wife, you know. She was called Agatha after my second cousin, once—"

"Yes, yes. Sorry. I call her Troy."

"Really? Quaint! I've formed the habit of thinking of her as Cousin Aggie. Well, the plan was that I'd be introduced to you as Grizel Locke and I should tell them afterwards if I recognized you or knew anything about you. They made me wear Grizel's clothes and paint my face, in case you'd heard about her or would be asked about her afterwards. And then, tomorrow, after the funeral we are meant to meet again and I'm to say I'm leaving for a trip to Budapest. If possible, you are to see me go. So that if a hue-and-cry goes out for Grizel Locke, you will support the story that she's left for Hungary. I'm to go as far as Marseilles and stay there until you're both out of the way. The factory has extensive connections in Marseilles. At the same time we're to give out that I, as myself, you know, have gone on holiday. How much longer have we got?"

"Twenty-one minutes."

"I've time, at least, to tell you quickly that whatever you're planning you mustn't depend too much upon me. You see, I'm one of them."

"You mean," Alleyn said, "you've formed the habit—?"

"I'm fifty. Sixteen years ago I was a good analytical chemist but terribly poor. They offered me a job on a wonderful salary. Research. They started me off in New York, and after the war they brought me over here. At first I thought it was all right and then gradually I discovered what was happening. They handled me on orthodox lines. A man, very attractive, and parties. I was always plain and he was experienced and charming. He started me on marihuana—reefers, you know—and I've never been able to break off. They see to it I get just enough to keep me going. They get me up here and make me nervous and then give me cigarettes. I'm very useful to them. When I smoke I get very silly. I hear myself saying things that fill me with bitter shame. But when I've got the craving to smoke and when *he's* given me cigarettes, I—well, you've seen. It wasn't all play-acting when I pretended to be Grizel Locke. We all get like that with Oberon. He has a genius for defilement."

"Why did you write as you did to Troy? I must tell you that we didn't realize what you were up to until yesterday."

"I was afraid you wouldn't. But I daren't be explicit. Their surveillance is terribly thorough and my letters might have been opened. They weren't, as turned out, otherwise you would have been recognized as my correspondent. I wrote—"

The voice, half vocal, half whispering, faltered. She pushed back her hood and tilted her tragic-comic face towards Alleyn's. "I began to write because of the girls like Ginny. You've seen me and you've seen Annabella Wells—frightful, aren't we? Grizel Locke was the same. Drug-soaked old horrors. We're what happens to the Ginnys. And there are lots and lots of Ginnys: bomb-children I call 'em. No moral stamina and no nervous reserve. Parents killed within the child's memory and experience. Sense of insecurity and impending disaster. The poor ones with jobs have the best chance. But the others—the rich Ginnys—if they run into our sort of set—whoof! And once they're made Daughters of the Sun it's the end of them. Too ashamed to look back or up or anywhere but at him. So when I saw in the English papers that my clever kinswoman had married *you*, I thought: 'I'll do it. I haven't the nerve or self-control to fight on my own but I'll try and hint.' So I did. I was a little surprised when Cousin Aggie replied as if to a man, but I did not correct her. Her mistake gave me a foolish sense of security. How long, now?"

"Just over seventeen minutes. Listen! Herrington and Ginny won't come back tonight. My chauffeur and I are replacing them. Can we get away with it? What happens in the ceremony?"

She had been talking eagerly and quickly, watching him with a bird-like attentiveness. Now it was as if his question touched her with acid. She actually threw up her hands in a self-protective movement and shrank away from him.

"I can't tell you. I've taken an oath of silence."

"All that dagger and fire and molten lead nonsense?"

"You can't know! How do you know? Who's broken faith?"

"Nobody. I hoped you might."

"Never!"

"A silly gimcrack rigmarole. Based on infamy."

"It's no good. I told you. I'm no good."

"My man's about Ginny's height and he's wearing the black robe. Has he a chance of getting by?"

"Not to the end. Of course not." She caught her breath in something that might have been a sob or a wretched giggle. "How can you dream of it?"

"Will anybody be asked to take this oath—alone?"

"No—I can tell you nothing—but—he—no. Why are you doing this?"

"We think the ceremony may give us an opportunity for an arrest on a minor charge. Not only that—" Alleyn hesitated. "I feel as you do," he said hurriedly, "about this wretched child. For one thing she's English and there's a double sense of responsibility. At the same time I'm not here to do rescue work, particularly if it prejudices the success of my job. What's more, if Oberon and Baradi suspect that this child and young Herrington have done a bolt, they'll also suspect a betrayal. They'll have the machinery for meeting such a crisis. All evidence of their interest in the racket will be destroyed and they'll shoot the moon. Whereas, if, by good luck, we can diddle them into thinking Ginny Taylor and Robin Herrington have returned to their unspeakable fold we may learn enough, here, tonight to warrant an arrest. We can then hold the principals, question the smaller fry and search the whole place."

"I'm small fry. How do you know I won't warn them?"

"I've heard you plead for Ginny."

"You've told me she's safe," whimpered Miss Garbel. She bit her finger-tips and looked at him out of the corner of her pale eyes. "That's all I wanted. You ask me to bring ruin on myself. I've warned you. I'm no good. I've no integrity left. In a minute I must smoke and then I'll be hopeless. You ask too much."

Alleyn said: "You're a braver woman than you admit. You've tried for months to get me here, knowing that if I succeed your job will be gone and you will have to break yourself of your drug. You risked try-

ing to tip me off yesterday morning and you risked coming to plead
with young Herrington here tonight. You're a woman of science with
judgment and curiosity and a proper scepticism. You know, positively,
that this silly oath of silence was taken under the influence of your
drug, that the threats it carries are meaningless, that it's your clear duty
to abandon it. I think you will believe me when I say that if you keep
faith with us tonight you will have our full protection afterwards."

"You can't protect me," she said, "from myself."

"We can try. Come! Having gone so far, why not all the way?"

"I'm so frightened," said Miss Garbel. "You can't think. So dreadfully frightened."

She clasped her claw-like hands together. Alleyn covered them with
his own. "All right," he said. "Never mind. You've done a lot. I won't
ask you to tell me about the rites. Don't go to the ceremony. Can you
send a message?"

"I must go. There must be seven."

"One for each point of the pentagram, with Oberon and the Black
Robe in the middle?"

"Did *they* tell you? Ginny and Robin? They wouldn't dare."

"Call it a guess. Before we separate I'm going to ask you to make one
promise tonight. Shall we say for Grizel Locke's sake? Don't smoke so
much marihuana that you may lose control of yourself and perhaps betray us."

"I shan't betray you. I *can* promise that. I don't promise not to smoke
and I implore you to depend on me for nothing more than this. I won't
give you away."

"Thank you a thousand times, my dear cousin-by-marriage. Before
the night is over I shall ask if I may call you Penelope."

"Naturally you may. In my bad moments," said poor Miss Garbel, "I
have often cheered myself up by thinking of you both as Cousins
Roddy and Aggie."

"Have you really?" Alleyn murmured and was saved from the necessity of further comment by the sound of a cascade of bells.

Miss Garbel was thrown into a great state of perturbation by the
bells which, to Alleyn, were reminiscent of the dinner chimes that tinkle through the corridors of ocean liners.

"There!" she ejaculated with a sort of wretched triumph. "The Temple bells! And here we are in somebody else's room and goodness *knows*
what will become of us."

"I'll see if the coast's clear," Alleyn said. He took up his stick and
then opened the door. The smell of incense hung thick on the air.
Evidently candles had been lit on the lower landing. The stair-well

sank into reflected light through which there rose whorls and spirals of scented smoke. As he watched, a shadow came up from below and the sound of bells grew louder. It was the Egyptian servant. Alleyn watched the distorted image of his tarboosh travel up the curved wall followed by that of his body and of his hands bearing the chime of bells. Alleyn stood firm, leaning on his stick with his hood over his face. The Egyptian followed his own shadow upstairs, ringing his little carillon. He crossed the landing, made a salutation as he passed Alleyn and continued on his way upstairs.

Alleyn looked back into the room. Miss Garbel stood there, biting her knuckles. He went to her.

"It's all right," he said. "You can go down. If you feel *very* brave and venturesome keep as close as you dare to the Black Robe and if he looks like he's making a mistake try and stop him. He only speaks French. Now, you'd better go."

She shook her head two or three times. Then, with an incredible suggestion of conventional leave-taking she began to settle herself inside her robe. She actually held out her hand.

"Goodbye. I'm sorry I'm not a braver woman," she said.

"You've been very brave for a long time and I'm exceedingly grateful," Alleyn said.

He watched her go and after giving her about thirty seconds, blew out the candle and followed her.

## II

The stairs turned three times about the tower before he came limping to the bottom landing. Here a lighted candelabrum stood near a door: the door he had noticed yesterday morning. Now it was open. The air was dense with the reek of incense so that each candle flame blossomed in a nimbus. His feet sank into the deep carpet and dimly he could make out the door into Oberon's room and the vista of wall-tapestries, receding into a passage.

Through the open door he saw four separate candlesticks, each with a lighted black candle. This, then, was the ante-room. Alleyn went in. The black velvet walls absorbed light and an incense burner hanging from the ceiling further obscured it. He could make out a partly opened curtain and behind this a rack of hanging robes. He could not be sure he was alone. Limping carefully, he made for the candles and took one up.

Remembering what Teresa had told him, he turned to the right and with his free hand explored the wall. The velvet surface was disagreeable to his touch. He moved along still pressing it and in a moment it yielded. He had found the swing-door into the temple.

There was an unwholesomeness about the silent obedience of the velvet door. It was as if everyday objects had begun to change their values. He followed his hand and walked, as it seemed, through the re-treating wall into the temple.

At first he was aware only of two candle flames below the level of his knees and some distance ahead, six glowing braziers. Then he saw a white robe, squatting not far from a candle and then a black robe, near a second flame. He felt the tessellated floor under his feet and, using his stick, tapped his way across. "All the same," he thought, "young Herrington's stick is rubber-shod."

By the light of his own candle he made out the shape of the giant pentagram in the mosaic of the floor. It had been let into the pavement and was traced in some substance that acted as a reflector. The five-pointed star was enclosed in a double circle and he saw that at each of the points there was a smaller circle and in this a black cushion and a brazier filled with glowing embers. It was on one of these cushions that the white robe squatted. He drew close to it. A recognizable hand crept out from under the sleeve. It was Miss Garbel's. He turned to the centre of the pentagram. Raoul was holding his candle under his own face. His hands and arms were gloved in black. He was seated, cross-legged on a black divan and in front of him was a brazier.

Alleyn murmured: "The lady behind you and to your right is not unfriendly. She knows who you are."

Raoul signalled an assent.

"Depend on me for nothing—nothing," admonished a ghost-whisper in French and then added in a sort of frenzy, "Not there! Not in the middle. Not yet. Like me. *There!*"

"Quick, Raoul. *There!*"

Raoul darted into the point of the pentagram in front of Miss Garbel's. He put down his candle on the floor and pulled forward his hood.

Alleyn moved to the encircled point opposite Miss Garbel's. He had seated himself on the cushion before his brazier and had laid down his stick and candle when a light danced across the facets of the pentagram. He sensed, rather than heard, the entrance of a new figure. It passed so close that he recognized Annabella Wells's scent. She moved into the encircled point on his right and seated herself facing outwards as he did. At the same time there was a new glint of candlelight and the sound of a subsidence behind and to the left of Alleyn. In a moment or two a figure, unmistakably Baradi's, swept round the pen-tagram and entered it between Annabella and Raoul. Alleyn guessed he had taken up his position at the centre. At the same time the bells cascaded close at hand. "Here we go," he thought.

The five candles and six braziers furnished light enough for him to get a fitful impression of the preposterous scene. By turning his head slightly and slewing round his eyes, he could see the neighbouring points of the great pentagonal star, each protected by its circle and each containing its solitary figure, seated before a brazier and facing outward. Outside the pentagram and facing the points occupied by Annabella and Raoul was the altar. Alleyn could see the glint of metal in the embroidered cloth and quite distinctly, could make out the shape of the great crystal sun-burst standing in the middle.

The sound of bells came close and then stopped. A door opened in the wall beside the altar and the Egyptian servant walked through. He wore only a loin cloth and the squarish head-dress of antiquity. Before each of the initiates he set down a little box. "More reefers," thought Alleyn, keeping his head down. "Damned awkward if he wants to light them for us."

But the Egyptian made no attempt to do so. He moved away and out of the tail of his eye, Alleyn saw Annabella Wells reach out to her brazier, take a pair of tongs and light her cigarette with a piece of charcoal. Alleyn found that his brazier, too, was provided with tongs.

Because of the form of the pentagram the occupants of the five points all had their backs turned to Baradi and their shoulders to each other. If Baradi was on his feet he would have a sort of aerial survey of their backs. If he was seated on the divan he would have a still less rewarding view. Alleyn reached out for a cigarette, hid it inside his robe and produced one of his own. This he lit with a coal from the brazier. He wondered if it had occurred to Raoul to employ the same ruse.

Little spires of smoke began to rise from the five points of the star. The Egyptian had retired to a dark corner beyond the altar and presently began to strike a drum and play a meandering air on some reed instrument. To Alleyn the scene was preposterous and phony. He remembered Troy's comment on the incident of the train window: hadn't she compared it to bad cinematography? Even the ritual, for what it was worth, was bogus: a vamped-up synthesis, he thought, of several magic formulae. The reedy phrase tricked on like a tourist-class advertisement for Cairo, the drum throbbed and presently he sensed a stir of excitement among the initiates. The Egyptian began to chant and to increase the pace and volume of his drumming. Drum and voice achieved a sort of crescendo at the peak of which a second voice entered with a long vibrant call, startling in its unexpectedness. It was Baradi's.

From that moment it was impossible altogether to dismiss the Rites of the Sun as cheap or ridiculous. No doubt they were both but they were also alarming.

Alleyn supposed that Baradi spoke Egyptian and that his chant was one of the set invocations of ritual magic. He thought he recognized the characteristic repetition of names: "O Oualbpaga! O Kammara! O Kamalo! O Karhenmou! O Amagaa! O Thoth! O Anubis!" The drum thumped imperatively. Small feral noises came from the points of the pentagram. Behind Alleyn, Carbury Glande began to beat with his palm on the floor. The other initiates followed, Alleyn with them. The Egyptian left his drum and running about the pentagram, threw incense on the braziers. Columns of heavily scented smoke arose amid sharp cries from the initiates. A gong crashed and there was immediate silence.

It was startling, after the long exhortations in an incomprehensible tongue to hear Baradi cry in a loud voice: "Children of the Sun in the Outer, turn inward, now turn in. Silence, silence, silence, symbol of the imperishable god protect us, silence. Turn inward now, turn in."

This injunction was taken literally by the initiates who reversed their positions on the cushions and thus faced Baradi and the centre of the pentagram. Looking across, diagonally, to the Black Robe, Alleyn saw that Raoul had not moved. The exhortations, being in English, had meant nothing to him. Alleyn dared not look up at Baradi. He could see his feet and his white robe, up to the knees. Between drifts of incense he caught sight of the other initiates, all waiting. It seemed as if an age went by before the Black Robe rose, turned and reseated itself. He saw Baradi's feet shift and his robe swing as he faced the altar.

Baradi intoned in a loud voice: "Here in the Names of Ra and Of the Sons of Ra—"

It was the oath Alleyn had read. Baradi gave it out phrase by phrase and the initiates repeated it after him. Alleyn spoke on the top register of his very deep voice. Raoul, of course, said nothing. Miss Garbel's thin pipe was unmistakable. Annabella's trained and vibrant voice rang out loudly. Carbury Glande's sounded unco-ordinated and hysterical.

"If I break this oath in the least degree," Baradi dictated and was echoed, "may my lips be burned with the fire that is now set before them." He gestured over his brazier. A tongue of flame darted up from it.

"May my eyes be put out by the knife that is now set before them."

With a suddenness that was extraordinarily unnerving, five daggers dropped from the ceiling and checked with a jerk before the five initiates' faces. A sixth, bigger, fell in front of Baradi, who seized and flourished it. The others hung glittering in the flamelight of the brazier. The women gave little whimpering febrile cries.

The oath of silence was taken through to its abominable conclusion. The flame subsided, the smaller daggers were drawn up to the ceiling, presumably by the Egyptian. The initiates turned outward again and Baradi settled down to a further exhortation, this time in English.

It was the blackest possible kind of affair, quite short and entirely infamous. Baradi demanded darkness and the initiates put out their candles. Alleyn dared not look at Raoul, but knew by the delayed flicker of light that he was a little slow with this. Then Baradi urged first of all the necessity of experiencing something called "the caress of the left hand of perfection" and went on to particularize in terms that would have appalled anyone who was not an alienist or a member of Mr. Oberon's chosen circle. The Egyptian had returned to his reed and drum and the merciless repetition of a single phrase had its own effect. Baradi began to pour out a stream of names: Greek, Jewish, Egyptian: Pan, Enlil, Elohim, Ra, Anubis, Seti, Adonis, Ra, Silenus, Ereschigal, Tetragrammaton, Ra. The recurrent "Ra" was presently taken up by the initiates, who began to bark it out with an enthusiasm, Alleyn thought, only to be equalled by the organized cheers of an American ball game.

"There are two signs," Baradi intoned. "There is the Sign of the Sun, Ra" ("Ra," barked the initiates), "and there is the sign of the Goat, Pan. And between the Sun and the Goat runs the endless cycle of the senses. Ra."

"*Ra!*"

"We demand a sign."

"*We demand a sign.*"

"What shall the sign be?"

"*The sign of the goat which is also the sign of the Sun which is also the sign of Ra.*"

"Let the goat come forth which is the Sun which is Ra."

"*Ra!*"

The drumming was increased to a frenzy. The initiates beat on the floor and clapped. Baradi must have thrown more incense on his brazier: the air was thick with billowing fumes. Alleyn could scarcely make out the shape of the altar. Now Baradi must be striking cymbals together.

The din was intolerable. The initiates, antic figures, half-masked by whorls of smoke, seemed to have gone down on all fours and to be flinging their hands high as they slapped the floor and cried out. Baradi broke into a chant, possibly in his own language, interspersed with further strings of names—Pan, Hylaesos, Lupercus, Silenos, Faunus—names that were caught up and shouted in a fury of abandon by the other voices. Alleyn, shouting with the rest, edged round on his knees, until he could look across the pentagram to Raoul. In the glow of the braziers he could just make out the black crouching figure and the black gloved hands rising and falling like drumsticks.

"A Sign, a Sign, let there be be a Sign!"

"*It comes.*"

"It comes."

"*It is here.*"

Again the well-staged crescendo that ended, this time, in a deafening crash of cymbals followed by a dead silence.

And across that silence: bathetic, ridiculous and disturbing, broke the unmistakable bleat of a billy goat.

The smoke eddied and swirled, and there, on the altar for all the world like one of old Marie's statuettes, it appeared, horned and shining, a silver goat whose hide glittered through the smoke. It opened its mouth sideways and superciliously bleated. Its pale eyes stared and it stamped and tossed its head.

"It's been shoved up there from the back," Alleyn thought. "They've treated it with fluorescent paint. *Ça s'illumine.*"

Baradi was speaking again.

"Prepare, prepare," he chanted. "The Sign is the Shadow of the Substance. The Goat-god is the precursor of the Man-god. The Man-god is the Bridegroom. He is the Spouse. He is Life. He is the Sun. Ra!"

There was a blare of light, for perhaps a second literally blinding in its intensity. "Flash-powder," thought Alleyn. "The Egyptian must be remarkably busy." When his eyes had adjusted themselves, the goat had disappeared and in its place the sun-burst blazed on the altar. "Car batteries," thought Alleyn, "perhaps. Flex soldered at the terminals. Well done, Mahomet or somebody."

"Ra! Ra! Ra!" the initiates ejaculated with Baradi as their cheerleader.

The door to the left of the altar had opened. It admitted a naked man.

He advanced through wreaths of incense and stood before the blazing sun-burst. It was, of course, Mr. Oberon.

*III*

Of the remainder of the ceremony, as far as he witnessed it, Alleyn afterwards prepared an official report. Neither this, nor a manual called *The Book of Ra*, which contained the text of the ritual, has ever been made public. Indeed, they have been stowed away in the archives of Scotland Yard where they occupy a place of infamy rivalling that of the *Book of Horus and the Swami Viva Ananda*. There are duplicates at the Sûreté. In the trial they were not put in as primary evidence, and the judge, after a distasteful glance, said that he saw no reason why the jury should be troubled to look at them.

For purposes of this narrative it need only be said that with the appearance of Oberon, naked, in the role of Ra or Horus, or both, the Rites took on the character of unbridled Phallicism. He stood on some raised place before the blazing sun-burst, holding a dagger in both hands. More incense burners were set reeking at his feet, and there he was, the nearest approach, Alleyn afterwards maintained, that he had ever seen, to a purely evil being.

His entry stung the initiates into their pitch of frenzy. Incredible phrases were chanted, indescribable gestures were performed. The final crescendo of that scandalous affair rocketed up to its point of climax. For the last time the Egyptian's drum rolled and Baradi clashed his cymbals. For the last time pandemonium gave place to silence.

Oberon came down from his eminence and walked towards the encircled pentagram. His feet slapped the tessellated pavement. His hair, lit from behind, was a nimbus about his head. He entered the pentagram and the initiates turned inwards, crouching beastily at the points. Oberon placed himself at the centre. Baradi spoke.

"Horus who is Savitar who is Baldur who is Ra. The Light, The Beginning and The End, The Life, The Source and The Fulfilment. Choose, now, Lord, O choose."

Oberon extended his arm and pointed his dagger at Raoul.

Baradi went to Raoul. He held out his hand. In the capricious glare from the sun-burst Alleyn could see Raoul on his knees, his shadow thrown before him towards Oberon's feet. His face was deeply hidden in his hood. Alleyn saw the gloved hand and arm reach out. Baradi took the hand. He passed Raoul across him with a dancer's gesture.

Raoul now faced Oberon.

Somewhere in the shadows the Egyptian servant cried out shrilly.

Baradi's dark hands, themselves seeming gloved, closed on the shoulders of Raoul's robe. Suddenly, with a flourish, and to a roll of the drum, he swept it free of its wearer. "Behold!" he shouted: "The Bride!"

And then, in the glare from the sun-burst, where, like an illustration from La Vie Parisienne, Mr. Oberon's victim should have been discovered; there stood Raoul in his underpants, black slippers and Ginny Taylor's gloves.

A complete surprise is often something of an anti-climax and so, for a moment or two, was this. It is possible that Annabella Wells and Carbury Glande were too fuddled with marihuana to get an immediate reaction. Miss Garbel, of course, had been prepared. As for Oberon and Baradi, they faced each other across the preposterous Thing they had unveiled and their respective jaws dropped like those of a pair of simultaneous comedians. Raoul himself merely cast a scandalized glance at Oberon and uttered in a loud apocalyptic voice the single word: *"Anathema!"*

It was then that Miss Garbel erupted in a single hoot of hysteria. It escaped from her and was at once cut off by her own hand clapped across her mouth. She squatted, heaving, in the corner of the pentacle, her terrified eyes staring over her knuckles at Baradi.

Baradi, in an unrecognizable voice and an unconscious quotation, said: "Which of you has done this?"

Oberon gave a bubbling cry: "I am betrayed!"

Raoul, hearing his voice, repeated: "Anathema!" and made the sign of the cross.

Oberon dragged Miss Garbel to her feet. He held her with his right hand; in his left was the dagger. She chattered in his face: "You can't! You can't! I'm protected. You can't!"

Alleyn advanced until he was quite close to them. Glande and Annabella Wells were on their feet.

"Is this your doing?" Oberon demanded, lowering his face to Miss Garbel's.

"Not mine!" she chattered. "Not this time. Not mine!"

He flung her off. Baradi turned on Raoul.

"Well!" Baradi said in French, "so I know you, now. Where's your master?"

"Occupy yourself with your own affairs, Monsieur."

"We are lost!" Oberon cried out in English.

His hand moved. The knife glinted.

*"Alors, Raoul!"* said Alleyn.

Raoul stooped and ran. He ran out of the pentacle and across the floor. The Egyptian darted out and was knocked sideways. His head struck the corner of the altar and he lay still. Raoul sped through the open door into Oberon's room. Oberon followed him. Alleyn followed Oberon and caught him up on the far side of the great looking-glass. He seized his right hand as it was raised. "Not this time," Alleyn grunted and jerked his arm. The dagger flew from Oberon's hand and splintered the great glass. At the same moment Raoul kicked. Oberon gave a scream of pain, staggered across the room and lurched against the window. With a whirr and a clatter the blind flew up and Oberon sank on the floor moaning. Alleyn turned to find Baradi facing him with the knife in his left hand.

"You," Baradi said. "I might have guessed. *You!*"

## IV

From the moment that the affair began, as it were, to wind itself up in Oberon's room, it became a straight-out conflict between Alleyn and Baradi. Alleyn had guessed that it would be so. Even while he sweated to remember his police training in unarmed combat he found time to consider that Oberon, naked and despicable, had at last become a negligible element. Alleyn was even aware of Carbury Glande and Annabella Wells teetering uncertainly in the doorway, and of Miss Garbel, who hovered like a spinsterly half-back on the edge of the scrimmage.

But chiefly he was aware of Baradi's dark infuriated body, smelling of sandalwood and sweat, and of the knowledge that he himself was the fitter man. They struggled together ridiculously and ominously, looking, in their white robes, like a couple of frenzied monks. There was, for Alleyn, a sort of pleasure in this fight. "I needn't worry. For once, I needn't worry," he thought. "For once the final arbitrament is as simple as this. I'm fitter than he is."

And when Raoul, absurd in his underpants and long gloves, suddenly hurled himself at Baradi and brought him down with a crash, Alleyn was conscious of a sort of irritation. He looked across the floor and saw that Raoul's foot, in its ridiculous sandal, had pinned down Baradi's left wrist. He saw Baradi's fingers uncurl from the knife-handle. He shoved free, landed a short-arm jab on the point of Baradi's jaw and felt him go soft. They had brought down the prayer wheel in their struggle. Alleyn reached for it and flung it at the window. It crashed through and he heard it fall with the broken glass on the railway line below. Oberon screamed out an oath. Alleyn fetched his breath and blew with all the wind he had on M. Dupont's police whistle. It trilled shrilly, like a toy, and was answered and echoed and answered again outside.

"The house is surrounded," Alleyn said, looking at Glande and Oberon. "I have a police authority. Anyone trying violence or flight will be dealt with out-of-hand. Stay where you are, all of you."

The glare from the sun-burst streamed through the doorway on clouds of incense. Alleyn bound Baradi's arms behind his back with the cord of his gown. Raoul tied his ankles together with the long gloves. Baradi's head lolled drunkenly and he made uncouth noises.

"I want to make a statement," Oberon said shrilly. "I am a British subject. I have my passport. I offer myself for Queen's evidence. I have my passport."

Annabella Wells, standing in the doorway, began to laugh. Carbury Glande said: "Shut up, for God's sake. This is IT."

Abruptly the room was lit. Wall-lamps, a bedside lamp and a standard lamp all came to life. By normal standards it was not a brilliant illumination, but it had the effect of reducing that unlikely interior to an embarrassing state of anti-climax. Glande, Annabella Wells and poor Miss Garbel, huddled in their robes, looked dishevelled and ineffectual. Baradi had a trickle of blood running from his nose into his moustache. The Egyptian servant staggered into the doorway, holding his head in his hands and wearing the foolish expression of a punch-happy pugilist. Oberon, standing before the cracked looking-glass as no doubt he had often done before: Oberon, naked, untactfully lit, was so repellent a sight that Alleyn threw the cover of the divan at him.

"You unspeakable monstrosity," he said, "get behind that."

"I offer a full statement. I am the victim of Dr. Baradi. I claim protection."

Baradi opened his eyes and shook the blood from his moustache.

"I challenge your authority," he said, blinking at Alleyn.

"Alleyn. Chief Detective-Inspector, C.I.D., New Scotland Yard. On loan to the Sûreté. My card and my authority are in my coat-pocket and my coat's in young Herrington's room."

Baradi twisted his head to look at Annabella. "Did you know this?" he demanded.

"Yes, darling," she said.

"You little—"

"Is that Gyppo for what, darling?"

"In a moment," Alleyn said, "the Commissioner of Police will be here and you will be formally arrested and charged. I don't know that I'm obliged to give you the customary warning but the habit's irresistible. Anything you say—"

Baradi and Annabella entirely disregarded him.

"*Why* didn't you tell me who he was?" Baradi said. "*Why?*"

"He asked me not to. He's got something. I didn't know he was here tonight. I didn't think he'd come back."

"Liar!"

"As you choose, my sweet."

"—may be used in evidence."

"You can't charge *me* with anything," Carbury Glande said. "I am an artist. I've formed the habit of smoking and I come to France to do it. I'm not mixed up in anything. If I hadn't had my smokes tonight I'd bloody well fight you."

"Nonsense," said Alleyn.

"I desire to make a statement," said Oberon, who was now wrapped in crimson satin and sitting on the divan.

"I wish to speak to you alone, Mr. Alleyn," said Baradi.

"All in good time."

"Garbel!" Baradi ejaculated.

"Shall I answer him, Roddy dear?"

"If you want to, Cousin Penelope."

"*Cousin!*" Mr. Oberon shouted.

"Only by marriage. I informed you," Miss Garbel reminded him, "of the relationship. And I think it only right to tell you that if it hadn't been for all the Ginnys—"

"My God," Carbury Glande shouted, "where are Ginny and Robin?"

"Ginny!" Oberon cried out. "Where is Ginny?"

"I hope," rejoined Miss Garbel, " 'in no place so unsanctified where such as thou mayst find her.' The quotation, cousin, is from *Macbeth*."

"And couldn't be more appropriate," murmured Alleyn, bowing to her. He sat down at Mr. Oberon's desk and drew a sheet of paper towards him.

"This woman," Baradi said to Alleyn, "is not in her right mind. I tell you this professionally. She has been under my observation for some time. In my considered opinion she is unable to distinguish between fact and fantasy. If you base your preposterous behaviour on any statement of hers—"

"Which I don't, you know."

"I am an Egyptian subject. I claim privilege. And I warn you, that if you hold me, you'll precipitate a political incident."

"My dear M. l'Inspecteur-en-Chef," said M. Dupont, coming in from the passage, "do forgive me if I am a little unpunctual."

"On the contrary, my dear M. le Commissaire, you come most punctually upon your cue."

M. Dupont shook hands with Alleyn. He was in tremendous form,

shining with leather and wax and metal: gloved, holstered and ba-
toned. Three lesser officers appeared inside the door.

"And these," said M. Dupont, touching his moustache and glancing
round the room, "are the personages. You charge them?"

"For the moment, with conspiracy."

"I am a naturalized British subject. I offer myself as Queen's evidence. I charge Dr. Ali Baradi with murder."

Baradi turned his head and in his own language shot a stream of
very raw-sounding phrases at his late partner.

"All these matters," said M. Dupont, "will be dealt with in an appropriate manner. In the meantime, Messieurs et Dames, it is required that
you accompany my officers to the *Poste de Police* in Roqueville where
an accusation will be formally laid." He nodded to his men, who advanced with a play of handcuffs.

Annabella Wells held her robe about her with one practiced hand
and swept back her hair with the other. She addressed herself in French
to Dupont.

"M. le Commissaire, do you recognize me?"

"Perfectly, Madame. Madame is the actress Annabella Wells."

"Monsieur, you are a man of the world. You will understand that I
find myself in a predicament."

"It is not necessary to be a man of the world to discover your predicament, Madame. It is enough to be a policeman. If Madame would care
to make some adjustment to her toilette—a walking costume, perhaps—I
shall be delighted to arrange the facilities. There is a *femme-agent de
police* in attendance."

She looked at him for a moment, seemed to hesitate, and then turned
on Alleyn.

"What are you going to do with me?" she said. "You've trapped me
finely, haven't you? What a fool I was! Yesterday morning I might
have guessed. And I kept faith! I didn't tell them what you were. God,
*what* a fool!"

"It's probably the only really sensible thing you've done since you
came here. Don't regret it."

"Is it wishful thinking or do I seem to catch the suggestion that I
may be given a chance?"

"Give yourself a chance, why not?"

"Ah," she said, shaking her head. "That'll be the day, won't it?"

She grinned at him and moved over to the door where Raoul waited.
Raoul stared at her with a kind of incredulity. He had kicked off his
sandals and wore only his pants and his St. Christopher medal and,
thus arrayed, contrived to look god-like.

"What a charmer!" she said in English. "Aren't you?"

"*Madame?*"

"*Quel charmeur vous êtes!*"

"*Madame!*"

She asked him how old he was and if he had seen many of her films. He said he believed he had seen them all. Was he a cinephile, then? "*Madame,*" Raoul said, "*Je suis un fervent—de vous!*"

"When they let me out of gaol," Annabella promised, "I shall send you a photograph."

The wreckage of her beauty spoke through the ruin of her make-up. She made a good exit.

"Ah, Monsieur," said Raoul. "What a tragedy! And yet it is the art that counts and she is still an artist."

This observation went unregarded. They could hear Annabella in conversation with the *femme-agent* in the passage outside.

"My dear Dupont," Alleyn murmured, "may I suggest that in respect of this woman we make no arrest. I feel certain that she will be of much greater value as a free informant. Keep her under observation, of course, but for the moment, at least—"

"But, of course, my dear Alleyn," M. Dupont rejoined, taking the final plunge into intimacy. "I understand perfectly, but perfectly."

Alleyn was not quite sure what Dupont understood so perfectly but thought it better merely to thank him. He said: "There is a great deal to be explained. May we get rid of the men first?"

Dupont's policemen had taken charge of the four men. Oberon, still wrapped in crimson satin, was huddled on his bed. His floss-like hair hung in strands over his face. Above the silky divided beard the naked mouth was partly open. The eyes stared, apparently without curiosity, at Alleyn.

Dupont's men had lifted Baradi from the floor, seated him on the divan and pulled his white robe about him. His legs had been unbound, but he was now handcuffed. He, too, watched Alleyn, but sombrely, with attentiveness and speculation.

Carbury Glande stood nearby, biting his nails. The Egyptian servant flashed winning smiles at anybody who happened to look at him. Miss Garbel sat at the desk with an air of readiness, like an eccentrically uniformed secretary.

Dupont glanced at the men. "You will proceed under detention to the *Commissariat de Police* at Roqueville. M. l'Inspecteur-en-Chef and I will later conduct an interrogation. The matter of your nationalities and the possibility of extradition will be considered. And now—forward."

Oberon said: "A robe. I demand a robe."

"Look here, Alleyn," Glande said, "what's going to be done about me? I'm harmless, I tell you. For God's sake tell him to let me get some clothes on."

"Your clothes'll be sent after you and you'll get no more and no less than was coming to you," Alleyn said. "In the interest of decency, my dear Dupont, Mr. Oberon should, perhaps, be given a garment of some sort."

Dupont spoke to one of his men, who opened a cupboard-door and brought out a white robe.

"If," Miss Garbel said delicately, "I might be excused. Of course, I don't know—?" She looked enquiringly from Alleyn to Dupont.

"This is Miss Garbel, Dupont, of whom I have told you."

"Truly? Not, as I supposed, the Honourable Locke?"

"Miss Locke has been murdered. She was stabbed through the heart at five thirty-eight yesterday morning in this room. Her body is in a coffin in a room on the other side of the passage-of-entry. Dr. Baradi was good enough to show it to me."

Baradi clasped his manacled hands together and brought them down savagely on his knees. The steel must have cut and bruised him, but he gave no sign.

Glande cried out: "Murdered! My God, they told us she'd given herself an overdose."

"Then the—pardon me, Mademoiselle, if I express it a little crudely —the third English spinster, my dear Inspecteur-en-Chef? The Miss Truebody?"

"Is to the best of my belief recovering from her operation in a room beyond a bridge across the passage-of-entry."

Baradi got clumsily to his feet. He faced the great cheval-glass. He said something in his own language. As he spoke, through the broken window, came the effeminate shriek of a train whistle followed by the labouring up-hill clank of the train itself. Alleyn held up his hand and they were all still and looked through the broken window. Alleyn himself stood beside Baradi, facing the looking-glass, which was at an angle to the window. Baradi made to move but Alleyn put his hand on him and he stood still, as if transfixed. In the great glass they both saw the reflexion of the engine pass by and then the carriages, some of them lit and some in darkness. The train dragged to a standstill. In the last carriage a lighted window, which was opposite their own window, was unshuttered. They could see two men playing cards. The men looked up. Their faces were startled.

Alleyn said: "Look, Baradi. Look in the glass. The angle of incidence is always equal to the angle of refraction, isn't it? We see their reflexion and they see ours. They see you in your white robe. They see your handcuffs. Look, Baradi!"

He had taken a paper-knife from the desk. He raised it in his left hand as if to stab Baradi.

The men in the carriage were agitated. Their images in the glass talked excitedly and gestured. Then, suddenly, they were jerked sideways and in the glass was only the reflexion of the wall and the broken window and the night outside.

"Yesterday morning, at five thirty-eight, I was in a railway carriage out there," Alleyn said. "I saw Grizel Locke fall against the blind and when the blind shot up I saw a man with a dark face and a knife in his right hand. He stood in such a position that the prayer wheel showed over his shoulder and I now know that I saw, not a man, but his reflexion in that glass and I know he stood where you stand and that he was a left-handed man. I know that he was you, Baradi."

"And really, my dear Dupont—" Alleyn said a little later, when the police-car had removed the four men and the two ladies had gone away to change—"really, this is all one has to say about the case. When I saw the room yesterday morning I realized what had happened. There was this enormous cheval-glass screwed into the floor at an angle of about forty-five degrees to the window. To anybody looking in from outside it must completely exclude the right-hand section of the room. And yet, I saw a man, apparently *in* the right-hand section of the room. He must, therefore, have been an image in the glass of a man in the left-hand section of the room. To clinch it, I saw part of the prayer wheel near the right shoulder of the image. Now, if you sit in a railway-carriage outside that window, you will, I think, see part of the prayer wheel, or rather, since I chucked the prayer wheel through the window, you will see part of its trace on the faded wall, just to your left of the glass. The stabber, it was clear, must be a left-handed man and Baradi is the only left-handed man we have. I was puzzled that his face was more shadowed than the direction of the light seemed to warrant. It is, of course, a dark face."

"It is perfectly clear," Dupont said, "though the verdict is not to be decided in advance. The motive was fear, of course."

"Fear of exposure. Miss Garbel believes that Grizel Locke was horrified when her young niece turned up at the Chèvre d'Argent. It became obvious that Ginny Taylor was destined to play the major role, opposite Oberon, in these unspeakable Rites. The day before yesterday it was announced that she would wear the Black Robe tonight. My guess is that Grizel Locke, herself the victim of the extremes of mood that agonize all drug-addicts, brooded on the affair and became frantic with—with what emotion? Remorse? Anxiety? Shame?"

"But jealousy? She is, after all, about to become the supplanted mistress, is she not? Always an unpopular assignment."

"Perhaps she was moved by all of these emotions. Perhaps, after a sleepless night or—God knows—a night of pleading, she threatened to expose the drug racket if Oberon persisted with Ginny Taylor. Oberon, finding her intractable, summoned Baradi. She threatened both of them. The scene rose to a climax. Perhaps—is it too wild a guess?—she hears the train coming and threatens to scream out their infamy from the window. Baradi reverts to type and uses a knife, probably one of the symbolic knives with which they frighten the initiates. She falls against the blind and it flies up. There, outside, is the train with a dimly lighted compartment opposite their own window. And, between the light and the window of the compartment is the shape of a man—myself."

Dupont lightly struck his hands together. "A pretty situation, in effect!"

"He no sooner takes it in than it is over. The train enters the tunnel and Baradi and Oberon are left with Grizel Locke's body on their hands. And within an hour I ring up about Miss Truebody. And by the way, I suggest we visit Miss Truebody. Here comes Miss Garbel who, I daresay, will show us to her room."

Miss Garbel appeared, scarcely recognizable, wearing an unsmart coat and skirt and no make-up. It was impossible to believe this was the woman who, an hour ago, had lent herself to the Rites of the Children of the Sun and who, yesterday morning, had appeared in pedal-pushers and a scarf on the roof-garden. Dupont looked at her with astonishment. She was very tremulous and obviously distressed. She went to the point, however, with the odd directness that Alleyn was learning to expect from her.

"You are yourself again, I see," he said.

"Alas, yes! Or not, of course altogether, alas. It is nice not having to pretend to be poor Grizel any more but, as you noticed, I found it only too easy, at certain times, to let myself go. I sometimes think it is a peculiar property of marihuana to reduce all its victims to a common denominator. When we are 'high,' as poor Grizel used to call it, we all behave rather in her manner. I am badly in need of a smoke now, after all the upset, which is why I'm so shaky, you know."

"I expect you'd like to go back to your own room in the Rue des Violettes. We'll take you there."

"I would like it of all things, but I think I should stay to look after

our patient, I've been doing quite a bit of the nursing—Mahomet and I
took it in turns with one of the maids. Under the doctor's instructions,
of course. Would you like to see her?"

"Indeed, we should. It's going to be difficult to cope with Miss
Truebody. Of course, they never sent for a nurse?"

"No, no! Too dangerous, by far. But I assure you every care has been
taken of the poor thing."

"I'll bet it has. They didn't want two bodies on their hands. M. le
Commissaire has arranged for a doctor and a nurse to come up by the
night train from St. Christophe. In the meantime, shall we visit
her?"

Miss Garbel led the way up to the front landing. M. Dupont indicated the wrought-iron door. "We discovered the key, my dear
Alleyn," he said gaily. "An excellent move!" They climbed to the roof-
garden and thence through a labyrinth of rooms to one of the bridge-
like extensions that straddled the outside passage-way.

They were half-way across this bridge when their attention was
caught by the sound of voices and of boots on the cobblestones below.

From the balustrade they looked down into a scene that might have
been devised by a film director. The sides of the house fell away from
moon-patched shadow into a deep blackness. At one point a pool of
light from an open door lay across the passage-way. Into this light
moved an incongruous company of foreshortened figures: the Egyptian
servant, Baradi and Oberon in their white robes, Carbury Glande bareheaded and in shorts, and six gendarmes in uniform. They shifted in
and out of the light, a curious pattern of heads and shoulders.

"*Alors*," said Dupont, looking down at them: "*Bon débarras!*"

His voice echoed stonily in the passage. One of the white hoods was
tilted backwards. The face inside it was thus exposed to the light but,
being itself dark, seemed still to be in shadow. Alleyn and Baradi
looked at each other. With a peck of his head Baradi spat into the night.

"*Pas de ça!*" said one of the gendarmes and turned Baradi about. It
was then seen that he was handcuffed to his companion.

"Mr. Oberon," Alleyn said, "will be delighted."

The procession moved off with a hollow clatter down the passage.
Raoul appeared in the doorway, rolling a cigarette, and watched them
go.

Miss Garbel made a curious and desolate sound but immediately afterwards said brightly: "Shall we—?" and led them indoors.

"Here we are!" she said and tapped. A door was opened by the
woman Alleyn had already seen at Miss Truebody's bedside.

"These are the friends of Mademoiselle," said Miss Garbel. "Is she awake?"

"She is awake but M. le Docteur left orders, Mademoiselle, that no one—" She saw Dupont's uniform and her voice faded.

"M. le Docteur," said Miss Garbel, "has reconsidered his order."

The woman stood aside and they went into the room. Dupont stayed by the door but Alleyn walked over to the bed. There, on the pillow, was the smooth, blunt and singularly hairless face he had remembered. She looked at him and smiled and this time she was wearing her teeth. They made a great difference.

"Why, it's Mr. Alleyn," she murmured in a thread-like voice. "How kind!"

"You're getting along splendidly," Alleyn said. "I won't tire you now, but if there is anything you want you'll let us know."

"Nothing. Much better. The doctor—too kind."

"There will be another doctor tomorrow and a new nurse to help these."

"Not—? But—Dr. Baradi—?"

"He has been obliged to go away," Alleyn said, "on a case of some urgency."

"Oh." She closed her eyes.

Alleyn and Dupont went outside. Miss Garbel came to the door.

"If you don't want me," she said, "I'll stay and take my turn. I'm all right, you know. Quite reliable until morning."

"And always," he rejoined warmly.

"Ah," she said, shaking her head. "That's another story."

She showed them where a stairway ran down to ground level and she peered after them, smiling and nodding over the banister.

"We must pay one more visit," Alleyn said.

"The third English spinster," Dupont agreed. He seemed to have a sort of relish for this phrase.

But when they stood in the whitewashed room and the raw light from an unshaded lamp now shone dreadfully on what was left of Grizel Locke, he looked thoughtful and said: "All three, each after her own fashion, may be said to have served the cause of justice."

"This one," Alleyn said drily, "may be said to have died for it."

## V

It was a quarter past two when Grizel Locke was carried in her coffin down to a mortuary van that shone glossily in the moonlight. Two hours later Alleyn and Dupont walked out of the Château de la Chèvre d'Argent. They left two men on guard and with Raoul went down the passage-way to the open platform. It was flooded in moonlight. The Mediterranean glittered down below and the hills reared themselves up fabulously against the stars. Robin Herrington's rakish car was parked at the edge of the platform.

Alleyn said: "These are our chickens come home to roost."

"Ah!" said M. Dupont cosily. "It is a night for love."

"Nevertheless, if you will excuse me—"

"But, of course!"

Alleyn, whistling tunelessly and tactfully, went over to the car. Robin was in the driver's seat with Ginny beside him. Her head was on his shoulder. He showed no particular surprise at seeing Alleyn.

"Good morning," Alleyn said. "So you had a breakdown."

"We did, sir, but we think we're under our own steam again."

"I'm glad to hear it. You will find the Chèvre d'Argent rather empty. Here's my card. The gendarme at the door will let you in. If you'd rather collect your possessions and come back to Roqueville, I expect we could get rooms for you both at the Royal."

He waited for an answer but it was perfectly clear to him that although they smiled and nodded brightly they had not taken in a word of his little speech.

Robin said: "Ginny's going to marry me."

"I hope you will both be *very* happy."

"We think of beginning again in one of the Dominions."

"The Dominions are, on the whole, both tolerant and helpful."

Ginny, speaking for the first time, said: "Will you please thank Mrs. Alleyn? She sort of did the trick."

"I shall. She'll be delighted to hear it." He looked at them for a moment and they beamed back at him. "You'll be all right," he said. "Get a tough job and forget you've had bad dreams. I'm sure it will work out."

They smiled and nodded.

"I'll have to ask you to come and see me later in the morning. At the Préfecture at eleven?"

"Thank you," they said vaguely. Ginny said: "You can't think how happy we are, all of a sudden. And just imagine, I was furious when the car broke down! And yet, if it hadn't, we might never have found out."

"Strange coincidence," said Alleyn, looking at Robin. And seeing that they were incapable of coming out of the moonlight he said: "Good morning and good luck to you both," and left them to themselves.

On the way down to Roqueville he and Dupont discussed the probable development of the case. "Oberon," Alleyn said, "has gone to pieces, as you see. He will try and buy his way out with information." "Callard also is prepared to upset the peas. But thanks to your admirable handling of the case we shall be able to dispense with such aids, and Oberon, I trust, will be tried with Baradi."

"Of the pair, Oberon is undoubtedly the more revolting," Alleyn said thoughtfully. "I wonder how many deaths could be laid at the door of those two. I don't know how you feel about it, Dupont, but I put their sort at the top of the criminal list. If they hadn't directly killed poor Grizel, by God, they'd still be mass murderers."

"Undoubtedly," said Dupont, stifling a yawn. "I imagine we take statements from the painter, the actress Wells and the two young ones and let it go at that. They may be more useful running free. Particularly if they return to the habit."

"The young ones won't. I'm sure of that. As for the others: there are cures."

In the front seat, Raoul, influenced no doubt by the moonlight and by his glimpse of Ginny and Robin, began to sing:

"*La nuit est faite pour l'amour.*"

"Raoul," Alleyn said in French for his benefit, "did a good job of work tonight, didn't he?"

"Not so bad, not so bad. We shall have you in the service yet, my friend," said Dupont. He leaned forward and struck Raoul lightly on the shoulder.

"No, M. le Commissaire, it is not my *métier*. I am about to settle with Teresa. And yet, if M. l'Inspecteur-en-Chef Alleyn should come back one day, who knows?"

They drove through the sleeping town to the little Square des Sarracins and put Alleyn down at the hotel.

Troy was fast asleep, with Ricky curled in beside her. The little silver goat illuminated himself on the bedside table. The French windows were wide open and Alleyn went out for a moment on the balcony. To the east the stars had turned pale and the first dawn cock was crowing in the hills above Roqueville.

# OVERTURE
# TO DEATH

# Contents

| Chapter I | The Meet at Pen Cuckoo | 441 |
|---|---|---|
| Chapter II | Six Parts and Seven Actors | 452 |
| Chapter III | They Choose a Play | 461 |
| Chapter IV | Cue for Music | 470 |
| Chapter V | Above Cloudyfold | 477 |
| Chapter VI | Rehearsal | 486 |
| Chapter VII | Vignettes | 494 |
| Chapter VIII | Catastrophe | 501 |
| Chapter IX | C. I. D. | 509 |
| Chapter X | According to Templett | 517 |
| Chapter XI | According to Roper | 526 |
| Chapter XII | Further Vignettes | 535 |
| Chapter XIII | Sunday Morning | 542 |
| Chapter XIV | According to the Jernighams | 551 |
| Chapter XV | Alleyn Goes to Church | 561 |
| Chapter XVI | The Top Lane Incident | 574 |
| Chapter XVII | Confession from a Priest | 587 |
| Chapter XVIII | Mysterious Lady | 597 |
| Chapter XIX | Statement from Templett | 607 |
| Chapter XX | According to Miss Wright | 617 |
| Chapter XXI | According to Mr. Saul Tranter | 628 |
| Chapter XXII | Letter to Troy | 638 |
| Chapter XXIII | Frightened Lady | 645 |
| Chapter XXIV | The Peculiarity of Miss P. | 654 |
| Chapter XXV | Final Vignettes | 667 |
| Chapter XXVI | Miss Prentice Feels the Draught | 674 |
| Chapter XXVII | Case Ends | 685 |

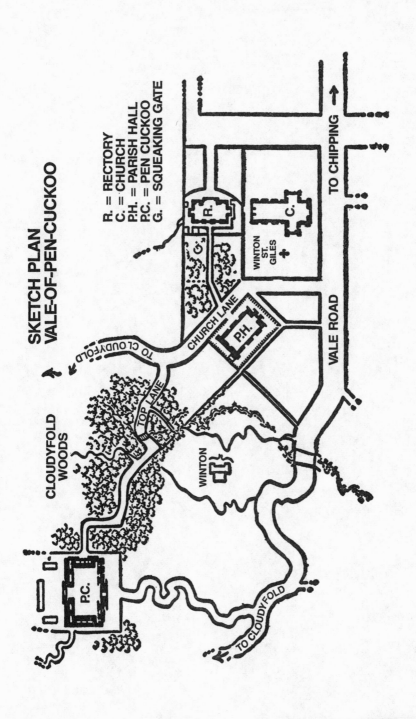

SKETCH PLAN
VALE-OF-PEN-CUCKOO

R. = RECTORY
C. = CHURCH
P.H. = PARISH HALL
P.C. = PEN CUCKOO
G. = SQUEAKING GATE

# CHAPTER I

# The Meet at Pen Cuckoo

## I

JOCELYN JERNIGHAM was a good name. The seventh Jocelyn thought so
as he stood at his study window and looked down the vale of Pen
Cuckoo towards that precise spot where the spire of Salisbury Cathedral could be seen through field-glasses on a clear day.

"Here I stand," he said, without turning his head, "and here my
forebears have stood, generation after generation, and looked over their
own tilth and tillage. Seven Jocelyn Jernighams."

"I'm never quite sure," said his son Henry Jocelyn, "what tilth and
tillage are. What precisely, Father, is a tilth?"

"There's no feeling for that sort of thing," said Jocelyn, angrily,
"among the present generation. Cheap sneers and clever talk that mean
nothing."

"But I assure you I like words to mean something. That is why I ask
you to define a tilth. And you say, 'the present generation.' You mean
my generation, don't you? But I'm twenty-three. There is a newer generation than mine. If I marry Dinah——"

"You quibble deliberately in order to lead our conversation back to
this absurd suggestion. If I had known——"

Henry uttered an impatient noise and moved away from the fireplace. He joined his father in the window and he too looked down into the darkling vale of Pen Cuckoo. He saw an austere landscape, adamant beneath drifts of winter mist. The naked trees slept soundly, the fields were dumb with cold; the few stone cottages, with their comfortable signals of blue smoke, were the only waking things in all the valley.

"I too love Pen Cuckoo," said Henry, and he added, with that tinge of irony which Jocelyn, who did not understand it, found so irritating: "I have all the pride of prospective ownership. But I refuse to be bully-ragged by Pen Cuckoo. I refuse to play the part of a Victorian young gentleman with a touch of Cophetua thrown in. I refuse to allow this conversation to run along the lines of ancient lineage. The proud father and self-willed heir stuff simply doesn't fit. We are not discussing a possible misalliance. Dinah is not a blushing maid of inferior station. She is part of the country, rooted equally with us. If we are going to talk about her in county terms, I can strike a suitable attitude and say there have been Copelands at the rectory for as many generations as there have been Jernighams at Pen Cuckoo."

"You are both much too young——" began Jocelyn.

"No, really, sir, that won't do. What you mean is that Dinah is too poor. If it had been somebody smarter and richer, you and my dear cousin Eleanor wouldn't have talked about youth. Don't let's pretend."

"And don't you talk to me like a damned sententious young puppy, Henry, because I won't have it."

"I'm sorry," said Henry, "I know I'm being tiresome."

"You're being extremely tiresome. Very well, I'll speak as plainly as you like. Pen Cuckoo means more to me and should mean more to you, than anything else in life. You know as well as I do that we're damned hard up. There are all sorts of things that should be done to the place. Those cottages up at Cloudyfold! Winton! Rumbold tells me that Winton'll leak like a basket if we don't fix up the roof. The point is——"

"I can't afford to make a poor marriage?"

"If you choose to put it like that."

"How else can one put it?"

"Very well, then."

"Well, since we must speak in terms of hard cash, which I assure you I don't enjoy, Dinah won't always be the poor parson's one ewe lamb."

"What d'you mean?" asked Jocelyn, uneasily, but with a certain air of pricking up his ears.

"I thought everybody knew Miss Campanula has left all her filthy lucre, or most of it, to the rector. Don't pretend, Father; you must have

heard that piece of gossip. The cook and housemaid witnessed the will
and the housemaid overheard Miss C. bawling about it to her lawyer.
Dinah doesn't want the money—nor do I—much—but that's what'll
happen to it eventually."

"Servant's gossip," muttered the squire. "Most distasteful. Anyway, it
may not—she may change her mind. It's *now* we're so damned hard-
up."

"Let me find a job of work," Henry said.

"Your job of work is here."

"What! with a perfectly good agent who looks upon me as a sort of
impediment in his agricultural speech?"

"Nonsense!"

"Look here, Father," said Henry gently, "how much of this has been
inspired by Eleanor?"

"Eleanor is as anxious as I am that you shouldn't make a bloody fool
of yourself. If your mother had been alive——"

"No, no," cried Henry, "let us not put ideas into the minds of the
dead. That is so grossly unfair. Let's recognize Eleanor's hand in this.
Eleanor has been too clever by half. I didn't mean to tell you about
Dinah until I was sure that she loved me. I am not sure. The scene,
which Eleanor so conveniently overheard yesterday at the rectory, was
purely tentative." He broke off, turned away from his father, and
pressed his cheek against the window pane.

"It is intolerable," said Henry, "that Eleanor should have spoiled the
memory of my first—my first approach to Dinah. To stand in the hall,
as she must have done, and to listen! To come clucking back to you like
a vulgar hen, agog with her news! As if Dinah were a housemaid with
a follower. No, it's too much!"

"You've never been fair to Eleanor. She's done her best to take your
mother's place."

"For God's sake," said Henry violently, "don't use that detestable
phrase! Cousin Eleanor has never taken my mother's place. She is an
aging spinster cousin of the worst type. It was not particularly kind of
her to come to Pen Cuckoo. Indeed, it was her golden opportunity. She
left the Cromwell Road for the glories of 'county.' It was the great moment of her life. She's a vulgarian."

"On her mother's side," said Jocelyn, "she's a Jernigham."

"Oh, my dear father!" said Henry, and burst out laughing.

Jocelyn glared at his son, turned purple in the face, and began to
stammer.

"You may laugh, but Eleanor—Eleanor—in bringing this information

—unavoidably overheard—no question of eavesdropping—only doing what she believed to be her duty."

"I'm sure she told you that."

"She did and I agreed with her. I am most strongly opposed to this affair with Dinah, and I am most relieved to hear that so far it is, as you put it, purely tentative."

"If Dinah loves me," said Henry, setting the Jernigham jaw, "I shall marry her. And that's flat. If Eleanor wasn't here to jog at your pride, Father, you would at least try to see my side. But Eleanor won't let you. She dramatizes herself as the first lady of the district. The squiress. The chatelaine of Pen Cuckoo. She sees Dinah as a sort of rival. What's more, I believe she's genuinely jealous of Dinah. It's the jealousy of a woman of her age and disposition, a jealousy rooted in sex."

"Disgusting balderdash!" said Jocelyn, angrily, but he looked uncomfortable.

"No!" cried Henry. "No, it's not. I'm not talking highbrow pornography. You must have seen what Eleanor is. She's an avid woman. She was in love with you until she found it was a hopeless proposition. Now she and her girl friend the Campanula are rivals for the rector. Dinah says all old maids always fall in love with her father. Everybody sees it. It's a recognized phenomenon with women of Eleanor's and Idris Campanula's type. Have you heard her on the subject of Dr. Templett and Selia Ross? She's nosed out a scandal there. The next thing that happens will be Eleanor feeling it her duty to warn poor Mrs. Templett that her husband is too fond of the widow. That is, if Idris Campanula doesn't get in first. Women like Eleanor and Miss Campanula are pathological. Dinah says——"

"Do you and Dinah discuss my cousin's attachment, which I don't admit, for the rector? If you do, I consider it shows an extraordinary lack of manners and taste."

"Dinah and I," said Henry, "discuss everything."

"And this is modern love-making!"

"Don't let's start abusing each other's generations, Father. We've never done that. You've been so extraordinarily understanding in so many ways. It's Eleanor!" said Henry. "It's Eleanor, Eleanor, Eleanor who is to blame for this!"

The door at the far end of the room was opened and against the lamplit hall beyond appeared a woman's figure.

"Did I hear you call me, Henry?" asked a quiet voice.

## II

Miss Eleanor Prentice came into the room. She reached out a thin hand and switched on the lights.

"It's past five o'clock," said Miss Prentice. "Almost time for our little meeting. I asked them all for half-past five."

She walked with small mincing steps towards the cherrywood table which, Henry noticed, had been moved from the wall into the center of the study. Miss Prentice began to place pencils and sheets of paper at intervals round the table. As she did this she produced, from between her thin closed lips, a dreary flat humming which irritated Henry almost beyond endurance. More to stop this noise than because he wanted to know the answer, Henry asked:

"What meeting, Cousin Eleanor?"

"Have you forgotten, dear? The entertainment committee. The rector and Dinah, Dr. Templett, Idris Campanula, and ourselves. We are counting on you. And on Dinah, of course."

She uttered this last phrase with additional sweetness. Henry thought, "She knows we've been talking about Dinah." As she fiddled with her pieces of paper Henry watched her with that peculiar intensity that people sometimes lavish on a particularly loathed individual.

Eleanor Prentice was a thin, colorless woman of perhaps forty-nine years. She disseminated the odor of sanctity to an extent that Henry found intolerable. Her perpetual half-smile suggested that she was of a gentle and sweet disposition. This faint smile caused many people to overlook the strength of her face, and that was a mistake, for its strength was considerable. Miss Prentice was indeed a Jernigham. Henry suddenly thought that it was rather hard on Jocelyn that both his cousin and his son should look so much more like the family portraits than he did. Henry and Eleanor had each got the nose and jaw proper to the family. The squire had inherited his mother's round chin and indeterminate nose. Miss Prentice's prominent gray eyes stared coldly upon the world through rimless pince-nez. The squire's blue eyes, even when inspired by his frequent twists of ineffectual temper, looked vulnerable and slightly surprised. Henry, still watching her, thought it strange that he himself should resemble this woman whom he disliked so cordially. Without a taste in common, with violently opposed views on almost all ethical issues, and with a profound mutual distrust, they yet shared a certain hard determination which each recognized in the other. In Henry this quality was tempered by courtesy and by a generous mind. She was merely polite and long-suffering. It was typical of her that although she had evidently overheard Henry's angry reiteration of her name, she accepted his silence and did not ask again why he had called her. Probably, he thought, because she had stood outside the door listening. She now began to pull forward the chairs.

"I think we must give the rector your arm-chair, Jocelyn," she said. "Henry, dear, would you mind? It's rather heavy."

Henry and Jocelyn helped her with the chair and, at her instruction, threw more logs of wood on the fire. These arrangements completed, Miss Prentice settled herself at the table.

"I think your study is almost my favorite corner of Pen Cuckoo, Jocelyn," she said brightly.

The squire muttered something, and Henry said, "But you are very fond of every corner of the house, aren't you, Cousin Eleanor?"

"Yes," she said softly. "Ever since my childhood days when I used to spend my holidays here (you remember, Jocelyn?) I've loved the dear old home."

"Estate agents," Henry said, "have cast a permanent opprobrium on the word 'home.' It has come to mean nothing. It is a pity that when I marry, Cousin Eleanor, I shall not be able to take my wife to Winton. I can't afford to mend the roof, you know."

Jocelyn cleared his throat, darted an angry glance at his son, and returned to the window.

"Winton is the dower-house, of course," murmured Miss Prentice.

"As you already know," Henry continued, "I have begun to pay my address to Dinah Copeland. From what you overheard at the rectory do you think it likely that she will accept me?"

He saw her eyes narrow but she smiled a little more widely, showing her prominent and unlovely teeth. "She's like a French caricature of an English spinster," thought Henry.

"I'm quite sure, dear," said Miss Prentice, "that you do not think I willingly overheard your little talk with Dinah. Far from it. I was very distressed when I caught the few words that——"

"That you repeated to father? I'm sure you were."

"I thought it my duty to speak to your father, Henry."

"Why?"

"Because I think, dear, that you two young people are in need of a little wise guidance."

"Do you like Dinah?" asked Henry abruptly.

"She has many excellent qualities, I am sure," said Miss Prentice.

"I asked you if you liked her, Cousin Eleanor."

"I like her for those qualities. I am afraid, dear, that I think it better not to go any further just at the moment."

"I agree," said Jocelyn from the window. "Henry, I won't have any more of this. These people will be here in a moment. There's the rectory car, now, coming round Cloudyfold bend. They'll be here in five minutes. You'd better tell us what it's all about, Eleanor."

Miss Prentice seated herself at the foot of the table.

"It's the Y.P.F.C.," she said. "We badly want funds and the rector suggested that perhaps we might get up a little play. You remember, Jocelyn. It was the night we dined there."

"I remember something about it," said the squire.

"Just among ourselves," continued Miss Prentice, "I know you've always loved acting, Jocelyn, and you're so good at it. So natural. Do you remember *Ici on Parle Français* in the old days? I've talked it all over with the rector and he agrees it's a splendid idea. Dr. Templett is *very* good at theatricals, especially in funny parts, and dear Idris Campanula, of course, is all enthusiasm."

"Good Lord!" ejaculated Henry and his father together.

"What on earth is *she* going to do in the play?" asked Jocelyn.

"Now, Jocelyn, we mustn't be uncharitable," said Miss Prentice, with a cold glint of satisfaction in her eye. "I dare say poor Idris would make quite a success of a small part."

"I'm too old," said Jocelyn.

"What nonsense, dear. Of course you're not. We'll find something that suits you."

"I'm damned if I'll make love to the Campanula," said the squire, ungallantly. Eleanor assumed her usual expression for the reception of bad language, but it was colored by that glint of complacency.

"Please, Jocelyn," she said.

"What's Dinah going to do?" asked Henry.

"Well, as dear Dinah is almost a professional——"

"She *is* a professional," said Henry.

"Such a pity, yes," said Miss Prentice.

"Why?"

"I am old-fashioned enough to think that the stage is not a very nice profession for a gentlewoman, Henry. But of course Dinah must act in our little piece. If she isn't too grand for such humble efforts."

Henry opened his mouth and shut it again. The squire said, "Here they are."

There was the sound of a car pulling up on the gravel drive outside, and two cheerful toots on an out-of-date klaxon.

"I'll go and bring them in," offered Henry.

*III*

Henry went out through the hall. When he opened the great front door the upland air laid its cold hand on his face. He smelt frost, dank earth, and dead leaves. The light from the house showed him three figures climbing out of a small car. The rector, his daughter Dinah, and a tall woman in a shapeless fur coat—Idris Campanula. Henry produced the right welcoming noises and ushered them into the house. Taylor, the butler, appeared, and laid expert hands on the rector's shabby overcoat. Henry, his eyes on Dinah, dealt with Miss Campanula's furs. The hall rang with Miss Campanula's conversation. She was a large arrogant spinster with a firm bust, a high-colored complexion, coarse gray hair, and enormous bony hands. Her clothes were hideous but expensive, for Miss Campanula was extremely wealthy. She was supposed to be Eleanor Prentice's great friend. Their alliance was based on mutual antipathies and interests. Each adored scandal and each cloaked her passion in a mantle of conscious rectitude. Neither trusted the other an inch, but there was no doubt that they enjoyed each other's company. In conversation their technique varied widely. Eleanor never relinquished her air of charity and when she struck, the blow always fell obliquely. But Idris was one of those women who pride themselves on their outspokenness. Repeatedly did she announce that she was a downright sort of person. She was particularly fond of saying that she called a spade a spade, and in her more daring moments would add that her cousin, General Campanula, had once told her that she went further than that and called it a "B. shovel." She cultivated an air of bluff forthrightness that should have deceived nobody, but actually passed as true currency among the simpler of her acquaintances. The truth was that she reserved to herself the right of broad speech, but would have been livid with rage if anybody had replied in kind.

The rector, a widower whose classic handsomeness made him the prey of such women, was, so Dinah had told Henry, secretly terrified of both these ladies who loomed so large in parochial affairs. Eleanor Prentice had a sort of coy bedside manner with the rector. She spoke to him in a dove-smooth voice and frequently uttered little musical laughs. Idris Campanula was bluff and proprietary, called him "my dear man" and watched him with an intensity that made him blink, and aroused in his daughter a conflicting fury of disgust and compassion.

Henry laid aside the fur coat and hurried to Dinah. He had known Dinah all his life, but while he was at Oxford and later, when he did a course with a volunteer air-reserve unit, he had seen little of her. When he returned to Pen Cuckoo, Dinah had finished her dramatic course, and had managed to get into the tail end of a small repertory company where she remained for six weeks. The small repertory company then fell to pieces and Dinah returned home, an actress. Three weeks ago he had met her unexpectedly on the hills above Cloudyfold, and with that encounter came love. He had felt as if he saw her for the first time. The bewildering rapture of discovery was still upon him. To meet her gaze, to speak to her, to stand near her, launched him upon a flood of bliss. His sleep was tinged with the color of his love and when he woke he found her already waiting in his thought. "She is my whole desire," he said to himself. And, because he was not quite certain that she loved him in return, he had been afraid to declare himself until yesterday, in the shabby, charming old drawing-room at the rectory, when Dinah had looked so transparently into his eyes that he began to speak of love. And then, through the open door, he had seen Eleanor, a still figure in the dark hall beyond. Dinah saw Eleanor a moment later and, without a word to Henry, went out and welcomed her. Henry himself had rushed out of the rectory and driven home to Pen Cuckoo in a white rage. He had not spoken to Dinah since then, and now he looked anxiously at her. Her wide gray eyes smiled at him.

"Dinah?"

"Henry?"

"When can I see you?"

"You see me now," said Dinah.

"Alone. Please?"

"I don't know. Is anything wrong?"

"Eleanor."

"Oh, Lord!" said Dinah.

"I must talk to you. Above Cloudyfold where we met that morning? To-morrow, before breakfast, Dinah, will you?"

"All right," said Dinah. "If I can."

Idris Campanula's conversation flowed in upon their consciousness. Henry was suddenly aware that she had asked him some sort of question.

"I'm so sorry," he began. "I'm afraid I——"

"Now, Henry," she interrupted, "where are we to go? You're forgetting your duties, gossiping there with Dinah." And she laughed her loud rocketing bray.

"The study, please," said Henry. "Will you lead the way?"

She marched into the study, shook hands with Jocelyn and exchanged pecks with Eleanor Prentice.

"Where's Dr. Templett?" she asked.

"He hasn't arrived yet," answered Miss Prentice. "We must always make allowances for our medical men, mustn't we?"

"He's up beyond Cloudyfold," said the rector. "Old Mrs. Thrinne is much worse. The third Cain boy has managed to run a nail through his big toe. I met Templett in the village and he told me. He said I was to ask you not to wait."

"Beyond Cloudyfold?" asked Miss Prentice sweetly. Henry saw her exchange a glance with Miss Campanula.

"Mrs. Ross doesn't have tea till five," said Miss Campanula, "which I consider a silly ostentation. We certainly will *not* wait for Dr. Templett. Ha!"

"Templett didn't say anything about going to Mrs. Ross's," said the rector, innocently, "though to be sure it is on his way."

"My dear good man," said Miss Campanula, "if you weren't a saint—however! I only hope he doesn't try and get her into our play."

"Idris, dear," said Miss Prentice. "May I?"

She collected their attention and then said very quietly:

"I think we are all agreed, aren't we, that this little experiment is to be just among ourselves? I have got several little plays here for five and six people and I fancy Dinah has found some too."

"Six," said Miss Campanula very firmly. "Five characters won't do, Eleanor. We've three ladies and three men. And if the rector——"

"No," said the rector, "I shall not appear. If there's any help I can give behind the scenes, I shall be only too delighted, but I really don't want to appear."

"Three ladies and three men, then," said Miss Campanula. "Six."

"Certainly no more," said Miss Prentice.

"Well," said the squire, "if Mrs. Ross is very good at acting, and I must say she's an uncommonly attractive little thing——"

"No, Jocelyn," said Miss Prentice.

"She is very attractive," said Henry.

"She's got a good figure," said Dinah. "Has she had any experience?"

"My dear child," said Miss Campanula loudly, "she's as common as dirt and we certainly don't want her. I may say that I myself have seen Eleanor's plays and I fully approve of *Simple Susan*. There are six characters: three men and three ladies. There is no change of scene, and the theme is suitable."

"It's rather old," said Dinah dubiously.

"My dear child," repeated Miss Campanula, "if you think we're going to do one of your modern questionable problem-plays you're very greatly mistaken."

"I think some of the modern pieces are really *not* quite suitable," agreed Miss Prentice gently.

Henry and Dinah smiled.

"And as for Mrs. Selia Ross," said Miss Campanula, "I believe in calling a spade a spade and I have no hesitation in saying I think we'll be doing a Christian service to poor Mrs. Templett, who we all know is too much an invalid to look after herself, if we give Dr. Templett something to think about besides——"

"Come," said the rector desperately, "aren't we jumping our fences before we meet them? We haven't appointed a chairman yet and so far nobody has suggested that Mrs. Ross be asked to take part."

"They'd better not," said Miss Campanula.

The door was thrown open by Taylor, who announced:

"Mrs. Ross and Dr. Templett, sir."

"What!" exclaimed the squire involuntarily.

An extremely well-dressed woman and a short rubicund man walked into the room.

"Hullo! Hullo!" shouted Dr. Templett. "I've brought Mrs. Ross along by sheer force. She's a perfectly magnificent actress and I tell her she's got to come off her high horse and show us all how to set about it. I know you'll be delighted."

# CHAPTER II

# Six Parts and Seven Actors

## I

IT WAS HENRY who rescued the situation when it was on the verge of becoming a scene. Neither Miss Campanula nor Miss Prentice made the slightest attempt at cordiality. The squire uttered incoherent noises, shouted "What!" and broke out into uncomfortable social laughter. Dinah greeted Mrs. Ross with nervous civility. The rector blinked and followed his daughter's example. But on Henry the presence of Dinah acted like a particularly strong stimulant and filled him with a vague desire to be nice to the entire population of the world. He shook Mrs. Ross warmly by the hand, complimented Dr. Templett on his idea, and suggested, with a beaming smile, that they should at once elect a chairman and decide on a play.

The squire, Dinah, and the rector confusedly supported Henry. Miss Campanula gave a ringing sniff. Miss Prentice, smiling a little more widely than usual, said:

"I'm afraid we are short of one chair. We expected to be only seven. Henry dear, you will have to get one from the dining-room. I'm so sorry to bother you."

"I'll share Dinah's chair," said Henry happily.

"Please don't get one for me," said Mrs. Ross. "Billy can perch on my arm."

She settled herself composedly in a chair on the rector's left and Dr. Templett at once sat on the arm. Miss Prentice had already made sure of her place on the rector's right hand and Miss Campanula, defeated, uttered a short laugh and marched to the far end of the table.

"I don't know whether this is where I am bidden, Eleanor," she said, "but the meeting seems to be delightfully informal, so this is where I shall sit. Ha!"

Henry, his father, and Dinah took the remaining chairs.

From the old chandelier a strong light was cast down on the eight faces round the table; on the squire, pink with embarrassment; on Miss Prentice, smiling; on Miss Campanula, like an angry mare, breathing hard through her nostrils; on Henry's dark Jernigham features; on Dinah's crisp and vivid beauty; on the rector's coin-sharp priestliness and on Dr. Templett's hearty undistinguished normality. It shone on Selia Ross. She was a straw-colored woman of perhaps thirty-eight. She was not beautiful but she was exquisitely neat. Her hair curved back from her forehead in pale waves. The thick white skin of her face was beautifully made-up and her clothes were admirable. There was a kind of sharpness about her so that she nearly looked haggard. Her eyes were pale and you would have guessed that the lashes were white when left to themselves. Almost every human being bears some sort of resemblance to an animal and Mrs. Ross was a little like a ferret. But for all that she had a quality that arrested the attention of many women and most men. She had a trick of widening her eyes, and looking slantways. Though she gave the impression of fineness she was in reality so determined that any sensibilities she possessed were held in the vice of her will. She was a coarse-grained woman but she seemed fragile. Her manner was gay and good-natured, but though she went out of her way to do kindnesses, her tongue was quietly malicious. It was clear to all women who met her that her chief interest was men. Dinah watched her now and could not help admiring the cool assurance with which she met her frigid reception. It was impossible to guess whether Mrs. Ross was determined not to show her hurts or was merely so insensitive that she felt none. "She *has* got a cheek," thought Dinah. She looked at Henry and saw her own thoughts reflected in his face. Henry's rather startlingly fierce eyes were fixed on Mrs. Ross and in them Dinah read both awareness and appraisal. He turned his head, met Dinah's glance, and at once his expression changed into one of such vivid tenderness that her heart turned over. She was drowned in a wave of emotion and was brought back to the world by the sound of Miss Prentice's voice.

"——to elect a chairman for our little meeting. I should like to propose the rector."

"Second that," said Miss Campanula, in her deepest voice.

"There you are, Copeland," said the squire, "everybody says 'Aye' and away we go." He laughed loudly and cast a terrified glance at his cousin.

The rector looked amiably round the table. With the exception of Henry, of all the company he seemed the least embarrassed by the arrival of Mrs. Ross. If Mr. Copeland had been given a round gentle face with unremarkable features and kind shortsighted eyes it would have been a perfect expression of his temperament. But ironical nature had made him magnificently with a head so beautiful that to most observers it seemed that his character must also be on a grand scale. With that head he might have gone far and become an important dignitary of the church, but he was unambitious and sincere, and he loved Pen Cuckoo. He was quite content to live at the rectory as his forebears had lived, to deal with parish affairs, to give what spiritual and bodily comfort he could to his people, and to fend off the advances of Idris Campanula and Eleanor Prentice. He knew very well that both these ladies bitterly resented the presence of Mrs. Ross, and that he was in for one of those hideously boring situations when he felt exactly as if he was holding down with his thumb the cork of a bottle filled with seething ginger-pop.

He said, "Thank you very much. I don't feel that my duties as chairman will be very heavy as we have only met to settle the date and nature of this entertainment, and when that is decided all I shall have to do is to hand everything over to the kind people who take part. Perhaps I should explain a little about the object we have in mind. The Young People's Friendly Circle, which has done such splendid work in Pen Cuckoo and the neighboring parishes, is badly in need of funds. Miss Prentice as president and Miss Campanula as secretary, will tell you all about that. What we want more than anything else is a new piano. The present instrument was given by your father, wasn't it, squire?"

"Yes," said Jocelyn. "I remember quite well. It was when I was about twelve. It wasn't new then. I can imagine it's pretty well a dead horse."

"We had a tuner up from Great Chipping," said Miss Campanula, "and he says he can't do anything more with it. I blame the scouts. Ever since the eldest Cain boy was made scout-master they have gone from bad to worse. He's got no idea of discipline, that young man. On

Saturday I found Georgie Biggins tramping up and down the keyboard in his boots and whanging the wires inside with the end of his pole. 'If I were your scout-master,' I said, 'I'd give you a beating that you'd not forget in a twelve-month.' His reply was grossly impertinent. I told the eldest Cain that if he couldn't control his boys himself he'd better hand them over to someone who could."

"Dear me, yes," said the rector hurriedly. "Young barbarians they are sometimes. Well now, the piano is of course not the sole property of the Y.P.F.C. It was a gift to the parish. But I have suggested that, as they use it a great deal, perhaps it would be well to devote whatever funds result from this entertainment to a piano fund, rather than to a general Y.P.F.C. fund. I don't know what you all think about this."

"How much would a new piano cost?" asked Dr. Templett.

"There's a very good instrument at Preece's in Great Chipping," said the rector. "The price is £50."

"We can't hope to make that at our show, can we?" asked Dinah.

"I tell you what," said the squire. "I'll make up the difference. The piano seems to be a Pen Cuckoo affair."

There was a general gratified murmur.

"Damned good of you, squire," said Dr. Templett. "Very generous."

"Very good indeed," agreed the rector.

Miss Prentice, without moving, seemed to preen herself. Henry saw Miss Campanula look at her friend and was startled by the singularly venomous glint in her eye. He thought, "She's jealous of Eleanor taking reflected glory from father's offer." And suddenly he was appalled by the thought of these two aging women united in so profound a dissonance.

"Perhaps," said the rector, "we had better have a formal motion."

They had a formal motion. The rector hurried them on. A date was fixed three weeks ahead for the performance in the parish hall. Miss Prentice, who seemed to have become a secretary by virtue of her seat on the rector's right hand, made quantities of notes. And all the time each of these eight people knew very well that they merely moved in a circle round the true matter of their meeting. What Miss Prentice called "the nature of our little entertainment" had yet to be determined. Every now and then someone would steal a covert glance at the small pile of modern plays in front of Dinah, and the larger pile of elderly French's acting editions in front of Miss Prentice. And while they discussed prices of admission, and dates, through each of their minds raced their secret thoughts.

## II

The rector thought, "I cannot believe it of Templett. A medical man with an invalid wife! Besides, there's his professional position. But what persuaded him to bring her here? He must have known how they would talk. I wish Miss Campanula wouldn't look at me like that. She wants to see me alone again. I wish I'd never said confession was recognized by the Church, but how could I not? I wish she wouldn't confess. I wish that I didn't get the impression that she and Miss Prentice merely use the confessional as a means of informing against each other. Six parts and seven people. Oh, dear!"

The squire thought, "Eleanor's quite right, I was good in *Ici on Parle Français*. Funny how some people take to the stage naturally. Now, if Dinah and Henry try to suggest one of those modern things, as likely as not there will be nothing that suits me. What I'd like is one of those charming not-so-young men in a Marie Tempest comedy. Mrs. Ross could play the Marie Tempest part. Eleanor and old Idris wouldn't have that at any price. I wonder if it's true that they don't really kiss on the stage because of the grease paint. Still, at rehearsals . . . I wonder if it's true about Templett and Mrs. Ross. I'm as young as ever I was. What the devil am I going to do about Henry and Dinah Copeland? Dinah's a pretty girl. Hard, though. Modern. If only the Copelands were a bit better off it wouldn't matter. I suppose they'll talk about me, both of them. Henry will say something clever. Blast and damn Eleanor! Why the devil couldn't she hold her tongue, and then I shouldn't have had to deal with it. Six parts and seven people. Why shouldn't she be in it, after all? I suppose Templett would want the charming not-so-young part and they'd turn me into some bloody comic old dodderer."

Eleanor Prentice thought, "If I take care and manage this well it will look as if it's Idris who is making all the trouble and he will think her uncharitable. Six parts and seven people. Idris is determined to stop that Ross woman at all costs. I can see one of Idris's tantrums coming. That's all to the good. I shall be forty-nine next month. Idris is more than forty-nine. Dinah should work in the parish. I wonder what goes on among actors and actresses. Dressing and undressing behind the scenes and traveling about together. If I could find out that Dinah had— If I married, Jocelyn would make me an allowance. To see that woman look at Templett like that and he at her! Dinah and Henry! I can't bear it. I can't endure it. Never show you're hurt. I want to look at him, but I mustn't. Henry might be watching. Henry knows. A parish priest should be married. His head is like an angel's head. No. Not an angel's. A Greek god. Prostrate before Thy throne to lie and gaze and gaze on Thee. Oh, God, let him love me!"

Henry thought, "To-morrow morning if it's fine I shall meet Dinah above Cloudyfold and tell her that I love her. Why shouldn't Templett have his Selia Ross in the play? Six parts and seven people to the devil! Let's find a new play. I'm in love for the first time. I've crossed the border into a strange country and never again will there be a moment quite like this. To-morrow morning, if it's fine, Dinah and I will meet up on Cloudyfold."

Dinah thought, "To-morrow morning, if it's fine, Henry will be waiting for me above Cloudyfold and I think he will tell me he loves me. There will be nobody in the whole wide world but Henry and me."

Templett thought, "I'll have to be careful. I suppose I was a fool to suggest her coming, but after she said she was so keen on acting it seemed the only thing to do. If those two starved spinsters get their teeth into us it'll be all up with the practice. I wish to God I was made differently. I wish to God my wife wasn't what she is. Perhaps it'd be all the same if she wasn't. Selia's got me. It's like an infection. I'm eaten up with it."

Selia Ross thought, "So far so good. I've got here. I can manage the squire easily enough, but he's got his eye on me already. The boy's in love with the girl, but he's a man and I think he'll be generous. He's no fool, though, and I rather fancy he's summed me up. Attractive, with those light gray eyes and black lashes. It might be amusing to take him from her. I doubt if I could. He's past the age when they fall for women a good deal older than themselves. I feel equal to the whole lot of them. It was fun coming in with Billy and seeing those two frost-bitten old virgins with their eyes popping out of their heads. They know I'm too much for them with my good common streak of hard sense and determination. They're both trying to see if Billy's arm is touching my shoulders. The Campanula is staring quite openly and the Poor Relation's looking out of the corner of her eyes. I'll lean back a little. There! Now have a good look. It's a bore about Billy's professional reputation and having to be so careful. I want like hell to show them all he's mine. I've never felt like this about any other man, never. It's as if we'd engulfed each other. I suppose it's love. I won't have him in their bogus schoolroom play without me. He might have a love scene with the girl. I couldn't stand that. Seven people and six parts. Now, then!"

And Idris Campanula thought, "If I could in decency lay my hands on that straw-colored wanton I'd shake the very life out of her. The infamous brazen effrontery! To force her way into Pen Cuckoo, without an invitation, under the protection of that man! I always suspected Dr. Templett of that sort of thing. If Eleanor had the gumption of a rabbit she'd have forbidden them the house. Sitting on the arm of her chair! A fine excuse! He's practically got his arm round her. I'll look straight at them and let her see what I think of her. There! She's smiling. She knows, and she doesn't care. It amounts to living in open sin with him. The rector *can't* let it pass. It's an open insult to me, making me sit at the same table with them. Every hand against me. I've no friends. They only want my money. Eleanor's as bad as the rest. She's tried to poison the rector's mind against me. She's jealous of me. The play was *my* idea and now she's talking as if it was hers. The rector must be warned. I'll ask him to hear my confession on Friday. I'll confess the unkind thoughts I've had of Eleanor Prentice and before he can stop me I'll tell him what they were and then perhaps he'll begin to see through Eleanor. Then I'll say I've been uncharitable about Mrs. Ross and Dr. Templett. I'll say I'm an outspoken woman and believe in look-ing facts in the face. He *must* prefer me to Eleanor. I ought to have married. With my ability and my money and my brains I'd make a suc-cess of it. I'd do the Rectory up and get rid of that impertinent old maid. Dinah could go back to the stage as soon as she liked, or if Eleanor's gossip is true, she could marry Henry Jernigham. Eleanor wouldn't care much for that. She'll fight tooth and nail before she sees another chatelaine at Pen Cuckoo. I'll back Eleanor up as far as Dr. Templett and his common little light-of-love are concerned, but if she tries to come between me and Walter Copeland she'll regret it. Now then, I'll speak."

And bringing her large, ugly hand down sharply on the table she said:

"May I have a word?"

"Please do," said Mr. Copeland nervously.

"As secretary," began Miss Campanula loudly, "I have discussed this matter with the Y.P.F.C. members individually. They plan an enter-tainment of their own later on in the year and they are *most* anxious that this little affair should be arranged *entirely* by ourselves. Just five or six, they said, of the people who are really interested in the Circle. They mentioned you, of course, rector, and the squire, as patron, and you Eleanor, naturally, as president. They said they hoped Dinah would not feel that our humble efforts were beneath her dignity and that she would grace our little performance. And you, Henry, they par-ticularly mentioned you."

"Thank you," said Henry solemnly. Miss Campanula darted a suspi-cious glance at him and went on:

"They seem to think they'd like to see me making an exhibition of myself with all the rest of you. Of course, I don't pretend to histrionic talent——"

"*Of course* you must have a part, Idris," said Miss Prentice. "We depend upon you."

"Thank you, Eleanor," said Miss Campanula; and between the two ladies there flashed the signal of an alliance.

"That makes five, doesn't it?" asked Miss Prentice sweetly.

"Five," said Miss Campanula.

"Six, with Dr. Templett," said Henry.

"We should be very glad to have Dr. Templett," rejoined Miss Prentice, with so cunningly balanced an inflection that her rejection of Mrs. Ross was implicit in every syllable.

"Well, a G.P.'s an awkward sort of fellow when it comes to rehearsals," said Dr. Templett. "Never know when an urgent case may not crop up. Still, if you don't mind risking it I'd like to take a part."

"We'll certainly risk it," said the rector. There was a murmur of assent followed by a deadly little silence. The rector drew in his breath, looked at his daughter who gave him a heartening nod, and said:

"Now, before we go any further with the number of performers, I think we should decide on the form of the entertainment. If it is going to be a play, so much will depend upon the piece chosen. Has anybody any suggestion?"

"I move," said Miss Campanula, "that we do a play, and I suggest *Simple Susan* as a suitable piece."

"I should like to second that," said Miss Prentice.

"What sort of play is it?" asked Dr. Templett. "I haven't heard of it. Is it new?"

"It's a contemporary of *East Lynne* and *The Silver King*, I should think," said Dinah.

Henry and Dr. Templett laughed. Miss Campanula thrust out her bosom, turned scarlet in the face, and said:

"In my humble opinion, Dinah, it is none the worse for that."

"It's so amusing," said Miss Prentice. "You remember it, Jocelyn, don't you? There's that little bit where Lord Sylvester pretends to be his own tailor and proposes to Lady Maude, thinking she's her own lady's maid. Such an original notion and so ludicrous."

"It has thrown generations of audiences into convulsions," agreed Henry.

"Henry," said the squire.

"Sorry, Father. But honestly, as a dramatic device——"

"*Simple Susan*," said Miss Campanula hotly, "may be old-fashioned in the sense that it contains no disgusting innuendoes. It does not depend on vulgarity for its fun, and that's more than can be said for most of your modern comedies."

"How far does Lord Sylvester go——" began Dinah.

"Dinah!" said the rector quietly.

"All right, Daddy. Sorry. I only——"

"How old is Lord Sylvester?" interrupted the squire suddenly.

"Oh, about forty-five or fifty," murmured Miss Prentice.

"Why not do *The Private Secretary?*" inquired Henry.

"I never thought *The Private Secretary* a very nice play," said Miss Prentice. "I expect I'm prejudiced." And she gave the rector a reverent smile.

"I agree," said Miss Campanula. "I always thought it in the worst of taste. I may be old-fashioned but I don't like jokes about the cloth."

"I don't think *The Private Secretary* ever did us much harm," said the rector mildly. "But aren't we wandering from the point? Miss Campanula has moved that we do a play called *Simple Susan*. Miss Prentice has seconded her. Has anybody else a suggestion to make?"

"Yes," said Selia Ross, "I have."

# CHAPTER III

# They Choose a Play

*I*

IF MRS. ROSS had taken a ticking bomb from her handbag and placed it on the table, the effect could have been scarcely more devastating. What she did produce was a small green book. Seven pairs of eyes followed the movements of her thin scarlet-tipped hands. Seven pairs of eyes fastened, as if mesmerized, on the black letters of the book cover. Mrs. Ross folded her hands over the book and addressed the meeting.

"I do hope you'll all forgive me for making my suggestion," she said, "but it's the result of a rather odd coincidence. I'd no idea of your meeting until Dr. Templett called in this afternoon, but I happened to be reading this play and when he appeared the first thing I said was, 'Some time or other we simply *must* do this thing.' Didn't I, Billy? I mean, it's absolutely marvelous. All the time I was reading it I kept thinking how perfect it would be for some of you to do it in aid of one of the local charities. There are two parts in it that would be simply ideal for Miss Prentice and Miss Campanula. The Duchess and her sister. The scene they have with General Talbot is one of the best in the play. It simply couldn't be funnier and you'd be magnificent as the General, Mr. Jernigham."

She paused composedly and looked sideways at the squire. Nobody spoke, though Miss Campanula wetted her lips. Selia Ross waited for a moment, smiling frankly, and then she said:

"Of course I didn't realize you had already chosen a play. Naturally I wouldn't have dreamt of coming if I had known. It's all this man's fault." She gave Dr. Templett a sort of comradely jog with her elbow. "He bullied me into it. I ought to have apologized and crept away at once, but I just couldn't resist telling you about my discovery." She opened her eyes a little wider and turned them on the rector. "Perhaps if I left it with you, Mr. Copeland, the committee might just like to glance at it before they quite decide. *Please* don't think I want a part in it or anything frightful like that. It's just that it *is* so good and I'd be delighted to lend it."

"That's very kind of you," said the rector.

"It's not a bit kind. I'm being thoroughly selfish. I just long to see you all doing it and I'm secretly hoping you won't be able to resist it. It's so difficult to find modern plays that aren't offensive," continued Mrs. Ross, with an air of great frankness, "but this really is charming."

"But what is the play?" asked Henry, who had been craning his neck in a useless attempt to read the title.

"*Shop Windows*, by Jacob Hunt."

"Good Lord!" ejaculated Dinah. "Of course! I never thought of it. It's the very thing."

"Have you read it?" asked Mrs. Ross, with a friendly glance at her.

"I saw the London production," said Dinah. "You're quite right, it would be grand. But what about the royalties? Hunt charges the earth for amateur rights, and anyway he'd probably refuse them to us."

"I was coming to that," said Mrs. Ross. "If you should decide to do it I'd like to stand the royalties if you'd let me."

There was another silence, broken by the rector.

"Now, that's very generous indeed," he said.

"No, honestly it's not. I've told you I'm longing to see it done."

"How many characters are there?" asked the squire suddenly.

"Let me see, I think there are six." She opened the play and counted prettily on her fingers.

"Five, six—no, there seem to be seven! Stupid of me."

"Ha!" said Miss Campanula.

"But I'm sure you could find a seventh. What about the Moorton people?"

"What about you?" asked Dr. Templett.

"No, no!" said Mrs. Ross quickly. "I don't come into the picture. Don't be silly."

"It's a damn' good play," said Henry. "I saw the London show too, Dinah. D'you think we could do it?"

"I don't see why not. The situations would carry it through. The three character parts are really the stars."

"Which are they?" demanded the squire.

"The General and the Duchess and her sister," said Mrs. Ross.

"They don't come on till the second act," continued Dinah, "but from then on they carry the show."

"May I have a look at it?" asked the squire.

Mrs. Ross opened the book and passed it across to him.

"Do read the opening of the act," she said, "and then go on to page forty-eight."

"May I speak?" demanded Miss Campanula loudly.

"Please!" said the rector hurriedly. "Please do. Ah—order!"

## II

Miss Campanula gripped the edge of the table with her large hands and spoke at some length. She said that she didn't know how everybody else was feeling but that she herself was somewhat bewildered. She was surprised to learn that such eminent authorities as Dinah and Henry and Mrs. Ross considered poor Pen Cuckoo capable of producing a modern play that met with their approval. She thought that perhaps this clever play might be a little too clever for poor Pen Cuckoo and the Young People's Friendly Circle. She asked the meeting if it did not think it would make a great mistake if it was over-ambitious. "I must confess," she said, with an angry laugh, "that I had a much simpler plan in mind. I did not propose to fly as high as West End successes and I don't mind saying I think we would be in a fair way to making fools of ourselves. And that's that."

"But, Miss Campanula," objected Dinah, "it's such a mistake to think that because the cast is not very experienced it will be better in a bad play than in a good one."

"I'm sorry you think *Simple Susan* a bad play, Dinah," said Miss Prentice sweetly.

"Well, I think it's very dated and I'm afraid I think it's rather silly," said Dinah doggedly.

Miss Prentice gave a silvery laugh in which Miss Campanula joined.

"I agree with Dinah," said Henry quickly.

"Suppose we all read both plays," suggested the rector.

"I have read *Shop Windows*," said Dr. Templett. "I must say I don't see how we could do better."

"We seem to be at a disadvantage, Eleanor," said Miss Campanula unpleasantly, and Miss Prentice laughed again. So, astonishingly, did the squire. He broke out in a loud choking snort. They all turned to look at him. Tears coursed each other down his cheeks and he dabbed at them absent-mindedly with the back of his hand. His shoulders quivered, his brows were raised in an ecstasy of merriment, and his cheeks were purple. He was lost in the second act of Mrs. Ross's play.

"Oh! Lord!" he said, "this is funny."

"Jocelyn!" cried Miss Prentice.

"Eh?" said the squire, and he turned a page, read half a dozen lines, laid the book on the table and gave himself up to paroxysms of unbridled laughter.

"Jocelyn!" repeated Miss Prentice. "Really!"

"What?" gasped the squire. "Eh? All right, I'm quite willing. Damn' good! When do we begin?"

"Hi!" said Henry. "Steady, Father! The meeting hasn't decided on the play."

"Well, we'd better decide on this," said the squire, and he leaned towards Selia Ross. "When he starts telling her he's got the garter," he said, "and she thinks he's talking about the other affair! And then when she says she won't take no for an answer. Oh, Lord!"

"It's heavenly, isn't it?" agreed Mrs. Ross, and she and Henry and Dinah suddenly burst out laughing at the recollection of this scene, and for a minute or two they all reminded each other of the exquisite facetiae in the second act of *Shop Windows*. The rector listened with a nervous smile; Miss Prentice and Miss Campanula with tightly-set lips. At last the squire looked round the table with brimming eyes and asked what they were all waiting for.

"I'll move we do *Shop Windows*," he said. "That in order?"

"I'll second it," said Dr. Templett.

"No doubt I am in error," said Miss Campanula, "but I was under the impression that my poor suggestion was before the meeting, seconded by Miss Prentice."

The rector was obliged to put this motion to the meeting.

"It is moved by Miss Campanula," he said unhappily, "and seconded by Miss Prentice, that *Simple Susan* be the play chosen for production. Those in favor——"

"Aye," said Miss Campanula and Miss Prentice.

"And the contrary?"

"No," said the rest of the meeting with perfect good humor.

"Thank you," said Miss Campanula. "*Thank you.* Now we know where we are."

"You wait till you start learning your parts in this thing," said Jocelyn cheerfully, "and you won't know whether you're on your heads or your heels. There's an awful lot of us three, isn't there?" he continued, turning the pages. "I suppose Eleanor will do the Duchess and Miss Campanula will be the other one—Mrs. Thing or whoever she is! Gertrude! That the idea?"

"That was my idea," said Mrs. Ross.

"If I may be allowed to speak," said Miss Campanula, "I should like to say that it is just within the bounds of possibility that it may not be ours."

"Perhaps, Jernigham," said the rector, "you had better put your motion."

But of course the squire's motion was carried. Miss Campanula and Miss Prentice did not open their lips. Their thoughts were alike in confusion and intensity. Both seethed under the insult done to *Simple Susan*, each longed to rise and, with a few well-chosen words, withdraw from the meeting. Each was checked by a sensible reluctance to cut off her nose to spite her face. It was obvious that *Shop Windows* would be performed whether they stayed in or flounced out. Unless all the others were barefaced liars, it seemed that there were two outstandingly good parts ready for them to snap up. They hung off and on, ruffled their plumage, and secretly examined each other's face.

### III

Meanwhile, with the enthusiasm that all Jernighams brought to a new project Jocelyn and his son began to cast the play. Almost a century ago there had been what Eleanor, when cornered, called an "incident" in the family history. The Mrs. Jernigham of that time was a plain silly woman and barren into the bargain. Her Jocelyn, the fourth of that name, had lived openly with a very beautiful and accomplished actress and had succeeded in getting the world to pretend that his son by her was his lawful scion, and had jockeyed his wife into bringing the boy up as her own. By this piece of effrontery he brought to Pen Cuckoo a dram of mummery, and ever since those days most of the Jernighams had had a passion for theatricals. It was as if the lovely actress had touched up the family portraits with a stick of rouge. Jocelyn and Henry had both played in the O.U.D.S. They both had the trick of moving about a stage as if they grew out of the boards, and they both instinctively bridged that colossal gap between the stage and the front row of the stalls. Jocelyn thought himself a better actor than he was, but Henry did not recognize how good he might be. Even Miss Prentice, a Jernigham, as the squire had pointed out, on her mother's side, had not escaped that dram of player's blood. Although she knew nothing about theater, mistrusted and disliked the very notion of the stage as a career for gentle people, and had no sort of judgment for the merit of a play, yet in amateur theatricals she was surprisingly composed and perfectly audible, and she loved acting. She knew now that Idris Campanula expected her to refuse to take part in *Shop Windows,* and more than half her inclination was so to refuse. "What," she thought. "To have my own play put aside for something chosen by that woman! To have to look on while they parcel out the parts!" But even as she pondered on the words with which she would offer her resignation, she pictured Lady Appleby of Moorton Grange accepting the part that Jocelyn said was so good. And what was more, the rector would think Eleanor herself uncharitable. That decided her. She waited for a pause in the chatter round Jocelyn, and then she turned to the rector.

"May I say just one little word?" she asked.

"Yes, yes, of course," said Mr. Copeland, "Please, everybody. Order!"

"It's only this," said Miss Prentice, avoiding the eye of Miss Campanula. "I do hope nobody will think I am going to be disappointed or hurt about my little play. I expect it *is* rather out-of-date, and I am only too pleased to think that you have found one that is more suitable. If there is anything that I can do to help, I shall be only too glad. Of course."

She received, and reveled in, the rector's beaming smile, and met Idris Campanula's glare with a smile of her own. Then she saw Selia Ross watching her out of the corners of her eyes and suddenly she knew that Selia Ross understood her.

"That's perfectly splendid," exclaimed Mr. Copeland. "I think it is no more than we expected of Miss Prentice's generosity, but we are none the less grateful." And he added confusedly, "A very graceful gesture."

Miss Prentice preened and Miss Campanula glowered. The others, vaguely aware that something was expected of them, made small appreciative noises.

"Now, how about casting the play?" said Dr. Templett.

## IV

There was no doubt that the play had been well chosen. With the exception of one character, it practically cast itself. The squire was to play the General; Miss Prentice, the Duchess; Miss Campanula, of whom everybody felt extremely frightened, was cast for Mrs. Arbuthnot, a good character part. Miss Campanula, when offered the part, replied ambiguously:

"Who knows?" she asked darkly. "Obviously, it is not for me to say."

"But you will do it, Idris?" murmured Miss Prentice.

"I have but one comment," rejoined Miss Campanula. "Wait and see." She laughed shortly, and the rector, in a hurry, wrote her name down opposite the part. Dinah and Henry were given the two young lovers, and Dr. Templett said he would undertake the French Ambassador. He began to read some of the lines in violently broken English. There remained the part of Hélène, a mysterious lady who had lost her memory, and who turned up in the middle of the first act at a country house-party.

"Obviously, Selia," said Dr. Templett, "you must be Hélène."

"No, *no,*" said Mrs. Ross, "that isn't a bit what I meant. Now do be quiet, Billy, or they'll all think I came here with an ulterior motive."

With the possible exception of the squire, that was precisely what they all did think, but not even Miss Campanula had the courage to say so. Having accepted Mrs. Ross's play they could do nothing but offer her the part, which, as far as lines went, was not a long one. Perhaps only Dinah realized quite how good Hélène was. Mrs. Ross protested and demurred.

"If you are quite sure you want me," she said, and looked sideways at the squire. Jocelyn, who had glanced through the play and found that the General had a love-scene with Hélène, said heartily that they wanted her very much indeed. Henry and Dinah, conscious of their own love-scenes, agreed, and the rector formally asked Mrs. Ross if she would take the part. She accepted with the prettiest air in the world. Miss Prentice managed to maintain her gentle smile and Miss Campanula's behavior merely became a degree more darkly ominous. The rector put on his glasses and read his notes.

"To sum up," he said loudly. "We propose to do this play in the Parish Hall on Saturday 27th, three weeks from tonight. The proceeds are to be devoted to the piano-fund and the balance of the sum needed will be made up most generously by Mr. Jocelyn Jernigham. The committee and members of the Y.P.F.C. will organize the sale of tickets and will make themselves responsible for the—what is the correct expression, Dinah?"

"The front of the house, Daddy."

"For the front of the house, yes. Do you think we can leave these affairs to your young folk, Miss Campanula? I know you can answer for them."

"My dear man," said Miss Campanula, "I can't answer for the behavior of thirty village louts and maidens, but they usually do what I tell them to. Ha!"

Everybody laughed sycophantly.

"My *friend*," added Miss Campanula, with a ghastly smile, "my *friend* Miss Prentice is president. No doubt, if they pay no attention to me, they will do anything in the world for her."

"Dear Idris!" murmured Miss Prentice.

"Who's going to produce the play?" asked Henry. "I think Dinah ought to. She's a professional."

"Hear, hear!" said Dr. Templett, Selia Ross and the squire. Miss Prentice added rather a tepid little, "Of course, yes." Miss Campanula said nothing. Dinah grinned shyly and looked into her lap. She was elected producer. Dinah had not passed the early stages of theatrical experience when the tyro lards his conversation with professional phrases. She accepted her honors with an air of great seriousness and called her first rehearsal for Tuesday night, November 9th.

"I'll get all your sides typed by then," she explained. "I'm sure Gladys Wright will do them, because she's learning and wants experience. I'll give her a proper part so that she gets the cues right. We'll have a reading and if there's time I'll set positions for the first act."

"Dear me," said Miss Prentice, "this sounds very alarming. I'm afraid, Dinah dear, that you will find us all very amateurish."

"Oh, no!" cried Dinah gayly. "I know it's going to be marvelous." She looked uncertainly at her father and added, "I should like to say, thank you all very much for asking me to produce. I do hope I'll manage it all right."

"Well, you know a dashed sight more about it than any of us," said Selia Ross bluntly.

But somehow Dinah didn't quite want Mrs. Ross so frankly on her side. She was aware in herself of a strong antagonism to Mrs. Ross and this discovery surprised and confused her, because she believed herself to be a rebel. As a rebel, she should have applauded Selia Ross. To Dinah, Miss Prentice and Miss Campanula were the hated symbols of all that was mean, stupid, and antediluvian. Selia Ross had deliberately given battle to these two ladies and had won the first round. Why, then, could Dinah not welcome her as an ally after her own heart? She supposed it was because, in her own heart, she mistrusted and disliked Mrs. Ross. This feeling was entirely instinctive and it upset and bewildered her. It was as if some dictator in her blood refused an allegiance that she should have welcomed. She could not reply with the correct comradely smile. She felt her face turning pink with embarrassment and she said hurriedly:

"What about music? We'll want an overture and an entr'acte."

And with those words Dinah unconsciously rang up the curtain on a theme that was to engulf Pen Cuckoo and turn *Shop Windows* from polite comedy into outlandish, shameless melodrama.

# CHAPTER IV

# Cue for Music

## I

As SOON AS DINAH had spoken those fatal words everybody round the table in the study at Pen Cuckoo thought of Rachmaninoff's Prelude in C-sharp minor, and with the exception of Miss Campanula, everybody's heart sank into his or her boots. For the Prelude was Miss Campanula's specialty. In Pen Cuckoo she had the sole rights in this composition. She played it at all church concerts, she played it on her own piano after her own dinner parties, and, unless her hostess was particularly courageous, she played it after other people's dinner parties, too. Whenever there was any question of music sounding at Pen Cuckoo, Miss Campanula offered her services, and the three pretentious chords would boom out once again: "Pom, *Pom*, POM" And then down would go Miss Campanula's foot on the left pedal and the next passage would follow in a series of woolly but determined jerks. She even played it as a voluntary when Mr. Withers, the organist, went on his holidays and Miss Campanula took his place. She had had her photograph taken, seated at the instrument, with the Prelude on the rack. Each of her friends had received a copy at Christmas. The rector's was framed, and he had not known quite what to do with it. Until three years ago when Eleanor Prentice had come to live at Pen Cuckoo, Idris Campanula and her Prelude had had it all their own way. But Miss Prentice also belonged to a generation when girls learned the pianoforte from their governesses, and she, too, liked to be expected to perform. Her *pièce de résistance* was Ethelbert Nevin's Venetian Suite, which she rendered with muffled insecurity, the chords of the accompaniment never quite synchronizing with the saccharine notes of the melody. Between the two ladies the battle had raged at parish entertainments, Sunday School services, and private parties.

They only united in deploring the radio and in falsely pretending that music was a bond between them.

So that when Dinah in her flurry asked, "What about music?" Miss Campanula and Miss Prentice both became alert.

Miss Prentice said, "Yes, of course. Now, couldn't we manage that amongst ourselves somehow? It's *so* much pleasanter, isn't it, if we keep to our own small circle?"

"I am afraid my poor wits are rather confused," began Miss Campanula. "Everything seems to have been decided out of hand. You must correct me if I'm wrong, but it appears that several of the characters in this delightful comedy—by the way, is it a comedy?"

"Yes," said Henry.

"Thank you. It appears that some of the characters do not appear until somewhere in the second act. I don't know which of the characters, naturally, as I have not yet looked between the covers."

With hasty mumbled apologies they handed the play to Miss Campanula. She said:

"Oh, thank you. Don't let me be selfish. I'm a patient body."

When Idris Campanula alluded to herself jocularly as a "body" it usually meant that she was in a temper. They all said, "No, no! Please have it." She drew her pince-nez out from her bosom by a patent extension and slung them across her nose. She opened the play and amidst dead silence she began to inspect it. First she read the cast of characters. She checked each one with a large bony forefinger, and paused to look round the table until she found the person who had been cast for it. Her expression, which was forbidding, did not change. She then applied herself to the first page of the dialogue. Still everybody waited. The silence was broken only by the sound of Miss Campanula turning a page. Henry began to feel desperate. It seemed almost as if they would continue to sit dumbly round the table until Miss Campanula reached the end of the play. He gave Dinah a cigarette and lit one himself. Miss Campanula raised her eyes and watched them until the match was blown out, and then returned to her reading. She had reached the fourth page of the first act. Mrs. Ross looked up at Dr.

Templett who bent his head and whispered. Again Miss Campanula raised her eyes and stared at the offenders. The squire cleared his throat and said:

"Read the middle bit of Act II. Page forty-eight, it begins. Funniest thing I've come across for ages. It'll make you laugh like anything."

Miss Campanula did not reply, but she turned to Act II. Dinah, Henry, Dr. Templett, and Jocelyn waited with anxious smiles for her to give some evidence of amusement, but her lips remained firmly pursed, her brows raised, and her eyes fishy. Presently she looked up.

"I've reached the end of the scene," she said. "Was that the funny one?"

"Don't you think it's funny?" asked the squire.

"My object was to find out if there was anybody free to play the entr'acte," said Miss Campanula coldly. "I gather that there is. I *gather* that the Arbuthnot individual does not make her first appearance until half-way through the second act."

"Didn't somebody say that Mrs. Arbuthnot and the Duchess appeared together?" asked Miss Prentice, to the accompaniment, every one felt, of the Venetian Suite.

"Possibly," said Miss Campanula. "Do I understand that I am expected to take this Mrs. Arbuthnot upon myself?"

"If you will," rejoined the rector. "And we hope very much indeed that you will."

"I wanted to be quite clear. I dare say I'm making a great to-do about nothing but I'm a person that likes to know where she is. Now I *gather*, and you must correct me if I'm wrong, that if I do this part there is no just cause or impediment," and here Miss Campanula threw a jocular glance at the rector, "why I should not take a little more upon myself and seat myself at the instrument. You *may* have other plans. You *may* wish to hire Mr. Joe Hopkins and his friends from Great Chipping, though on a Saturday night I gather they are rather more undependable and tipsy than usual. *If* you have other plans then no more need be said. If not, I place myself at the committee's disposal."

"Well, that seems a most excellent offer," the poor rector began. "If Miss Campanula——"

"May I?" interrupted Miss Prentice sweetly. "May I say that I think it very kind indeed of dear Idris to offer herself, but may I add that I do also think we are a little too inclined to take advantage of her generosity. She will have all the young folk to manage and she has a large part to learn. I do feel that we should be a little selfish if we also expected her to play for us on that dreadful old piano. Now, as the new instrument is to be in part, as my cousin says, a Pen Cuckoo affair, I think the very least I can do is to offer to relieve poor Idris of this un-welcome task. If you think my little efforts will pass muster I shall be very pleased to play the overture and entr'acte."

"Very thoughtful of you, Eleanor, but I am quite capable——"

"Of course you are, Idris, but at the same time——"

They both stopped short. The antagonism that had sprung up be-tween them was so obvious and so disproportionate that the others were aghast. The rector abruptly brought his palm down on the table and then, as if ashamed of a gesture that betrayed his thoughts, clasped his hands together and looked straight before him.

He said, "I think this matter can be decided later."

The two women glanced quickly at him and were silent.

"That is all, I believe," said Mr. Copeland. "Thank you, everybody."

## II

The meeting broke up. Henry went to Dinah who had moved over to the fire.

"Ructions!" he said under his breath.

"Awful!" agreed Dinah. "You'd hardly believe it possible, would you?"

They smiled secretly and when the others crowded about Dinah, ask-ing if they could have their parts before Monday, what sort of clothes would be needed, and whether she thought they would be all right, neither she nor Henry minded very much. It did not matter to them that they were unable to speak to each other, for their thoughts went forward to the morning, and their hearts trembled with happiness. They were isolated by their youth, two scatheless figures. It would have seemed impossible to them that their love for each other could hold any reflection, however faint, of the emotions that drew Dr. Templett to Selia Ross, or those two aging women to the rector. They would not have believed that there was a reverse side to love, or that the twin-op-posites of love lay dormant in their own hearts. Nor were they to guess that never again, as long as they lived, would they know the rapturous expectancy that now possessed them.

Miss Prentice and Miss Campanula carefully avoided each other. Miss Prentice had seized her opportunity and had cornered Mr. Cope-land. She could be heard offering flowers from the Pen Cuckoo green-houses for a special service next Sunday. Miss Campanula had tackled Jocelyn about some enormity committed on her property by the local fox-hounds. Dr. Templett, a keen follower of hounds, was lugged into the controversy. Mrs. Ross was therefore left alone. She stood a little to one side, completely relaxed, her head slanted, a half-smile on her lips. The squire looked over Idris Campanula's shoulder, and caught that half-smile.

"Can't have that sort of thing," he said vaguely. "I'll have a word with Appleby. Will you forgive me? I just want——"

He escaped thankfully and joined Mrs. Ross. She welcomed him with an air that flattered him. Her eyes brightened and her smile was intimate. It was years since any woman had smiled in that way at Jocelyn, and he responded with Edwardian gallantry. His hand went to his mustache and his eye brightened.

"You know, you're a very alarming person," said Jocelyn.

"Now what precisely do you mean by that?" asked Mrs. Ross.

He was delighted. This was the way a conversation with a pretty woman ought to start. Forgotten phrases returned to his lips, waggishly nonsensical phrases that one uttered with just the right air of significance. One laughed a good deal and let her know one noticed how damned well-turned-out she was.

"I see that we have a most important scene together," said Jocelyn, "and I shall insist on a private rehearsal."

"I don't know that I shall agree to that," said Selia Ross.

"Oh, come now, it's perfectly safe."

"Why?"

"Because you are to be the very charming lady who has lost her memory. Ha, ha, ha! Damn' convenient, what!" shouted Jocelyn, wondering if this remark was as daring as it sounded. Mrs. Ross laughed very heartily and the squire glanced in a gratified manner round the room, and encountered the astonished gaze of his son.

"This'll show Henry," thought Jocelyn. "These modern pups don't know how to flirt with an attractive woman." But there was an unmistakably sardonic glint in Henry's eye, and the squire, slightly shaken, turned back to Mrs. Ross. She still looked roguishly expectant and he thought, "Anyway, if Henry's noticed *her*, he'll know I'm doing pretty well." And then Dr. Templett managed to escape Miss Campanula and joined them.

"Well, Selia," he said, "if you're ready I think I'd better take you home."

"Doesn't like me talking to her!" thought the squire in triumph. "The little man's jealous."

When Mrs. Ross silently gave him her hand, he deliberately squeezed it.

"*Au revoir*," he said. "This is your first visit to Pen Cuckoo, isn't it? Don't let it be the last."

"I shouldn't be here at all," she answered. "There have been no official calls, you know."

Jocelyn made a slightly silly gesture and bowed.

"We'll waive all that sort of nonsense," he said. "Ha, ha, ha!"

Mrs. Ross turned to say good-by to Eleanor Prentice.

"I have just told your cousin," she said, "that I've no business here. We haven't exchanged calls, have we?"

If Miss Prentice was at all taken aback, she did not show it. She gave her musical laugh and said, "I'm afraid I am very remiss about these things."

"Miss Campanula hasn't called on me either," said Mrs. Ross. "You must come together. Good-by.

"Good-by, everybody," said Mrs. Ross.

"I'll see you to your car," said the squire. "Henry!"

Henry hastened to the door. Jocelyn escorted Mrs. Ross out of the room and, as Dr. Templett followed them, the rector shouted after them:

"Just a minute, Templett. About the youngest Cain."

"Oh, yes. Silly little fool! Look here, rector——"

"I'll come out with you," said the rector.

Henry followed and shut the door behind them.

"Well!" said Miss Campanula. "Well!"

"*Isn't it?*" said Miss Prentice. "*Isn't it?*"

### III

Dinah, left alone with them, knew that the battle of the music was postponed in order that the two ladies might unite in abuse of Mrs. Ross. That it was postponed and not abandoned was evident in their manner, which reminded Dinah of stewed fruit on the turn. Its sweetness was impregnated by acidity.

"Of course, Eleanor," said Miss Campanula, "I can't for the life of me see why you didn't show her the door. I should have refused to receive her. I should!"

"I was simply dumbfounded," said Miss Prentice. "When Taylor announced them, I really couldn't believe my senses. I am deeply disappointed in Dr. Templett."

"Disappointed! The greatest piece of brazen effrontery I have ever encountered. He shan't have my lumbago! I can promise him that."

"I really should have thought he'd have known better," continued Miss Prentice. "It isn't as if we don't know who he is. He should be a gentleman. I always thought he took up medicine as a *vocation*. After all, there have been Templetts at Chippingwood for——"

"For as long as there have been Jernighams at Pen Cuckoo," said Miss Campanula. "But, of course, you wouldn't know that."

This was an oblique hit. It reminded Miss Prentice that she was a newcomer and not, strictly speaking, a Jernigham of Pen Cuckoo. Miss Campanula followed it up by saying, "I suppose in your position you could do nothing but receive her; but I must say I was astonished that you leaped at her play as you did."

"I did not leap, Idris," said Miss Prentice. "I hope I took the dignified course. It was obvious that everybody but you and me was in favor of her play."

"Well, it's a jolly good play," said Dinah.

"So we have been told," said Miss Campanula. "Repeatedly."

"I was helpless," continued Miss Prentice. "What could I do? One can do nothing against sheer common persistence. Of course she has triumphed."

"She's gone off now, taking every man in the room with her," said Miss Campanula. "Ha!"

"Ah, well," added Miss Prentice, "I suppose it's always the case when one deals with people who are *not quite*. Did you hear what she said about our not calling?"

"I was within an ace of telling her that I understood she received men only."

"But, Miss Campanula," said Dinah, "we don't know there's anything more than friendship between them, do we? And even if there is, it's their business."

"Dinah, *dear!*" said Miss Prentice.

"As a priest's daughter, Dinah——" began Miss Campanula.

"As a priest's daughter," said Dinah, "I've got a sort of idea charity is supposed to be a virtue. And, anyway, I think when you talk about a parson's family it's better not to call him a priest. It sounds so scandalous, somehow."

There was a dead silence. At last Miss Campanula rose to her feet.

"I fancy my car is waiting for me, Eleanor," she said. "So I shall make my adieux. I am afraid we are neither of us intelligent enough to appreciate modern humor. Good night."

"Aren't we driving you home?" asked Dinah.

"Thank you, Dinah, no. I ordered my car for six, and it is already half-past. Good night."

# CHAPTER V

# Above Cloudyfold

*1*

THE NEXT MORNING was fine. Henry woke at six and looked out of his window at a clear, cold sky with paling stars. In another hour it would begin to get light. Henry, wide awake, his mind sharp with anticipation, leaped back into bed and sat with the blankets caught between his chin and his knees, hugging himself. A fine winter's dawn with a light frost and then the thin, pale sunlight. Down in the stables they would soon be moving about with lanterns to the sound of clanking pails, shrill whistling, and boots on cobblestones. Hounds met up at Moorton Park to-day, and Jocelyn's two mounts would be taken over by his groom to wait for his arrival by car. Henry spared a moment to regret his own decision to give up hunting. He had loved it so much: the sound, the smell, the sight of the hunt. It had all seemed so perfectly splendid until one day, quite suddenly, as if a new pair of eyes had been put into his head, he had seen a mob of well-fed expensive people, with red faces, astraddle shiny quadrupeds, all whooping ceremoniously after a very small creature which later on was torn to pieces while the lucky ones sat on their horses and looked on, well satisfied. To his violent annoyance, he had found that he could not rid himself of this unlovely picture and, as it made him feel slightly sick, he had given up everything but drag-hunting. Jocelyn had been greatly upset and had instantly accused Henry of pacifism. Henry had just left off being a pacifist, however, and assured his father that if England was invaded he would strike a shrewd blow before he would see Cousin Eleanor raped by a foreign mercenary. Hugging his knees, he chuckled at the memory of Jocelyn's face. Then he gave himself four minutes to revise the conversation he had planned to have with Dinah. He found that the thought of Dinah sent his heart pounding, just as it used to pound in the old days before he took his first fence. "I suppose I'm hunting again," he thought, and this primitive idea gave him a curiously exalted sensation. He jumped out of bed, bathed, shaved and dressed by lamplight, then he stole downstairs out into the dawn.

It's a fine thing to be abroad on Dorset hills on a clear winter's dawn. Henry went round the west wing of Pen Cuckoo. The gravel crunched under his shoes and the dim box-borders smelled friendly in a garden that was oddly remote. Familiar things seemed mysterious as if the experience of the night had made strangers of them. The field was rimmed with silver, the spinney on the far side was a company of naked trees locked in a deep sleep from which the sound of footsteps among the dead leaves and twigs could not awaken them. The hillside smelled of cold earth and frosty stones. As Henry climbed steeply upwards, it was as if he left the night behind him down in Pen Cuckoo. On Cloudyfold, the dim shapes took on some resolute form and became rocks, bushes and posts, expectant of the day. The clamor of faraway cock-crows rose vaguely from the valley like the overlapping echoes of dreams, and with this sound came the human smell of wood smoke.

Henry reached the top of Cloudyfold and looked down the vale of Pen Cuckoo. His breath made a small cold mist in front of his face, his fingers were cold and his eyes watered, but he felt like a god as he surveyed his own little world. Half-way down, and almost sheer beneath him, was the house he had left. He looked down into the chimney-tops, already wreathed in thin drifts of blue. The servants were up and about. Farther down, and still drenched in shadow, were the roofs of Winton. Henry wondered if they really leaked badly and if he and Dinah could ever afford to repair them. Beyond Winton his father's land spread out into low hills and came to an end at Selwood Brook. Here, half-screened by trees, he could see the stone façade of Chippingwood which Dr. Templett had inherited from his elder brother who had died in the Great War. And separated from Chippingwood by the hamlet of Chipping was Miss Campanula's Georgian mansion, on the skirts of the village but not of it. Farther away, and only just visible over the downlands that separated it from the Vale, was Great Chipping, the largest town in that part of Dorset. Half-way up the slope, below Winton and Pen Cuckoo, was the church, Winton St. Giles, with the rectory hidden behind it. Dinah would strike straight through their home copse and come up the ridge of Cloudyfold. If she came! Please God, make it happen, said Henry's thoughts as they used to do when he was a little boy. He crossed the brow of the hill. Below him, on the far side, was Moorton Park Road and Cloudyfold Village, and there, tucked into a bend in the road, was Duck Cottage, with its scarlet door and window frames, newly done up by Mrs. Ross. Henry wondered why Selia Ross had decided to live in a place like Cloudyfold. She seemed to him so thoroughly urban. For a minute or two he thought of her, still snugly asleep in her renovated cottage, dreaming perhaps of Dr. Templett. Farther away over the brow of a hill was the Cains' farm, where Dr. Templett must drive to minister to the youngest Cain's big toe.

"They're all down there," thought Henry, "tucked up in their warm houses, fast asleep; and none of them knows I'm up here in the cold dawn waiting for Dinah Copeland."

He felt a faint warmth on the back of his neck. The stivered grass was washed with color, and before him his own attenuated shadow appeared. He turned to the east and saw the sun. Quite near at hand he heard his name called, and there, coming over the brow of Cloudyfold, was Dinah, dressed in blue with a scarlet handkerchief round her neck.

Henry could make no answering call. His voice stuck in his throat. He raised his arm, and the shadow before him sent a long blue pointer over the grass. Dinah made an answering gesture. Because he could not stand dumbly and smile until she came up with him, he lit a cigarette, making a long business of it, his hands cupped over his face. He could hear her footsteps on the frozen hill, and his own heart thumped with them. When he looked up she was beside him.

"Good morning," said Henry.

"I've no breath left," said Dinah; "but good morning to you, Henry. Your cigarette smells like heaven."

He gave her one.

"It's grand up here," said Dinah. "I'm glad I came. You wouldn't believe you could be hot, would you? But I am. My hands and face are icy and the rest of me's like a hot-cross bun."

"I'm glad you came, too," said Henry. There was a short silence. Henry set the Jernigham jaw, fixed his gaze on Miss Campanula's chimneys, and said, "Do you feel at all shy?"

"Yes," said Dinah. "If I start talking I shall go on and on talking, rather badly. That's a sure sign I'm shy."

"It takes me differently. I can hardly speak. I expect I'm turning purple, and my top lip seems to be twitching."

"It'll go off in a minute," said Dinah. "Henry, what would you do if you suddenly knew you had dominion over all you survey? That sounds Biblical. I mean, suppose you could alter the minds—and that means the destinies—of all the people living down there—what would you do?"

"Put it into Cousin Eleanor's heart to be a missionary in Polynesia."

"Or into Miss Campanula's to start a nudist circle in Chipping."

"Or my father might go surrealist."

"No, but honestly, what would you do?" Dinah insisted.

"I don't know. I suppose I would try and simplify them. People seem to me to be much too busy and complicated."

"Make them kinder?"

"Well, that might do it, certainly."

"It would do it. If Miss Campanula and your Cousin Eleanor left off being jealous of each other, and if Dr. Templett was sorrier for his wife, and if Mrs. Ross minded more about upsetting other people's apple-carts, we wouldn't have any more scenes like the one last night."

"Perhaps not," Henry agreed. "But you wouldn't stop them falling in love, if you can call whatever they feel for each other, falling in love. I'm in love with you, as I suppose you know. It makes me feel all noble minded and generous and kind; but, just the same, if I had a harem of invalid wives, they wouldn't stop me telling you I loved you, Dinah. Dinah, I love you so desperately."

"Do you, Henry?"

"You'd never believe how desperately. This is all wrong. I'd thought out the way I'd tell you. First we were to have a nice conversation and then, when we'd got to the right place, I was going to tell you."

"All elegant like?"

"Yes. But it's too much for me."

"It's too much for me, too," said Dinah.

They faced each other, two solitary figures. All their lives they were to remember this moment, and yet they did not see each other's faces very clearly, for their sight was blurred by the agitation in their hearts.

"Oh, Dinah," said Henry. "Darling, darling Dinah, I do love you so much."

He reached out his hand blindly and touched her arm. It was a curious tentative gesture. Dinah cried out: "Henry, my dear."

She raised his hand to her cold cheek.

"Oh, God!" said Henry, and pulled her into his arms.

Jocelyn's groom, hacking quietly along the road to Cloudyfold, looked up and saw two figures locked together against the wintry sky.

## II

"We must come back to earth," said Dinah. "There's the church clock. It must be eight."

"I'll kiss you eight times to wind up the spell," said Henry. He kissed her eyes, her cheeks, the tips of her ears, and he kissed her twice on the mouth.

"There!" he muttered. "The spell's wound up."

"Don't!" cried Dinah.

"What, my darling?"

"Don't quote from Macbeth. It couldn't be more unlucky!"

"Who says so?"

"In the theater everybody says so."

"I cock a snook at them! We're not in the theater: we're on top of the world."

"All the same, I'm crossing my thumbs."

"When shall we be married?"

"Married?" Dinah caught her breath, and Henry's pure happiness was threaded with a sort of wonder when he saw that she was no longer lost in bliss.

"What is it?" he said. "What has happened? Does it frighten you to think of our marriage?"

"It's only that we *have* come back to earth," Dinah said somberly. "I don't know when we'll be married. You see, something pretty difficult has happened."

"Good Lord, darling, what are you going to falter in my ear? Not a family curse, or dozens of blood relations stark ravers in lunatic asylums?"

"Not quite. It's your Cousin Eleanor."

"Eleanor!" cried Henry. "She scarcely exists."

"Wait till you hear. I've got to tell you now. I'll tell you as we go down."

"Say first that you're as happy as I am."

"I couldn't be happier."

"I love you, Dinah."

"I love you, Henry."

"The world is ours," said Henry. "Let us go down and take it."

## III

They followed the shoulder of the hill by a path that led down to the rectory garden. Dinah went in front, and their conversation led to repeated halts.

"I'm afraid," Dinah began, "that I don't much care for your Cousin Eleanor."

"You astonish me, darling," said Henry. "For myself, I regard her as a prize bitch."

"That's all right, then. I couldn't mention this before you'd declared yourself, because it's all about us."

"You mean the day before yesterday when she lurked outside your drawing-room door? Dinah, if she hadn't been there, what would you have done?"

This led to a prolonged halt.

"The thing is," said Dinah presently, "she must have told your father."

"So she did."

"He's spoken to you?"

"He has."

"Oh, Henry!"

"That sounds as if you were settling a quotation. Yes, we had a grand interview. 'What is this I hear, sir, of your attentions to Miss Dinah Copeland?' 'Forgive me, sir, but I refuse to answer you.' 'Do you defy me, Henry?' 'With all respect, sir, I do!' That sort of thing."

"He doesn't want it?"

"Eleanor has told him he doesn't, blast her goggling eyes!"

"Why? Because I'm the poor parson's daughter, or because I'm on the stage, or just because he hates the sight of me?"

"I don't think he hates the sight of you."

"I suppose he wants you to marry a proud heiress."

"I suppose he does. It doesn't matter a tuppenny button, my sweet Dinah, what he wants."

"But it does. You haven't heard. Miss Prentice came to see Daddy last night."

Henry stopped dead and stared at her.

"She said—she said——"

"Go on."

"She told him we were meeting, and that you were keeping it from your father, but he'd found out and was terribly upset and felt we'd both been very underhand and—oh, she must have been absolutely foul! She must have sort of hinted that we were——" Dinah boggled at this and fell silent.

"That we were living in roaring sin?" Henry suggested.

"Yes."

"My God, the minds of these women! Surely the rector didn't pay any attention.

"She's so loathsomely plausible. Do you remember the autumn day, weeks ago, soon after I came back, when you drove me to Moorton Bridge and we picnicked and didn't come back till the evening?"

"Every second of it."

"She'd found out about that. There was no reason why the whole world shouldn't know, but I hadn't told Daddy about it. It had been such a glowing, marvelous day that I didn't want to talk about it."

"Me, too."

"Well, now, you see, it looks all fishy and dubious, and Daddy feels I have been behaving in an underhand manner. When Miss Prentice had gone he took me into his study. He was wearing his beretta, a sure sign that he's feeling his responsibilities. He spoke more in sorrow than in anger, which is always rather toxic, and the worst of it is, he really was upset. He got more and more feudal and said we'd always been—I forget what—almost fiefs or vassals of this man's-man of the Jernighams, and had never done anything disloyal, and here was I behaving like a housemaid having clandestine assignations with you. On and on and on; and Henry, my dear darling, ridiculous though it sounds, I began to feel shabby and common."

"He didn't believe——?"

"No, of course he didn't believe that. But, all the same, you know he's frightfully muddled about sex."

"They all are," said Henry, with youthful gloom. "And with Eleanor and Idris hurling their inhibitions in his teeth——"

"I know. Well, anyway, the upshot was, he forbade me to see you alone. I said I wouldn't promise. It was the first really deadly row we've ever had. I fancy he prayed about it for hours after I'd gone to bed. It's very vexing to lie in bed knowing somebody in the room below is praying away like mad about you. And, you see, I adore the man. At one moment I thought I would say my own prayers, but the only thing I could think of was the old Commination Service. You know: 'Cursed is he that smiteth his neighbor secretly. Amen.'"

"One for Eleanor," said Henry appreciatively.

"That's what I thought, but I didn't say it. But what I've been trying to come to is this: I can't bear to upset Daddy permanently, and I'm afraid that's just what would happen. No, please wait, Henry. You see,

I'm only nineteen, and he can forbid the bans—and, what's more, he'd do it."

"But why?" said Henry. "Why? Why? Why?"

"Because he thinks that we shouldn't oppose your father and because, secretly, he's got a social inferiority complex. He's a snob, poor sweet. He thinks if he smiled on us it would look as if he was all agog to make a grand match for me, and was going behind the squire's back to do it."

"Absolutely driveling bilge!"

"I know, but that's how it goes. It's just one of those things. And it's all due to Miss Prentice. Honestly, Henry, I think she's positively evil. *Why* should she mind about us?"

"Jealousy," said Henry. "She's starved and twisted and a bit dotty. I dare say it's physiological as well as psychological. I imagine she thinks you'll sort of dethrone her when you're my wife. And, as likely as not, she's jealous of your father's affection for you."

They shook their heads wisely.

"Daddy's terrified of her," said Dinah, "*and* of Miss Campanula. They *will* ask him to hear their confessions, and when they go away he's a perfect wreck."

"I'm not surprised, if they tell the truth. I expect what they really do is to try to inform against the rest of the district. Listen to me, Dinah. I refuse to have our love for each other messed up by Eleanor. You're mine. I'll tell your father I've asked you to marry me, and I'll tell mine. I'll *make* them see reason; and if Eleanor comes creeping in—my God, I'll, I'll, I'll——"

"Henry," said Dinah, "how magnificent!"

Henry grinned.

"It'd be more magnificent," he said, "if she wasn't just an unhappy, warped middle-aged spinster."

"It must be awful to be like that," agreed Dinah. "I hope it never happens to me."

"You!"

There was another halt.

"Henry," said Dinah suddenly. "Let's ask them to call an armistice until after the play."

"But we must see each other like this. Alone."

"I shall die if we can't; but all the same I feel, somehow, if we said we'd wait until then, that Daddy might sort of begin to understand. We'll meet at rehearsals, and we won't pretend we're not in love, but I'll promise him I won't meet you alone. It'll be—it'll be kind of dignified. Henry, *do* you see?"

"I suppose so," said Henry unwillingly.

"It'd stop those hateful old women talking."

"My dear, nothing would stop them talking."

"Please, darling Henry."

"Oh, Dinah."

"Please."

"All right. It's insufferable, though, that Eleanor should be able to spoil a really miraculous thing like Us."

"Insufferable."

"She's so completely insignificant."

Dinah shook her head.

"All the same," she said, "she's a bad enemy. She creeps and creeps, and she's simply brimful of poison. She'll drop some of it into our cup of happiness if she can."

"Not if I know it," said Henry.

# CHAPTER VI

# Rehearsal

*I*

THE REHEARSALS were not going any too well. For all Dinah's efforts, she hadn't been able to get very much concerted work out of her company. For one thing, with the exception of Selia Ross and Henry, they would *not* learn their lines. Dr. Templett even took a sort of pride in it. He was forever talking about his experiences in amateur productions when he was a medical student.

"I never knew what I was going to say," he said cheerfully. "I'm capable of saying almost anything. It was always all right on the night. A bit of cheek goes a long way. One can bluff it out with a gag or two. The great thing is not to be nervous."

He himself was not at all nervous. He uttered such lines of the French Ambassador's as he remembered, in a high-pitched voice, made a great many grimaces, waved his hands in a foreign manner, and was never still for an instant.

"I leave it to the spur of the moment," he told them. "It's wonderful what a difference it makes when you're all made-up, with funny clothes on. I never know where I ought to be. You can't do it in cold blood."

"But, Dr. Templett, you've got to," Dinah lamented. "How can we get the timing right or the positions, if at one rehearsal you're on the prompt and at the next on the o.p.?"

"Don't you worry," said Dr. Templett. "We'll be all right. Eet vill be —'ow you say?—so, so charmante."

Off-stage he continually spoke his lamentable broken English, and when he dried up, as he did incessantly, he interpolated his: "'ow you say?"

"If I forget," he said to the rector, who was prompting, "I'll just walk over your side and say, ''ow you say?' like that, and then you'll know."

Selia Ross and he had an irritating trick of turning up late for rehearsals. Apparently the youngest Cain's big toe still needed Dr. Templett's attention, and he explained that he picked up Mrs. Ross and brought her to rehearsals on his way back from Cloudyfold. They would walk in with singularly complacent smiles, half an hour late, while Dinah was reading both their parts and trying to play her own. Sometimes she got her father to read their bits, but the rector intoned them so carefully and slowly that everybody else was thrown into a state of deadly confusion.

Miss Campanula, in a different way, was equally troublesome. She refused to give up her typewritten part. She carried it about with her and read each of her speeches in an undertone during the preceding dialogue, so that whenever she was on the stage the others spoke through a distressing mutter. When her cue came she seldom failed to say, "Oh. Now it's me," before she began. She would often rattle off her lines without any inflection, and apparently without the slightest regard for their meaning. She was forever telling Dinah that she was open to correction, but she received all suggestions in huffy grandeur, and they made not the smallest difference to her performance. Worse than all these peculiarities were Miss Campanula's attempts at characterization. She made all sorts of clumsy and ineffective movements over which she herself seemed to have little control. She continually shifted her weight from one large foot to the other, rather in the manner of a penguin. She wandered about the stage and she made embarrassing grimaces. In addition to all this, she had developed a frightful cold in her nose, and rehearsals were made hideous by her catarrhal difficulties.

Jocelyn was the type of amateur performer who learns his lines from the prompter. Unlike Miss Campanula, he did not hold his part in his hand. Indeed, he had lost it irrevocably immediately after the first rehearsal. He said that it did not matter, as he had already memorized his lines. This was a lie. He merely had a vague idea of their sense. His performance reminded Dinah of divine service, as he was obliged to repeat all his lines, like responses, after the rector. However, in spite of this defect, the squire had an instinctive sense of the theater. He did not fidget or gesticulate. With Dr. Templett tearing about the stage like a wasp, this was particularly refreshing.

Miss Prentice did not know her part either, but she was a cunning bluffer. She had a long scene in which she held a newspaper open in her hands. Dinah discovered that Miss Prentice had pinned several of her sides to the sheets of the *Times*. Others were left in handy places about the stage. When, in spite of these maneuvers, she dried up, Miss Prentice stared in a gently reproachful manner at the person who spoke after her, so that everybody thought it was her *vis-à-vis* who was at fault.

Mrs. Ross had learned her part. Her clear, hard voice had plenty of edge. Once there, she worked, tried to follow Dinah's suggestions, and was very good-humored and obliging. If ever anything was wanted, Mrs. Ross would get it. She brought down to the Parish Hall her cushions, her cocktail glasses and her bridge table. Dinah found herself depending more and more on Mrs. Ross for "hand props" and odds and ends of furniture. But, for all that, she did not like Mrs. Ross, whose peals of laughter at all Dr. Templett's regrettable antics were extremely irritating. The determined rudeness with which Miss Prentice and Miss Campanula met all Mrs. Ross's advances forced Dinah into making friendly gestures which she continually regretted. She saw, with something like horror, that her father had innocently succumbed to Mrs. Ross's charm, and to her sudden interest in his church. This, more than anything else she did, inflamed Miss Campanula and Eleanor Prentice against Selia Ross. Dinah felt that her rehearsals were shot through and through with a mass of ugly suppressions. To complete her discomfort, the squire's attitude towards Mrs. Ross, being ripe with Edwardian naughtiness, obviously irritated Henry and the two ladies almost to breaking point.

Henry had learned his part and shaped well. He and Dinah were the only members of the cast who gave any evidence of team work. The others scarcely even so much as looked at each other, and treated their speeches as if they were a string of interrupted recitations.

## II

The battle of the music had raged for three weeks. Miss Prentice and Miss Campanula, together and alternately, had pretended to altruistic motives, accused each other of selfishness, sulked, denied all desire to perform on the piano, given up their parts, relented, and offered their services anew. In the end Dinah, with her father's moral support behind her, seized upon a moment when Miss Campanula had said she'd no wish to play on an instrument with five dumb notes in the treble and six in the bass.

"All right, Miss Campanula," said Dinah, "we'll have it like that. Miss Prentice has kindly volunteered, and I shall appoint her as pianist. As you've got the additional responsibility of the Y.P.F.C. girls in the front of the house, it really does seem the best idea."

After that Miss Campanula was barely civil to anybody but the rector and the squire.

Five days before the performance, Eleanor Prentice developed a condition which Miss Campanula called "a Place" on the index finger of the left hand. Everybody noticed it. Miss Campanula did not fail to point out that it would probably be much worse on the night of the performance.

"You'd better take care of that Place on your finger, Eleanor," she said. "It's gathering, and to me it looks very nasty. Your blood must be out of order."

Miss Prentice denied this with an air of martyrdom, but there was no doubt that the Place grew increasingly ugly. Three days before the performance it was hidden by an obviously professional bandage, and everybody knew that she had consulted Dr. Templett. A rumor sprang up that Miss Campanula had begun to practice her Prelude every morning after breakfast.

Dinah had a private conversation with Dr. Templett.

"What about Miss Prentice's finger? Will she be able to play the piano?"

"I've told her she'd better give up all idea of it," he said. "There's a good deal of inflammation, and it's very painful. It'll hurt like the devil if she attempts to use it, and it's not at all advisable that she should."

"What did she say?"

Dr. Templett grinned.

"She said she wouldn't disappoint her audience, and that she could rearrange the fingering of her piece. It's the 'Venetian Suite,' as usual, of course?"

"It is," said Dinah grimly. "'Dawn' and 'On the Canal' for the overture, and the 'Nocturne' for the entr'acte. She'll never give way."

"Selia says she wouldn't mind betting old Idris has put poison in her girl friend's gloves like the Borgias," said Dr. Templett, and added: "Good Lord, I oughtn't to have repeated that! It's the sort of thing that's quoted against you in a place like this."

"I won't repeat it," said Dinah.

She asked Miss Prentice if she would rather not appear at the piano.

"How thoughtful of you, Dinah, my dear," rejoined Miss Prentice, with her holiest smile. "But I shall do my little best. You may depend upon me."

"But, Miss Prentice, your finger!"

"Ever so much better," said Eleanor in a voice that somehow suggested that there was something slightly improper in mentioning her finger.

"They are waiting to print the programs. Your name——"

"Please don't worry, dear. My name may appear in safety. Shall we just not say any more about it, but consider it settled?"

"Very well," said Dinah uneasily. "It's very heroic of you."

"Silly child!" said Eleanor playfully.

## III

And now, on Thursday, November the 25th, two nights before the performance, Dinah stood beside the paraffin heater in the aisle of the Parish Hall, and with dismay in her heart prepared to watch the opening scenes in which she herself did not appear. There was to be no music at the dress rehearsal.

"Just to give my silly old finger time to get *quite* well," said Miss Prentice.

But Henry had told Dinah that both he and his father had seen Eleanor turn so white after knocking her finger against a chair that they thought she was going to faint.

"You won't stop her," said Henry. "If she has to play the bass with her feet, she'll do it."

Dinah gloomily agreed.

She had made them up for the dress rehearsal and had attempted to create a professional atmosphere in a building that reeked of parochial endeavor. Even now her father's unmistakably clerical voice could be heard beyond the green serge curtain, crying obediently:

"Beginners, please."

In front of Dinah, six privileged Friendly Young Girls, who were to sell programs and act as ushers at the performance, sat in a giggling row to watch the dress rehearsal. Dr. Templett and Henry were their chief interest. Dr. Templett was aware of this and repeatedly looked round the curtain. He had insisted on making himself up, and looked as if he had pressed his face against a gridiron and then garnished his chin with the hearth-brush. Just as Dinah was about to ring up the curtain, his head again bobbed round the corner.

"Vy do you, 'ow you say, gargle so mooch?" he asked the helpers. A renewed paroxysm broke out.

"Dr. Templett!" shouted Dinah. "Clear stage, *please.*"

"Ten thousand pardons, Mademoiselle," said Dr. Templett. "I vaneesh." He made a comic face and disappeared.

"All ready behind, Daddy?" shouted Dinah.

"I think so," said the rector's voice doubtfully.

"Positions, everybody. House lights, please." Dinah was obliged to execute this last order herself, as the house lights switch was in the auditorium. She turned it off and the six onlookers yelped maddeningly.

"Ssh, please! Curtain!"

"Just a minute," said the rector dimly.

The curtain rose in a series of uneven jerks, and the squire, who should have been at the telephone, was discovered gesticulating violently to someone in the wings. He started, glared into the house, and finally took up his position.

"Where's that telephone bell?" demanded Dinah.

"Oh, dear!" said the rector's voice dismally. He could be heard scuffling about in the prompt-corner and presently an unmistakable bicycle bell pealed. But Jocelyn had already lifted the receiver and, although the bell, which was supposed to summon him to the telephone, continued to ring off-stage, he embarked firmly on his opening lines:

"Hallo! Hallo! Well, who is it?"

The dress rehearsal had begun.

Actors say that a good dress rehearsal means a bad performance. Dinah hoped desperately that the reverse would prove true. Everything seemed to go wrong. She suspected that there were terrific rows in the dressing-rooms, but as she herself had no change to make, she stayed in front whenever she was not actually on the stage. Before the entrance of the two ladies in the second act, Henry came down, and joined her.

"Frightful, isn't it?" he asked.

"It's the end," said Dinah.

"My poor darling, it's pretty bad luck for you. Perhaps it'll pull through to-morrow."

"I don't see how—— Dr. Templett!" roared Dinah. "What are you doing? You ought to be up by the fireplace. Go back, please."

Miss Prentice suddenly walked straight across the stage, in front of Jocelyn, Selia Ross and Dr. Templett, and out at the opposite door.

"*Miss Prentice!*"

But she had gone, and could be heard in angry conversation with Georgie Biggins, the call-boy, and Miss Campanula.

"You're a very naughty little boy, and I shall ask the rector to forbid you to attend the performance."

"You deserve a sound whipping," said Miss Campanula's voice. "And if I had my way——"

The squire and Dr. Templett stopped short and stared into the wings. "What is it?" Dinah demanded.

Georgie Biggins was thrust on the stage. He had painted his nose carmine, and Miss Prentice's hat for the third act was on his head. He had a water-pistol in his hand. The girls in the front row screamed delightedly.

"Georgie," said Dinah with more than a suspicion of tears in her voice, "take that hat off and go home."

"I never——" began Georgie.

"Do what I tell you."

"Yaas, Miss."

Miss Prentice's arm shot through the door. The hat was removed. Dr. Templett took Georgie Biggins by the slack of his pants and dropped him over the footlights.

"Gatcha!" said George and bolted to the back of the hall.

"Go on, please," said poor Dinah.

Somehow or another they got through. Dinah took them back over the scenes that had been outstandingly bad. This annoyed and bored them all very much, but she was adamant.

"It'll be all right on the night," said Dr. Templett.

"Saturday's the night," said Dinah, "and it won't."

At midnight she sat down in the third bench and said she supposed they had better stop. They all assembled in one of the Sunday School rooms behind the stage and gathered round a heater, while Mrs. Ross gave them a very good supper. She had insisted on making this gesture and had provided beer, whiskey, coffee and sandwiches. Miss Campanula and Miss Prentice had both offered to make themselves responsible for this supper, and were furious that Mrs. Ross had got in first.

Dinah was astounded to learn from their conversation that they thought they had done quite well. The squire was delighted with himself; Dr. Templett still retained his character as a Frenchman; and Selia Ross said repeatedly that she thought both of them had been marvelous. The other two ladies spoke only to Mr. Copeland, and each waited until she could speak alone. Dinah saw that her father was bewildered and troubled.

"Oh, Lord!" thought Dinah. "What's brewing now?" She wished that her father was a stronger character, that he would bully or frighten those two venomous women into holding their tongues. And suddenly, with a cold pang she thought: "If he should lose his head and marry one of them!"

Henry brought her a cup of black coffee.

"I've put some whiskey in it," he said. "You're as pale as a star, and you look frightened. What is it?"

"Nothing. I'm just tired."

Henry bent his dark head and whispered:

"Dinah?"

"Yes."

"I'll talk to father on Saturday night when he's flushed with his dubious triumphs. Did you get my letter?"

Dinah's hand floated to her breast.

"Darling," whispered Henry. "Yours, too. We can't wait any longer. After to-morrow?"

"After to-morrow," murmured Dinah.

# CHAPTER VII

# Vignettes

## I

"I HAVE SINNED," said Miss Prentice, "in thought, word and deed by my fault, by my own fault, by my most grievous fault. Especially I accuse myself that since that last confession, which was a month ago, I have sinned against my neighbor. I have harbored evil suspicions of those with whom I have come in contact, accusing them in my heart of adultery, unfaithfulness and disobedience to their parents. I have judged my sister-woman in my heart and condemned her. I have listened many times to evil reports of a woman, and because I could not in truth say that I did not believe them——"

"Do not seek to excuse rather than to condemn yourself," said the rector from behind the Norman confessional that his bishop allowed him to use. "Condemn only your own erring heart. You have encouraged and connived at scandal. Go on."

There was a brief silence.

"I accuse myself that I have committed sins of omission, not performing what I believed to be my bounden Christian duty to the sick, not warning one whom I believe to be in danger of great unhappiness."

The rector heard Miss Prentice turn a page of the notebook where she wrote her confessions. "I know what she's getting at," he thought miserably. But because he was a sincere and humble man, he prayed: "Oh, God, give me the strength of mind to tackle this woman. Amen."

Miss Prentice cleared her throat in a subdued manner and began again. "I have consorted with a woman whom I believe to be of evil nature, knowing that by doing so I may have seemed to connive at sin."

"Our Lord consorted with sinners and was sinless. Judge not that you be not judged. The sin of another should excite only compassion in your heart. Go on."

"I have had angry and bitter thoughts of two young people who have injured someone who is——"

"Stop," said the rector. "Do not accuse others. Accuse only yourself. Examine your conscience. Be sure that you have come here with a contrite and humble heart. If it holds any uncharitable thoughts, repent and confess them. Do not try to justify your anger by relating the cause. God will judge how greatly you have been tempted."

He waited. There was no response at all from his penitent. The church, beyond the confessional, seemed to listen with him for the next whisper.

"My daughter, I am waiting," said the rector, and was horrified when he was answered by a harsh, angry sobbing.

## II

In spite of her cold, Miss Campanula was happy. She was about to make her confession, and she felt at peace with the world and quite youthful and exalted. The terrible black mood that had come upon her when she woke up that morning had vanished completely. She even felt fairly good-humored when she thought of Eleanor playing her "Venetian Suite" at the performance to-morrow evening. With that Place on her finger, Eleanor was likely enough to make a hash of the music, and then everybody would think it was a pity that she, Idris Campanula, had not been chosen. That thought gave her a happy, warm feeling. Nowadays she was never sure what her mood would be. It changed in the most curious fashion from something like ecstasy to a dreadful irritation that came upon her with such violence and with so little provocation that it quite frightened her. It was as if, like the people in the New Testament, she had a devil in her, a beast that could send her thoughts black and make her tremble with anger. She had confessed these fits of rage to Father Copeland (she and Eleanor called him that when they spoke of him together), and he had been kind and had prayed for her. He had also, rather to her surprise, suggested that she should see a doctor. But there was nothing wrong with her health, she reflected, except lumbago and the natural processes attached to getting a little bit older. She pushed that thought away quickly, as it was inclined to make her depressed, and when she was depressed the beast took advantage of her.

Her chauffeur drove her to church, but she was a few minutes early, so she decided that she would look in at the Parish Hall and see if the committee of the Y.P.F.C. had begun to get it ready for to-morrow night. The decorating, of course, would all be done in the morning under her supervision; but there were floors to be swept, forms shifted and tables moved. Perhaps Eleanor would be there—or even Father Copeland on his way to church. Another wave of ecstasy swept over her. She knew why she was so happy. He would perhaps be at Pen Cuckoo for this ridiculous "run through for words" at five o'clock; but, better than that, it was Reading Circle night in the rectory dining-room, and her turn to preside. After it was over she would look in at the study, and Father Copeland would be there alone and would talk to her for a little.

Telling her chauffeur to wait, she marched up the graveled path to the hall.

It was locked. This was irritating. She supposed those young people imagined they had done enough for one day. You might depend upon it, they had made off, leaving half the work for to-morrow. She was just going away again when dimly, from within, she heard the sound of strumming. Someone was playing "Chopsticks" very badly, with the loud pedal on. Miss Campanula felt a sudden desire to know who had remained inside the hall to strum. She rattled the doors. The maddening noise stopped immediately.

"Who's in there?" shouted Miss Campanula, in a cold-infected voice, and rattled again.

There was no answer.

"The back door!" she thought. "It may be open." And she marched round the building. But the back door was shut, and although she pounded angrily on it, splitting her black kid gloves, nobody came to open it. Her face burned with exertion and rising fury. She started off again and completed the circuit of the hall. The frosted windows were all above the level of her eyes. The last one she came to was open at the bottom. Miss Campanula returned to the lane and saw that her chauffeur had followed her in the car from the church.

"Gibson!" she shouted. "Gibson, come here!"

He got out of the car and came towards her. He was a wooden-faced man with a fine physique; very smart in his dark maroon livery and shiny gaiters. He followed his mistress round the front of the hall to the far side.

"I want you to look inside that window," said Miss Campanula. "There's somebody in there who's behaving suspiciously."

"Very good, miss," said Gibson.

He gripped the window sill. The muscles under his smart tunic swelled as he raised himself until his eyes were above the sill.

Miss Campanula sneezed violently, blew her nose on her enormous handkerchief drenched in eucalyptus, and said, "Cad you see annddything?"

"No, miss. There's nobody there."

"But there *bust* be," insisted Miss Campanula.

"I can't see any one, miss. The place is all tidied up, like, for to-morrow."

"Where is the piano?"

"Down on the floor, miss, in front of the stage."

Gibson lowered himself.

"They bust have gone into one of the back rooms," muttered Miss Campanula.

"Could whoever it was have come out at the front door, miss, while you were round at the back?"

"Did you see addybody?"

"Can't say I did, miss. Not round the hall. But I was turning the car. They might have gone round the bend in the lane before I would notice."

"I consider it bost peculiar and suspicious."

"Yes, miss. There's Miss Prentice just coming out of church, miss."

"Is she?" Miss Campanula peered short sightedly down the lane. She could see the south porch of St. Giles and a figure in the doorway.

"I mustn't be late," she thought. "Eleanor has got in first, as usual." And she ordered Gibson to wait for her outside the church. She crossed the lane and strode down to the lych-gate. Eleanor was still in the porch. One did not stop to gossip when going to confession, but she gave Eleanor her usual nod and was astonished to see that she looked ghastly.

"There's something wrong with her," thought Miss Campanula, and somewhere, in the shifting hinterland between her conscious and unconscious thoughts, lay the warm hope that the rector had been displeased with Eleanor at confession.

Miss Campanula entered the church with joy in her heart.

## III

At the precise moment when Miss Prentice and Miss Campanula passed each other in the south porch, Henry, up at Pen Cuckoo, decided that he could remain indoors no longer. He was restless and impatient. He and Dinah had kept their pact, and since their morning on Cloudyfold had not met alone. Henry had announced their intention to his father at breakfast while Eleanor Prentice was in the room.

"It's Dinah's idea," he said. "She calls it an armistice. As our affairs seem to be so much in the public eye, and as her father has been upset by the conversation you had with him last night, Cousin Eleanor, Dinah thinks it would be a good thing if we promised him we would postpone what you have described as our clandestine meetings for three weeks. After that I shall speak to the rector myself." He had looked directly at Miss Prentice and added: "I shall be very grateful if you would not discuss the matter with him in the meantime. After all, it is primarily our affair."

"I shall do what I believe to be my duty, Henry," Miss Prentice said; and Henry had answered, "I'm afraid you will," and walked out of the room.

He and Dinah had written to each other. Henry had found Miss Prentice eyeing Dinah's first letter as it lay beside his plate at breakfast. He had put it in the breast pocket of his coat, rather shocked at the look he had surprised in her face. After that morning he had come down early to breakfast.

During the three weeks' truce, Jocelyn never spoke to his son of Dinah, but Henry knew very well that Miss Prentice nagged at the squire whenever a chance presented itself. Several times Henry had walked into the study to find Eleanor closeted with Jocelyn. The silence that invariably followed his entrance, his father's uncomfortable attempts to break it, and Miss Prentice's tight smile as she glided away, left Henry in no doubt as to the subject of their conversation.

This afternoon, Jocelyn was hunting. Miss Prentice would come back from church before three, and Henry could not face the prospect of tea alone with his cousin. She had refused a car, and would return tired and martyred. Although Jocelyn had taught her to drive, it was her infuriating custom to refuse a car. She would walk to church after dark, on pouring wet nights, and give herself maddening colds in the head. Today, however, was fine with glints of watery sunlight. He took a stick and went out.

Henry walked through the trees into a lane that came out near the church. Perhaps there would be a job of work to be done at the hall. If Dinah was there she would be surrounded by helpers, so that would be all right.

But about half-way down he walked round a sharp bend in the lane and found himself face to face and alone with Dinah.

For a moment they stood and stared at each other. Then Henry said, "I thought I might be able to help in the hall."

"We finished for today at two o'clock."

"Where are you going?"

"Just for a walk. I didn't know you'd—I thought you'd be——"

"I didn't know, either. It was bound to happen sooner or later."

"Yes, I suppose so."

"Your face is white," said Henry, and his voice shook. "Are you all right?"

"Yes. It's only the shock. Yours is white, too."

"Dinah!"

"No, no. Not till to-morrow. We promised."

As if moved by some compulsion outside themselves, they moved like automatons into each other's arms.

When Miss Prentice, dry-eyed but still raging, came round the bend in the lane, Henry was kissing Dinah's throat.

## IV

"I can't see," said Selia Ross, "that it matters what a couple of shocking, nasty old church-hens choose to say."

"But it does," answered Dr. Templett. He kicked a log on the fire. "Mine is one of the few jobs where your private life affects your practice. Why it should be so, the Lord alone knows. And I can't afford to lose my practice, Selia. My brother went through most of what was left when my father died. I don't want to sell Chippingwood, but it takes me all my time to keep it up. It's a beastly situation, I know. Other things being equal, I still couldn't ask Freda to divorce me. Lying there from one year's end to another! Spinal paralysis isn't much fun and—she's still fond of me."

"My poor darling," said Mrs. Ross softly. Templett's back was towards her. She looked at him speculatively. Perhaps she wondered if she should go to him. If so, she decided against it and remained, exquisitely neat and expensive, in a high-backed chair.

"Only just now," muttered Templett, "old Mrs. Cain said something about seeing my car outside. I've noticed things. They're beginning to talk, damn their eyes. And with this new fellow over at Penmoor I can't afford to take chances. It's all due to those two women. Nobody would have thought anything about it if they hadn't got their claws into me. The other day, when I fixed up old Prentice's finger, she asked after Freda, and in almost the same breath she began to talk about you. My God, I wish she'd get gangrene! And now this!"

"I'm sorry I told you."

"No, it was much better you should. I'd better see the damn' thing."

Mrs. Ross went to her writing-desk and unlocked a drawer. She took out a sheet of note-paper and gave it to him. He stared at six lines of black capitals.

"You are given notice to leave the district. If you disregard this warning, your lover shall suffer."

"When did it come?"

"This morning. The postmark was Chipping."

"What makes you think it's her?"

"Smell it."

"Eucalyptus, my God!"

"She's drenched in it."

"She probably carried it in her bag?"

"That's it. You'd better burn it, Billy."

Dr. Templett dropped the paper on the smoldering log and then snatched it up again.

"No," he said. "I've got a note from her at home. I'll compare the paper."

"Surely hers has a printed address."

"This might be a plain sheet for the following on. It's good paper."

"She'd never be such a fool."

"The woman's pathological, my dear. She might do anything. Anyway, I'll see."

He put the paper in his pocket.

"In my opinion," said Selia Ross, "she's green with jealousy because I've rather got off with the parson and the squire."

"So am I."

"Darling," said Mrs. Ross, "you can't think how pure I am with them."

Templett suddenly burst out laughing.

# CHAPTER VIII

# Catastrophe

## I

At ten minutes to eight on the night of Saturday, November 27th, the Parish Hall at Winton St. Giles smelled of evergreens, wet mackintoshes, and humanity. Members of the Young People's Friendly Circle, harried and dragooned by Miss Campanula, had sold all the tickets in advance, so, in spite of the appalling weather, every seat was occupied. Even the Moorton Park people had come over with their house-party, and sat in the front row of less uncomfortable chairs at two shillings a head. Behind them were ranged the church workers including Mr. Prosser, chemist of Chipping, and Mr. Blandish, the police superintendent, both churchwardens. The Women's Institute was there with its husbands and children. Farther back, in a giggling phalanx, were those girls of the Friendly Circle who were not acting as ushers, and behind them, on the back benches, the young men of the farms and villages, smelling of hair-grease and animal warmth. In the entrance, Miss Campanula had posted Sergeant Roper, of the Chipping Constabulary, and sidesman of St. Giles. His duties were to collect tickets and subdue the backbenchers, who were inclined to guffaw and throw paper pellets at their girls. At the end of the fourth row from the front, on the left of the center aisle, sat Georgie Biggins with his parents. He seemed strangely untroubled by his dethronement from the position of call-boy. His hair was plastered down with water on his bullet-shaped head, his face shone rosily, and there was an unholy light in his black boot-button eyes, which were fixed on the piano.

The piano, soon to achieve a world-wide notoriety, stood beneath the stage and facing the center aisle. One of the innumerable photographs that appeared in the newspapers on Monday, November 29th, shows a museum piece, a cottage pianoforte of the nineties, with a tucked silk panel, badly torn, in the front. It has a hard-bitten look. It would not be too fanciful to compare it to a spinster, dressed in dilapidated moth-eaten finery, still retaining an air of shabby gentility, but given over to some very dubious employment. This air is enhanced by the presence of five aspidistras, placed in a row on the top of the bunting, which has been stretched across the top, over the opening and the turned-back lid, tightly fixed to the edges with drawing pins, and allowed to fall in artistic festoons down the sides and in a sort of valance-like effect across the front. At ten to eight on the night of the concert, there on the fretwork rack under the valance of bunting was Miss Prentice's "Venetian Suite," rather the worse for wear, but ready for her attention.

There was a notice in the programs about the object of the performance, a short history of the old piano, a word of thanks to Jocelyn Jernigham, Esq., of Pen Cuckoo, for his generous offer to make up the sum of money needed for a new instrument. The old piano came in for a lot of attention that evening.

At eight o'clock Dinah, sick with apprehension in the prompt-corner, turned on the stage lights. Sergeant Roper, observing this signal, leaned across the row of boys on the back bench and switched off the house lights. The audience made noises of pleasurable anticipation.

Improvised footlights shone upwards on the faded green curtain. After a moment's pause, during which many people in the audience said, "Ssh!" an invisible hand drew the curtain aside and the rector walked through. There was a great burst of applause in the second row, and the reporter from the *Chipping Courier* took out his pad and pencil.

Mr. Copeland's best cassock was green about the seams, the toes of his boots turned up because he always neglected to put trees in them. He was actually a good-looking, rather shabbily-dressed parish priest. But, lit dramatically from beneath, he looked magnificent. It was the head of a medieval saint, austere and beautiful, sharp as a cameo against its own black shadow.

"He ought to be a bishop," said old Mrs. Cain to her daughter.

Behind the curtain, Dinah took a final look at the set. The squire, satisfactory in plus-fours and a good clean make-up, was in his right position up-stage, with a telegram in his hand. Henry stood off-stage at the prompt entrance, very nervous. Dinah moved into the wings with the bicycle bell in her hands.

"He ought to be a bishop," said old Mrs. Cain to her daughter.

Behind the curtain, Dinah took a final look at the set. The squire, satisfactory in plus-fours and a good clean make-up, was in his right position up-stage, with a telegram in his hand. Henry stood off-stage at the prompt entrance, very nervous. Dinah moved into the wings with the bicycle bell in her hands.

"Don't answer the telephone till it's rung twice," she hissed at Jocelyn.

"All right, all right, all right."

"Clear, please," said Dinah severely. "Stand by."

She went into the prompt box, seized the curtain lines and listened to her father.

"—So you see," the rector was saying, "the present piano is almost a historical piece, and I'm sure you will be glad to hear that this old friend will be given an honorable place in the small recreation room at the back of the stage."

Sentimental applause.

"I have one other announcement. You will see on your programs that Miss Prentice of Pen Cuckoo, in addition to taking a part, was to play the overture and entr'acte this evening. I am sorry to say that Miss Prentice has—ah—has—ah—an injured finger which has given—and I am sorry to say is still giving her—a great deal of pain. Miss Prentice, with her customary pluck and unselfishness"—Mr. Copeland paused hopefully and was awarded a tentative outbreak of clapping—"was anxious not to disappoint us and was prepared, up to a minute or two ago, to play the piano. However, as she has an important rôle to fill later on in the evening, and as her hand is really not fit, she—ah—Dr. Templett has—ah—has taken matters in hand and ordered her not to—to play."

The rector paused again while the audience wondered if it should applaud Dr. Templett's efficiency, but decided that, on the whole, it had better not.

"Now, although you will be disappointed and will sympathize, I am sure, with Miss Prentice, we all know we mustn't disobey doctor's orders. I am happy to say that we shall still have our music—and very good music, too. Miss Idris Campanula, at literally a moment's notice, has consented to play for us. Now, I think this is particularly generous and sporting of Miss Campanula, and I'll ask you all to show your appreciation in a really——"

Deafening applause.

"Miss Campanula," ended Mr. Copeland, "will play Rachmaninoff's 'Prelude in C-sharp minor.' Miss Campanula."

He led her from the wings, handed her down the steps to the piano, and returned to the stage through the side curtains.

It was wonderful to see Idris Campanula acknowledge the applause with an austere bend, smile more intimately at the rector, descend the steps carefully and, with her back to the aisle, seat herself at the instrument. It was wonderful to see her remove the "Venetian Suite," and place her famous Prelude on the music rack, open it with a masterly flip, deal it a jocular slap, and then draw out her pince-nez from the tucked silk bosom that so closely resembled the tucked silk bosom of the instrument. Miss Campanula and the old piano seemed to face each other with an air of understanding and affinity. Miss Campanula's back hollowed as she drew up her bosom until it perched on the top of her stays. She leaned forward until her nose was within three inches of the music, and she held her left hand poised over the bass. Down it came.

Pom. *Pom.* POM.

The three familiar pretentious chords.

Miss Campanula paused, lifted her big left foot and planked it down on the soft pedal.

## II

The air was blown into splinters of atrocious clamor. For a second nothing existed but noise—hard racketing noise. The hall, suddenly thick with dust, was also thick with a cloud of intolerable sound. And, as the dust fell, so the pandemonium abated and separated into recognizable sources. Women were screaming. Chair legs scraped the floor, branches of evergreens fell from the walls, the piano hummed like a gigantic top.

Miss Campanula fell forward. Her face slid down the sheet of music, which stuck to it. Very slowly and stealthily she slipped sideways to the keys of the piano, striking a final discord in the bass. She remained there, quite still, in a posture that seemed to parody the antics of an affected virtuoso. She was dead.

## III

Lady Appleby in her chair by the piano turned to her husband as if to ask him a question and fainted.

George Biggins screamed like a whistle.

The rector came through the curtain and ran down the steps to the piano. He looked at that figure leaning on the keys, wrung his hands and faced the audience. His lips moved, but he could not be heard.

Dinah came out of the prompt-corner and stood transfixed. Her head was bent as if in profound meditation. Then she turned, stumbled past the curtain, calling, "Henry! Henry!" and disappeared.

Dr. Templett, in his appalling make-up, came through from the opposite side of the curtain. He went up to the rector, touched his arm and then descended to the piano. He bent down with his back to the audience, stayed so for a moment and then straightened up. He shook his head slightly at the rector.

Mr. Blandish, in the third row, pushed his way to the aisle and walked up to the stage.

He said, "What's all this?" in a loud, constabulary tone, and was heard. The hall went suddenly quiet. The voice of Mr. Prosser, the Chipping organist, said all by itself: "It was a gun. That's what it was. It was a gun."

Mr. Blandish was not in uniform, but he was dressed in authority. He examined the piano and spoke to Dr. Templett. There was a screen masking the corner on the prompt side between the stage and the wall. The two men fetched it and put it round the piano.

The rector mounted the steps to the stage and faced his parishioners.

"My dear people," he said in a trembling voice, "there has been a terrible accident. I beg of you all to go away quietly to your own homes. Roper, will you open the door?"

"Just a minute," said Mr. Blandish. "Just a minute, if *you* please, sir. This is an affair for the police. Charlie Roper, you stay by that door. Have you got your notebook on you?"

"Yes, sir," said Sergeant Roper.

"All right." Mr. Blandish raised his voice. "As you pass out," he roared, "I'll ask you to leave your names and addresses with the sergeant on duty at the door. Anybody who has had anything to do with this entertainment," continued Mr. Blandish with no trace of irony in his voice, "either in the way of taking part or decorating the hall or so forth, will kindly remain behind. Now move along quietly, please, there's no need to rush. The back benches first. Keep your seats till your turn comes."

To the rector he said, "I'd be much obliged if you'd go to the back door, sir, and see nobody leaves that way. If it can be locked and you've got the key, lock it. We'll have this curtain up, if you please. I'm going to the telephone. It's in the back room, isn't it? Much obliged."

He went through the back of the stage, passing Dinah and Henry, who stood side by side in the wings.

"Good evening, Mr. Jernigham," said the superintendent. "Do you mind raising the curtain?"

"Certainly," said Henry.

The curtain rose in a series of uneven jerks, revealing to the people still left in the hall a group of four persons: Jocelyn Jernigham, Selia Ross, Eleanor Prentice and the rector, who had returned from the back door with the key in his hand.

"I can't believe it," said the rector. "I simply cannot believe that it has happened."

"Is it murder?" asked Mrs. Ross sharply. Her voice pitched a note too high, sounded shockingly loud.

"I—I can't believe——" repeated Mr. Copeland.

"But see here, Copeland," interrupted the squire, "I don't know what the devil everybody's driving at. Shot through the head! What d'you mean? Somebody must have seen something. You can't shoot people through the head in a crowded hall without being spotted."

"The shot seems to have come from—from——"

"From where, for heaven's sake?"

"From inside the piano," said the rector unhappily. "We mustn't touch anything; but it seems to have come from inside the piano. You can see through the torn silk."

"Good God!" said Jocelyn. He looked irritably at Miss Prentice, who rocked to and fro like a middle-aged marionette and moaned repeatedly.

"Do be quiet, Eleanor," said the squire. "Here! Templett!"

Dr. Templett had again gone behind the screen, but he came out and said, "What?" in an irascible voice.

"Has she been shot through the head?"

"Yes."

"How?"

"From inside the piano."

"I never heard such a thing," said Jocelyn. "I'm coming to look."

"Yes. But, I say," objected Dr. Templett, "I don't think you ought to, you know. It's a matter for the police."

"Well, you've just been in there."

"I'm police surgeon for the district."

"Well, by God," said the squire, suddenly remembering it, "I'm Acting Chief Constable for the county."

"Sorry," said Dr. Templett. "I'd forgotten."

But the squire was prevented from looking behind the screen by the return of Mr. Blandish.

"That's all right," said the superintendent peaceably. He turned to the squire. "I've just rung up the station and asked for two chaps to come along, sir."

"Oh, yes. Yes. Very sensible," said Jocelyn.

"Just a minute, Blandish," said Dr. Templett. "Come down here, would you?"

They disappeared behind the screen. The others waited in silence. Miss Prentice buried her face in her hands. The squire walked to the edge of the stage, looked over the top of the piano, turned aside, and suddenly mopped his face with his handkerchief.

Blandish and Templett came out and joined the party on the stage.

"Lucky, in a way, your being here on the spot, sir," Blandish said to Jocelyn. "Your first case of this sort since your appointment, I believe."

"Yes."

"Very nasty affair."

"It is."

"Yes, sir. Well, now, with your approval, Mr. Jernigham, I'd just like to get a few notes down. I fancy Mr. Henry Jernigham and Miss Copeland are with us."

He peered into the shadows beyond the stage.

"We're here," said Henry.

He and Dinah came on the stage.

"Ah, yes. Good evening, Miss Copeland."

"Good evening," said Dinah faintly.

"Now," said Blandish, looking round the stage, "this is the whole company of performers, I take it. With the exception of the deceased, of course."

"Yes," said Jocelyn.

"I'll just make a note of the names."

They sat round the stage while Blandish wrote in his notebook. A group of ushers and two youths were huddled on a bench at the far end of the hall under the eyes of Sergeant Roper. Dinah fixed her gaze on this group, on Blandish, on the floor, anywhere but on the top of the piano jutting above the footlights and topped with pots of aspidistra. Far down through the aspidistra, heavily shadowed by the screen, and not quite covered by the green and yellow bunting they had thrown over it, was Miss Campanula's body, face down on the keys of the piano. Dinah found herself wondering who was responsible for the aspidistras. She had meant to have them removed. They must mask quite a lot of the stage from the front rows.

"Don't look at them," said her mind. She turned quickly to Henry.

He took her hands and pulled her round with her back to the footlights.

"It's all right, Dinah," he whispered, "it's all right, darling."

"I'm not panicked or anything," said Dinah.

"Yes," said Blandish, "that's all the names. Now, sir—— Well, what is it?"

A uniformed constable had come in from the front door and stood waiting in the hall.

"Excuse me," said Blandish, and went down to him. There was a short rumbling conversation. Blandish turned and called to the squire.

"Can you spare a moment, sir?"

"Certainly," said Jocelyn, and joined them.

"Can you beat this, sir?" said Blandish, in an infuriated whisper. "We've had nothing better than a few old drunks and speed merchants in this place for the last six months or more, and now, tonight, there's got to be a breaking and entering job at Moorton Park with five thousand pounds' worth of her ladyship's jewelry gone and Lord knows what else besides. Their butler rang up the station five minutes ago, and this chap's come along on his motor bike and he says the whole place is upside down. Sir George and her ladyship and the party haven't got back yet. It looks like the work of the gang that cleaned up a couple of jobs in Somerset a fortnight back. It'll be a big thing to tackle. Now what am I to do, sir?"

Jocelyn and Blandish stared at each other.

"Well," said Jocelyn at last, "you can't be in two places at once."

"That's right, sir," said Blandish. "It goes against the grain when we've scarcely got started, but it looks as if it'll have to be the Yard."

# CHAPTER IX

# C. I. D.

## I

FIVE HOURS AFTER MISS CAMPANULA struck the third chord of the Prelude, put her foot on the soft pedal, and died, a police car arrived at the parish hall of Winton St. Giles. It had come from Scotland Yard. It contained Chief Detective-Inspector Alleyn, Detective-Inspector Fox, Detective-Sergeant Bailey, and Detective-Sergeant Thompson.

Alleyn, looking up from his road map, saw a church spire against a frosty, moonlit hill, trees against stars, and nearer at hand the lighted windows of a stone building.

"This looks like the hidden treasure," he said to Thompson who was driving. "What's the time?"

"One o'clock, sir."

As if in confirmation a clock, outside in the night, chimed for the hour and tolled one.

"Out we get," said Alleyn.

The upland air was cold after the stuffiness of the car. It smelled of dead leaves and frost. They walked up a graveled path to the front of the building. Fox flashed a torch on the brass plate.

"Winton St. Giles Parish Hall. The Gift of Jocelyn Jernigham Esquire of Pen Cuckoo, 1805. To the Glory of God. In memory of his wife Prudence Jernigham who passed away on May 7th, 1801."

"This is the place, sir," said Fox.

"Sure enough," said Alleyn, and rapped smartly on the door.

It was opened by Sergeant Roper, bleary-eyed after a five hours' vigil.

"Yard," said Alleyn.

"Thank Gawd," said Sergeant Roper.

They walked in.

"The super asked me to say, sir," said Sergeant Roper, "that he was very sorry not to be here when you arrived, but seeing as how there's been a first-class breaking and entering up to Moorton Park——"

"That's all right," said Alleyn. "What's it all about?"

"Murder," said Roper. "Will I show you?"

"Do."

They walked up the center aisle between rows of empty benches and chairs. The floor was littered with programs.

"I'll just turn on the other lights, sir," said Roper. "Deceased's behind the screen."

He trudged up the steps to the stage. A switch clicked and Dinah's improvised foot and proscenium lights flooded the stage. Bailey and Thompson pulled the screen to one side.

There was Miss Campanula with her face on the keyboard of the piano, waiting for the expert, the camera, and the pathologist.

"Good Lord!" said Alleyn.

Rachmaninoff's (and Miss Campanula's) Prelude was crushed between her face and the keys. A dark crimson patch had seeped out towards the margin of the music, but the title showed clearly. A hole had been blown through the center. Without touching the music, Alleyn could see several penciled reminders. After the last of the opening chords was an emphatic "S.P." The left hand had been pinned down by the face but the right had fallen, and hung inconsequently at the end of a long purple arm. The face itself was hidden. They stared down at the back of the head. Its pitiful knot of gray hair, broken and loosened, hung over a dark hole. Weepers of stained hair stuck to the thin neck.

"Through the back of the skull," said Fox.

"That's the wound of exit," said Alleyn. "We shall have to find the bullet."

Bailey turned away and began to search along the aisle.

Alleyn shone his torch on the tucked silk front of the piano. There was a rent exactly in the center extending above and below the central hole made by the bullet. Inside the hole, but quite close to the surface, the light picked up a shining circle. Alleyn leaned forward, peering, and uttered a soft exclamation.

"That's the gun that did the job, sir," said Roper. "Inside the piano."

"Has it been touched?"

"No, sir, no. The super was in the audience and he took over immediately, did super. Except for doctor, not a soul's been near."

"The doctor. Where is he?"

"He's gone home, sir. Dr. Templett it is, up to Chippingwood. He's police surgeon. He was here when it happened. He said would I ring him up when you came and if you wanted him he'd be over. It's only a couple of miles off."

"I think he'd better come. Ring him up now, will you?"

When Roper had gone, Alleyn said, "This is a rum go, Fox."

"Very peculiar, Mr. Alleyn. How's it been worked?"

"We'll take a look-see when we've got some pictures. Take every angle, Thompson."

Thompson had already begun to set up his paraphernalia. Soon the flashlight threw Miss Campanula into startling relief. For the second and last time she was photographed, seated at the instrument.

Roper came back from the telephone and watched the experts with avid interest.

"Funniest go you ever did see," he said to Bailey, who had moved to the end of the aisle. "I was on the spot. The old lady sits down at the piano in her bold way and wades into it. Biff, biff, plonk, and before you know where you are the whole works go off like a packet of crackers and she's lying there a corpse."

"Cuh!" said Bailey and stooped swiftly to the floor. "Here we are, sir," he said. "Here's the bullet."

"Got it? I'll look at it in a minute."

Alleyn marked the position of the head and arm and squatted on the floor to run a chalk line round the feet.

"Size eight," he murmured. "The left foot looks as if it's slipped on the soft pedal. Now, I wonder. Well, we'll soon find out. Got gloves on, all of you? Good. Go carefully, I should, and keep away from the front. Will you, sergeant—what is your name, by the way?"

"Roper, sir."

"Right. Will you clear the stuff off the top?"

Roper shifted the aspidistras and began to unpin the bunting. Alleyn went up to the stage and squatted over the footlights like a sort of presiding deity.

"Gently does it, the thing's tottering. Look at that!"

He pointed at the inside of the top lid, which was turned back.

"Wood-rot. No wonder they wanted a new one. Good Lord!"

"What, sir?"

"Come and look at this, Fox."

Alleyn shone his torch in at the top. The light glinted on a steel barrel. He slipped in his gloved fingers. There was a sharp click.

"I've just snicked over the safety-catch on a perfectly good automatic. Now, then."

Roper pulled away the bunting.

"Well, I'll be damned!" said Fox.

## II

"Very fancy, isn't it?" said Alleyn.

"A bit too fancy for me, sir. How does it work?"

"It's a Colt. The butt's jammed between the pegs, where the wires are made fast, and the front of the piano. The nozzle fits into a hole in this fretwork horror in front of the silk bib. The bib's rotten with age and bulging. It could be tweaked in front of the nozzle. Anyway, the music would hide it. Of course the top was smothered in bunting and vegetables."

"But what pulled the trigger?"

"Half a second. There's a loop of string round the butt and over the trigger. The string goes on to an absurd little pulley in the back of the inner case. Then forward to another pulley on a front strut. Then it goes down." He moved his torch. "Yes, now you can see. The other end of the string is fixed to the batten that's part of the soft pedal action. When you use the pedal the batten goes backwards. Moves about two inches, I fancy. Quite enough to give a sharp jerk to the string. We'll have some shots of this, Thompson. It's a bit tricky. Can you manage?"

"I think so, Mr. Alleyn."

"It looks like a practical joke," said Fox.

Alleyn looked up quickly.

"Funny you should say that," he said. "You spoke my thoughts. A small boy's practical joke. The Heath Robinson touch with the string and pulleys is quite in character. I believe I even recognize those little pulleys, Fox. Notice how very firmly they've been anchored. My godson's got their doubles in one of those building sets, an infernal dithering affair that's supposed to improve the mind, and nearly sent me out of mine. 'Twiddletoy,' it's called. Yes, and by George, Brer Fox, that's the sort of cord they provide; thin green twine, very tough, like fishing line, and fits nicely into the groove of the pulley."

"D'you reckon some kid's gone wild and rigged this for the old girl?" asked Fox.

"A child with a Colt .32?"

"Hardly. Still, he might have got hold of one."

Alleyn swore softly.

"What's up, sir?" asked Fox.

"It's the whole damn' layout of the thing! It's exactly like a contraption they give in the book of the works of these toys. 'Fig. 1. Signal.' It's no more like a signal than your nose. Less, if anything. But you build it on this principle. I made the thing for my godson. The cord goes up in three steps to pulleys that are fixed to a couple of uprights. At the bottom it's tied to a little arm and at the top to a bigger one. When you push down the lower arm, the upper one waggles. I'll swear it inspired this job. You see how there's just room for the pulley in the waist of the Colt at the back? They're fiddling little brutes, those pulleys, as I know to my cost. Not much bigger than the end of a cigarette. Hole through the middle. Once you've threaded the twine it can't slip out. It's guarded by the curved lips of the groove. You see, the top one's anchored to the wires above that strip of steel. The bottom one's tied to a strut in the fretwork. All right, Thompson, your witness."

Thompson maneuvered his camera.

A car drew up outside the hall. A door slammed.

"That'll be the doctor, sir," said Roper.

"Ah, yes. Let him in, will you?"

Dr. Templett came in. He had removed his make-up and his beard and had changed the striped trousers and morning coat proper to a French Ambassador, for a tweed suit and sweater.

"Hullo," he said. "Sorry if I kept you waiting. Car wouldn't start."

"Dr. Templett?"

"Yes, and you're from Scotland Yard, aren't you? Didn't lose much time. This is a nasty business."

"Beastly," said Alleyn. "I think we might move her now."

They brought a long table from the back of the hall and on it they laid Miss Campanula. She had been shot between the eyes.

"Smell of eucalyptus," said Alleyn.

"She had a cold."

Dr. Templett examined the wounds while the others looked on. At last he straightened up, took a bottle of ether from his pocket, and used a little to clean his hands.

"There's a sheet in one of the dressing-rooms, Roper," he said. Roper went off to get it.

"What've you got there?" Templett asked Alleyn.

Alleyn had found Miss Prentice's Venetian Suite behind the piano. He turned it over in his hands. Like the Prelude, it was a very jaded affair. The red back of the cover had a discolored circular patch in the center. Alleyn touched it. It was damp. Roper returned with the sheet.

"Can't make her look very presentable, I'm afraid," said Dr. Templett. "Rigor's fairly well advanced in the jaw and neck. Rather quick after five hours. She fell at an odd angle. I didn't do more than look at her. The exit wound showed clearly enough what had happened. Of course, I assured myself she was dead."

"Did you realize at once that it was a wound of exit?"

"What? Yes. Well, after a second or two I did. Thought at first she'd been shot through the back of the head and then I noticed characteristics of an exit wound, direction of the matted hair and so on. I bent down and tried to see the face. I could just see the blood. Then I noticed the hole in the music. The frilling round the edge of the hole showed clearly enough which way the bullet had come."

"Very sound observation," said Alleyn. "You knew, then, what had happened?"

"I was damn' puzzled and still am. When we'd rigged up the screen I had another look and spotted the nozzle of the revolver or whatever it is, behind the silk trimmings. I told Blandish, the local superintendent, and he had a look too. How the devil was it done?"

"A mechanical device that she worked herself."

"Not suicide?"

"No, murder. You'll see when we open the piano."

"Extraordinary business."

"Very," agreed Alleyn. "Bailey, you might get along with your department now. When Thompson's finished, you can go over the whole thing for prints and then dismantle it. In the meantime, I'd better produce my notebook and get a few hard facts."

They carried the table into a corner and put the screen round it. Roper came down with a sheet and covered the body.

"Let's sit down somewhere," suggested Dr. Templett. "I want a pipe. It's given me a shock, this business."

They sat in the front row of stalls. Alleyn raised an eyebrow at Fox who came and joined them. Roper stood in the offing. Dr. Templett filled his pipe, Alleyn and Fox opened their notebooks.

"To begin with," said Alleyn, "who was this lady?"

"Idris Campanula," said Templett. "Spinster of this parish."

"Address?"

"The Red House, Chipping. You passed it on your way up."

"Have the right people been told about this?"

"Yes. The rector did that. Only the three maids. I don't know about the next-of-kin. Somebody said it was a second cousin in Kenya. We'll have to find that out. Look here, shall I tell you the story in my own words?"

"I wish you would."

"I thought I'd find myself in the double rôle of police surgeon and eye-witness, so I tried to sort it out while I waited for your telephone call. Here goes. Idris Campanula was about fifty years of age. She came to the Red House as a child of twelve to live with her uncle, General Campanula, who adopted her on the death of her parents. He was an old bachelor and the girl was brought up by his acidulated sister, whom my father used to call one of the nastiest women he'd ever met. When Idris was about thirty, the general died, and his sister only survived him a couple of years. The house and money, a lot of money by the way, were left to Idris, who by that time was shaping pretty much like her aunt. Nil nisi and all that, but it's a fact. She never had a chance. Starved and repressed and hung about with a mass of shibboleths and Victorian conversation. Well, here she's stayed for the last twenty years, living on rich food, good works and local scandal. Upon my word, it's incredible that she's gone. Look here, I'm being too diffuse, aren't I?"

"Not a bit. You're giving us a picture in the round which is what we like."

"Well, there she was until tonight. I don't know if you've heard from Roper about the play."

"We haven't had time," said Alleyn, "but I hope to get volumes from him before dawn."

Roper looked gratified and drew nearer.

"The play was got up by a group of local people."

"Of whom you were one," said Alleyn.

"Hullo!" Dr. Templett took his pipe out of his mouth and stared at Alleyn. "Now, did any one tell you that, or is this the real stuff?"

"I'm afraid it's not even up to Form 1 at Hendon. There's a trace of grease paint in your hair. I wish I could add that I have written a short monograph on grease paint."

Dr. Templett grinned.

"I'll lay you ten to one," he said, "that you can't deduce what sort of part I had."

Alleyn glanced sideways at him.

"We are not allowed to show off," he said, "but with Inspector Fox's austere eye on me, I venture to have a pot shot. A character part, possibly a Frenchman, wearing a rimless eyeglass. Any good?"

"Did we bet in shillings?"

"It was no bet," said Alleyn apologetically.

"Well, let's have the explanation," said Templett. "I enjoy feeling a fool."

"I'm afraid I'll feel rather a fool making it," said Alleyn. "It's very small beer indeed. In the words of all detective heroes, you only need to consider. You removed your make-up in a hurry. Spirit gum, on which I have not written a monograph, leaves its mark unless removed with care and alcohol. Your chin and upper lip show signs of having been plucked and there's a very remote trace of black crêpe hairiness. Only on the tip of your chin and not on your cheeks. Ha! A black imperial. The foreign ambassadorial touch. A sticky reddish dent by the left eye suggests a rimless glass, fixed with more spirit gum. The remains of a heated line across the brow suggests a top hat. And, when you mentioned your part, you moved your shoulders very slightly. You were thinking subconsciously of your performance. Broken English. ''Ow you say?' with a shrug. That sort of thing. For heaven's sake say I'm right."

"By gum!" said Sergeant Roper, devoutly.

"Amen," said Dr. Templett. "In the words of Mr. Holmes——"

"—of whom nobody shall make mock in my presence. Pray continue your most interesting narrative," said Alleyn.

# CHAPTER X

# According to Templett

*I*

"——AND SO YOU SEE," concluded Templett, "there is absolutely nothing about any of us that is at all out of the ordinary. You might find the same group of people in almost any of the more isolated bits of English countryside. The parson, the squire, the parson's daughter, the squire's son, the two church hens and the local medico."

"And the lady from outside," added Alleyn, looking at his notes. "You have forgotten Mrs. Ross."

"So I have. Well, she's simply a rather charming newcomer. That's all. I'm blessed if I can see who, by the wildest flight of imagination, could have wanted to kill this very dull middle-aged frumpish spinster. I shouldn't have thought she had an enemy in the world."

"I wouldn't say that," said Sergeant Roper, unexpectedly. Alleyn looked up at him.

"No?"

"No, sir, I wouldn't say that. To speak frankly, she was a very sharp-tongued lady. Mischievous like. Well, overbearing. Very curious, too. Proper nosey-parker. My missus always says you couldn't change your mind without it being overheard at the Red House. My missus is friendly with the cook up to Red House, but she never says anything she doesn't want everybody in the village to hear about. Miss Campanula used to order the meals and then wait for the news, as you might say. They call her the Receiving Set in Chipping."

"Do they, indeed?" murmured Alleyn.

"You don't murder people for being curious," said Templett.

"You do sometimes, I reckon, doctor," said Roper.

"I can't imagine it with Miss Campanula."

"I don't reckon anybody *did* want to murder Miss Campanula," said Roper, stolidly.

"Hullo!" Alleyn ejaculated. "What's all this?"

"I reckon they wanted to murder Miss Prentice."

"Good God!" said Templett. "I never thought of that!"

"Never thought of what?" said Alleyn.

"I forgot to tell you. Good Lord, what a fool! Why didn't you remind me, Roper? Good Lord!"

"May we hear now?" asked Alleyn patiently.

"Yes, of course."

In considerable confusion, Templett explained about Miss Prentice's finger and the change of pianists.

"This is altogether another kettle of fish," said Alleyn. "Let's get a clear picture. You say that up to twenty minutes to eight Miss Prentice insisted that she was going to do the overture and entr'acte?"

"Yes. I told her three days ago she'd better give it up. There was this whitlow on her middle finger and she mucked about with it and got some sort of infection. It was very painful. D'you think she'd give in? Not a bit of it. Said she'd alter the fingering of her piece. Wouldn't hear of giving it up. I asked her tonight if she'd let me look at it. Oh, no! It was 'much easier'! She'd got a surgical stall over it. At about twenty to eight I passed the ladies' dressing-room. The door was half open and I heard a sound like somebody crying. I could see her in there alone, rocking backwards and forwards holding this damned finger. I went in and insisted on looking at it. All puffed up and as fiery as hell! She was in floods of tears but she still said she'd manage. I put my foot down. Dinah Copeland came in, saw what was up, and fetched her father who's got more authority over these women than anybody else. He made her give in. Old Idris, poor old girl, had turned up by then and was all agog to play the famous Prelude. She's played it in and out of season for the last twenty years, if it's been written as long as that. Somebody was sent off to the Red House for the music and a dress; she was dressed up for her part, you see. The rector said he'd make an announcement about it. By that time Miss Prentice had settled down to being a martyr and—but, look here, I'm being most amazingly indiscreet. Now, don't go and write all this down in that notebook and quote me as having said it."

Dr. Templett looked anxiously at Fox whose notebook was flattened out on his enormous knee.

"That's all right, sir," said Fox blandly. "We only want the essentials."

"And I'm giving you all the inessentials. Sorry."

"I didn't say that, now, doctor."

"We can take it," Alleyn said, "that, in your opinion, up to twenty to eight everybody, including Miss Campanula and Miss Prentice, believed the music would be provided by Miss Prentice."

"Certainly."

"And this Venetian Suite was Miss Prentice's music?"

"Yes."

"Nobody could have rigged this apparatus inside the piano after seven-forty?"

"Lord, no! The audience began to arrive at about half-past seven, didn't it, Roper? You were on the door."

"The Cains turned up at seven-twenty," said Roper, "and Mr. and Mrs. Biggins and that young limit Georgie, were soon after them. I was on duty at seven. Must have been done before then, sir."

"Yes. What about the afternoon and morning? Anybody here?"

"We were all in and out during the morning," said Dr. Templett. "The Y.P.F.C. girls did the decorating and fixed up the supper arrangements and so on, and we got our stuff ready behind the scenes. Masses of people."

"You'd been rehearsing here, I suppose?"

"Latterly. We did most of the rehearsing up in the study at Pen Cuckoo. It was too cold here until they got extra heaters in. We had our dress rehearsal here on Thursday night. Yesterday afternoon at five, Friday I mean, we went up to Pen Cuckoo and had what Dinah calls a run-through for words."

"What about this afternoon before the performance?"

"It was shut up during the afternoon. I called in at about three o'clock to drop some of my gear. The place was closed then and the key hung up between the wall of the outside place and the main building. We'd arranged that with Dinah."

"Did you notice the piano?"

"Now, did I? Yes. Yes, I did. It was where it is now, with bunting all over the top and a row of pot plants. They'd fixed it up like that in the morning."

"Did anybody else look in at three o'clock while you were here?"

"Let me think. Yes, Mrs. Ross was there with some foodstuff. She left it in the supper-room at the back of the stage."

"How long were you both in the place?"

"Oh, not long. We—talked for a minute or two and then came away."

"Together?"

"No. I left Mrs. Ross arranging sandwiches on plates. By the way, if you want anything to eat, do help yourselves. And there's some beer under the table. I provided it, so don't hesitate."

"Very kind of you," said Alleyn.

"Not a bit. Be delighted. Where were we? Oh, yes. I had a case over near Moorton and I wanted to look in at the cottage hospital. I wasn't here long."

"Nobody else came in?"

"Not then."

"Who was the first to arrive in the evening?"

"I don't know. I was the last. Had an emergency case at six. When I got home I found my wife not so well again. We didn't get here till half-past seven. Dinah Copeland thought I wasn't going to turn up and had worked herself into a frightful stew. She'd be able to tell you all about times of arrival. I bet she got here long before the rest of the cast. Dinah Copeland. That's the parson's daughter. She produced the play."

"Yes. Thank you."

"Well, I suppose you don't want me any longer. Good Lord, it's nearly two o'clock!"

"Awful, isn't it? We shall be here all night, I expect. No, we won't bother you any more, Dr. Templett."

"What about moving the body? Shall I fix up for the mortuary van to come along as early as possible?"

"I wish you would."

"I'll have to do the P.M., I suppose?"

"Yes. Yes, of course."

"Pretty plain sailing, it'll be, poor old girl. Well, good night or good morning, er—I don't know your name, do I?"

"Alleyn."

"What, Roderick Alleyn?"

"Yes."

"By George, I've read your book of criminal investigation. Damned good. Fascinating subject, isn't it?"

"Enthralling."

"For the layman, what? Not such fun for the expert."

"Not quite such fun."

Dr. Templett shook hands, turned to go, and then paused.

"I tell you what," he said. "I'd like to see how this booby-trap worked."

"Yes, of course. Come and have a look."

Bailey was at the piano with an insufflator and a strong lamp. Thompson stood by with his cameras.

"How's it going, Bailey?" asked Alleyn.

"Finished the case, sir. Not much doing. Somebody must have dusted the whole show. We may get some latent prints but I don't think there's a chance, myself. Same with the Colt. We're ready to take it down."

"All right. Go warily, we don't want to lose any prints if they're there. I'll move the front of the piano off and you hold the gun."

Bailey reached a gloved hand inside the top.

"I'll take off the pulley on the front panel, sir."

"Yes. That'll give us a better picture than if you dismantled the twine altogether."

Fox undid the side catches and Alleyn lifted away the front of the piano and put it on one side.

"Hullo," he said, "this silk paneling seems as though it's had water spilled on it. It's still dampish. Round the central hole."

"Blood?" suggested Dr. Templett.

"No. There's a little blood. This was water. A circular patch of it. Now, I wonder. Well, let's have a look at the works."

The Colt, supported at the end of the barrel by Bailey's thumb and forefinger, was revealed with its green twine attachments. The butt was still jammed against the pegs at the back. Alleyn picked up the detached pulley and held it in position.

"Good God!" said Dr. Templett.

"Ingenious, isn't it?" Alleyn said. "I think we'll have a shot of it like this, Thompson. It'll look nice and clear for the twelve good men and true."

"Is the safety catch on?" demanded Dr. Templett, suddenly stepping aside.

"It is. You've dealt with the soft pedal, haven't you, Bailey?" He stooped and pressed the left pedal down with his hand. The batten with its row of hammers moved towards the string. The green twine tightened in the minute pulleys.

"That's how it worked. You can see where the pressure comes on the trigger."

"A very neat-fingered person, wouldn't you say, Mr. Alleyn?" said Fox.

"Yes," said Alleyn. "Neat and sure fingers."

"Oh, I don't know," said Templett. "It's amazingly simple, really. The only tricky bit would be passing the twine through the trigger guard, round the butt, and through the top pulley. That could be done before the gun was jammed in position. No, it's simpler than it looks."

"It's like one of these affairs in books," said Bailey disgustedly. "Someone trying to think up a new way to murder. Silly, I call it."

"What do you say, Roper?" said Alleyn.

"To my way of thinking, sir," said Sergeant Roper, "these thrillers are ruining our criminal classes."

Dr. Templett gave a shout of laughter. Roper turned scarlet and stared doggedly at the wall.

"What d'you mean by that, my lad?" asked Fox, who was on his knees, staring into the piano.

Thompson, grinning to himself, touched off his flashlight.

"What I mean to say, Mr. Fox," said Roper. "It puts ideas in their foolish heads. And the talkies, too. Especially the young chaps. They get round the place talking down their noses and making believe they're gangsters. Look at this affair! I bet the chap that did this got the idea of it out of print."

"That's right, Roper, stick to it," said Dr. Templett. Roper disregarded him. Templett repeated his good nights and went away.

"Go on, Roper. It's an idea," said Alleyn when the door had slammed. "What sort of print do you imagine would inspire this thing?"

"One of those funny drawings with bits of string and cogs and umbrellas and so forth?" suggested Thompson.

"Heath Robinson? Yes."

"Or more likely, sir," said Roper, "one of the fourpenny boys' yarns in paper covers like you buy at the store in Chipping. I used to buy them myself as a youngster. There's always a fat lad and a comic lad and the comical chap plays off the fat one. Puts lighted crackers in his pants and all that. I recollect trying the cracker dodge under the rector's seat at Bible class, and he gave me a proper tanning for it, too, did rector."

"The practical joke idea again, you see, Fox," said Alleyn.

"Well," said Fox, stolidly. "Do we start off reading the back numbers of a boys' paper, or what?"

"You never know, Brer Fox. Have you noticed the back of the piano where the bunting's pinned down? There are four holes in the center drawing pin and three to each of the others. Will you take the Colt out now, and all the rest of the paraphernalia? I'm going to take a look round the premises. We'll have to start seeing these people in the morning. Who the devil's that?"

There was a loud knock at the front entrance.

"Will I see?" asked Sergeant Roper.

"Do."

Roper tramped off down the center aisle and threw open the doors.

"Good morning," said a man's voice outside. "I wonder if I can come in for a moment. It's raining like Noah's half-holiday and I'd like to have a word with——"

"Afraid not, sir," said Roper.

"But I assure you I want to see the representative from Scotland Yard. I've come all the way from London," continued the voice plaintively. "I have, indeed. I represent the *Evening Mirror.* He'll be delighted to see me. Is it by any chance——"

"Yes, it is," said Alleyn loudly and ungraciously. "You can let him in, Roper."

A figure in a dripping mackintosh and streaming hat made a quick rush past Roper, gave a loud exclamation expressive of delight, and hurried forward with outstretched hand.

"I am *not* pleased to see you," said Alleyn.

"Good morning, Mr. Bathgate," said Fox. "Fancy it being you."

"Yes, just fancy!" agreed Nigel Bathgate. "Well, well, well! I never expected to find the old gang. Bailey, too, and Thompson. It's like the chiming of old bells to see you all happily employed together."

"How the blue hell did you get wind of this?" inquired Alleyn.

"The gentleman who does market and social notes for the *Chipping Courier* was in the audience tonight and like a bright young pressman he rang up the Central News. I was in the office when it came through and you couldn't see my rudder for the foam. Down here in four hours with one puncture. God bless my soul, now, what's it all about?"

"Sergeant Roper will perhaps spare a moment to throw you a bone or two. I'm busy. How are you?"

"Grand. Angela would send her love if she knew I was here, and your godson wants you to put him down for Hendon. He's three on Monday. Is it too late?"

"I'll inquire. Roper, you will allow Mr. Bathgate to sit quietly in a corner somewhere. I'll be back in a few minutes. Coming, Fox?"

Alleyn and Fox went up on the stage, looked round the box-set, and explored the wings.

"We'll have to go over this with a toothcomb," Alleyn said, "looking for Lord knows what, as usual. Miss Dinah Copeland seems to have gone to a lot of trouble. The scenery's been patched up. Improvised footlights, you see, and I should think the two big overheads are introduced."

He went into the prompt-corner.

"Here's the play. *Shop Window,* by Hunt. Rather a good comedy. Very professional, with all the calls marked and so on. A bicycle bell. Probably an adjunct of the telephone on the stage. Let's have a look behind."

A short flight of steps on each side of the back wall led down into a narrow room that ran the length of the stage.

"Mrs. Ross's supper arrangements all laid out on the table. Lord, Fox, those sandwiches look good."

"There's a lot more in this basket," said Fox. "Dr. Templett did say——"

"And beer under the table," murmured Alleyn. "Brer Fox?"

"A keg of it," said Fox, who was exploring. "Dorset draught beer. Very good, Dorset draught."

"You're right," said Alleyn after an interval. "It's excellent. Hullo!" He stooped and picked something out of a box on the floor.

"Half a Spanish onion. Any onion in your sandwiches?"

"No."

"Nor in mine. It's got flour or something on it." He put the onion on the table and began to examine the plates of sandwiches. "Two kinds only, Fox. Ham and lettuce on the one hand, cucumber on the other. Hullo, here's a tray all set out for a stage tea. Nobody eats anything. Wait a bit."

He lifted the lid of the empty silver teapot and sniffed at the inside.

"The onion appears to have lived in the teapot. Quaint conceit, isn't it? Very rum, indeed. Come on."

They explored the dressing-rooms. There were two on each side of the supper-room.

"Gents to the right, ladies to the left," said Alleyn. He led the way into the first room on the left. He and Fox began a methodical search through the suitcases and pockets.

"Not quite according to Cocker, perhaps," Alleyn remarked, peering at Miss Prentice's black marocain on the wall. "But I think we'll ask afterwards. Anyway, I'm provided with a blank search warrant so we're all right. Damn this onion, my hand stinks of it. This must be the two spinsters' rooms, judging by the garments."

"Judging by the pictures," said Fox, "it's a Bible classroom in the ordinary way."

"Yes. The Infant Samuel. What about next door? Ah, rather more skittish dresses. This will be Dinah Copeland and Mrs. Ross. Dr.

Templett seemed rather self-conscious about Mrs. Ross, I thought. Miss Copeland's grease paints are in a cardboard box with her name on it. They've been used a lot. Mrs. Ross's, in a brand new japanned tin affair and brand new themselves, from which, inspired by Dorset draught, I deduce that Miss Copeland may be a professional, but Mrs. Ross undoubtedly is not. Here's a card in the new tin box. 'Best luck for tonight, B.' A present, by gum! Who's B., I wonder. Now for the men's rooms."

They found nothing of interest in the men's rooms until Alleyn came to a Donegal tweed suit.

"This is the doctor's professional suit," he said. "It reeks of surgery. Evidently the black jacket is not done in a country practice. I suppose, in the hubbub, he didn't change but went home looking like a comic-opera Frenchman. He must have——"

Alleyn stopped short. Fox looked up to see him staring at a piece of paper.

"Found something, sir?"

"Look."

It was a piece of plain blue paper. Fox read the lines of capitals:

"YOU ARE GIVEN NOTICE TO LEAVE THE DISTRICT. IF YOU DISREGARD THIS WARNING, YOUR LOVER SHALL SUFFER."

"Where did you find this, Mr. Alleyn?"

"In a wallet. Inside breast pocket of the police surgeon's suit," said Alleyn. He dropped it on the dressing-table and then bent down and sniffed at it.

"It smells of eucalyptus," he said.

# CHAPTER XI

# According to Roper

## *I*

"That's awkward," grunted Fox, after a pause.

"Couldn't be more awkward."

"'Your *lover* shall suffer,'" quoted Fox. "That looks as if it was written to a woman, doesn't it?"

"It's not common usage nowadays the other way round, but it's English. Common enough in the mixed plural."

"He's a married man," Fox remembered.

"Yes, it sounded as if his wife's an invalid, didn't it? This may have been written to his mistress or possibly to him, or it may have been shown him by a third person who is threatened and wants advice."

"Or he may have done it himself."

"Yes, it's possible, of course. Or it may be the relic of a parlor game. Telegrams, for instance. You make a sentence from a string of letters. He'd hardly carry that about next to his heart, though, would he? Damn! I'm afraid we're in for a nasty run, Brer Fox."

"How did the doctor strike you, Mr. Alleyn?"

"What? Rather jumpy. Bit too anxious to please. Couldn't stop talking."

"That's right," agreed Fox.

"We'll have to flourish the search warrant a bit if we work on this," said Alleyn. "It'll be interesting to see if he misses it before we tackle him about it."

"He's doing the P.M."

"I know. We shall be present. Anyway, the lady was shot through the head. We've got the weapon and we've got the projectile. The post-mortem is not likely to be very illuminating. Hullo, Bailey, what is it?"

Bailey had come down the steps from the stage.

"I thought you'd better know, sir. This chap Roper's recognized the automatic. Mr. Bathgate ran him down to the station and they've checked up the number."

"Where is he?"

"Out in the hall." A reluctant grin appeared on Bailey's face. "I reckon he still thinks it's great to be a policeman. He wants to tell you himself."

"Very touching. All right. Bailey, I want you to test this paper for prints. Do it at once, will you, and put it between glass when you've finished. And, Bailey, have a shot at the teapot out there. Inside and out."

"Teapot, sir?"

"Yes. Also the powdered onion on the table. I dare say it's quite immaterial, but it's queer, so we'd better tackle it."

They returned to the hall where they found Roper standing over the automatic with something of the air of a clever retriever.

"Well, Roper," said Alleyn, "I hear you've done a bit of investigation for us."

"Yes, sir, I have so. I've recognized the lethal weapon, sir."

"Well, whose is it?"

"I says to myself when I see it," said Roper, "I know you, my friend, I've had you in my hands, I said. And then I remembered. It was when we checked up on firearms licenses six months ago. Now, I suppose a hundred weapons must have passed under my notice that time, this being a sporting part of the world, so I reckon it's not surprising I didn't pick this affair as soon as I clapped eyes on her. I reckon that's not surprising, and yet she looked familiar, you understand?"

"Yes, Roper, I quite understand. Who is the owner?"

"This weapon, sir, is a Colt .32 automatic, the property of Jocelyn Jernigham, Esquire, of Pen Cuckoo."

"Is it, indeed?" murmured Alleyn.

"This gentleman, Mr. Bathgate, ran me down to the station, sir, and it didn't take me over and above five minutes to lay my fingers on the files. You can take a look at the files, sir, and——"

"I shall do so. Now, Roper, see if you can give me some model answers. Short, crisp, and to the point. When did you see the automatic? Can you give me the date?"

"In the files!" shouted Sergeant Roper, triumphantly. "May 31st of the current year."

"Where was it?"

"In the study at Pen Cuckoo, sir, that being the room at the extreme end of the west wing facing the Vale."

"Who showed it to you?"

"Squire, himself, showed it to me. We'd checked up all the weapons in the gun-room, of which there was a number, and squire takes me into his study and says, 'There's one more,' he says, and he lays his hand on a wooden box on the table and opens the lid. There was this lethal masterpiece laying on her side, with a notice written clear in block letters. 'Loaded.' 'It's all right,' says Mr. Jernigham, seeing me step aside as he takes her out. 'The safety catch is on,' he says. And he showed me. And he says, 'It went all through the war with me,' he says, 'and there's half a clip left in it. I'd fired two shots when I got my Blighty one,' he says, 'and I've kept it like this ever since. I let it be known there's a loaded automatic waiting at Pen Cuckoo for anybody that feels like coming in uninvited.' We'd had some thieving in the district at that time, same as we've got it now. He told me this weapon had lain loaded in that box for twenty years, did squire."

"Was the box locked?"

"No, sir. But he said all the maids was warned about it."

"Anybody else in the room?"

"Yes, sir. Mr. Henry was there, and Miss Prentice, sitting quietly by the fire and smiling, pussy-like, same as she always does."

"Don't you like Miss Prentice?"

"I think she's all right, but my missus says she's proper sly. My missus is a great one for the institute and Miss Prentice is president of same."

"I see. Any local gossip about Miss Prentice?"

Roper expanded. He placed his hands in his belt with the classic heaving movement of all policemen. He then appeared to remember he was in the presence of authority and rearranged himself in an attitude of attention.

"Aye," he said, "they talk all right, sir. You see, Miss Prentice, she came along, new to the Vale, on three years back when Mrs. Jernigham died. I reckon the late Mrs. Jernigham was nigh-on the best liked lady in this part of Dorset. A Grey of Stourminster-Weston she was, Dorset born and bred, and a proper lady. Now, this Miss Prentice, for all she's half a Jernigham, is a foreigner as you might say, and she doesn't know our ways here. Mrs. Jernigham was welcome everywhere, cottage and big houses alike, and wherever she went she was the same. Never asking questions or if she did, out of real niceness and not nosey-parkishness. Now, folk about here say Miss Prentice is the other way round. Sly. Makes trouble between cottages and rectory, or would if she could. Cor!" said Roper, passing his ham of a hand over his face. "The way that old maiden got after rector! My missus says—well, my missus is an outspoken woman and come off a farm."

Alleyn did not press for a repetition of Mrs. Roper's agricultural similes.

"There was only one worse than her," continued Roper, "and that was the deceased. She was a dragon after rector. And before Miss Prentice came, Miss Campanula had it all her own way, but I reckon Miss Campanula kind of lost driving power when t'other lady got going with her insinuating antics."

"How did they get on together?"

"Fast as glue," said Roper. "Thick as thieves. My missus says they knew too much about each other to be anything else. Cook up to Red House, she says Miss Campanula was jealous fair-to-bust of Miss Prentice, but she was no match for her, however, being the type of woman that lets her anger be seen and rages out in the open, whereas Miss Prentice, with her foxy ways, goes quiet to work. Cook told my missus that deceased was losing ground daily and well-nigh desperate over it."

"How do you mean, losing ground?"

"With rector."

"Dear me," murmured Alleyn. "How alarming for the rector."

"Reckon he picks his way like that chap in Bible," said Roper. "He's a simple sort of chap is rector but he's a Vale man and he suits us. His father and grandfather were rectors here before him and he knows our ways."

"Quite so, Roper," said Alleyn, and lit a cigarette.

"No. But the rector met his match in those two ladies, sir, and it's a marvel one of them hasn't snapped him up by this time. Likely he holds them off with holy conversation, but I've seen the hunted look in the man's eyes more than once."

"I see," said Alleyn. "Do you think it generally known that Mr. Jernigham kept this loaded automatic in the study?"

"I should say it was, sir. If I make so bold, sir, I'd say it was never squire that did this job. He's peppery, is Mr. Jernigham, but I'd bet my last penny he's not a murderer. Flares up and forgets all about it the next minute. Very outspoken. Mr. Henry, now, he's deeper. A nice young fellow but quiet-like. You never know what he's thinking. Still, he's got no call to kill anybody, and wouldn't if he had."

"Who is Mrs. Ross of Duck Cottage, Cloudyfold?"

"Stranger to these parts. She only came here last April." Roper's blue eyes became hard and bright.

"Young?" asked Alleyn.

"Not what you'd say so very young. Thin. Pale hair, done very neat, and very neat in her dressing. Her clothes look different to most ladies. More like the females in the talkies only kind of simpler. Dainty. She's dressed very quiet, always, but you notice her." Roper paused, six-foot-two of dim masculine appreciation. "I reckon she's got It," he said at last. "It's not my place to say so, but I suppose a chap always knows her sort. By instinct."

There was an odd little silence during which the other five men stared at Sergeant Roper.

"Dr. Templett does, anyway," he said at last.

"Oh," said Alleyn. "More local gossip?"

"The women-folk. You know what they are, sir. Given it a proper thrashing, they have. Well, there's a good deal of feeling on account of Mrs. Templett being an invalid."

"Yes, I suppose so. Let me see, that's all the cast of the play, isn't it? Except Miss Copeland."

"Miss Dinah? She'll be in a taking-on, I make no doubt. After all the work she's given to this performance for it to go up, as you might say, in a cloud of dust. Still, she's courting, that'll be a kind of comfort to the maid. Mr. Henry was watching over her after the tragedy, holding her hand for all to see. They're well-matched and we're hoping to hear it's a settled matter any time now. My missus says it'll be one in the eye for Miss Prentice."

"Why on earth?"

"She won't be fancying another lady at Pen Cuckoo. I saw her looking blue murder at them even while deceased was lying, you might say, a corpse at their feet. She's lucky it wasn't her. Should be thanking her Creator she's still here to make trouble."

"Miss Prentice," said Nigel, "seems to be a very unpleasant cup of tea. Perhaps her sore finger was all a bluff and she rigged the tackle for the girl-friend."

"Dr. Templett said it was no bluff, Mr. Bathgate," said Fox. "He said she held out till the last moment that she was going to play."

"That's right enough, sir," said Roper. "I went round to the back to see Miss Dinah just before it had happened and there was Miss Prentice crying her eyes out, with her finger looking that unwholesome it'd turn your stomach, and Miss Dinah telling her she was ruining the paint on her face and the doctor saying, 'I absolutely forbid it. Your finger's in a very nasty state and if you weren't playing this part tonight,' he said, 'I'd open it up.' Yes, he threatened her with the knife, did doctor. Mr. Henry says, 'You'll make a mess of Mr. Nevin's ecstasies.' Her piece was composed by a chap of that name as you'll see in the program. 'You'll never stay the course, Cousin Eleanor,' says Mr. Henry. 'I know it's hurting you like stink,' says Mr. Henry, 'because you're crying,' he says. But no, she wouldn't give in till Miss Dinah fetched her father. 'Come,' he says, 'we all know how you feel about it, but there are times when generosity is better than heroism.' She looked up at rector, then, and she said, 'If you say so, Father,' and with that Miss Campanula says, 'Now, who'll go and get my music? Where's Gibson?' Which is the name of her chauffeur. So she give in, but very reluctant."

"A vivid enough picture of the rival performances, isn't it?" said Alleyn. "Well, there's the history of the case. It's getting on for three o'clock. I think, on second thought, Fox, we won't wait for the light of day. We'll make a night of it. This place must be overhauled sometime and it looks as though we'll have a busy day to-morrow. You can turn in if you like, Roper. Some one can relieve us at seven."

"Are you going to search the premises, sir?"

"Yes."

"Reckon I'd like to give a hand if it's agreeable to you."

"Certainly. Fox, you and Thompson make sure we've missed nothing in the dressing-rooms and supper-room. Bailey, you can take Roper with you on the stage. Go over every inch of it. I'll tackle the hall and join you if I finish first."

"Are you looking for anything in particular?" asked Nigel.

"The usual unconsidered trifles. Spare bits of Twiddletoy, for instance. Even a water-pistol."

"Not forgetting any kid's annuals that happen to be lying round," added Fox.

"Poor things!" said Nigel. "Back to childhood's day, I see. Is there a telephone here?"

"In a dressing-room," said Alleyn. "But it's only an extension."

"I'll ring up the office from a pub, then. In the meantime, I may as well write up a pretty story."

He took out his pad and settled himself at a table on the stage.

Police investigation is for the most part a dull business. Nothing could be more tedious than searching for things. Half a detective's life is spent in turning over dreary objects, finding nothing, and replacing them. Alleyn started in the entrance porch of the parish hall and began a meticulous crawl over dusty surfaces. He moved like a snail, across and across, between the rows of benches. He felt cold and dirty and he smelled nothing but dust. He could not allow his thoughts to dwell pleasantly on his own affairs, his coming marriage, and the happiness that kept him company nowadays; because it is when his thoughts are abstracted from the business in hand that the detective misses the one small sign events have set in his path. Sometimes the men on the stage heard a thin whistling down in the hall. Sergeant Roper's voice droned interminably. At intervals the church clock sweetly recorded the journey of the hours. Miss Campanula lay stealthily stiffening behind a red baize screen, and Nigel Bathgate recorded her departure in efficient journalese.

Alleyn had passed the benches and chairs and was groveling about in the corner with an electric torch. Presently he uttered a soft exclamation. Nigel looked up from his writing and Bailey, who had the loose seat of a chair in his hands, shaded his eyes and peered down into the corner.

Alleyn stood by the stage, on the audience's left. He held a small shining object between finger and thumb. His hand was gloved. One of his eyebrows was raised and his lips were pursed in a soundless whistle.

"Struck a patch, sir?" asked Bailey.

"Yes, I rather think so, Bailey."

He walked over to the piano.

"Look."

Bailey and Nigel came to the footlights.

The shining object Alleyn held in his hands was a boy's water-pistol.

## II

"As you said yourself, Bathgate, back to childhood days."

"What's the idea, sir?" asked Bailey.

"It seems to be a recurrent idea," said Alleyn. "I found this thing stuffed away in a sort of locker under the stage over there. It was poked in a dark corner, but there's little or no dust on it. The rest of the stuff in the locker's smothered in dirt. Look at the butt, Bailey. Do you see that shiny scratch? It's rather a super sort of water-pistol, isn't it? None of your rubber bulbs that you squeeze—but a proper trigger action. Fox!"

Fox and Thompson appeared from the direction of the supper-room.

Alleyn went to the small table where Bailey had placed the rest of the exhibits, lifted the covering cloth and laid his find beside the Colt automatic.

"The length is the same to within a fraction of an inch," he said; "and there's a mark on the butt of the Colt very much like the mark on the butt of the water-pistol. That, I believe, is where it was rammed in the piano, between the steel pegs where the strings are fastened."

"But what the devil," asked Nigel, "is the explanation?"

Alleyn pulled off his gloves and fished in his pockets for his cigarette-case.

"Where's Roper?"

"Out at the back, sir," said Bailey. "He'll be back shortly with a new set of reminiscences. His super ought to issue a gag to that chap."

"This is a rum go," said Fox profoundly.

"'Jones Minor' all over it," said Alleyn. "You were right, Bailey, I believe, when you suggested the death-trap in the piano was too elaborate to be true. It *is* only in books that murder is quite as fancy as all this. The whole thing carries the hallmark of the booby-trap and the signature of the practical joker. It is somehow difficult to believe that a man or woman would, as Bailey has said, think up murder on these lines. But what if a man with murder in his heart came upon this booby-trap, this water-pistol aimed through a hole in the torn silk bib? What if this potential murderer thought of substituting a Colt for the water-pistol? It becomes less farfetched, then, doesn't it? What's more, there are certain advantages. The murderer can separate himself from his victim and from the *corpus delicti*. The spadework has been done. All the murderer has to do is remove the water-pistol, jam in the Colt and tie the loose end of twine round the butt. It's not his idea, it's Jones Minor's."

"He'd want to be sure the Colt was the same length," said Fox.

"He could measure the water-pistol."

"And then go home and check up his Colt?"

"Or somebody else's Colt," said Bailey.

"One of the first points we have to clear up," Alleyn said, "is the accessibility of Jernigham's war souvenir. Roper says he thinks everybody knew about it, and apparently it was there in the study for the picking up. They've all been rehearsing in the study. They were there last night—Friday night, I mean. It's Sunday now, heaven help us."

"If Dr. Templett recognized the Colt," observed Fox, "he didn't let on."

"No more he did."

The back door banged and boots resounded in the supper-room.

"Here's Roper," said Fox.

"Roper!" shouted Alleyn.

"Yes, sir?"

"Come here."

Sergeant Roper stumbled up the steps and appeared on the stage.

"Come and have a look at this."

"Certainly, sir."

Roper placed his palm on the edge of the stage and vaulted deafeningly to the floor. He approached the table with an air of efficiency and contemplated the water-pistol.

"Know it?" asked Alleyn.

Roper reached out his hand.

"Don't touch it!" said Alleyn sharply.

"'T, 't, 't!" said Fox and Bailey.

"Beg pardon, sir," said Roper. "Seeing that trifling toy, and recognizing it in a flash, I had a natural impulse, as you might say——"

"Your natural impulses must be mortified if you want to grow up into a detective," said Alleyn. "Whose water-pistol is this?"

"Mind," said Roper warningly, "there may be two of this class in the district, sir. Or more. I'm not taking my oath there aren't. But barring that eventuality, I reckon I can put an owner on it. And seeing he had the boldness to take a shot at me, outside the Jernigham Arms, me being in uniform——"

"Roper," said Alleyn, "it is only about three hours to the dawn. Don't let the sun rise on your parentheses. Whose water-pistol is this?"

"George Biggins's," said Roper.

# CHAPTER XII

# Further Vignettes

*I*

AT SEVEN O'CLOCK the Yard car dropped Alleyn and Fox at the Jernigham Arms.

The rain had stopped, but it was a dank, dreary morning, and so cloudy that only a mean thinning of the night, a grudging disclosure of vague, wet masses, gave evidence that somewhere beyond the Vale there was dawnlight.

Bailey and Thompson drove off for London. Alleyn stared after the tail light of the car while Fox belabored the front door of the Jernigham Arms.

"There's *somebody* moving about in there," he grumbled.

"Here they come."

It was the pot-boy, very tousled and peepy, and accompanied by a gust of stale beer. Alleyn thought that he looked like all pot-boys at dawn throughout time and space.

"Good morning," Alleyn said. "Can you give us rooms for a day or two, and breakfast in an hour? There's a third man on his way here."

"I'll ask Missus," said the pot-boy. He gaped at them, blinked, and went off down a passage. They could hear him calling with the cracked uncertainty of adolescence:

"Missus! 'Be detec-er-tives from Lunnon, along of Miss Campanula's murder, likely. Mrs. Pe-e-each! Missus!"

"The whole place is buzzing with it," said Alleyn.

## II

At seven o'clock Henry found himself suddenly awake. He lay still, wondering for a moment why this day would be different from any other day. Then he remembered. He saw with precision a purple heap, the top of a head, the nape of a neck laced with dark, shining streaks. He saw a sheet of music, crumpled, pinned to the keys of a piano by the head. The picture was framed in aspidistras like a nightmarish valentine and across the lower margin was the top of a piano.

"I have looked down at a murdered woman." And for a time his thoughts would not move beyond this sharp memory, so that he found himself anxiously retracing the pattern of the head, the neck, the white sheet of music, and the fatuous green leaves. Then the memory of Dinah's cold fingers crept into his hands. He closed his hands on the memory, clenching them as he lay in bed, and the whole idea of Dinah came into his mind.

"If it had been Eleanor, there would have been an end to our troubles."

He pushed this thought away from him, telling himself it was horrible, but it returned repeatedly, and at last he said, "It is stupid to pretend otherwise. I do wish it had been Eleanor." He began to think of all that happened after Idris Campanula died; of how his father went aside with Superintendent Blandish, and of the solemn, ridiculous look on his father's face. He remembered Dr. Templett's explanations and Miss Prentice's moans which had irritated them all very much. He remembered that when he looked at Mr. Copeland he saw that his lips were moving, and realized, with embarrassment, that the rector was at prayer. He remembered Mrs. Ross's almost complete silence and the way she and Templett had not spoken to each other. And again his thoughts returned to Dinah. He had walked to the rectory with Dinah and her father, and on the threshold he had kissed her openly, the rector seeming scarcely aware of it. On the way home to Pen Cuckoo, the squire had not forgotten that, in the absence of Sir George Dillington, he was Chief Constable, and had discoursed solemnly on the crime, saying again and again that Henry was to treat everything he heard as confidential, and relating how, with Blandish, he had come to a decision to call in Scotland Yard. When they were indoors at last, Eleanor Prentice had fainted, and the squire had forced brandy down her throat with such an uncertain hand that he had half-asphyxiated her. They helped her to her room and Jocelyn, nervously assiduous, had knocked the bandaged finger so that she screamed with pain. Henry and his father had a solemn drink together in the dining-room, Jocelyn still discoursing on his responsibilities.

Henry went cold all over, his heart dropped like a plummet, and he faced the worst memory of all, the one that he had been pushing away ever since he woke.

It was when Jocelyn told him how, strong in his position of Acting Chief Constable, he had peered through the hole in the tucked silk front, and had seen the glimmer of a firearm.

"A revolver," Jocelyn had said, "or else an automatic."

At that moment the picture of the box in the study had risen in Henry's imagination. He had hurried his father to bed, but when he was alone had been afraid to go into the study and lift the lid of the box. Now he knew that he must do it. Quickly, before the servants were up. He leaped out of bed, threw on his dressing-gown, and crept downstairs through the dark house. There was an electric torch in the hall. He found it and made his way to the study.

The box was empty. The notice "LOADED" in block capitals lay at the bottom.

Henry turned away with panic in his heart, and a minute later he was knocking at his father's door.

### III

Selia Ross had been awake for a very long time. She was wondering when she could telephone to Dr. Templett or whether it would be altogether too unsafe to get into touch with him. She knew the telephone rang at his bedside until eight o'clock in the morning, and that he slept far enough away from his wife's room for it not to disturb her. Mrs. Ross wanted to ask him what he had done with the anonymous letter. She knew that he had put it in his wallet, and that he kept the wallet in his breast pocket. She remembered that after the catastrophe he had not changed back into his ordinary suit, and she was hideously afraid that the letter might still be in his coat at the hall. He was very forgetful and careless about such things, and had once left one of her letters, open, on his dressing-table, only remembering it later on in the day.

She had no knowledge of what the police would do. She had a sort of an idea she had read in a criminal novel that they were not allowed to search through private houses without a permit of some kind. But did that apply to a public hall? And surely if the body of a murdered person was there, in the hall, they would hunt everywhere. What would they think if they found that letter? She wanted to warn Dr. Templett to be ready with an answer.

But he himself was an official.

But he had almost certainly remembered the letter.

Would it be better to say he knew the author to be someone else—his wife, even? Any one but one of those two women.

Her thoughts, needle-sharp, darted in and out of the fabric of her terror.

Perhaps if he went down early . . .

Perhaps she should have telephoned an hour ago.

She switched on her bedside lamp and looked at her clock. It was five minutes to eight.

Perhaps she was too late.

In a panic she reached for the telephone and dialed his number.

## IV

Miss Prentice's finger had kept her awake, but it is doubtful if she would have slept even if it had not throbbed all night. Her thoughts were too hurried and busy, weaving backwards and forwards between the rector, herself and Idris Campanula, who was murdered. She thought of all sorts of things: of how when she first came to Pen Cuckoo she and Idris had been such friends, confiding the secrets of their bosoms to each other like schoolgirls. She remembered all the delicious talks they had had together, talks full of exciting conjectures about the behavior of other people in the village and the county. There would be nobody now who would speak her language and discuss things and people in that way. They had been so intimate until Idris grew jealous. That was the form Miss Prentice gave to their differences: Idris grew jealous of her friend's rising influence in the village and in church affairs.

She would not think yet of Mr. Copeland. The memory of the things he had said to her at confession must be thrust down into oblivion, and that other memory, that other frightful revelation of Idris's perfidy.

No. Better to remember the old friendly days and to think of Idris's will. It had been a very simple will. A lot for Mr. Copeland, a little for the distant nephew, and seven thousand for Eleanor herself. Idris had said she'd never had a real friend until Eleanor came, and that if she died first she would be happy in the thought that she had been able

to do this. Eleanor even then rather resented her friend's air of pa-
tonage.

But it was true that if she had this money she would no longer be so
dependent on Jocelyn.

Mr. Copeland would be very well off indeed, for Idris was an extremely rich woman.

Dinah would be an heiress.

She had not thought of that before. There would be no worldly
reason now why Dinah and Henry should not marry.

If she were to withdraw her opposition quickly, before the will was
known—would not that seem generous and kind? If she could only
stifle the recollection of that scene on Friday afternoon. Dinah limp in
Henry's arms, lost in rapture. It had nearly driven Eleanor mad. How
could she unsay all that she had said before she turned away and stumbled up the lane, escaping from so much agony? But with Dinah married to Henry, then her father would be lonely. A rich lonely man, fifty
years old, and too dignified to look for a young wife. Surely, then!

Then! Then!

The first bell, calling the people to eight o'clock service, roused her
from her golden plans. She rose, dressed and went out into the dark
morning.

## V

The rector was astir at seven. It was Sunday, and he would be in
church in an hour. He dressed hurriedly, unable to lie thinking any
longer of the events of the night that was past. All sorts of recollections
flocked into his thoughts, and in all of them the murdered woman was
present, turning them into nightmares. He felt as if he was dyed in
guilt, as if he would never rid himself of his dreadful memories. His
thoughts were chaotic and quite uncontrollable.

Long before the warning bell sounded for early celebration, he stole
out of the house and walked, as he had done every Sunday for twenty
years, down the drive, through the nut walk and over the stile into the
churchyard.

When he was alone inside the dark church he fell on his knees and
tried to pray.

## VI

Somewhere, a long way off, somebody was knocking at a door. Bang,
bang, *bang*. Must be old Idris pounding away at that damned lugu-

brious tune. Blandish needn't have locked Eleanor up inside the piano. As Deputy Chief Constable, I object to that sort of thing; it isn't cricket. Let her out! If she knocks much louder she'll blow the place up, and then we'll have to get in the Yard. Bang, bang—

The squire woke with a sickening leap of his nerves.

"Wha-a-a?"

"Father, it's me! Henry! I want to speak to you."

## VII

When Dinah heard her father go downstairs long before his usual hour, she knew that he hadn't slept, that he was miserable, and that he would go into church and pray. She hoped that he had remembered to wear a woolen cardigan under his cassock, because he seemed to catch cold more easily in church than anywhere else. She knew last night that she was in for a difficult time with him. For some extraordinary reason, he had already begun to blame himself for the tragedy, saying that he had been weak and vacillating, not zealous enough in his duties as a parish priest.

Dinah was unable to follow her father's reasoning, and with a sinking heart she had asked him if he suspected any one as the murderer of Idris Campanula. That was when they got home last night and she was fortified by Henry's kiss.

"Daddy, do you think you know?"

"No, darling, no. But I haven't helped them as I should. And when I did try, it was too late."

"But what do you mean?"

"You mustn't ask me, darling."

And then she had realized that he was thinking of the confessional. What on earth had Idris Campanula told him on Friday? What had Eleanor Prentice told him? Something that had upset him very much, Dinah was sure. Well, one of them was gone and wouldn't make mischief any more. It was no good trying to be sorry. She wasn't sorry, she was only frightened and filled with horror whenever she thought of the dead body. It was the first dead body Dinah had ever seen.

Of course it was obvious to everybody that the trap had been set for Eleanor Prentice. Her father must realize that. Who, then, had a motive to kill Eleanor Prentice?

Dinah sat up in bed, cold with terror. She remembered the meeting in the lane on Friday afternoon, the things Eleanor Prentice had said in a breathless whisper, and the answer Henry had made.

"If she tells them what he said," thought Dinah, "they'll say Henry had a motive."

And with her whole soul she tried to send out a warning message to Henry.

But Henry, at that moment, was pounding his father's bedroom door, and into his startled mind there came no warning message from Dinah. There was no need for one, for already he was afraid.

## VIII

Dr. Templett was dreamlessly and peacefully asleep when the telephone rang at his bedside. At once, and with the accuracy born of long practice, he reached out in the half-light for the receiver.

"Dr. Templett here," he said, as he always did when the telephone rang at an ungodly hour. He remembered that young Mrs. Cartwright might be now in labor.

But it was Selia Ross.

"Billy? Billy, have you got that letter?"

"What!"

He lay there quite still, holding the receiver to his ear and listening to his own thumping heart.

"Billy! Are you there?"

"Yes," he said, "yes. It's all right. There's nothing to worry about. I'll look in some time to-day."

"Do, for God's sake."

"All right. Good-by."

He hung up the receiver and lay staring at the ceiling. What had he done with that letter?

# CHAPTER XIII

# Sunday Morning

*I*

ALLEYN AND FOX were at breakfast and Nigel was still asleep when Superintendent Blandish walked in. He was blue about the chin and his eyes and nose were watery.

"You must wonder if there is anybody except that jabbering chap Roper in the Great Chipping Constabulary," he said as he shook hands. "I'm sorry to have neglected you like this; but we're in for a picnic, and no mistake, with this case up at Moorton Park."

"Damn' bad luck, the two cases cropping up at the same time," said Alleyn. "Of course, you'd have liked to handle our business yourself. Have you had breakfast?"

"Haven't taken a look at food since six o'clock yesterday."

Alleyn went to the hatch and shouted:

"Mrs. Peach! Another lot of eggs and bacon, if you can manage it."

"Well, I won't say no," said Blandish, and sat down. "And I won't say I wouldn't have liked to try my hand at this business. But there you are: never rains but it pours, does it?"

"That's right," agreed Fox. "We get the same thing at the Yard. Though lately it's been quietish—hasn't it, Mr. Alleyn?"

Blandish chuckled. "Maybe that's why we've been honored with the topnotchers," he said. "Well, Mr. Alleyn, it will be quite an experience for us to see you working. Needless to say, we'll give you all the help we can."

"Thank you," said Alleyn. "We'll need it. This is a remarkably rum business. You were in the audience, weren't you?"

"I was, and I can give you my word I got a fright. Thought the whole place had exploded. The old piano went on buzzing for Lord knows how long. By gum, it took all my self-control not to have a peep inside the lid before I went off to Moorton. But, 'No,' I thought. 'You're handing over, and you'd better not meddle.'"

"Extraordinarily considerate. We breathed our fervent thanks, didn't we, Fox? I suppose that conversation piece you've got for a sergeant has told you all about it?"

Blandish pulled an expressive grimace.

"I shut him up after the second recital," he said. "He wants sitting on, does Roper, but he's got his wits about him. I'd like to hear your account."

While he devoured his eggs and bacon, Alleyn gave him the history of the night. When he came to the discovery of the message in Dr. Templett's coat, Blandish laid down his knife and fork and stared at him.

"Glory!" he said.

"I know."

"This is hell," said Blandish. "I mean to say, it's awkward."

"Yes."

"Not to put too fine a point on it, Mr. Alleyn, it's bloody awkward."

"It is."

"By gum, I'm not so sure I do regret being out of it. It may not be anything, of course, but it can't be overlooked. And I've been associated with the doctor I don't know how many years."

"Like him?" asked Alleyn.

"Do I like him? Well, now, yes. I suppose I do. We've always got on very pleasantly, you know. Yes, I—well, I'm accustomed to him."

"You'll know the questions we're going to ask. In this sort of affair we have to batten on local gossip."

Alleyn went to the corner of the dining-room, got his case and took from it the anonymous letter. It was flattened between two sheets of glass joined, at the edges, with adhesive tape. The corner, back and sides of the paper bore darkened impressions of fingers.

"There it is. We brought up three sets of latent prints. One of them corresponds with a print taken from a powder box in the dressing-room used by the victim and Miss Prentice. It has been identified as the victim's. A second has its counterpart on a new japanned make-up box, thought to be the property of Mrs. Ross. The third is repeated on other papers in the wallet, and is obviously Dr. Templett's."

"Written by deceased, sent to Mrs. Ross and handed by her to the doctor?"

"It seems indicated. Especially as two of Mrs. Ross's prints, if they are hers, appear to be superimposed on the deceased's prints, and one of Dr. Templett's lies across two of the others. We'll get more definite results when Bailey develops his photographs."

"This is an ugly business. You mentioned local gossip, Mr. Alleyn. There's been a certain amount in this direction, no denying it, and the two ladies in question were mainly responsible, I fancy."

"But is it a motive for murder?" asked Fox of nobody in particular.

"Well, Brer Fox, it might be. A doctor, in a country district especially, doesn't thrive on scandal. Is Templett a wealthy man, do you know, Blandish?"

"No, I wouldn't say he was," said Blandish. "They're an old Vale family, and the doctor's a younger son. His elder brother was a bit of a rip. Smart regiment before the war, and expensive tastes. It's always been understood the doctor came in for a white elephant when he got Chippingwood. I'd say he needs every penny he earns. He's a hunting man, too, and that costs money."

"What about Mrs. Ross?"

"Well, there you are! If you're to believe everything you hear, they are pretty thick. But gossip's not evidence, is it?"

"No, but it's occasionally based on some sort of foundation, more's the pity. Ah, well! It indicates a line and we'll follow the pointer. Now, about the automatic. It's Mr. Jernigham's all right."

"I've heard all about that, Mr. Alleyn, and that's not too nice either, though I wouldn't believe, if I saw the weapon smoking in his hand, that the squire would shoot a woman, let alone plan to murder his own flesh and blood. Unlikely enough people have turned out to be murderers, as we all know, and I suppose that it is not beyond the possibilities that Mr. Jernigham might kill his man in hot blood; but I've known him all my life, and I'd stake my reputation he's not the sort to do an underhand fantastic sort of job like this. The man's not got it in him. That's not evidence, either——"

"It's expert opinion, though," said Alleyn, "and to be respected as such."

"The squire's Acting Chief Constable while Sir George Dillington's away."

"We seem to be on official preserves wherever we turn," said Alleyn.

"I'll call at Pen Cuckoo later in the morning. The mortuary van came before it was light. Dr. Templett's doing the post-mortem this afternoon. Either Fox or I will be there. I think our first job now is to call on Mr. Georgie Biggins."

"Young limb of Satan? You'll find him in the last cottage on the left, going out of Chipping. The station's in Great Chipping, you know—only five miles from here. Roper and a P-c. enjoy their midday snooze at a substation in this village. Both are at your service."

"Is there a car of sorts I could hire for the time being? You'll need the official bus for your own work, of course."

"As a matter of fact, I'm afraid we shall. It's a tidy stretch over to Moorton Park, and we'll be going backwards and forwards. No doubt about our men being Posh Jimmy & Co. Typical job. Funny how they stick to their ways, isn't it? About a car. As a matter of fact, the Biggins have got an old Ford they hire."

"Splendid. An admirable method of approaching Mr. Georgie. How old is he?"

"In years," said Blandish, "he's about thirteen. In sin he's a hundred. A limb, if ever there was one. Nerve of a rhinoceros."

"We'll see if we can shake it," said Alleyn.

The superintendent departed, lamenting the amount of work that lay before him.

## II

Alleyn and Fox lit their pipes and walked through Chipping. By daylight it turned out to be a small hamlet with a row of stone cottages on each side of the road, a general store, a post office, and the Jernigham Arms. Even the slope of Cloudyfold, rising steeply above it from the top of Pen Cuckoo Vale, did not rob Chipping of its upland character. It felt high in the world, and the cold wind blew strongly down the Vale road.

The Biggins's cottage stood a little apart from the rest of the village, and had a truculent air. It was one of those bare-faced Dorset cottages, less picturesque than its neighbors, and more forbidding.

As Alleyn and Fox approached the front door, they heard a woman's voice:

"Whatever be the matter with you, then, mum-budgeting so close to my apron strings? Be off with you!"

Silence.

"To be sure," continued the voice, "if you wasn't so strong as a young foal, Georgie Biggins, I'd think something ailed you. Stick out your tongue."

Silence.

"As clean as a whistle. Stick it in again, then. Standing there like you was simple Dick with your tongue lolling! I never see! What ails you?"

"Nuthun," said a small voice.

"Nuthun killed nobody."

Alleyn tapped on the door.

Another silence was broken by a sharp whispering and an unmistakable scuffle.

"Do what I tell you!" ordered the voice. "Me in my working apron, and Sunday morning! Go *on* with you."

There was a sound of rapid retreat and then the door opened three inches to disclose a pair of boot-button eyes and part of a very white face.

"Hullo," said Alleyn. "I've come to see if I can hire a car. This is Mr. Biggins's house, isn't it?"

"Uh."

"Have you got a car for hire?"

"Uh."

"Well, how about opening the door a bit wider and we can talk about it?"

The door opened very slowly to another five inches. Georgie Biggins stood revealed in his Sunday suit. His moonface was colorless and he had the look of a boy who may bolt without warning.

Alleyn said, "Now, what about this car? Is your father at home?"

"Along to pub corner," said Georgie in a stifled voice. "Mum's comeun."

The cinema has made all little boys familiar with the look of a detective. Alleyn kept a change of clothes in the Yard in readiness for sudden departures. His shepherd's plaid coat, flannel trousers and soft hat may have reassured George Biggins, but when the boot-button eyes ranged farther afield and lit on Inspector Fox, in his dark suit, mackintosh and bowler, their own uttered a yelp of pure terror, turned tail and charged into his mother, who had at that moment walked out of the bedroom. She was a large woman, and she caught her son with a practised hand.

"Now!" she said. "That's enough and more, for sure. What's the meaning of these goings-on? You wait till your Dad comes home. I never see!"

She advanced to the door, bringing her son with her by the scruff of the neck.

"I'm sure I'm sorry to keep you waiting," she said.

Alleyn asked about the car and was told he could have it. Mrs. Biggins examined both of them with frank curiosity and led the way round the house to a dilapidated shed where they found a Ford car, six years old, but, as Alleyn cheerfully remarked, none the worse for that. He paid a week's rental in advance. Mrs. Biggins kept a firm but absent-minded grip on her son's shirt-collar.

"I'll get you a receipt," she said. "Likely you're here on account of this terrible affair."

"That's it," said Alleyn.

"Are you from Scotland Yard, then?"

"Yes, Mrs. Biggins, that's us." Alleyn looked good naturedly at Master Biggins. "Is this Georgie?" he asked.

The next second, Master Biggins had left the best part of his Sunday collar in his mother's hand and had bolted like a rabbit, only to find himself held as if in a vice by the terrible man in the mackintosh and bowler.

"Now, now, now," said Fox. "What's all this?"

The very words he had so often heard on the screen.

"Georgie!" screamed Mrs. Biggins in a maternal fury. Then she looked at her son's face and at the hands that held him.

"Here you!" she stormed at Fox. "What are you at, laying your hands on my boy?"

"There's nothing to worry about, Mrs. Biggins," said Alleyn. "Georgie may be able to help us, that's all. Now, look here, wouldn't it be better if we went indoors out of sight and sound of your neighbors?"

The shot went home.

"Mighty me!" said Mrs. Biggins, still almost as white as her child, but rallying. "Mighty me, it's true enough they spend most of the Lord's Day minding other folks' business and clacking their tongues. Georgie Biggins, if you don't hold your noise I'll have the skin off you. Do us go in, then."

### III

In a cold but stuffy parlor, Alleyn did his best with mother and son. Georgie was now howling steadily. Mrs. Biggins's work-reddened hands pleated and repleated the folds of her dress. But she listened in silence.

"It's just this," said Alleyn. "Georgie is in no danger, but we believe he's in a position to give us extremely important information."

Georgie checked a lamentable roar and listened.

Alleyn took the water-pistol from his pocket and handed it to Mrs. Biggins.

"Do you recognize it?"

"For sure," she said slowly. "It's his'en."

George burst out again.

"Young Biggins," said Alleyn, "is this your idea of being a detective? Come here."

Georgie came.

"See here, now. How would you like to help the police bring a murderer to justice? How would you like to work with us? We're from Scotland Yard, you know. It's not often you'll get the chance to work with the Yard, is it?"

The black eyes fastened on Alleyn's and brightened.

"What are the other chaps going to think if you, if you"—Alleyn hunted for the right phrase—"if you solve the problem that has baffled the greatest sleuths of all time?" He glanced at his colleague. Fox, looking remarkably bland, closed one eye.

"If you come in with us," Alleyn continued, "you'll be doing a man's job. How about it?"

A faintly hard-boiled expression crept over Georgie Biggins's undistinguished face.

"Okay," he said in a treble voice still fuddled with tears.

"Good enough." Alleyn took the water-pistol from Mrs. Biggins. "This is your gun, isn't it?"

"Yaas," said Georgie; and, remembering James Cagney the week before last at Great Chipping Plaza, he added with a strong Dorset accent: "Sure it's my gat."

"You fixed that water-pistol in the piano at the hall, didn't you?"

"So what?" said Georgie.

This was a little too much for Alleyn. He contemplated the child for a moment and then said:

"Look here, Georgie, never you mind about the pictures. This is real. There's somebody about who ought to be locked up. You're an Englishman, a man of Dorset, and you want to see right done, don't you? You thought it would be rather fun if Miss Prentice got a squirt of water in the eye when she put her foot on the soft pedal. I'm afraid I agree. It would have been funny."

Georgie grinned.

"But how about the music? You'd forgotten about that, hadn't you?"

"Nah, I had not. My pistol's proper strong pistol. 'Twould have bowled over the music, for certain, sure."

"You may be right," said Alleyn. "Did you try it after you had fixed it up?"

"Nah."

"Why not?"

"'Cause something happened."

"What happened?"

"Nuthing! Somebody made a noise. I went away."

"Where did you get the idea?" said Alleyn after a pause. "Come on, now."

"I'll be bound I know, the bad boy," interrupted his mother. "If our Georgie's been up to such-like capers, it's out of one of the claptrappy tales he's always at. Ay, only last week he tied an alarm clock under faather's chair and set 'un for seven o'clock when he takes his nap, and there was the picture in this rubbish to give him away."

"Was it out of a book, Georgie?"

"Yaas. Kind of."

"I see. And partly out of your Twiddletoy model, wasn't it?"

Georgie nodded.

"When did you do it?"

"Froiday."

"What time?"

"Aafternoon. Two o'clock, about."

"How did you get into the hall?"

"Was there with them girls and I stayed behind."

"Tell me about it. You must have been pretty smart for them not to see what you were up to."

Georgie, it seemed, had slipped into a dark corner as the Friendly Young People left at about a quarter past two. His idea had been to shoot at them with his water-pistol as they passed; but at the last moment a more amusing notion occurred to him. He remembered the diverting tale of a piano booby-trap which he had read with the greatest enjoyment in the last number of *Bingo Bink's Weekly*. He had some odds and ends of Twiddletoy in his pockets, and as soon as the front door slammed he got to work. First he silently examined the piano and made himself familiar with the action of the pedals. At this juncture his mother told Alleyn that Georgie was of a markedly mechanical turn of mind and had made many astonishing models from Twiddletoy all of which could be made to revolve or even propel. Georgie had gone solidly to work. Stimulated by Alleyn's ardent attention, he described his handiwork. When it was finished he played a triumphant stanza or two of "Chopsticks," taking care to use the loud pedal only.

"And nobody came?"

The devilish child turned white again.

"Nobody saw," he muttered. "They never saw nuthun. Only banged at door and shouted."

"And you didn't answer? I see. Know who it was?"

"I never seen 'em."

"All right. How did you leave?"

"By front door. I shut 'un behind me."

There was a brief silence. Georgie's face suddenly twisted into a painful grimace, his lip trembled again, and he looked piteously at Alleyn.

"I never meant no harm," he said. "I never meant it to kill her."

"That's all right," said Alleyn. He reached out a hand and took the child by the shoulder.

"It's nothing to do with you, young Biggins," said Alleyn.

But over the boy's head he saw the mother's stricken face and knew he could not help her so easily.

# CHAPTER XIV

# According to the Jernighams

## I

ALLEYN WENT ALONE TO PEN CUCKOO. He left Fox to visit Miss Campanula's servants, find out the name of her lawyers, and pick up any grain of information that might be the fruit of his well-known way with female domestics.

The Biggins's car chugged doggedly up the Vale Road in second gear. It was a stiff grade. The Vale rises steeply above Chipping, mounting past Winton to Pen Cuckoo Manor and turned into Cloudyfold Rise at the head of the valley. It is not an obviously picturesque valley, but it has a charm that transcends mere prettiness. The lower slopes of Cloudyfold make an agreeable pattern, the groups of trees are beautifully disposed about the flanks of the hills, and the scattered houses, being simple, seem to have grown out of the country, as indeed they have, since they are built of Dorset stone. It is not a tame landscape, either. The four winds meet on Cloudyfold, and in winter the small lake in Pen Cuckoo grounds holds its mask of ice for days together.

Alleyn noticed that several lanes came down into the Vale Road. He could see that at least one of them led crookedly up to the Manor, and one seemed to be a sort of bridle path from the Manor down to the church. He drove on through the double gates, up the climbing avenue and out on the wide sweep before Pen Cuckoo house.

A flood of thin sunshine had escaped the heavy clouds, and Pen Cuckoo looked its wintry best, an ancient and gracious house, not so very big, not at all forbidding, but tranquil. "A happy house," thought Alleyn, "with a certain dignity."

He gave his card to Taylor.

"I should like to see Mr. Jernigham, if I may."

"If you will come this way, sir."

As he followed Taylor through the west wing, he thought: "With any luck, it'll be the study."

It was, and the study was empty.

As soon as the door had shut behind Taylor, Alleyn looked for the box described by Sergeant Roper. He found it on a table underneath one of the windows. He lifted the lid and saw that the box was empty. He looked closely at the notice "LOADED," which was printed in block capitals. Alleyn gently let fall the lid and walked over to the french window. It was not locked. It looked across the end of the graveled sweep and over the tops of the park trees right down Pen Cuckoo Vale to Chipping and beyond.

Alleyn was still tracing the course of the Vale Road as it wound through the valley when the squire walked in.

Jocelyn looked fresh and composed. Perhaps his eyes were a little more prominent than usual and his face a little less red, but he had the look of a man who has come to a decision, and there was a certain dignity and resolution in his manner.

"I'm glad to see you," he said as he shook hands. "Sit down, won't you? This is a terrible affair."

"Yes," said Alleyn. "It's both terrible and bewildering."

"Good God, I should think it was bewildering! It's the most damned complicated, incomprehensible business I ever want to come up against. I suppose Blandish has told you that in Dillington's absence I've got his job?"

"As Chief Constable? Yes, sir, he told me. That's partly my reason for calling on you."

The squire stared solemnly into the fire and said, "Quite."

"Blandish says you were present when the thing happened."

"Good God, yes. I don't know why it happened, though, or exactly how. As soon as we decided to call you in, Blandish was all for leaving things severely alone. Be damn' glad if you'd explain."

Alleyn explained. Jocelyn listened with his eyes very wide open and his mouth not quite closed.

"Beastly, underhand, ingenious sort of thing," he said. "Sounds more like a woman's work to me. I don't mean to say I think women are particularly underhand, you know; but when they do turn nasty, in my opinion they are inclined to turn crooked-nasty."

He laughed unexpectedly and uncomfortably.

"Yes," agreed Alleyn.

"Sort of inverse ratio or something, what?" added the squire dimly.

"That's it, sir. Now, the first thing we've got to tackle is the ownership of the Colt. I don't know——"

"Wait a bit," said Jocelyn. He stood up, drove his hands into his breeches pockets and walked over to the french windows.

"It's mine," he said.

Alleyn did not answer. The squire turned and looked at him. Seeing nothing but polite attention in Alleyn's face, he made a slight inarticulate noise, strode to the table under the window and opened the box.

"See for yourself," he said. "It's been in that box for the last twenty years. It was there last week. Now it's gone."

Alleyn joined him.

"Hellish unpleasant," said Jocelyn, "isn't it? I only found out this morning. My son was thinking about the business, it seems, and suddenly remembered that the Colt is always lying there, loaded. He came downstairs and looked, and then he came to my room and told me. I'm wondering if I ought to resign my position as C.C."

"I shouldn't do that, sir," said Alleyn. "With any luck, we ought to be able to clear up the disappearance of the automatic."

"I feel pretty shaken up about it, I don't mind telling you."

"Of course you do. As a matter of fact, I've brought the Colt up here to show you. May I just fetch it? I can slip out to the car this way."

He went straight through the french windows and returned with his case, from which he took the automatic wrapped in a silk handkerchief.

"There's really no need for all these precautions," said Alleyn as he unwrapped it. "We've been all over it for prints and found none. My fingerprint man travels with half a laboratory in his kit. This thing's been dusted, peered at and photographed. It was evidently very thoroughly cleaned after it was put in position."

He laid the automatic in the box. It exactly fitted the indentation in the green baize lining.

"Seems a true bill," said Alleyn.

"How many rounds gone?" asked Jocelyn.

"Three," answered Alleyn.

"I fired the first two in 1917," said Jocelyn; "but I swear before God I'd nothing to do with the third."

"I hope you'll at least have the satisfaction of knowing who had," said Alleyn. "Did you write this notice, 'Loaded,' sir?"

"Yes," said Jocelyn. "What of it?"

Alleyn paused for a fraction of a second before he said, "Only routine, sir. I was going to ask if it always lay on top of the Colt."

"Certainly."

"Do you mind, sir, if I take this box away with me? There may be prints; but I'm afraid your housemaids are too well trained."

"I hope to God you find something. Do take it. I tell you, I'm nearly worried to death by the whole thing. It's a damned outrage that this blasted murderer—"

The door opened and Henry came into the room.

"This is my son," said Jocelyn.

## II

From an upstairs window Henry had watched the arrival of Alleyn's car. Ever since his visit to the study at dawn and his subsequent interview with the abruptly awakened Jocelyn, Henry had been unable to think coherently, to stay still, or to do anything definite. It struck him that he was in very much the same condition as he had been last night while waiting in the wings for the curtain to go up. He had telephoned to Dinah and arranged to see her at the rectory. He had prowled miserably about the house. At intervals he had tried to reassure his father, who had taken the news well, but was obviously very shaken. He had wondered what they would do with Eleanor when she chose to appear. She had gone straight to her room on her return from church, and was reported to be suffering from a headache.

When Jocelyn went downstairs to meet Alleyn, Henry's condition became several degrees more uncomfortable. He imagined his father making a bad job of the automatic story, getting himself further and further involved, and finally losing his temper. The Yard man would probably be maddeningly professional and heavy handed. Henry pictured him seated on the edge of one of the study chairs, staring at his father with sharp, inhuman eyes set in a massive policeman's face. "He will carry his bowler in with him and his boots will be intolerable," thought Henry. "A mammoth of officialdom!"

At last his own idleness became insupportable, and he ran downstairs and made for the study.

He could hear his father's voice raised, as it seemed, in protest. He opened the door and walked in.

"This is my son," said Jocelyn.

Henry's first thought was that this was some stranger, or perhaps a friend of Jocelyn's arrived with hideous inconvenience to visit them. He saw an extremely tall man, thin, and wearing good clothes, with an air of vague distinction.

"This is Mr. Alleyn," said Jocelyn, "from Scotland Yard."

"Oh," said Henry.

He shook hands, felt suddenly rather young, and sat down. His next impression was that he had seen Mr. Alleyn before. He found himself looking at Alleyn in terms of a pencil drawing. A drawing that might have been done by Dürer with a sharp, hard pencil and then washed delicately with blue-blacks and ochres. "A grandee turned monk," thought Henry, "but retaining some amusing memories." And he sought to find a reason for this impression which seemed more like a recollection. The accents of the brows, the winged corners to the mouth and eyes, the sharp insistence of the skull—he had seen them all before.

"Henry!" said his father sharply.

Henry realized that Alleyn had been speaking.

"I'm so sorry," he said. "I'm afraid I didn't—— I'm very sorry."

"I was only asking," said Alleyn, "if you could help us with this business of the Colt. Your father says it was in its box last week. Can you get any nearer to it than that?"

"It was there on Friday afternoon at five," said Henry.

"How d'you know?" demanded the squire.

"You'll scarcely credit it," said Henry slowly, "but I've only just remembered. It was before you came down. I was here with Cousin Eleanor waiting for the others to come in for Dinah's run-through for words. They all arrived together, or within two or three minutes of each other. Somebody, Dr. Templett, I think, said something about the burglaries in Somerset last week. Posh Jimmy and his Boys, and all that. We wondered if they'd come this way. Miss Campanula talked about burglar alarms and what she'd do if she heard stealthy footsteps in the small hours. I told them about your war relic, Father, and we all looked at it. Mrs. Ross said she didn't think it was safe to have a loaded firearm lying about. I showed her that the safety catch was on. Then we talked about something else. You came in and we started the rehearsal."

"That's a help," said Alleyn. "It narrows the time down to twenty-seven hours. That was Friday evening. Now, did either of you go to the hall on Friday afternoon?"

"I was hunting," said Jocelyn. "I didn't get back till five, in time for this run-through."

Alleyn looked at Henry.

"I went for a walk," said Henry. "I left at about half-past two. I remember now. It was half-past two."

"Did you go far?"

Henry looked straight before him.

"No. About halfway down to the church."

"How long were you away?"

"About two hours."

"You stopped somewhere, then?"

"Yes."

"Did you speak to anybody?"

"I met Dinah Copeland." Henry looked at his father. "*Not* by appointment. We talked. For some time. Then my cousin, Eleanor Prentice, came up. She had been to church. If it's of any interest, I remember hearing the church clock strike three when she came up. After that Dinah went back to the rectory and I struck up a path to Cloudyfold. I came home by the hill path."

"At what time did you get home?"

"Tea-time. About half-past four."

"Thank you. Now for Friday at five, when the company met here and you showed them the automatic. Did they all leave together?"

"Yes," said Henry.

"At what time?"

"Soon after six."

"Nobody was alone in here at any time before they left?"

"No. We rehearsed in here. They all went out by the french window. It saves trailing through the house."

"Yes. Is it always unlocked?"

"During the day it is."

"I lock it before we go to bed," said Jocelyn, "and fasten the shutters. Lock up the whole place."

"You did this on Friday night, sir?"

"Yes. I was in here reading, all Friday evening."

"Alone?"

"I was here part of the time," Henry said. "Something had gone wrong with one of Dinah's light plugs in the hall and I'd brought it up here to mend. I started in here, and then went to my own room where I had a screwdriver. I tried to ring Dinah up, but our telephone was out of order. A branch had fallen across it in Top Lane."

"I see. Now, how about yesterday? Any visitors?"

"Templett came up in the morning to borrow an old four-in-hand tie of mine," said Jocelyn. "He seemed to think he'd like to wear it in the play. He offered to look at my cousin's finger, but she wouldn't come down."

"She was afraid he'd tell her she couldn't play her filthy 'Venetian Suite,'" said Henry. "Do you admire the works of Ethelbert Nevin, Mr. Alleyn?"

"No," said Alleyn.

"They're gall and wormwood to me," said Henry gloomily. "And I suppose we'll have them here for the rest of our lives. Not that I like the bloody Prelude much better. Do you know what the Prelude is supposed to illustrate?"

"Yes, I think I do. Isn't it——"

"Burial," said Henry. "It's supposed to be a man buried alive. Bump, bump, bump on the coffin lid. Well, I suppose it's not so frightfully inappropriate."

"Not so frightfully," agreed Alleyn rather grimly. "Now, about yesterday's visitors."

But Henry and his father were rather vague about yesterday's visitors. The squire had driven into Great Chipping in the morning.

"And Miss Prentice?" asked Alleyn.

"Same thing. She went with us. She was in the hall all the morning. They were all there."

"All?"

"Well, not Templett," said Henry. "He called in here as we've described, at about ten o'clock, and my father gave him the tie. And a pretty ghastly affair it is, I may add."

"They were damn' smart at one time," said the squire hotly. "I remember I wore that tie——"

"Well, anyway," said Henry, "he got the tie. I didn't see him. I was hunting up my own clothes. We all went out soon after he'd gone. You saw him off, didn't you, Father?"

"Yes," said the squire. "Funny sort of fellow, Templett. First I knew about him was that Taylor told me he was in here and wanted the four-in-hand. I told Taylor to hunt it up and came down and found Templett. We talked for quite a long time and I'm blessed if, when I walked out with him to the car, poor little Mrs. Ross wasn't sitting there. Damn' funny thing to do," said Jocelyn, brushing up his mustache. "'Pon my word, I think the fellow wanted to keep her to himself."

Alleyn looked thoughtfully at him.

"How was Dr. Templett dressed?" he asked.

"What? I don't know. Yes, I think I do. Donegal tweed."

"An overcoat?"

"No."

"Bulging pockets?" asked Henry, with a grin at Alleyn.

"I don't think so. Why? Good Lord, you don't suppose he took my Colt, do you?"

"We've got to explore the possibilities, sir," said Alleyn.

"My God," said Jocelyn, "I suppose they're all under suspicion! What?"

"Including us," said Henry. "You know," he added, "theoretically one wouldn't put it past Templett. Eleanor's been poisonous about his alleged—notice how I protect myself, Mr. Alleyn—his alleged affair with Selia Ross."

"Good God!" shouted Jocelyn angrily, "haven't you got more sense than to talk like that, Henry? This is a damn' serious business, let me tell you, and you go blackening Mr.—Mr. Alleyn's mind against a man who—"

"I spoke theoretically, remember," said Henry. "I don't really suppose Templett is a murderer, and as for Mr. Alleyn's mind—"

"It doesn't blacken very readily," said Alleyn.

"And after all," Henry continued, "you might make out just as bad a case against me. If I thought I could murder Cousin Eleanor in safety I dare say I should undertake it. And I should think Mr. Copeland would feel sorely tempted after the way she's—"

"Henry!"

"But, my dear Father, Mr. Alleyn is going to hear all the local gossip if he hasn't done so already. Of course, Mr. Alleyn will suspect each of us in turn. Even dear Cousin Eleanor herself is not above suspicion. She may have infected her finger in the approved manner with a not too deadly toxin. Or made it up to look septic. Why not? There were the grease paints. True, she overdid it a bit, but that may have been pure artistry."

"Damn' dangerous twaddle," shouted Jocelyn. "It was hurting her like hell. I've known Eleanor since we were children, and I've never seen her cry before. She's a Jernigham."

"A good deal of it was straight-out annoyance at not being able to perform the 'Venetian Suite,' if you ask me. Tears of anger, they were, and the only sort you'll ever wring from Eleanor's eyes. Did she cry when they yanked out her gall-bladder? No. She's a Jernigham."

"Be quiet, sir," stormed Jocelyn.

"As far as I can see, the only one of us who could *not* have set the trap is poor old Idris Campanula. Oh, God!"

Alleyn, watching Henry, saw him turn very white before he moved away to the window.

"All right," Henry said to the landscape. "One's got to do something about it. Can't go on all day thinking of an old maid with her brains blown out. Might as well be funny in our hard, decadent modern way."

"I remember getting the same reaction in the war," said Alleyn vaguely. "As they say in vaudeville, 'I had to laugh.' It's not an uncommon rebound from shock."

"I don't suppose I was being anything but excessively commonplace," said Henry tartly.

## III

"Then you don't know if anybody came while you were out yesterday morning?" asked Alleyn, after some considerable time spent in collecting the attention of the two Jernighams.

"I'll ask the servants," said Jocelyn importantly, and rang for Taylor.

As Alleyn expected, the evidence of the servants was completely inconclusive. Nobody had actually rung the door bells, but on the other hand anybody might have walked into the study and done anything. They corroborated Jocelyn and Henry's statements about their own movements and Taylor remembered seeing Miss Prentice come in at four on Friday afternoon. When the last maid had gone Alleyn asked if they had all been at Pen Cuckoo for some time.

"Lord, yes," said the squire. "Out of the question they should have anything to do with this affair. No motive, no opportunity."

"And not nearly enough sense," added Henry.

"In addition to which," said Alleyn, "they have provided each other with alibis for the whole day until they all went down in a solid body to the church hall at seven-thirty."

"I understand the entertainment provided," said Henry, "caused cook to vomit three times on the way home, and this morning, Father, I am told, the boot-boy heaved everything he had into the tops of your hunting boots."

"Well, that's a nice thing!" began Jocelyn crossly.

Alleyn said, "You told me it is out of the question that the automatic could have been substituted for the water-pistol during yesterday morning."

"Unless it was done under the noses of a bevy of Friendly Young People and most of the company," said Henry.

"How about the afternoon?"

"It was locked up then and the key, instead of being at the rectory as usual, was hidden, fancifully enough, behind the outside lavatory," said Henry. "Dinah invented the place of concealment, and announced it at rehearsal. Cousin Eleanor was too put-out to object. Nobody but the members of the cast knew about it. As far as I know, only Templett and Mrs. Ross called in during the afternoon."

"What did you do?" asked Alleyn.

"I went for a walk on Cloudyfold. I met nobody," said Henry, "and I can't prove I was there."

"Thank you," said Alleyn mildly. "What about you, sir?"

"I went round the stables with Rumbold, my agent," said Jocelyn, "and then I came in and went to sleep in the library. I was waked by my cousin at five. We had a sort of high tea at half-past six and went down to the hall at a quarter to seven."

"All three of you?"

"Yes."

"And now, if you please," said Alleyn, "I should like to see Miss Prentice."

# CHAPTER XV

# Alleyn Goes to Church

*I*

MISS PRENTICE CAME IN LOOKING, as Henry afterwards told Dinah, as much like an early Christian martyr as her clothes permitted. Alleyn, who had never been able to conquer his proclivity for first impressions, took an instant dislike to her.

The squire's manner became nervously proprietary.

"Well, Eleanor," he said, "here you are. We're sorry to bring you down. May I introduce Mr. Alleyn? He's looking into this business for us."

Miss Prentice gave Alleyn a forebearing smile and a hand like a fish. She sat on the only uncomfortable chair in the room.

"I shall try not to bother you too long," Alleyn began.

"It's only," said Miss Prentice, in a voice that suggested the presence of Miss Campanula's body in the room, "it's only that I hope to go to church at eleven."

"It's a few minutes after ten. I think you'll have plenty of time."

"I'll drive you down," said Henry.

"Thank you, dear, I think I should like to walk."

"I'm going, anyway," said Jocelyn.

Miss Prentice smiled at him. It was an approving, understanding sort of smile, and Alleyn thought it would have kept him away from church for the rest of his life.

"Well, Miss Prentice," he said, "we are trying to see daylight through a mass of strange circumstances. There is no reason why you shouldn't be told that Miss Campanula was shot by the automatic that is kept in a box in this room."

"Oh, Jocelyn!" said Miss Prentice, "how terrible! You know, dear, we *have* said it wasn't really quite advisable, haven't we?"

"You needn't go rubbing it in, Eleanor."

"Why wasn't it advisable?" asked Henry. "Had you foreseen, Cousin Eleanor, that somebody might pinch the Colt and rig it up in a piano as a lethal booby-trap?"

"Henry dear, please! We just said sometimes that perhaps it wasn't very wise."

"Are you employing the editorial or the regal 'we'?"

Alleyn said, "One minute, please. Before we go any further I think, as a matter of pure police routine, I would like to see your finger, Miss Prentice."

"Oh, dear! It's very painful. I'm afraid——"

"If you would rather Dr. Templett unwrapped it——"

"Oh, no. No."

"If you will allow me, I think I can do a fairly presentable bandage."

Miss Prentice raised her eyes to Alleyn's and a very peculiar expression visited her face, a mixture of archness and submission. She advanced her swathed hand with an air of timidity. He undid the bandage very quickly and lightly and exposed the finger with a somewhat battered stall drawn over a closer bandage. He peeled off the stall and completely unwrapped the finger. It was inflamed, discolored and swollen.

"A nasty casualty," said Alleyn. "You should have it dressed again. Dr. Templett——"

"I do not wish Dr. Templett to touch it."

"But he could give you fresh bandages and a stall that has not been torn."

"I have a first-aid box. Henry, would you mind, dear?"

Henry was dispatched for the first-aid box. Alleyn redressed the finger very deftly. Miss Prentice watched him with a sort of eager concentration, never lowering her gaze from his face.

"How beautifully you manage," she said.

"I hope it will serve. You should have a sling, I fancy. Do you want the old stall?"

She shook her head. He dropped it in his pocket and was startled when she uttered a little coy murmur of protestation, for all the world as if he had taken her finger-stall from some motive of gallantry.

"You deserve a greater reward," she said.

"Lummy!" thought Alleyn in considerable embarrassment. He said, "Miss Prentice, I am trying to get a sort of time-table of everybody's movements from Friday afternoon until the time of the tragedy. Do you mind telling me where you were on Friday afternoon?"

"I was in church."

"All the afternoon?"

"Oh, no," said Eleanor, softly.

"Between what hours were you there, please?"

"I arrived at two."

"Do you know when the service was over?"

"It was not a service," said Miss Prentice with pale forbearance.

"You were there alone?"

"It was confession," said Henry, impatiently.

"Oh, I see." Alleyn paused. "Was anybody else there besides yourself and—and your confessor?"

"No. I passed poor Idris on my way out."

"When was that?"

"I think I remember the clock struck half-past two."

"Good. And then?"

"I went home."

"Directly?"

"I took the top lane."

"The lane that comes out by the church?"

"Yes."

"Did you pass the Parish Hall?"

"Yes."

"You didn't go in?"

"No."

"Was any one there, do you think?"

"The doors were shut," said Miss Prentice. "I think the girls only went in for an hour."

"Were the keys in their place of concealment on Friday?" asked Alleyn.

Miss Prentice instantly looked grieved and shocked. Henry grinned broadly and said, "There's only one key. I don't know if it was there on Friday. I think it was. Dinah would know about that. Some of the committee worked there on Friday, as Cousin Eleanor says, but none of us. They may have returned the key to the rectory. I only went halfway down."

"At what part of the top lane on Friday afternoon did you meet Mr. Henry Jernigham and Miss Copeland, Miss Prentice?"

Alleyn heard her draw in her breath and saw her turn white. She looked reproachfully at Henry and said:

"I'm afraid I do not remember."

"I do," said Henry. "It was at the sharp bend above the foot-bridge. You came round the corner from below."

She bent her head. Henry looked as if he dared her to speak.

"There's something damned unpleasant about this," thought Alleyn.

He said, "How long did you spend in conversation with the others before you went on to Pen Cuckoo?"

An unlovely red stained her cheeks.

"Not long."

"About five minutes, I should think," said Henry.

"And you arrived home, when?"

"I should think at about half-past three. I really don't know."

"Did you go out again on Friday, Miss Prentice?"

"No," said Miss Prentice.

"You were about the house? I'm sorry to worry you like this, but you see I really do want to know exactly what everybody did on Friday."

"I was in my room," she said. "There are two little offices that Father Copeland has given us for use after confession."

"Oh, I see," said Alleyn, in some embarrassment.

## II

Alleyn waded on. Miss Prentice's air of patient martyrdom increased with every question, but he managed to get a good deal of information from her. On Saturday, the day of the performance, she had spent the morning in the parish hall with all the other workers. She left when the others left, and, with Jocelyn and Henry, returned to Pen Cuckoo for lunch. She had not gone out again until the evening but had spent the afternoon in her sitting-room. She remembered waking the squire at tea-time. After tea she returned to her room.

"During yesterday morning you were all at the hall?" said Alleyn. "Who got there first?"

"Dinah Copeland, I should think," said Jocelyn promptly. "She was there when we arrived. She was always the first."

Alleyn made a note of it and went on, "Did any of you notice the position and appearance of the piano?"

They all looked very solemn at the mention of the piano.

"I think I did," said Miss Prentice in a low voice. "It was as it was for the performance. The girls had evidently arranged the drapery and pot-plants on Friday. I looked at it rather particularly as I was—I was to play it."

"Good Lord!" ejaculated the squire, "you were strumming on the damned thing. I remember now."

"Jocelyn, dear, please! I did just touch the keys, I believe, with my right hand. Not my left," said Miss Prentice with her most patient smile.

"This was yesterday morning, wasn't it?" said Alleyn. "Now, please, Miss Prentice, try to remember. Did you use the soft pedal at all when you tried the piano?"

"Oh, dear, now I wonder. Let me see. I did sit down for a moment. I expect I did use the soft pedal. I always think soft playing is so much nicer. Yes, I should think almost without doubt I used the soft pedal."

"Was anybody by the piano at the time?" asked Alleyn.

Miss Prentice turned a reproachful gaze upon him.

"Idris," she whispered. "Miss Campanula."

"Here, wait a bit," shouted Jocelyn. "I've remembered the whole thing. Eleanor, you sat down and strummed about with your right hand and she came up and asked you why you didn't try with your left to see how it worked."

"So she did," said Henry, softly. "And so, of course, she would."

"And you got up and went away," said the squire. "Old Camp—well, Idris Campanula—gave a sort of laugh and dumped herself down and—"

"And away went the Prelude!" cried Henry. "You're quite right, Father. 'Pom. *Pom!* POM!!' And then down went the soft pedal. That's it, sir," he added, turning to Alleyn. "I watched her. I'll swear it."

"Right," said Alleyn. "We're getting on. This was yesterday morning. At what time?"

"Just before we packed up," said Henry. "About midday."

"And—I know I've been over this before, but it's important—you all left together?"

"Yes," said Henry. "We three drove off in the car. I remember that I heard Dinah slam the back door just as we started. They were all out by then."

"And none of you returned until the evening? I see. When you arrived at a quarter to seven you found Miss Copeland there."

"Yes," said Jocelyn.

"Where was she?"

"On the stage with her father, putting flowers in vases."

"Was the curtain down?"

"Yes."

"What did you all do?"

"I went to my dressing-room," said the squire.

"I stayed in the supper-room and talked to Dinah," said Henry. "Her father was on the stage. After a minute or two I went to my dressing-room."

"Here!" ejaculated Jocelyn, and glared at Miss Prentice.

"What, dear?"

"Those girls were giggling about in front of the hall. I wonder if any of them got up to any hanky-panky with the piano."

"Oh, my dear Father!" said Henry.

"They were strictly forbidden to touch the instrument," said Miss Prentice. "Ever since Cissie Drury did such damage."

"How long was it before the others arrived? Dr. Templett and Mrs. Ross?" asked Alleyn.

"They didn't get down until half-past seven," said Henry. "Dinah was in a frightful stew and so were we all. She rang up Mrs. Ross's cottage in the end. It took ages to get through. The hall telephone's an extension from the rectory and we rang for a long time before anybody at the rectory answered and at last, when it was connected with Mrs. Ross's house, there was no reply, so we knew she'd left."

"She came with Dr. Templett?"

"Oh, yes," murmured Miss Prentice.

"The telephone is in your dressing-room, isn't it, Mr. Jernigham?"

"Mine and Henry's. We shared. We were all there round the telephone."

"Yes," said Alleyn. He looked from one face to another. Into the quiet room there dropped the Sunday morning sound of chiming bells. Miss Prentice rose.

"Thank you so much," said Alleyn. "I think I've got a general idea of the two days now. On Friday afternoon Miss Prentice went to church, Mr. Jernigham hunted, Mr. Henry Jernigham went for a walk. On her return from church, Miss Prentice met Mr. Henry Jernigham and Miss Copeland, who had themselves met by chance in the top lane. That was at about three. Mr. Henry Jernigham returned home by a circuitous route, Miss Prentice by the top lane. Miss Prentice went to her room. At five you had your rehearsal for words in this room, and everybody saw the automatic. You all three dined at home and remained at home. It was also on Friday afternoon that some helpers worked for about an hour at the hall, but apparently they had finished at two-thirty when Miss Prentice passed that way. On Saturday (yesterday) morning Dr. Templett and Mrs. Ross called here for the tie. You all went down to the hall and you, sir, drove to Great Chipping. You all returned for lunch. By this time the piano was in position with the drapery and aspidistras on top. In the afternoon Mr. Henry Jernigham walked up to Cloudyfold and back. As far as we know, only Dr. Templett and Mrs. Ross visited the hall yesterday afternoon. At a quarter to seven you all arrived there for the performance."

"Masterly, sir," said Henry.

"Oh, I've written it all down," said Alleyn. "My memory's hopeless."

"What about your music, Miss Prentice? When did you put it on the piano?"

"Oh, on Saturday morning, of course."

"I see. You had it here until then?"

"Oh, no," said Miss Prentice. "Not *here*, you know."

"Then, where?"

"In the hall, naturally."

"It lives in the hall?"

"Oh, no," she said, opening her eyes very wide, "why should it?"

"I'm sure I don't know. When did you take it to the hall?"

"On Thursday night for the dress-rehearsal, of course."

"I see. You played for the dress-rehearsal?"

"Oh, no."

"For the love of heaven!" ejaculated Jocelyn. "Why the dickens can't you come to the point, Eleanor. She wanted to play on Thursday night but her finger was like a bad sausage," he explained to Alleyn.

Miss Prentice gave Alleyn her martyred smile, shook her head slightly at the bandaged finger, and looked restlessly at the clock.

"H'm," she said unhappily.

"Well," said Alleyn. "The music was in the hall from Thursday onwards and you put it in the rack yesterday morning. And none of you went into the hall before the show last night. Good."

Miss Prentice said, "Well—I think I shall just—Jocelyn, dear, that's the first bell, isn't it?"

"I'm sorry," said Alleyn, "but I should like, if I may, to have a word with you, Miss Prentice. Perhaps you will let me drive you down. Or if not——"

"Oh," said Miss Prentice, looking very flurried, "thank you. I think I should prefer—I'm afraid I really can't——"

"Cousin Eleanor," said Henry, "I will drive you down, father will drive you down, or Mr. Alleyn will drive you down. You might even drive yourself down. It is only twenty-five to eleven now and it doesn't take more than ten minutes to *walk* down, so you can easily spare Mr. Alleyn a quarter of an hour."

"I'm afraid I do fuss rather, don't I, but you see I like to have a few quiet moments before——"

"Now, look here, Eleanor," said the squire warmly, "this is an investigation into murder. Good Lord, it's your best friend that's been killed, my dear girl, and when we're right in the thick of it, damme, you want to go scuttling off to church."

"*Jocelyn!*"

"Come on, Father," said Henry. "We'll leave Mr. Alleyn a fair field."

## III

"——you see," said Alleyn, "I don't think you quite realize your own position. Hadn't it occurred to you that you were the intended victim?"

"It is such a dreadful thought," said Miss Prentice.

"I know it is, but you've got to face it. There's a murderer abroad in your land and as far as one can see his first coup hasn't come off. It's been a fantastic and horrible failure. For your own, if not for the public's good, you must realize this. Surely you want to help us."

"I believe," said Miss Prentice, "that our greatest succor lies in prayer."

"Yes," said Alleyn slowly, "I can appreciate that. But my job is to ask questions, and I do ask you, most earnestly, if you believe that you have a bitter enemy among this small group of people."

"I cannot believe it of any one."

Alleyn looked at her with something very like despair. She had refused to sit down after they were alone, but fidgeted about in the center of the room, looked repeatedly down the Vale, and was thrown into a fever of impatience by the call of the church bells.

A towering determined figure, he stood between Eleanor and the window, and concentrated his will on her. He thought of his mind as a pin-pointed weapon and he drove it into hers.

"Miss Prentice. Please look at me."

Her glanced wavered. Her pale eyes traveled reluctantly to his. Deliberately silent until he felt he had got her whole attention, he held her gaze with his own. Then he spoke. "I may not try to force information from you. You are a free agent. But think for a moment of the position. You have escaped death by an accident. If you had persisted in playing last night you would have been shot dead. I am going to repeat a list of names to you. If there is anything between any one of these persons and yourself which, if I knew of it, might help me to see light, ask yourself if you should not tell me of it. These are the names:

"Mr. Jocelyn Jernigham?

"His son, Henry Jernigham?

"The rector, Mr. Copeland?"

"No!" she cried, "no! Never! Never!"

"His daughter, Dinah Copeland?

"Mrs. Ross?"

He saw the pale eyes narrow a little.

"Dr. Templett?"

She stared at him like a mesmerized rabbit.

"Well, Miss Prentice, what of Mrs. Ross and Dr. Templett?"

"I can accuse nobody. Please let me go."

"Have you ever had a difference with Mrs. Ross?"

"I hardly speak to Mrs. Ross."

"Or with Dr. Templett?"

"I prefer not to discuss Dr. Templett," she said breathlessly.

"At least," said Alleyn, "he saved your life. He dissuaded you from playing."

"I believe God saw fit to use him as an unworthy instrument."

Alleyn opened his mouth to speak and thought better of it. At last he said, "In your own interest, tell me this. Has Mrs. Ross cause to regard you as her enemy?"

She wetted her lips and answered him with astounding vigor:

"I have thought only as every decent creature who sees her must think. Before she could silence the voice of reproach she would have to murder a dozen Christian souls."

"Of whom Miss Campanula was one?"

She stared at him vacantly and then he saw she had understood him.

"That's why he wouldn't let me play," she whispered.

On his way back, Alleyn turned off the Vale road and drove up past the church to the hall. Seven cars were drawn up outside St. Giles and he noticed a stream of villagers turning in at the lych-gate.

"Full house, this morning," thought Alleyn grimly. And suddenly he pulled up by the hall, got out, and walked back to the church.

"The devil takes a holiday," he thought, and joined in with the stream.

He managed to elude the solicitations of a sidesman and slip into a seat facing the aisle in the back row where he sat with his long hands clasped round his knee. His head looked remotely austere in the cold light from the open doors.

Winton St. Giles is a beautiful church and Alleyn, overcoming that first depression inseparable from the ecclesiastical smell, and the sight of so many people with decorous faces, found pleasure in the tranquil solidity of stone shaped into the expression of devotion. The single bell stopped. The organ rumbled vaguely for three minutes, the congregation stood, and Mr. Copeland followed his choir into church.

Like everybody else who saw him for the first time, Alleyn was startled by the rector's looks. The service was a choral Eucharist and he wore a cope, a magnificent vestment that shone like a blazon in the candle light. His silver hair, the incredible perfection of his features, his extreme pallor, and great height, made Alleyn think of an actor admirably suited for the performance of priestly parts. But when the time came for the short sermon, he found evidence of a simple and unaffected mind with no great originality. It was an unpretentious sermon touched with sincerity. The rector spoke of prayers for the dead and told his listeners that there was nothing in the teaching of their church that forbade such prayers. He invited them to petition God for the peace of all souls departed in haste or by violence, and he commended meditation and a searching of their own hearts lest they should harbor anger or resentment.

As the service went on, Alleyn, looking down the aisle, saw a dark girl with so strong a resemblance to the rector that he knew she must be Dinah Copeland. Her eyes were fixed on her father and in them Alleyn read anxiety and affection.

Miss Prentice was easily found, for she sat next the aisle in the front row. She rose and fell like a ping-pong ball on a water jet, sinking in solitary genuflexions and crossing herself like a sort of minor soloist. The squire sat beside her. The back of his neck wore an expression of indignation and discomfort, being both scarlet and rigid. Much nearer to Alleyn, and also next the aisle, sat a woman whom he recognized as probably the most fashionable figure in the congregation. Detectives are trained to know about clothes and Alleyn knew hers were impeccable. She wore them like a Frenchwoman. He could only see the thin curve of her cheek and an immaculate wing of straw-colored hair, but presently, as if aware of his gaze, she turned her head and he saw her face. It was thinnish and alert, beautifully made-up, hard, but with a look of amused composure. The pale eyes looked into his and widened. She paused with unmistakable deliberation for a split second, and then turned away. Her luxuriously gloved hand went to her hair.

"That was once known as the glad eye," thought Alleyn.

Under cover of a hymn he slipped out of church.

## IV

He crossed the lane to the hall. Sergeant Roper was on duty at the gate and came smartly to attention.

"Well, Roper, how long have you been here?"

"I relieved Constable Fife an hour ago, sir. The super sent him along soon after you left. About seven-thirty, sir."

"Anybody been about?"

"Boys," said Roper, "hanging round like wasps and as bold as brass with that young Biggins talking that uppish you'd have thought he was as good as the murderer, letting on as he was as full of inside knowledge as the Lord Himself, not meaning it in the way of blasphemy. I subdued him, however, and his mother bore him off to church. Mr. Bathgate took a photograph of the building, and asked me to say, sir, that he'd look back in a minute or two in case you were here."

"I dare say," grunted Alleyn.

"And the doctor came along, too, in a proper taking on. Seems he left one of his knives for slashing open the body in the hall last night, and he wanted to fetch her out for to lay bare the youngest Cain's toe. I went in with the doctor but she was nowhere to be found, no not even in the pockets of his suit which seemed a strange casual spot for a naked blade, no doubt so deadly sharp as 'twould penetrate the very guts of a man in a flash. Doctor was proper put about by the loss and made off without another word."

"I see. Any one else?"

"Not a living soul," said Roper. "I reckon rector will have brought this matter up in his sermon, sir. The man couldn't well avoid it, seeing it's his job to put a holy construction on the face of disaster."

"He did just touch on it," Alleyn admitted.

"A ticklish affair and you may be sure one that he didn't greatly relish, being a timid sort of chap."

"I think I'll have a look round the outside of the hall, Roper."

"Very good, sir."

Alleyn wandered round the hall on the lane side, his eyes on the graveled path. Roper looked after him wistfully until he disappeared at the back. He came to the rear door, saw nothing of interest, and turned to the outhouses. Here, in a narrow gap between two walls, he found a nail where he supposed the key had hung yesterday. He continued his search round the far side of the building and came at last to a window, where he stopped.

He remembered that they had shut this window last night before they left the hall. It was evidently the only one that was ever opened. The others were firmly sealed in accumulated grime. Alleyn looked at the wall underneath it. The surface of the weathered stone was grazed in many places, and on the ground he discovered freshly detached chips. Between the graveled path and the side of the building was a narrow strip of grass. This bore a rectangular impress that the night's heavy rain had softened but not obliterated. Within the margin of the impress he found traces of several large footprints and two smaller ones. Alleyn returned to a sort of lumbershed at the back and fetched an old box. The edges at the open end bore traces of damp earth. He took it to the impression and found that it fitted exactly. It also covered the lower grazes on the wall. He examined the box minutely, peering into the joints and cracks in the rough wood. Presently he began to whistle. He took a pair of tweezers from his pocket, and along the edge, from a crack where the wood had split, he pulled out a minute red scrap of some springy substance. He found two more shreds caught in the rough surface of the wood, and on a projecting nail. He put them in an envelope and sealed it. Then he replaced the box. He measured the height from the box to the window sill.

"Good morning," said a voice behind him. "You must be a detective."

Alleyn glanced up and saw Nigel Bathgate leaning over the stone fence that separated the parish hall grounds from a path on the far side.

"What a fascinating life yours must be," continued Nigel.

Alleyn did not reply. Inadvertently he released the catch on the steel tape. It flew back into the container.

"Pop goes the weasel," said Nigel.

"Hold your tongue," said Alleyn, mildly, "and come here."

Nigel vaulted over the wall.

"Take this tape for me. Don't touch the box if you can help it."

"It would be pleasant to know why."

"Five-foot-three from the box to the sill," said Alleyn. "Too far for Georgie, and in any case we know he didn't. That's funny."

"Screamingly."

"Go to the next window, Bathgate, and raise yourself by the sill. If you can."

"Only if you tell me why."

"I will in a minute. Please be quick. I want to get this over before the hosts of the ungodly are upon us. Can you do it?"

"Listen, Chief. This is your lucky day. Look at these biceps. Three months ago I was puny like you. By taking my self-raising course——"

Nigel reached up to the window sill, gave a prodigious heave, and cracked the crown of his head smartly on the sill.

"Great strength rings the bell," said Alleyn. "Now try and get foothold."

"Blast and damn you!" said Nigel, scraping at the wall with his shoes.

"That will do. I'm going into the hall. When I call out, I want you to repeat this performance. You needn't crack your head again."

Alleyn went into the hall, forced open the second window two inches, and went over to the piano.

"Now!"

The shape of Nigel's head and shoulders rose up behind the clouded glass. His collar and tie appeared in the gap. Alleyn had a fleeting impression of his face.

"All right."

Nigel disappeared and Alleyn rejoined him.

"Are we playing Peep Bo or what?" asked Nigel sourly.

"Something of the sort. I saw you all right. Yes," continued Alleyn, examining the wall. "The lady used the box. We will preserve the box. Dear me."

"At least you might say I can come down."

"I'm so sorry. Of course. And your head?"

"Bloody."

"But unbowed, I feel sure. Now I'll explain."

# CHAPTER XVI

# The Top Lane Incident

## I

ALLEYN GAVE NIGEL HIS EXPLANATION as they walked up Top Lane by
the route Dinah had taken on Friday afternoon. They walked briskly,
their heads bent, and a look of solemn absorption on their faces. In a
few minutes they crossed a rough bridge and reached a sharp turn in
the lane.

"It was here," said Alleyn, "that Henry Jernigham met Dinah Copeland on Friday afternoon. It was here that Eleanor Prentice found
them on her return from the confessional. I admit that I am curious
about their encounters, Bathgate. Miss Prentice came upon them at
three, yet she left the church at half-past two. Young Jernigham says he
was away two hours. He left home at two-thirty. It can take little more
than five minutes to come down here from Pen Cuckoo. They must
have been together almost half an hour before Miss Prentice arrived."

"Perhaps they are in love."

"Perhaps they are. But there is something that neither Miss Prentice
nor Master Henry cares to remember when one speaks of this meeting.
They turn pale. Henry becomes sardonic and Miss Prentice sends out
waves of sanctimonious disapproval in the manner of a polecat."

"What can you mean?"

"It doesn't matter. She left the church at three. She only spent five minutes here with the others and yet she did not reach Pen Cuckoo till after four. There seems to be a lot of time to spare. Henry struck up this path to the hilltop. Miss Copeland returned by the way we have come, Miss Prentice went on to Pen Cuckoo. I have a picture of three specks of humanity running together, exploding, and flying apart."

"There are a hundred explanations."

"For their manner of meeting and parting? Yes, I dare say there are, but not so many explanations for their agitation when the meeting is discussed. Say that she surprised them in an embrace, Master Henry might feel foolish at the recollection, but why should Miss Prentice go white and trembly?"

"She's an old maid, isn't she? Perhaps it shocked her."

"It may have given her a shock."

Alleyn was searching the wet lane.

"The rain last night was the devil. This great bough must have been blown down quite recently. Master Henry told me that their telephone was dumb on Friday night. He said it was broken by a falling bough in Top Lane. There are the wires and it almost follows as the night the day that this is the bough. It's protected the ground. Wait, I believe we've struck a little luck."

They moved the still unwithered bough.

"Yes. See here, Bathgate, here is where they stood. How much more dramatic footprints can be than the prints of hands. Look, here are Dinah Copeland's, if indeed they are hers, coming round the bend into the protection of the bank. The ground was soft but not too wet. Coming downhill we pick *his* prints up, as they march out of the sodden lane into the lee of the bank and overlapping trees. Surface water has seeped into them but there they are. And here, where the bough afterwards fell, they met."

"And what a meeting!" ejaculated Nigel, looking at the heavy impressions of overlapping prints.

"A long meeting. Yes, and a lover's meeting. She looks a nice girl. I hope Master Henry——"

He broke off.

"Here we are, by George. Don't come too far. Eleanor Prentice must have rounded the corner, taken two steps or so, and stopped dead. There are her feet planted side by side. She stood for some time in this one place, facing the others and then—what happened? Ordinary conversation? No, I don't think so. I'll have to try to get it from the young ones. *She* won't tell me. Yes, there are her shoes, no doubt of it. Blackcalf with pointed toes and low heels. Church hen's shoes. She was wearing them this morning."

Alleyn squatted by the two solitary prints, reached out a long finger and touched the damp earth. Then he looked up at Nigel.

"Well, it's proved one thing," he said.

"What?"

"If these are Eleanor Prentice's prints, and I think they are, it wasn't Eleanor Prentice who tried to see in at the window of the parish hall. Wait here, will you, Bathgate? I'm going down to the car for my stuff. We'll have a cast of these prints."

## II

At half-past twelve Alleyn and Nigel arrived at the Red House, Chipping. An elderly parlor maid told them that Mr. Fox was still there, and showed them into a Victorian drawing-room which, in the language of brassware and modernish silk Japanese panels, spoke unhappily of the late General Campanula's service in the East. It was an ugly room, over-furnished and unfriendly. Fox was seated at a writing desk in the window and before him were many neat stacks of papers. He rose and looked placidly at them over the tops of his glasses.

"Hullo, Brer Fox," said Alleyn. "How the hell are you getting on?"

"Fairly comfortably, thank you, sir. Good morning, Mr. Bathgate."

"Good morning, inspector."

"What have you got there?" asked Alleyn.

"A number of letters, sir, none of them very helpful."

"What about that ominous wad of foolscap, you old devil? Come on, now; it's the will, isn't it?"

"Well, it is," said Fox.

He handed it to Alleyn and waited placidly while he read it.

"This was a wealthy woman," said Alleyn.

"How wealthy?" demanded Nigel, "and what has she done with it?"

"Nothing that's for publication."

"All right, all right."

"She's left fifty thousand. Thirty of them go to the Reverend Walter Copeland of Winton St. Giles in recognition of his work as a parish priest and in deep gratitude for his spiritual guidance and unfailing wisdom. Lummy! He is to use the money as he thinks best but she hopes that he will not give it all away to other people. Fifteen thousand to her dear friend, Eleanor Jernigham Prentice, four thousand to Eric Campanula, son of William Campanula, and second cousin to the testatrix. Last heard of in Nairobi, Kenya. A stipulation that the said four thousand be invested by Miss Campanula's lawyers, Messrs. Waterworth, Waterworth and Biggs, and the beneficiary to receive the interest at their hands. The testatrix adds the hope that the beneficiary will not spend the said interest on alcoholic beverages or women, and will think of her and mend his ways. One thousand to be divided among the servants. Dated May 21st, 1938."

"There was a note enclosed dated May 21st of this year," said Fox. "Here it is, sir."

Alleyn read aloud with one eyebrow raised:

"To all whom it may concern. This is my last Will and Testament so there's no need for anybody to go poking about among my papers for another. I should like to say that the views expressed in reference to the principal beneficiary are the views I hold at the moment. If I could add anything to this appreciation of his character to make it more emphatic, I would do so. There have been disappointments, and friends who have failed me, but I am a lonely woman and see no reason to alter my Will. Idris Campanula."

"She seems to have been a very outspoken lady, doesn't she?" asked Fox.

"She does. That's a nasty jab in the eye for her dear friend, Eleanor Prentice," said Alleyn.

"Well, now," said Nigel briskly, "do you think either of these two have murdered her? You always say, Alleyn, that money is the prime motive."

"I don't say so in this instance," Alleyn said. "It may be, but I don't think it is. Well, there we are, Fox. We must get hold of the Waterworths and Mr. Biggs, before they read about it in the papers."

"I've rung them up, Mr. Alleyn. The parlormaid knew Mr. Waterworth senior's private address."

"Excellent, Fox. Anything else?"

"There's the chauffeur, Gibson. I think you might like to talk to him."

"All right. Produce Gibson."

Fox went out and returned with Miss Campanula's chauffeur. He wore his plum-colored breeches and shining gaiters and had the air of having just crammed himself into his tunic.

"This is Gibson, sir," said Fox. "I think the chief inspector would like to hear about this little incident on Friday afternoon, Mr. Gibson."

"Good morning," said Alleyn. "What's the incident?"

"It concerns deceased's visit to church at two-thirty, sir," Fox explained. "It seems that she called at the hall on her way down."

"Really?" said Alleyn.

"Not to say called, sir," said Gibson. "Not in a manner of speaking, seeing she didn't go in."

"Let's hear about it?"

"She used to go regular, you see, sir, to the confessing affair. About every three weeks. Well, Friday, she orders the car and we go down, getting there a bit early. She says, drive on to the hall, so I did and she got out and went to the front door. She'd been in a good mood all the morning. Pleased at going down to church and all, but soon as I saw her rattling the front door I knew one of her tantrums was coming on. As I was explaining to Mr. Fox, sir, she was a lady that was given to tantrums."

"Yes."

"I watched her. Rattle, rattle, rattle! And then I heard her shouting, 'Who's in there! Let me in!' I thought I could hear the piano, too. Off she goes round to the back. I turned the car. When I looked out again she had come round the other side, the one away from the lane. Her face was red, and, Gawd help us, I thought, here we go, and sure enough she starts yelling out for me to come. 'There's someone in there behaving very suspicious,' she says. 'Take a look through that open window.' I hauled myself up and there wasn't a blooming thing to be seen. 'Where's the piano?' Well, I told her. The piano was there right enough down on the floor by the stage. I knew she was going to tell me to go to the rectory for the key, when I see Miss Prentice coming out of the church. So I drew her attention to Miss Prentice and she was off like a scalded cat, across the lane and down to the church. I followed along slow, it's only a couple of chain or so, and pulled up outside the church."

"What about the box?"

"Pardon, sir?"

"Didn't you get a box out of the shed at the back of the hall for Miss Campanula to stand on in order to look through the window?"

"No, sir. No."

Nigel grinned and whistled softly.

"All right," said Alleyn. "It's no matter. Anything else?"

"No, sir. Miss Prentice came out looking very upset, passed me, and went up the lane. I reckon she was going home by Top Lane."

"Miss Prentice looked upset?"

"She did so, sir. It's my belief Mr. Copeland had sent her off with a flea in her ear, if you'll excuse the liberty."

"Did you watch her go? Look after her, I mean?"

"No, sir, I didn't like, seeing she was looking so queer."

"D'you mean she was crying?"

"She wasn't actually that way, sir. Not shedding tears or anything, but she looked queer. Upset, very down in the mouth."

"You don't know if she went to the hall?"

"No, sir, I can't say. I did have a look in the driving mirror and I saw her cross the road as soon as she'd gone a few steps, but she'd do that, anyway, sir, very likely."

"Gibson, can you remember exactly how the piano looked? Describe it for me as accurately as you possibly can."

Gibson scraped his jaw with his mechanic's hand.

"Down on the floor where it was in the evening, sir. Stool in front of it. No music on it. Er—let's see now. It wasn't quite the same. No, that's right. It *was* kind of different."

Alleyn waited.

"I got it," said Gibson loudly. "Yes, by gum, I got it."

"Yes?"

"Those hot plants was on the edge of the stage and the top of the piano was open."

"Ah," said Alleyn, "I hoped so."

### III

"What's the inner significance of all that?" demanded Nigel when Gibson had gone. "What about this box? Is it the one you had under the window?"

"It is." Alleyn spoke to Fox. "At some time since Gibson hauled himself up to look in at the window, somebody has put an open box there and stood on it. It's left a deep rectangular scar overlapping one of Gibson's prints. I found the box in the outhouse. It wasn't young Georgie. He used the door, and anyway the window would have been above his eye-level. The only footprints are Miss C.'s and some big ones, no doubt Gibson's. They trod on the turf. The box expert must have come later, perhaps on Saturday, and only stood on the gravel. We'll try the box for prints, but I don't think we'll do any good. When I heard Gibson's story I expected we would find that Miss Campanula had used it. Evidently not. It's a tedious business but we'll have to clear it up. Have you said much to the maids?"

"It looks as if deceased was a proper tartar," said Fox. "I've heard enough to come to the conclusion. Mary, the parlormaid, you saw just now, sir, seems to have acted as a kind of lady's-maid as well. Miss Campanula had a very open way with Mary when she was in the mood. Surprising some of the things she used to tell her."

"For instance, Brer Fox?"

"Well, Mr. Alleyn, to Mary's way of thinking, Miss C. was a bit queer on the subject of Mr. Copeland. Potty on him is the way Mary puts it. She says that about the time the rector walks through the village of a morning, deceased used to go and hang about under one pretext or another until she could meet him."

"Oh Lord!" said Alleyn distastefully.

"Yes, it's kind of pitiful, sir, isn't it? Mary says she'd dress herself up, very particularly, walk up to Chipping, and go into the little shop. She'd keep the women there talking, while she bought some trifle or another, and all the time she'd be looking through the glass door. If the rector showed up, Miss Campanula would be off like lightning. She was a very uncertain tempered lady, and when things went wrong she used to scare the servants by the wild way she talked, saying she'd do something violent, and so on."

"This is getting positively Russian," said Alleyn, "and remarkably depressing. Go on."

"It wasn't so bad till Miss Prentice came. She had it her own way in the parish till then. But Miss Prentice seems to have put her in the shade, as you might say. Miss Prentice beat her to all the top places. She's president of this Y.P.F.C. affair and Miss C. was only secretary. Same sort of thing with the Girl Guides."

"She's never a Girl Guide!" Alleyn ejaculated.

"Seems like it, and she beat Miss C. hands down, teaching the kids knots and camp cookery. Got herself decorated with badges and so on. Started at the bottom and swotted it all up. The local girls didn't fancy it much, but she kind of got round them; and when Lady Appleby gave up the Commissioner's job Miss Prentice got it. Same sort of thing at the Women's Circle and all the other local affairs. Miss P. was too smart for Miss C. They were as thick as thieves; but Mary says sometimes Miss C. would come back from a Friendly meeting or something of the sort, and the things she'd say about Miss Prentice were surprising."

"Oh, Lord!"

"She'd threaten suicide and all the rest of it. Mary knew all about the will. Deceased often talked about it, and as short time back as last Thursday, when they had their dress rehearsal, she said it'd serve Miss Prentice right if she cut her out, but she was too charitable to do that, only she hoped if she did go first the money would be like scalding water on Miss Prentice's conscience. On Friday, Mary says, she had one of her good days. Went off to confession and came back very pleased. Same thing after the five o'clock affair at Pen Cuckoo, and in the evening she went to some Reading Circle or other at the rectory.

She was in high feather when she left, but she didn't get back until eleven—very much later than usual. Gibson says she didn't speak on the way back, and Mary says when she came in she had a scarf pulled round her face and her coat collar turned up and—"

"It wasn't her," said Nigel. "Miss Prentice had disguised herself in Miss C.'s clothes in order to have a look at the will."

"Will you be quiet, Bathgate. Go on, Fox."

"Mary followed her to her room; but she said she didn't want her, and Mary swears she was crying. She heard her go to bed. Mary took in her tea first thing yesterday morning, and she says Miss Campanula looked shocking. Like an Aunt Sally that had been left out in the rain, was the way Mary put it."

"Graphic! Well?"

"Well, she spent yesterday morning at the hall with the others, but when she came back she wrote a note to the lawyers and gave it to Gibson to post; but she stayed in all yesterday afternoon."

"I knew you had something else up your sleeve," said Alleyn. "Where's the blotting paper?"

Fox smiled blandly.

"It's all right, as it turns out, sir. Here it is."

He took a sheet of blotting paper from the writing-table and handed it to Alleyn. It was a clean sheet with only four lines of writing. Alleyn held it up to an atrocious mirror and read:

"De S
        K dly    nd   our   presentative  to   ee  me  at   our
arliest  on enience
                        ours faithfully
                        RIS C MP NULA."

"Going to alter her will," said Nigel over Alleyn's shoulder.

"Incubus!" said Alleyn. "Miserable parasite! I wouldn't be surprised if you were right. Anything else, Fox?"

"Nothing else, sir. She seemed much as usual when she went down to the performance. She left here at seven. Not being wanted till the second act, she didn't need to be so early."

"And they know of nobody, beyond the lawyers, whom she should inform?"

"Nobody, Mr. Alleyn."

"We'll have some lunch and then visit the rectory. Come on."

When they returned to the Jernigham Arms they found that the representative of the *Chipping Courier* had been all too zealous. A

crowd of young men wearing flannel trousers and tweed coats greeted
Nigel with a sort of wary and suspicious cordiality, and edged round
Alleyn. He gave them a concise account of the piano and its internal
arrangements, said nothing at all about the water-pistol, told them the
murder appeared to be motiveless, and besought them not to follow him
about wherever he went.

"It embarrasses me and it's no use to you. I'll see that you get photographs of the piano."

"Who's the owner of the Colt, chief inspector?" asked a pert young
man wearing enormous glasses.

"It's a local weapon, thought to have been stolen," said Alleyn. "If
there's anything more from the police, gentlemen, you shall hear of it.
You've got enough in the setting of the thing to do your screaming
worst. Off you go and do it. Be little Pooh Bahs. No corroborative details required. The narrative is adequately unconvincing, and I understand artistic verisimilitude is not your cup of tea."

"Try us," suggested the young man.

"*Pas si bête*," said Alleyn, "I want my lunch."

"When are you going to be married, Mr. Alleyn?"

"Whenever I get a chance. Good morning to you."

He left them to badger Nigel.

Alleyn and Fox finished their lunch in ten minutes, left the inn by
the back door, and were off in Biggins' car before Nigel had exhausted
his flow of profanity. Alleyn left Fox in the village. He was to seek our
Friendly Young People, garner more local gossip, and attend the post-
mortem. Alleyn turned up the Vale Road, and in five minutes arrived
at the rectory.

## IV

Like most clerical households on Sunday, the rectory had a semi-
public look about it. The front door was wide open. On a hall table
Alleyn saw a neat stack of children's hymn-books. A beretta lay beside
them. In a room some way down the hall they heard a female voice.

"Very well, Mr. Copeland. Now the day is over."

"I think so," said the rector's voice.

"Through the night of doubt and sorrow," added the lady brightly.
"Do they like that?"

"Aw, they love it, Mr. Copeland."

"Very well," said the rector wearily. "Thank you, Miss Wright."

A large village maiden came out into the hall. She gathered the hymn-books into a straw bag and bustled out, not neglecting to look pretty sharply at Alleyn.

Alleyn rang the bell again, and presently an elderly maid appeared.

"May I see Mr. Copeland?"

"I'll just see, sir. What name, please?"

"Alleyn. I'm from Scotland Yard."

"Oh! Oh, yes, sir. Will you come this way, please?"

He followed her through the hall. She opened a door and said: "Please, sir, the police."

He walked in.

Mr. Copeland looked as if he had sprung to his feet. At his side was the girl whom Alleyn had recognized as his daughter. They were indeed very much alike, and at this moment their faces spoke of the same mood: they looked startled and alarmed.

Mr. Copeland, in his long cassock, moved forward and shook hands.

"I'm so sorry to worry you like this, sir," said Alleyn. "It's the worst possible day to badger the clergy, I know; but, unfortunately, we can't delay things."

"No, no," said the rector, "we are only too anxious. This is my daughter. I'm afraid I don't——"

"Alleyn, sir."

"Oh, yes. Yes. Do sit down. Dinah, dear?"

"Please don't go, Miss Copeland," said Alleyn. "I hope you may be able to help us."

Evidently they had been sitting with the village maiden in front of the open fireplace. The chairs, drawn up in a semi-circle, were comfortably shabby. The fire, freshly mended with enormous logs, crackled companionably and lent warmth to the faded apple-green walls, the worn beams, the rector's agreeable prints, and a pot of bronze chrysanthemums from the Pen Cuckoo glasshouses.

They sat down, Dinah primly in the center chair, Alleyn and the rector on either side of her.

Something of Alleyn's appreciation of this room may have appeared in his face. His hand went to his jacket pocket and was hurriedly withdrawn.

"Do smoke your pipe," said Dinah quickly.

"That was very well observed," said Alleyn. "I'm sure you will be able to help us. May I, really?"

"Please."

"It's very irregular," said Alleyn; "but I think I might, you know."

And as he lit his pipe he was visited by a strange thought. It came into his mind that he stood on the threshold of a new friendship, that he would return to this old room and again sit before the fire. He thought of the woman he loved, and it seemed to him that she would be there, too, at this future time, and that she would be happy. "An odd notion!" he thought, and dismissed it.

The rector was speaking: "——Terribly distressed. It is appalling to think that among the people one knows so well there should have been one heart that nursed such dreadful anger against a fellow-creature."

"Yes," said Alleyn. "The impulse to kill, I suppose, is dormant in most people; but when it finds expression we are so shockingly astonished. I have noticed that very often. The reaction after murder is nearly always one of profound astonishment."

"To me," said Dinah, "the most horrible thing about this business is the grotesque side of it. It's like an appalling joke."

"You've heard the way of it, then?"

"I don't suppose there's a soul within twenty miles who hasn't," said Dinah.

"Ah," said Alleyn. "The industrious Roper."

He lit his pipe and, looking over his thin hands at them, said, "Before I forget, did either of you put a box outside one of the hall windows late on Friday or sometime on Saturday?"

"No."

"No."

"I see. It's no matter."

The rector said, "Perhaps I shouldn't ask, but have you any idea at all of who——"

"None," said Alleyn. "At the moment, none. There are so many things to be cleared up before the case can begin to make a pattern. One of them concerns the key of the hall. Where was it on Friday?"

"On a nail between an outhouse and the main building," said Dinah.

"I thought that was only on Saturday."

"No. I left it there on Friday for the Friendly Circle members who worked in the lunch hour. They moved the furniture and swept up, and things. When they left at two o'clock they hung the key on the nail."

"But Miss Campanula tried to get in at about half-past two and couldn't."

"I don't think Miss Campanula knew about the key. I told the girls, and I think I said something about it at the dress rehearsal in case the others wanted to get in, but I'm pretty sure Miss Campanula had gone by then. We've never hung it there before."

"Did you go to the hall on Friday?"

"Yes," said Dinah. "I went in the lunch hour to supervise the work. I came away before they had quite finished, and returned here."

"And then you walked up Top Lane towards Pen Cuckoo?"

"Yes," said Dinah in surprise, and into her eyes came that same guarded look he had seen in Henry's.

"Was Georgie Biggins in the hall when you left at about two o'clock?"

"Yes. Making life hideous with his beastly water-pistol. He *is* a naughty boy, Daddy," said Dinah. "I really think you ought to exorcise Georgie. I'm sure he's possessed of a devil."

"Then you haven't heard about Georgie?" murmured Alleyn. "Roper has his points."

"What about Georgie?"

Alleyn told them.

"I want," he said, "to make as little as possible of the obvious implication. There seems to be little doubt that Georgie, plus Twiddletoy, and his water-pistol made the bullets that the murderer subsequently fired. It's an unpleasant responsibility to lay on a small boy's shoulders, however bad he may be. I'm afraid it must come out in evidence, but as far as possible I think we ought to try and avoid village gossip."

"Certainly," said the rector. "At the same time, he knew he was doing something wrong. The terrible consequences——"

"Are disproportionately terrible, don't you think."

"I do. I agree with you," said Dinah.

Alleyn, seeing priest's logic in the rector's eye, hurried on.

"You will see," he said, "that the substitution of the Colt for the water-pistol must have taken place after two o'clock on Friday when Georgie was flourishing his pistol. I know he stayed behind on Friday and rigged it up. He has admitted this. Miss Campanula's chauffeur, at her request, looked through the open window at two-thirty and saw the piano with the top open. His story leads us to believe that at that time Georgie was hiding somewhere in the building. Georgie did not tell me that at all willingly, and I confess I am afraid the memory of Miss Campanula, banging at the doors and demanding admittance, is likely to become a childish nightmare. I don't pretend to understand child psychology."

"The law," said Dinah, "in the person of her officer, seems to be surprisingly merciful."

Alleyn disregarded this.

"So that gives us two-thirty on Friday as a starting-off point. You, Miss Copeland, walked up Top Lane and by chance encountered Mr. Henry Jernigham."

"What?" the rector ejaculated. "Dinah!"

"It's all right," said Dinah in a high voice. "It *was* by accident, Daddy. I did meet Henry and we did behave as you might have expected. Our promise was almost up. It's my fault. I couldn't help it."

"Miss Prentice arrived some time later, I believe," said Alleyn. *"Has she told you that?"*

"Mr. Henry Jernigham told me and Miss Prentice agreed. Do you mind, Miss Copeland, describing what happened at this triple encounter?"

"If they haven't told you," said Dinah, "I won't."

# CHAPTER XVII

# Confession from a Priest

*I*

"Won't you?" said Alleyn mildly. "That's a pity. We shall have to do the Peer Gynt business."

"What's that?"

"Go round about. Ask servants about the relationship between Miss Prentice and her young cousin. Tap the fabulous springs of village gossip—all that."

"I thought," flashed Dinah, "that nowadays the C.I.D. was almost a gentleman's job."

"Oh, no!" said Alleyn. "You couldn't be more mistaken."

Her face was scarlet. "That was a pretty squalid remark of mine," said Dinah.

"It was inexcusable, my dear," said her father. "I am ashamed that you have been capable of it."

"I find no offense in it at all," Alleyn said cheerfully. "It was entirely apposite."

But Mr. Copeland's face was pink with embarrassment, and Dinah's still crimson with mortification. The rector addressed her as if she was at children's service. His voice became more markedly clerical, and in the movement of his head Alleyn recognized one of his pulpit mannerisms.

He said, "You have broken a solemn promise, Dinah, and to this fault you add a deliberate evasion and an ill-bred and entirely unjustifiable impertinence. You force me to make Mr. Alleyn some sort of explanation." He turned to Alleyn. "My daughter and Henry Jernigham," he said, "have formed an attachment of which his father and I do not approve. Dinah suggested that they should give their word not to meet alone for three weeks. Friday was the final day of the three weeks. Miss Prentice was also of our mind in this matter. If she came upon them at a moment when, as Dinah has admitted, they had completely forgotten or ignored this promise, I am sure she was extremely disappointed and distressed."

"She wasn't!" exclaimed Dinah, rallying a little. "She wasn't a bit like that. She was absolutely livid with rage and beastliness."

"Dinah!"

"Oh, Daddy, *why* do you shut your eyes? You must know what she's like—you of all people!"

"Dinah, I must insist—"

"No!" cried Dinah. "No! First you say I've been underhand; and then, when I go all upperhand and open, you don't like it any better. I'm sorry in a way that Henry and I didn't stay the course; but we nearly did, and I *won't* think there was anything very awful about Friday afternoon. I won't have Henry and me made seem grubby. I'm sorry I was rude to Mr. Alleyn and I—well, I mean, it's quite obvious it wasn't only rude, but silly. I mean, it's obvious from the way he's taken it—I mean—oh, hell! Oh, Daddy, I'm sorry."

Alleyn choked down a laugh.

The rector said, "Dinah! Dinah!"

"Yes, well, I *am* sorry. And now Mr. Alleyn will think heaven knows what about Friday afternoon. I may as well tell you, Mr. Alleyn, that in Henry's and my opinion Miss Prentice is practically ravers. It's a well-known phenomenon with old maids. She's tried to sublimate her natural appetites and—and—work them off in religion. I can't help it, Daddy, she *has*. And it's been a failure. She's only repressed and repressed, and when she sees two natural, healthy people making love to each other she goes off pop."

"It is I," said the rector, looking hopelessly at his child, "who have been a failure."

"Don't. You haven't. It's just that you don't understand these women. You're an angel, but you're not a modern angel."

"I should be interested to know," said Alleyn, "how an angel brings himself up to date. Streamlined wings, I suppose."

Dinah grinned.

"Well, you know what I mean," she said. "And I'm right about these two. If you had heard Miss Prentice! It was simply too shaming and hideous. She actually shook all over and sort of gasped. And she said the most ghastly things to us. She threatened at once to tell you, Daddy, and the squire. She suggested—oh, she was beyond belief. What's more, she dribbles and spits."

"Dinah, my dear!"

"Well, Daddy, she *does*. I noticed the front of her beastly dress, and it was *disgusting*. She either dribbles and spits, or else she spills her tea. Honestly! And, anyway, she was perfectly *sceptic*, the things she said."

"Didn't either of you try to stop her?" asked Alleyn.

"Yes," said Dinah. She turned rather white and added quickly: "In the end she just blundered past us and went on up the lane."

"What did you do?"

"I went home."

"And Mr. Jernigham?"

"He went up to Cloudyfold, I think."

"By the steep path? He didn't walk down with you?"

"No," said Dinah. "He didn't. There's nothing in that."

## II

"I cannot see," said the rector, "that this unhappy story can have any bearing on the tragedy."

"I think I can promise," said Alleyn, "that any information found to be irrelevant will be completely blotted out. We are, quite literally, not interested in any facts that cannot be brought into the pattern."

"Well, that can't," Dinah declared. She threw up her chin and said loudly:

"If you think, because Miss Prentice made us feel uncomfortable and embarrassed, it's a motive for murder, you're quite wrong. We're not in the least afraid of Miss Prentice or anything she may say or do. It can't make any difference to Henry and me." Dinah's lower lip trembled and she added: "We simply look at her from a detached analytical angle and are vaguely sorry for her. That's all." She uttered a dry sob.

The rector said: "Oh, my darling child, what nonsense," and Dinah walked over to the window.

"Well," said Alleyn mildly, "let's go on being detached and analytical. What did you both do on Saturday afternoon? That's yesterday."

"We were both in here," said Dinah. "Daddy went to sleep. I went over my part."

"What time did you get to the hall last evening?"

"We left here at half-past six," answered Mr. Copeland, "and walked over by the path through our garden and wood."

"Was anybody there?"

"Yes. Yes, Gladys Wright was there, wasn't she, Dinah? She is one of our best workers and was in charge of the programs. She was in the front of the hall. I think the other girls were either there, or came in soon after we did."

"Can you tell me exactly what you did up to the time of the catastrophe?"

"I can, certainly," rejoined the rector. "I saw that the copy of the play and the bicycle bell I had to ring were in their right places, and then I sat in an armchair on the stage to keep out of the way and see that nobody came in from the front of the hall. I was there until Dinah came for me to speak to Miss Prentice."

"Did you expect Miss Prentice would be unable to play?"

"No, indeed. On the contrary, she told me her finger was much better. That was soon after she arrived."

"Had you much difficulty in persuading Miss Prentice not to play?"

"Yes, indeed I had. She was most determined about it, but her finger was really very bad. It was quite impossible, and I told her I should be very displeased if she persisted."

"And apart from that time you never left the stage?"

"Oh! Oh, yes, I *did* go to the telephone before that, when they were trying to get Mrs. Ross's house. That was at half-past seven. The telephone is an extension of ours and our maid, Mary, is deaf and takes a long time to answer."

"We were all frantic," said Dinah, from the window. "The squire and Henry and father and I were all standing round the telephone, with Miss Campanula roaring instructions, poor old thing. The squire hadn't got any trousers on, only pink woolen underpants. Miss Prentice came along, and when she saw him she cackled like a hen and flew away, but no one else minded about the squire's pants, not even Miss C. We were all in a flat spin about the others being late, you see. Father was just coming over to ring from here, when we got through."

"I returned to the stage then," said the rector.

"I can't tell you exactly what I did," said Dinah. "I was all over the place." She peered through the window. "Here's Henry now."

"Why not go and meet him?" suggested Alleyn. "Tell him how I've bullied you."

"You haven't, but I will," said Dinah.

She opened the window and stepped over the low sill into the garden.

"I'm so sorry," said Alleyn, when the window had slammed.

"She's a good child, really," said the rector sadly.

"I'm sure she is. Mr. Copeland, you see what a strange position we are in, don't you? If Miss Prentice was the intended victim we must trace her movements, her conversation—yes, and if we could, even her thoughts during these last days. We are in the extraordinary position of having, apparently, a living victim in a case of homicide. There is even the possibility that the murderer may make a second attempt."

"No! No! That's too horrible."

"I am sure that, as your daughter says, you know a great deal about these two ladies—the actual and, as far as we know, the intended victim. Can you tell me anything, anything at all, that may throw a glint of light on this dark tangle of emotions?"

The rector clasped his hands and stared into the fire.

"I am very greatly troubled," he said. "I cannot see my way."

"Do you mean that you have got their confidence, and that under ordinary circumstances you would never speak of your knowledge?"

"Let me make myself clear. As no doubt you already know, I have heard the confessions of many of my parishioners. Under no condition will I break the seal of the confessional. That goes without saying. Moreover, it would serve no purpose if I did. I tell you this lest you should think I hold a key to the mystery."

"I recognize the position," said Alleyn, "and I shall respect it."

"I'm glad of that. There are many people, I know, who regard the sacrament of confession in the Anglo-Catholic Church as an amateurish substitute for the Roman use. It is no such thing. The Romans say, 'You must,' the Protestant Nonconformists say, 'You must not,' the Catholic Church of England says, 'You may!' "

But Alleyn was not there for doctrinal argument, and wouldn't have welcomed it under any circumstances.

He said, "I realize that a priest who hears confession, no matter what faith he professes, must regard the confessional as inviolate. That, I take, is not what troubles you. Do you perhaps wonder if you should tell me something that you have heard from one of your penitents outside the confessional?"

The rector gave him a startled glance. He clasped his hands more tightly and said:

"It is not that I believe it would be any help. It's only that I am burdened with the memory and with a terrible doubt. You say that this murderer may strike again. I don't believe that is possible. I am sure it is not possible."

"Why?" asked Alleyn in astonishment.

"Because I believe that the murderer is dead," said the rector.

### III

Alleyn turned in his chair and regarded Mr. Copeland for some seconds before he answered.

At last he said: "You think she did it herself?"

"I am sure of it."

"Will you tell me why?"

"I suppose I must. Mr. Alleyn, I am not, unfortunately, a man of strong character. All my life I have avoided unpleasantness. I know this very well and try to conquer my weakness. I have vacillated when I should have insisted; temporized when I should have taken definite action. Because of these veritable sins of omission I believe I am morally responsible, or at any rate in part responsible, for this terrible crime."

He paused, still looking at the fire. Alleyn waited.

"On Friday night," said Mr. Copeland, "the Reading Circle met in the rectory dining-room. It usually meets in St. Giles Hall; but because of the preparations for the play they all came here instead. It was Miss Campanula's turn to preside. I went in for a short time. Dinah read a scene from *Twelfth Night* for them, and after that they went on with their book. It is G. K. Chesterton's *The Bull and the Cross*, and Miss Campanula had borrowed my copy. When they had finished she came in here to return it. I was alone. It was about a quarter past ten."

"Yes?"

"Mr. Alleyn, it is very difficult and disagreeable for me to tell you of this incident. Really, I—I—don't know quite how to begin. You may not be familiar with parochial affairs, but I think many clergy find that there is an unfortunately rather common type of church worker who is always a problem to her parish priest. I don't know if you will understand me when I say that one finds this type among—dear me—among ladies who are not perhaps very young and who have no other interests."

The rector was now very pink.

"I think I understand," said Alleyn.

"Do you? Well, I am sorry to say poor Miss Campanula was really an advanced—er—specimen of this type. Poor soul, she was lonely and she had a difficult temperament which I am sure she did her best to discipline, but at times I could not help thinking that she needed a doctor as well as a priest to help her. I have even suggested as much."

"That was very wise advice, sir."

"She didn't take it," said the rector wistfully. "She stuck to me, you see, and I'm afraid I failed her."

"About Friday night?" Alleyn reminded him gently.

"Yes, I know. I'm coming to Friday night; but, really, it's *very* difficult. There was a terrible scene. She—I think she had got it into her head that if Dinah married or went away again—Dinah is on the stage, you know—I should be as lonely as she was. She said as much. I was very much startled and alarmed and I was at a loss how to reply. I think she misunderstood my silence. I really can't quite remember the order of events. It was rather like a bad dream, and still is. She was trembling dreadfully and looking at me with such a desperate expression in her eyes that I—I—I——"

He shut his eyes tight and added in a great hurry: "I patted her hand."

"That was quite a natural thing to do, wasn't it?"

"You wouldn't have said so if you'd seen the result."

"No?"

"No, indeed. The next moment she was, to be frank, in my arms. It was without any exception the most awful thing that has ever happened to me. She was sobbing and laughing at the same time. I was in agony. I couldn't release myself. We never draw our blinds in this room, and there was I in this appalling and even ludicrous situation. I was obliged actually to—to support her. And I was so sorry for her, too. It was so painfully evident that she had made a frightful mistake. I believe she was hysterically delighted. It makes me feel ashamed and, as we used to say when I was young, caddish to repeat all this."

"It's beastly for you," said Alleyn; "but I'm sure you should tell me."

"I would have preferred, before doing so, to take the advice of one of my brother clergy, but there is no one who—— However, that is beside the point. You are being very patient."

"How did it end?"

"Very badly," said the rector, opening his eyes wide. "It couldn't have ended worse. When she had quietened down a little—and it was a long time before she did—I hastened to release myself, and I am afraid the first thing I did was to draw the curtains. You see, some members of the Reading Circle might still have been about. Their young men come up to meet them. Worse than that, Miss Prentice rang up in the morning and said she wanted to speak to me that evening. While Miss Campanula was still with me she telephoned to say she was not coming.

"Well, I wouldn't. She's the sort that's always called a man's woman."

"It's rather a stupid sort of phrase," said Henry.

"It simply means," said Dinah, "that she's nice to men and would let a woman down as soon as look at her!"

"I should have thought it just meant that she was too attractive to be popular with her own sex."

"Darling, that's simply a masculine cliché," said Dinah. "I don't think so."

"There are tons of devastating women who are enormously popular with their own sex."

Henry smiled.

"Do you think she's attractive?" asked Dinah casually.

"Yes, very. I dare say she's rather a little bitch, but she is pleasing. For one thing, her clothes fit her."

"Yes, they do," said Dinah somberly. "They must cost the earth."

Henry kissed her.

"I'm a low swine," he muttered. "I was being tiresome. You're my dear darling and I'm no more fit to love you than a sweep, but I do love you so much."

"We must never be jealous," whispered Dinah.

"Dinah!" called the rector in the hall below.

"Yes, Daddy?"

"Where are you?"

"In the schoolroom."

"May I go up, do you think?" asked a deep voice.

"That's Alleyn," said Henry.

"Come up here, Mr. Alleyn," called Dinah.

# CHAPTER XVIII

# Mysterious Lady

### I

"Sit down, Mr. Alleyn," said Dinah. "The chairs are all rather rickety in this room, I'm afraid. You know Henry, don't you?"

"Yes, rather," said Alleyn. "I'll have this, if I may."

He squatted on a stuffed footstool in front of the fire.

"I told Henry how rude I'd been," said Dinah.

"I was horrified," said Henry. "She's very young, poor girl."

"You couldn't by any chance just settle down and spin us some yarns about crime?" suggested Dinah.

"I'm afraid not. It would be delightful to settle down, but you see we're not allowed to get familiar when we're on duty. It looks impertinent. I've got a monstrous lot of things to do before to-night."

"Do you just collect stray bits of evidence," asked Henry, "and hope they'll make sense?"

"More or less. You scavenge and then you arrange everything and try and see the pattern."

"Suppose there's no pattern?"

"There must be. It's a question of clearing away the rubbish."

"Any sign of it so far?" asked Dinah.

"Not a great many signs."

"Do you suspect either of us?"

"Not particularly."

"Well, we didn't do it," said Dinah.

"Good."

"Cases of homicide," said Henry, "must be different from any other kind. Especially cases that occur in these sorts of surroundings. You're not dealing with the ordinary criminal classes."

"True enough," said Alleyn. "I'm dealing with people like yourselves who will be devastatingly frank up to a certain point—far franker than the practical criminal, who lies to the police from sheer force of habit— but who will probably bring a good deal more *savoir faire* to the business of withholding essentials. For instance, I know jolly well there's something more to that meeting you both had with Miss Prentice on Friday afternoon; but it's no good saying to you, as I would to Posh Jimmy: 'Come on, now. It's not you I'm after. Tell me what I want to know and perhaps we'll forget all about that little job over at Moorton.' Unfortunately, I've nothing against you."

"That's exactly what I mean," said Henry. "Still, you can always go for my Cousin Eleanor."

"Yes. That's what I'll have to do," agreed Alleyn.

"Well, I hope you don't believe everything she tells you," said Dinah, "or you *will* get in a muddle. Where we're concerned she's as sour as a quince."

"And, anyway, she's practically certifiable," added Henry. "It's a question which was dottiest: Eleanor or Miss C."

"Lamentable," said Alleyn vaguely. "Mr. Jernigham, did you put a box outside one of the hall windows after 2.30 on Friday?"

"No."

"What is this about a box?" asked Dinah.

"Nothing much. About the piano. When did those aspidistras make their appearance?"

"They were there on Saturday morning, anyway," said Dinah. "I meant to have them taken away. They must have masked the stage from the audience. I think the girls put them there after I left on Friday."

"In which case Georgie moved them off to rig his pistol."

"And the murderer," Henry pointed out, "must have moved them again."

"Yes."

"I wonder when," said Henry.

"So do we. Miss Copeland, did you see Miss Campanula on Friday night?"

"Friday night? Oh, I saw her at the Reading Circle meeting in the dining-room."

"Not afterwards?"

"No. As soon as I got out of the dining-room I came up here. She went into the study to see Daddy. I could just hear her voice scolding away as usual, I should think, poor thing."

"The study is beneath this room, isn't it?"

"Yes. I wanted to have a word with Daddy, but I waited until I heard her and the other person go."

Alleyn only paused for a second before he said:

"The other person?"

"There was somebody else in the study with Miss C. I can't help calling her 'Miss C.' We all did."

"How do you know there was someone else there?"

"Well, because they left after Miss C.," said Dinah impatiently. "It wasn't Miss Prentice, because she rang up from Pen Cuckoo just about that time. Mary called me to the telephone, so I suppose it must have been Gladys Wright. She's leader of the Reading Circle. She lives up the lane. She must have gone out by the window in the study, because I heard the lane gate give a squeak. That's how I knew she'd been here."

Alleyn walked over to the window. It looked down on a graveled path, a lawn, and a smaller earthen path that led to a rickety gate and evidently ran on beyond it through a small plantation to the lane.

"I suppose you always go that way to the hall?" asked Alleyn.

"Oh, yes. It's much shorter than going round the house from the front door."

"Yes," said Alleyn, "it would be."

He looked thoughtfully at Dinah and said, "Did you hear this other person's voice?"

"Hi!" said Dinah. "What *is* all this? No, I didn't. Ask Daddy. He'll tell you who it was."

"Stupid of me," said Alleyn. "Of course he will."

## II

He didn't ask the rector, but before he left he crunched boldly round the gravel path and walked across the lawn to the gate. It certainly creaked very loudly. It was one of those old-fashioned gates that has a post stile beside it. The path was evidently used very often. There was no hope of finding anything useful on its hard but greasy surface. There had been too much rain since Friday night. "Much too much rain," sighed Alleyn. But just inside the gate he found two softened but unmistakable depressions. Horseshoe-shaped holes about two inches in diameter that had held water. "Heels," he thought, "but not a hope of saying whose. Female. Stood there a long time facing the house." He could see the rector crouched over the study fire. "Oh, well," he said, and plunged into the little wood. "Nothing at all that's to the purpose. Nothing."

He saw that the hall was only a little way up on the other side from where this path came out on the lane. He returned, circled the rectory, perfectly aware that Dinah and Henry watched him from the schoolroom window. As he got into the car Henry opened the window and leaned out.

"I say," he shouted.

"Shut up," said Dinah's voice behind him. "*Don't*, Henry."

"What is it?" called Alleyn, squinting up through his driving-window.

"It's nothing," said Dinah. "He's gone ravers, that's all. Good-by."

Henry's head shot out of sight and the window slammed.

"Now I wonder," thought Alleyn, "if Master Henry has got the same idea as I have."

He drove away.

At the Jernigham Arms he found Nigel, but no Fox.

"Where are you going?" Nigel demanded when Alleyn returned to the car.

"To call on a lady."

"Let me come."

"Why the devil?"

"I won't go in with you if you'd rather not."

"Naturally. All right. I can do with some comic relief."

"Oh, God, your only jigmaker," said Nigel and got in. "Now, who's the lady?" he said. "Speak up, dearie."

"Mrs. Ross."

"The mysterious stranger."

"Why do you call her that?"

"It's the part she played in their show. I've got a program."

"So it is," said Alleyn.

He turned the car up the Vale Road and presently he began to talk. He went over the history of the case from midday on Friday. As far as he could, he traced the movements of the murdered woman and each of her seven companions. He correlated their movements and gave Nigel a time-table he had jotted down in his notebook.

"I hate these damn' things," Nigel grumbled. "They shatter my interest; they remind me of a Bradshaw, and they are therefore completely unintelligible."

"It's a pity about you," said Alleyn dryly. "Look at the list at the bottom."

Nigel looked and read:

"Piano. Drawing-pin holes. Automatic. Branch. Onion. Chopsticks. Key. Letter. Creaky gate. Window. Telephone."

"Thank you," said Nigel. "Now, of course, I see the whole thing in a blinding flash. It's as clear as the mud in your eye. The onion is particularly obvious, and as for the drawing-pins— It's ludicrous that I didn't spot the exquisite reason of the drawing-pins."

He returned the paper to Alleyn.

"Go on," he continued acidly. "Say it. 'You have the facts, Bathgate. You know my methods, Bathgate. What of the little gray cells, Bathgate?' Sling in a quotation; add: 'Oh, my dear chap,' and vanish in a fog of composite fiction."

"This is Cloudyfold," said Alleyn. "Cold, isn't it? They had twelve degrees of frost on the pub thermometer last night."

"Oh, Mr. Mercury, how you did startle me!"

"That must be Mrs. Ross's cottage down there."

"Can't I come in as your stenographer?"

"Very well. I may send you out on an errand into the village."

Duck Cottage stands in a bend of the road before it actually reaches Cloudyfold Village. It is a typical Dorset cottage, plain fronted, well proportioned, cold-gray and weather-worn. Mrs. Ross had smartened it up. The window sashes and sills and the front door were painted vermilion, and a vermilion tub with a Noah's Ark tree stood on each side of the entrance which led straight off the road.

Alleyn gave a double rap on the shiny brass knocker.

The door was opened by a maid, all cherry-red and muslin. Mrs. Ross was at home. The maid took Alleyn's card away with her and returned to usher them in.

Alleyn had to stoop his head under the low doorway, and the ceilings were not much higher. They walked through a tiny ante-room, down some uneven steps and into Mrs. Ross's parlor. She was not there. It was a charming parlor looking out on a small formal garden. There were old prints on the walls, one or two respectable pieces of furniture, a deep carpet, some very comfortable chairs, and a general air of chintz, sparkle and femininity. It was a delicate little room. Alleyn looked at a bookcase filled with modern novels. He noticed one or two works by authors whose sole distinction had been conferred by the censor, and at three popular collections of famous criminal cases. They all had startling wrappers and photographic illustrations. Within their covers one would find the cases of Brown and Kennedy, Bywaters, Seddon, and Stinie Morrison. Their style would be characterized by a certain arch taciturnity. Alleyn grinned to himself and took one of them from the shelf. He let it fall open in his hands and a discourse on dactylography faced him. The groove between the pages was filled with cigarette ash. A photograph of prints developed and enlarged from a letter illustrated the written matter. A woman's voice sounded. Alleyn returned the book to its place. The door opened and Mrs. Ross came in.

She was the lady Alleyn had noticed in church. This did not surprise him much, but it made him feel wary. She greeted him with a sensible good-humored air, shook hands and then gave him a slanting smile.

"This is Mr. Bathgate," said Alleyn. He noticed that Nigel's fingers had flown to his tie.

She settled them by the fire with the prettiest air in the world, and he saw her glance at the little cupid clock on the mantelpiece.

"I do think all this is too ghastly," she said. "That poor wretched old creature! How anybody could!"

"It's a bad business," said Alleyn.

She offered them cigarettes. Alleyn refused and Nigel, rather unwillingly, followed suit. Mrs. Ross took one and leaned towards Alleyn for a light.

"*Chanel, Numéro Cinq,*" thought Alleyn.

"I've never been 'investigated' before," said Mrs. Ross. "Dear me, that sounds rather peculiar, doesn't it? I don't mean what you mean."

She chuckled. Nigel uttered rather a flirtatious laugh, caught Alleyn's eye and was silent.

Alleyn said, "I shan't bother you for long, I hope. We've got to try and find out where everybody was from about midday on Friday up to the moment of the disaster."

"Heavens!" said Mrs. Ross. "I'll never be able to remember that; and if I do, it's sure to sound too incriminating for words."

"I hope not," said Alleyn sedately. "We've got a certain amount of it already. On Friday you went to a short five o'clock rehearsal at Pen Cuckoo, didn't you?"

"Yes. Apart from that, I was at home all day."

"And Friday evening?"

"Still at home. We aren't very gay in Cloudyfold, Mr. Alleyn. I think I've dined out twice since I came here. The county is simply rushing me, as you see."

"On Saturday evening I suppose you joined the others at the hall?"

"Yes. I carted down one or two things they wanted for the stage. We towed them in a trailer behind Dr. Templett's Morris."

"Did you go straight to the hall?"

"No. We called at Pen Cuckoo. I'd quite forgotten that. I didn't get out of the car."

"Dr. Templett went into the study?"

"He went into the house," she said lightly. "I don't know which room."

"He didn't return by the french window?"

"I don't remember." She paused and then added: "The squire, Mr. Jernigham, came and talked to me. I didn't notice Dr. Templett until he was actually at the car window."

"Ah, yes. You came back here for lunch?"

"Yes."

"And in the afternoon?"

"Saturday afternoon. That's only yesterday, isn't it? Heavens, it seems a lifetime! Oh, I took the supper down to the hall."

"At what time?"

"I think it was about half-past three when I got there."

"Was the hall empty?"

"Yes. No, it wasn't. Dr. Templett was there. He arrived just after I did. He'd brought down his clothes."

"How long did you stay there, Mrs. Ross?"

"I don't know. Not long. It might have been half an hour."

"And Dr. Templett?"

"He left before I did. I was putting out sandwiches."

"And cutting up onions?"

"*Onions!* Good Lord, why should I do that? No, thank you. I'm sick at the sight of one, and I have got some respect for my hands."

They were luxurious little hands. She held them to the fire.

"I'm sorry," said Alleyn. "There was an onion in the supper-room."

"I don't know how it got there. The supper-room was all scrubbed out on Friday."

"It's no matter. Did you look at the piano on Saturday afternoon?"

"No, I don't think so. The curtain was down, so I suppose if anything had been out of order I shouldn't have noticed. I didn't go to the front of the hall. The one key opens both doors."

"And only Dr. Templett came in?"

"Yes."

"Could any one have come unnoticed into the front of the hall while you were in the supper-room?"

"I suppose they might have. No. No, of course they couldn't. We had the key and the front door was locked."

"Did Dr. Templett go into the auditorium at all?"

"Only to shut the window."

"Which window was open?"

"It's rather odd," she said quickly. "I'm sure I shut it in the morning."

### III

"It's the window on the side away from the lane, nearest the front," continued Mrs. Ross after a pause. "I remember that, just as we were leaving, I pulled it down in case the rain blew in. That was at midday."

"Were you the last to leave at noon?"

"No. Well, we all left together; but I think Dr. Templett and I actually walked out first. The Copelands always leave by the back door."

"So presumably someone reopened the window?"

"Presumably."

"Were you on the stage when Dr. Templett shut the window?"

"Yes."

"What were you doing there?"

"We—I tidied it up and arranged one or two ornaments I'd brought."

"Dr. Templett helped you?"

"He—well, he looked on."

"And all this time the window was open?"

"Yes, I suppose so. Yes, of course it was."

"Did you tell him you thought you had shut it?"

"Yes."

"You don't think somebody pushed it open from outside?"

"No," she said positively. "We were certain they didn't. The curtain was up. We'd have seen."

"I thought you said the curtain was down."

"Oh, how stupid of me. It was up when we got there, but we let it down. It was supposed to be down. I wanted to try the effect of a lamp I'd taken."

"Did you lower the curtain before or after you noticed the window?"

"I don't remember. Oh. Yes, please, I think it was afterwards."

She leaned forward and looked at Nigel, who had been making notes.

"It's simply petrifying to see all this going down," she said to him. "Do I read it over and sign it?"

"It would have to go into longhand first," said Nigel.

"Do let me see."

He gave her his notes.

"They look exactly like journalists' copy," said Mrs. Ross.

"That's our cunning," said Nigel boldly, but rather red in the face. She laughed and gave them back to him.

"Mr. Alleyn thinks we're terribly flippant, I can see," she said. "Don't you, inspector?"

"No," said Alleyn. "I regard Bathgate as a zealous and serious-minded young officer."

Nigel tried to look zealous and serious-minded. He was a little shaken.

"You mustn't forget that telegram, Bathgate," added Alleyn. "I think you'd better go into Cloudyfold and send it. You can pick me up on the way back. Mrs. Ross will excuse you."

"Very good, sir," said Nigel and left.

"What a very charming young man," said Mrs. Ross, with her air of casual intimacy. "Are all your officers as Eton and Oxford as that?"

"Not quite all," rejoined Alleyn.

What a curious trick she had of widening her eyes! The pupils actually seemed to dilate. It was as if she was aware of something, recognized it, and gave just that one brief sign. Alleyn read into it a kind of polite wantonness. "She proclaims herself," he thought, "by that trick. She is a woman with a strong, determined appetite." He knew very well that, for all her impersonal manner, she had made small practised signals to him, and he wondered if he should let her see he had recognized these signals.

He leaned forward in his chair and looked deliberately into her eyes.

"There are two more questions," he said.

"Two more? Well?"

"Do you know whose automatic it was that shot Miss Campanula between the eyes and through the brain?"

She sat quite still. The corners of her thin mouth drooped a little. Her short blackened lashes veiled her light eyes.

"It was Jocelyn Jernigham's, wasn't it?" she said.

"Yes. The same Colt that Mr. Henry Jernigham showed you on Friday evening."

"That's awful," she said and looked squarely at him. "Does it mean that you suspect one of us?"

"By itself, it doesn't amount to so much. But it was his automatic that killed her."

"*He'd* never do it," she said contemptuously.

"Did you put a box outside one of the hall windows at any time after 2.30 on Friday?" asked Alleyn.

"No. Why?"

"It's of no importance."

Alleyn put his hand in the breast pocket of his coat and took out his note-book.

"Heavens!" said Selia Ross. "What next?"

His long fingers drew out a folded paper. That trick with her eyes must after all be unconscious. She looked slantways at the paper and the lines of block capitals, painstakingly executed by Inspector Fox. She took it from Alleyn, raising her eyebrows, and handed it back.

"Can you tell me anything about this?" asked Alleyn.

"No."

"I think perhaps I should tell you we regard it as an important piece of evidence."

"I've never seen it before. Where did you find it?"

"It just cropped up," said Alleyn.

Somebody had come into the adjoining room. There came the sound of stumbling feet on the uneven steps. The door burst open. Alleyn thought, "Blast Bathgate!" and glanced up furiously.

It was Dr. Templett.

# CHAPTER XIX

# Statement from Templett

*I*

"Selia?" said Dr. Templett, and stopped short.

The paper dangled from Alleyn's fingers.

"Hullo, chief inspector," said Templett breathlessly. "I thought I might find you here. I've just done the P.M."

"Yes?" said Alleyn. "Anything unexpected?"

"Nothing."

Alleyn held out the paper.

"Isn't this your letter?"

Templett stood absolutely still. He then shook his head, but the gesture seemed to repudiate the implication rather than the statement.

"Were you not looking for it this morning in the breast pocket of your coat?"

"Is it yours, Billy?" Selia said. "Who's been writing comic letters to you?"

The skin of his face seemed to tighten. Two sharp little cords sprang up from his nostrils to the corners of his mouth. He turned to the fire and stooped as if to warm his hands. They trembled violently and he thrust them into his pockets. His face was quite without color, but the firelight dyed it crimson.

Alleyn waited.

Mrs. Ross lit a cigarette.

"I think I'd like to speak to Mr. Alleyn alone," said Templett.

"Can you come back to Chipping with me?" asked Alleyn.

"What? Yes. Yes, I'll do that."

Alleyn turned to Mrs. Ross and bowed.

"Good evening, Mrs. Ross."

"Is it so late? Good-by. Billy, is anything wrong?"

Alleyn saw him look at her with a sort of wonder. He shook his head and walked out. Alleyn followed him.

Nigel was sitting in the Biggins's car. Alleyn signaled quickly to him and followed Templett to his Morris.

"I'll come with you, if I may," said Alleyn.

Templett nodded. They got in. Templett turned the car and accelerated violently. Cloudyfold Rise leapt at them. They crossed the hilltop in two minutes. It was already dusk and the houses down in the Vale were lit. A cold mist hung about the hills.

"God damn it," said Dr. Templett, "you needn't watch me like that! I'm not going to take cyanide."

"Of course not."

As they skidded round Pen Cuckoo corner, Templett said, "I didn't do it."

"All right."

At the church lane turning the car skated twenty yards on the greasy road, and fetched up sideways. Alleyn held his peace and trod on imaginary brakes. They started off again more reasonably, but entered Chipping at forty miles an hour.

"Will you stop outside the Jernigham Arms for a minute?" asked Alleyn.

Templett did not slow down until they were within two hundred yards of the inn. They shot across the road and stopped with screaming brakes. The pot-boy came running out.

"Is Mr. Fox there? Ask him to come out, will you?" called Alleyn cheerfully. "And when Mr. Bathgate arrives, send him on to the police station at Great Chipping. Ask him to bring my case with him."

Fox came out, bareheaded.

"Pop in at the back, Brer Fox," said Alleyn. "We're going into Great Chipping. Dr. Templett will take us."

"Good evening, doctor," said Fox, and got in.

Dr. Templett put in his clutch and was off before the door shut. Alleyn's arm hung over the back of the seat. He twiddled his long fingers eloquently.

They reached the outskirts of Great Chipping in ten minutes, and here Templett seemed to come to his senses. He drove reasonably enough through the narrow provincial streets and pulled up at the police station.

Blandish was there. A constable showed them into his office and stood inside the door.

"Good evening, gentlemen," said the superintendent, who seemed to be in superb form. "Some good news for me, I hope? Glad to say we're getting on quite nicely with our little job, Mr. Alleyn, I wouldn't be surprised if we won't be able to give the City a bit of very sound information by to-morrow. The bird's flown to Bermondsey, and we ought to be able to pull him in. Very gratifying. Well, now, sit down, all of you. Smith! The chair by the door."

He bustled hospitably, caught sight of Templett's face and was abruptly silent.

"I'll make a statement," said Templett.

"I think perhaps I should warn you——" said Alleyn.

"I know all that. I'll make a statement."

Fox moved up to the table. Superintendent Blandish very startled and solemn, shoved across a pad of paper.

## II

"On Friday afternoon," said Dr. Templett, "on my return from hunting, an anonymous letter came into my possession. I believe the police now have this letter. Inspector Alleyn has shown it to me. I attached very little importance to it. I do not know who wrote it. I put it in my pocket-book in the inside breast pocket of my coat. I intended to destroy it. At five o'clock on Friday I attended a rehearsal at Pen Cuckoo. On my return home I was immediately called out on a difficult case. I did not get back until late night. I forgot all about the letter. Yesterday, Saturday, wearing the same suit, I left my house at about 8.30, having only just got up. I collected some furniture from Duck Cottage, called at Pen Cuckoo, went on to the hall, where I left the furniture. She was with me. The rest of Saturday was spent on my rounds. I was unusually busy. They gave me some lunch at the cottage hospital. In the afternoon I called at the hall. I was only there for about half an hour. I did not go near the piano and I didn't remember the letter. I was not alone at the hall at any time. I arrived there for the evening performance at half-past seven, or possibly later. I went straight to my dressing-room and changed, hanging up my coat on the wall. Henry Jernigham came in and helped me. After the tragedy I did not change until I got home. At no time did I remember the letter. The next time I saw it was this afternoon when Inspector Alleyn showed it to me. That's all."

Fox looked up.

Blandish said, "Make a full transcript of Inspector Fox's notes, Smith."

Smith went out with the notes.

Alleyn said, "Before we go any further, Dr. Templett, I think I should tell you that the letter I showed you was a copy of the original and made on identical paper. The original is in our possession and it is in my bag. Fox, do you mind seeing if Bathgate has arrived?"

Fox went out and in a minute returned with Alleyn's case.

"Have you," Alleyn asked Templett, "as far as your memory serves, given us the whole truth in the statement you have just made?"

"I've given you everything that's relevant."

"I am going to put several questions to you. Would you like to wait until your lawyer is present?"

"I don't want a lawyer. I'm innocent."

"Your answers will be taken down and——"

"And may be used in evidence. I know."

"—And may be used in evidence," Alleyn repeated.

"Well?" asked Templett.

"Have you shown the letter to any one else?"

"No."

"Did you receive it by post?"

"Yes."

Alleyn nodded to Fox, who opened the case and took out the original letter between its two glass cover-sheets.

"Here it is," said Alleyn. "You see, we have developed the prints. There are three sets—yours, the deceased's, and another's. I must tell you that the unknown prints will be compared with any that we find on the copy which Mrs. Ross has held in her hands. You can see, if you look at the original, that one set of prints is superimposed on the other two. Those are your own. The deceased's prints are the undermost."

Templett did not speak.

"Dr. Templett, I am going to tell you what I believe to have happened. I believe that this letter was sent in the first instance to Mrs. Ross. The wording suggests that it was addressed to a woman rather than a man. I believe that Mrs. Ross showed it to you on Saturday, which was yesterday morning, and that you put it in your pocket-book. If this is so, you know as well as I do that you will be ill-advised to deny it. You have told us the letter came by post. Do you now feel it would be better to alter this statement?"

"It makes no difference."

"It makes all the difference between giving the police facts instead of fiction. If we find what we expect to find from the fingerprints, you will not help matters by adding your misstatement to the one that was made at Duck Cottage."

Alleyn paused and looked at the undistinguished, dogged face.

"You have had a great shock," he said, and added in a voice so low that Blandish put his hand to his ear like a deaf rustic: "It's no good trying to protect people who are ready at any sacrifice of loyalty to protect themselves."

Templett laughed.

"So it seems," he said. "All right. That's how it was. It's no good denying it."

"Mrs. Ross gave you the letter on Saturday?"

"I suppose so. Yes."

"Did you guess at the authorship?"

"I *guessed.*"

"Did you notice the smell of eucalyptus?"

"Yes. But I'm innocent. My God, I tell you I had no opportunity. I can give you an account of every moment of the day."

"When you were at the hall with Mrs. Ross, did you not leave her to go down to the auditorium?"

"Why should I?"

"Mrs. Ross told me you shut one of the windows."

"Yes. I'd forgotten. Yes, I did."

"But if Mrs. Ross says she had shut this window herself in the morning?"

"I know. We couldn't make it out."

"You noticed the open window, shut it, returned to the stage, and lowered the curtain?"

"*Did she tell you that!*"

Templett suddenly collapsed into the chair behind him and buried his face in his hands. "My God," he said, "I've been a fool. *What* a fool!"

"They say it happens once to most of us," said Alleyn unexpectedly and not unkindly. "Did Mrs. Ross not mention at the time that she thought she had already shut the window?"

"Yes, yes, yes. She said so. But the window was *open.* It was opened about three inches. How can I expect you to believe it? You think I lowered the curtain, went to the piano, and fixed this bloody trap. I tell you I didn't."

"Why did you lower the curtain?"

Templett looked at his hands.

"Oh, God," he said. "Have we got to go into all that?"

"I see," said Alleyn. "No, I don't think we need. There was a scene that would have compromised you both if anybody had witnessed it?"

"Yes."

"Did you at any time speak about the letter?"

"She asked me if I'd found out—I may as well tell you I've got a note somewhere from Miss Campanula. I thought I'd compare the paper. I'd been so rushed during the day I hadn't had time. That's why I didn't destroy the thing."

"When you opened the window did you look out?"

"What? Yes. Yes. I think I did." There was a curious note of uncertainty in his voice.

"Have you remembered something?"

"What's the good! It sounds like something I've made up at the last moment."

"Let us have it anyway."

"Well, she caught sight of the window. She noticed it first; saw it over my shoulder, and got an impression that there was something that dodged down behind the sill. It was only a flash, she said. I thought it was probably one of those damned scouts. When I got to the window I looked out. There was nobody there."

"Were you upset by the discovery of an eavesdropper?"

Templett shrugged his shoulders.

"Oh, what's the good!" he said. "Yes, I suppose we were."

"Who was this individual?"

"I can't tell you."

"But didn't Mrs. Ross say who it was? She must have had some impression."

"Ask her if you must," he said violently. "I can't tell you."

"When you looked out they had gone," murmured Alleyn. "But you looked out."

He watched Dr. Templett, and Blandish and Fox watched him. Fox realized that they had reached a climax. He knew what Alleyn's next question would be, he saw Alleyn raise one eyebrow and screw his mouth sideways before he asked his question.

"Did you look down?" asked Alleyn.

"Yes."

"And you saw?"

"There was a box under the window."

"Ah!" It was the smallest sigh. Alleyn seemed to relax all over. He smiled to himself and pulled out his cigarette case.

"That seemed to suggest," said Templett, "that somebody had stood there, using the box. It wasn't there when I got to the hall because I went round that way to get the key."

Alleyn turned to Fox.

"Have you asked them about the box?"

"Yes, sir. Mr. Jernigham, Miss Prentice, every kid in the village, *and* all the helpers. Nobody knows anything about it."

"Good," said Alleyn, heartily.

For the first time since they got there, Dr. Templett showed some kind of interest.

"Is it important?" he asked.

"Yes," said Alleyn. "I think it's of the first importance."

### III

"You knew about this box?" asked Templett after a pause.

"Yes, why don't you smoke, Dr. Templett?" Alleyn held out his case.

"Are you going to charge me?"

"No. Not on present information."

Templett took a cigarette and Alleyn lit it for him.

"I'm in a hell of a mess," said Templett. "I see that."

"Yes," agreed Alleyn. "One way and another you've landed yourself in rather a box." But there was something in his manner that drove the terror out of Templett's eyes.

Smith came in with the transcript.

"Sergeant Roper's outside, sir," he said. "He came down with Mr. Bathgate and wants to see you particular."

"He can wait," said Blandish. "He's wanted to see me particular about ten times a day ever since we got busy."

"Yes, sir. Will I leave this transcript?"

"Leave it here," said Blandish, "and wait outside."

When Smith had gone Blandish spoke to Dr. Templett for the first time that evening.

"I'm very sorry about this, doctor."

"That's all right," said Templett.

"I think Mr. Alleyn will agree with me that if it's got no bearing on the case we'll do our best to bury it."

"Certainly," said Alleyn.

"I don't care much what happens," said Templett.

"Oh, come now, doctor," said Blandish uncomfortably, "you mustn't say that."

But Alleyn saw a gay little drawing-room with a delicate straw-colored lady, whose good nature did not stretch beyond a very definite point, and he thought he understood Dr. Templett.

"I think," he said, "you had better give us a complete time-table of your movements from two-thirty on Friday up to eight o'clock last night. We shall check it, but we'll make the process an impersonal sort of business."

"But for those ten minutes in the hall, I'm all right," said Templett. "God, I was with her all the time, until I shut the window. Ask her how long it took! I wasn't away two minutes over the business. Surely to God she'll at least bear me out in that. She's nothing to lose by it."

"She shall be asked," said Alleyn.

Templett began to give the names of all the houses he had visited on his rounds. Fox took them down.

Alleyn suddenly asked Blandish to find out how long the Pen Cuckoo telephone had been disconnected by the falling branch. Blandish rang up the exchange.

"From eight-twenty until the next morning."

"Yes," said Alleyn. "Yes."

Dr. Templett's voice droned on with its flat recital of time and place.

"Yes, I hunted all day Friday. I got home in time to change and go to the five o'clock rehearsal. The servants can check that. When I got home again I found this urgent message. . . . I was out till after midnight. Mrs. Bains at Mill Farm. She was in labor twenty-four hours . . . yes. . . ."

"May I interrupt?" asked Alleyn. "Yesterday morning, at Pen Cuckoo, Mrs. Ross did not leave the car?"

"No."

"Were you shown into the study?"

"Yes."

"You were there alone?"

"Yes," said Templett, showing the whites of his eyes.

"Dr. Templett, did you touch the box with the automatic?"

"Before God, I didn't."

"One more question. Last night did you use all your powers of authority and persuasion to induce Miss Prentice to allow Miss Campanula to take her place?"

"Yes, but—she wouldn't listen to me."

"Will you describe again how you found her?"

"I told you last night. I came in late. I thought Dinah would be worried and after I'd changed, I went along to the women's dressing-room to show her I was there. I heard some one sniveling and moaning, and through the open door I saw Miss Prentice in floods of tears, rocking backwards and forwards and holding her hand. I went in and looked at it. No doctor in his senses would have let her thump the piano. She *couldn't* have done it. I told her so, but she kept on saying, 'I will do it. I will do it.' I got angry and spoke my mind. I couldn't get any further with her. It was damned near time we started and I wasn't even made-up."

"So you fetched Miss Copeland and her father, knowing the rector would possibly succeed where you had failed."

"Yes. But I tell you it was physically impossible for her to use the finger. I could have told her that——"

He stopped short.

"Yes? You could have told her that, how long ago?" said Alleyn.

"Three days ago."

## IV

Smith returned.

"It's Sergeant Roper, sir. He says it's very particular indeed and he knows Mr. Alleyn would want to hear it."

"Blast!" said Blandish. "All right, all right."

Smith left the door open. Alleyn saw Nigel crouched over an anthracite stove and Roper, sweating and expectant, in the middle of the room.

"Right-o, Roper," said Smith audibly. Roper hurriedly removed his helmet, cleared his throat, and marched heavily into the room.

"Well, Roper?" said Blandish.

"Sir," said Roper, "I have a report." He took his official note-book from a pocket in his tunic and opened it, bringing it into line with his nose. He began to read very rapidly in a high voice.

"This afternoon, November 28th, at 4 p.m. being on duty at the time outside the parish hall of Winton St. Giles I was approached and accosted by a young female. She was well-known to me being by name Gladys Wright (Miss) of Top Lane, Winton. The following conversation eventuated. Miss Wright inquired of me if I was waiting for my girl or my promotion. Myself (P.S. Roper): I am on duty, Miss Wright, and would take it kindly if you would pass along the lane. Miss Wright: Look what our cat's brought in. P.S. Roper: And I don't want no lip or saucy boldness. Miss Wright: I could tell you something and I've come along to do it, but seeing you're on duty maybe I'll keep it for your betters. P.S. Roper: If you know anything, Gladys, you'd better speak up for the law comes down with majesty on them that aids and abets and withholds. Miss Wright: What will you give me? The succeeding remarks are not evidence and bear no connection with the matter in hand. They are therefore omitted."

"What the hell did she tell you?" asked Blandish. "Shut that damned book and come to the point."

"Sir, the girl told me in her silly way that she came down to the hall at six-thirty on yesterday evening being one of them selected to usher. She let herself in and finding herself the first to arrive, living nearby and not wishing to return home, the night being heavy rain with squalls and her hair being artificially twisted up with curls which to my mind—"

"*What did she tell you?*"

"She told me that at six-thirty she sat down as bold as brass and played 'Nearer my Gawd to Thee' with the soft pedal on," said Roper.

# CHAPTER XX

# According to Miss Wright

## I

SERGEANT ROPER, SWEATING LIGHTLY, allowed an expression of extreme gratification to suffuse his enormous face. The effect of his statement on his superiors left nothing to be desired. Superintendent Blandish stared at his sergeant like a startled codfish, Detective-Inspector Fox pushed his glasses up his forehead and brought his hands down smartly on his knees. Dr. Templett uttered in a whisper a string of amazing blasphemies. Chief Inspector Alleyn pulled his own nose, made a peculiar grimace, and said:

"Roper, you shall be hung with garlands, led through the village, and offered up at the Harvest Festival."

"Thank you, sir," said Roper.

"Where," asked Alleyn, "is Gladys Wright?"

Roper flexed his knees and pointed with his thumb over his shoulder.

"Stuck to her like glue, I have. I telephoned Fife from the hall to relieve me, keeping the silly maiden under observation the while. I brought her here, sir, on the bar of my bike, all ten stones of her, and seven miles if it's an inch."

"Magnificent. Bring her in, Roper."

Roper went out.

oner in the court on trial for murder. Please think very carefully indeed. Would you make this statement on oath?"

"Oh *yass*," said Miss Wright.

"Thank you," said Alleyn. He looked at Templett. "I don't think we need keep you, Dr. Templett, if you are anxious to get home."

"I—I'll drive you back," said Templett.

"That's very nice of you—I shan't be long." He turned back to Gladys Wright. "Did any one come in while you were playing?"

"I stopped when I heard them coming. Cissie Dewry come first and then all the other girls."

"Did you notice any of the performers?"

"No. We was all talking round the door, like." She rolled her eyes at Roper. "That was when you come, Mr. Roper."

"Well, Roper?"

"They were in the entrance, sir, giggling and cackling in their female manner, sure enough."

"Oo you *are*," said Miss Wright.

"And had any of the company arrived at that time?"

"Yes, sir," said Roper. "Miss Copeland was there ahead of me, but she went to the back door same as all the performers, I don't doubt. And the Pen Cuckoo party was there, sir, but I didn't know that till I went round to back of stage when I found them bedizening their faces in the Sunday-school rooms."

"So that there was a moment when the ladies were at the front door, talking, and the Pen Cuckoo party and Miss Copeland were behind the scenes?"

"That's right, sir."

"They were ringing and ringing at the telephone," interjected Miss Wright, "all the time us girls was there."

"And you say, Miss Wright, that none of the performers came into the front of the hall."

"Not one. Truly."

"Sure?"

"Yass. Certain sure. We would have seen them. Soon after that the doors were open and people started to come in."

"Where did you stand?"

"Up top by the stage, ushering the two shillingses."

"So if anybody had come down to the piano from the stage you would have seen them?"

"Nobody came down. Not ever. I'd take another Bible oath on that," said Miss Wright, with considerable emphasis.

"Thank you," said Alleyn. "That's splendid. One other question.

You were at the Reading Circle meeting at the rectory on Friday night. Did you go home by the gate into the wood. The gate that squeaks?"

"Oo *no!* None of us girls goes that way at night." Miss Wright giggled, extensively. "It's too spooky. Oo, I wouldn't go that way for anything. The others, they all went together, and my young gentleman, he took me home by lane."

"So you're sure nobody used the gate?"

"Yass, for sure. They'd all gone," said Miss Wright, turning scarlet, "before us. And we used lane."

"You passed the hall, then. Were there any lights in the hall?"

"Not in front."

"You couldn't see the back windows, of course. Thank you so much, Miss Wright. We'll get you to sign a transcript of everything you have told us. Read it through carefully, first. If you wouldn't mind waiting in the outer office I think I can arrange for you to be driven home."

"Oo well, thanks ever so," said Miss Wright, and went out.

## II

Alleyn looked at Templett.

"I ought to apologize," he said, "I've given you a damned bad hour."

"I don't know why you didn't arrest me," said Templett with a shaky laugh. "Ever since I realized I'd left that bloody note in the dressing-room I've been trying to think how I could prove I hadn't rigged the automatic. There seemed to be no possible proof. Even now I don't see—— Oh, well, it doesn't matter. Nothing much matters. If you don't mind, I'll wait outside in the car. I'd like a breath of fresh air."

"Certainly."

Dr. Templett nodded to Blandish and went out.

"Will I shadow the man?" asked Roper, earnestly.

Blandish's reply was unprintable.

"You might ask Mr. Bathgate to drive your witness home, Roper," said Alleyn. "Let her sign her statement first. Tell Mr. Bathgate I'm returning with Dr. Templett. And Roper, as tactfully as you can, just see how Dr. Templett's getting on. He's had a shock."

"Yes, sir."

Roper went out.

"He's got about as much tact as a cow," said Blandish.

"I know, but at least he'll keep an eye on Templett."

"The lady let him down, did she?"

"With a thump that shook the crockery."

"S-s-s-s!" said Blandish appreciatively. "Is that a fact?"

"He's had two narrow escapes," said Fox, "and *that's* a fact. The lady's let him down with a jerk and he's lucky the hangman won't follow suit."

"Fox," said Alleyn, "you have the wit of a Tyburn broadsheet, but there's matter in it."

"I don't know where I am," said Blandish. "Are we any nearer to an arrest?"

"A good step," said Alleyn. "The pattern emerges."

"What does that mean, Mr. Alleyn?"

"Well," said Alleyn, apologetically, "I mean all these mad little things like the box, and the broken telephone, and the creaking gate— I'm not so sure of the onion——"

"The onion!" cried Fox, triumphantly. "I know all about the onion, Mr. Alleyn. Georgie Biggins is responsible for that, the young limb. I saw him this afternoon and asked him, as well as every other youngster in the village, about the box. He's going round as pleased as punch, letting on he's working at the case with the Yard. Answers me as cool as you please, and when I'm going he says, 'Did you find an onion in the teapot, mister?' Well, it seems that they had a tea-party on the stage, with Miss Prentice and Miss Campanula quarreling about which should pour out. If the young devil didn't go and put an onion in the pot. It seems they each had to take the lid off and look in the pot and this was another of George's bright ideas. I suppose someone found it in time and threw it into the box on the floor, where you picked it up."

"Dear little Georgie," said Alleyn. "Dear little boy! We've had red herrings before now, Fox, but never a Spanish onion. Well, as I was saying, all these mad little things begin to bear some sort of relationship."

"That's nice, Mr. Alleyn," said Fox, woodenly. "You're going to tell us you know who did it, I suppose?"

"Oh, yes," said Alleyn looking at him in genuine surprise. "I do *now*, Brer Fox. Don't you?"

### III

When a man learns that his mistress, faced with putting herself in a compromising position, will quite literally see him hanged first, he is not inclined for conversation. Templett drove slowly back towards Chipping and was completely silent until the first cottage came into view. Then he said, "I don't see how any one could have done it. The piano was safe at six-thirty. The girl used the soft pedal. It was safe."

"Yes," agreed Alleyn.

"I suppose, putting the pedal down softly, the pressure wasn't enough to pull the trigger?"

"It's a remarkably light pull," said Alleyn. "I've tried."

Templett brushed his hand across his eyes. "I suppose my brain won't work."

"Give the thing a rest."

"But how could anybody fix that contraption inside the piano after half-past six when those girls were skylarking about in the front of the house? It's impossible."

"If you come down to the hall to-morrow night, I'll show you."

"All right. Here's your pub. What time's the inquest? I've forgotten. I'm all to pieces." He pulled up the car.

"Eleven o'clock to-morrow."

Alleyn and Fox got out. It was a cold windy evening. The fine weather had broken again and it had begun to rain. Alleyn stood with the door open and looked at Templett. He leaned heavily on the wheel and stared with blank eyes at the windscreen.

"The process of convalescence," said Alleyn, "should follow the initial shock. Take heart of grace, you will recover."

"I'll go home," said Templett. "Good night."

"Good night."

He drove away.

They went upstairs to their rooms.

"Let's swap stories, Brer Fox," said Alleyn. "I'll lay my case, for what it's worth, on the dressing-table. I want a shave. You can open your little heart while I'm having it. I don't think we'll unburden ourselves to Bathgate just yet."

They brought each other up-to-date before they went downstairs again in search of a drink.

They found Nigel alone in the bar parlor.

"I'm not going to pay for so much as half a drink and I intend to drink a very great deal. I've had the dullest afternoon of my life and all for your benefit. Miss Wright smells. When I took her to her blasted cottage she made me go in to tea with her brother who turns out to be the village idiot. Yes, and on the way back from Duck Cottage, your lovely car sprang a puncture. Furthermore——"

"Joe!" shouted Alleyn. "Three whiskies-and-sodas."

"I should damn well think so. What are you ordering for yourselves?"

Nigel calmed down presently and listened to Alleyn's account of the afternoon. Mrs. Peach, a large flowing woman, told them she had a proper juicy steak for their dinner and there was a fine fire in the back parlor. They moved in, taking their drinks with them. It was pleasant, when the curtains were drawn and the red-shaded oil lamp was lit, to hear the rain driving against the leaded windows and to listen to the sound of grilling steak beyond the kitchen slide.

"Not so many places left like this," said Fox. "Cozy, isn't it? I haven't seen one of those paraffin lamps for many a long day. Mrs. Peach says old Mr. Peach, her father-in-law, you know, won't have electricity in the house. He's given in as far as the tap-room's concerned but nowhere else. Listen to the rain! It'll be a wild night again."

"Yes," said Alleyn. "It's strange, isn't it, to think of the actors in this silly farfetched crime, all sitting over their fires, as we are now, six of them wondering what the answer is, and the seventh nursing it secretly in what used to be known as a guilty heart."

"Oo-er," said Nigel.

Mrs. Peach's daughter brought in the steak.

"Are you going out again?" asked Nigel after an interval.

"I've got a report to write," answered Alleyn. "When that's done I think I might go up to the hall."

"Whatever for?"

"Practical demonstration of the booby-trap."

"I might come," said Nigel. "I can ring up the office from there."

"You'll have to square up with the Copelands if you do. The hall telephone is on an extension from the rectory. Great hopping fleas!" shouted Alleyn, "why the devil didn't I think of that before!"

"What!"

"The telephone."

"Excuse him," said Nigel to Fox.

## IV

"We'll take half an hour's respite," said Alleyn, when the cloth had been drawn and a bottle of port, recommended by old Mr. Peach, had been set before them. "Let's go over the salient features."

"Why not?" agreed Nigel, comfortably.

Alleyn tried the port, raised an eyebrow, and lit a cigarette.

"It's respectable," he said. "An honest wine and all that. Well, as I see it, the salient features are these. Georgie Biggins rigged his booby-trap between two and three on Friday afternoon. Miss Campanula rattled on the door just before two-thirty. Georgie was in the hall, but must have hidden, because when Gibson looked through the window, the top of the piano was open and Georgie nowhere to be seen. Miss Campanula didn't know that the key was hung up behind the outhouse. The rest of the company were told but they are vague about it. Now George didn't test his booby-trap because, as he says, 'somebody came.' I think this refers to Miss Campanula's onslaught on the door. I'm afraid Miss Campanula is a nightmare to George. He won't discuss her. I'll have to try again. Anyway, he didn't test his booby-trap. But *somebody* did, because the silk round the hole made by the bullet was still damp last night. That means something was on the rack, possibly Miss Prentice's 'Venetian Suite' which seems to have been down in the hall for the last week. It has a stain on the back which suggests that the jet of water hit it and splayed out, wetting the silk. Now, Georgie left the hall soon after the interruption, because he finished up by playing "Chopsticks" with the loud pedal on, and Miss Campanula overheard this final performance. The next eighteen hours or so are still wrapped in mystery but, as far as we know, any of the company may have gone into the hall. Miss Prentice passed it on her way home from confession, the Copelands live within two minutes of the place. Master Henry says that after his meeting with Dinah Copeland he roamed the hills most of that unpleasantly damp afternoon. He may have come down to the hall. Jernigham senior seems to have hunted all day and so does Templett, but either of them may have come down in the evening. Miss Prentice says that she spent the evening praying in her room, Master Henry says he tinkered with a light plug in his room, the squire says he was alone in the study. It takes about eight minutes to walk down Top Lane to the hall and perhaps fifteen to return. On Friday night the rector had an agonizing encounter in his own study. I'll tell you about it."

Alleyn told them about it.

"Now the remarkable thing about this is that I believe he spoke the truth, but his story is made so much nonsense if Dinah Copeland was right in thinking there was a third person present. Miss C. would hardly make passionate advances and hang herself round the rector's neck, with a Friendly Helper to watch the fun. Dinah Copeland bases her theory on the fact that she heard the gate opposite the study window squeak, as if somebody had gone out that way. She tells us it couldn't have been Miss Prentice because Miss Prentice rang up a few minutes later to say she wasn't coming down. We know Miss Prentice was upset when she left confession that afternoon. The rector had ticked her off and given her a penance or something and he thinks that's why she didn't come. It wasn't any of the readers. Who the devil was it?"

"The rector himself," said Nigel promptly, "taking a short cut to the hall."

"He says that after Miss C. left him he remained a wreck by his fireside."

"That may not be true."

"It may be as false as hell," agreed Alleyn. "There are one or two points about this business. I'll describe the layout again and repeat the rector's story."

When he had done this he looked at Fox.

"Yes," said Fox. "Yes, I think I get you there, Mr. Alleyn."

"Obviously, I'm right," said Nigel, flippantly. "It's the reverend."

"Mr. Copeland's refusing the money, Mr. Bathgate," said Fox. "I was telling the chief, just now. I got that bit of information this afternoon. Mr. Henry told the squire in front of the servants and it's all round the village."

"Well, to finish Friday," said Alleyn. "Dr. Templett spent the best part of the night on a case. That can be checked. Mrs. Ross says she was at home. Tomorrow, Foxkin, I'll get you to use your glamor on Mrs. Ross's maid."

"Very good, sir."

"Now then. Some time before noon yesterday, the water-pistol disappeared, because at noon Miss P. strummed with her right hand and used the soft pedal. Nothing happened."

"Perhaps George's plan didn't work," suggested Nigel.

"We are going to see presently if George's plan works. Whether it works or not, the fact remains that somebody found the water-pistol, removed and hid it, and substituted the Colt."

"That must have been later still," said Nigel.

"I agree with you, but not, I imagine, for the same reason. Dr. Templett's story seems to prove that the box was placed outside the window while he and Mrs. Ross were in the hall. He got the impression that someone dodged down behind the sill. Now this eavesdropper was not Miss Campanula because the servants agree that she didn't go out yesterday afternoon. Miss Prentice, the squire, Dinah Copeland and her father were all in their respective houses, but any of them could have slipped out for an hour. Master Henry was again roving the countryside. None of them owns to the box outside the window. Fox has asked every soul in the place and not a soul professes to know anything about the box."

"That's right," said Fox. "I reckon the murderer was hanging about with the Colt and had a look in to see who was there. He'd see the cars in the lane but he'd want to find out if the occupants were in the

hall or had gone that way into the vicarage. On the far side of the hall
he'd have been out of sight, and he'd have plenty of time to dodge if
they sounded as if they were coming round that way. But they never
would, of course, seeing it's the far side. He'd be safe enough. Or she,"
added Fox with a bland glance at Nigel.

"That's how I read it," agreed Alleyn. "Now, look here."

He took an envelope from his pocket, opened it, and, using tweezers,
took out four minute reddish-brown scraps, when he laid on a sheet of
paper.

"Salvage from the box," he said.

Nigel prodded at them with the tweezers.

"Rubber," said Nigel.

"Convey anything?"

"Somebody wearing galoshes. Miss Prentice, by gosh. I bet she
wears galoshes. Or Miss C. herself. Good Lord," said Nigel, "perhaps
the rector's right. Perhaps it is a case of suicide."

"These bits of rubber were caught on a projecting nail and some
rough bits of wood inside the box."

"Well, she might have trodden inside the box before she picked it
up."

"You have your moments," said Alleyn. "I suppose she might."

"Galoshes!" said Fox and chuckled deeply.

"Here!" said Nigel, angrily. "Have you got a case?"

"The makings of one," said Alleyn. "We're not going to tell you just
yet, because we don't want to lower our prestige."

"We like to watch your struggles, Mr. Bathgate," said Fox.

"We are, as it might be," said Alleyn, "two experts on a watch-tower
in the middle of a maze. 'Look at the poor wretch,' we say as we nudge
each other, 'there he goes into the same old blind alley. Jolly comical,'
we say, and then we laugh like anything. Don't we, Fox?"

"So we do," agreed Fox. "But never you mind, Mr. Bathgate, you're
doing very nicely."

"Well, to hell with you anyway," said Nigel. "And moreover what
about Gladys Wright putting her splay foot on the soft pedal an hour
and a half before the tragedy?"

"Perhaps she wore galoshes," said Fox, and for the first time in these
records he broke into a loud laugh.

# CHAPTER XXI

# According to Mr. Saul Tranter

## I

ALLEYN FINISHED HIS REPORT by nine o'clock. At a quarter-past nine they were back in the Biggins's Ford, driving through pelting rain to the hall.

"I'll have to go up to the Yard before this case is many hours older," said Alleyn. "I telephoned the A.C. this morning but I think I ought to see him and there are a lot of odd things to be cleared up. Perhaps tomorrow night. I'd like to get to the bottom of that meeting between Master Henry, Dinah Copeland and Miss Prentice. I rather think Master Henry wishes to unburden himself and Miss Dinah won't let him. Here we are."

Once more they crunched up the gravel path to the front door. The shutters had been closed and they and the windows were all locked. P.C. Fife was on duty. He let them in and being an incurious fellow retired thankfully when Alleyn said he would not be wanted for two hours.

"I'll ring up the Chipping station when we're leaving," said Alleyn.

The hall smelt of dying evergreens and varnish. It was extremely cold. The piano still stood in its old position against the stage. The hole in the faded silk gaped mournfully. The aspidistras drooped a little in their pots. A fine dust had settled over everything. The rain drove down steadily on the old building and the wind shook the shutters and howled desperately under the eaves.

"I'm going to light these heaters," said Nigel. "There's a can of paraffin in one of the back rooms. This place smells of mortality."

Alleyn opened his case and took out Georgie Biggins's water-pistol. Fox wedged the butt between steel pegs in the iron casing. The nozzle fitted a hole in the fretwork front. They had left the cord and pulleys in position.

"On Friday," said Alleyn, "there was only the long rent in the tucked silk. You see there are several of them. The material has rotted in the creases. No doubt Georgie arranged the silk tastefully behind the fretwork, so that the nozzle didn't catch the light. We'll have a practical demonstration from Mr. Bathgate, Fox. Now, if you fix the front pulley, I'll tie the cord round the butt of the pistol. Hurry up. I hear him clanking in the background."

They had just dropped a sheet of newspaper on the rack when Nigel reappeared with a large can.

"There's some fairly good beer in that room," said Nigel. He began to fill the tank of the heater from his can.

Alleyn sat down at the piano, struck two or three chords, and began to vamp *"Il état une Bérgère."*

"That's odd, Fox," he said.

"What's wrong, Mr. Alleyn?"

"I can't get the soft pedal to budge. You try. Don't force it."

Fox seated himself at the piano and picked out "Three Blind Mice," with a stubby forefinger.

"That's right," he said. "It makes no difference."

"What's all this?" demanded Nigel, and bustled forward.

"The soft pedal doesn't work."

"Good Lord!"

"It makes no difference to the sound," said Fox.

"You're not using it."

"Here," said Nigel, "let me try."

Fox got up. Nigel took his place with an air of importance.

"Rachmaninoff's Prelude in C-sharp minor," he said. He squared his elbows, raised his left hand and leaned forward. The voice of the wind mounted in a thin wail and seemed to encircle the building. Down came Nigel's left hand like a sledge-hammer.

"Pom. *Pom.* POM!"

Nigel paused. A violent gust shook the shutters so impatiently that, for a second, he raised his head and listened. Then he trod on the soft pedal.

The newspaper fell forward on his hands. The thin jet of water caught him between the eyes like a cold bullet. He jerked backwards, uttered a scandalous oath, and nearly lost his balance.

"It does work," said Alleyn.

But Nigel did not retaliate. Above all the uneasy clamor of the storm, and like an echo of the three pretentious chords, sounded a loud triple knock on the front door.

"Who the devil's that?" said Alleyn.

He started forward, but before he could reach the door it crashed open, and on the threshold stood Henry Jernigham with streaks of rain lacing his chalk-white face.

## II

"What the hell's happening in here?" demanded Henry.

"Suppose you shut the door," said Alleyn.

But Henry stared at him as if he had not heard. Alleyn walked past him, slammed the door, and secured the catch. Then he returned to Henry, took him by the elbow, and marched him up the hall.

Fox waited stolidly. Nigel wiped his face with his handkerchief and stared at Henry.

"Now what is it?" demanded Alleyn.

"My God!" said Henry, "who played those three infernal chords?"

"Mr. Bathgate. This is Mr. Bathgate, Mr. Jernigham, and this is Detective-Inspector Fox." Henry looked dimly at the other two and sat down suddenly.

"Oh, Lord," he said.

"I say," said Nigel. "I'm most extraordinarily sorry if I gave you a shock, but I assure you I never thought——"

"I'd come into the lane," said Henry, breathlessly, "the rectory trees were making such a noise in the wind that you couldn't hear anything else."

"Yes?" said Alleyn.

"Don't you see? I'd come up the path and just as I reached the door a great gust of wind and rain came screeching round the building like the souls of the damned. And then, when it dropped, those three chords on a cracked piano! My God, I tell you I nearly bolted."

Henry put his hand to his face and then looked at his fingers.

"I don't know whether it's sweat or rain," he said, "and that's a fact.

Sorry! Not the behavior of a pukka sahib. No, by Gad, sir. Blimp wouldn't think anything of it."

"I can imagine it was rather trying," said Alleyn. "What were you doing there, anyway?"

"Going home. I stayed on to supper at the rectory. Only just left. Mr. Copeland's in such a hoo that he's forgotten all about choking me off. When I occurred at cold supper he noticed me no more than the High Church blanc-mange. I say, sir, I am sorry I made such an ass of myself. Honestly! How I could!"

That's all right," said Alleyn. "But why did you turn in here?"

"I thought if that splendid fellow Roper held the dog-watch, I might say, 'Stand ho! What hath this thing appeared?' and get a bit of gossip out of him."

"I see."

"Have a cigarette?" said Nigel.

"Oh, thank you. I'd better take myself off."

"Would you like to wait and see a slight experiment?" asked Alleyn.

"Very much indeed, sir, if I may."

"Before we begin, there's just one thing I'd like to say to you, as you are here. I shall call on Miss Prentice tomorrow and I shall use every means within the law to get her to tell me what took place on that encounter in Top Lane on Friday. I don't know whether you'd rather give me your version first."

"I've told you already, she's dotty," said Henry with nervous impatience. "It's my belief she is actually and literally out of her senses. She looks like death and she won't leave her room except for meals, and then she doesn't eat anything. She said at dinner tonight that she's in danger, and that in the end she'll be murdered. It's simply ghastly. God knows whom she suspects, but she suspects somebody, and she's half dead with fright. What sort of sense will you get out of a woman like that?"

"Why not give us a sane version first?"

"But it's nothing to do with the case," said Henry, "and if you feel like saying 'tra-la,' I'd be grateful if you'd restrain yourselves."

"If it turns out to be irrelevant," said Alleyn, "it shall be treated as such. We don't use irrelevant statements."

"Then why ask for them?"

"We like to do the winnowing ourselves."

"Nothing happened in Top Lane."

"You mean Miss Prentice stood two feet away from you both, stared into your face until her heels sank an inch into the ground, and then walked away without uttering a word?"

"It was private business. It was altogether our affair."

"You know," said Alleyn, "that won't do. This morning at Pen Cuckoo, and this afternoon at the rectory, frankness was the keynote of your conversation. You have said that you wouldn't put it past Miss Prentice to do murder, and yet you boggle at repeating a single word that she uttered in Top Lane. It looks as though it's not Miss Prentice whom you wish to protect.

"Hasn't Miss Copeland insisted on your taking this stand because she's nervous on your account? What were you going to call out to me this afternoon when she stopped you?"

"Well," said Henry unexpectedly, "you're quite right."

"See here," said Alleyn, "if you are innocent of murder, I promise you that you are not going the right way to make us think so. Remember that in a little place like this we are bound to hear of all the rifts and ructions and this thing only happened twenty-six hours ago. We've scarcely touched the fringe of local gossip, and already I know that Miss Prentice is opposed to your friendship with Miss Dinah Copeland. I know very well that to you police methods must seem odious and——"

"No, they don't," said Henry. "Of course, you've got to do it."

"Very well, then."

"I'll tell you this much, and I dare say it's no more than you've guessed: My Cousin Eleanor was thrown into a dither by finding us there together, and our conversation consisted of a series of hysterical threats and embarrassing accusations on her part."

"And did you make no threats?"

"She'll probably tell you I did," said Henry, "but, as I have said six or eight times already, she's mad. And I'm sorry, sir, but that's all I can tell you."

"All right," said Alleyn with a sigh. "Let's get to work, Fox."

### III

They removed the water-pistol and set up the Colt in its place. Alleyn produced the "Prelude" from his case and put it on the rack. Henry saw the hole blown through the center and the surrounding ugly stains. He turned away and then, as if he despised this involuntary revulsion, moved closer to the piano and watched Alleyn's hands as they moved inside the top.

"You see," said Alleyn, "all the murderer had to do was exactly what

I'm doing now. The Colt fits into the same place, and the loose end of cord which was tied round the butt of the water-pistol is tied round the butt of the Colt. It passes across the trigger. It is remarkably strong cord, rather like fishing line. I've left the safety catch on. Now look."

He sat on the piano stool and pressed the soft pedal. The two pulleys stood out rigidly from their moorings, the cord tautened as the dampers moved towards the strings and checked.

"It's stood firm," said Alleyn. "Georgie made sure of his pulleys. Now."

"By gum!" ejaculated Nigel, "I never thought of——"

"I know you didn't."

Alleyn reached inside and released the safety catch. Again he trod lightly on the soft pedal. This time the soft pedal worked. The cord tightened in the pulleys and the trigger moved back. They all heard the sharp click of the striker.

"Well, there you are for what it's worth," said Alleyn lightly.

"Yes, but last night the top of the piano was smothered in bunting and six he-men aspidistras," objected Henry.

"So you think it was done last night," said Alleyn.

"I don't know when it was done, and I don't think it could have been done last night, unless it was before we all got to the hall."

Alleyn scowled at Nigel, who was obviously pregnant with a new theory.

"It's perfectly true," said Nigel defiantly. "Nobody could have moved those pots after 6.30."

"I so entirely agree with you," said Alleyn. A bell pealed distantly. Henry jumped.

"That's the telephone," he said and started forward.

"I'll answer it, I think," said Alleyn. "It's sure to be for me."

He crossed the stage, found a light switch and made his way to the first dressing-room on the left. The old-fashioned manual telephone pealed irregularly until he lifted the receiver.

"Hullo?"

"Mr. Alleyn? It's Dinah Copeland. Somebody wants to speak to you from Chipping."

"Thank you."

"Here you are," said Dinah. The telephone clicked and the voice of Sergeant Roper said, "Sir?"

"Hullo?"

"Roper, sir. I thought I should find you, seeing as how Fife is still asleep here. I have a small matter in the form of a recent arrest to bring before your notice, sir."

"In *what* form?"

"By name Saul Tranter, and by employment as sly a poacher as ever you see; but we've cotched him very pretty, sir, and the man's sitting here at my elbow with guilt written all over him in the form of two fine cock-pheasants."

"What the devil——?" began Alleyn, and checked himself. "Well, Roper, what about it?"

"This chap says he's got a piece of information that'll make the court think twice about giving him the month's hard he's been asking for these last two years. He won't tell me, sir, but in his bold way he asks to be faced with you. Now, we've got to get him down to the lock-up some time and——"

"I'll send Mr. Bathgate down, Roper. Thank you." Alleyn hung up the receiver and stared thoughtfully at the telephone.

"I'll have to see about you," he told it and returned to the front of the hall.

"Hullo," he said, "where's Master Henry?"

"Gone home," said Fox. "He's a funny sort of young gentleman, isn't he?"

"Rather a bumptious infant, I thought," said Nigel.

"He's about the same age as you were when I first met you," Alleyn pointed out, "and not half as bumptious. Bathgate, I'm afraid you'll have to go into Chipping and get a poacher."

"A poacher!"

"Yes. Treasure-trove of Roper's. Apparently the gentleman wishes to make a blunderbuss about his impending sentence. He says he's got a story to unfold. Bring Fife with him. Stop at the pub on the way back and get your own car, and let Fife drive the Ford here and he can use it afterwards to deliver this gentleman to the lock-up. We'll clear up this place tonight."

"Am I representative of a leading London daily or your odd-boy?"

"You know the answer to that better than I do. Away you go."

Nigel went, not without further bitter complaint. Alleyn and Fox moved to the supper-room.

"All this food can be thrown away to-morrow," said Alleyn. "There's something else I want to see down here, though. Look, there's the tea-tray ready to be carried on in the play. Mrs. Ross's silver, I dare say. It looks like her. Modern, expensive and streamlined."

He lifted the lid of the teapot.

"It reeks of onion. Dear little Georgie."

"I suppose someone spotted it and threw it out. You found it lying on the floor here, didn't you, Mr. Alleyn?"

"In that box over there. Yes. Bailey has found Georgie's and Miss P.'s prints in the pot, so presumably Miss P. hawked out the onion."

He stooped down and looked under the table.

"You went all over here last night, didn't you, Fox? Last night! This morning! 'Little Fox, we've had a busy day.'"

"All over it, sir. You'll find the onion peel down there. Young Biggins must have skinned it and then put it in the teapot."

"Did you find any powder in here?"

"Powder? No. No, I didn't. Why?"

"Or flour?"

"No. Oh, you're thinking of the flour on the onion."

"I'll just get the onion."

Alleyn fetched the onion. He had put it in one of his wide-necked specimen bottles.

"We haven't had time to deal with this as yet," he said. "Look at it, Fox, it's pinkish. That's powder, not flour."

"Perhaps young Biggins fooled round with it in one of the dressing-rooms."

"Let's look at the dressing-rooms."

They found that on each dressing-table there was a large box of theatrical powder. They were all new, and it looked as if Dinah had provided them. The men's boxes contained a yellowish powder, the women's a pinkish cream. Mrs. Ross, alone, had brought her own in an expensive-looking French box. In the dressing-room used by Miss Prentice and Miss Campanula, some of their powder had been spilled across the table. Alleyn stopped and sniffed it.

"That's it," he said. "Reeks of onion." He opened the box. "But this doesn't. Fox, ring up Miss Copeland and ask when the powder was brought into these rooms. It's an extension telephone. You just turn the handle."

Fox plodded away. Alleyn, in a sort of trance, stared at the top of the dressing-table, shook his head thoughtfully and returned to the stage. He heard a motor-horn, and in a minute the door opened. Roper and Fife came in shepherding between them a pigmy of a man who looked as if he had been plunged in a water-butt.

Mr. Saul Tranter was an old man with a very bad face. His eyes were no bigger than a pig's and they squinted, wickedly close together, on either side of his mean little nose. His mouth was loose and leered uncertainly, and his few teeth were objects of horror. He smelled very strongly indeed of dirty old man, dead birds and whisky. Roper thrust him forward as if he was some fabulous orchid, culled at great risk.

"Here he be, sir," said Roper. "This is Saul Tranter, sure enough, with all his wickedness hot in his body, having been taken in the act with two of squire's cock-pheasants and his gun smoking in his hands. Two years you've dodged us, haven't you, Tranter, you old fox? I thought I'd come along with Fife, sir, seeing I've got the hang of this case, having brought my mind to bear on it."

"Very good of you, Roper."

"Now, then, Tranter," said Roper, "speak up to the chief inspector and let him have the truth—if so be it lies in you to tell it."

"Heh, my sonnies!" said the poacher in a piping voice. "Be that the instrument that done the murder?" And he pointed an unspeakably dirty hand at the piano.

"Never you mind that," ordered Roper. "That's not for your low attention."

"What have you got to tell us, Tranter?" asked Alleyn. "Good Lord, man, you're as wet as a water-rat!"

"Wuz up to Cloudyfold when they cotched me," admitted Mr. Tranter. He drew a little closer to the heater and began stealthily to steam.

"Ay, they cotched me," he said. "Reckon it do have to happen so soon or so late. Squire'll sit on me at court and show what a mighty man he be, no doubt, seeing it's his woods I done trapped and shot these twenty year. 'Od rabbit the man, he'd change his silly, puffed-up ways if he knew what I had up my sleeve for 'un."

"That's no way to talk," said Roper severely, "you, with a month's hard hanging round your neck."

"Maybe. Maybe not, Charley Roper." He squinted up at Alleyn. "Being I has my story to tell which will fix the guilt of this spring-gun on him as set it, I reckon the hand of the law did ought to be light on my ancient shoulders."

"If your information is any use," said Alleyn, "we might put in a word for you. I can't promise. You never know. I'll have to hear it first."

"'Tain't good enough, mister. Promise first, story afterwards, is my motter."

"Then it's not ours," said Alleyn coolly. "It looks as though you've nothing to tell, Tranter."

"Is threats nothing? Is blasting words nothing? Is a young chap caught red-handed same as me, with as pretty a bird as ever flewed into a trap, nothing?"

"Well?"

Fox came down into the hall, joined the group round the heater and stared with a practiced eye at Tranter. Nigel arrived and took off his streaming mackintosh. Tranter turned his head restlessly and looked sideways from one face to another. A trickle of brown saliva appeared at the corner of his mouth.

"Well?" Alleyn repeated.

"Sour, tight-fisted men be the Jernighams," said Tranter. "What's a bird or two to them! I'm up against all damned misers, and so be all my side. Tyrants they be, and narrow as the grave, father and son."

"You'd better take him back, Roper."

"Nay, then, I'll tell you. I'll tell you. And if you don't give me my dues, dang it, if I don't fling it in the faces of the J.P.s. Where be your pencils and papers, souls? This did oughter go down in writing."

# CHAPTER XXII

# Letter to Troy

## I

"ON FRIDAY AFTERNOON," SAID MR. TRANTER, "I were op to Cloudy-fold. Never mind why. I come down by my own ways, and proper foxy ways they be, so quiet as moonshine. I makes downhill to Top Lane. Never mind why."

"I don't in the least mind," said Alleyn. "Do go on."

Mr. Tranter shot a doubtful glance at him and sucked in his breath.

"A'most down to Top Lane, I wuz, when I heard voices. A feymell voice and a man's voice, and raised in anger. 'Ah,' thinks I. 'There's somebody down there kicking up Bob's-a-dying in the lane and, that being the case, the lane's no place for me, with never-mind-what under my arm and never-mind-what in my pockets, neither.' So I worms my way closer, till at last I'm nigh on bank above lane. There's a great ancient beech tree a-growing theer, and I lays down and creeps forward, so cunning as a serpent, till I looks down atwixt the green stuff into the lane. Yass. And what do I see?"

"What *do* you see?"

"Ah! I sees young Henry Jernigham, as proud as death and with the devil himself in his face, and rector's wench in his arms."

"That's no way to talk," admonished Roper. "Choose your words."

"So I will, and mind your own business, Charley Roper. And who do I see standing down in lane a-facing of they two with her face so sickly as cheese and her eyes like raging fires and her limbs trimbling like a trapped rabbit. Who do I see?"

"Miss Eleanor Prentice," said Alleyn.

Mr. Tranter, who was now steaming like a geyser and smelling like a polecat, choked and blinked his eyes.

"She's never told 'ee?"

"No. Go on."

"Trimbling as if to take a fit, she was, and screeching feeble, but uncommon venomous. Threating 'em with rector, she was, and threating 'em with squire. She says she caught 'em red-handed in vice and she'd see every decent critter in parish heard of their goings-on. And more besides. You'd never believe that old maiden had the knowledge of sinful youth in her, like she do seem to have. Nobbut what she don't tipple."

"Really?" Alleyn ejaculated.

"Aye. One of them hasty secret drinkers, she is. She'd sloshed her tipple down her bosom, as I clearly saw. No doubt that's what'd inflamed the old wench and caused her to rage and storm at 'em. She give it 'em proper hot and sizzling, did Miss Prentice. And when she was at the full blast of her fury, what does t' young spark do but round on 'er. Aye, t' young toad! Grabs her by shoulders and hisses in 'er face. If she don't let 'em be, 'e says, and if she tries to blacken young maid's name in eyes of the world, he says, he'll stop her wicked tongue for good an' all. He were in a proper rage, more furious than her. Terrible. And rector's maid, she says, 'Doan't, Henry, doan't!' But young Jernigham 'e take no heed of the wench, but hammer-and-tongs he goes to it, so white as a sheet and blazing like a furnace. Aye, they've all got murderous, wrathy, passionate tempers, they Jernighams, as is well known hereabouts; I've heard the manner of this bloody killing, and I reckon there's little doubt he set his spring-gun for t'one old hen and catched t'other. Now!"

## II

"Damn!" said Alleyn, when Mr. Tranter had been removed. "What a *bloody* business this is."

"Is it what you expected?" asked Nigel.

"Oh, I half expected it, yes. It was obvious that something pretty dramatic had happened on Friday afternoon. Miss Prentice and Henry Jernigham showed the whites of their eyes whenever it was mentioned, and the rector told me that he and the squire and Miss Prentice had all been opposed to this match. Why, the Lord alone knows. She seems a perfectly agreeable girl, rather a nice girl, blast it. And look at the way Master Henry responded to inquiry! Fox, did you ever know such a case? One cranky spinster is enough, heaven knows; and here we have two, each a sort of Freudian prize packet, and one a corpse on our hands."

"The whole thing seems very unlikely sort of stuff to me, Mr. Alleyn, and yet there it is. She *was* murdered. If that kid had never read his comic paper, and if he hadn't had his Twiddletoy outfit, it wouldn't have happened."

"I believe you're right there, Brer Fox."

"I suppose, sir, that was what Miss Prentice wanted to see the rector about on Friday evening. The meeting in Top Lane, I mean."

"Yes, I dare say it was. Oh, hell, we'll have to tackle Miss Prentice in the morning. What did Dinah Copeland say about the face-powder?"

"She brought it down with her last night. Georgie Biggins wasn't behind the scenes at all last night. He made such a nuisance of himself that they gave him the sack. He was call-boy at the dress rehearsal, but the tables and dressing-rooms have all been scrubbed out since then. That powder must have been spilled after half-past six last evening. And another thing: Miss Dinah Copeland never heard about the onion —or says she didn't."

"That makes sense, anyway!"

"*Does it?*" said Nigel bitterly. "I don't mind owning that I fail to see the faintest significance in anything you've been saying. Why this chat about an onion?"

"Why, indeed," sighed Alleyn. "Come on. We'll pack up and go home. Even a policeman must sleep."

## III

But before Alleyn went to sleep that night he wrote to his love.

*The Jernigham Arms*
*November 29th.*

MY DARLING TROY,

What a chancey sort of lover you've got. A fly-by-night who speaks to you at nine o'clock on Saturday evening, and soon after midnight is down in Dorset looking at lethal pianos. Shall you mind this sort of thing when we are married? You say not, and I suppose and hope not. You'll turn that dark head of yours and find your husband gone from your side. "Off again, I see," you'll say, and fall to thinking of the picture you are to paint next day. My dear and my darling Troy, you shall disappear, too, when you choose, into the austerity of your work, and never, never, never shall I look sideways, or disagreeably, or in the manner of the martyred spouse. Not as easy a promise as you might think, but I make it.

This is a disagreeable and unlikely affair. You will see the papers before my letter reaches you, but in case you'd like to know the official version, I enclose a very short account written in Yard language, and kept as colorless as possible. Fox and I have come to a conclusion, but are hanging off and on, hoping for a bit more evidence to turn up before we make an arrest. You told me once that your only method in detection would be based on character: and a very sound method, too, as long as you've got a flair for it. Now, here are our seven characters for you. What do you make of them?

First, the squire, Jocelyn Jernigham of Pen Cuckoo, and Acting Chief Constable to make it more difficult. He's a reddish, baldish man, with a look of perpetual surprise in his rather prominent light eyes. A bit pomposo. You would always know from the tone of his voice whether he spoke to a man or a woman. I think he would bore you and I think you would frighten him. The ladies, you see, should be gay and flirtatious and winsome. You are not at all winsome, darling, are you? They should make a man feel he's a bit of a dog. He's not altogether a fool, though, and, I should think, has a temper of his own. I think his cousin, Eleanor Prentice, frightens him, but he's full of family pride, and probably considers that even half a Jernigham can't be altogether wrong.

Miss Eleanor Prentice is half a Jernigham. She's about forty-nine or fifty, and I think rather a horrid woman. She's quite colorless and she's got buck teeth. She disseminates an odor of sanctity. She smiles a great deal, but with an air of forbearance as if hardly anything was really quite nice. I think she's a religious fanatic, heavily focussed on the rector. This morning when I interviewed her she was thrown into a perfect fever by the sound of church bells. She could scarcely listen to the simplest question, much less return a reasonable answer, so ardent and impatient was her longing to go to church. Now, in your true religious that's understandable enough. If you believe in the God Christ preached, you must be overwhelmed by your faith, and in time of trouble turn, with a heart of grace, to prayer. But I don't think Eleanor Prentice is that sort of religious. God knows I'm no psychoanalyst, but I imagine she'd be meat and drink to any one who was. Does one talk about a sex-fixation? Probably not. Anyway, she's gone the way modern psychology seems to consider axiomatic with women of her age and condition. This opinion is based partly on the statements of Henry Jernigham and Dinah Copeland and partly on my own impression of the woman.

Henry Jernigham is a good-looking young man. He's dark, with a jaw, gray eyes and an impressive head. He adopts the conversational manner of the moment, ironic and amusing, and gives the impression that he says whatever comes . . . into his head. But I don't believe any one has ever done that. How deep are our layers of thought, Troy. So deep that the thought of thought is terrifying to most of us. After many years, or perhaps only a few years, you and I may sometimes guess at each other's thoughts before they are spoken; and how strange that will seem to us. "A proof of our love!" we shall cry.

This young Jernigham is in love with Dinah Copeland. Why didn't we meet when I was his age and you were a solemn child? Should I have loved you when you were fourteen and I was twenty-three? In those days I seem to remember I had a passion for full-blown blondes. But, without doubt, I would have loved and you would have never noticed it. Well, Henry loves Dinah, who is a nice, intelligent child and vaguely on the stage, as almost all of them seem to be nowadays. I long to drivel on about the damage that magnificent chap Irving did to his profession when he made it respectable. No art should be fashionable, Troy, should it? But Dinah is evidently a serious young actress and probably quite a good one. She adores Master Henry.

Dr. Templett, as you will see, looks very dubious. He could have taken the automatic, he could have fixed it in position, he has a motive, and he used all his authority to bring about the change of pianists. But he didn't get down to the hall until the audience had arrived, and he was never alone from the time he arrived until the time of the murder. To meet, he's a commonplace enough fellow. Under ordinary circumstances, I think he'd be tiresomely facetious. There is no doubt that he was infected with a passion for Mrs. Selia Ross, and woe betide the man who loves a thin straw-colored woman with an eye to the main chance. If she doesn't love him she'll let him down, and if she does love him she'll suck away his character like a leech. He'll develop anemia of the personality. Mrs. Ross, as you will have gathered, *is* a thin, straw-colored woman, with the sort of sex appeal that changes men's faces when they speak of her. Their eyes turn bright and at the same time guarded, and the muscle from the nostril to the corner of the mouth becomes accentuated. Do you think that a very humorless observation? It's very true, my girl, and if you ever want to draw a sensualist, draw him like that. Trust a policeman: old Darwin found it out in spite of those whiskers. Mrs. Ross could have nipped out of the car and dodged through the french window into the squire's study while Templett was handing his hat and coat to the butler. Had you thought of that? But she came down to the hall with Templett for the evening performance.

The rector, Walter Copeland, B.A. Oxon.: The first thing you think of is his head. He's an amazingly fine-looking fellow. Everything the photographer or the producer ordered for a magnificent cleric. Silver hair, dark eyebrows, saintly profile. It's like a head on a coin or a statue, and much too much like any magazine illustration of "A Handsome Man." He seems to be less startling than his looks, and appears, in fact, to be a conscientious priest, rather disinclined for difficult jobs, but capable, suddenly, of digging in his toes. He is High Church, and I am sure very sincerely so. I should say that, if his belief came into question, he could be obstinate and even ruthless, but the general impression is of gentle vagueness.

The murdered woman seems to have been an arrogant, lonely, hysterical spinster. She and Miss Prentice might be taken as the positive and negative poles of parochial fanaticism with the rector as the needle. Not a true analogy. The general opinion is that she was a tartar.

It's midnight. I didn't get to bed last night, so I must leave you now. Troy, shall we have a holiday cottage in Dorset? A small house with a stern gray front, not too picturesque, but high up in the world so that you could paint the curves of the hills and the solemn changing cloud shadows that hurry over Dorset? Shall we have one? I'm going to marry you next April, and I love you with all my heart.

Good night,

R.

IV

Alleyn laid down his pen and stretched his cramped fingers.

He was, he supposed, the only waking being in the inn, and the silence of a country dwelling at night flowed in upon his mind. The wind had dropped again, and he realized that for some time there had been no sound of rain. The fire had fallen into a glow. The timbers of the inn cracked abruptly and startled him. He was suddenly weary. His body was a stranger to his mind and he looked at it in wonder. He stood as if in a trance, alarmed at meeting himself as a stranger, yet aware of this experience which was not new to him. As always, some part of his mind tried to step across the threshold of the unknown, but was unable to give purpose to his whole thought. He returned to himself and, rousing, lit his candle, turned out the lamp, and climbed the stairs to his room.

His window looked up the Vale. High above him he could see a light. "They are late at bed at Pen Cuckoo," he thought, and opened the window. The sound of water dripping from the eaves came into the room and the smell of wet grass and earth. "Perhaps it will be fine tomorrow," he thought, and went happily to bed.

# CHAPTER XXIII

# Frightened Lady

## I

"—LET ME REMIND YOU, GENTLEMEN," said the coroner, looking severely at Mr. Prosser, "that you are not concerned with theories. It is your duty to decide how this unfortunate lady met with her death. If you find you are able to do so, you must then make up your minds whether you are to return a verdict of accident, suicide or murder. If you are unable to arrive at this second decision, you must say so. Now, there is no difficulty in describing the manner of death. On Friday afternoon a small boy, after the manner of small boys, set an ingenious booby-trap. At some time before Saturday night, someone interfered with this comparatively harmless piece of mechanism. A Colt automatic was substituted for a water-pistol. You have heard that this automatic, the property of Mr. Jocelyn Jernigham, was in a room which is accessible from outside all day and every day. You have heard that it was common knowledge that the weapon was kept loaded in this room. You realize, I am sure, that on Saturday it would have been possible for anybody to enter the room through the french window and take the automatic. You have listened to a lucid description of the mechanism of this death-trap. You have examined the Colt automatic. You have been told that at 6.30 Miss Gladys Wright used the left-hand pedal of the piano, and that nothing untoward occurred. You have heard her say that from 6.30 until the moment of the catastrophe the front of the hall was occupied by herself, her fellow-helpers and, as they arrived, the audience. You have been shown photographs of the piano as it was at 6.30. The open top was covered in bunting which was secured to the sides by drawing-pins. On top of the piano and standing on the bunting, which stretched over the turned-back lid, were six pot plants. You realize that up to within fifteen minutes of the tragedy, every member of the company of performers, and every person in the audience, believed that it was Miss Prentice who was to play the overture. You may therefore have formed the opinion that Miss Prentice, and not Miss Campanula, was the intended victim. This need not affect your decision and, as a coroner's jury, does not actually concern you. If you agree that at eight o'clock Miss Campanula pressed the left-hand or soft pedal and was killed by a charge from the automatic and that somebody had put the automatic in the piano with felonious intent, in short with intent to murder, and if you consider there is no evidence to show who this person was—why, then, gentlemen, you may return a verdict to this effect."

"O upright beak!" said Alleyn as Mr. Prosser and the jury retired. "O admirable and economic coroner! Slap, bang, and away they go. Slap, bang, and here they are again."

They had indeed only gone into a huddle in the doorway, and returned looking rather as if they had all washed their faces in rectitude.

"Yes, Mr. Prosser?"

"We are all agreed, sir."

"Yes?"

"We return a verdict of murder," said Mr. Prosser, looking as if he feared he hadn't got it quite as it ought to be, "against person or persons unknown."

"Thank you. The only possible conclusion, gentlemen."

"I should like to add," said the smallest juryman, suddenly, "that I think them water-pistols ought to be put down by law."

## II

Immediately after the inquest, Fox in the Ford left for Duck Cottage. Alleyn's hand was on the door of Nigel's car, when he heard his name called. He turned and found himself face to face with Mrs. Ross.

"Mr. Alleyn—I'm sorry to bother you, but may I come and see you? I've remembered something that I think you ought to know."

"Certainly," said Alleyn. "Now, if it suits you."

"You're staying at the Jernigham Arms, aren't you? May I come there in ten minutes?"

"Yes, of course. I shall drive straight there."

"Thank you so much."

Alleyn replaced his hat and climbed into the car.

"*Now,* what the devil?" he wondered. "It's fallen out rather well, as it happens. Fox will have a longer session with the pretty housemaid."

Nigel came out and drove him to the inn. Alleyn asked Mrs. Peach if he could use the back parlor as an office for an hour. Mrs. Peach was volubly agreeable.

Nigel was told to take himself off.

"Why should I? Who are you going to see?"

"Mrs. Ross."

"Why can't I be there?"

"Because I think she'll speak more freely if she sees me alone."

"Well, let me sit in the next room with the slide a crack open."

Alleyn looked thoughtfully at him.

"Very well," he said, "you may do that. Take notes. It can't be used in evidence, but it may be handy. Wait a second. You've got your camera?"

"Yes."

"See if you can get a shot of her as she comes in. Careful about it. Get there quickly. She'll arrive in a second."

Nigel was only just in time. In five minutes the pot-boy announced Mrs. Ross, who came in looking much more like the Ritz than the Jernigham Arms.

"It is nice of you to see me," she said. "Ever since I remembered it, I've been so worried about this thing. I felt very bold, accosting you outside the hall of justice or whatever it was. You must be rushed off your feet."

"It's my job to listen," said Alleyn.

"May I sit down?"

"Please. I think this is the most comfortable chair."

She sat down with a pretty air of intimacy. She drew off her gloves, rummaged in her bag for her cigarettes, and then accepted one of his. Alleyn remained standing.

"You know," said Mrs. Ross, "you're not a bit my idea of a detective."

"No?"

"Not a *bit.* That enormous man who drives about with you looks much more the thing done at the Yard."

"Perhaps you would rather see Inspector Fox?"

"No, I'd much rather see you. Don't snub me."

"I'm sorry if I seemed to do that. What is it you would like to tell me?"

She leaned forward. Her manner lost its flippancy and took on an air of practical concern, but it also managed to suggest that she knew he would understand and sympathize with her motive in coming to him.

"You'll think I was such a fool not to remember it before," she said; "but the whole thing's been rather a shock. I suppose I simply had a blank moment or something. Not that I had any affection for the poor old thing; but, for all that, it was rather a shock."

"I'm sure it was."

"When you came to see me yesterday I had a ghastly headache and could hardly think. Did you ask me if I went out on Friday night?"

"Yes. You told me you were at home."

"I *thought* I did. Honestly, I don't know what I could have been thinking about. I *was* at home practically all the evening, but I went out for about half an hour. I drove from here to post a letter. I quite forgot."

"That's not very serious."

"I'm extremely relieved to hear you say so," she said, and laughed. "I was afraid you'd be *angry* with me."

She had a comical trick of over-emphasis, as if she parodied her own conversation. She drew out the word *angry*, making a grimace over it and opening her eyes very wide.

"Is that the whole story?" asked Alleyn.

"No, it's not," she said flatly. "The thing is, on my way down I came by Church Lane, past the hall. Church Lane goes on over the hills, you know, and comes out close to my cottage."

"Yes."

"Well, there was a light in one of the dressing-rooms."

"What time was this?"

"It was eleven when I got back. Say about twenty to eleven. No, a little earlier."

"Which dressing-room was it, do you know?"

"Yes. I've worked it out. It was too far away to be either of the women's rooms, and anyway they've got blinds. Miss Prentice, who is a very pure woman, thought it wasn't quite nice for us not to have blinds. The one Billy Templett uses has its window on the far side. It must have been the squire's. Mr. Jernigham's. But the funny thing about it was that it only flashed on for a few seconds and then went out again."

"Are you quite sure it wasn't the reflection of your headlights?"

"Absolutely positive. It was much too far to my right, and anyway it wasn't a bit like that. The glass is that thick stuff. No, a yellow square just popped up and popped out again."

"I see."

"It may not be anything at all, but it was on my conscience, so I thought I'd own up, and *come clean* and all that. I didn't think anything of it at the time. It might have been Dinah Copeland messing about over there, or any old thing; but as every moment after Friday seems important——"

"It's much better to let the police know of anything you remember that may have even the smallest significance," said Alleyn.

"I hoped you'd say that. Mr. Alleyn, I'm so terribly worried, and you're so human and unofficial, I wonder if I dare ask you something rather awkward."

Alleyn's manner could scarcely have been more formal as he replied: "I am here as a policeman, you know."

"Yes, I know. Well, when in doubt, ask a policeman." She grinned charmingly. "No, but honestly I'm in a horrid—awful muddle. It's about Billy Templett. I'm sure you've already heard all the local gossip, and you'll have found out for yourself that the charming people in this aristocratic part of the world have got minds like sinks and worse. No doubt they've told you all the local lies about Billy Templett and me. Well, we *are* great friends. He's the only soul in the entire district with an idea beyond hunting and other people's business, and we've got a lot in common. Of course, as a doctor, he's not supposed to look on women as anything but sets of insides and collections of complaints. I never dreamed it might actually do his practice no good if he saw rather more of me than old Mrs. Cain and the oldest inhabitant. Oh, dear, this *is* difficult. May I have another cigarette, please?"

Alleyn gave her another cigarette.

"I may as well choke it out before I lose my nerve altogether. Do you suspect Billy of this beastly crime?"

"As the case stands," said Alleyn, "it appears to be quite impossible that Dr. Templett should have had any hand in it."

"Is that true?" she asked, and her voice was as sharp as a knife.

"It is a very serious offense for a policeman to set traps or deliberately mislead his witnesses."

"I'm sorry. I know that. It was just the relief. You remember that letter you showed me yesterday? The anonymous letter?"

"Yes."

"It was written to me."

"Yes."

"I knew I hadn't taken you in. You are a clever beast, aren't you?" She laughed again. Alleyn wondered how many people had told her she laughed like a gamine and whether she ever forgot it.

"Do you want to amend your statement about the letter?" he asked.

"Yes, please. I want to explain. I showed the letter to Billy and we discussed it and decided to take no notice. When you showed it to me I supposed you'd picked it up somewhere in the hall, and as I knew it had nothing to do with this murder, and I wanted to protect poor old Billy, I said I didn't know anything about it. And then he came in and I thought he'd take his cue from me and—well, it went wrong."

"Yes," said Alleyn, "it went very wrong."

"Mr. Alleyn, what did he tell you last evening when he went away with you? Was he—was he angry with me? He didn't realize I'd tried to help him, did he?"

"I don't think so."

"He might have known! It's one of those hideous things that turn into a muddle."

"I'm afraid your explanation has gone equally astray."

"What do you mean?"

"I mean that you knew where Dr. Templett put the letter and that it is very unlikely we picked it up in the hall. I mean that yesterday you spoke instinctively and with the object of getting out of an awkward position. You have since remembered that there is a fingerprint system, so you come to me with a story of altruistic motives. When I told you Dr. Templett is not, on the evidence we have, a likely suspect you regretted that you had shown your hand. I think I know a frightened woman when I see one, and yesterday you were very frightened, Mrs. Ross."

She had let her cigarette burn down to her fingers. Her hand jerked and she dropped the butt on the floor. He picked it up and threw it in the fire.

"You're wrong," she said. "I did it for *him*."

Alleyn made no answer.

She said, "I thought she'd written it. The murdered woman. And I thought old Prentice was going to play."

"Dr. Templett didn't tell you on Saturday morning that it would be a physical impossibility for Miss Prentice to play?"

"We didn't discuss it. Billy didn't do it and neither did I. We didn't get to the place till nearly eight o'clock."

"You arrived soon after 7.30," Alleyn corrected her.

"Well, anyway, it was too late to do anything to the piano. The hall was packed. We were never alone."

"Mrs. Ross, when I asked you yesterday about the episode of the window, why did you not tell me you saw someone dodge down behind the sill?"

She seemed startled but not particularly alarmed at this. She looked at him, as he thought, speculatingly, as though she deliberately weighed his question and pondered the answer. At last she said:

"I suppose Billy told you that. It was only an impression, through the thick glass. The window was only open about two inches."

"I suggest that you were alarmed at the idea of an eavesdropper. I suggest that you noticed this shadow at the window only after you had been for some little time on the stage with Dr. Templett, and that enough had taken place in that time for you to be seriously compromised. I suggest that you told Dr. Templett to shut the window and that you lowered the curtain to insure privacy."

She tilted her head to one side and looked at him under her lashes.

"You really ought to join the Women's Circle. They'd adore that story at a tea-party."

"I shall work," said Alleyn, "on the theory that you said nothing more to Dr. Templett of this shadowy impression, as you did not wish to alarm him, but that it was not too shadowy or too fleeting for you to recognize the watcher at the window."

That shot did go home. Her whole face seemed to sharpen and she made a quick involuntary movement of her hands. She waited for a moment, and he knew that she was mustering her nerves. Then in one swift movement she was on her feet, close to him, her hands on his coat.

"You don't believe I'd do anything like that, do you? You're not such a fool. I don't even understand how it worked, and I've never been able to tie a knot in my life. Mr. Alleyn? Please?"

"If you are innocent you're in no danger."

"Do you promise that?"

"Certainly."

Before he could move she dropped her head against him and clung to his coat. She murmured broken phrases. Her hair was scented. He felt her uneven breathing.

"No, no," he said, "this won't do."

"I'm sorry—you've frightened me. Don't be nervous. I'm not trying to seduce you. I'm only rather shaken. I'll be all right in a moment."

"You're all right now," said Alleyn. He took her wrists and held her away from him. "That's better."

She stood before him with her head bent down. She achieved a look of helpless captivity. Her whole posture seemed to proclaim her subjection. When she raised her face it wore a gamine grin.

"You're either made of dough," she said, "or else you're afraid I'll compromise you. Poor Mr. Alleyn."

"You would have been wiser to call on Mr. Jernigham," said Alleyn. "He's Acting Chief Constable, you know."

### III

When she had been gone some minutes, Nigel looked cautiously into the back parlor.

"Hell knows no fury," he said.

"An intensely embarrassing lady," said Alleyn. "Did you get a shot of her?"

"Yes. Ought to be all right. I got her as she came in."

"Let me have the film or plate, or whatever it is."

"Do explain all this, Alleyn."

"It's as plain as daylight. She's got a genius for self-preservation. When I showed her the anonymous letter she was hell-bent on keeping out of suspicion, and on the spur of the moment denied all knowledge of it. She'd do her best for Templett up to a point, but a charge of homicide is definitely beyond that point. Yesterday she let him down with a thud. Now she's regretting it. I think she's probably as much in love with him as she could be with anybody. She's read a popular book on criminal investigation. She remembered that she'd handled the letter and realized we'd find her prints. So she hatched up this story. Now she knows we're not after Templett she'll try to get him back. But she's a sensible woman, and she wouldn't hang for him."

"I wonder if he'll believe her," said Nigel.

"Probably," said Alleyn. "If she gets a chance to see him alone."

Fox came in.

"I've seen Mrs. Ross's maid, sir. There's nothing much, except that Mrs. Ross did go out on Friday night. It was the maid's night off, but her boy had a cold and it was raining, so she stayed in. She only mentioned this to Mrs. Ross this morning."

"And Mrs. Ross mentioned it to me in case the maid got in first."

"Is that a fact, sir?"

"It is, Brer Fox. You shall hear of our interview."

Fox listened solemnly to the account of the interview.

"Well," he said, "she's come off worst in that bout, sir. What'll she do now?"

"I think she'd like to have a shot at old Jernigham. She's frightened and rattled. A shrewd woman, but not really clever."

"Does she think you suspect her, Mr. Alleyn?"

"She's afraid I might."

"*Do* you suspect her?" asked Nigel.

"Of all sorts of things," said Alleyn lightly. He sniffed at his coat. "Blast the woman. I stink of Chanel No. 5."

Nigel burst out laughing.

"Don't you think she's attractive?" he said. "I do."

"Fortunately I don't. I can see she might be; but she gives me house-maid's creeps. What do you think, Fox?"

"Well, sir, under more favorable conditions I dare say she'd be quite an experience in a way. There's something about her."

"You licentious old article."

"She's not very comfortable, if you know what I mean. More on the frisky side. I'd say she's one of these society ladies who, if they were born in a lower walk of life, would set up for themselves in a rather ex-clusive way, but well within the meaning of the act."

"Yes, Fox."

"What do we do now, Mr. Alleyn?"

"We lunch. After lunch we have a word together. And tonight I think we play a forcing hand, Fox. We've got about as much informa-tion as we'll ever screw out of them by separate interviews. Let's see how we get on with a mixed bunch. There's a fast train from Great Chipping in an hour. I think I'll catch it. Will you see the telephone people? Have one more stab at the villagers for Saturday afternoon. The person who stood at the box and peeped through the window. Ask if any one saw anybody about the place. You won't get anything, but we've got to try. Arrange the meeting with Jernigham senior. I'd better see him myself before hand. There are one or two things—— Go care-fully with him, Fox. And telephone me at the Yard before half-past five."

"I'll come up with you, if I may," said Nigel.

"Do. There's a good train that gets to Great Chipping at 8.15. I'll re-turn by that, and send a car ahead with two people and clanking chains, in case we feel like arresting somebody. All right?"

"Very good, sir," said Fox.

"Then we'd better lunch."

# CHAPTER XXIV

# The Peculiarity of Miss P.

## I

"It's no good taking it like this, Eleanor," said the squire, laying down his napkin and glaring at his cousin. "How do you suppose we feel? You won't help matters by starving yourself."

"I'm sorry, Jocelyn, but I cannot eat."

"You can't go on like this, my dear girl. You'll get ill."

"Would that matter very much?"

"Don't be an ass, Eleanor. Henry, give her some apple tart."

"No, thank you, Henry."

"What you want, Cousin Eleanor," said Henry from the side table, "is a good swinging whisky."

"Please, dear. I'm sorry if I'm irritating you both. It would be better if I didn't come down to lunch."

"Good Gad, woman," shouted the squire. "Don't talk such piffling drivel. We simply don't want you to kill yourself."

"It's a pity," said Miss Prentice stonily, "that I wasn't killed. I realize that. It would have been a blessed release. They say poor Idris didn't feel anything. It's the living who suffer."

"Cousin Eleanor," said Henry, returning with a loaded plate, "have you ever read *Our Mutual Friend?*"

"No, Henry."

"Because you're giving a perfectly brilliant impersonation of Mrs. R. W."

"Was she very irritating?"

"Very."

"That'll do, Henry," said the squire. He darted an uncomfortable glance at Miss Prentice, who sat upright in her chair with her head bowed. At intervals she drew in her breath sharply and closed her eyes.

"Is your finger hurting you?" demanded Jocelyn after a particularly noticeable hiss from the sufferer. She opened her eyes and smiled palely.

"A little."

"You'd better let Templett see it again."

"I'm not very likely to do that, Jocelyn."

"Why not?" asked Henry. "Do you think he's the murderer?"

"Oh, Henry, Henry," said Miss Prentice. "Some day you'll be sorry you have grieved me so much."

"Upon my word," said Henry, "I can't for the life of me see why that should grieve you. One of us is a murderer. I only asked if you thought it might be Templett."

"You are fortunate to be able to speak so lightly of this terrible, terrible tragedy."

"We're as much worried as you are," protested Jocelyn with an appealing glance at his son. "Aren't we, boy?"

"Of course we are," said Henry cheerfully.

"As a matter of fact, I've asked Copeland to come up here and talk the whole thing over."

Miss Prentice clasped her hands and gave a little cry. A dull flush stained her cheeks and her eyes brightened.

"Is he coming? How wise of you, Jocelyn! He is so wonderful. He will help us all. It will all come out right. It will come out quite, quite all right."

She laughed hysterically and clapped her hands.

"When is he coming?"

Jocelyn looked at her with positive terror.

"This evening," he said. "Eleanor, you're not well."

"And is dear Dinah coming, too?" asked Miss Prentice shrilly.

"Hullo!" said Henry. "Here's a change." And he stared fixedly at his cousin.

"Henry," said Miss Prentice very rapidly. "Shall we forget our little differences? I have your happiness so much at heart, dear. If you had been more candid and straightforward with me——"

"Why should I?" asked Henry.

"—I think you would have found me quite understanding. Shall we let bygones be bygones? You see, dear, you have no mother to——"

"Will you excuse me, sir?" said Henry. "I feel slightly sick." And he walked out of the room.

"I thought," said Miss Prentice, "that I had been deeply enough injured already. So deeply, deeply injured. I am sorry I am rather excited, Jocelyn dear, but, you see, when someone is waiting down at St. Giles to shoot you—— *Jocelyn, is that somebody coming?*"

"What the devil's the matter, Eleanor?"

"It's that woman! It was her car! I saw it through the window. Jocelyn, I won't meet that woman. She'll do me an injury. She's wicked, wicked, wicked. A woman of Babylon. They're all the same. All bad, horrible creatures."

"Eleanor, be quiet."

"You're a man. You don't understand. *I will not meet her.*"

Taylor came in.

"Mrs. Ross to see you, sir."

"Damnation!" said the squire. "All right. Take her to the study."

## II

The squire was worried about Eleanor. She was really very odd indeed, far odder than even these uncomfortable circumstances warranted. There was no knowing what she'd say next. If he didn't look out, she'd land him in a pretty tight corner with one of these extraordinary statements of hers. She'd got such a damned knowing look in her eye. When she thought he wasn't noticing her, she'd sit in a corner watching him, with an expression which could only be described as a leer. If she was going mad! Well, there was one thing: mad people couldn't give evidence. Perhaps the best thing would be to ask an alienist down for the weekend. He hoped to heaven she wouldn't take it into her head to come raging into the study and go for poor little Mrs. Ross. His thoughts raced through his head as he crossed the hall, passed through the library and entered his study. Anyway, it'd be a relief to talk to an attractive woman.

She did look very attractive. Pale-ish, but that was understandable. She wore her clothes like a Frenchwoman. He'd always liked black. Damn' good figure and legs. He took the little hand in its delicate glove and held it tightly.

"Well," he said, "this *is* nice of you."

"I simply had to see you. You'll think me a most frightful bore, coming at this time."

"Now you knew that wasn't true before you said it."

The little hand started in his.

"Have I hurt you?" asked the squire. "I am a clumsy brute."

"No. Not really. Only you are rather strong, aren't you? It's just my ring."

"I insist on investigating."

He peeled back the soft glove and drew it down.

"Look at that! A red mark on the inside of your finger. Now, what can be done about that?"

A subdued laugh. He separated the white fingers and kissed them.

"Ha-ha, my boy!" thought the squire, and led her to a chair.

"You've done me good already," he said. "Do you realize that, madam?"

"Have I?"

"Don't you think you're rather an attractive little thing?"

"What am I supposed to say to that?"

"You know it damned well, so you needn't say anything. Ha, ha, ha!"

"Well, I *have* heard something like it before."

"How often?" purred the squire.

"Never you mind."

"Why are you so attractive?"

"Just made that way."

"Little devil," he said and kissed the hand again. He felt quite excited. Everything was going like clockwork.

"Oh, dear," whispered Mrs. Ross. "You're going to be simply livid with me."

"Simply furious?" he asked tenderly.

"Yes. Honestly. I don't want to tell you; but I must!"

"Don't look at me like that or I shall have to kiss you."

"No, please. You must listen. Please."

"If I listen I expect to be rewarded."

"We'll see about that," she said.

"Promise?"

"Promise."

"I'm listening," said the squire, rather feverishly.

"It's about this awful business. I want to tell you first of all, very, very sincerely that you've nothing to fear from me."

"Nothing——?"

He still held her hand, but his fingers relaxed.

"No," she said, "nothing. If you will just trust me——"

Her voice went on and on. Jocelyn heard her to the end, but when it was over he did not remind her of her promise.

## III

When Alleyn left the assistant commissioner and returned to his own office, he found Bailey there.

"Well, Bailey?"

"Well, sir, Thompson's developed Mr. Bathgate's film. He's got a couple of shots of the lady."

He laid the still wet prints on the desk.

There was Mrs. Ross in profile on the front step of the Jernigham Arms, and there she was again full face as she came up the path. Nigel must have taken his snapshots through the open window. Evidently she had not seen him. The pointed chin was set a little to one side, the under lip projected very slightly, and the thin mouth was drawn down at the corners. They were not flattering photographs.

"Any luck?" asked Alleyn.

With his normal air of mulish disapproval Bailey laid a card beside the prints. On it was mounted a double photograph. Sharp profile, thin mouth, pointed chin; and the front view showed the colorless hair, drawn back in two immaculate shining wings, from the rather high forehead.

Alleyn muttered: "Sarah Rosen. Age 33. Height 5 ft. 5¼ ins. Eyes, light blue. Hair, pale blonde. Vey well dressed, cultured speech, usually poses as widow. Detained with Claude Smith on blackmailing charge, 1931. Subsequently released—insufficient evidence. Claude got ten years, didn't he?"

"That's right, sir. They stayed at the Ritz as brother and sister."

"I remember. What about the prints?"

"They're good enough."

"Blackmail," said Alleyn thoughtfully.

"I've looked up the case. She was in the game all right, but they hadn't a thing on her. She seems to have talked her way out."

"She would. Thank you, Bailey. I wish I'd known this a little earlier. Oh, well, no matter, it fits in very prettily."

"Anything else, Mr. Alleyn?"

"I'm going to my flat for half an hour. If Fox rings up before I'm back, tell him I'm there. The car ought to leave now. I'll fix that up. We'd better take a wardress, I suppose. All right, Bailey. Thank you."

## IV

Henry wondered what the devil Mrs. Ross had to say to his father. He had watched with extreme distaste their growing intimacy. "How sharper than a serpent's tooth it is," he thought, "to have a prancing parent." When Jocelyn spoke to Mrs. Ross his habit of loud inexplicable laughter, his manner of leaning backwards, of making a series of mysterious little bows, the curious gesture he employed, the inclination his eyes exhibited towards protuberance, and the naked imbecility of his conversation, all vexed and embarrassed his son to an almost insupportable degree. If Jocelyn should marry her! Henry had no particular objection to Mrs. Ross, but the thought of her as a stepmother struck dismay to his heart. His affection for his father was not weakened by Jocelyn's absurdities. He loved him deeply, he realized, and now the thought that his father might be making a fool of himself in there with that woman was more than he could endure. Miss Prentice had, no doubt, gone to her room; Dinah was out; there was nothing to do.

He wandered restlessly into the library, half-hoping that the door into the study would be open. It was closed. He could hear the murmur of a woman's voice. On and on. What the hell could she have to say? Then a baritone interjection in which he read urgency and vehemence. Then a long pause.

"My God!" thought Henry. "If he has proposed to her!"

He whistled raucously, took an encyclopedia from the shelves, banged the glass door and slammed the book down on the table.

He heard his father exclaim. A chair castor squeaked and the voices grew more distant. They had moved to the far end of the room.

Henry flung himself into an armchair, and once again the conundrum of the murder beset him. Who *did* the police believe had tried to murder Eleanor Prentice? Which would they say had the greatest reason for wishing Eleanor dead? With the thud of fear that came upon him whenever he thought of this, he supposed that he himself had most reason for wishing Eleanor out of the way. Was it possible that Alleyn suspected him? Whom *did* Alleyn suspect? Not Dinah, surely, not the rector, not his own father. Templett, then? Or—yes—Mrs. Ross? But, Alleyn would surely reason, if Templett was the murderer, it was a successful murder, since it was Templett who insisted that Eleanor shouldn't play the piano. Alleyn would wonder if Templett had told Mrs. Ross he would not allow Eleanor to play. Did Dinah's tirade against Mrs. Ross mean that Dinah suspected her? Had the police any idea who could have gone to the piano after there were people in the hall, and yet not be seen? Already the story of Gladys Wright had reached Pen Cuckoo. And as a final conjecture, perhaps they would ask themselves if Eleanor Prentice in some way had faked her finger and set the trap for her bosom enemy. Or might they agree with the rector and call it a case of attempted murder and suicide?

He leaped to his feet. There was no longer a sound of voices in the study. They must have gone out by the french window.

Henry opened the door and walked in. No. They were still there. Mrs. Ross sat in the window with her back to the light. Jocelyn Jernigham faced the door. When Henry saw Jocelyn he cried out: "Father, what's the matter?"

Jocelyn said, "Nothing's the matter."

Mrs. Ross said, "Hullo! Good afternoon."

"Good afternoon," said Henry. "Father, are you ill?"

"No. Don't come bursting into the room asking people if they're ill. It's ridiculous."

"But your face! It's absolutely ashen."

"I've got indigestion."

"I don't believe it."

"I thought he looked pale," said Mrs. Ross solicitously.

"He's absolutely green."

"I'm nothing of the sort," said Jocelyn angrily. "Mrs. Ross and I are talking privately, Henry."

"I'm sorry," said Henry stubbornly, "but I know there's something wrong here. What is it?"

"There's nothing wrong, my dear boy," she said lightly.

He stared at her.

"I'm afraid I still think there is."

"Well, I very much hope you won't still think there is when we tell you all about it. At the moment I'm afraid it's a secret." She looked up at Jocelyn. "Isn't it?"

"Yes. Of course. Go away, boy, you're making a fool of yourself."

"Are you sure," Henry asked slowly, "that nobody is making a fool of you?"

Taylor came in. He looked slightly disgruntled.

"Inspector Fox to see you, sir. I told him——"

"Good afternoon, sir," said a rumbling voice, and the bulk of Inspector Fox filled the doorway.

## V

Henry saw the squire look quickly from the open window to Mrs. Ross. Taylor stood aside and Fox walked in.

"I hope you'll excuse me coming straight in like this, sir," said Fox. "Chief Inspector Alleyn asked me to call. I took the liberty of following your butler. Perhaps I ought to have waited."

"No, no," said Jocelyn. "Sit down, er——"

"Fox, sir. Thank you very much, sir."

Fox placed his bowler on a nearby table. He turned to Henry.

"Good afternoon, sir. We met last night, didn't we?"

"This is Inspector Fox, Mrs. Ross," said Henry.

"Good afternoon, madam," said Fox tranquilly. Then he sat down. As Alleyn once remarked to Nigel, there was a certain dignity about Fox.

Mrs. Ross smiled charmingly.

"I must take myself off," she said, "and not interrupt Mr. Fox. Don't move, anybody, please."

"If it's not troubling you too much, Mrs. Ross," said Fox, "I'd be obliged if you'd wait for a moment. There are one or two little routine questions for general inquiry, and it will save me taking up your time later on."

"But I'm longing to stay, Mr. Fox."

"Thank you, madam."

Fox took out his spectacles and placed them on his nose. Then he drew his note-book from an inside pocket, opened it and stared at it.

"Yes," he said. "Now, the first item's a small matter, really. Did anybody present find the onion in the teapot?"

"*What!*" Henry ejaculated.

Fox fixed his eyes on him.

"The onion in the teapot, sir."

"Which onion in what teapot?" demanded Jocelyn.

Fox turned to him.

"Young Biggins, sir, has admitted that he put a Spanish onion in the teapot used on the stage. We'd like to know who removed it."

Mrs. Ross burst out laughing.

"I'm so sorry," she said, "but it *is* rather funny."

"It sounds rather a ridiculous sort of thing, doesn't it, madam?" agreed Fox gravely. "Do you know anything about it?"

"I'm afraid not. I think Mr. Alleyn has already accused me of an onion."

"Did you happen to hear anything of it, sir?"

"Good Lord, no," said Jocelyn.

"And you, Mr. Henry?"

"Not I," said Henry.

"The next matter," said Fox, making a note, "is the window. I understand you found it open on Saturday afternoon, Mrs. Ross."

"Yes. We shut it."

"Yes. You'd already shut it once, hadn't you? At midday?"

"Yes, I had."

"Who opened it?" inquired Fox, and he looked first at Jocelyn and then at Henry. They both shook their heads.

"I should think it was probably Miss Prentice. My cousin," said Henry. "She has a deep-rooted mania——" He checked himself. "She's a fresh-air fiend of the worst variety, and continually complained that the hall was stuffy."

"I wonder if I might ask Miss Prentice?" said Fox. "Is she at home, sir?"

The squire looked extremely uncomfortable.

"I think she's—ah—she's—ah—in. Yes."

"Do you want me any longer, Mr. Fox?" asked Mrs. Ross.

"I think that will be all for the present, thank you, madam. The chief inspector would be much obliged if you could come down to the hall at about 9.15 this evening."

"Oh? Yes, very well."

"Thank you very much, madam."

"I'll see you out," said the squire hurriedly.

They went out by the french window.

Henry offered Fox a cigarette.

"No. Thank you very much, all the same, sir."

"Mr. Fox," said Henry. "What do you think of the rector's theory? I mean, the idea that Miss Campanula set the trap for my cousin, and that something happened to make her so miserable that when she was asked to play she thought: 'Oh, well, this settles it. Here goes!'"

"Would you have said the deceased lady seemed very unhappy, sir?"

"Well, you know, I didn't notice her very much. But I've been thinking it over, and—yes—she was rather odd. She was damned odd. For one thing, she's evidently had a colossal row with my cousin. Or rather my cousin seemed friendly enough, but Miss C. wouldn't say a word to her. She was a cranky old cup of tea, you know, and we none of us took much notice. Know what I mean?"

"I understand, sir," said Fox looking hard at Henry. "Perhaps if I could just have a word with Miss Prentice."

"Oh, Lord!" said Henry ruefully. "Look here, Mr. Fox, you'll find her pretty rum. You'll think we specialize in eccentric spinsters in this part of the world, but I promise you I think the shock of this business has pushed her off at the deep end. She seems to think the murderer's made a mess of the first attempt, and sooner or later will have another go at her."

"That's not unnatural, is it, sir? Perhaps the lady would feel more comfortable with police protection."

"I pity the protector," said Henry. "Well, I suppose I'd better see if she'll come down."

"If you wouldn't mind that, sir," said Fox comfortably.

In some trepidation, Henry mounted the stairs and tapped on Miss Prentice's door. There was no answer. He tapped again. The door opened suddenly and Miss Prentice was revealed with her fingers to her lips, like some mysterious bucktoothed sibyl.

"What's happened!" she whispered.

"Nothing's happened, Cousin Eleanor. It's simply one of the men from Scotland Yard with a rather childish question to ask you."

"Is that woman there? I won't meet that woman."

"Mrs. Ross has gone."

"Henry, is that true?"

"Of course it's true."

"Now I've made you angry again. You're very unkind to me, Henry."

"My dear Cousin Eleanor!"

Her hand moved restlessly across the bosom of her dress.

"Yes, you are. So unkind. And I'm so fond of you. It's only for your own good. You're young and strong and handsome. All the Jernighams are very strong and beautiful. Don't listen to women like that, Henry. Don't listen to any woman. They'll do you harm. Except dear Dinah."

"Will you come down and speak to Inspector Fox?"

"It's not a trap to make me meet that woman? Why is it a different man? Fox? Where's the other man? He was a gentleman. So tall! Taller than Father Copeland."

He saw with astonishment that the movement of her hand traced a definite pattern on her bosom. She was crossing herself.

"This man is perfectly harmless," said Henry. "Do come."

"Very well. My head's splitting. I suppose I must come."

"That's better," said Henry. He added awkwardly: "Cousin Eleanor, your dress is undone."

"Oh!" She blushed crimson and, to his horror, laughed shrilly and turned aside her head. Her fingers fumbled with the fastening of her dress. Then she shrank past him and, with a kind of coquettishness in her gait, hurried downstairs.

Henry followed with a sinking heart and escorted her to the study. His father had returned and stood before the fire. Jocelyn glared uncomfortably at Miss Prentice.

"Hullo, Eleanor, here you are. This is Inspector Fox."

Miss Prentice offered her hand and, as soon as Fox touched it, snatched it away. Her eyes were downcast, her hands pleated a fold in her dress. Fox looked calmly at her.

"I'm sorry to trouble you, Miss Prentice. I only wanted to ask if you opened one of the hall windows as you left at noon on Saturday."

"Oh, yes," she whispered. "Was that the unpardonable sin?"

"I beg your pradon, miss?"

"Did I let it in?"

"Let what in, Miss Prentice?"

"You know. But I only opened it the least little bit. A tiny crack. Of course it can make itself very small, can't it?"

Fox adjusted his spectacles and made a note.

"You did open the window?" he said.

"You shouldn't keep on asking. You know I did."

"Miss Prentice, did you find anything in the teapot you were to use on the stage?"

"Is that where it hid?"

"Where what hid?"

"The unpardonable sin. You know. The thing she did!"

"You're talking nonsense, Eleanor," said Jocelyn. He got behind her and made violent grimaces at Fox.

"I'm sorry if I irritate you, Jocelyn."

"You don't know anything about an onion that a small boy put in the teapot, Miss Prentice?"

She opened her eyes very wide and shaped her mouth like an O. Then she slowly shook her head. Once started, she seemed unable to leave off shaking her head, but went on and on until the movement lost all meaning.

"Well," said Fox, "I think that's all I need trouble you about, thank you, Miss Prentice."

"Henry," said Jocelyn. "See your cousin upstairs."

She went out without another word. Henry hurried after her. Jocelyn turned to Fox.

"See how it is!" he said. "The shock sent her out of her mind. There are no two ways about it. See for yourself. Have to get a specialist. Better not believe a word she says."

"She's never been like this before, sir?"

"Good God, no."

"That's very distressing, sir, isn't it? The chief inspector asked me to speak to you, sir, about this evening. He thinks it would be a good idea to see, at the same time, all the people who were in the play, and he wonders if you would be good enough to send your party down to the hall."

"I must say I don't quite see—— As a matter of fact, I've asked the Copelands for dinner to talk things over."

"That will fit in very nicely, then, won't it, sir? You can come on to the hall."

"Yes, but I don't see what good it'll do."

"The chief inspector will explain when he comes, sir. He asked me to say he'd be very much obliged if you would give the lead in this little matter. In view of your position in the county, sir, he thought you would prefer to come before the others. You've two cars, haven't you, sir?"

"I suppose I'd better." Jocelyn stared very hard at a portrait of his actress-ancestress and said, "Have you got any idea who it is?"

"I couldn't say what the chief intends just at the moment, sir," answered Fox so blandly that the evasion sounded exactly like a direct answer. "No doubt he will report to you himself, sir. Would nine o'clock suit you at the hall, Mr. Jernigham?"

"What? Oh, yes. Yes, certainly."

"I'm much obliged, sir. I'll say good afternoon."

"Good afternoon," said Jocelyn restlessly.

## VI

"This is Miss Bruce," said the supervisor. "She was on duty on Friday night, but I doubt if she'll be able to help you."

Fox looked placidly at Miss Bruce and noted that she seemed a bright young person.

He said, "Well, Miss Bruce, we'll be very pleased if you can put us right in this little matter. I understand you were on duty as an operator at ten o'clock on Friday evening."

"Yes, that's right."

"Yes. Now the call we're interested in came through somewhere round about 10.30. It was to the rectory, Winton St. Giles. It's a party line with the old manual telephones and a long extension. Not many of those left, are there?"

"They'll be gone by this time next year," said the supervisor.

"Is that a fact?" said Fox comfortably. "Well, well. Now, Miss Bruce, can you help us?"

"I don't remember any calls on the rectory phone on Friday night," said Miss Bruce. "Chipping 10, the number is. I'm in the Y.P.F.C., so I know. We always have to ring a long time there, because the old housemaid Mary's a bit deaf, and Miss Dinah's room's away upstairs, and the rector never answers until he's fetched. It's a line that's used a lot, of course."

"It would be."

"Yes. Friday was Reading Circle night, and they're usually over at the hall, so everybody knows not to ring up on Friday, see, because they won't be in. Actually, last Friday it was at the rectory because of the play; but people wouldn't know that, see. They'd think: 'Well, Friday. It's no use ringing on Friday.'"

"So you're sure nobody rang?"

"Yes. Yes, I'm sure of it. I'd swear to it if that's what's wanted."

"If the extension was used you wouldn't know, I suppose?"

"I wouldn't know anything about that."

"No," agreed Fox. "Well, thank you very much, miss. I'm greatly obliged. Good afternoon."

"Pleasure, I'm sure," said Miss Bruce. "Ta-ta."

# CHAPTER XXV

# Final Vignettes

## I

THE EXPRESS FROM LONDON roared into Great Chipping station. Alleyn, who had been reading the future in the murky window pane, rose hurriedly and put on his overcoat.

Fox was on the platform.

"Well, Brer Fox?" said Alleyn when they reached the Biggins's Ford.

"Well, sir, the Yard car's arrived. They're to drive up quietly after we've all assembled. Alison can come into the supper-room with his two men and I'll wait inside the front door."

"That'll be all right. I'd better give you all a cue to stand by, as Miss Copeland would say. Let's see. I'll ask Miss Prentice if she's feeling the draught. We'll sit on the stage round that table so there'll probably be a hell of a draught. How did you get on at Pen Cuckoo?"

"She was there."

"Not?"

"Ross or Rosen. You had a lucky strike there, Mr. Alleyn. Fancy her being Claude Smith's girl. We were on the Quantock case at that time, weren't we?"

"We weren't at the Yard, anyway. I've never seen her before this."

"More've I. Well, she was there. Something up—between him and her—I should say."

"Between who and her, Mr. Fox?" asked Nigel. "You're very dark and cryptic this evening."

"Between Jernigham senior and Mrs. Ross, Mr. Bathgate. When I arrived he was looking peculiar, and Mr. Henry seemed as if he thought something was up. She was cool enough, but I'd say the other lady was a case for expert opinion."

"Miss Prentice?" murmured Alleyn.

"That's right, sir. Young Jernigham went and fetched her. She owned up to opening the window as sweet as you please, and then began to talk a lot of nonsense about letting in the unpardonable sin. I took it all down, but you'd be surprised how silly it was."

"The unpardonable sin? Which one's that, I wonder?"

"Nobody owned to the onion," said Fox gloomily.

"I think onions, in any form, the unpardonable sin," said Nigel.

"I reckon you're right about the onion, Mr. Alleyn."

"I think so, Fox. After all, on finding onions in teapots, why not exclaim on the circumstance? Why not say, 'Georgie Biggins for a certainty,' and raise hell?"

"That's right, sir. Well, from the way they shaped up to the question, you'd say none of them had ever smelled one. Mr. Jernigham's talking about getting a doctor in. Do you know what? I think he's sweet on her. On Rosen, I mean."

Fox changed into second gear for Chipping Rise and said, "The telephone's right. I told you that when I rang up, didn't I?"

"Yes."

"And I've seen the four girls who helped Gladys Wright. Three of them are ready to swear on oath that nobody came down into the hall from the stage, and the fourth is certain nobody did, but wouldn't swear, as she went into the porch for a minute. I've rechecked the movements of all the people behind the scenes. Mr. Copeland sat facing the footlights from the time he got there until he went in to Mr. Jernigham's room, when they tried to telephone to Mrs. Ross. He went back to the stage and didn't leave it again until they all crowded round Miss Prentice."

"I think it's good enough, Fox."

"I think so, too. This Chief Constable business is awkward, isn't it, Mr. Alleyn?"

"It is, indeed. I know of no precedent. Oh, well, we'll see what the preliminary interview does. You arranged that?"

"Yes, sir, that's all right. Did you dine on the train?"

"Yes, Fox. The usual dead fish and so on. Mr. Bathgate wants to know who did the murder."

"I do know," said Nigel in the back seat; "but I won't let on."

"D'you want to stop at the pub, Mr. Alleyn?"

"No. Let's get it over, Brer Fox, let's get it over."

## II

At Henry's suggestion, they had invited Dinah and the rector to dinner.

"You may as well take Dinah and me for granted, father. We're not going to give each other up, you know."

"I still think—however!"

And Henry, watching his father, knew that the afternoon visit of Miss Campanula's lawyers to the rectory was Vale property. Jocelyn boggled and uttered inarticulate noises; but already, Henry thought, his father was putting a new roof on Winton. It would be better not to speak, thought Henry, of his telephone conversation with Dinah after Fox had gone. For Dinah had told Henry that her father felt he could not accept the fortune left him by Idris Campanula.

Henry said, "I don't suppose you suspect either the rector or Dinah, do you, even though they do get the money? They don't suspect us. Cousin Eleanor, who suspects God knows who, is in her room and won't appear until dinner."

"She ought not to be alone."

"One of the maids is with her. She's quietened down again and is quite normally long-suffering and martyred."

Jocelyn looked nervously at Henry.

"What do you think's the matter with her?"

"Gone ravers," said Henry cheerfully.

The Copelands accepted the invitation to dinner. Sherry was served in the library, but Henry managed to get Dinah into the study, where he had made up a large fire and had secretly placed an enormous bowl of yellow chrysanthemums.

"Darling Dinah," said Henry, "there are at least fifty things of the most terrific importance to say to you, and when I look at you I can't think of one of them. May I kiss you? We're almost publicly betrothed, aren't we?"

"Are we? You've never really asked for my hand."

"Miss Copeland—may I call you Dinah?—be mine. Be mine."

"I may not deny, Mr. Jernigham, that my sensibilities, nay, since I will not dissemble, my affections are touched by this declaration. I cannot hear you unmoved."

Henry kissed her and muttered in her ear that he loved her very much.

"All the same," said Dinah, "I do wonder why Mr. Alleyn wants us to go down to the hall tonight. I don't want to go. The place gives me the absolute horrors."

"Me, too. Dinah, I made such a fool of myself last night."

He told her how he had heard the three chords of the "Prelude" as he came through the storm.

"I would have died of it," said Dinah. "Henry, *why* do they want us tonight? Are they—are they going to arrest someone?"

"Who?" asked Henry.

They stared solemnly at each other.

"Who indeed," said Dinah.

### III

"I tell you, Copeland, I'm pretty hard hit," said the squire, giving himself a whisky-and-soda. "It's so beastly uncomfortable. Have some more sherry? Nonsense, it'll do you good. You're not looking particularly happy yourself."

"It's the most dreadful thing that has ever happened to any of us," said the rector. "How's Miss Prentice?"

"That's partly what I want to talk about. I ought to warn you——"

The rector listened with a steadily blanching face to Jocelyn's account of Miss Prentice.

"Poor soul," he said, "poor soul."

"Yes, I know, but it's damned inconvenient. I'm sorry, rector, but it—well, it's—it's—— Oh, God!"

"Would you like to tell me?" asked the rector, and if he spoke at all wearily, Jocelyn did not notice it.

"No," said Jocelyn, "no. There's nothing to tell. I'm simply rather worried. What d'you suppose is the meaning of this meeting tonight?"

The rector looked curiously at him.

"I thought you probably knew. Your position, I mean——"

"As the weapon happens to be my property, I felt it better to keep right out of the picture. Technically, I'm a suspect."

"Yes. Dear me, yes." The rector sipped his sherry. "So are we all, of course."

"I wonder," said the squire, "what Alleyn is up to."

"You don't think he's going to—to arrest anybody?"

They stared at each other.

"Dinner is served, sir," said Taylor.

## IV

"Good night, dear," said Dr. Templett to his wife. "I expect you'll be asleep when I get home. I'm glad it's been a good day."

"It's been a splendid day," said that steadfastly gallant voice. "Good night, my dear."

Templett shut the door softly. The telephone pealed in his dressing-room at the end of the landing. The hospital was to ring before eight. He went to his dressing-room and lifted the receiver.

"Hullo?"

"Is that you, Billy?"

He sat frozen, the receiver still at his ear.

"Billy? Hullo? Hullo?"

"Well?" said Dr. Templett.

"Then you are alive," said the voice.

"I haven't been arrested, after all."

"Nor, strangely enough, have I, in spite of the fact that I've been to Alleyn and taken the whole responsibility of the letter——"

"Selia! Not on the telephone!"

"I don't much care what happens to me now. You've let me down. Nothing else matters."

"What do you mean? No, don't tell me! It's not true."

"Very well. Good-by, Billy."

"Wait! Have you been told to parade at the hall this evening?"

"Yes. Have you?"

"Yes." Dr. Templett brushed his hand across his eyes. He muttered hurriedly: "I'll call for you."

"What?"

"If you like I'll drive you there."

"I've got my own car. You needn't bother."

"I'll pick you up at nine."

"And drop me a few minutes later, I suppose?"

"That's not quite fair. What do you suppose I thought when——?"

"You obviously don't trust me. That's all."

"My God——!" began Dr. Templett. The voice cut in coolly:

"All right. At nine. Why do you suppose he wants us in the hall? Is he going to arrest someone?"

"I don't know. What do you think?"

"I don't know."

## V

The church clock struck nine as the police car drew up outside the hall. Alleyn and Fox got out, followed by Detective-Sergeant Alison and two plain-clothes men. At the same moment, Nigel drove up in his own car with Sergeant Roper. They all went in through the back door. Alleyn switched on the stage lights and the supper-room light.

"You see the lie of the land, don't you," he said. "Two flights of steps from the supper-room to the stage. We'll have the curtain down, I think, Fox. You can stay on the stage. So can you, Bathgate, in the wings, and with not a word out of you. You know when to go down and what to do?"

"Yes," said Nigel nervously.

"Good. Alison, you'd better move to the front door, and you others can go into the dressing-rooms. They'll come straight through the supper-room and won't see you. Roper, you're to go outside and direct them to the back door. Then come in. But quietly, if you don't want me to tear your buttons off and half kill you. The rest of you can stay in the dressing-rooms until the company's complete. When it is complete, I'll slam both doors at the top of the steps. You can then come into the supper-room and sit on the steps. The piano's in position, isn't it, Fox? And the screens? Yes. All right, down with the curtain."

The curtain came down in three noisy rushes, releasing a cloud of dust.

With the front of the hall shut out, the stage presented a more authentic appearance. Dinah's box set, patched and contrived though it was, resembled any touring company's stock scenery, while Mrs. Ross's chairs and ornaments raised the interior to still greater distinction. The improvised lights shone bravely enough on chintz and china. The stage had taken on a sort of eerie half-life and an air of expectancy. On the round table Alleyn laid the anonymous letter, the "Prelude in C minor," the "Venetian Suite," the pieces of rubber in their box, the onion, the soap-box and the teapot. He then covered this curious collection with a cloth.

Fox and Alison brought extra chairs from the dressing-rooms and put one of the paraffin lamps on the stage.

"Eight chairs," counted Alleyn. "That's right. Are we ready? I think so."

"Nothing else, sir?"

"Nothing. Remember your cue. Leave on the supper-room lights. Here he comes, I think. Away you go."

Fox walked over to the prompt corner. Nigel went through the opposite door and sat out of sight in the shadow of the proscenium. Alison went down to the auditorium, the two plain-clothes men disappeared into the dressing-rooms, and Roper, breathing stertorously, made for the back door.

"Shock tactics," muttered Alleyn. "Damn, I hate 'em. So infernally unfair, and they look like pure exhibitionism on the part of the police. Oh, well, can't be helped."

"I don't hear a car," whispered Nigel.

"It's coming."

They all listened. The wind howled and the rain drummed on the shutters.

"I'll never think of this place," said Nigel, "without hearing that noise."

"It's worse than ever," said Fox.

"Here he is," said Alleyn.

And now they all heard the car draw up in the lane. A door slammed. Boots crunched up the gravel path. Roper's voice could be heard. The back door opened. Roper, suddenly transformed into a sort of major-domo, said loudly:

"Mr. Jernigham senior, sir."

And the squire walked in.

# CHAPTER XXVI

# Miss Prentice Feels the Draught

*I*

"—SO YOU SEE," SAID ALLEYN, "I was led to wonder if, to speak frankly, the object of her visit was blackmail."

The squire's face was drained of all its normal color, but now it flushed a painful crimson.

"I cannot believe it."

"In view of the record—"

The squire made a violent, clumsy gesture with his right hand. Standing in the center of the stage under those uncompromising lights, he looked at once frightened and defiant. Alleyn watched him for a moment and then he said:

"You see, I think I know what she had to say to you."

Jernigham's jaw dropped.

"I don't believe you," he said hoarsely.

"Then let me tell what I believe to be her hold on you."

Alleyn's voice went on and on, quietly, dispassionately. Jernigham listened with his gaze on the floor. Once he looked up as though he would interrupt, but he seemed to think better of this impulse and fell to biting his nails.

"I give you this opportunity," said Alleyn. "If you care to tell me now——"

"There is nothing to tell you. It's not true."

"Mrs. Ross did not come this afternoon with this story. She did not make these very definite terms with you?"

"I cannot discuss the matter."

"Even," said Alleyn, "in view of this record?"

"I admit nothing."

"Very well. I was afraid you would take this line."

"In my position——"

"It was because of your position I gave you this opportunity. I can do no more."

"I can't see why you want this general interview."

"Shock tactics, sir," said Alleyn.

"I—I don't approve."

"If you wish, sir, I can hand my report in and you may make a formal complaint at the Yard."

"No."

"It would make no difference," said Alleyn. "I think the others have arrived. This is your last word?"

"I have nothing to say."

"Very well, sir."

Roper tapped at one of the supper-room doors.

"Hullo!" shouted Alleyn.

"Here they be, sir, every living soul, and all come together."

"All right, Roper. Show them in."


## II


Miss Prentice came in first, followed by Dinah, the rector and Henry. Alleyn asked Miss Prentice to sit in the most comfortable chair, which he had placed on the prompt side of the table. When she dithered, he was so crisply polite that she was there before she realized it. She looked quickly towards the rector, who took the chair on her right. Dinah sat on her father's right with Henry beside her. The squire looked furtively at Alleyn.

"Will you sit down, sir?" invited Alleyn.

"What! Yes, yes," said the squire convulsively, and sat beside Henry.

Mrs. Ross came in. She was dressed in black and silver, a strangely exotic figure in those surroundings. She said: "Good evening," with her customary sidelong smile, bowed rather more pointedly to Alleyn, and sat beside the squire. Templett, seeming ill at ease and shamefaced, followed her.

Miss Prentice drew in her breath and began to whisper:

"No, no, no! Never at the same table. I can't——!"

Alleyn sat on her left in the one chair remaining vacant and said, "Miss Prentice—please!"

His voice had sufficient edge to silence Miss Prentice and call the others to a sort of guarded alertness.

His long hands lay clasped before him on the table. He leant forward and looked with deliberation round the circle of attentive faces.

He said, "Ladies and gentlemen, I shall not apologize for calling you together tonight. I am sure that most—not all, but most—of you are only too anxious that this affair should be settled, and I may tell you that we have now collected enough evidence to make an arrest. Each of you in turn has provided evidence; each of you has withheld evidence. From the information you have given, and from the significance of your several reticences, has emerged a pattern which, as we read it, has at its center a single person: the murderer of Miss Idris Campanula."

They sat as still as figures in a tableau, and the only sound, when Alleyn paused, was the sound of rain and the uneasy stirring of the wind outside.

"From the beginning, this strange affair has presented one particularly unusual problem: the problem of the murderer's intention. Was it Miss Idris Campanula for whom this trap was set, or was it Miss Eleanor Prentice? If it was indeed Idris Campanula, then the number of possible suspects was very small. If it was Miss Prentice, the field was a great deal wider. During most of yesterday and part of today my colleague, Inspector Fox, interviewed the people who have known and come into contact with both these ladies. He could find no motive for the murder of either of them, outside the circle of people we have found motive. Money, jealousy, love and fear are the themes most usually found behind homicide. All four appeared in this case if Miss Campanula was the intended victim: the last three, if the intended victim was Miss Prentice. The fact that on Friday evening at five o'clock Mr. Henry Jernigham showed the automatic to all of you, except his father, who is the owner, was another circumstance that suggested one of you as the guilty person."

Henry rested his head on his hand, driving his fingers through his hair. Templett cleared his throat.

"At the inquest this morning you all heard the story of the water-pistol. The booby-trap was ready at 2.30 on Friday. The water-pistol was no longer in position at noon on Saturday when Miss Prentice used the soft pedal. Yet some time between Friday at 2.30 and noon on Saturday, somebody sat at the piano and used the soft pedal and the booby-trap worked."

Alleyn lifted the cloth from the table. Miss Prentice gave a nervous yelp. He took up the "Venetian Suite" and pointed to the circular blister and discolored splashes on the back.

"Five hours after the catastrophe, this was still damp. So was the torn silk round the hole in the front of the piano. Miss Prentice has told us that her music was left on the piano earlier in the week. All Saturday morning the hall was occupied. It seems, therefore, that the water-pistol was removed before Saturday morning, and presumably by the guilty person, since an innocent person would not have kept silent about the booby-trap. On Friday afternoon and evening the hall was deserted. At this stage I may say that Mr. Jernigham and Dr. Templett both have alibis for Friday afternoon, when they hunted up till a short time before the rehearsal-for-words at Pen Cuckoo. Dr. Templett has an alibi for Friday and well into Saturday morning, during which time he was occupied with professional duties. It is hardly conceivable that he would enter the hall in the small hours of Saturday morning to play the piano. The helpers arrived soon after nine o'clock on Saturday, and by that time the pistol had been removed.

"Now for the automatic. If, as we suppose, the water-pistol was discovered on Friday, it is of course possible that the automatic was substituted before Saturday. This possibility we consider unlikely. It was known that the helpers would be in the hall all Saturday morning, and the murderer would have run the risk of discovery. It was only necessary for someone to disarrange the rotten silk in the front of the piano to reveal the nozzle of the Colt. True, this piece of music was on the rack; but it might have been removed. Somebody might have dusted the piano. It is also true that nobody was likely to look in the top, as the person who removed the water-pistol had taken pains to refasten the bunting with drawing-pins and to cover the top with heavy pot plants. Still, there would have been considerable risk. It seems more probable that the murderer would leave the setting of the automatic until as late as possible. Say about four o'clock on Saturday afternoon."

Templett made a sudden movement, but said nothing.

"For four o'clock on Saturday afternoon," said Alleyn, "none of you has an alibi that would stand up to five minutes' cross-examination."

"But——"

"I've told you——"

"I explained yesterday——"

"Do you want me to go into this? Wait a little and listen. At about half-past three, Mrs. Ross arrived at the hall. Dr. Templett got there a few minutes later. She had come to complete the supper arrangements, he to put his acting clothes in his dressing-room. They had both called at Pen Cuckoo in the morning. Mrs. Ross tells us that while Dr. Templett went into the house she remained in the car. I imagine there is no need to remind you all of the french window into the study at Pen Cuckoo."

"I knew," whispered Miss Prentice. "I knew, I knew!"

"You're going beyond your duty, Mr. Alleyn," said Mrs. Ross.

"No," said Alleyn. "I merely pause here to point out how easy it would have been for any of you to come up Top Lane and slip into the study. To return to the 3.30 visit to the hall. Dr. Templett has given what I believe to be a true account of this visit. He has told us that he arrived to find Mrs. Ross already there and occupied with the supper arrangements. After a time they came here on to this stage. They noticed that the last window on the right, near the front door, was a few inches open. Mrs. Ross, who first noticed this, told Dr. Templett that she saw someone dodge down behind the sill. To reach the window this on-looker used a box."

He turned the cloth farther back and the dilapidated soap-box was revealed. Miss Prentice giggled and covered her mouth with her hand.

"This is the box. It fits into the marks under the window. Do you recognize it, Dr. Templett?"

"Yes," said Templett dully, "I remember that splash of white on the top. I saw it as I looked down."

"Exactly. I should explain that when Dr. Templett reached the window he looked out to see if he could discover anybody. He saw nobody, but he noticed the box. He tells me it was not there when he arrived. Now Mrs. Ross said that she did not recognize this person. But I have experimented, and have found that if one sees anybody at all under the conditions she has described, one stands a very good chance of recognizing them. One would undoubtedly know, for instance, whether it was a man or a woman whose image showed for a moment and disappeared behind the sill. It will be urged by the police that Mrs. Ross did, in fact, recognize this person." Alleyn turned to Templett.

"Mrs. Ross did not tell you who it was?"

"I didn't know who it was," said Mrs. Ross.

"Dr. Templett?"

"I believe Mrs. Ross's statement."

Alleyn looked at the squire.

"When you saw Mrs. Ross alone this afternoon, sir, did she refer to this incident?"

"I can't answer that question, Alleyn," muttered the squire. Henry raised his head and looked at his father with a sort of wonder.

"Very well, sir," said Alleyn. "I must remind you all that you are free to refuse answers to any questions you may be asked. The police may not set traps, and it is my duty to tell you that we have established the identity of the eavesdropper." He took the lid from a small box.

"One of those fragments of rubber," he said, "was found on the point of a nail on the inside of the box. The others were caught behind projecting splinters also on the inside of the box."

He opened an envelope and from it he shook a torn surgical finger-stall.

"The fragments of rubber," he said, "correspond with the holes in this stall."

Miss Prentice electrified the company by clapping her hands with great violence.

"Oh, inspector," she cried shrilly, "how perfectly, perfectly wonderful you are!"

### III

Alleyn turned slowly and met her enraptured gaze. Her prominent eyes bulged, her mouth was open, and she nodded her head several times with an air of ecstasy.

"Then you acknowledge," he said, "that you put this box outside the window on Saturday afternoon?"

"Of course!"

"And that you stood on it in order to look through the window?"

"Alas, yes!"

"Miss Prentice, why did you do this?"

"I was guided."

"Why did you not admit you recognized the box when Inspector Fox asked you about it?"

With that unlovely air of girlishness she covered her face with her fingers.

"I was afraid he would ask me what I saw."

"This is absolute nonsense!" said Templett angrily.

"And why," continued Alleyn, "did you tell me you were indoors all Saturday afternoon?"

"I was afraid to say what I'd done."

"Afraid? Of whom?"

She seemed to draw herself inwards to a point of venomous concentration. She stretched out her arm across the table. The finger pointed at Mrs. Ross.

"Of *her*. She tried to murder me. She's a murderess. I can prove it. I can prove it."

"No!" cried the squire. "No! Good God, Alleyn—"

"Is there any doubt in your mind, Mr. Alleyn," said Mrs. Ross, "that this woman is mad?"

"I can prove it," repeated Miss Prentice.

"How?" asked Alleyn. "Please let this finish, Mr. Jernigham. We shall see daylight soon."

"She knew I saw her. She tried to kill me because she was afraid."

"You hear that, Mrs. Ross? It is a serious accusation. Do you feel inclined to answer it? I must warn you, first, that Dr. Templett has made a statement about this incident."

She looked quickly at Templett.

He said, "I thought you hadn't considered me over the other business. I told the truth."

"You fool," said Mrs. Ross. For the first time she looked really frightened. She raised her hands to her thin neck and touched it surreptitiously. Then she hid her hands in her lap.

"I do not particularly want to repeat the gist of Dr. Templett's statement," said Alleyn.

"Very well." Her voice cracked, she took a breath and then said evenly, "Very well. I recognized Miss Prentice. I've nothing whatever to fear. One doesn't kill old maids for eavesdropping."

"Mr. Jernigham," said Alleyn, "did Mrs. Ross tell you of this incident this afternoon?"

The squire was staring at Mrs. Ross as if she was a sort of Medusa. Without turning his eyes, he nodded.

"She suggested that Miss Prentice had come down to the hall with the intention of putting the automatic in the piano?"

"So she had. I'll swear," said Mrs. Ross.

"Mr. Jernigham?"

"Yes. Yes, she suggested that."

"She told you, perhaps, that you could trust her?"

"Oh, my God!" said the squire.

"I arrived too late at this place," said Mrs. Ross, "to be able to do anything to the piano." She looked at Dinah. "You know that."

"Yes," said Dinah.

"It was soon after that," said Miss Prentice abruptly, "that she began to set traps for me, you know. Then I saw it all in a flash. She must have seen me through a glass darkly, and because I witnessed the unpardonable sin she will destroy me. You understand, don't you, because it is very important. She is in league with The Others, and it won't be long before one of them catches me."

Templett said, "Alleyn, you must see. This has gone on long enough. It's perfectly obvious what's wrong here."

"We will go on, if you please," said Alleyn. "Mr. Copeland, you told me that on Friday night you expected Miss Prentice at the rectory."

The rector, very pale, said, "Yes."

"She didn't arrive?"

"No. I told you. She telephoned."

"At what time?"

"Not long after ten."

"From Pen Cuckoo?"

"It was my hand, you know," said Miss Prentice rapidly. "I wanted to rest my hand. It was so *very* naughty. The blood tramped up and down my arm. Thump, thump, thump. So I said I would stay at home."

"You rang up from Pen Cuckoo?"

"I took the message, Mr. Alleyn," said Dinah. "I told you."

"And what do you say, Miss Copeland, if I tell you that on Friday night the Pen Cuckoo telephone was out of order from 8.20 until the following morning?"

"But—it couldn't have been."

"I'm afraid it was." He turned to Henry Jernigham. "You agree?"

"Yes," said Henry without raising his head.

"You can thank The Others for that," said Miss Prentice in a trembling voice.

"The Others?"

"*The Others*, yes. They are always doing those sort of tricks; and she's the worst of the lot, that woman over there."

"Well, Miss Copeland?"

"I took the message," repeated Dinah. "Miss Prentice said she was at home and would remain at home."

"This contradiction," said Alleyn, "takes us a step further. Mrs. Ross, on Friday night you drove down to Chipping by way of Church Lane?"

"Yes."

"You have told me that you saw a light in this hall."

"Yes."

"You think it was in Mr. Jernigham's dressing-room?"

"Yes."

"The telephone is in that room, Miss Dinah, isn't it?"

"Yes," whispered Dinah. "Oh, yes."

Alleyn took a card from his pocket and scribbled on it. He handed it over to Henry.

"Will you take Miss Dinah to the rectory?" he said. "In half an hour I want you to ring through to here on the extension. Show this card to the man at the door and he will let you out."

Henry looked fixedly at Alleyn.

"Very well, sir," he said. "Thank you."

Henry and Dinah went out.

## IV

"Now," said Alleyn, "we come to the final scene. I must tell you— though I dare say you have heard it all by now—that at 6.30 Miss Gladys Wright used the piano and pressed down the soft pedal. Nothing untoward happened. Since it is inconceivable that anybody could remove the pot plants and rig the automatic after 6.30, we know that the automatic must have been already in position. The safety-catch, which Mr. Henry Jernigham showed to all of you, and particularly to Mrs. Ross, accounts for Gladys Wright's immunity. How, then, did the guilty person manage to release the safety-catch after Gladys Wright and her fellow-helpers were down in the front of the hall? I will show you how it could have been done."

He went down to the footlights.

"You notice that the curtain falls on the far side of the improvised footlights and just catches on the top of the piano. Now, if you'll look."

He stooped and pushed his hand under the curtain. The top of the piano, with its covering of green and yellow bunting, could just be seen.

"This bunting is pinned down as it was on Saturday. It is stretched tight over the entire top of the piano. The lid is turned back, but of course that doesn't show. The pot plants stand on the inside of the lid. I take out the center drawing-pin at the back and slide my hand under the bunting. I am hidden by the curtain, and the pot plants also serve as a mask for any slight movement that might appear from the front of the hall. My fingers have reached the space beyond the open lid. Inside the opening they encounter the cold, smooth surface of the Colt. Listen."

Above the sound of rain and wind they all heard a small click.

"I have pushed over the safety-catch," said Alleyn. "The automatic is now ready to shoot Miss Campanula between the eyes."

"Horrible," said the rector violently.

"There is one sequence of events about which we can be certain," said Alleyn. "We know that the first person to arrive was Gladys Wright. We know that she entered the hall at 6.30, and was in front of the curtain down there with her companions until and after the audience came in. We know that it would have been impossible for anybody to come down from the stage into the front of the hall unnoticed. Miss Wright is ready to swear that nobody did this. We know that Miss Dinah Copeland arrived with her father soon after Gladys Wright, and was here behind the scenes. We know Mr. Copeland sat on the stage until he made his announcement to the audience, only leaving it for a moment to join the others at the telephone, and once again when he persuaded Miss Prentice not to play. Mr. Copeland, did you at any time see anybody stoop down to the curtain as I did just then?"

"No. No! I am quite certain that I didn't. You see, my chair faced the exact spot."

"Yes, therefore we know that unless Mr. Copeland is the guilty person, the safety-catch must have been released during one of his two absences. But Mr. Copeland believed, up to the last moment, that Miss Prentice was to be the pianist. We are satisfied that Mr. Copeland is not the guilty person."

The rector raised one of his large hands in a gesture that seemed to repudiate his immunity. The squire, Miss Prentice, Mrs. Ross and Templett kept their eyes fixed on Alleyn.

"Knowing the only means by which the safety-catch might be released, it seems evident that Miss Prentice was not the intended victim. Miss Prentice, you are cold. Do you feel a draught?"

Miss Prentice shook her head, but she trembled like a wet dog and looked not unlike one. There was a faint sound of movement behind the scenes. Alleyn went on:

"When you were all crowded round her and she gave in and consented to allow Miss Campanula to play, it would have been easy enough to come up here and put the safety-catch on again. Why run the risk of being arrested for the murder of the wrong person?"

Alleyn's level voice halted for a moment. He leaned forward, and when he spoke again it was with extreme deliberation:

"No! The trap was set for Miss Campanula. It was set before Miss Prentice yielded her right to play, and it was set by someone who knew she would not play. The safety-catch was released at the only moment when the stage was empty. The moment when you were all crowded round the telephone. Then the murderer sat back and waited for the catastrophe to happen. Beyond the curtain at this moment someone is sitting at the piano. In a minute you will hear the opening chords of the 'Prelude' as you heard them on Saturday night. If you listen closely you will hear the click of the trigger when the soft pedal goes down. That will represent the report of the automatic. Imagine this guilty person. Imagine someone whose hand stole under the curtain while the hall was crowded and set that trap. Imagine someone who sat, as we sit now, and waited for those three fatal chords."

Alleyn paused.

As heavy as lead and as loud as ever the dead hand had struck them out, in the empty hall beyond the curtain, thumped the three chords of Miss Campanula's "Prelude."

"Pom. *Pom*. POM!"

And very slowly, in uneven jerks, the curtain began to rise.

As it rose, so did Miss Prentice. She might have been pulled up by an invisible hand in her hair. Her mouth was wide open, but the only sound she made was a sort of retching groan. She did not take her eyes from the rising curtain, but she pointed her hand at the rector and waved it up and down.

"*It was for you*," screamed Miss Prentice. "*I did it for you!*"

And Nigel, seated at the piano, saw Alleyn take her by the arm.

"Eleanor Prentice, I arrest you——"

# CHAPTER XXVII

# Case Ends

## I

HENRY AND DINAH sat by the fire in the rectory study and watched the clock.

"*Why* does he want us to ring up?" said Dinah for perhaps the sixth time. "I don't understand."

"I think I do. I think the telephoning's only an excuse. He wanted us out of the way."

"But why?"

Henry put his arm round her shoulders and pressed his cheek against her hair.

"Oh, Dinah," he said.

"What, darling?"

Dinah looked up. He sat on the arm of her chair and she had to move a little in his embrace before she could see his eyes.

"Henry! What is it?"

"I think we're in for a bad spin."

"But—isn't it Mrs. Ross?"

"I don't think so."

Without removing her gaze from his face she took his hand.

"I think it's Eleanor," said Henry.

*"Eleanor!"*

"It's the only answer. Don't you see that's what Alleyn was driving at all the time?"

"But she *wanted* to play. She made the most frightful scene over not playing."

"I know. But Templett said two days before that she'd never be able to do it. Don't you see, she worked it so that we should find her crying and moaning, and insist on her giving up?"

"Suppose we hadn't insisted?"

"She'd have left the safety-catch on or not used the soft pedal, or perhaps she'd have 'discovered' the automatic and accused Miss C. of putting it there. That would have made a glorious scene."

"I can't believe it."

"Can you believe it of any one else?"

"Mrs. Ross," said Dinah promptly.

"No, darling. I rather think Mrs. Ross has merely tried to blackmail my papa. It is my cousin who is a murderess. Shall you enjoy a husband of whom every one will say: 'Oh, yes, Henry Jernigham! Wasn't he the Pen Cuckoo murderess's nephew or son or something?"

"I shall love my husband and I shan't hear what they say. Besides, you don't know. You're only guessing."

"I'm certain of it. There are all sorts of things that begin to fit in. Things that don't fit any other way. Dinah, I know she's the one."

"Anyway, my dear darling, she's mad."

"I hope so," said Henry. "God, it's awful, isn't it?"

He sprang up and began to walk nervously up and down.

"I can't stand this much longer," said Henry.

"It's time we rang up."

"I'll do it."

But as he reached the door they heard voices in the hall.

The rector came in, followed by Alleyn and the squire.

"Dinah! Where's Dinah?" cried the rector.

"Here she is," said Henry. "Father!"

The squire turned a chalk-white face to his son.

"Come here, old boy," he said. "I want you."

"That chair," said Alleyn quickly.

Henry and Alleyn put the squire in the chair.

"Brandy, Dinah," said the rector. "He's fainted."

"No, I haven't," said Jocelyn. "Henry, old boy, I'd better tell you——"

"I know," said Henry. "It's Eleanor."

Alleyn moved back to the door and watched them. He was now a detached figure. The arrest came like a wall of glass between himself and the little group that hovered round Jocelyn. He knew that most of his colleagues accepted these moments of isolation. Perhaps they were scarcely aware of them. But, for himself, he always felt a little like a sort of Mephistopheles, who looked on at his own handiwork. He didn't enjoy the sensation. It was the one moment when his sense of detachment deserted him. Now, as they remembered him, he saw in the faces turned towards him the familiar guarded antagonism of herded animals.

He said, "If Mr. Jernigham would like to see Miss Prentice, it shall be arranged. Superintendent Blandish will be in charge."

He bowed, and was going when Jocelyn said loudly:

"Wait a minute."

"Yes, sir?" Alleyn moved quickly to the chair. The squire looked up at him.

"I know you tried to prepare me for this," he said. "You guessed that woman had told me. I couldn't admit that until—until it was all up—I wouldn't admit it. You understand that?"

"Yes."

"I'm all to blazes. Think what to do in the morning. Just wanted to say I appreciate the way you've handled things. Considerate."

"I would have avoided the final scene, sir, if I had seen any other way."

"I know that. Mustn't ask questions, of course. There are some things I don't understand—— Alleyn, you see she's out of her mind?"

"Dr. Templett, I'm sure, will advise you about an alienist, sir."

"Yes. Thank you."

The squire blinked up at him and then suddenly held out his hand.

"Good night."

"Good night, sir."

Henry said, "I'll come out with you."

As they walked to the door, Alleyn thought there were points about being a Jernigham of Pen Cuckoo.

"It's queer," said Henry. "I suppose this must be a great shock to us; but at the moment I feel nothing at all. Nothing. I don't realize that she's—— Where is she?"

"The Yard car is on the way to Great Chipping. She'll need things from Pen Cuckoo. We'll let you know what they are."

Henry stopped dead at the rectory door. His voice turned to ice.

"Is she frightened?"

Alleyn remembered that face with the lips drawn back from the projecting teeth, the tearless bulging eyes, the hands that opened and closed as if they had let something fall.

"I don't think she is conscious of fear," he said. "She was quite composed. She didn't weep."

"She can't. Father's often said she never cried as a child."

"I remembered your father told me that."

"I hated her," said Henry. "But that's nothing now. She's insane. It's strange, because there's no insanity in the family. What happens? I mean, when will they begin to try her. We—what ought we to do?"

Alleyn told him what they should do. It was the first time he had ever advised the relatives of a person accused of murder, and he said, "But you must ask your lawyer's advice first of all. That is really all I may tell you."

"Yes. Yes, of course. Thank you, sir." Henry peered at Alleyn. He saw him against rods of rain that glinted in the light from the open door.

"It's funny," said Henry jerkily. "Do you know, I was going to ask you about Scotland Yard—how one began."

"Did you think seriously of this?"

"Yes. I want a job. Hardly suitable for the cousin of the accused."

"There's no reason why you shouldn't try for the police."

"I've read your book. Good Lord, it's pretty queer to stand here and talk like this."

"You're more shocked than you realize. If I were you I should take your father home."

"Ever since yesterday, sir, I've had the impression I'd seen you before. I've just remembered. Agatha Troy did a portrait of you, didn't she?"

"Yes."

"It was very good, wasn't it? Rather a compliment to be painted by Troy. Is she pleasant or peculiar?"

"I think her very pleasant indeed," said Alleyn. "I have persuaded her to say she will marry me. Good night."

He smiled, waved his hand and went out into the rain.

## II

Nigel had driven his own car over to the rectory, and he took Alleyn to Great Chipping.

"The others have only just got away," said Nigel. "She fainted after you left, and Fox had to get Templett to deal with her. They're picking the wardress up at the substation."

"Fainted, did she?"

"Yes. She's completely dotty, isn't she?"

"I shouldn't say so. Not completely."

"Not?"

"The dottiness has only appeared since Saturday night. She's probably extremely neurotic. Unbalanced, hysterical, all that. In law, insanity is very closely defined. Her counsel will probably go for moral depravity, delusion, or hallucination. If he can prove a history of disturbance of the higher levels of thought, he may get away with it. I'm afraid poor old Copeland will have to relate his experiences. They'll give me fits for your performance on the piano, but I've covered myself by warning the listeners. I don't mind betting that even if lunacy is not proved, there'll be a recommendation for mercy. Of course, they may go all out for 'not guilty' and get it."

"You might give me an outline, Alleyn."

"All right. Where are we? It's as dark as hell."

"Just coming into Chipping. There's the police car ahead."

"Ah, yes. Well, here's the order of events as we see it. On Friday, by 2.40, Georgie had set the booby-trap. Miss Campanula tried to get into the hall before he left it. He hid while the chauffeur looked through the window. When the chauffeur had gone, Georgie repinned the bunting over the open top of the piano, replaced the aspidistras and decamped. At a minute or two after half-past two, Miss C. passed Miss P. in the church porch. Miss P. was seen by Gibson. She crossed Church Lane and would pass the hall on her way to Top Lane. In Top Lane she met Dinah Copeland and Henry Jernigham at three o'clock.

"Apparently she had taken half an hour to walk a quarter of a mile. We did it yesterday in five minutes. Our case is that she'd gone into the hall in a great state of upset because the rector had ticked her off at confession. She must have sat at the piano, worked the booby-trap and got the jet of water full in the face. She removed the pistol, and probably the first vague idea of her crime came into her head, because she kept quiet about the booby-trap. Perhaps she remembered the Colt and wondered if it would fit. We don't know. We only know that at three o'clock she had the scene in Top Lane with Henry and Dinah, the scene that was watched and overheard by that old stinker, Tranter. Tranter and Dinah noticed that the bosom of her dress was wet. That, with the lapse in time, are the only scraps of evidence we've got so far to give color to this bit of our theory, but I'd like to know how else the front of her bodice got wet, if not from the pistol. It wasn't raining, and anyhow rain wouldn't behave like that. And I'd like to know how else you can account for her arrival, as late as three, at a spot five minutes away."

"Yes, it'll certainly take a bit of explaining."

"The butler remembered she got back at four. At five Henry explained the mechanism of the Colt to the assembled company, stressing and illustrating the action of the safety-catch. Miss P. had told the rector she wanted to see him that evening. Of course, she wanted to give him a distorted and poisonous version of the meeting between Henry and his Dinah. She was to come to the rectory after the Reading Circle activities. About ten o'clock, that would be. Now, soon after ten, Miss C. flung herself into the rector's arms in the rectory study."

"Christopher!"

"Yes. I hope for his sake we won't have to bring this out; but it's a faint hope. The curtains were not drawn, and anybody on the path to the hall could have seen. Round about 10.15, Miss Dinah heard the gate into the wood give its customary piercing shriek. She thought somebody had gone out that way and believed it was Miss C. We contend it was Miss P. coming in for her appointment. We contend she stood inside the gate transfixed by the tableau beyond the window, that she put the obvious interpretation on what she saw, and fell a prey to whatever furies visit a woman whose aging heart is set on one man and whose nerves, desires and thoughts have been concentrated on the achievement of her hope. We think she turned, passed through the post-stile and returned to Church Lane. To help this theory we've got two blurred heel-prints, the statements that nobody else used the gate that night, and the fact that Miss P. rang up shortly afterwards from the hall."

"How the devil d'you get that?"

"The telephone operator is prepared to swear nobody rang up the rectory. But Miss P. rang up and the old housemaid called Dinah Copeland, who went to the telephone. She evidently didn't notice it was an extension call. Miss P. said she was speaking from Pen Cuckoo. Miss P. has admitted she rang up. The hall telephone is an extension and doesn't register at the exchange. Mrs. Ross saw a light in the hall telephone room, at the right moment. It's the only explanation. Miss P. didn't know the Pen Cuckoo telephone was out of order and thought she was safe enough to establish a false alibi. She probably got the water-pistol that night and took it away with her to see if the Colt was the same length. It was an eleventh of an inch shorter, which meant that the nozzle would fit in the hole without projecting. Now we come to Saturday afternoon. She told me she was in her room. Mrs. Ross recognized her through the hall window, and we've got the scraps of rubber to prove that she handled the box. She looked through the hall window to see if the coast was clear. I imagine Templett was embracing his dubious love, who saw the onlooker over his shoulder. Miss P.

took to cover, leaving the box. When they'd gone, she crept into the hall and put the Colt in position. She'd had four emotional shocks in twenty-six hours. The rector had given her fits. She'd seen Henry making ardent love to Dinah. She'd seen Idris Campanula, apparently victoriously happy, in the rector's arms, and she'd watched Templett and Mrs. Ross in what I imagine must have been an even more passionate encounter. And though I do *not* consider her insane in law, I do consider that these experiences drove her into an ecstasy of fury. Since it is the rector with whom she herself is madly and overwhelmingly in love, Idris Campanula was the object of her hatred. It was Idris who had robbed her of her hopes. Incidentally, it is Idris who left her a fortune. Georgie Biggins had shown her the way. It's worth noting here that she won a badge for tying knots, and taught the local Guides in this art. At half-past four she was back at Pen Cuckoo and waked the squire in time for tea. This account, too, sounds like conjecture, but the finger-stall proves she lied once, the telephone proves she lied three times."

"In the teapot?"

"I'll explain them in a minute."

They reached the top of Great Chipping Rise, and the lights of the town swam brokenly beyond the rain.

"There's not much more," said Alleyn. "The prosecution will make the most of this last point. The only time the stage was deserted, after they arrived in the evening, was when all the others stood round the telephone trying to get through to Mrs. Ross and Dr. Templett. Only Miss Prentice was absent. She appeared for a moment, saw the squire in his underpants, scuttled off to the stage and did her stunt with the safety-catch. Our case really rests on this. We can check and double-check the movements of every one of them from half-past six onwards. The rector sat on the stage, and will swear nobody touched the piano from that side. Gladys Wright and her helpers were in the hall and will swear nobody touched it from that side. The only time the catch could have been moved was when they were all round the telephone, and Miss P. was absent. She is literally the only person who could have moved the catch."

"By George," said Nigel, "she must be a cold-blooded creature! What a nerve!"

"It's given way a little since the event," said Alleyn grimly. "I think she found she wasn't as steady as she expected to be, so she allowed her hysteria to mount into the semblance of insanity. Her nerve had gone at the shock of her dear friend's death, you see. Now she's going to work the demented stunt for all it's worth. I wonder when she first began to be afraid of me. I wonder if it was when I put the finger-stall in my pocket. Or was it at the first tender mention of the onion?"

"The onion!" shouted Nigel. "Where the devil does the onion come in?"

"Georgie Biggins put the onion in the teapot. We found it in a cardboard box in the corner of the supper-room. It had pinkish powder on it. There was pinkish powder on the table in Miss P.'s dressing-room. It smelled of onion. The dressing-rooms were locked while Georgie was in the hall, so he didn't drop the onion in Miss P.'s powder. My theory is that Miss P. found the onion in the teapot, which she had to use, took it to her dressing-room and put it down on the table amongst the spilled powder. The teapot has her prints on the inside, and hers and Georgie's on the outside."

"But what the suffering cats did she want with an onion? She wasn't going to make Irish stew."

"Haven't you heard that she has never been known to shed tears until Saturday night, when floods were induced by sheer pain and disappointment because she couldn't play the piano? She took a good sniff at the onion, opened her dressing-room door, swayed to and fro, moaned and wept and wept and wept until Dr. Templett heard her and behaved exactly as she knew he would behave. Later on she chucked the onion into the débris in the supper-room. She ought to have returned it to the teapot."

"I boggle at the onion."

"Boggle away, my boy. If it was an innocent onion, why didn't she own to it? There are her powder and her prints. Nobody else extracted it from the teapot. But it doesn't matter. It's only another corroborative detail."

"The whole thing sounds a bit like Pooh Bah."

"It's a beastly business. I detest it. She's a horrible woman, not a generous thought in her make-up; but that doesn't make much odds. If Georgie Biggins hadn't set his trap she'd have gone on to the end of her days, most likely, hating Miss C., scheming, scratching, adoring. Everybody will talk psychiatry and nonsense. Her *idée fixe* will be pitchforked about the studios of the intelligentsia. That old fool Jernigham, who's a nice old fool, and his son, who's no fool at all, will go through hell. The rector, who supplied the *idée fixe,* will blame himself; and God knows he's not to blame. Templett will hover on the brink of professional odium, but he'll be cured of Mrs. Ross."

"What of Mrs. Ross?"

"At least she's scored a miss in the Vale of Pen Cuckoo. No hope now of blackmailing old Jernigham into matrimony, or out of hard cash. We'll catch the Rosen sooner or later, please heaven, for she's a nasty bit of work, and that's a fact. She would have seen Templett in the dock before she'd have risked an eyelash to clear him, and yet I imagine she's very much attracted by Templett. As soon as she knew we thought him innocent, she was all for him. Here we are."

Nigel pulled up outside the police station.

"May I come in with you?" he asked.

"If you like, certainly."

Fox met Alleyn in the door.

"She's locked up," said Fox. "Making a great old rumpus. The doctor's gone for a straitjacket. Here's a letter for you, Mr. Alleyn. It came this afternoon."

Alleyn looked at the letter and took it quickly. The firm small writing of the woman he loved brought the idea of her into his mind.

"It's from Troy," he said.

And before he went into the lighted building he looked at Nigel.

"If one could send every grand passion to the laboratory, do you suppose, in each resulting formula, we should find something of Dinah and Henry's young idyll, something of Templett's infatuation, something of Miss P.'s madness, and even something of old Jernigham's foolishness?"

"Who knows?" said Nigel.

"Not I," said Alleyn.